Isle of Canes

A Historical Novel

Elizabeth Shown Mills

Ancestry®

Library of Congress Cataloging-in-Publication Data

Mills, Elizabeth S.
  Isle of Canes / by Elizabeth Shown Mills.
    p. cm.
  ISBN 1-59331-175-3 (alk. paper)
  1. African American families—Fiction. 2. Louisiana—Fiction. 3. Islands—Fiction. 4. Racism—Fiction. I. Title.
  PS3613.I568I85 2004
  813'.54—dc22

                                                    2004000055

Published by:
MyFamily.com, Inc.
360 West 4800 North
Provo, UT 84604

Cover design by Robert Davis

Cover photos:
"Melrose" courtesy of Guillet Photography,
Natchitoches, Louisiana. Used with permission.

"Cane River" courtesy of Jennifer Browning. Used with permission.

Portraits of Marie Carmelite "Melite" Anty and Auguste Metoyer, oil on canvas,
painted ca. 1836 by Feuille. Photographs courtesy of Northwestern State University
of Louisiana, Watson Memorial Library, Cammie G. Henry Research Center.
Used with permission.

10 9 8 7 6 5 4 3 2 1

Printed in the United States of America.

To

Family

Theirs, mine, and all of ours.

Family is our beginning and our end. It is who we are and why we are. Amid its roots we can find an understanding of the problems our world has inherited, and amid the intertwining of its branches we can see hope for a better world in the generations to come.

Publisher's Note

The story that follows is a real one, well known to tens of thousands of Americans whose roots go back to the Isle of Canes—and to a myriad of others who have been lured there, once or often, by the Isle's fabled heritage. Every effort has been made to present the lives of the Islanders as accurately as possible. Due to the complexity of documented detail and the sheer size of the family involved, some simplification of circumstances and timeline has been necessary. However, the reader may be assured that the historical integrity of all events and characters has been respectfully preserved.

Contents

Illustrations

Foreword

Cane River stole my heart in 1970. As a young wife and mother, I went there to find my children's roots, never suspecting that a bout of curiosity would turn into a lifelong love affair.

I found its people to be a puzzle. Cloutiers, Derbannes, Duprés, La Cours and Le Courts, Lecomtes, Prudhommes, and Rachals. They came in many shades. They gave their children the same names. They worshipped in the same churches but, curiously, in different wings—one for whites, one for blacks, and one for those considered to be neither. They shared not only the same river but the same records, challenging modern researchers to sort them out. Among them, like the glue that held them all together, lived the Metoyers, a family that intrigued me although I could find no place for them on our family charts.

Cane River fever spread within our household. My husband, a young historian, was duly cautioned by his department head "not to get involved with genealogy or his career would be ruined"—a warning common to the era but one he proceeded to ignore. My mother-in-law took me back to Cloutierville and taught me the way her people thought—they and the neighbors who shared their lives and some of the same ancestral lines. As I gathered their stories and struggled to chart out their connections on mammoth rolls of newsprint, my three-year-old joined me on the floor to "write Rachals," as she put it. Her affinity for that family name was not surprising. It was the one we had, perhaps with premonition, given her at birth.

In 1972, my hobby became a profession. The Association for the Preservation of Historic Natchitoches had been gifted with the estate grounds of a plantation steeped in lore and wracked with controversy. If legend could be believed, it dated to the colonial era, during which it had been founded by a freed slave woman variously known as Marie Thérèse or Coincoin. My charge was to document its history. The hope was to earn a slot on the National Register of Historic Places. As often was the case, the legend strayed here and there from the facts of history, like partners in a waltz who touch and twirl together then swing away to tease and flirt with others before coming back into each other's arms. Yet the story that emerged from thousands of records scattered across six nations, was even more incredible. By the time the project ended, the fabled plantation actually founded by Coincoin's son Louis—and known now as Melrose on the Cane—was proclaimed a National Historic Landmark.

Even then, Cane River and its Isle still held the Millses in their grip. Bridging the traditional divide between academic and family history, my husband adopted the Isle for his doctoral dissertation. The parish of Natchitoches continued to be our "other home," and the Metoyers who carved a civilization out of the canebrakes became our "adopted family." Inevitably, Gary's career would take him elsewhere, but mine would stay rooted along that mystic river.

Gary's dissertation, which Louisiana State University Press published in 1977 as *The Forgotten People: Cane River's Creoles of Color,* reconstructs the socio-economic history of the Isle from the naked bones of the documentary record. Beyond those bones, however, there was a heart throbbing with family stories left untold, a soul formed by the society that spawned rich traditions, and the flesh of historical context that was colored by all the families with whom the Metoyers lived, worked, loved, and feuded. Here now, in the *Isle of Canes,* the heart, soul, flesh, and bones are made one.

Three decades of research on any subject leave one owing many debts. The first and greatest is surely to the late Arthur Chopin Watson who, as legal counsel to the Association for the Preservation of Historic Natchitoches, persuaded me to take on that research project in 1972 and then opened doors that neither Gary nor I might have entered on our own. The guidance, hospitality, and support of Arthur, his wife Gene Hickman Watson, and their friends—particularly Eddie and Jean Mahan—were priceless. Over the years, Carol Wells and John Price of the Watson Library, Northwestern State University; Irby Knotts, his staff, and their successors at the Natchitoches Parish Courthouse; a succession of priests in all the parishes; the late Lee Etta Vaccarini Couti, Lewis E. and Gloria Sers Jones, and Tillman and Armeline Roque Chelettre of the Isle; Dr. Harlan Mark

Guidry of Houston; and the Natchitoches historian and preservationist Robert B. DeBlieux were all valuable touchstones. Amid this year's whirlwind schedule of production, Northwestern's Mary Linn Wernet, who heads the Cammie G. Henry Research Center, and Sonny Carter, the Center's digital imaging specialist, surely worked overtime to share the Center's artwork for the book's final design. Beyond that treasure trove of history, all who share my fascination with Cane River's past are blessed to have a new resource at their disposal, Northwestern's Louisiana Creole Heritage Center, ably run by two professionals deeply rooted in the Isle, Janet Colson and Louise Llorens.

And now, as I write *finis* upon this labor of love, I owe my final thanks to Ancestry, its officers, and its editors—to Loretto Dennis Szucs, vice-president of publishing, who believed in this story from the start; to Tom Stockham, president and CEO of Ancestry's parent company MyFamily.com, and André Brummer, its senior vice president of product, who found within these pages a world they did not know or expect, and then understood why this story needed telling; and to Matt Wright, Jennifer Utley, Rob Davis, and the other members of the Ancestry editorial and graphics team who gently but wisely helped me shape the final manuscript.

To these friends, to their offspring and my own, and to all who now give me an irreplaceable part of their lives—that is, the hours they spend in reading the *Isles of Canes*—I offer this story in hopes it helps to create a better understanding and a keener appreciation of the rich, complex, and often-conflicting cultures that have shaped America.

—Elizabeth Shown Mills

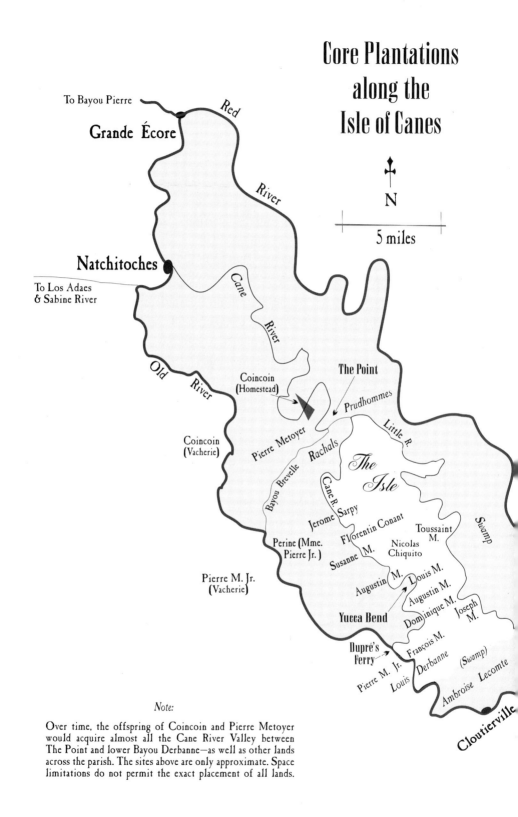

Core Plantations along the Isle of Canes

To Bayou Pierre

Grande Écore

Red River

N

5 miles

Natchitoches

To Los Adaes & Sabine River

Cane River

Old River

Coincoin (Homestead)

The Point

Coincoin (Vacherie)

Prudhommes

Pierre Metoyer

Little R.

Rachals

The Isle

Bayou Brevelle

Cane R.

Perine (Mme. Pierre Jr.)

Jerome Sarpy

Florentin Conant

Toussaint M.

Swamp

Nicolas Chiquito

Susanne M.

Pierre M. Jr. (Vacherie)

Augustin M.

Louis M.

Augustin M.

Dominique M.

Joseph M.

Yucca Bend

Dupré's Ferry

Pierre M. Jr.

François M.

Louis Derbanne

(Swamp)

Ambroise Lecomte

Cloutierville

Note:

Over time, the offspring of Coincoin and Pierre Metoyer would acquire almost all the Cane River Valley between The Point and lower Bayou Derbanne—as well as other lands across the parish. The sites above are only approximate. Space limitations do not permit the exact placement of all lands.

The Families

The First Generation
François and Fanny
The African artisan and his princess, captured into slavery and brought to the wilds of Louisiana in 1735. He accepted their fate and insisted that she accept it, too.

The Second Generation
Coincoin
Beautiful, talented, and fiery, she swore over the dead bodies of her parents that one day their family would be free, rich, and proud. She kept her vow.

The Third Generation
Augustin
Half-African, half-French, he ruled over the Isle of Canes as patriarch of a legendary colony of *creoles de couleur* who lived in pillared mansions yet toiled beside the 500 slaves who tilled their 18,000 acres.

The Fourth Generation
Perine
Born to riches, she died in shame; but she never forgot the heritage of her family or the brutal Civil War that destroyed it. Through the persecutions of Reconstruction and Jim Crow, hers was a different vow: *Never* would her family forget who they were, until the day came that they could—and *would*—reclaim their pride and their Isle. She, too, kept her promise.

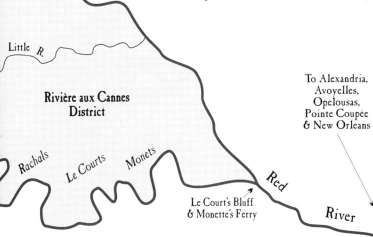

The Original Family*

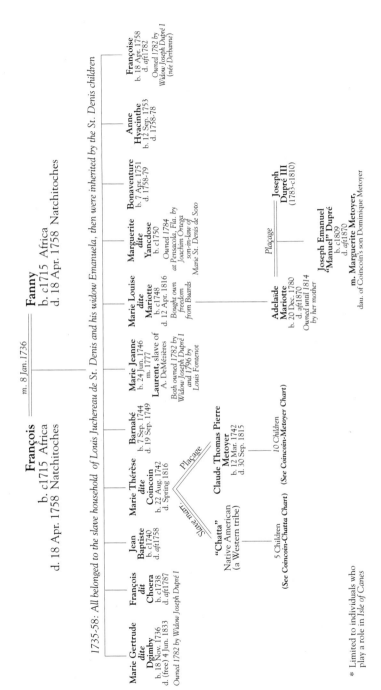

François —— m. 8 Jan. 1736 —— **Fanny**
b. c1715 Africa   b. c1715 Africa
d. 18 Apr. 1758 Natchitoches   d. 18 Apr. 1758 Natchitoches

1735-58: All belonged to the slave household of Louis Juchereau de St. Denis and his widow Emanuela, then were inherited by the St. Denis children

Marie Gertrude dite Dgimby
b. 18 Nov. 1736
d. (free) 4 Jun. 1833
Owned 1782 by Widow Joseph Dupré I

François dit Choera
b. c1738
d. aft1787

Jean Baptiste
b. c1740
d. aft1758

Marie Thérèse dite Coincoin
b. 22 Aug. 1742
d. Spring 1816

Placage

Slave marr.

"Chatta"
Native American
(a Western tribe)

5 Children
(See Coincoin-Chatta Chart)

Claude Thomas Pierre Metoyer
b. 12 Mar. 1742
d. 30 Sep. 1815

10 Children
(See Coincoin-Metoyer Chart)

Barnabé
b. 7 Sep. 1744
d. 19 Sep. 1749

Marie Jeanne
b. 24 Jan. 1746
m. 1777
Laurent, slave of
A. DeMézières
Both owned 1782 by Widow Joseph Dupré I and 1796 by Louis Fontenot

Marie Louise dite Mariotte
b. c1748
d. 12 Apr. 1816
Bought own freedom from Buards

Marguerite dite Yancdose
b. c1750
Owned 1784 at Pensacola, Fla. by Joachim Ortega son-in-law of Marie St. Denis de Soto

Bonaventure
b. 7 Apr. 1751
d. 1758-79

Anne Hyacinthe
b. 12 Sep. 1753
d. 1758-78

Françoise
b. 18 Apr. 1758
d. aft1782
Owned 1782 by Widow Joseph Dupré I (née Derbanne)

Adelaide Mariotte
b. 20 Dec. 1780
d. aft1870
Owned until 1814 by her mother

Plaçage

Joseph Dupré III
(1783–c1810)

Joseph Emanuel "Manuel" Dupré
b. c1809
d. aft1870

m. Marguerite Metoyer,
dau. of Coincoin's son Dominique Metoyer

* Limited to individuals who
play a role in *Isle of Canes*

The
St. Denis - De Mézières Family *

Louis Juchereau de St. Denis
Chevalier & Commandant
(1676 Canada - 1744 Natchitoches)

Marie-Josephe Minard
(1697-1768, France)

Unidentified Natchitoches Indian

Emanuela Sanchez y Navarre
(c1697-1758)

Claude Christophe Mauguet de Mézieres
(Nobleman & Attorney, 1689-1734)

Louis Béraud de la Haye de Riou
(Marquise, 1677-1754)

Children of Louis Juchereau de St. Denis and Unidentified Natchitoches Indian

Louise Marguerite
m. (1) Pierre Couteleau Duplessis
 └ Pierre-Louis Duplessis
m. (2) Martin Goutierrez

Children of Louis Juchereau de St. Denis and Emanuela Sanchez y Navarre

Rose de St. Denis
m. Jacques de la Chaise

Louis Antoine de St. Denis
m. Louise Marguerite Derbanne

Gertrude de St. Denis

Petronille de St. Denis
m. Athanase de Mézières

Dolores de St. Denis
m. César de Blanc, Commandant
 └ Louis Charles de Blanc, Commandant

Marie des Neiges de St. Denis
m. Manuel Bermudez y de Soto
 └ Manuela de Soto
   m. Athanase Poissot

Pierre Antoine de St. Denis

Children of Claude Christophe Mauguet de Mézieres

Marie Françoise Felicité Mauguet de Mézières
m. 2ierre César Ducrest, Marquis de St. Aubin
 └ Caroline Stéphanie Félicité Ducrest de St. Aubin aka "Madame Genlis"
   m. Charles Alexis Brulart, Count de Genlis

Athanase Christophe Fortunat Mauguet de Mézières
Chevalier, commandant, Tejas governor
(1719, France-1779, San Antonio)
 └ **Elisabeth Marie Felicité Nepomucene de Mézières**

By 2nd wife, Pelagie Fazende
 └ **Athanase de Mézières Jr.**
   Placage w/ Marie Bernard, his slave
    └ **Fanny Mézières**
      └ Flavie Mézières m. Gassion Metoyer, grandson of Coincoin

Children of Louis Béraud de la Haye de Riou

Charlotte Jeanne de la Haye aka "Madame Montesson"
m. (1) Jean Baptiste, Marquis de Montesson
m. (2) Louis Philippe, Duke of Orleans
   (Nephew of Louis XIV)

---

* Limited to individuals who play a role in *Isle of Canes*

The Family of Coincoin & "Chatta" *

Marie Thérèse dite Coincoin
St. Denis-De Soto slave
22 Aug. 1742 - Spring 1816
Freed 1778 by Pierre Metoyer

1758-1765 ═══ **"Chatta," a Plains Indian**
De Soto Slave
Left Natchitoches c1765
Identified only by legend

Marie Louise
b. 7 Sep 1759 Natchitoches
freed 1786-95 by Coincoin
(*No known surviving offspring*)

Thérèse
b. 23 Sep 1761 Natchitoches
d. 4 Feb 1831 Opelousas
Freed 1790-95 by Coincoin

    José Mauricio
    b. 1781, Opelousas - d. *aft*1795

Françoise "Fanchon"
b. Jul 1763 Natchitoches
d. *aft*1804 Rivière aux Cannes

Nicolas Chiquito
b. c1764/65 Natchitoches
d. 11 Apr 1850 Cane River
Freed 1793-97 by Coincoin &
her son Augustin Metoyer
(*No known surviving offspring*)

**Jean Joseph
aka Jeannot Metoyer**
b. 20 February 1766
Purchased by Metoyer, 1776
Left Natchitoches as an adult,
reputedly for Indian country

All were slaves of Louise Marguerite Lecomte & her husbands Jean Baptiste Dupré and Louis Monet until 1825

Remy
b. c1779

**Marie Louise
Lecomte**
b. 26 Nov. 1781
Child of Ambroise Lecomte
Freed 1835 by son Louis

Charles
b. c1783

Marie Jeanne
b. c1785
d. young

Henry
b. 20 Oct. 1787

Hortense
b. 1789-93
(*Left offspring*)

Pierre
b. 1789-93

**François Nicolas
Monette**
b. cSep 1795
Child of Louis Monet
Free by 1835

Marie Jeanne
b. 1797
(*Left offspring*)

Thérèse
b. 20 Aug. 1799

Rose
b. 1801
(*Left offspring*)

    Louis Monette
    b. 25 Dec. 1802
    Child of Louis Monet
    Freed 1825 by his father's widow

    Marie Zelia Monette
    b. 1820
    Slave of Gen. F. Gaienné
    Freed 1835 by her father

*Limited to individuals who play a role in *Isle of Canes

The
Family of
Coincoin & Pierre*

Marie Thérèse *dite* Coincoin ══ 1766-1784 ══ **Claude Thomas Pierre Metoyer**
St. Denis-De Soto slave | b. 12 Mar. 1744 France
22 Aug. 1742 - Spring 1816 | d. 30 Sep. 1815 Cane River
Freed 1778 by Pierre Metoyer | m. 13 Oct. 1788 Marie Thérèse Buard

---

Nicolas Augustin
b. 22 Jan. 1768
d. 19 Dec. 1856
m. 22 Aug. 1792
Marie Agnes Poissot

- Marie Modeste
  b. 1793 - d. young
- J. Baptiste-Augustin
  1795-1855
  m. M. Suzette Anty
  • Barbe
    m. B. Dauphine
    & C.N. Rocques
- Marie Louise
  1797-1847
  m. Florentin Conant
- J. B. Maxille
  1798-1830
  m. M. Aspasie Anty
- Auguste Augustin
  1800-1830
  m. M. Thérèse Carmelite
  "Melite" Anty
- Marie Pompose
  1802-1845
  m. Charles N. Rocques
- Joseph Augustin
  c1804-1851
  m. Antoinette Coindet
- Marie Susette
  1806-1864
  m. (1) Elisée Rocques
     (2) Louis A. Morin
- François-Gassion
  c1809-1865
  m. (1) Flavie Mézières†
     • F. G. N. A. "Gus"
       m. Estelle Morin
     (2) Rosine Carles
     (3) Perine Metoyer

Marie Susanne
b. 22 Jan. 1768
d. 28 Jan. 1838
Plaçages
Dr. Joseph Conant &
Jean Baptiste Anty

Plaçage c1792–95
Dr. Joseph Conant

- Florentin Conant
  1794-aft1860
  m. M. Louise Metoyer

Plaçage c1797-c1807
Jean Baptiste Anty

- Marie Suzette
  b. 1797-aft1860
  m. J. B. A. Metoyer
- Marie Aspasie
  1800-aft1850
  m. Maxille Metoyer
  & Octave Deronce
- Marie Arsene
  1803-1836
  m. Manuel Llorens
- Unnamed son
  1805-1805
- Valsain
  1806-1814
- Marie Thérèse
  Carmelite "Melite"
  1807-aft1860
  m. Auguste Metoyer

Louis
b. c1770
d. 11 Mar. 1832
m. 9 Feb. 1801
Marie Thérèse Lecomte
(French & Canneci Indian)

- Jean Baptiste Louis
  1800-1838
  m. Marie Susanne Metoyer
  (dau. of Pierre II)
  • Théophile Louis

Liaison c1789-93
Françoise Lecomte

- Marie Louise
  "Catiche"
  b. 1790-aft1870
  m. F. M. Mulon
  Liaison Étienne Carles
- Marie Rose
  b. 1793-aft1860
  Liaisons
  • J. B. Baltazar, "griffe"
  • J. A. Coindet
  • Dr. J. A. Z. Carles
  • James Hurst, Esq.

Liaison c1796-97
Madeleine Grappe, "griffe"

- Thérèse
  b. 1797
  m. Augustin Cloutier

Liaison c1812-13
Marie "Babe"

- Antoine Louis

Pierre II
b. c1772
d. 25 Jun. 1833
m. 1802 & 1818
Perine Lecomte &
Henriette Cloutier

By Perine Lecomte

- Marie Susanne
  1804-aft1870
  m. J. B. Louis Metoyer
- Pierre III
  1806 - 1860-70
  m. Desneiges Metoyer
  • Perine
    m. Gassion Metoyer
    & Joseph E. Dupré
- Athanase Vienne
  1813-aft1860
  m. M. Emelia Metoyer

By Henriette Cloutier

- Marie Osite
  1816-aft1870
  m. J. B. N. Le Court†
- Neres Pierre
  1817-aft1901
  m. M. Elise Rocques
- Marie Eliza
  1819-aft1866
  m. Belisaire Llorens
- J. B. Delores
  1821-died young
- Auguste Dorestan
  1823-aft1848

Dominique
b. c1774
d. 30 Apr. 1839
m. 19 Jan. 1795
Marguerite Lecomte

- Dominique
  1796-1796
- J. B. Dominique I
  1797-1850
  m. Adelaïde Rachal
- Joseph Dominique
  1799-1816
- Marie Susanne
  1801-aft1870
  m. J. B. E. Rachal
- Marie Perine
  1803-aft1830
  m. Pre. Mission Rachal
- Narcisse Dominique
  1805-aft1836
  m. M. Cephalide David
- J. B. Dominique II
  1808-aft1860
  m. Doralise Dupré
- Marie Silvie
  1809-aft1860
  m. J. V. B. Le Court†
- Louis Florentin
  1811-aft1870
  m. Théotise Chagneau
- Marie Celine
  1813-c1842
  m. J. Eloy Le Court†
- Joseph Ozeme
  1815-aft1870
  m. Catherine David

---

† Denotes offspring of French nobility. The term *griffe* signified part-Indian ancestry.
The fourth generation here is limited to individuals who play a role in *Isle of Canes*.

The
Family of
Coincoin & Pierre *

| Marie Thérèse *dite* Coincoin | 1766-1784 | Claude Thomas Pierre Metoyer |

Marie Thérèse *dite* Coincoin
St. Denis-De Soto slave
22 Aug. 1742 - Spring 1816
Freed 1778 by Pierre Metoyer

Claude Thomas Pierre Metoyer
b. 12 Mar. 1744 France
d. 30 Sep. 1815 Cane River
m. 13 Oct. 1788 Marie Thérèse Buard

Dominique
(Continued)

Eulalie
b. 14 Jan. 1776
d. young

Antoine Joseph
b. 26 Jan. 1778
d. 9 Oct. 1838
m. 1 Jun. 1801
Pelagie Le Court†

Marie Françoise Rosalie
b. 9 Dec. 1780
d. young

Pierre Toussaint
b. 10 Oct. 1782
d. 17 Feb. 1863
Never married

François
b. 26 Sep. 1784
d. 28 Dec. 1862
m. 1804 & 1815
Marguerite La Fantasy
& Arthemise Dupart

M. Marguerite
1817-1899
m. J. Emanuel Dupré
• **Joseph E., Jr.**
(1834-c.1900)
m. Elise Antonia Metoyer
& Perine Metoyer

Ambroise Chastain Dominique
b. 1819-*aft*1870
m. Osine LaBaume†

Marie Cephalide
1821-c1842
m. J. B. Mariotte
dit St. Ville

Marie Louise Théotise
1824/25-*aft*1851
m. Marin Rachal

Marguerite "Zelmie" Artemise
1826 - 1850-60
m. F. Vilcour Metoyer

Marie Lise
1828-*aft*1870
m. L. T. B. Le Court†

Marie Susanne
1802-1803

Marie Aspasie
b. 1804 - 1850-60
m. Seraphin Llorens

Marie Desneiges
b. 1806-*aft*1870
m. Pierre Metoyer III

Joseph Jr.
b. 1807-*bef*1860
m. Doralise Coindet
& Lodoiska Llorens

Separated c1808-17

Joseph Zenon
b. 1818-*bef*1838

Marie Elina
b. 1821-*aft*1867
m. Théophile
Louis Metoyer

Marie Celina
b. c1821/23-c1852/53
m. Augustin
Maximin Metoyer

St. Sibor Hypolite
b. 1827-*aft*1861
m. Julia Chevalier

By Marguerite La Fantasy

Marie Adelaïde
c1805-*aft*1860
m. Jerome Sarpy Sr.

Joseph François I
1807-*aft*1870
m. Desirée Cotonmaïs

By Arthemise Dupart

Marie Susette
1816-*aft*1850

Joseph François II
aka **Joseph Clervil**
1819-*aft*1870
(1) M. Cécile Chevalier
(2) M. Louise Vienne

Le Court-Lecomte-Rachal[*]
Connections

Étienne Le Roy
(Soldier) b. Paris
d. 1742-47 Natchitoches

m.
c1734 Louisiana

Louise Françoise Guillot
("Casket girl") b. Paris
d. 19 Oct. 1756 Natchitoches

Pierre Rachal *dit* St. Denis
(Soldier) b. 37 Jan. 1698 Ile d'Oléron, Fr.
d. 19 Apr 1756 Natchez, Miss. River

m.
c1721 Louisiana

Marianne Benoist
("Casket girl") b. 1697 Palace of Versailles
d. 15 Nov. 1754 Natchitoches

Jeanne Le Roy
b. *c* Oct. 1735 Natchitoches
d. 3 Nov. 1777 Rivière aux Cannes
Plaçage 1757-65, then marriage to the noble
Lt. Louis Matthias Le Court de Prelle
b. 24 Feb. 1717 Corantine-Quimper, Bretagne
d. 1783 Rivière aux Cannes

└ **Barthelemy Le Court** (1763-1833)
Liaison:
1783 Marie Magdeline Lecomte
└ **Pelagie**, who m. **Joseph Metoyer**

Plaçages:
1790-c1813 Ursulle (Canneci Indian)
1817-c1825 Adelaïde Mariotte (Coincoin's niece)

Marguerite Le Roy
b. 31 Jan. 1741 Natchitoches
d. c1804 Rivière aux Cannes
m. 3 Jul. 1756
Jean Baptiste Lecomte (French soldier)
d. 28 May 1784 Rivière aux Cannes
(*See Lecomte Slave Roots Chart*)

├ **Ambroise Lecomte** (1760-1830)
m. Hélène Cloutier
(*See Lecomte Slave Roots Chart*)
└ **Marie Françoise Lecomte** (1702-1806)
m. 1780 Joseph Dupré
(*See Lecomte-Dupré-Poissot Chart*)
m. 1780 Alexis Cloutier

Marie Louise Le Roy
b. 19 Apr. 1738 Natchitoches
d. Fall 1788 Rivière aux Cannes
m. 23 Jul 1753 Louis Rachal

Marie Elisabeth Rachal
b. May 1729 Natchitoches
m. 6 Jun 1748
Mathieu Monet (French soldier)
└ **Louis Monet** (1753-1804)
By liaisons, father of:
Dorothée, whose dau. m. **Pierre Metoyer**
Nicolas François, born to Coincoin's Fanchon
Louis, b. to Fanny's dau. M. Louise Lecomte
(*See Lecomte Slave Roots Chart*)

m. 2 Mar 1767 Pointe Coupée
J. B. Alexis Cloutier (Canadian)
Settled at Rivière aux Cannes

├ **Hélène Cloutier** (1767-1825)
m. **Ambroise Lecomte** (1760-1830)

└ **Alexis Cloutier** (1769-1836)
m. Marie Françoise Lecomte
Liaison 1796 with Dorothée Monet
└ **Henriette**, who m. **Pierre Metoyer**

Louis Rachal
b. c1733 Natchitoches
d. aft Aug 1815 Rivière aux Cannes
├ **Julien Rachal** (1760-1810)
└ **Jean Baptiste Louis Rachal** (1777-aft1820)
Placage: 1796-c1816 Françoise Lecomte
(See *Lecomte Slave Roots Chart*)

---

*Limited to individuals who play a role in *Isle of Canes*
All Metoyers listed on this chart of sons of Coincoin

The
Lecomte-Dupré-Poissot*
Connections

Jean Baptiste Lecomte
(Soldier) b. France
d. 28 May 1784 Rivière aux Cannes

m.
3 Jul 1756
Marguerite Le Roy
b. 31 Jan 1741 Natchitoches
d. c1804 Rivière aux Cannes

**Anne Marie Philippe
Tedt *dite* Scoup**
b. 18 Jun. 1709 Ittlingen, Germany
d. 21 Sep. 1781 Natchitoches

Jacques Dupré
(Soldier) b. c1700 Paris
d. 1736 Natchitoches

Lt. Remy Poissot
b. 1706 Dijon, France
d. 1788 Natchitoches

Louise Marguerite Lecomte
b. Apr 1757 Natchitoches
d. *aft* Jan 1825 Rivière aux Cannes
m. 1769 Jean Baptiste Dupré
 1786 Louis Monet
  (*See Le Court-Lecomte-Rachal Chart*)
  By *liaison* with dau. of Coincoin's Fanchon
  └─**Louis Monette,** freed by his father's widow

Jean Baptiste Dupré
b. 1731 German Coast of Louisiana
d. 1781 Rivière aux Cannes
Owned Fanchon, dau. of Coincoin

Ambroise Lecomte
b. 1760 Rivière aux Cannes
d. 1830 Shallow Lake, Cane River
m. 1783 Hélène Cloutier
(*See Le Court-Lecomte-Rachal Chart*)
 └─ Jean Baptiste Lecomte
   └─ **Ambroise Lecomte**
      (b. 1807)
By liaisons, Ambrose fathered
Thérèse, who m. **Louis Metoyer**
Marie Louise, mother of Louis Monette
(*See Lecomte Slave Roots Chart*)

Marie Catherine Dupré
m. 1743 P. J. F. B. Vildec *dit* Perot
 └─ **Remy Perot**
   b. 1765, Bayou Pierre

Joseph Dupré I
b. 1735 Natchitoches
d. 1782 Rivière aux Cannes
m. 1757 Marie de l'Incarnacion Derbanne
 Owned 3 children of François & Fanny
 (Dgimby, Choera, & Jeanne)

Marie Françoise Lecomte
b. 1762 Rivière aux Cannes
d. Jul 1806 Rivière aux Cannes
m. 1780 Joseph Dupré II
 1788 Alexis Cloutier
  (*See Le Court-Lecomte-Rachal Chart*)
  By *liaison* with Dorothée Monet (dau. of Louis Monet)
  └─**Henriette,** who m. **Pierre Metoyer II**

Joseph Dupré II
m. Marie Françoise Lecomte
 └─**Joseph Dupré III**
   Plaçage with Adelaïde Mariotte
   (g-dau. of François & Fanny)

By liaisons, Jean Baptiste Lecomte fathered
Magdeleine, whose dau. m. **Antoine Joseph Metoyer**
Françoise, whose dau. m. **Pierre Metoyer II**
(*See Lecomte Slave Roots Chart*)

Athanase Poissot

Liaison c1770-72
Françoise
slave of Pierre Derbanne

m. 12 Apr. 1773
Manuela de Soto
dau. of *Marie de St. Denis*
(*See St. Denis Chart*)

 └─ **M. Agnes Poissot**
   b. c1770-72
   d. 1839 Isle of Canes
   m. 1792 **Nicolas Augustin Metoyer**

*Limited to individuals who play a role in *Isle of Canes*
All Metoyers listed on this chart are sons of Coincoin

The
Lecomte Slave Roots *

Jean Baptiste Lecomte
(d. 1784)

Note: Lecomte married in 1756, but his wife quit bearing children in 1762 at the age of 21.

Ambroise Lecomte
(1760-1830)

Note: This only son of Jean Baptiste Lecomte & Marguerite Le Roy wed Hélène Cloutier in 1783.

Liaison

Victoire Marguerite
"Negro," apparently African, purchased from his wife's sister, Mme. Louis Le Court

Magdeleine Lecomte, "mulatto"
b. 14 January 1769
Liaison, **Barthelemy Le Court**
└─ **Pelagie Le Court**, "quadroon"
b. 2 Apr. 1781, freed by father
m. 1 June 1801 **Joseph Metoyer**

Françoise Lecomte, "mulatto"
b. c1771
└─ **Perine Lecomte**, "mulatto"
b. 1786, father unidentified
Given by Widow Lecomte to her grandson, Joseph Dupré III
Freed by Augustin Metoyer, 1801
m. 1802 **Pierre Metoyer II**

Liaison, **Louis Metoyer**
└─ **Catiche**, "pardo"
Freed by Coincoin, 1794

Rose, "pardo"
Freed by Augustin Metoyer, 1800
Plaçage, c1796-1816, **J. B. Louis Rachal**

Liaison

Marie
"Negro," purchased from his brother-in-law, Joseph Trichel, just after Marguerite's birth

Marguerite Lecomte, "mulatto"
b. cMay 1780
Freed by Coincoin, 1794
m. 19 Jan. 1795, **Dominique Metoyer**

Athanase Lecomte, "mulatto"
b. 15 Dec. 1781

Liaison

Thérèse
Canneci Indian, slave of Ambroise's uncle, Lt. Le Court

Jacques Ambroise Lecomte
b. 1779 (lived as white)
Freed and well provided-for by Ambroise, himself
m. (elopement) 23 June 1808
Natchez, Mississippi
Silvie Brosset (French)
└─ **Tranqueline Lecomte**

Thérèse Lecomte
b. c1781 (lived as "colored")
Apparently freed by Lecomtes
m. 9 Feb. 1801, **Louis Metoyer**

Liaison

Françoise "Fanchon"
"Griffe," dau. of Coincoin & Chatta owned by Ambroise's sister, the wife of Jean Baptiste Dupré

Marie Louise Lecomte, "mulatto"
b. 26 Nov. 1781
Freed by son Louis, 1835
Liaison, 1802, **Louis Monet** (her master)
└─ **Louis Monette**, "quadroon"
b. 25 Dec. 1802
Freed by his father's widow
(Ambroise's sister),
Marguerite Lecomte, 1825

Ethnic terms used in French and Spanish records:
griff(e) = Indian-African; or Indian-African-white
mulatto = ½ African, ½ white
pardo = light brown
quadroon = ¼ African, ¾ white

* Limited to individuals who play a role in *Isle of Canes*
All Metoyers listed on this chart are sons of Coincoin

PROLOGUE

Circa 1900

The Memory-Keeper

A pall, as insensible as death itself, gripped the crowd that ringed the old plantation manse. Walls quivered and flames belched through scores of broken panes as the inferno caged inside Augustin Manor threatened to explode two solid feet of massive brick laid by long-forgotten slaves. Then a rumble rose deep from the belly of the relic and its inner walls collapsed, taking with them floors of parqueted hardwood that once had shone like Cane River under an August moon. The mansion from which the Isle of Canes had once been ruled would see no more balls, no more satin slippers, no more upswept curls coiled around tea roses and hibiscus blossoms. Tonight only the flames danced, reddening the evening sky with frenzied sweeps and bows in mockery of the *fais-do-dos* of those who had lived inside those walls, and the hoedowns of those who had lived and labored on its lands.

Above the rumbling, seething crackle, a baby's wail pierced the miasma. Somewhere a man laughed nervously, shucking some edge of remorse he was not used to feeling.

"Good riddance!" he muttered. "That dilapidated eyesore should have been pulled down a long time ago." Around him some faces stared, masking the hostility they dared not show, but most murmured their assent.

The spell was broken. Here and there a few somber figures clustered, cemented by memories they shared but could not speak. In other circles, hushed whispers turned to chatter and the *coup de grâce* of the old showplace became just another spectacle—a brief reprieve to the restlessness that cankered this stretch of river where newcomers and their ways had displaced all that was sacred.

In the moss-draped shadows of the live oak that had reigned as long as she remembered, an old woman stood mutely planted, with a slender stripling of a lad clutching at her gnarled hands.

"Tante Perine?"

She did not seem to hear him. For her, for just this moment, there was no crowd, no callous chitchat, just the tinkle of laughter as children played Nip 'n Tuck on Easter mornings. There was no inferno, but the coziness of a marble fireplace on chilly evenings as young ones gathered around Grandpère's rocker and he wove a spell that swept them back to a different time when Louisiana belonged to France and Spain.

"Look at that!" A low voice came from somewhere outside the shadows. Perine heard the voice, but she could not put a face with it. It did not fit into her past.

"Would you just look at that, Ada Bell?" the voice repeated. "That old darkie's crying!"

Perine's reverie was broken. Ada Bell. Ada Bell Mackey. Perine knew all the Mackeys. Pain, real pain, sliced into the heart she thought this inferno would char forever.

"Shhh." Ada Bell's stage-whisper shushed her friend. " 'Course she's crying, darling, but don't call her a *darkie!*"

"But I thought that's what you Southerners called them."

"Oh, you ninny! That's *Tante Perine* you're talking about. She's no darkie. She's a *Metoyer!*"

"A what?"

"A *Metoyer.* They're the people who built this place. That's why she's crying. She lived here when she was young—back before that war y'all started."

"*We* started?" The stranger's voice rose in pique, but then he laughed. "You'll not get me riled again, Ada Bell. I will just let that one pass. Still, I'll admit I don't understand you Southerners at all. Black or white. You talk like you despise each other, but at times you really seem to care. Here you are feeling sorry for that old woman, and there she is crying over the house of white folks who kept her a slave."

"Do *what?* A slave? Darling! Wherever did you go to school? No, don't tell me! You already did. You went to one of those fancy places Up East where everybody goes but nobody learns anything—leastways, not about the South. Honey, I've just gotta sit you down and give you a history lesson!"

The stranger's voice cut Ada Bell off with another low laugh. "But not now, *dahlin',*" he murmured. "The moon is ripe and there's a scent of magnolias all around us that even the smoke can't hide...." His voice grew softer, huskier. Perine could not hear the rest of his words, just Ada Bell's giggle.

"Tante Perine?" The little boy tried again. "You alright, Tante Perine?"

For a while, still, she was silent, immobilized by too many years and too many dreams that seemed gone forever, like Grandpère's house now was. But then the ancient shoulders squared, her jaw jutted forward, and her eyes softened as they always did when little Gustin came around.

"*Oui, cher.* Come. Let's go home, child. There is nothing we can do here."

They trudged along the moss-strewn road that wound down Cane River, the din of the crowd trailing off behind them. Again, it was Gustin who broke the silence.

"Tante Perine, why didn't folks try t' save it? When ol' Mr. Mackey's kitchen catched itself on fire las' year, everbody lined up gettin' water from the river. They put out *his* fire."

Perine groped for an answer, one the child could understand. Gustin was so full of questions no one liked to hear, much less answer. But, then, that was one of the reasons she loved this child so much more than any of the dozens who called her *tante.* It was not just that he was prettier. *Sur ma foi!* He was a beautiful boy, with skin the color of broth into which a bit of olive oil had been stirred and blue eyes that danced like cloud puffs on a breezy morn. He was smart, too, even though his grammar clearly showed that he spent far more time in the fields than the schoolroom.

Non, Gustin was different because he *cared.* More than any other child who carried the name *Metoyer,* he *cared.* When Perine looked at Gustin, she saw hope. All the fires and wars and droughts and floods and *people* God had sent to test them would never wipe out what used to be—what could be again—as long as it lived on in hearts like hers and young Gustin's.

"*Ah, mon cher,*" the old woman sighed as they turned up the narrow path that led to her little cabin. "Grandpère's house burned today because our people have lost hope and others just do not care. That is why the *étrangers* who own Grandpère's land now let his house run down. It means nothing to them. That is why those there tonight made no move to put out the fire. They do not care either—or maybe they just do not know—how Grandpère's door and Grandpère's heart were open to everyone, even *étrangers.* You see, child, *no one cares now about the way things used to be.* Those outsiders, they have looked all these years at Grandpère's Big House and they've seen just another relic, of no use for anything but firewood, taking up land on which they could plant more cotton."

Only her flip of the latch on the old iron gate, a bit more forceful than it needed to be, betrayed the anger Perine tried to wash from her soul every Sabbath eve in St. Augustin's confessional. Thirty years had passed since she had closed the door to Grandpère's mansion-house, resolutely handed the key to that *outsider* who had paid the overdue taxes, and moved Grandpère's best things through this little door she opened now for Gustin. Time had not eased the pain of that day, nor the feeling that she did not belong here, inside these walls that once had housed a family of their slaves. *Non!* This hut of bousillage with its baked-clay hearth was but a stage in time, a place to regroup—but never rest—until her family recovered the life that was their birthright.

"But we coulda saved it, Tante Perine. There wuz lots o' us there. I seen Oncle Pierre an' François an' Colas an' cousin Noel an'...."

Perine lit the old kerosene lamp that had stood so long on Grandpère's *bibliothèque*, and by the flare of its light Gustin read his own answer in her weary face. Still, she answered him, carefully measuring her words while she rekindled enough coals to warm their supper.

"Gustin, your *oncles,* the old ones, they are losing hope. The older they get and the more time passes, the less they remember. The less they *believe* that things can be right for us again. And you young ones? Ah, *cher!* You children grow up knowing nothing but the way life is around you. Every time you have to say 'Yes, sir' and 'No, ma'am' to the Mackeys, it makes you forget that your blood is just as good. Or better.

"*Non*, child, it just does not seem real to any of you now when I tell you it is *our* Big House the Mackeys live in at Yucca Bend! It was ours before the Mackeys ever came to Natchitoches Parish or to the Isle. It could be ours again one day if we all set our minds to it."

"Wuz that what *she* used t' say, Tante Perine?"

"*Hehn?* Who, child?"

"Grandpère's mother. The one you talked about t'other night to papa, when he tol' you he wuz gonna start croppin' for the Mackeys."

She could not stop it, the sudden rush of images that swept her back into Grandpère's stories and turned her hoary two-room cabin into another. One that smelled, always, of gardenias, with wood shavings in a corner basket and a freshly carved doll or toy or trinket on the mantel waiting to surprise the next set of wee ones who stopped in to see their Mère Coincoin. Then the cabin grew and spread until it was Grandpère's Big House and there was a life-sized doll of crackled ebony, lifeless in a green sateen dress, lying in state in the middle of Grandpère's big four-poster—the bed a distant forebear had once carved for his princess. But then the smell of gumbo, bubbling in the old iron kettle behind the hearth, chased away those memories and brought Perine back to the present.

"Oui, mon petit. Coincoin was her name, and that is what she taught us. We can be anything we want to be, do anything we want to do, if we *believe.* Grandpère believed, and he made himself the greatest man this Isle has ever known. You can, too. You have his name, child. You have his heart. You have that same way of staring into life head-on and searching for its answers."

"What'd she look like, Tante Perine?" Gustin persisted, once he emptied the bowl she had set before him. "I see Grandpère's big picture every time I come here, and I seen all the others ol' Miz Mackey shows off to everybody like she done painted 'em all herself. But I ain't never seed one for Coincoin. Did she look like them? Or you? Or me?"

Perine smiled in spite of herself and shook her head. *"Non,* child. She was just as beautiful as you, but in a different way. Coincoin was as black as that little colt you helped your *oncle* foal last year—and just as frisky and bold. She was born a slave, but they could never make her *feel* like one. They could tie her up but they could not fence her in, because she was born to be free, just like your colt."

"But he ran off…," the child began, a shadow flickering across his finely chiseled face.

"Oui, cher. He did. In that way, Coincoin was different, too. She would not run. She never ran from any person or any fight, and she taught her children not to, either. That is what we are all doing wrong now, child! We are running from our problems. We have given in. Too many of us have just plain given in!"

Perine's old voice trembled from the weight of nearly a half-century of hurt and hunger. Heaving herself from the old rosewood chair that once graced Grandpère's library, she began to clear the table—the cheap, pine slab that served as one. For the thousandth time, she chastised herself for giving in when Mrs. Mackey pleaded for Grandpère's fine old mahogany table, shipped all the way from France, with its massive revolving tray built into the center. Another family treasure gone. And for a basket of store-bought food.

"Sur ma foi!" Perine exclaimed, as much to herself as to the child. "We have let the Mackeys and all their kind do it to us. Your *oncles* have, your papa and

mama, even I have. But do not let them do it to you, *cher!* Do not settle for what the world expects of *darkies,* as that man called us, when you know you are a *Metoyer!* Do not let yourself lose sight of all the good you can do for your people and the world itself. Coincoin never did! And her children never did. That is how the Metoyers became so great back before the war."

Even by the lantern light, she could see the fine blond hairs knit themselves across his slender brow. "But how'd they do it, Tante? How'd Coincoin get free if'n she didn't run 'way? An' why didn't she have to say 'Yas'm' to the Mackeys?"

She almost smiled then, at the simpleness with which children see the world. As she wiped the crumbs of corn bread he had dropped from his plate, one gnarled hand, spotted with years, tousled his rumpled curls affectionately, reassuring herself as much as this boy before her.

"*Ah, chien-chien!* The Mackeys were not even here then. But there were others just like them."

Gustin's eyes did not yield, and the old woman sighed. I am too old, she thought. No wonder the young ones do not understand me any more. I talk about worlds they have never known. Things they simply cannot imagine.

She wavered. He stared. And then, for an aching moment, life almost broke the soul of Marie Perine Metoyer Metoyer Dupré. *Madame* François Gassion Metoyer, she had once been to all who called at her door, hat in hand. The chatelaine of Augustin Manor. She, whose family owned and filled the front pews of the Church of St. Augustin, while the white planters and their wives rented the pews behind them. Indeed, that last was the memory that made the gravity of their fall almost more than even she could bear.

And so, Perine tossed her dishcloth down onto the old sideboard, turned her back on the pan of soapy dishes and a lifetime of habit, and settled into the old rocker that had been Grandpère's and Coincoin's before him. Making space beside her on the cushion she had patched a dozen times, she beckoned Gustin to join her.

"Come, *cher.* It is long past time for me to tell you about Coincoin and Grandpère and the Metoyers and this Isle that once was ours. Tonight, Gustin, you need to know—before the world turns you into what others want you to be, instead of what you are."

Augustin Manor

This sketch, made from a photograph taken shortly before its burning, depicts a home about 130 feet long by 80 feet deep, constructed of slave-made bricks, with walls two feet thick. By the time this image was captured in the late-nineteenth century, the walls were crumbling and their original crown of cypress shingles had been supplanted by a roof of tin. Doors of carved oak and etched glass had been stripped and sold, replaced by cheap slabs and wire screens. Windows had been boarded, and the moss-draped oaks that once stood sentinel had been rooted from the soil so the estate grounds could be profitably planted in the South's "white gold."

PART ONE

1742–1758

The Promise

Baptism of Marie Thérèse dite Coincoin, 1742
Parish of St. François des Natchitoches

L'an mil sept cent quarante deux le vingt quatre août, je soussigné prêtre Capucin ai baptisé Marie Thérèse, Negritte appartenant à Mr. de St. Denis, Commandant de ce poste. Le parrain a été Mr. de Lachaise et la marraine Damoiselle Marie de St. Denis, en foi de quoi j'ai signé. Pᵉ Arcange, Capucin.

"In the year seventeen hundred and forty two, the twenty-fourth of August, I, the undersigned Capuchin priest, have baptized Marie Thérèse, an infant Negro girl belonging to Mr. de St. Denis, Commandant of this post. The godfather has been Mr. de la Chaise and the godmother, Demoiselle Marie de St. Denis. In testimony whereof, I have signed. Father Arcange, Capuchin."

⚖ 1 ⚖

24 August 1742

In nómine Patris, et Fílii, et Spíritus Sancti…

Through the stillness of the early morning, François could hear the prayers of Père Arcange droning to a close as they crossed the *place d'armes* and stopped before the door of the church. The infant stirred in his arms. Her small black face nudged hungrily against his breast, and he passed the child to its mother.

Dóminus vobíscum…

The ritual blessing of the priest wafted through the open doorway, and his flock softly responded *et cum spíritu tuo.*

François paced the stones that paved the entrance way, his body a stocky, tightly wound coil of steel-laced muscle. Again he felt it as he passed the open door, that uneasiness that nagged him every time he knelt at Sunday Mass with M'sieur's family, every time Madame called her *nègres* and her children into her little chapel for their catechism. In seven winters François had learned the tongues these people spoke and all but forgotten his own, but the gods his grandfather taught him had not been replaced by the one these milk-white people bowed before.

Ite, Missa est. Vade in pace. The Mass is ended, go in peace.

Wooden rosaries clicked, skirts rustled, and the recessional began. A typical daily Mass, François mused, as the faithful filed through the broad double doorway. A dozen or so women, all aged, except for Madame and her children. The commandant's family always filled his pew, with or without him. But usually without him.

"*Hé!*" The niggling doubts that always seemed to hover just beyond François's sight suddenly came into focus. *That* was why this God had no meaning for him! The religion of the white men was not the white *men's* faith. It belonged to the women. The men built this house of communion, but they came only for celebrations. The men cried *Mon Dieu* with every other breath, but it was their womenfolk who bowed their heads in daily prayer. Their priest was a man, but even he wore long skirts and denied himself his very manhood!

St. François Church
Poste St. Jean Baptiste des Natchitoches

When Commandant Louis Juchereau de St. Denis inventoried church property on 9 May 1738, he described the chapel: "Twenty feet long and twenty-four wide, built on nine foot logs, with double beams filled in between with mud. The same Church has six windows with shutters and iron work, a big double door with iron work, a small door with a lock. The said building is roofed with shingles on planks without fancy work. Everything being new." Also inventoried was the "thirteen and a half pound bell, set up aside the church."

The church bell tolled the end of Mass, but the pride that swelled each time he heard its peal gave way now to an empty truth. He had taken the iron the Reverend Père had ordered up from New Orleans and he had molded it into music, but the god he honored when he forged that churchyard bell could never be *his* own.

The infant whimpered softly, and its mother began to croon the song Madame had taught her. *Ave María, grátia plena, Dóminus tecum.* Unbidden, his loins tightened as he gazed upon his wife and the child she had just borne him. His woman was strong, a statuesque goddess of deepest ebony, with a high, queenly forehead below her close-sheared crown of plush black nap. Her nose flared nobly, and her deep-ruby mouth was full and generous, softly shaped now as she sang her song of mother-love. But François knew the power and heat that burned inside those lips.

Oui, Fanny was strong. Still it was not a physical strength that had brought her from her bed, just hours after childbirth, to see her infant baptized at the holy font. It was faith. Simple, unquestioning faith. Fanny could believe in the god of this new world. She did believe. But he could not.

"Time, François," she had promised him. "Time will make the difference. I came here as a girl. You came as a man. In a year, two years, you will see the power of this God, and you will believe." But François knew now no time could bridge the chasm. He would never believe because he was a *man,* because here there was no god in which *men* believed.

"*Bonjour,* Fanny. François."

The stridency of the voice startled François from his musing. For a moment he almost lost the composure that long since had won for him the respect of his master and the suspicion of his master's wife. His eyes hardened, then hooded themselves with caution, as his mistress glided toward them, moving with a grace curious for so plump a form. Emanuela María Stefania Sanchez-Navarro Juchereau de St. Denis was shorter than most women at the post. Yet she managed to look down upon everyone she met, and the inches her stature lacked were well augmented by the raven braids she piled above her higher than the triple-crowned tiaras of the bishops she had known in Mexico.

"Père is almost ready for the baptism," Emanuela announced. "Monsieur de la Chaise is coming now from the *magazin.* Your child has been very honored, you know, by his consent to be her godfather. It is not every slave child who has an

15

important official for its *parraine.*" Emanuela's fan fluttered in the stale summer air, sweeping away the fly that buzzed in and out of the folds of her mantilla.

"But of course we will still wait for Monsieur. He takes these matters very seriously, I assure you. The management of this frontier is never so heavy a burden that he would neglect the spiritual needs of the souls we hold in trust for God. As I tell you and our other *nègres* so often, it is *such an honor* that God has chosen us to be the instrument of your salvation!"

Emanuela's chatter rolled on. Three times before, François thought, his Fanny had produced an infant for the greater fortune of M'sieur de St. Denis and the greater glory of Madame's god. Three times before, he had taken that infant to the Reverend Père for baptism as the law prescribed, and each time Madame had told him how *honored* she was that God had blessed her and the great M'sieur so generously.

By now, François could recite by heart the story of her childhood, the years she had been taught her catechism in a school she called a *convent,* and the end-less prayers she had raised to heaven that her god would find a way to use her for his glory. And again, as her litany invoked his own searing memories of the Mexican port in which he had been sold, his heart argued that she was using *him*—for far more than the mere toil a slave was expected to provide.

"Ah, my man François!"

A booming voice cut into Emanuela's prattle, and François masked a smile at the sight that greeted him. Sieur Louis Juchereau de St. Denis was as resplendent as usual. Most men at this frontier outpost went about in frayed shirts of coarse linen and breeches of ticking, but M'sieur le Commandant never let himself be seen without his braid-trimmed surtout and India breeches, his silken hose and silver knee buckles. Even on so routine a matter as the baptism of another slave child, the commandant's only concession to the August heat was the substi-tution of a pale blue taffeta with silver trim for his preferred surtouts of scarlet damask and golden braid.

"What do we have here this time, my man? Another son to whom you can teach your many skills—or a daughter with her mother's sable beauty?"

"A girl-child, M'sieur," François replied, with a nod of deference prompted more by a respect for the man than by a fear of the master.

"Hehn? Another daughter! Well, what do we call this one? As I recollect, I named your first one Gertrude after my own saintly babe, God rest her soul,

but you insist upon calling your child Dgimby or something of the sort. You know, the Reverend Père is scandalized over that. Every time you bring that girl to church he reminds me that no saint ever lived by such a name and declares me derelict in my Christian duty because I humor you."

François was not surprised that his master's tone mocked the reproof his words contained. He well knew by now that M'sieur lost no sleep over chastisement from a priest. A string of clerics had come and gone on this frontier while St. Denis remained entrenched—and it was no coincidence that their departures followed an occasion when their crucible crossed with the commandant's sword.

"Ah, too," St. Denis continued with his small talk while Père Arcange dismissed the last of his lingering flock. "It seems to me we named your firstborn François, the same honorable saint's name I gave you at baptism, but you insist upon calling the boy Choera. Eh?"

"There's less confusion that way, M'sieur," François parried with a shrug.

"*Oui, oui.* You have a point, François. You have a point. So, for the sake of less confusion, what do you plan to call this child?"

"With your leave, M'sieur… Coincoin*. In the tongue of our people, it is the name given to all second-born daughters."

"Then Coincoin it is. Unofficially, of course. She'll still need a Christian name. I assume Madame has told you that Mademoiselle Marie will be this babe's godmother? Madame feels it will be good spiritual training for our daughter." His voice lowered discreetly. "Of course, just between us, I suspect the child has not the slightest notion of what a baptism is all about."

"*Possible,* M'sieur. But perhaps both of you are right. When one is eight years old, one sees a baby as a plaything, not a soul." François carefully turned off all expression from his face as he continued. "Still, I am sure that Madame will find a way to teach ma'mselle something from this occasion…."

Pax vobis… Peace be with you.

The chatter ceased as Père Arcange intoned the opening words of ceremony from the doorway of the mud and cypress cabin someone had grandly named L'Eglise de St. François. His voice was low and soft, a rhythmic monotone with no trace of monotony, and François's tension eased in spite of himself. Of all the traits of this religion he had cataloged to date, the hypnotic intonations of a language spoken only by the priest was the only one that stirred his soul.

---

*Pronounced KońKwṅ, the name is from the Glidzi dialect of the Ewe people of Togo.

Quo nómine vocáris?

"Marie Thérèse, Your Reverence," the godfather responded as he took the sleeping babe from her mother's arms and presented her at the doorway, routinely assuming the spiritual role of surrogate father.

"If, then, you wish to enter into life," Père Arcange droned over the sleeping infant, "keep the commandments: You shall love the Lord your God with your whole heart, and with your whole soul, and with your whole mind, and your neighbor as yourself."

Three times the rotund priest blew into the infant's face. "Depart from her, unclean spirit, and give place to the Holy Spirit, the Consoler. Receive the mark of the cross on your forehead and within your heart. So live that you will indeed be a temple of God."

The air hung still and humid as they moved, then, into the sacristy of white-washed *bousillage*. Through the unpaned windows, a fierce sun probed all the corners, stretched toward the altar, and then beamed as it saw its own reflection in the golden monstrance and silver chalice that adorned the antipedium of the altar. Inside, François shifted his weight, restlessly, checking the impulse to settle comfortably upon his haunches.

"*C'est impropre!*" Madame had once admonished him. "You may *kneel* in church, at the proper moments, but you must not *squat.*"

Accípite sal sapiéntiae: propitiátio sit tibi in vitam aetérnam. Receive salt, which is the symbol of wisdom. May it bring you God's favor for life everlasting.

The infant stirred as the grain was placed into her mouth. François could almost taste its bitterness. Seven Holy Seasons had come and gone since the Christmas he had been brought into this chapel for his own baptism. A *brut nègre* they had called him, a black man thrust among whites, bewildered by a world for which nothing in his own had prepared him. That grain of salt had brought him the promised wisdom, but as yet he had seen no sign of favors from this god.

Marie Thérèse, credis in Deum Patrem omnipoténtem, creatórem coeli et terrae? Do you believe in God, the Father Almighty, creator of heaven and earth?

"I do believe," the infant's godfather answered in her stead, as ritual required.

Marie Thérèse, credis in Jesum Christum, Fílium ejus únicum, Dóminum nostrum, natum, et passum? Do you believe in Jesus Christ, his only Son, our Lord, who was born into this world and who suffered?

Again, the ceremonial reply, "I do believe."

But what if she doesn't? François argued mutely. You can answer for her now, M'sieur de la Chaise, just as M'sieur the surgeon answered for me that Christmas when I was as ignorant of your god as my girl-child is today. But when we meet your god—if we meet your god!—we must answer for ourselves. How will we answer then?

Viz baptizari? Do you wish to be baptized?

"I do." Again the godfather intoned the expected answer, as the little godmother twisted her damp locks and looked about her for a place to sit. Madame frowned. Her child stiffened.

Ego te baptízo in nómine Patris, et Fílii, et Spíritus Sancti. I baptize you in the name of the Father and of the Son and of the Holy Spirit.

The infant cried, lustily, as the stream of water from an upturned urn traced a cross upon her forehead. Fanny's grip tightened on François's arm, and he saw a tear wind down her face. He had not seen her cry since the morning they had first stood together in this church, two weeks after his arrival at the post, and exchanged vows with words he could not understand but whose meaning was clear enough. She had cried tears of sorrow then, but this was one of joy. That much he understood, although there was much else about this woman he could not fathom. He had sired four children by her since M'sieur bought her from Sergeant Rachal and gave her to him as his wife. She had moved into his bed upon command—and unexpectedly into his heart—but he still did not understand her any more than he could grasp this god Madame had taught her to love.

Accípite vestem candidam, quam pérferas immaculátam… et irrepresehensibílis custódi baptísmum tuum. Receive this white garment. Never let it become stained… and keep the grace of your baptism throughout a blameless life.

The wee *marraine,* short and plump in the way of her mother, tugged upon the blanket that wrapped the newborn child. Smiling, De la Chaise lowered the fretting babe for little Marie to see. A tiny black fist flailed and caught a pudgy white one, as the godmother tiptoed to her highest and kissed her godchild's cheek. The whimpering ceased. The little church grew still. And the child's father fought back tears of his own.

∽ 2 ∽
November 1743

François rapped discreetly on the commandant's office door, lifted the latch, and stepped inside without waiting for his master to bid him enter. Rusting iron creaked as the slab of splintered cypress closed behind him, and he made a mental note to grease the hinges the first free moment he might have.

It was an endless battle he waged—they all waged—against the elements here at the westernmost outpost of France's colonial empire. A quarter-century had passed since King Louis's troops had invaded the lands of the Natchitoches Indians and cleared this stretch of Red River they called the Cane. They had thrown up buildings to punctuate the point that the Natchitoches nation was now off-limits to missionaries from Mexico and that the Red River was a line crusading Spaniards should not cross. But the God of Nature that had ruled Red River for eons longer had proved their greatest foe. Spring floods and summer fevers respected nothing. They permeated every token of civilization the Frenchmen planted in their soil, and were it not for the will of a single man and the respect he earned from those who both feared and followed him, Poste Jean Baptiste des Natchitoches would have long since surrendered to rust and rot.

"You sent for me, M'sieur?"

"*Oui,* François." The old commandant turned from the window as he spoke and limped slowly back to his desk.

The arthritis is getting worse, François noted with a twinge of worry…. *M'sieur's troubles weigh more heavily on him every day.* But then he snorted to himself at the irony of life. *M'sieur may be a nobleman and master of everything in sight, but man is never so exalted that the gods cannot find a way to humble him. This proud peacock the Indians once called* belles jambes, *beautiful legs, will soon be a helpless cripple.*

"François, my man." St. Denis barely paused as he heaved his frame into the oversized chair François had carved for him two winters before, then nodded in the general direction of the fireplace. "This gentleman is Señor Delago, senior aide to His Excellency, Justo Boneo y Morales, the new governor of *Tejas*. Señor Delago and I have an assignment for you tonight—one of considerable importance to us all."

François's eyebrows almost cocked at the exuberance in his master's voice,

an enthusiasm the old commandant rarely showed these days. "*Certainement,*
M'sieur.*" François turned as he spoke, dutifully acknowledging the presence
of his master's guest with the bow that had been one of the first "refinements"
St. Denis had insisted upon his learning. "Seenyor Deel-agha...?" his tongue
tripped hesitantly over the Spaniard's name, and the visitor's taut mouth curled
into scorn.

"*No habla español, esclavon?*" The sneer in Delago's clipped Castillian was
plain as he raised his eyebrows at his host. "This is the Negro who is to handle
our transaction tonight, Señor?"

"I would have no other, Delago. I assure you, François is a trusted servant."

The Spaniard shrugged, while his reed-thin, white-gloved hand plucked lint
from the suit of unrelieved black he affected after the manner of continental
grandées. "It is certainly not my place to tell a man of your reputation how he
should conduct his affairs."

"Nor would I expect you to," St. Denis retorted, and the Mexican emissary
smiled back this time—a flash of perfect teeth that did nothing to soften the sting
of his thinly veiled sarcasm. Flinging his cape across girlish shoulders, Delago
stepped forward to extend his hand, forcing the old commandant to rise again,
and St. Denis clutched his desk for support as he leaned across it to return the
visitor's limp shake.

"*Con su permisso,*" Delago continued smoothly. "I believe we have concluded
our discussion, Señor. Since I have arrangements of my own to make before
tonight, I must ask your leave."

"Of course," St. Denis replied with strained civility, and François could not
help but notice the now-familiar note of weariness creeping back into his master's
voice. "Please give your illustrious governor my regards, and those of Madame
as well. She still recalls him fondly from her childhood, and it was a happy day
for both of us when we learned of his appointment to Los Adaës. Do tell our
old friend that we eagerly await his first visit."

"*Sí, señor.* The frontier is truly a lonely place for men of our rank, no?"
Delago simpered. "The company of rabble and *negros*—even comely ones—does
grow boresome."

"On the contrary, Delago. No man is boring, and station and color make
no difference."

21

The thin gash that marked the Spaniard's mouth twitched at the older man's terse rebuke. "I must say, Señor de San Denis, it has been an interesting morning. It is not often one has the opportunity to meet an adversary whose legend has spread throughout every capital city on the continent."

"Adversary, Delago? I thought you came here today in friendship?"

"*Mas o menos, señor.* Shall we say that I have come as the emissary of your friend and my governor? But the crown of Spain and the crown of France know better than to trust each other, even on this frontier."

Polished boot heels squeaked across the rough flooring as the envoy wheeled toward the door. "*A díos, señor comandante!*"

"God be with you, too," St. Denis echoed, but it was a snort he gave to François as Delago closed the door behind himself. "High heels, no less! A bantam who has to stand on a perch before he can hold his own with roosters is a man of little self-esteem and much deceit."

"I suspect you're right, M'sieur," François agreed politely.

"What's more, he thinks me a fool as well."

"Oh, no, M'sieur…"

"Oh, yes, François. But that's to my advantage, rest assured. Right now that little popinjay is wondering how I've managed to rule these borderlands for thirty years. The Indians love me, the Spaniards fear me, and he thinks me a senile old fool who puts his trust in ignorant *nègres.*" The commandant's weathered face cracked into a grin. "But, then, he does not know you yet, does he, my man?"

A sudden draft of chilled November air cut through the open shutters, and François hastily moved to latch them when he saw his master shiver.

"Delago tells me that the storehouses at Los Adaës are almost empty," St. Denis went on idly. "They didn't harvest enough corn there this fall to feed the soldiers through the winter, much less the settlers or the mission Indians. In fact, he says there is not enough to last the month, and I don't doubt it. Every year those damn fool Spaniards try to farm their red clay hills, and the more they plant the less they have. Governor Boneo's spies have reported the good crop we made here on the river, so he hopes we'll fill their grain bins for them."

"The regulations have been eased, M'sieur?" François asked warily.

"*Sacrebleu!* Those fools in Paris don't care what happens in the colony, so long as their pockets are lined. *Non,* François," St. Denis went on wearily, "trade between the Spanish post and ours is just as illegal as it ever was. Still, I can't sit here with a full storehouse while others starve a few leagues away."

"No, M'sieur."

"And besides, Delago has offered a generous price. Three *pesos* per bushel."

François whistled in appreciation, then quickly straightened his face as his master scowled. "Beg pardon, M'sieur," he mumbled.

M'sieur did not answer. Instead he rummaged deep in the drawer of his desk, and then his scowl grew darker as he shook the flask he had retrieved and realized it was empty.

"You finished that last week, M'sieur, when the *ordinateur* from New Orleans was here. Shall I go to the brandy shop for more?"

St. Denis tossed the empty bottle back into the drawer and slammed it shut. "No, never mind. Besides, I did not empty it *while* that prattling fool was here. I waited politely until he left. If I had gotten drunk before I shoved his pirogue down the river, I would have told him what I think of his damned governor and the council and their accursed refusal to pay me for all the presents I have to give these Indians. It takes more than a handful of trinkets to buy peace out here on King Louis's frontier."

"*Oui,* M'sieur," François murmured.

"*Merde,* François! That's why I took the Spaniard's offer for that grain. I'm not greedy, and I don't condone breaking rules without good reason. Last week I'd have *given* Boneo what he needs to keep that poor post from starving, but so long as my own governor forces me to buy the loyalty of all the western tribes out of my own pocketbook, then I have to have funds to do it. Last year alone put me twenty thousand *livres* in debt."

"*Oui,* M'sieur," François repeated, before proceeding cautiously. "About tonight, M'sieur?"

"*Mais oui...* tonight." The old Frenchman leaned forward thoughtfully, lightly juggling in his big gnarl of a hand the pouch of coins Delago had tossed onto his desk. "*Oui,* François. Tonight we make the first shipment."

"The first?"

"Even my governor has his spies—and even in my district. Prudence calls for several small deliveries. Delago's men will meet you in the woods behind my barns with three strings of pack mules, an hour past sundown. One hundred and fifty bushels should go overland by them. Get Caesar and a couple of his boys to help you."

"Joseph and Noël, M'sieur?"

"*Oui.* They'll do. On second thought, use Zenon, too. It will take three pirogues to haul the other hundred and fifty bushels I promised Delago for tonight. Let Caesar and his boys man those."

"And I, M'sieur?"

Coins jingled softly again as St. Denis resumed his absentminded juggling of the pouch. "You'll see that everything goes as planned, François, and collect the other half of my money. Delago paid 450 pesos in advance. He'll give you the balance after the grain is loaded into the government storehouse at Los Adaës."

"*Oui,* M'sieur," François hesitated momentarily before venturing to inquire. "And you trust him?"

"Not at all—under any other circumstance. But we have the upper hand in this matter, François. We have what he needs." Still, the old man's brows furrowed as he read the uneasiness lurking on his *nègre's* face. "You're skeptical?"

"For a man who needs what you have, M'sieur," François parried, "the Spaniard shows a considerable lack of deference."

The commandant cackled. "*Ma foi!* Strange you should say that! Did I ever tell you that Madame says the same about you? In her opinion, you show too great an inclination to judge your masters."

François stood there, blandly, and St. Denis grinned back, his humor now restored. For two decades he had maneuvered the French and the Spanish and a dozen tribes—all men of the same ilk, priests and politicians and hunters and warriors alike, regardless of the cut of their clothes or the color of their skin—across the untamed borderlands like human pawns on an undrawn chessboard and he had done it with one sole skill: his ability to read in men's eyes what their mouths did not say. As short as François might be on deference, he was long on loyalty and had damned good instincts of his own. That, alone, was worth more to Louis Juchereau de St. Denis than all the fancy work his Togo slave did with wood and metal.

And so, indulgently, the Frenchman leaned back in his chair and lit one of the long *cigarros* the Spanish governor had sent as a token of his goodwill.

"*Ça va,* François, tell me something. You're a man of some learning and worldly experience—granted, your world was much different from this one—but tell me anyway. How does this Señor Delago strike you?"

François's face tightened, hinting at a bitter memory. "In fact, M'sieur, the señor reminds me very much of my world…."

"Oh?"

"…and the jackal in the markets of Dakar who spit on my wares when I offered them to him at a fair price—then sent his henchmen to steal them from me that night because he knew mine was the finest metalwork there was."

"But in this case, François, the man in the marketplace has offered more than a fair price, and the goods are as much as his. What is there for him to steal?"

François shrugged, and his face went expressionless. "I'm only a *nègre*, M'sieur. Undoubtedly, I am wrong and you are right."

"*Zut*, François! Don't play that role with me. We respect each other too much for that. Still, if you're willing to gamble, you might load on some of that tobacco you grow in your spare time and see what kind of bargain you can strike for yourself."

François could not suppress the grin. "But, M'sieur! A French-speaking *nègre* in a nest of Spaniards? I am sure to be rooked!"

"*Mi negro pobre*," his master chuckled back. "If Delago has assumed that, he's in for a surprise, *verdad?*"

"*Verdad!*"

᥄ 3 ᥆

At Los Adaës

"*Mon Dios, negro!* Are you questioning my honor?" Delago spat at François. The hawks that perched inside his eyes were clearly ready to pounce. Even by the candlelight of the adobe warehouse, François could see the man's taut muscles straining to hold in check his birds of prey.

"No, Señor," François replied politely, with no trace of the clumsiness he had used to address the man that morning at Natchitoches. As the Spaniard caught the subtle difference in François's accent, his brow arched and François smiled. His feigned ignorance of the Spanish tongue had well served its purpose once again. He had ridden mutely in their midst down the whole seven leagues of El Camino Real that linked the French post to the Spanish one, and he had not been surprised by what he overheard. They had cursed their laden asses up every hill and damned the French on the downslopes in between. Assuming he spoke no Spanish, they had used no discretion, and their careless chatter had confirmed his own suspicions. Delago's concern for the hungry at Los Adaës was far less sincere than St. Denis's had been.

"Four pesos per bushel!" Delago had reported to the Spanish governor on his return from Natchitoches. "Twelve hundred pesos total! That is the price set by that French *ladron* who holds this frontier under his oppressive thumb. Others there would have sold me the grain we need so badly at three pesos per bushel, but the Great Thief of Natchitoches would skin anyone who encroached upon his monopoly of border trade. As you instructed, Señor, I left the pouch of four hundred and fifty pesos as a pledge, but I was forced to promise delivery of seven hundred and fifty more tonight."

Aha! François had reckoned to himself as he followed their clipped Spanish. Delago collects another seven hundred and fifty pesos from his governor. He gives me the four hundred and fifty for M'sieur, and he pockets the rest. Still, François had not anticipated the full measure of the Spaniard's chicanery, not until the pouch of coins actually passed into his hands.

"No, Señor," he repeated now, weighing his words as carefully as he weighed the sack of gold he held. *"Yo no tengo no duda sobre su honor."*

This time the Spaniard's lips curled as he realized that St. Denis and his slave had duped him.

"I have no doubts about your honor," François repeated, blunting his barb with the civil tone his situation required. "However, the light is poor in here, Señor. Perhaps that explains how someone miscounted the coins in this pouch."

"Negro, I have said the pouch contains five hundred pesos. Four hundred and fifty for your master and fifty for you—fifty pesos I generously offered for your wormy tobacco."

"Señor, the light does deceive you. No tobacco I grow is wormy. I concede I am in no position to debate the generosity of your price, but I do have an obligation to my master. I must return to him full value for the goods he entrusted to my care."

"Por Díos! Then you do question my honesty, *esclavon!"* Delago hissed.

"Señor, I am a metal worker and the son of one. I am well acquainted with the weights of all the metals. It is as much a part of my training as diplomacy is yours. This bag, Señor, could not possibly contain five hundred pesos, and I insist I must count the coins before we conclude this transaction."

Instinctively, Delago reached for his sword to settle the insult in the manner that long had been his habit. François calmly parried the threat.

"Señor, your Toledo is an instrument for gentlemanly combat. I am sure you would not dishonor it by using it on a slave."

The blade eased slowly back into its sheath until only the silver hilt was visible, and a thin smile slit the Spaniard's face. "You are quite right, *negro!* The taste of leather would be far more fitting for you than the taste of steel."

"Juan?" Delago called to the muleteer who stood watch in the doorway. His summons was unhurried, his tone offhanded, his eyes calculating how long he would need to toy with the San Denis *negro* before the brute's nerves disintegrated.

"Juan, I think we have just caught this *esclavon* in the very act of plundering our warehouse. Should he not pay the penalty of our law before we drag him home?"

"*Sí, señor,*" the peasant grinned, brown juice from a wad of tobacco oozing down the stubble of his unshaven chin. "*Mierda!* Here I stand making knots with the rope from his tobacco. Shall I use it to string him over a beam?"

"*Sí,* Juan. *Sí.*" Delago's usual staccato had slowed to a deliberate drawl as he punctuated each word with a hint of the sting his lash would inflict. François forced his voice to respond with the same coolness it had shown all night.

"Señor, my master expects me to return with his pesos, not your stripes."

"But, *negro mío,*" the Spaniard purred, "you shall have both. In fact, Juan will be happy to drag you back himself. Then he can explain to your commandant how we caught you pilfering our storehouse after we paid you and sent you on your way—and you can explain to your master why it is that the bag of gold we entrusted to you is one hundred pesos short."

November's wind cut through the open storehouse as the ticking coat was ripped from François's back, but his blood ran hot with the fear he refused to show. Not since he had been herded onto the ship at Dakar, after the vile Egyptian had stolen his wares and sold him into slavery, had he felt the sting of a whip. His wounds were still festering when St. Denis bought him off the block at the port of Tampico, and the old Frenchman had treated them himself and waited for his recovery before setting François astride a pack mule and heading northward with him across Tejas to the frontier of French Louisiana.

Knotted leather snapped now across his bare back, splitting the flesh, but no sound came from François's lips. It was only his heart that screamed *Where are you, O god who sees all? Are you as just as Père Arcange says? Or do you serve only those whose skin is white?*

Slashed nerve ends rippled pain through every muscle. *Where are you, O son of God?* François mutely cried as his back split open again and again. *If you endured the whip as Madame says, why won't you save others from this agony?*

Still the lash crackled and seared its endless rhythm. *Where are you, Caesar? Where are you and your sons? Aren't you through loading the rest of the grain into this bastard's barn? O Lord... Jesus... Caesar...* François prayed through clenched jaws until his prayers and his pain blurred into one and all was darkness.

The moon had settled, briefly, behind a screen of clouds by the time they emerged from the little barn below Delago's house. Caesar blinked and flexed his aching shoulders.

"Lordy, but I'm gittin' too old f'r dis kind o' work," he mumbled to himself. "Ain't nobody wid a stron' enuf back t' do dis f'rever."

The older guard jabbed him forward, his pistol moving far less surely than the flask of *aguardiente* he and his *compadre* had shared the past two hours. Shrugging, Caesar nodded to his sons, and they followed him across the plaza toward the government warehouse.

It was then amid the soft chorus of the night, amid the chatter of crickets and the croaks of bullfrogs the starving post had not yet skewered, that he sensed the whoosh-zing every slave feels deep inside his soul. It was muffled at first, but grew louder with each step they took across the open square. The big, yellow slave tensed and groped behind him in the dark, passing a silent alert to his nearest son. As they turned the front corner of the government office, Caesar glimpsed through the lantern light of the open storehouse the sight he knew he would see; but his pair of Spanish guards were too deep into their flasks to notice—or to care. Three steps more and the Negroes rounded the back corner of the government house, with their tipsy escorts lagging a bit too far behind. As the Spaniards stumbled around the same corner, eight arms greeted them, and they crumpled into the clay.

Within seconds, Caesar and his sons closed the distance between them and the open doorway. But Delago and his henchman were oblivious to their arrival.

"*Perdón, negro!*" the Castillian hissed as his whip cracked again across a back into which red rivers already had been cut, and Juan cackled his approval. "Say it you black son of a bitch. Just one little word! *Perdón!* Say it, or this will be the last time you ever question the honor of a Spaniard!"

"You say it, mista," Caesar challenged quietly from the doorway. "Seems t' me, yo de one w'at owes dat 'pology."

The Spaniard spun. "*Jesu Cristo!*" he breathed, disbelieving, as he stared down the barrels of the pistols Caesar and his sons had appropriated from the fallen guards. "What kind of insolence does San Denis teach his slaves?"

"Not ins'lence, mista. De old man te'ch justice. Yo know w'at dat word mean, *hunh?*" Underscoring his point, Caesar cocked his purloined weapon and nodded toward the beam from which François hung. "Now cut 'im down."

Delago merely leaned against the broad side of the crib behind him, idly rolling the stock of the whip between his hands.

"*Esclavon,* I suggest you reappraise your situation. I do not take orders from a slave. You hold a *pistola*, but you dare not use it. One shot, just one shot fired, and you rouse the post. There would be a dozen men out before you and your whelps can reach the stockade. We would cut you down before you made it over the top."

"Mista," Caesar growled, "mebbe you better redraw yo own picture. If'n I die, I'll take yo soul t' hell wid me. But I don't has t' shoot you, no." His leathered face broke into a broad grin. "Go right on, mista. Holler f'r help, an' we die shoutin' t' yo hungry friends dat we jes loaded gov'ment corn into yo private barn."

The whip slipped silently from Delago's hand. "You black bastard!"

"You jes part right, mista. I's a bastid, for sure. But I's jes half black. My daddy, he was de Car'lina overseer w'at raped my mama—and she say he wuz a real bastid. Now, mista, you cut my frien' loose!"

Delago nodded sullenly to his henchman.

"Un-unh, peasant!" Caesar barked before the muleteer could move. "The mista's gonna take François down hisself, an' he gonna do it nice 'n gently. I wanna see 'im cradle my frien' real sof' like in his arms."

"May the gods damn me, if I touch him!"

"Hunh?" The big mulatto stared the Spaniard squarely in the eye until Delago shifted. "You want w'at I call de gov'nor t' help, mista?"

"*Maldito sea!*" Delago raged. But this time he moved. Warily. Still eyeing the pistols that Caesar and his sons seemed quite capable of using, he eased the dagger from the folds of his blouse and sliced the cords that bound François's wrists to the cypress rafters. Then his lips curled as he watched the bloody form crumple into a pile of mule dung some stable hand had neglected to shovel out.

"One day, my half-black man," he snarled, "we shall meet again under different odds."

"Sure 'nuff, mista. But jes now, you still owe my frien' dat apology w'at you ast him for."

Castillian pride flared again. "I'll see the both of you in hell before I apologize to a *negro!*"

Caesar's broad grin grew wider. "Oh? Well den, we jes hav' t' fin' ourselves s'm ot'er way t' humble yo a bit. Noël! Zenon! Hang up dese gent'men real tight like, jes de way dey hang up François."

The pair of younger boys sprang forward, leaving Caesar and his eldest with their pistols aimed straight into two Spanish guts.

"Yo be sure t' cry, mista, if'n dey pull de ropes too tight," Caesar mocked, as the end of each cord was looped over the rafters. Delago loosed another stream of curses and the muleteer fired his own wad of tobacco juice. But the big man's grin never wavered.

"Whaddayo say, boys? Dese gent'men are dressed up too fin', hunh? Ruffled shirts don' look ri't on men in dat position."

The hawk eyes widened in the first signs of fear, as the silk of his blouse ripped under Zenon's yank. "You would not dare use the whip on me," Delago hissed.

"Yo right ag'in, mista," Caesar grimaced. "I wouldn't. But I sure would dare t' rid yo o' yo pants. Dat's it, Zenon, all the way down t' dat goat-milk skin w'at the fine mista hides from de sun wid his *parasol*. All the way, Zenon! Lessee w'at kin' of balls he's got… Woooey! Would yo jes look, boys! Yo mama churns up bigger curds 'n *dat!*"

The first gusts of winter whistled in appreciation, raising goosebumps on Delgado's thighs, and Caesar grinned anew. "W'at a fin' figure o' a chicken yo make, mista, but yo do look a trifle nak'd wit'out yo feathers!"

Caesar's sons guffawed, but from the muck beneath them, François moaned and the grin faded from Caesar's face.

"Noël! Zenon! Hoist François 'tween yo an' let's git. It'll be daylight in 'n hour. We better git out o' here."

The spate of Spanish oaths resumed and the sight of the pair, strung and plucked like hens in a street market, drew from Caesar one last taunt. "In the meanw'ile, mista, yo got 'bout 'n hour left 'fore daylight t' conjure up sum expl'nation for yo predic'ment. *Bye now!*"

The big mulatto bowed grandiosely, picked up the leather pouch from the worktable, blew out the flickering lantern, and quietly shut the warehouse door behind him.

∽ 4 ∽

François sank back groggily onto his mattress, onto the scratchy ticking stuffed with moss and pine needles, and his face contorted at the pungent smell of the potion only Fanny could have concocted. "*Sacrebleu* woman! What have you done to me?"

"God does not like profanity, François," Fanny chided. "Besides, what *I* have done is not the question. What have *you* been doing? You leave here before supper without a word, and Caesar brings you back in this shape in the middle of morning, mumbling some wild tale about a bear hunt. I know bear wounds when I see them, and no bear did this."

"You're right, Fanny. It was a jackal."

"A jackal? *Que?* François, you are still not giving me a straight story! There are no jackals in this country."

"There are jackals everywhere," François growled. "Some places just have more of them than others."

"You are delirious, man. I swear you look sane, but you are talking crazy. Are you going to tell me what happened or no?"

He told her. Never had François kept from her the past assignments St. Denis had put to him. He had seen no need to then and he saw none now. Whatever he told Fanny, he knew, would never go past their door. This wife was not like other women, black or white, who chattered constantly without weighing the worth of what they said.

It's in her blood, he thought. That's what sets her apart from others. She was taken from her people as a child but she can't forget that her father was a king. That memory is a wall around her no one can breach. Sixteen years she's been a slave, and she still feels different from other *nègres*. Even me. I talk as good as she does, but she still thinks she's better—that life has something more in store for her, if she just bides her time. *Ah, Fanny!* François muttered to himself what he dared not say aloud. *That destiny you dream of is nothing but a torment to your soul!*

From her corner pallet, little Coincoin cried, reminding her mother that it was time for a supper feeding. Fanny picked up the infant and returned to François's bedside with long, graceful strides.

A lissome gazelle, François mused. A beautiful, delicate animal, even in her trap. *Ça,* Fanny! It's a good thing you believe in that promised kingdom Madame preaches, because it's the only one you'll ever know!

"Man, I just do not understand you, and I never will," Fanny declared as she unbuttoned her blouse and gave a ripe breast to her whimpering child. François made no reply. There was no way to explain in terms that Fanny would understand.

"Why, François? Why would you invite this whipping? Why did you not just take that Spaniard's pouch and bring it back? It is not our place to question whether one white man is honest with the other.

"You could have taken that pouch of money and disappeared, François! You are a *man,* you can survive out there in the woods, or in those great plains past Los Adaës that you told me about. With a sack of gold and your fine skills, the way you learn so easily the tongues of the Spanish and the *indiens,* you could live anywhere and fool anybody into believing you are *free.* I swear, François! You are the most intelligent *nègre* I have known here, but in some ways you are the dumbest!"

"If it were the will of the gods, Fanny, I would be free." This was the simplest explanation he could muster. "They made me a slave. This is my destiny. It's what the gods meant for me, and I must do it well."

"There are no *gods,* François!" Fanny exclaimed in exasperation. "There is just one God and He gives us free will to *choose* what we want to do and be. Just because other men get in our way with their own designs, it does not mean we have to accept what they do to us."

"You haven't changed *your* life yet," François said gently, hating to cauterize her own wounds.

"Ah, but it is not yet my time," she sighed eventually. "God also made me a mother. I cannot run from this post with four babes, and you know I could never go without them."

Little Coincoin's hunger had abated, and she began to doze. Fanny rose with her child, pacing the small and sparsely furnished room that was their home. Like a lioness with her cub, François thought. A bold queen-cat ready to prowl her kingdom but biding time until the cub could make its way alone.

"You wonder why I cried that day we married?" Fanny continued softly, opening one small chink in the wall that guarded her secrets. "It was not because someone else picked my husband for me. Among my own people, my father would have done that, too. *Non,* I cried because I did not want a husband at all. When a woman takes a man, she bears children, and children put stronger chains on a woman than any master can. That's why I cried, François! Because I knew those vows we said in church would tie me to this place until all my children are born and grown and I am as old as Isabella the Bambara!"

"But has it been so bad, Fanny? M'sieur puts few restraints upon us. And Madame? Well, she's haughty. It's her Spanish blood. But her words have never hurt us."

"Ah, man! It is just knowing what we are and what we should be. Besides, it is not the words Madame says that hurts. It is the words I have to say to her... *Oui, Madame. Non, Madame. Whatever you say, Madame.* Man, I am the daughter of a *king!* People bowed down before my family. I was not born to bow to others!"

"Well, my proud princess, if you'll pace over here to the bed, I'd be happy to bow down before your altar," François teased, raising himself on one elbow before searing pain sliced through him again.

"Ayyyy," he winced and eased back upon the mattress, deciding on second thought that her humble servant would have to wait a few days before he could pay his overdue respects.

"*Mon Dieu,* François! Be still!" The voice of St. Denis bellowed from the doorway that Fanny had opened to let in the afternoon sun. "Fanny's salve can't work its miracle if you keep tearing open those sores. Oh, by the way, pardon me if I am intruding on a private discussion."

His eyebrows cocked in Fanny's direction, as her own narrowed warily. How much had the old M'sieur heard? Until now, he had never raised more than his voice to her, but never had he heard her say such things as what she had said just now! He seems unperturbed, she reassured herself, calling to mind some of his indulgences in the past. But would he tell *Madame?* Masking the chaos of her thoughts, Fanny put the child to bed, closed the shutters against the sharpening evening breeze, and slipped outside to call her brood together for the night.

"François. My ever-faithful François," the old commandant continued soberly. "Once again, you haven't disappointed me. But I am clearly in your debt for the pain you're suffering. Caesar told me what happened, or at least as much as he knew. The payment he delivered was short a hundred pesos, so I assume that Delago's treatment of you had something to do with the financial settlement of last night's affair?"

"*Oui,* M'sieur." François tried to turn so that he could talk directly to his master, but he flinched again as a ripped muscle scratched the coarse homespun beneath him.

"Be still, François. You're no good to me in that shape. If you don't stay off those cuts you'll lose two weeks of work," St. Denis admonished with mock severity. "Now tell me what happened."

Again, François repeated the story, and the commandant's face drew more haggard all the while. The matter was worse than he had dared to hope. Not that he worried about reprisals toward his men. Delago would not dare report the incident. They knew the details of his duplicity. Still....

"It's obvious," he finally said aloud. "There can be no further deals with this administration at Los Adaës. What happened to you last night can't happen again."

"Perhaps, M'sieur, another man might deal more effectively with the Spaniard—perhaps M'sieur Duplessis, your... your notary." François had almost said *your son-in-law,* but checked himself. It was true that M'sieur le Commandant openly showed his affection for the notary's wife and allowed her to use his name. Yet the relationship between the old French cavalier and the young half-breed who wed the post's new notary was not a matter anyone dared to openly discuss.

"*En fer,* François! I don't need a better man to deal for me at Los Adaës. I need a better man at Los Adaës to deal with! No, there will be no further rendezvous with Señor Delago. Only if the governor comes to me himself, as one old friend to another, only then will I consider the rest of those grain sales—and only if he brings his pack horses openly. I am far too old to skulk around, and I have chastised myself for doing so this time."

"But, M'sieur," François reminded him hesitantly. "The sale would still be illegal, no? Your soldiers would never arrest you, but what about your governor?"

"Vaudreuil be hanged! There's no love between us anyway. Right now, if he dared question me on this I'd leave this godforsaken frontier to his mismanagement. Consequences be damned!"

The old commandant sat morosely in the shadows of the darkened hut. Wretched quarters! He thought to himself without breaking the stride of his conversation with François. This *nègre* and his proud wife do deserve better than what the government provides here. *Mon Dieu!* but life is ironical. All I wanted at Tampico was a big *brut nègre* for a blacksmith. I paid for a strong back and brought home a wizard. I demand only obedience, and he gives me loyalty. *Sur ma foi!* Emanuela would resent him if she knew that in eight short years this black man has come to mean as much to me as our own sons.

St. Denis's eyes softened, though his voice was bitter as he continued to muse aloud. "For more than two decades, François, the French and Spanish soldiers have stood their ground on this frontier, with only fifteen miles of hills between us, and I have tried to stave off a boundary war in every way possible. I've made friends of all the Indian nations, so their power will be on our side and the Spanish will fear to attack us. I've tried to keep this fort strong and our economy healthy, so we won't be at the mercy of anyone in this hell-hole of a wilderness."

François merely nodded. The old man didn't need or expect his affirmation.

"But most of all, I've tried to be friends with the Spanish at that post. I've helped them in every need, even when I had to skirt our own laws to do it. Still, I have to honestly say, I've bent those rules gladly, because the blunderheads in Paris can't fathom what survival demands out here. And the dunces in New Orleans are no better."

François still said nothing. What could he say? In his other life, eons away, his peers had sought his counsel and shared their confidences. He had even known slaves, there, who were the confidants of their masters. But nothing in his years of servitude among these people had prepared him for now.

"Times have changed, François," the old man continued, talking as much to himself as to his servant. "Each new administration at Los Adaës is more corrupt than the one before it. If they would move the capital of Tejas over into the plains across the Sabine and let Los Adaës be a simple frontier outpost, with administrators of less ambition and greed, then cooperation between us might be possible. But I will not be here to see that. I won't be here that long."

"M'sieur," François began. His master silenced him.

"I've made up my mind, François. I'm resigning, if the government will let me and if God wills that I should live until then. Madame has wanted me to for years. When I settle my debts here, we plan to join her family in Mexico."

"Speaking of debts…," St. Denis pulled from his surtout a purse of leather, richly tooled but meagerly filled, and he counted out five coins. "You are due fifty pesos for your tobacco."

"No, M'sieur," François protested. "I failed the assignment and caused you a loss. I cannot take your money."

"Nonsense! My loss was no fault of yours. I'm the one Delago tricked, but he won't do it again." St. Denis dropped the coins into the wooden trunk next to the bed, a small but intricate chest François had carved for his family's few belongings.

"And François…" More coins clinked into the corner of the chest. "Here are another fifty for your pain, not to mention your loyalty."

A lump in his throat silenced François as he thought of all the debts this old commandant had accumulated to maintain peace along the troubled borderlands. Then he thought of the aborted plans for more grain sales to Los Adaës that would have helped St. Denis recover some of that loss.

"M'sieur," he began. "A slave does not need money. But you are a free man and a master. You have to provide for both your family and mine."

The Frenchman limped to the door; but as his hand raised the latch, he paused. "Yes, François. You need the money. When I leave this post, you won't go with me—unless you choose to go and, somehow, I do not think you would care for Mexico. But, in any case, when I leave, François, you, too, will be a free man with a family to support."

⟋ 5 ⟍
12 June 1744

Fanny's scream broke through the rhythm of François' hammer, shattering the solitude he cherished. As always, when his master did not need him elsewhere, he had come early to his smithy—rising even before the cock's crow so that he could watch the birth of dawn. When he had closed behind him the door to their mud hut within the fort, Fanny had been frying leftover grits to feed the little ones. Within minutes, she would have nursed and swaddled Coincoin, and left them all in the care of the old Bambara before letting herself into Madame's household to begin her day. *How long had it been since he left? What could have wrought that scream? Had terror struck his house or the master's?* Dropping the fence spike he had been shaping, François turned toward Fanny's voice. Then fixing on its location, he loped the length of the hill that descended from St. Denis's blacksmith shop down to the fort.

"François!" Fanny wailed again, hysterically, as their paths collided. Instinctively, his arms wrapped around her but she flung them off and collapsed amid the red mud left by a month of rain. François floundered, unsure of what to say or do. In nine years, he had never known anything or anyone to erode her composure—until now.

"Fanny?" He knelt beside her, cradling her, though she seemed not to notice. She was as tall as he. Yet curled into a ball now, she seemed as small and helpless as she must have been the day warring tribesmen tore her from her family and sold her to the slavers. "There now, Fanny." He could think of nothing else to say and so those same words became a chant until, at last, she pulled herself from the shell into which she had retreated.

"He's dead," Fanny whispered dully, as though she had lost all will to live herself.

"Dead?" François's voice rose as images of both their sons flashed to mind. "Who, Fanny?"

"M'sieur! Last night. The new priest found him when he went in to prepare for morning Mass. M'sieur was in church, all alone, kneeling in his pew, with his hands folded in prayer! *Frozen* in prayer! He was already *cold*, François!"

The rest of Fanny's words were lost in the cacophony inside his head. All François heard then was his own pulse and the thrashing of his own questions:

M'sieur, dead? In church? In prayer? But it is not even Sunday!

"François! Did you hear me?"

She was shaking him. Or was he shaking on his own? Unsure, he clutched her tighter until her gasp brought him back into the present. "I heard the first part, Fanny. Tell me the rest again."

So she spilled her pain again, wincing at every slight she had felt, while mocking the ignorance of those who had scorned her. It was all the surgeon's fault. Even Madame had said so. Vaguely, now, François recalled her concern of the night before—a concern, God help him, he had not taken seriously. M'sieur had been running a fever and she had offered to treat him. Madame had been uncertain. Perhaps they should consult the surgeon. Then that nitwit had forbidden her to go near the sickbed. Her medicine might work on slaves, he had told Madame, but a man of the rank of Chevalier de St. Denis should not be subjected to *heathen potions!* He had actually used those words to Madame, not even caring that Fanny heard him, and Madame had let him have his way.

"He killed him, François." Fanny moaned, quieter now, though shudders still rippled between her breaths as she recalled the treatment the *butcher* had prescribed. "He killed M'sieur by *leeching* him! He drained the lifeblood from a man who had no strength left at all! Then he forced M'sieur's mouth open and poured down gum camphor mixed with cayenne pepper, saying that would *burn the fever out!*"

"*Hehn?*"

"Oh, François!" Fanny rushed on, fueled by the torment spilling from her gut. "When I left last night, M'sieur was sweating something awful. Madame says he fell asleep about half-past nine, and then she dozed off on the chaise. Dozed! *Ha!* She was on her third glass of Madeira when I left! If she had only dozed, she would have heard him leave. She would have stopped him. She could have saved him. But no! She sent me home, and drank herself to sleep, and no one even missed him until the priest came at six and woke the household! Oh, François!" she wailed anew. "What do we do now?"

It was that question, not her litany of slights and faults, that shook him from his fugue. "We, Fanny?"

"*Oui,*" she choked, clinging now to her husband for support as she had never done in nine years of marriage. "What do we do now? M'sieur was going to free us when he left here, but Madame never will!"

Calmly, so calmly that not a muscle on his face betrayed the tumult of his thoughts, François unwrapped her long arms from around his neck and pulled her upright onto her own broad feet. "I'll tell you what *I'm* going to do. *I'm* going back up that hill and make my master the kind of burial box he deserves."

As Fanny gaped behind him, François trudged back to his workshop at the crest of St. Denis Hill. A few cattle lolled placidly around the barns, too hot or too lazy to join the herd that ranged through the woods beyond. A mare neighed coyly, spying her stallion across the cleared swath of pasture. But as the sun rose upon the hill, beginning its westward roll toward Los Adaës, no human presence intruded again upon François's solitude—and he was glad. If ever he needed to be alone, it was now. He had to sort through this news Fanny had delivered, this death that had overturned his life. It was not the fact that M'sieur had died. He knew that was coming soon, and M'sieur did, too. It was the *way* in which the old commandant had chosen to die that shook François's soul.

I thought I had these white men figured out, he repeated over and again, as he measured and sawed the boards of cherrywood he had been hoarding. *I thought I understood these men and the god they mock one day and call upon the next. Man cannot mock the god in which he believes. Or can he?*

Mindlessly, François's chisel notched and grooved and joined the pieces, as he mentally measured the man who had been his master, his mentor, and, in some curious way, his friend. M'sieur had been no more pious than any man at the post, François told himself. *Remember the Sabbath and keep it holy,* Madame preached to all of them. But M'sieur remembered the Sabbath only when Madame reminded him. *Thou shalt not commit adultery or fornication!* Every priest who came here thundered that commandment, but everyone at the post knew that Mme. Duplessis was the commandant's own love child. Surely M'sieur broke the precepts that Madame and all the priests invoked. Yet he chose to die in the pew he seldom occupied, on pain-wracked knees in a humility he rarely showed, praying to a god in which, François had thought, a *man* could not believe.

"*Mon Dieu,*" he whispered finally, his head falling upon his fresh-built coffin as the churchyard bell began its toll. "*My God! Are you my God?*"

ᘉ 6 ᘒ

In the long hours that followed

"Thank you, Père Barnabé, Padre Ballejo. I could never have borne this day without you." Behind her thin veil, Emanuela's eyes seemed suitably swollen, but the iron in her voice belied her words as she greeted the latest round of mourners. That was what galled Fanny the most. As she squeezed her way through the crowded rooms, tending the needs of guests who had come and gone since morning, she seethed with an anger she knew was most unchristian and for once she barely cared. M'sieur was *dead*, and this woman showed no pain at all! It was *she, Fanny*, who truly grieved—not so much for M'sieur, God forgive her!—but for her own life that would never be, the destiny she would never know, the future her children would never have.

But anger blinds, and so it was that Fanny's judgments failed her. Madame was not just calm, she was oblivious—to the heat, the stench of so many bodies in such proximity on a summer day, to everything, that is, but the role she knew she had to play.

"Père Barnabé," her litany of thanks went on. "I will be forever grateful to you for the honor you have done us, by burying Monsieur within the sacristy itself."

"But, of course, Madame," the French Capuchin murmured, giving the widow her due even as he mopped at the perspiration that dripped from his florid face. "It was only fitting, Madame, that he be laid to rest under the pew in which he died. By the very manner in which Monsieur chose to spend his last minutes on this earth, he set an example that will long inspire both sides of this frontier. Is that not so, Padre Ballejo?"

Beside him, the Reverend Francisco Ballejo, president of Mexico's eastern missions, had been otherwise preoccupied. In fact, he had been shocked to see the means in which the fabled Frenchman—a Chevalier of the Order of St. Louis, mind you!—had spent his last years. As the widow had chattered on, Ballejo had idled away his tedium with calculations of the cubic feet of air space this hovel offered to the fifty or so souls now packed inside. It was shocking, *shocking!* Was this French colony so impoverished that it could afford no better quarters for the officials who governed it?

"Padre Ballejo?" Through the din, Fanny heard the voice of her mistress rise in concern. "Padre! You look faint! Quick, Fanny! More cool wine for the Reverend Fathers!"

"*Oui,* Madame," Fanny responded, with far more grace than she really felt. The baby she carried high under her breasts was getting far too heavy, and the tension of the day had eaten her nerves raw. Still, she was glad Emanuela had ordered her to stay through the funeral. It spared her from having to *think,* to weigh the havoc this death had wrought for her and her offspring.

By the time she retrieved the fresh carafe from the mud-walled cooler, both the padre and Emanuela seemed to have recovered their aplomb. Ballejo was unctuously reassuring her that he, himself, had been honored by her invitation to co-celebrate Señor's Requiem Mass. The crowd, mercifully, had begun to drift away, back to their own galleries for supper.

Fanny had kept the doors and windows open all that day, begging for a breeze, but the air was rank with stale wine and sweet cigars, as well as sweat and heat. A fresh wave of nausea sent her rushing now for the doorway and there she collided with a late arrival. A Spaniard, obviously, judging from the muttered oath with which he brushed off her apologies. Then she heard his voice turn dulcet as he passed on inside.

"*Cara!*"

Emanuela turned to the voice, raising a quizzical gaze to the level at which she usually found most males, but she had to drop them again to meet the eyes of the dapperling who approached her.

"*Cara!*" he repeated, squeezing her a bit too tightly as his clipped moustache brushed her cheek. "Emanuela! Dear playmate of my childhood! How it saddens me that we should meet again under circumstances so tragic."

"Justo?" she parried hesitantly. "Justo Boneo y Morales?"

Of course, Justo, Fanny muttered, recalling Madame's reaction when a visitor told her that the man had called upon the government house to pay his respects. Madame had seemed truly bewildered. Why *there?* Why not *here?* Why had he not come to *her?* The guest had only stared, chalking up her reaction to her grief. But Fanny had heard enough whispered tales between her mistress and the woman's sister who came monthly from Los Adaës to visit. It was Emanuela the adolescent Justo had pushed in the peach-tree swing, declaring his love for her forever. It was Emanuela who had been the lure when he scaled the convent wall on a steamy May evening and earned for the both of them a month of penance from the bishop himself. And it was Justo who had become a governor, while M'sieur had remained a commandant.

"Ah, Justo!" Emanuela's sigh barely veiled the hurt that ate at her. "Ever since we heard you were Tejas's new governor, we have looked forward to a visit from you. Only Monsieur's ill health kept us from making the trip over to Los Adaës to spend time with you. *Sí,* Justo, I do wish Monsieur had lived to see you again!"

"And I share that sorrow," Boneo proclaimed. "It is only a small comfort I can offer you now, *cara,* but I have requested a Mass to be said for the soul of your beloved husband and my dear friend."

"*Hé!*" Fanny scarcely bothered to check her snort as the grandée's honeyed words flowed on. Your valet told a better tale, just now, out in the kitchen—how one of your spies had dashed back to Los Adaës with the news and you had cackled to your aide, "Thank God! Delago. St. Denis is dead!" Well, at least you had the decency not to bring The Jackal with you!

"And now, *cara,*" His Excellency's sympathy had already run its course. "I truly regret that I must cut this visit short. The other guests have left and it is growing late. You need rest, and El Camino Real is said to be a treacherous way at night. Padre Ballejo and I should be on our way."

"Of course, *mi amigo. Gracias por todos,* Padre, Justo. *Vaya con Díos.*"

Fanny could hear the weariness creeping into Emanuela's voice as she bade the Spaniards good-bye. The rituals of society have ended now, Fanny mused. Madame will go to bed alone tonight—to face some grief, I hope—while I'll go back to François to face my own.

The baby kicked hard against her liver as she stooped to pick up a fallen goblet, reminding her of the curious pronouncement François had made when she took him his midday meal. "If that's a son you are carrying, Fanny," he had said, staring at her swollen belly, "if that is a son, his name shall be Barnabé."

She had been so startled that she almost dropped the dish she carried, but the look on his face forestalled her and she left without uttering the question that had plagued her ever since. *Why would he pick a Christian name this time? Why Barnabé?* The only Barnabé either of them knew was this new priest.

A timid knock broke the stillness that had at last descended upon the household. As Fanny hesitated, still half lost to reverie, her young master moved to open the door.

Louis Juchereau de St. Denis, *fils*, at twenty-six, was the image of his father's long-forgotten youth—tall of frame, with skin of light olive and a mass of curls the color of mahogany cascading around his thick and powerful neck. But the young Louis lacked the bearing that had set his father apart from other men. Beneath his skin, Fanny had long since decided, he was his mother's son. Imperious and impetuous. Only more so. Emanuela's restlessness had been curbed by a convent that was blind to rank and privilege, but her son had been indulged by a frontier where no law was obeyed save that of his own father. Throughout the tedious *visite de condoléances* of all his father's friends and subjects this day, he had paced endlessly and drank heavily, but neither that nor the departure of their guests had relieved his tension.

"Louis, sir?" Fanny heard a husky murmur as her young master opened the outside door. "I came as quickly as I could, Louis. Señor Gutierrez had invited my little Louis-Pierre and me to Los Adaës to share his saint's day. It was there I heard about papa, that he had been sick with the fever, but I did not believe it! Not at first! I only left here yesterday. Why did no one tell me that he was ill?" The low voice was clearly distraught. "I had a right to know. Now he's not only dead but buried—without me!"

"Madame Widow Duplessis!" Louis's retort was so palpable that the sound of it crawled down Fanny's spine. "In this household, Madame Duplessis, you have no rights!"

Even in the dusk, Fanny could see the poor girl blanch as her new master launched into his rant. "How dare you speak to me of a father! You never had one—or maybe you had a dozen. Who knows? The only certainty you have, woman, is this: just because my father, in his dotage, had pity on a half-breed orphan bastard, don't think this grieving family will suffer your insult forever!"

A swarthy hand flew to the young woman's mouth to stifle a gasp. Her doe eyes darted from Louis to the chaise on which his mother lounged, begging, it seemed to Fanny, for some sign that her existence could be forgiven amid their shared grief. If that was her hope, it was wasted. Beside her in the doorway, the slender stripling she had named for both her father and her husband shuffled uncomfortably, and Fanny herself cringed as she recalled the past expletives young St. Denis had used to describe this nephew he never would acknowledge.

"You're no St. Denis, Madame," Louis ploughed on, "The only name you have is the one your late husband gave you in exchange for his sinecure. And you have no moral right to use even that, now that you've exchanged your widow's weeds for a party dress so soon after his death. You want family? Well, take your whelp and move in with the Señor Gutierrez. Just don't expect us to pay for another man to marry you!"

The heavy cypress door slammed hard in the face of its two visitors, and the new head of the Juchereaus de St. Denis walked calmly back into the breast of his family, his tension assuaged at last by the long-anticipated assault upon the bastard sister he neither claimed nor wanted.

"A little more wine, Maman?" he inquired solicitously, as Emanuela sank at last onto her chaise. She smiled, wearily, continuing to ignore the *débat* she obviously overheard, and Fanny knew she would not rebuke her eldest son. M'sieur Louis's denunciation had been as much for her benefit as for his own. Emanuela may never have voiced to him her feelings about Louise Marguerite Duplessis, but she did not have to. She and her firstborn understood each other perfectly.

"*Non,* Louis," she replied at last. "Let's not waste the good Madeira on me. That may be our last."

"Ah, Maman! Don't be so pessimistic. I know Papa didn't leave us much, but this embarrassment is just temporary. De la Chaise takes over now until a new commandant is sent up from New Orleans. I'd say things have worked to our advantage, Maman. Had the governor not refused Papa's resignation, there would be a new commandant here already. As it is, De la Chaise will be happy to extend a little credit to the family of his dearly departed bride."

Emanuela winced as she labored to raise her plump feet upon the stool François had carved for her. Dutifully, Fanny bent over her swollen belly to loosen Madame's laces, but she knew the woman's wince was not just because she had vainly laced her shoes too tight.

Louis never noticed. "De La Chaise is recommending me for an *enseigne's* commission in the Royal Marines, and of course, we are requesting that I be stationed here. Dolores and Petronille are both grown enough. With their pedigrees, we should have no problem marrying them off well—and soon. See? That leaves us with only Marie and little Pierre-Antoine to provide for."

"Louis!" Emanuela mildly scolded, as her daughters gasped. "You should not speak of your sisters as though they were cattle being auctioned to the highest bidder."

"I'm only being practical, Maman. We have to be. As for your reference to auctions, that is another recourse, you know. Some of our slaves would bring a handy sum."

O God! Fanny almost burned herself with the candle she was using to light the sconces for the evening. For the first time in years she met real fear and the smell of it sickened her again. *O God!* When M'sieur died, I wished it had been Madame! The tears I cried were for my own dreams, not my master's soul. But I did not think of *this!* O Mary, Mother of Jesus! Hear this poor mother's plea and pray for us all! Don't let God punish François and our children for my unchristian thoughts!

Emanuela, when she at last replied, was stern.

"Louis, you will not talk of auctioning anyone. Our *nègres* are human beings, not animals. They have wives and husbands and children. You know as well as I, the law forbids the sale of any husband from his wife or any child from its mother."

"The law?" Louis demurred. "What the law says and what people do are often not the same, Maman."

"That law has never been violated here," his mother retorted. "Your father would never have allowed it. We never have and never will break up servants whom God has joined, and no one at this post could afford to buy an entire family."

Emanuela paused, her bosom heaving in distress, and young St. Denis circled his mother's chaise. Softly, cajolingly, his fingers kneaded her plump shoulders, but his mother well knew his ploys.

When she spoke again, weariness had crept back into her voice. Still her words were final. "Louis, our *nègres* are a responsibility God has entrusted to us. That has not changed. The subject is closed."

Jesus, Mary, and Joseph! Fanny exhaled—not a profane oath, but a prayer of thanks.

"Fanny?"

"*Oui,* Madame?" She answered quickly, but she could not force herself to look her mistress in the face.

"Fanny, you look faint. I should not have kept you here so long when your time is almost upon you. Go home. See about your own family and go to bed. I can manage now."

"*Oui,* Madame." Quickly, Fanny let herself out the door and fled into the night, not toward home and François, but toward the always-open door of the little church across the square. Tonight it was Fanny who needed to rethink her life.

∽ 7 ∾

Spring 1749

Dusk had at last descended upon St. Denis Hill. The coral glow of twilight no longer tinged the tree tops that wrapped the backside of the knoll. The pungent fragrance of jasmine and quince in first bloom wafted upwards through the cool evening breeze and sweetened the aroma of the deer Fanny was roasting over an open pit. Across the cleared slope that rolled lazily through the meadow to the post, the cows lowed, crooning a bovine lullaby to their offspring.

From his vantage point upon the crest, François squatted on his haunches and watched the lights flare within the stockade of the post as sentries lit the bear oil in the lamps. In the southwest corner, small cookfires glistened, casting eerie lights on the faces of the *negresses* as they patted out their family's corn cakes or added *filé* to a pot of gumbo they had concocted from an unlucky rabbit, a deep dark roux, a pot of water, and their own secret blend of herbs. Behind them, their menfolk smoked and children chased each other around the wretched huts the government provided as quarters for the servants of post officials.

Why is it, François wondered to himself, that Providence smiles upon some men and grinds others under her heel? For a *nègre,* he had been treated well enough by that divine goddess, much better than the Africans down there in the post. The death of his master had been a blow to both him and Fanny, each in a different way. Yet things had turned out better than they feared, despite the fact that Fanny's prediction had come true. Madame had not given them their freedom as M'sieur had promised.

At first, François had expected Fanny to be crushed, but she accepted the disappointment with a complacency he never thought he'd see her wear. As always, he attributed the change to the nobleness of her birth, but still it worried him that she seldom spoke now of her heritage or the freedom that once she had considered to be both her birthright and her destiny.

46

Fort St. Jean Baptiste des Natchitoches

The fort François beheld, as he gazed down from St. Denis Hill, has been reconstructed at its original site along the banks of Cane River. Within the stockade, visitors can see the wretched, thatched-roof huts in which the frontier government housed its slaves and the soldiers' barracks that were little better, as well as the common kitchen, the commandant's office, the church, and governmet warehoues—all rebuilt from the design put to paper in 1733 by the Crown's engineer-architect François Broutin.

Even more puzzling had been the lassitude that overcame Emanuela in the wake of her husband's death. Her iron resolve, the only thing about her that he ever did admire, crumbled under the weight of her widow's veil. Señor Sanchez-Navarro had asked his sister to move her family to Los Adaës. Now that her French husband had departed, he had pointed out to Emanuela one sultry afternoon while Fanny massaged her mistress's ever-aching head, it was only fitting that his sister rejoin her own people. But Emanuela had simply fluttered a pudgy hand and made some excuse about the dangers of rash actions. She needed time to make her plans.

Weeks had stretched into months, and no plans seemed in the offing. St. Denis's successor had been forced to remind the widow that the commandant's house went with the appointment, but Emanuela put him off again and again. Not once did she give him a reason, but Fanny knew what it was.

St. Denis's lands were generous, stretching far beyond the crude settlement that now ringed the fort. It was that distance that filled Madame with fear. That and the memory of a sight both she and Fanny had beheld out there on St. Denis Hill. It was in the years before François came to the post, Fanny told him—back during the troubles the colony had with the Natchez Indians. After they massacred the settlers on the Mississippi, the French Crown had vowed to exterminate the tribe. The Natchez had then scattered and their remnants had ended up on the banks of Red River, where they besieged the fort at Natchitoches.

While the frontier families huddled inside the stockade, the Natchez had raised a cross high on the hill so all the French could see. To that cross, they had nailed a Frenchwoman, a captive taken during their bloody massacre, and then they had lit a fire beneath that godforsaken soul. It was that sight, that smell, those screams Emanuela could not forget.

Still, she had no choice. And so, in mid-November, when young Louis returned from some clandestine mission among the Tuokani of Tejas, Emanuela relented. The commandant could have his house. She would move her family to the hill where her husband already had his barns and storehouses.

The tobacco had been cured, the corn shucked and stored. The Christmas season lay ahead and the *nègres* had looked forward to a long, slow winter when Emanuela issued her decree. Before spring planting, they would move. François must put the hands to work immediately on the construction of the family home and the servant cabins up on the hill. Still, two more weeks of clear, late-autumn weather had been wasted while Emanuela and her offspring quarreled over the house they would erect.

"*Un grande maison!*" Petronille insisted petulantly. "It's high time we had a proper home. I declare! I don't know why Papa permitted us to live in such indignity! Here I am, swooning over the *noble* Athanase Christophe Fortunat Mauguet de Mézières. *Ma foi!* How can I land a nobleman if my family lives in a *hut?*"

"Nobleman, indeed!" her brother Louis had retorted, and François had chuckled when Fanny repeated M'sieur's description of the latest officer sent out by the Crown. "De Mézières may be of noble stock, but he cavorts like a baseborn jackass!"

It was no secret, even to the *nègres,* that the young cadet Petronille de St. Denis adored was a scoundrel, or that his own mother had asked the king to exile her son to the colonies. Even after the man's poor mother had a change of heart and pleaded for the order to be revoked, the king still told the governor to keep the rascal and his *lettre de cachet* as far from France as possible. A continued stay in the colonies, His Majesty's minister supposedly had said, might make a useful soldier out of the rogue. If not, Louis XV would at least have one less troublemaker to mar the idyll he thought his kingdom was.

Ma'mselle Dolores, of course, had her own ideas of how the new house should look. "Maman!" she had wailed when her mother mused about a Spanish *casa* with high, private walls around their gardens. "*Grand Dieu!* Maman! It's bad enough to be stuck off on that hill away from everybody! A walled garden? You might as well put me in a cloister. No one will ever see me!"

"I don't know, *chien-chien,*" her mother had begun, wavering as she did now with every issue, and Petronille pressed on.

"Oh, Maman. We have to have a big broad gallery all the way around so I can sit out and appreciate the natural beauty of the hill. Then when young *gallants* come by, they can appreciate *my* natural beauty. Oh, Maman…."

"That's quite enough, Dolores!" Louis had cut in. "The females of our family do not expose themselves to every ruffian who comes by to gawk. Whatever charms you think you have will be appreciated soon enough by a gentleman of breeding, if you are not rash enough to advertise yourself."

"Oh, Louis!" his sister had wailed, but it was Louis who had the final word and there seemed to be no end to the litany of orders he proceeded to give.

"You will build a Creole-style *maison,* François," he decreed. "There have to be spacious galleries on all sides. This climate demands them. When you prepare the bousillage for the walls, I want only deer hair mixed with the mud. No moss, mind you. And be sure the mix is of proper consistency, so it will not crack at first freeze. I want the framework of cypress only. We can't have it rotting in a year's time. And every upright post must be imbedded deep, with cross timbers fitted so tightly a hair can't even pass between them."

"*Oui,* M'sieur Louis."

"I also want a stone fireplace at each end of the broad salon, and one in each of the chambers that flank the rear. We'll have to forego the luxury of panes for the windows, temporarily of course, but the shutters must be finely louvered."

"*Oui,* M'sieur Louis."

"In fact, that goes for all the woodwork. I will not tolerate rough-hewn timbers," Louis added, curtly and quite unnecessarily. "The roof shingles and the double door at the front should be of cypress also, and I expect you to carve those doors to whatever design Madame gives you. This one touch of Spain she does insist upon."

"But M'sieur Louis," François had been forced to remind his new master. "Cypress is too hard a wood to carve into the intricacies your mother will envision. Perhaps this should be of black oak?"

"*Ah, bien, nègre,* whatever you say. St. Denis men aren't trained in manual crafts."

Still, Louis had not been done with his instructions. "When you build the *nègre* camp, make sure you put it to the north of the Big House. At a *proper* distance, of course, but not too far way."

"*Oui,* M'sieur." François did not need to inquire what the *proper* distance might be. He had overheard enough Frenchmen spout their views on slave camps. Cabins go to the north or northeast because winds seldom blew from there in this latitude. That way, the master's family was less likely to be *offended* by the *odor* they claimed to smell when Angolas or Congos or Aradas lived in the camps. The *proper* distance, of course, was far enough away that no scent would waft its way downwind when a breeze did come from that direction, but close enough to maintain constant oversight.

"I want the camp enclosed with palisades and a door," Louis had continued, oblivious to—or unconcerned about—the feelings his majordomo masked behind the blue-black marble of his face. "I'll need a lock and key for this, of course."

"*Oui,* M'sieur."

"And in the center of the camp, I want a bathing pond. The residents of this post have never bothered to install them, but we're getting far too many *nègres* here for them to bathe in Red River without making it unsuitable for us to swim in."

"*Mais oui,* M'sieur." By this point, François had barely cared whether his resentment showed. Still, force of habit had held his tongue, and his face had not betrayed his thought that such fastidiousness was quite unnecessary: men here were more than willing to mingle with their *nègres. Sur ma foi!* François had snorted to himself. The whole post gossips now about the nightly visits of white males to the cabins of the young slave women, an occasion for gossip that never occurred while M'sieur le Commandant governed this frontier.

"Oh, yes, one thing more. The hut for you and Fanny can have two rooms—three, if you want to work on that in your own time. Father told me before his death that he intended you to have a better situation. It's only proper that I honor his desire."

Louis paused for emphasis. "But build your place outside the camp, immediately behind our back gallery. Madame's health is very frail now, and she insists that Fanny must at all times be within an arm's reach, figuratively speaking, of course."

"Of course, M'sieur. *Merci.*" François muttered the expected thanks, but anger seared him as he thought of his own nubile Dgimby who would also be within arm's reach of their young master.

The building had progressed rapidly, with Caesar and his sons responsible for most of the construction. The burly Carolinian needed little supervision from François, leaving the younger artisan free to devote himself to Emanuela's doors and the carving of the delicate mantels and other interior woodwork that had become obsessions for his mistress.

The family had moved into the Big House, as hoped, in time for Petronille's betrothal to the Sieur de Mézières, a celebration that was to precede the actual wedding by the *proper* number of months. But then Fanny had surprised François one spring night by reporting that Madame had cancelled all festivities, and the next morning the entire post had buzzed with the gossip that Madame's sixteen-year-old Pet and the girl's *roué* had eloped the night before to Los Adaës. So it was that, instead of an engagement party, the first occasion François's pious mistress celebrated in her new home, four and a half months later, was a baptism.

Madame was crushed, Fanny had confided to François, but no one at her splendid *fête* could have guessed the Spanish woman's shame. She had rallied from her lassitude and was every inch the doting grandmother and imperious *doña*. Not one spiteful tongue had dared to risk a catty jibe or quip that afternoon, either to Emanuela's face or behind her back.

That little triumph of will had been short-lived. Petronille had died in the blustery winter of 1747–48, and her death had wounded Emanuela far more than had her child's "unfortunate disgrace." Madame had lost three daughters since her arrival at the post, but she had borne the other losses with a fortitude that brooked no pity. Now she lolled and murmured to Fanny or herself—it mattered little—how she had borne five daughters and had tried to rear them all in virtue. "Haven't I, Fanny?" she invariably asked, like a hurt child seeking reassurance that she had been good.

"*Oui,* Madame," Fanny would demur, waiting for the line she knew would follow.

"Then how could God take three babies from me? He has spared all of yours! Except for Barnabé. How could He be so cruel to *me?*"

This question Fanny could never, would never, answer and so Madame would cry softly over her lovely and fiery Marie Rose, conceived on her idyllic honeymoon with her beloved Louis down on the Río Grande and born amid the tears of the year-long separation that international politics had forced upon them. It was not fair, she whimpered, that Marie Rose should have died in the fullness of her own sweet love, leaving a shattered husband and two infants.

Again, Fanny would murmur sympathetically, and then Madame would wail anew at the thought of her beloved Gertrude who had been snatched from her and M'sieur as an innocent bud, never given the chance to bloom. But always her thoughts came back to Pet, and then her eyes would haze, and her musings would start to wander to the kingdom where her babies now waited for their *maman*.

Fanny had always told François that Madame was torn between two worlds, Louisiana and New Spain. Now she had been lulled into a third, as her mind dwelled more and more upon those daughters who had left the earthly world behind. There had been no more talk of the day Madame might move her children to the Spanish side of the frontier. If she left Natchitoches now, Fanny feared, she would go alone, cutting all ties with her earthbound children, her slaves, and all other worldly baggage.

"What will happen to us then?" Fanny fretted aloud one night, and François dared not answer. He, too, dreaded the day young Louis would take control of the St. Denis *nègres*.

Considering Madame's ill health, François thought now, as he watched Fanny baste the deer he had tracked and killed that morning, it was even more surprising that she had ordered Fanny to Los Adaës tomorrow. Yet Madame had been adamant, Fanny reported to him glumly. Madame's sister's husband had the fever and Emanuela was determined he would not die like her own beloved Louis, at the mercy of continental doctors who knew nothing about the *mysteries* of tropical diseases.

"But Madame," Fanny had dared to protest, "what if they don't let me tend him? Like before?"

"This time they will! Padre Ballejo vowed so today when he rode over, God bless him. My sister sent him here to ask for you, and I have promised that you will go. Ballejo guarantees that you will be given full control. No surgeon will interfere. Padre's word at Los Adaës carries more weight than anyone's, you know. Even the governor's."

Fanny had dutifully packed her medicines, while François railed at the thought of a separation from his woman, even one of only a few miles and a few days. In fourteen years of marriage, there had been only one night, the night after their master died, that François had slept without his ebony princess molded into the curve of his loins, his face all but buried in the velvet flock that crowned her head.

Time had been gentle to his princess, he mused now as she bent to remove a deer leg from the spit. The six children she had borne him had ripened her lithe form. At the birth of their son Barnabé, which came so soon after their master's death, François had been tempted to pray to this new God that Fanny would be ridden of her fertility. That birthing had been a terrible one, the only hard one his fecund wife had ever known. At times amid her agony, he had wondered if Fanny's spirit had been broken by their lost freedom, if she had lost her will to live as well. But she had rallied, packed all her strength into one bone-melting shriek, and pushed their Barnabé into the world. Two days later she pulled herself from her childbed, two weeks after that she welcomed him into her arms, and within two years she effortlessly brought forth yet another soul for the greater glory of their mistress and the greater profit of their young master.

While the moon sprayed its first glimmers across the hill, Fanny called the children from their play, in the age-old rite of the mother hen bringing her little ones under her wings for the night. François grinned as Choera and Jean Baptiste tumbled quickly from a nearby hayloft—the boys never needed a second call to supper. Dgimby came giggling from the woods, poking fun at the younger Coincoin who shepherded the babies home in guileless mimicry of her mother.

It was not right to compare his children the way he did and fault one in favor of the other. François knew that. Yet every time he thought of these two daughters he could not help it. It was adolescent Dgimby, short and plump but physically a woman now, who was still a child in heart and mind, totally innocent and maddeningly irresponsible, while the little Coincoin, who had not yet seen her eighth saint's day, seemed to have sprung from her mother's womb with the wisdom of Isis.

François shook his head, in wonder and in worry, as he watched her now. She was as tall as Dgimby, but slender and lissome. God had gifted his Coincoin with her mother's height and grace and beauty, and her spirit as well. But He also gave her François's own probing, forever-restless mind. Truly, their second-born daughter, this goddess in the making, had inherited the best of both of them, and there had to be a reason.

François knew that reason, although he had never uttered it to Fanny. The two of them had been born free, and they would die as slaves. Their children had been born in slavery; but in his heart, François knew that God had in store for one of them the greater destiny their mother could only dream of.

☾ 8 ☽

Ten days later

A trail of ants marched in formation toward the apple core that lay forgotten on the window sill near Emanuela's chaise, a long and undulating thread of crusty red, vaguely observed but undisturbed. Then one soldier-worker sensed

new booty and strayed off to explore the chaise's arm, along with the pudgy
fingers that draped across it—all ten of them tipped with the sticky nectar of
an overripe pear. It was the fire ant's nip that stung Emanuela from the reverie
in which she had spent her morning after little Marie and Pierre Antoine had
gone off to Monsieur Dupain's weekly grammar school.

Isabella! Emanuela's bellow would have curled the ears of any other servant, but the elderly Bambara whom she had brought in from the nursery to
replace the absent Fanny had long since learned that her age could excuse poor
hearing when the mistress roused from her chaise and began to bark a litany
of orders.

Blasted *nègres!* Emanuela muttered to herself for want of anyone else upon
whom she could vent the frustrations of her past ten days. She had fed and
clothed and *cared for* the old Bambara for the whole quarter-century they both
had spent at this godforsaken outpost. And *this* was the woman's gratitude! Pine
straw plainly littered the parlor floor around her, blown in through the windows
they still could not afford to pane, and no one had yet bothered to sweep it
out. The noon-day sun had already peaked and Dgimby was not yet back from
the post, where she had been sent to fetch a batch of Perot's meat pies for the
household's lunch. How many times, Emanuela fumed, had she tried to instill
upon her servants that *discipline* was a duty God expected of all of them? And
now, just because she was too ill to oversee their every action and Fanny was
elsewhere, they were treating themselves to sloth and indolence and who knows
what other vices!

Isabella! Manon! Crystal tinkled on the sideboard with each bark but no
doors slammed in response from the outside kitchen or the laundry hut and no
feet scurried in to do her bidding. Only the distant clipclop of some beast of
burden mounting the hill broke the maddening silence as Emanuela peevishly
heaved herself from the chaise to flip the offending apple core through the open
shutters. It was then that she spied them—the Spaniard with his rail-thin arms
wrapped around Fanny while the woman disgracefully shared his saddle—and
utter relief unnerved her. By the time Fanny could dismount and let herself in,
followed peremptorily by the governor's aide, Emanuela had collapsed again
upon her chaise.

Delago, of course, had wasted his trip. Emanuela made that clear, once
Fanny's ministrations had revived her enough that she could do her duty as

hostess to this uninvited guest. "I am sorry, Señor," she retorted rather curtly when the man announced why he had personally brought her servant back from Los Adaës. "I could not even consider your offer."

"Then I will double it, Madame," he responded, tapping his gold-tipped cane upon the hardwood floor with obvious impatience. "Fifteen hundred pesos is far more than the woman is worth…"

His spiel went on endlessly. Checking her impatience, Emanuela heard him through. Of course, he admitted that Fanny's medical skill was unsurpassed. Of course, the whole of Los Adaës was grateful for the miracles she had wrought with all the sick ones while she was there. Even so, Delago simpered, fifteen hundred pesos was an unheard-of price—a fact that even Madame would surely have to admit.

"I do, Delago, and that is precisely why I am wondering what prompts you to offer it."

The Spaniard coughed, flushing behind his goatee, not merely because of the sharpness with which he had been answered but also because of the implications behind the St. Denis woman's words. Distracted though she had been by all her tribulations during Fanny's absence, Emanuela had not missed the suggestiveness of the position in which the man had placed Fanny when he brought her home—not discreetly behind him, sitting backward, as decent women rode when forced to share a mount with a man, but in front of him so that his arms, as they wrapped around her to control the reins, lay flagrantly across her breasts. Obviously, Emanuela snorted to herself, he had put her there so that with every jolt of the pinto's gait, his manhood would jab into her rump; and in spite of herself, she winced. *She* had ridden just that way with her Louis across the plains of Tejas, when he had brought her to Natchitoches as a bride. She *knew* what that position did to a man and, in her mind, that memory grossly magnified Delago's blatant insult.

Emanuela's disgust could not have been plainer, and so Delago groped for a stronger card to deal in his game of sympathy.

"You see, Madame, my wife died just six months ago. God rest her soul. She left me with children. One day—for their sake, of course—I may overcome my grief enough to take another wife; but in the meantime, I need someone I can trust to run my home without constant supervision, since I would only be there at night."

That, precisely, is what concerns me, Emanuela thought grimly to herself. There is not a wagging tongue at Los Adaës that has not discussed your abuse of servant women. *The bigger, the blacker, the better. That's the reputation you have earned for yourself, Señor.* As she took in the too-tight cut of his breeches and the foppish handkerchief tucked into the sleeve of his summer blouse, Emanuela could easily imagine him just as her sister had depicted in her latest round of gossip from the Spanish post—how he had been caught wearing his dead wife's dressing gown while the drummer boy pleasured him on a pallet of feedsacks in the back of the government storehouse. Woman or boy, to Delago it apparently did not matter.

"My contacts here at Natchitoches," Delago continued smoothly, "tell me that Fanny is capable of anything, anything at all. That is why I am willing to offer a price so generous."

"I assume your contacts have informed you that she has a husband and children who also need her. Do you wish to purchase them as well?"

"Ah, Madame, of course I have considered that." Delago smiled, a twitch playing upon the corners of his mouth. "I also understand that her husband— François is his name, *no?*—is a somewhat unusual *negro* and I am sure it would be most gratifying to own him. But I have absolutely no need for a pack of wolf-cubs, and prudence tells me I would best serve my needs by purchasing only the wife."

Undoubtedly, Señor, *sin duda!* Still Emanuela kept the thought to herself. There were far more discreet reasons for refusing Delago's offer.

"Señor, the answer is still *no*. Fanny is not for sale. I am sure I need not point out to you that Louisiana's *Code Noir*, our colony's whole law of slavery, forbids separating families by sale. Certainly you have had enough dealings with officials here to know that."

"Of course, Madame. But we all know that the bureaucrats abroad who make our laws have no idea of the trials we endure here in the colonies. Your esteemed late husband was acutely aware of this problem, and if he were still alive to counsel you…"

"My esteemed late husband was acutely aware of the problems of humanity as well as those of bureaucracy," Emanuela interrupted shortly, "and if he were alive he would point out to you that the sacredness of the family is inviolate to all who honor God."

"But, Madame," Delago countered, frustration cutting through his unctuousness at last. "After all, we are discussing *negros*."

"Señor, I am discussing *people*. Men, women, and children. Christians. I have taught my servants to love their Creator and to fear his wrath if they break his commandments. Never would I break one that would cause them injury, even if my purse might suffer as a result."

Delago cleared his throat again. "Madame," he began hesitantly, dealing his last card in a final bid to trump her stubbornness.

"I am glad you brought up that subject, my lady, since I promised your son a while ago that I would not. I understand that the royal neglect of Louisiana causes even its best families to suffer financial embarrassment. Your son has intimated that a sale of this woman for so generous a price would ease your own situation. Perhaps if you consulted him…"

Emanuela stopped him coldly. "Señor, in this household I do not consult anyone, and you were ill-advised to speak to my son behind my back. I suffer no embarrassment, only self-reproach for having let this conversation continue to this point."

"Fanny!" Emanuela raised her voice but slightly, confident that her *négresse* would be hovering within earshot of the whole exchange. "Fanny, show Señor Delago the way out."

"That will not be necessary, Madame," the Castillian shot back, his voice brittle with rage. "A blind beggar could find his way out of this hovel." High heels clicking, Delago wheeled then from the room, ignoring all civilities of leavetaking. As she watched him go, likening him to the kind of cur that would back off but never tuck tail between his legs as he ran, Emanuela sank into her chaise, the last of her energy spent.

I was a fool to let Fanny go! she chided herself for the thousandth time in the past ten days. *My sister could have found some other nurse. She was just playing me to her own ends, like she always has. That was why she sent Padre Ballejo to plead for her.*

I'm too soft! That's my real problem. I am much too old to fall for such tricks—and much too old to deal with all I've put up with in Fanny's absence! Isabella has balked at everything, whining that she was trained to be a *lady's lady*, not for menial tasks like *sweeping*. Sure, that old Bambara came back into the household eagerly enough, huffing mightily and mumbling protestations that a good woman never got too old to be a *lady's lady*, and if she was now clumsy it was only a lack of practice at being a *lady's lady*—which wasn't her fault either, because she hadn't asked to be turned out years ago so Fanny could take her place. And on and on! Then comes Manon's complaints about Isabella interfering in the kitchen. And Nanette's complaints of Isabella interfering in the laundry.

Desperate. That's what I was! I had to be desperate to call in Fanny's daughter to wait on me. That lollygagging Dgimby's no better than the fat, old Bambara. She may be Fanny's girl, but she will never be good for anything but field work. It's no wonder, after all these trifling feuds and needless frustrations, I absolutely flew to the window in joy at the sight of Fanny riding up the hill in the arms of Justo's popinjay! What was it Louis told me that François once called the Spaniard? Ah, yes, Señor Jackal. *Ma foi!* The *nègre* had certainly sized up that man right!

As always, it was Fanny now who eased Emanuela back into the present, helping her confront the troubles the world kept throwing before her, unbidden and demanding to be dealt with. Sighing resignedly as her *négresse* raised her swollen feet onto the tabouret and began the nightly massage that made it possible for her to walk each morning, Emanuela continued her thoughts aloud.

"Undoubtedly, you overheard this wearisome *débat.*" It was a statement, not a question, and so Fanny made no effort to answer. Nor did Emanuela wait for her response.

"Impertinent *imbécile,* to say the least. I should have dismissed him sooner. Still, he had brought you home and spared my sister's family all that trouble, so I was loathe to be ungracious. I *was* gracious, up to the very last, was I not, Fanny?"

This time it definitely was a question, another of those querulous lead-ins to another round of self-pity, and so Fanny murmured the agreement that was expected. She need not have bothered. Emanuela had slipped back into that long-ago, whose memory had overtaken her the moment she spied the way Fanny sat upon Delago's mount.

A quarter century? Had it really been that long? she wondered now. How could it be, when I can still feel Louis's arms around me that whole ride through those scorching plains of Texas, and our torrid nights under the open sky. *Where exactly was that Asanai village we stayed in?* The one in which Louis had to ply some diplomacy or another with that awful Indian woman who all but ruled the place? *Angelina. Angelique,* yes! That's what Louis called her. Years before, the chit had followed Louis to Mexico, on his first trading venture with the Spanish. After that, she had taken Louis's manservant, Dumont, as her husband. And then she had lorded it over me the whole time we were there—as though Louis had been the servant and Dumont the master!

Ma foi! How could the gods be so unfair! My own son, every time he comes back from Tejas now, talks of the Río Angelina. To think that my people actually named a river for that woman! How could they, while *I,* the scion of Spanish governors, waste away among these French who never let me forget I'm not one of them? Bless Louis, he did try to name *this* river for me after he heard what they called the other one—the *Rivière Emanuelle* it would have been. Such a melodious ring! But some ruffian had made a joke of it and brayed that what the commandant's wife really needed was not her name upon the river but some of its canes upon her rump!

"Madame?" The sound of Fanny's voice, tinged a bit with worry, brought her back into the present; and she sighed, reminding herself that all these injustices and countless more were just crosses she must bear along the road to the Eternal Kingdom where she would find her true rewards.

"Fanny, I have a little confession to make," Emanuela went on at last, contritely, while her *négresse* continued to work miracles upon her feet. "Would you believe me if I told you I was tempted by Señor's offer of so much money? After all, I was not born to live in poverty such as this! My family controlled most of two *estados* in Mexico. Even M'sieur's people were the lords of *seigneuries* in Canada and in France, too, in ancient times. Oh, Fanny! How could I end up in such a lot as I'm reduced to at this post?"

That question hung there in the lengthening shadows of the evening, as Fanny pondered whether, this time, Madame expected an answer or was simply lost in thought. Before she could decide that quibble, her own memories of her own past—all those she had struggled to hold in chains since the death of the old M'sieur—rushed upon her and she snapped.

"Destiny does strange things to us, Madame. I was not born to this station, either. *My father was a king!*"

There! she had said it! She had stripped years of resentment to their core and, stricken now by her own audacity, she waited for the backlash from this woman who *owned* her—body, soul, and offspring.

Curiously, Emanuela seemed not to notice her servant's outburst. "*Oui,* Fanny," she murmured, with a flutter of a hand momentarily lifted from its resting place on her forehead. "M'sieur said something about that once. But of course we are not talking about the same thing at all, Fanny. An African 'king' and Spanish noblemen are worlds apart."

Fanny exhaled, a long hard rasp that seemed to flush from her all the fears that had chained her soul and tied her tongue since the day the slavers grabbed her from the woods into which she had wandered in childish play. Stranger still, the new breath that replaced that scalding one was filled with a sense of empowerment she had never felt in this woman's presence. Deliberately, she set Emanuela's feet back to the floor and walked away to clean the crumbs that still littered the windowsill and to brush away the ants that were still carrying them off, bite by bite.

"Yes, our birthrights were worlds apart, Madame," Fanny responded at last, choosing her words carefully but bluntly as she tested the bounds of their relationship. "So what difference does it make now? Neither of us will ever know those privileges again."

Again Emanuela took no notice of the brashness of her tone. "Perhaps you are right," she finally murmured, her voice trailing off into some other thoughts she did not bother to speak aloud.

"Is there anything more you need this evening, Madame?" Fanny demanded, as she closed the shutters for the night.

"No, Fanny. Go home to your family now. They've missed you.... Ah, yes!" Suddenly, Emanuela roused from the other world into which she had again begun to sink. "Before you go, there is something else you should know. There was an accident while you were gone."

Fanny froze.

"Your little Coincoin, sweet child! She tried to be a perfect mother to your babies, but yesterday they became so restless that she took them to the woods to pick pawpaws. Your youngest child—Jeanne, is it?—jumped into a bed of leaves for a moment's frolic, and there was a copperhead beneath the pile."

Fanny's throat jammed. Like the primeval dam of logs that jammed Red River above Natchitoches, like the flow of waters from the western mountains that could not break through the logjam, the question she tried to ask, the one she had to ask, just could not spill out aloud.

"Oh! I didn't mean to frighten you!" Emanuela went on lightly, fluttering her hand again to dismiss that thought. "Your child's all right now. You see, little Coincoin handled everything just the way you would have! She grabbed a broken chinaberry limb and flailed at the snake until it slithered back into the pile, and then she grabbed up the baby and ran home.

"Of course, no one was there," Emanuela continued, smiling at some thought she must have thought was funny. "I had sent François down to the post, and your boys were rounding up the cattle. Not a soul knew what had happened until Coincoin knocked on my door and calmly announced that she had tourniqueted the baby's leg, cut the wound just as she saw you do last year when old Isabella was bitten, then sucked the poison from the blood and bathed it with a wash of oil and hartshorn.

"So, there was only one thing she wanted from me," Emanuela added, chuckling at the punch line to come. "She wanted some *spirits* to put the child to sleep!"

The marrow began to gel again within Fanny's bones. Emanuela did not notice. Or did not care. "Tomorrow, Fanny, bring Coincoin with you when you come to work. I can see we have been wasting that child's talents! You simply must teach her everything you know. If I am ever deprived of you for another spell like this one, I'll need her to help me survive."

Fanny only nodded as she turned to go, still doubting that her voice would work and fearful of what would come out now if it did.

"And Fanny…"

The *négresse* froze, caught again on the tenterhook of a mistress who rarely saw beyond her own needs.

"To be completely honest with you, Fanny, I never could have sold you to Señor Jackal, no matter how much the money tempted me. He had personal reasons I disapprove of, but I had one of my own. I simply could not live without you."

Emanuela chuckled again to herself, holding on to that thought a moment more, and then she mused, "Do you think, Fanny, when I die, God will let me take you with me?" She was still toying with that thought when Fanny pulled the door behind her, drank in a deep draught of the night, and hurried home.

◯ 9 ◯

Summer 1750

Marie peered down at the odd-looking plant, then quickly over her shoulder at her young companion. Only three minutes in the woods and already she had found something! "Look, Coincoin!" she called out. "Here's a rattlesnake herb. See, it's tall and has long pointed spikes and hard prickles. Admit it now, Coincoin! I'm getting better, aren't I?"

Delighted with her prowess, the adolescent Ma'mselle de St. Denis deposited herself on a nearby stump, delicately lifting her skirt from under her so she would not rumple it. As she waited idly for the younger girl to dig the bulbous root, she patted her ringlets and tugged at the ribbon that held those unruly curls off her short, plump neck. "Is my bow still straight, Coincoin?"

"Of course. You haven't done anything yet to mess it up," the child sassed.

In the year Coincoin had spent with her mother in the St. Denis household, a curious tie had bound the child to her fifteen-year-old godmother, a chumminess with limits of its own that went unspoken. Both girls knew the older one's rank was born of race as well as years, although Marie pooh-poohed that thought as being much too *Louis* for her taste. To *him,* a St. Denis was better than everybody at this post and it was *improper* for her to associate with common riffraff—which, of course, meant all the other French girls of her age. And so, the lonely Marie had never known companionship until Fanny's precocious child was brought into her home.

Marie had, in fact, expected Louis to complain about Coincoin, as well, and she had the perfect retort already planned. Why, brother dear! she'd tell him, Coincoin is of *royal* blood! But then Louis exasperated her even more by paying no attention whatsoever to her new friendship, as though it were beneath his notice. So it was that, in one short year, the slave child had become not just a companion but, almost, the little sister Marie had never had.

"Besides," Coincoin went on disdainfully, "you still can't tell one plant from another, even if you are older than me. In four trips to the woods, Mama taught me every plant out here, but you've been coming with me to gather herbs every Monday since the daffodils first bloomed, and you still can't remember that a rattlesnake herb has shorter spikes with red spots underneath. That plant you found," Coincoin sniffed, "is *esquine.* It's good for nothing but making hair grow!"

"Really?" Marie giggled. "Maybe we ought to take some back for the old man Dolores married yesterday. He sure could use some hair. The top of his head is as round and shiny as the belly of his surtout!"

"Now, Ma'mselle!" Coincoin scolded, suppressing her own giggles. "Even a fine lady like you ought to show more respect for the new commandant! Why Mama said it was a great honor for him to pick your sister for his wife."

"Ha!" Marie retorted. "It was an honor to that old goat for Dolores to marry him, and she wouldn't have done it if Louis had not made her. I don't know why she didn't just refuse. Reverend Père could not have married them if Dolores had said she did not want to. That's church law, you know."

"But, M'sieur Louis...."

"Oh, Louis be hanged! I can promise you one thing, Coincoin. He's not picking my husband for me. I won't marry any old goat just 'cause he's the commandant, and a nobleman, and has a good *reputation.* And I told him so!"

Truth was, Marie had said a good bit more. It was positively mean, she thought, the way Louis kept praising the old De Blanc, while making snide remarks about the "rapscallion" Pet had married—especially since poor Pet was dead and couldn't defend the handsome noble she had swooned over for a year and a half before she did what she had to do to catch him! And so Marie had told her brother exactly what she knew Pet would have told him had she been there. If M'sieur de Blanc had a better reputation than Pet's rapscallion, then it was only because the old goat was too decrepit to do anything rapscallious anyway! Ohhhh, Louis had almost had a conniption at *that.*

Marie tittered at the recollection, and Coincoin bit her bottom lip to hold back the comment she knew she should not make.

"Naturally," Marie chattered on, "big brother got all puffed up and started lecturing me about saying things that might compromise my honor. So I reminded him that it hasn't been a year since De Blanc's old wife died. If you ask me, it's Louis who compromised our honor with his haste to marry off Dolores—just because the geezer's rich and politically important. That's what I told him!"

Coincoin grinned in spite of herself, at the thought of this family set-to. She didn't much like M'sieur Louis either, although Fanny had warned her sternly not to ever say how she felt. "What did he say then?"

"Oh, he just got mad and ordered me to my room. That's Louis's answer to everything I say and do. He just dismisses me as if I were a child. Well, I'm not!"

"No, ma'am. You sure aren't," Coincoin quipped, baiting her young mistress with a knowing look that was totally out of place on so innocent a face. Marie did not miss it, either.

"Why, whatever do you mean, child?" she asked indignantly, patting at her curls again.

Coincoin pondered for a moment weighing just how much she dared to say and how she ought to say it. Fanny had lectured her day in and night out as to what was *proper* for her to do and say when she was around Madame and M'sieur and all the other white masters at the post. But much of it never seemed to fit the situations she got into with Ma'mselle Marie. They weren't quite playmates, but there really did not seem to be a word that fit their teasing and their games and the fun they had even when the both of them had their chores to do. The problem now was that these trips into the woods didn't fit what their mamas harped on either. Despite their banter, she knew Marie did not come with her to pick plants because she cared about herbs or medicine. Nor was she worried about Coincoin getting lost out here all by herself like she claimed to be.

"Ummh," she finally ventured into the thicket of the problem. "I was just thinking about M'sieur Baptiste—and wondering what M'sieur Louis or your mama would say if I accidentally mentioned him."

Marie jumped frantically from her stump, stamping her slippered feet to little effect against the leaves that had carpeted those virgin woods since time primeval. "You wouldn't dare, you naughty child! When I get ready to tell Maman, I'll tell her. But you shan't! Wait! Come back here! Don't you run away from me before we settle this!"

"You'd better hurry up and tell her," Coincoin threw her retort over her shoulders as she darted between the persimmons and the poplars, squealing with all the glee of a little sister who is at last besting her bossy sibling. But then she stopped and her face went serious, "If you don't it'll be *your* honor that gets compromised!"

"Oh?" Marie huffed, as she caught up with her. "What would a child like you know about 'compromising honor'?"

"Mmmh, enough!" Coincoin teased. "Enough to notice you're so careful not to muss your pretty dress and your fine shoes that are too good to wear out here anyway. At least you don't muss them before M'sieur Baptiste just happens by. But after you go for your little walk with him, you sure come back with your ruffles mussed up then, ma'am."

"Why you impertinent little thing! Just because my skirts got caught once in the brambles...."

"Un-hunh," Coincoin broke in, thoroughly enjoying her chance to tease the older girl. "That's the excuse Dgimby used when Mama got all over her about *compromising her honor* with Zenon. 'Now Dgimby,' Mama told her, 'it's not proper for a young girl....'"

"Proper, proper, proper!" Marie shot back, tiring now of Coincoin's game. Goodness gracious! Sometimes the child and her mama sounded just like old Louis and Maman. *Proper!* That's all she seemed to hear out of any grown-up ever since she turned thirteen and got her monthlies. Especially from Louis. Especially since he'd gotten his last promotion to lieutenant! Outdone at the very thought of him, Marie pursed her lips and plopped her fists squarely on her hips, trying to look stern as she thought of the direst threat she could possibly make. "If you ever use that word around me again, child, I'll take away that nice Christian name I gave you at baptism and rename you *Louis!*"

Coincoin grinned, and Marie's straight face fell into one of pure frustration. "You just don't know what it's like!" she wailed, as she flounced onto another stump and wrapped her arms dejectedly around her drawn-up knees. "That's all I hear out of Louis every time he opens his mouth. *Thou shalt act proper!* You'd think he was a general already, the way his chest puffs up and he goes around passing out orders. He has more 'Thou shalt nots' than God himself!"

"Ma'mselle!"

"Well, it's true! 'I am thy brother and thy protector, *thou shalt not* disobey me!'" Marie mimicked. "And that's just the beginning. Every time I set foot out of the house, he wags his finger at me and bellows, '*Thou shalt not compromise your honor*, or I won't be able to find you a husband!' Well, ol' General God needn't worry about that! I'm perfectly capable of finding my own husband. And he won't be old and fat and *honorable*, either!"

Even in the shadows of the glade, Coincoin could see, but could not understand, the glow that suddenly brightened her Ma'mselle's face.

"No... he'll be young and handsome and naughty, like De Mézières." Her voice lowered to a whisper, "In fact, he *is* young and handsome and naughty!"

"Uh-oh," the child giggled, her eyes still wide. "M'sieur Louis will never let you marry him."

"Oh, yes, he will!" Marie retorted. "I've made sure of that." But then the gold flecks faded from her eyes and her cheeks seemed to pale a shade in the dappled light that filtered through the canopy of the trees. *Feeling* a difference she didn't understand, Coincoin pondered for a moment the mysteries of being fifteen and a half.

"You what?" she prompted.

At first, there was no answer. But then a twig crackled beyond them, and Marie shot up from her stump. "Oh, you ask too many questions, child! Go pick your herbs. I'm going for a walk with M'sieur Baptiste." With that she flew into the little grove of poplars to join her young and handsome and naughty lover.

◌ 10 ◌

Marie was wrong, and Coincoin was right. Louis did not let his sister marry her young, handsome, and naughty lover. Whatever plan the impetuous Marie had concocted obviously did not work. That much was clear to her young god-child as gloom descended upon the Big House. Coincoin had grown accustomed, these past few months, to the regimen Fanny enforced in Emanuela's household, so unlike the riot of her own little cabin where a half-dozen children jostled for space in less than half that many rooms. But in the week that followed Coincoin's last trip into the woods with Ma'mselle, the St. Denis parlor turned funereal—its pall relieved only by the ravings of Marie's older brother.

Just what M'sieur Louis's curses meant, Coincoin was not sure, since so many of his words were ones she had never heard before. Besides, Fanny kept finding more and more work for her to do outside the Big House, at least while M'sieur was there. Eventually, it was through Fanny herself that the child pieced together the matter that had upended the family and would, eventually, decide the course of Coincoin's life itself.

At night, in the privacy of her own bed, Fanny would report to François the histrionics that played out around her in the Big House while she moved among her masters with the muteness of those whose duty is to serve, not judge. Her whispered tales lacked the turbulence of Louis's rants, and her words were far more carefully chosen. But only a thin wall partitioned the bed Fanny shared with François from the pallet Coincoin shared with Jeanne, and so the precocious Coincoin lay awake each night, cataloging things she was not meant to hear.

Oh, *mais oui!* Marie really had *compromised her honor!* That much was clear, although Coincoin still puzzled over what those grave words meant. She had, just that spring, heard Fanny warning Dgimby not to *compromise her honor,* and she knew it wasn't just that Dgimby's boyfriend was a low-class *nègre* who couldn't even speak good French. *Non,* it had something to do with *kissing,* but just *what* was the puzzle Coincoin could not figure out.

Maybe it *was* who the fellow was, she decided when Fanny described M'sieur's tirades after Marie named her beau. A *je ne sais quoi!* Louis had called him; and Coincoin thought it funny that M'sieur Louis called M'sieur Baptiste an *I-don't-know-what,* because if there was one thing she had learned during her months in the Big House, it was that M'sieur Louis *always* knew what to call *everybody!*

Eventually, the chaos of the household found its rhythm, thanks primarily to the commandant's dispatch of Louis upon another mission to the Indians of Spanish Tejas. In his absence, the household was left to run itself, or rather left to Fanny. Emanuela rarely mustered the strength to leave her bed and Marie now stayed in hers, as well. Crying and eating, eating and crying, the young girl did little else from dawn to dusk and well into each night. Within weeks, her pretty face had puffed and blurred and her little frame, already plump, became quite fat. It was then that Emanuela forbade her daughter to leave the house at all, even for Sunday Mass.

To Coincoin, that was the most curious thing about this whole affair—next to Marie's acceptance of the maternal edict. She could see the bitterness that seethed inside Ma'mselle, even when she gave in, but her innocence offered Coincoin nothing by which she could explain the meaning of Marie's behavior. She only knew that the feisty playmate who had romped with her and played pranks upon her, who had seriously whispered the most inconsequential secrets into her ear, had turned cold and cutting.

It was a frigid, blustery November when the truth erupted. Winter had come early to Red River, blanketing the landscape with a rare autumn snow. For a week, the wind had howled mercilessly, blasting down the flue of the great, stone fireplace François had built in the big room that doubled as living quarters for his family and a bedroom for himself and Fanny. Dead embers froze that night where a fire had crackled less than two hours before and Fanny shivered, snuggling closer to her husband in the big four-poster that overwhelmed the front room of their cabin.

What a bed! Fanny had actually gaped in wonder when he hauled it in and set it up. One whole summer François had spent in carving it, working by moonlight after his day's labor was done. A tribute to his princess, he had called it. The altar of their love, he sometimes jested. And a work of art, it was. That was what had truly frightened her the day M'sieur Louis barged in and found it standing there. He had stared at it, but he did not say what all of them were thinking: that the home of the master held nothing half so fine. No one, not even Madame, had broached the subject since, and Fanny knew they dared not. Master and slave they were. Each knew their place. But they also knew who and what it was that held together this little fiefdom on St. Denis Hill while M'sieur Louis pursued his politics and his trade among the Tejas Indians.

Beside her now, Fanny's newest babe began to whimper in her cradle, and so she brought it to their bed to warm it between herself and François. It was then, just as she was drifting off to sleep again, that she heard the pounding on her door and Louis's high-pitched frenzy. Intuitively, she knew what her master wanted. It was much too early. The young Ma'mselle should have another month to go and by then, Fanny had hoped, M'sieur would be gone as well. But Marie's time had surely come against all predictions of the learned doctor and amidst all the rage of her dishonored brother. The assault upon Fanny's door did not abate as she returned Marie Louise to the cradle and shivered into her dress. Then, throwing a deer skin over her head and shoulders, she braced herself against the fury of both the night and her master.

Nothing but the wind cut their silence as Louis stormed across to the back gallery of the Big House, with Fanny behind him, stumbling to hold her own against the raging gusts. "M'sieur, the doctor?" she inquired discreetly, as they stepped at last inside.

"Doctor? There is no doctor, woman! The damn fool is on another drunk. That's all they ever send to this colony. Damned drunks and butchers! All the scum who have disgraced themselves in France and can no longer make a living there. The refuse of our beloved, mother country! That's all this hell-hole gets. Fitting, though, isn't it?" Louis sneered.

M'sieur was obviously deep into his own cups, Fanny thought as she surveyed the situation she would have to deal with. A fire crackled at both ends of the long room, but the air was frigid. From a pile of comforters on the chaise, Emanuela whimpered, stretching out one arm to her *négresse* while the other pressed at wrinkles on her forehead. "Fanny! Oh, Fanny! I need you."

Fanny had no pity. "Get up, Madame! There's nobody here to help me with Ma'mselle, except you and your two sons, and a birthing-room is no place for menfolk." Marching into Emanuela's chamber, she yanked open the armoire and grabbed a faded robe. "Here," she ordered, throwing it on the chaise. "Put that on, so we can tend your child."

"*Oui*, Fanny," Emanuela murmured dutifully. She stumbled from her chaise, but only stood, dazed, as though she still could not comprehend what was at hand. From Marie's chamber, a low moan rose into a shriek; and from the fireplace behind them, where Louis stood, came another string of curses.

The next twenty-four hours were a blur for Fanny. The storm outside subsided, but within the Big House life still spent its fury. The little Marie, so plump of flesh but so small of bone, slipped in and out of consciousness, as the infant forced its way into her narrow pelvis. Fanny's decoction of St. John's Wort helped to ease the ripping pain, and the little mother, herself a child, begged for long, great draughts; but her nurse would give her only sips. Too great a dose would ease not just the pain but also the contractions. And that urgent force had to hold if this infant and its mother were to survive.

Beyond their chamber, voices rose and fell, as the family came and went. Emanuela hurried the young Pierre Antoine from the house as soon as he awoke, telling him to take Caesar's sons into the woods to hunt for game. Marianne brought the family breakfast from the lean-to kitchen, surveyed the situation, and fetched Nanette from the wash room to help Fanny—whereupon their mistress collapsed again upon her chaise.

Midmorning, Dolores tripped up the hill from the post to gossip with her mother, and then stayed to suffer with her, in more ways than one. Five months married, Dolores still showed no signs of pregnancy, and her aging husband had already begun to question the fertility of his young bride. Then, as night fell again, De Blanc came in search of his wife and stayed to help the now thoroughly sodden Louis mourn the family's loss of honor.

"Damned to hell!" Louis exclaimed as Fanny became aware again of his rising pitch. Although the heavy door between the salon and Marie's chamber was firmly closed, it did little to contain his rage. All day long, Emanuela had tried to shush her elder son, sternly forbidding his angry oaths, but she had succeeded only in reducing them to a mutter. Bolstered now by the presence of another male and a fresh bottle of *tafia*, Louis unleashed the rage that had seethed inside him ever since Marie confidently announced that she had picked her own husband and Louis had no choice but to agree. So she thought!

"Damned to hell!" Louis said it again. "My chances of ever arranging a decent marriage for that little chit are damned once and for all!"

"Louis!" his mother pleaded. "You cannot speak about poor Marie that way!"

"Madame *mère*, I will not be silenced," he sneered. "My words are not nearly so disgusting as your daughter's behavior. Our sainted Marie Rose was the wife of the *subdélégué* of this post, and dear Dolores is now the wife of our commandant, no less. Even Petronille...."

Louis's lip curled, "Well, at least Pet did wed an officer and a nobleman, in spite of the circumstances. But who does Marie pick to destroy the family honor? A raunchy smile and a big lewd body with no brains or family name. Then she had the gall to think she could force me to allow such a *mésalliance!* At least if she had sullied herself with some man of *class*, had the rogue not been willing to wed her as well as bed her, I might have found an officer to give her bastard a name in return for all this family has. But your *poor* daughter, Madame *mère*, did not even have the decency to choose well when she hiked her skirts!"

Marie moaned as another pain tore through her loins. Her eyelids fluttered, and she floated back once more into the conscious world. Quickly, Fanny gave her another draught, chancing a deeper one this time, as she cradled Marie in her arms and began to croon. She had brought this girl-child into the world, and now she sat with her as Marie, herself, descended into that valley-of-the-shadow-of-death that claims so many mothers. The last thing this poor child needed, Fanny thought, was to hear those ravings of her brother. She had little enough will to live already.

Marie floated away again, and Fanny checked once more beneath the comforter. The infant's head was visible now, a thin patch of dark wet hair against a rosy skull. With a little more prayer and less profanity, Fanny thought, this miracle of birth might be wrought this night after all.

"To be fair, dear brother, one could also say this problem is partly your own doing." Dolores's voice was barely audible through the closed doorway, but Fanny could hear its sharpness. "Did it not occur to you, *mon Louis,* that you could have let her marry the boy? Then her child would have had both a name and a father."

"A peasant's name!" Louis hissed. "Never has the noble name of Juchereau de St. Denis been coupled in holy wedlock with the name of a peasant, a churl of mean ancestry—another savage *mestizo* probably, judging from his swarthiness."

"Mean? Now, Louis!" Again, it was his sister's chide. "He didn't seem so mean to me. Each time he looked at Marie, that night he came to share responsibility for their action, I thought his eyes were rather full of love." Dolores's voice choked slightly, her words barely audible, but the dreams the young matron had forsaken when she accepted her brother's marital edict came through clearly to her old nurse, even if her words did not.

"Full of love? *Mon Dieu!* You mean lust and greed!" Louis sneered. "I'm sure your husband will agree that Marie's adventurer had his profit as well as his pleasure. It did not take much urging to persuade the rogue that five hundred *sols* could take him far enough way to find another dalliance."

Dolores's gasp could be heard even above Marie's fresh moans. "So that's why he disappeared! And poor Marie thought he left her of his own accord!"

"She'll recover from that little disappointment—a lot faster than her reputation will."

This time it was a scream, not a moan, that burst all the way from the young girl's womb. And then the swelling moved, perceptively, downward under the fresh linen that covered her. Fanny leaped to the foot of the bed, and her long hands cradled the infant as it came into the world. Pushing the reddened comforter aside, she raised to the candlelight this new, frail gift of God.

Another girl-child, Fanny thought. Another girl-child whose honor M'sieur can worry over. Another girl-child to be sold to the highest or most important bidder, no matter how old, how fat, how ugly, or how mean he might be. Then Fanny laughed—if such a primordial caw could ever be called a laugh—as a new thought struck her. It's not just *nègres* who are enslaved. For a woman, it mattered little whether she was black or white. They were all somebody's property.

With a will Fanny did not think the little mother had left in her, Marie survived the ordeal of those two days. From the moment Fanny placed into her arms the little infant she had borne, Marie adored her tiny, swarthy replica of Baptiste. Softly, she kissed its cheek and ran her fingers, exploringly, through its wet, black hair. Then, with a virginal embarrassment that made Fanny smile at last, Marie drew the infant closer to her under the cover and offered it one of her waiting breasts.

Somehow, Fanny made it through the day that followed. As evening fell, Nanette put her own family to bed in their little cabin in the camp and hastened back to the Big House to relieve Fanny for the night. Gratefully, Fanny left instructions and then plodded into the moonlit snow toward her own cabin and her husband's comfort.

From the little chamber behind the big room, Coincoin heard her mother but resisted the impulse to bound from her pallet. It had been three nights since M'sieur Louis had awakened them and taken Fanny away, and Coincoin knew her mother would be exhausted. There would be time enough in the morning, she told herself, to tell her how much she had been missed—and to pry from her an explanation of why she had been gone so long and why François had ordered Coincoin to stay at home.

"Marie Louise needs your care," her father had told her that first morning of Fanny's absence, with a look that forbade all questions and refueled her curiosity. But Coincoin knew that the little "Mariotte," as she liked to call this newest babe, was doing quite well under Dgimby's watch. *Non,* whatever was happening at the Big House, Coincoin's instincts argued, it was Fanny who could have used her help.

Through the wall beside her bed, Coincoin could hear her mother slip between the covers without taking the time to eat the supper François had left warming on the embers. From the curtained bed on the other side of the wall, she could hear the usual murmurs. Then two words came through with stark clarity and she bolted upright, oblivious to the cold as she pressed her ear to the wall. What was that about Ma'mselle's *bastard child?*

An eerie tingling almost took her breath away. Never before, to her recollection, had Coincoin heard the word *bastard,* but she certainly knew what a *child* was, and never in her wildest fantasies about Marie had she thought of *that.*

So *that's* what Ma'mselle did! she said to herself over and again that night after she crawled back under her comforter, shivering as much from shock as from the cold. Just how Marie had managed to do *that* was still unclear, but somehow she had done *that* without a husband, and Coincoin had never known anyone who had a child without a husband—except Sainte Marie, the Mother of God, for whom she and Ma'mselle and most other little Christian girls were named.

The next morning, Fanny calmly brought up the subject that Coincoin had not yet mustered courage enough to broach. As she squatted before the hearth, frying for their breakfast a generous portion of the bear Choera had trapped while she was gone, Fanny quietly announced that Coincoin would return with her to the Big House that morning.

Madame was impressed, Fanny told her second-born daughter, with the way Coincoin tended her own little brothers and sisters, and the way she had mastered the medicines Fanny had taught her. Now Madame had a new duty for her that was even more important than taking care of Mariotte. Then Fanny explained, just as though it was the most natural thing in the world, Coincoin thought, that God had blessed Ma'mselle Marie with the most precious gift he ever gave a woman. A child. And Madame had decided that Coincoin should be its nurse.

The new assignment did not awe her. She simply stood there, debating whether she should first ask her mother *why* God had given Ma'mselle the child or why Ma'mselle's baby was more important than Baby Mariotte. But for these and all her questions there would be no answer. Fanny would give the child no chance to ask them. To Coincoin's vexation, her mother silenced her with that look adults always used to hide the important things in life; and it took some doing for Coincoin to stand respectfully through Fanny's latest litany of do's and don'ts.

When they returned to the Big House, Fanny cautioned, Coincoin could no longer act like a child in any way. Politely, Coincoin interjected the expected, "Yes ma'am."

Nor could Coincoin continue to treat Ma'mselle as a playmate, her mother admonished. Ma'mselle Marie was now an adult, and in the adult world there was no room for friendship between a mistress and her slave.

"Yes, ma'am."

Above all, Fanny continued, Coincoin must never, *ever* ask foolish questions about things that were none of her business. Whatever she needed to know, her mother or Madame would tell her. All she had to do was just what she was told.

Again, the wooden "Yes, ma'am" acknowledged her instructions and, for a fleeting moment, Fanny allowed herself to feel her daughter's struggle with the dumb, mute role that was their lot in life.

Coincoin did not merely return to the Big House that day. She *moved* into it. She, her three dresses, her two chemises, her two changes of rough and scratchy underwear and well-darned stockings, her one pair of shoes, and the little wooden doll that François had carved for her on a long-ago Christmas. All these belongings were layered into a little basket and set in the *cabinet* behind Marie's chamber, next to the moss mattress that had been put there for Coincoin to sleep on.

It bothered the child, at first, seeing her mother only in the day hours when Fanny was so busy, and scarcely ever seeing François and Dgimby and Jean Baptiste or little Jeanne and Mariotte and the playmates she had left behind. Still, the new duties were far heavier than she expected, leaving little time for loneliness. There were diapers to change and wash, and sugar teats to fill, itching gums to rub with oil of cloves through sleepless nights, and cries to rock away so Ma'mselle could get her rest.

It was those nights that overwhelmed Coincoin the most, as she snatched bits of sleep between the baby's feedings, its changes, and its colic. None of this was a surprise to her, of course; Fanny had trained her well. But Jeanne and Mariotte had still been just her *doll babies,* to play with in the pasture and tuck in at nighttime before she went to bed herself, knowing that their mama would listen for their whimpers the long night through.

Now it was *she*—barely nine but no longer a child—who bore the brunt of motherhood, while Ma'mselle played with Eleanore until she tired and gave her mother's milk until it dried. Soon, the tiny Eleanore, not quite white enough to fit into the world in which she had been born, became in Coincoin's mind not so much Ma'mselle's baby as her own. And then, the graceful wooden doll François had carved for her, of the blackest walnut he could find, lay forgotten at the bottom of Coincoin's little basket of belongings.

∽ 11 ∽

2 June 1754

A fly buzzed incessantly around the netting that covered her mattress, beating at the thin gauze folds as it chased an army of spineless mosquitoes back into the corners to hide until another night. Beneath the netting, Coincoin flounced restlessly, wide awake and sticky wet from the sweat that soaked her ticking. The first rays of dawn barely crept through the open shutters, but the heat was already stultifying. Slipping from her bed, she swatted the fly before its droning could wake the little Eleanore, who slept in the crib beside her.

Today! Ma'mselle's wedding day! Again, Coincoin felt that curious shiver of excitement and dread as she shimmied into the thin muslin dress she had inherited from Dgimby and fumbled to fasten the laces across her budding breasts. The bodice was too tight already, and Coincoin could not help giggling as she recalled the perplexed looks her mama gave her lately. It was positively indecent, Fanny kept saying. Here this child was not quite twelve, and already she was more developed than her teenaged sister. Positively indecent!

Indecent! Coincoin grinned to herself. That was a word she had heard a lot of these past few years, ever since Ma'mselle quit going to the woods with her to gather herbs—and to meet her boyfriend. *Indecent* was the word that had replaced *proper* in everyone's admonishments.

Had that really been just four years ago? Coincoin asked herself this sweltering morning, as she turned to spread the plain cotton coverlet over the little bed that Madame finally had set up for her. As always, Coincoin noticed that the coverlet was worn and frayed and brown and ugly and had no embroidery and no lace tester as Marie's bed did. But she could not blame her young ma'mselle. The poor girl had no say-so about anything that went on in the Big House. To Emanuela and Louis she was still a mindless child. Only Coincoin really knew how much Ma'mselle had changed.

Rarely now did the yellow sparks dance impishly in Ma'mselle's eyes, as they had when Fanny first began taking Coincoin to the Big House. That firelight had turned cold and hard. Sometimes she softened when Coincoin did her a special favor, or when little Eleanore laughed and threw back her head the way Baptiste used to do. But when any of the family approached Marie, the voice that answered them was caustic.

Even Ma'mselle Dolores—Madame de Blanc, as Coincoin kept forgetting to call her—lectured Marie about how she never would find a husband if she constantly acted as though she was made of kumquats instead of ripened plums. Naturally, that only made Ma'mselle madder, and her voice turned even sharper when she informed her older sister very curtly that she had not the slightest interest in any man.

That was all before this spring, though. Before the young Spaniard appeared in Natchitoches. Commandant de Blanc had been the one who brought him to the Big House, with some story about his having fled from Tejas. To the family's surprise, Ma'mselle had been amused, and Coincoin could not stifle her own grin as she recalled her Ma'mselle's old infatuation with rapscallions.

The Spaniard's name was Don Manuel Antonio Bermudez y de Soto and he had served as secretary to the Spanish governor before the unfortunate discovery of certain dealings he had with the French. Naturally, since the man was well acquainted with Spanish justice, he had seen the wisdom of leaving Tejas. And it was just as natural that he should expect asylum from his allies. Not that he said so directly, of course, when he entertained the commandant and M'sieur Louis and Madame, and Ma'mselle as well, with a wildly improbable tale of fleeing from Spanish soldiers and hostile Indians.

While others laughed, De Blanc had assured the Spaniard that his "crime" really was not so bad. In fact, the French greatly appreciated his assistance. Under the circumstances, the least they could do would be to offer him a guarantee of safety and the hospitality of the St. Denis home.

Emanuela had not been so sure. *She's never really sure of anything any more!* Coincoin had tittered, thinking of all the ways everybody used that now to their advantage. Being a Spaniard, Madame had seemed to think perhaps she should not openly help a Spanish fugitive. Patiently, confidently, persistently, De Blanc had then persuaded his mother-in-law that they owed the man their aid for all he had done for them in the past. Without his assistance, in fact, Louis's recent mission to sway the Tejas Indians to French allegiance might have failed. Where else, De Blanc insisted, could Don Manuel go now and be safe, except the home of the late commandant whose very name still made Spanish knees tremble?

Coincoin had not said so, after all Fanny had told her to mind her own business while she was in the Big House, but it did seem obvious that the old commandant had another reason for leaving Don Manuel on St. Denis Hill. Only Madame did not see it. M'sieur Louis did not see it either, and that was strange. He should have thought of it himself! And so, while he still ranted that he never would find a husband for his sullied sister, he failed to notice that she spent little time now in her chamber with Eleanore and a lot more time in the salon with her family and their guest.

It was no coincidence, either, Coincoin knew, that Ma'mselle ordered Nanette to make her two new dresses, or suddenly decided that her old hairdo was too childish. Perhaps she ought to put her tresses up in braids instead of curls, Marie had mused one spring evening as the fragrance of hibiscus wafted through the open shutters, surrounding them with its opiate. Or, maybe fasten her locks up off her neck with a *sophisticated* comb? What did Coincoin think?

"The comb, Ma'mselle," she had agreed offhandedly, squelching her own precocious thoughts that her mistress had not yet dared to voice.

By the next week, Marie's questions had become bolder. Was not Don Manuel the most handsome man in all the post? Again Coincoin nodded coolly, but this time her stifled giggles broke, Marie tittered back, and four strained years of playing roles that neither of them wanted gave way to one last afternoon in which they were chums again. Bouncing on the corner of Marie's big bed, they mooned over the Spaniard's dark and sinful eyes, his arrogant nose, the jut of his jaw, and the slim and muscular body that was just perfect, even though he was almost as short as Ma'mselle herself.

Within the week De Blanc had scurried back up the hill, waving a letter he had received from the Tejas governor. Conveniently, Don Manuel was out. Emanuela, as usual, lounged upon her chaise and Louis, as usual, sprawled at the old oak secretary he despised for its frontier crudeness, muttering once more over the accounts his mother and sister had run up at Rambin's Shop. From their chamber, Coincoin and Marie clearly heard the conversation that ensued, since the commandant made no effort to spare the sensibilities of the sister-in-law whose life he now openly planned.

"Barrios knows that De Soto is here and says he must conclude one of two things. Either we are unaware of the warrant for the man's arrest, or else we are partners to his treason.

"Naturally," De Blanc continued, "Barrios demands that we return De Soto for trial. That leaves us with just two choices, Louis. Either we give up the man, which seems a shame considering how useful he has been, or else we have to find a way to justify our refusal."

"And I assume you have already found that justification?" Louis had inquired.

"Mais oui," the commandant smiled. "In fact, I'm surprised you have not thought of this yourself, since it solves a little problem that's bothered you for several years."

Louis was now attentive, bills forgotten.

"It's perfectly logical, Louis. Don Manuel becomes the brother-in-law of the commandant of this post and the son-in-law of its revered founder. That gives him a reason to want to stay here and us a reason to support him, without any of us having to admit to anything the Spaniards may suspect."

Both Coincoin and Marie had heard Louis's long, low whistle. *"Parbleu!* You are right! And De Soto would not dare refuse such a convenient solution to his problem."

"Of course not," De Blanc had purred. Madame had murmured something they could not hear and Marie, behind the closed door to her chamber, with no one to see her but her handmaid, had fainted from sheer giddiness. Her brother had once again decided her life for her, but this time she did not mind at all.

Don Manuel agreed, naturally. What he actually said, neither Marie nor Coincoin knew, because that discussion was held elsewhere. But, within three hours, Louis had marched into his sister's chamber and announced to her that Bermudez y de Soto had asked for her hand in marriage and that he had given it. To Louis's utter surprise, his sister calmly agreed and asked that Reverend Père be told to announce the banns immediately.

Coincoin had barely made it behind the cabinet door before she loosed a flood of giggles. Ma'mselle had won this battle with her brother after all! Just as she had sworn, that day out in the woods, Marie had not let Louis marry her off to an old important dullard. *Non,* Ma'mselle had gotten herself a rapscallion after all.

Père Eustache had announced the banns promptly, as Louis ordered. Yesterday, the third and last of them had been read, and today at noon Marie would become Doña de Soto. In her excitement, Coincoin had tossed half the night, before drifting off into her dreams. Even then, she had slept fitfully, until finally she had given up and slipped out of bed—her anticipation tainted somehow with something akin to dread.

The future Coincoin saw that morning left her sad, scared, and more than a little lonely. Ma'mselle would continue to live in the Big House, with Don Manuel, and Coincoin would continue to serve her; but the camaraderie they had shared these past five years would, after noon today, be forever gone.

"Coincoin, are you up yet?" Marie's call shattered her reverie, and she could not miss its edge of petulance. "Come help me fix my hair. Oh, damn these curls! Coincoin!"

"Coming, Ma'mselle," she replied. Quickly smoothing her own cropped velvet with a touch of rose oil to stave off the summer frizzies, Coincoin lifted her shoulders high to claim another smidgen of the height that had become her one advantage over her young mistress. Then, donning her mother's mien, she glided into Ma'mselle's chamber in a perfect imitation of Fanny's long and sylphlike stride.

It was Marie's wedding day, not her own, but for the rest of her life, Coincoin would remember the second of June 1754 as the day that she, too, ceased to be a child. Mimicking the poise that was her mother's crown and mantle, she picked up the boar's hair brush and quietly set to work, coaxing Marie's unruly locks as she had done a hundred times before and would do a thousand times again, before the day that another young man with olive skin would finally, irrevocably, come between them.

15–19 April 1758

The laughter of the children tinkled in the breeze as they tumbled across the broad meadow, poking fat fingers into scattered patches of golden daffodils, peering solemnly beneath each leaf that lay moldering where last autumn's breeze had blown it. A triumphant squeal announced Eleanore's discovery and a flurry of pudgy legs, some white, some black, descended upon her clump of clover. Then little arms again flailed wildly in search of another egg. Two weeks had passed, almost, since Easter; but the magic of that special day still held the little ones enthralled—not the mystery of the Resurrection but the enchantment of the childish, pagan games to which the Christian world still clung.

"Another hunt, Coincoin! Make us another hunt!" The seven-year-old

Eleanore had begged when they found the fallen bird's nest that morning, with its tiny, speckled eggs intact. And so Coincoin, almost as eagerly as the rest of her little flock, had boiled them, dyed three yellow with ayac wood and the rest red with achechy juice, and hid them in the meadow while twelve sets of fingers pretended to cover six eager faces. Knowingly, Coincoin had rewarded the expected peeks with a dramatic show of hiding those seven eggs behind every generous clump of greenery in the meadow.

At sixteen, Coincoin was a woman now. As she sat amidst the grass, her sculpted arms wrapped around long, lean legs that stretched immodestly beyond her too-short skirt, there came to mind a memory—or was it a dream?—of another hunt years before on this same hill. Fanny was there, just as she had been at every Easter hunt before this year. And there was Ma'mselle Marie and her now-dead sisters, and Dgimby and Choera, too. Only they were younger, a different mix of squeals and giggles, but the same blend of innocence that had just begun to see the differences between castes and classes, black and white.

She was there, too. It had to be her. But this other her could barely walk, and everyone else kept finding all the eggs—until He came, the big man that she remembered so starkly. A shiny coat. A big square jaw and a mahogany mane of hair. And He bent down and took her little hand and led her to the special spot where the biggest egg of all had been tucked away from sight.

That same image came back this April afternoon as Coincoin sat on the lush carpet of St. Denis Hill, freshly mowed by a herd of cows, and watched the children frolic. Instead of Mama hiding the eggs, it is now me, she thought, secretly coveting this new passing of the guard, bittersweet though it was. Instead of Dgimby and Choera giving in when Ma'mselle Marie and Pet claimed an egg as theirs, it is now Mama's newest babies that give way to Ma'mselle's little girls. Only He is missing—that big, magnificent man with the light olive face and the tender gray-green eyes that could look right into your heart and read your secret wishes.

Sometimes she had almost asked her mother who He was, but always she stopped herself. Fanny just never talked about the past. Once Coincoin had inquired about the strange red dots that marked the little circle on her mother's forehead, but Fanny's eyes had clouded and she just walked away. Then Coincoin had asked François, only to be told that one day, when the time was right, her mother would talk. Until then, she should not ask.

So Coincoin did not pry, yet no day passed that she did not wonder. About many things. About the mark. About the big man who had read her secret longing. About herself, why her skin was the blue-black of a raven and Marie's was the color of cream. About why her Mama's children had to give in when Marie's children claimed the eggs.

That last night before Fanny and François left, for an eerie moment, Coincoin had the feeling that her mother was about to tell her. The moment had both chilled and warmed her, hinting that the door to her past was about to open and then slam shut forever. But Madame had called Fanny, and that had ended *that*. When her mother returned, she had nothing more to say; and Coincoin had not dared to press her because she knew Fanny's heart weighed heavily that night. Fanny's and François's both.

Neither of them liked going to Los Adaës. Coincoin knew that, though she had no idea why. Fortunately they did not often go. Madame was almost always ill now and rarely felt up to the trip; but whenever her melancholy lifted and she remembered the family of her birth, she had Fanny pack her bags, her medicine, and herself into her little buggy. Then François drove them the fifteen miles down El Camino Real that took them across the border into Spanish Tejas.

This trip would be no different, as far as Emanuela knew. She had awakened Good Friday morning in a mood of gaiety that definitely did not suit the mournfulness of that holy day; and she had announced just after breakfast that they—she, Fanny, and François—would spend their Easter holy days at Los Adaës.

"Yes, Madame," was all that Fanny murmured, but Coincoin did not miss the flash that shot through her mother's eyes. What would it matter to Madame, after all, that Jeanne was to make her First Communion this Easter Sunday? Or that François had carved for the occasion a wooden Rosary, just as he had done for Coincoin's first Communion four Easters past? Or that Fanny had made a new dress for her daughter's celebration, working by the firelight every night until the embers lost their glow? Coincoin knew the old Madame well enough to know that all this mattered naught.

And so, again, Fanny and François had left without complaint, and they had missed the Easter processional with Jeanne in her new white gown, with the chain of wooden beads so intricately carved, wrapped in prayer around her virginal fingers as she tasted for the first time of the Body and Blood of the Risen Savior.

Lost in her thoughts, Coincoin did not hear at first the wild creaking of wheels, or the frantic pounding of hooves from Emanuela's matched pair of Spanish pacers, or the cracking of the whip in empty air. It was not until her father's crisp *Ay-yie-yie-iiee!* cut through the children's mirth that she noticed the carriage careening wildly up the hill, with François standing before the driver's seat, goading Madame's prized stallions to untried limits. Behind him, in the half-closed buggy, only Fanny's bent back was visible, as she knelt over the floor. Madame was no where to be seen.

The vehicle screeched to a halt before the front gallery, as Coincoin flew up the hill with her flock scrambling willy-nilly behind her. Fanny jumped into the dust, her bag of medicine in tow, calling for Marie. Then François stepped upon the carriage, bent deep, and gently raised Emanuela in his arms, heedless of the blackness that trickled from her mouth and across his sleeve.

"Maman!"

As Coincoin crested the hill, she could hear Marie's scream, and the anguish in that wail was real. Eight years of bitterness had sat daily at the table between the old Madame and her rebellious daughter, Coincoin thought; but the love was there, just as though it never had been tried.

"No, Ma'mselle! Wait!" Quickly Fanny stepped into Marie's pathway, as her young mistress flew from the kitchen to the carriage with her newest baby at her breast. "Don't touch her, Ma'mselle. Not her! Not me!"

With Emanuela in his arms, François crossed the broad gallery in two strides, kicked open the heavy oaken door, and disappeared inside. Slowly, walking backwards, Fanny edged toward the Big House to join him, her arm still outstretched, palm first, in that age-old gesture that plainly says, *Come no further.*

"The fever," Fanny croaked. "It's the fever. Last night, the first man died at Los Adaës, and Madame insisted we had to leave. But we left too late. Your mama's face was flushed before we loaded her into the buggy. She insisted upon coming home, but she was too weak, and the road too hard."

Before her, Coincoin watched a miracle happen. The giddy Marie, twenty-two and still an untried child, as frivolous and irresponsible as the infants she had borne, became a woman. "Fanny, the fever must not spread past this hill. We cannot have an epidemic at both posts." Marie's voice was calm, her eyes steely, as, for the first time, she tried on the cloak of authority and clearly liked it.

"Coincoin! Take the children to the fort and stay with them. Madame de

Blanc will make room for you and for Don Manuel. Don't let him come until I send for all of you, and do not send the doctor or the priest. They would only spread the plague. If Fanny cannot save Maman, no one can. If she doesn't, well, Maman has said enough prayers already to buy her way to heaven."

"Marianne!" Marie turned to her cook, who had followed her from the kitchen. "Go back to the camp. We'll get our own meals, here. Fanny, you need help, so I'm staying. And François stays. If it's God's will, we will survive."

"Ma'mselle, please!" Fanny's upraised hand still held off her young mistress. Her voice was as curt as ever, so curt Coincoin feared it would dissolve the sudden mettle in Marie's backbone.

"Ma'mselle! I need the help of somebody with *know-how*—that's Coincoin, not you. Besides, your babies need a mother. Take them on down to your sister's house and stay there." For a moment, Fanny paused, then plowed on, no longer bothering to weigh her words. "You might even try *praying* for a change. Then, if it is God's will, *some* of us may survive."

Marie wavered, and Coincoin's heart ached for her, for the courage that seemed to wither in the face of Fanny's verbal lashing. But then Marie stiffened and she nodded. "You're right, Fanny. As always, I'd be just a hindrance. We will go."

Quietly, Marie stooped and picked up her little Manuela in her empty arm and started down the hill with Eleanore trailing mutely behind her, bewildered by the speed with which an afternoon of frolic had turned into one of fear. At the crest of the hill, Marie hesitated, then turned, quickly calling back to Fanny, who was disappearing through the front door of the Big House.

"One day, Fanny," Marie called, her voice choking, as her *négresse* reappeared upon the gallery. "One day, I will make this up to you, Fanny. I promise." Then she turned again and trudged on down the hill.

It was not God's will to spare them, not all of them. Fanny drugged her mistress heavily with flat root, the strongest sudorific that she knew, yet the fever raged. Emanuela sweated until it seemed no moisture could be left within her. Deep folds of flab replaced her puffy cheeks, yet the fever would not break. Her once-obsidian pupils turned gray and crackled like weathered wood, and the lustrous whites of her Spanish eyes yellowed and took on a web of crimson threads. At daybreak, she woke, while Coincoin again was changing her sodden sheets. Feverish arms flailed, as she sought the comfort of her nurse.

"Fanny, where are you!"

"Here, Madame."

"Don't leave me, Fanny! I cannot live without you. You know that, Fanny!"

"Yes, Madame."

"Promise me, Fanny." Emanuela insisted hoarsely. "Promise me!"

Fanny sat down beside the bed and took one of Emanuela's scalding hands in both her own. "Madame, do you know what day this is?"

"What, Fanny?" It was barely a whisper.

"It is Good Shepherd Sunday. Remember, Madame, how many times you read us today's Gospel? I can recite it by heart."

Rhythmically, Fanny began her soft, consoling chant. "I am the Good Shepherd. The good shepherd lays down his life for his sheep. But the hireling, who is not a shepherd, whose own the sheep are not, sees the wolf coming and leaves the sheep and flees. The wolf snatches and scatters the sheep, but the hireling flees because he is a hireling and has no concern for the sheep." Fanny paused, deliberately, and then continued, "Madame, I am no hireling. I will not flee."

For a moment, Emanuela seemed to rally. Pulling her hand from Fanny's, she stretched out both her arms, grasping Fanny's elbow in a deathlike squeeze. It was, surely, a gesture of love and Fanny did not feel the pain. She only heard the words, "You are no shepherd either, Fanny. You are a queen."

Those were the last words she said. Behind them, there came another spew of blood and Emanuela María Stefania Sanchez-Navarro Juchereau de St. Denis was gone. Again, Fanny and Coincoin bathed her, and François feverishly built another coffin. Not the fine one he had made for his old master those years before, but a rude and hasty box.

For the Widow de St. Denis, there would be no wake. Her contagious corpse could not lie in state, receiving the homage of all at both posts, white, black, and red, as her husband's remains had done. There could be no ceremonious burial in the church, or even in the sacred earth of the adjacent churchyard. In the spongy valley of the Cane, where water coursed a few feet beneath every footstep, no plague-ridden body could be interred within its bosom to be washed by water that people would drink another day.

For the proud, pious Spanish doña, the funeral procession was a stark one. Her small box, plain and unadorned and almost square in size, was borne into the post astride the broad shoulders of François's sons. The prayers were few and hasty. The grains of earth Père Eustache spread over her were only the symbolic ones that ritual demanded, and then the sexton heaped upon Emanuela, as she lay in her crude coffin atop the ground, a massive, foreboding mound of stone.

Up on the hill, the fever raged anew. The preventative doses Fanny had prescribed for herself, François, and Coincoin had been small. Heavily dosed they would have been unable to attend their mistress. The medicine came too late now—at least for the older couple in whom the plague had, for days, been germinating.

François was the first to fall. Together, Fanny and Coincoin carried him to his bed. Were he to die, it had to be in his own home, not Madame's. Dgimby, now fat from birthing her first child and lazier than ever, wailed at the sight of her stricken father, fearing not for him nor for the safety of the children in her care, but for herself. Wearily, Fanny ordered her family to the back chamber and, to Dgimby's relief, she sternly forbade any of them to approach the sickroom. She neither needed nor wanted any help but Coincoin's.

By Monday noon, Fanny's eyes were bloodshot and her lips as parched as François's, but she ignored Coincoin's pleas for her to go to bed. The proud African princess, still lithe in spite of her once-more-swollen belly, her face taut and resolute despite her pain, refused to relinquish her control.

While François slipped in and out of consciousness, his fever undulating between Fanny's doses of flat root and Coincoin's bowls of gruel laced with sweetgum balm, Fanny's fever rose. The evening air chilled their mud-walled cabin, but her thin dress clung to her limbs, saturated with the sweat and stench of her own fever. Soon, even François's skin seemed cool to her heavy touch and she did not notice when his fever rose again, not until Coincoin seated herself beside the bed and quietly began to bathe her father with an astringent of fermented yapon and passion thorn.

"No, child! That is my job!" Fanny tried to protest, but her voice lost its timbre and she reached for the bedpost to brace herself. Only for a moment, she told herself, and the giddiness would pass.

Coincoin did not budge, as she turned aside her mother's protest. "Right now, Mama, he doesn't know my touch from yours. Go to bed until he wakes, Mama. I'll call you then."

Fanny did not answer. The silence hung there, before the reality of the moment struck Coincoin and she turned to see her mother's face go ashen. The wide, lustrous, almond eyes bulged apopletically, and Fanny slithered down the bedpost to the floor. A tide of bloody flux spewed from her lips, and Coincoin could not stop it.

The baby that was not yet due, sensing the urgency of its plight, began its fight to come into the world, but Fanny's breath choked within her, her heart gave up the struggle, and the pulsations of her womb died as well. Dry-eyed and numb, Coincoin turned to her father's chest, found the slender blade with which he had carved Jeanne's rosary three weeks before, and with the tenderness of a practiced surgeon she took the child from her mother's body, there on the rough cypress floor of their cabin.

While François tossed and flailed in his fitful coma, Coincoin bathed her newborn sister in a fresh bowl of the same astringent she had mixed for her father, and called Dgimby from the back room where she still cowered.

Dgimby came, slowly waddling and loudly wailing, but her cries turned to pleas when she realized what her sister had in mind. How could she give suck to this infant from their mother's plague-ridden body? That creature would kill them all! Coldly, Coincoin plunked the squalling baby into Dgimby's arms, spun her sister around like a ball on a tether, and kicked her broad backside toward the door from which she had emerged.

As morning dawned, Coincoin washed her mother's stiffening corpse, called her brothers to make another coffin, and again, for the second time, they descended to the post—two black couriers of death, carrying their grim news upon their shoulders.

The sun rose and brightly lit the hill, but few rays filtered through the still-closed shutters of the death cabin in which François lay. Midmorning, he stirred again, calling in his sleep for his wife, his lover, his friend.

"It's me, Papa," Coincoin whispered, as his fingers grasped her own and caressed them slowly, but François did not hear.

"...so soft, and tender, and gentle," he murmured. "I've always loved your hands, Fanny. They always know how to comfort me, no matter where I ache."

The vice closed tighter around Coincoin's heart. How could she tell him what had happened while his consciousness had hovered in another world?

"Fanny… Fanny…," François began again, and Coincoin said the only thing she could. "No, Papa, it's me."

That time he heard her. The thick wool of his brows, clumped now with blood and sweat, knitted for a moment and he queried, slowly, struggling to pull words from some distant place. "Where's Mama, child?"

Coincoin could not force herself to answer. His eyes hazed again, and he answered his own question. "Of course, Madame must have called her and she had to go."

"Yes, Papa," Coincoin answered quickly. In his feverishness he had forgotten about Madame's death, and she was glad. Still, it was not a lie, she reassured herself. In a sense, Madame *had* called Fanny and she had gone to her, for the last time ever.

Then Coincoin actually laughed, not her usual trill but a sound she barely recognized as her own, a bark undercut with a bitterness she did not know that she could feel. It had become a joke between her mistress and her mother, a macabre jest that had made her shiver every time she heard it. Hardly a week had passed that Madame had not said how she could never manage without Fanny, and then Fanny would retort that Madame would probably take her with her when she died. Was it really sport, Coincoin wondered now, or premonition?

The harshness of her laugh cut through François's torpor, and he remembered. Madame was gone. It was Coincoin's face that hovered over him now, not Fanny's. But it was a face he had not seen his daughter wear and he knew what caused it, even though she could not say. Fanny was gone, and he was about to join her.

"Destiny…," he mumbled. Coincoin could barely hear him, but then he really had not been talking to her at all.

"What, Papa?"

François did not answer. He could not grasp the thoughts he tried to form. What was it Fanny used to say about destiny? That all of us make our own? He had not believed. He had been complacent, a stalk of wheat, pliant, yielding, never questioning the winds as to why they bent him double or made him bow before their might. Because of him, Fanny had ceased to dream. Because of him, she never found her destiny and died without her birthright! If only he had shared her faith, instead of making her disbelieve, then he would not face death now, knowing that he left nothing to his seed but the hopelessness of bondage.

"Papa? More gruel? We must keep up your strength."

François barely heard the words. His mouth moved mechanically as the warm mush was injected, but his mind struggled feverishly to find some meaning to his life.

Coincoin. His little goddess. His and Fanny's gift to a world that had given them so little. Long ago—or was it yesterday?—he had sat out on the edge of a broad hill and watched his little girl grow up. No, she didn't grow up, either. She had always been grown. What was it he had thought that night? That Destiny surely had greater things in mind when she created this woman-child? Yes! Fanny's destiny was not dead! She had bequeathed it to this daughter, and Coincoin would fulfill it! Only she didn't know! Fanny had not told her!

A rash of words then spilled from his swollen lips as he gave his second-born daughter answers to all the questions he and Fanny had never let her ask; as he bared to her his soul, his sins, his failings, as though she were a priest administering to him the last holy rites; as he sang for her the praises of his princess that were not sung at her ignominious burial and then lay before Coincoin the key to her past and the door to her future.

As suddenly as it had come, the tempest from François's soul subsided and he lay still. For hours, or minutes—it could have been either—Coincoin sat in the shadows of the great four-poster that ruled over the little cabin they called home. Death this day had wrenched from her the only meaning her life had known, the very source from which she had sprung. Yet, for what it took, it gave a measure in return. Over and again her mind repeated a single line from the communion prayer that the reverend father chanted at each Sunday's Mass: *Dying, he gave new life. Dying, he gave new life.* And in her grief, Coincoin felt no sense of sacrilege at this blurring of the image of her father and her Savior.

She rose, slowly, as tall and graceful as the goddess he thought she was. Bending across the big bed, she kissed her father good-bye. No fear of mortal plague could come between them at this last parting for she, too, shared her father's knowledge that the hour of her destiny had not yet come. She still lived, because she was meant for something more in life than that which life had given them. The vague ache she had always known deep within her soul had a name now, and she knew its meaning and her mission.

"One day… Papa… Mama!" she cried, thrusting her face toward heaven as she pounded with both hands on the bed post where Fanny had fallen. "One day, Mama's dream will happen! One day, we shall be free again! Free! And proud! And noble! And men will bow before us, and we will never have to say 'Yes, Madame' or 'No, Madame' to anyone unless we choose to. We… will… be… *free!* This, *I promise!*"

PART TWO
1765–1781

The Price

B

Claude Thomas Pierre
Metoyer

Baptism of Claude Thomas Pierre Metoyer, 1744

St. Sauveur Parish, La Rochelle, France

On the fourteenth of March in the year seventeen hundred and forty-four, I, the undersigned lecturer of divinity, have baptized Claude Thomas Pierre, born the twelfth of the current month, legitimate son of Nicolas François Metoyer, merchant, and of his wife Marie Anne Draperon. The Godfather has been Pierre Draperon, merchant, and the godmother Jeanne Draperon, both of whom are present and have signed. Jaillot, Curate of St. Sauveur.

In the fall of 1765

Impatiently, Claude Thomas Pierre Metoyer dabbed at the sweat that trickled down his muscular neck, curling the mahogany locks that were much too long for the climate. It was autumn on Red River, but the pestilential heat that had greeted him that summer in New Orleans had not let up. His pirogue came aground in the mud that gave the river its name and he climbed ashore, sinews rippling almost indecently beneath his sodden shirt and breeches.

Pierre squinted westward into the savage sun, his green eyes narrowing to slits as he surveyed first the broad meadow with its small plots of tobacco and Indian corn. Then, beneath the bridge of his nose, crooked lips smiled sardonically, contemptuously, as he took in the low bluff that lay before him, crowned by a fort of rotting palisades and a row of crude houses that composed this royal Poste de St. Jean Baptiste des Natchitoches, on the part of Red River they called the Cane.

Why had he come to this hell-hole in the first place? Pierre asked himself as the other pirogues came aground behind him. After two months of gut-sick ocean passage and three mosquito-plagued weeks on the Red River, he could barely recall the spirit of adventure that had lured him from his native France. Of course, the nice inheritance that had come his way, for investment in some worthy enterprise, had robbed him temporarily of his senses. For a month, he had eased his grief and celebrated his good fortune in the grog shops and taverns that lined La Rochelle's Bay of Biscay, but in the end it was the rum that had made him vulnerable to the fantasies and schemes of his old friend, Étienne Pavie.

While Pierre had seduced every half-willing barmaid, Étienne had seduced him, verbally, with glorious accounts of a tropical paradise where native women wore no clothes and a small fortune could be turned into a big one faster than a *putain* could tag him with a bastard. A quick in and out and they could be back in France with enough riches to live a life of ease. Eventually, when no new barmaids remained to be conquered and the pursuit of the same ones had lost its challenge, Pierre had succumbed to the lure of Étienne's promised land. Not out of any interest in the naked natives, he hastily assured his friend. Dusky heathens were for men of less discriminating tastes. But gold and silver? *Mais oui!* These deserved lust wherever they might be found.

Now, as the young rake stood in the midst of his friend's illusion, his nostrils rebelling against the stench of alligator urine that had for three weeks permeated his clothes, his skin, and even his food, he silently cursed the greed that had brought him to this purgatory.

"Eh, Pierre, are you coming with me to the town, or not? We'll make no fortune off these goods as long as you stand there daydreaming."

"Daydreaming? *Merde,* Étienne! This is a nightmare. No wonder the king decided to just give this colony to Spain. If you ask me, he's smarter than any of us gave him credit for."

"Pierre the Pessimist!" Étienne chided blithely as he pulled a fresh shirt from his trunk, donned it, and then retied his long blond curls against the nape of his slender neck.

"Look, man!" Étienne continued. "Consider yourself a missionary like your Oncle Jorge. He brings the Word of God to those who need it, and you're bringing the comforts of civilization to those who sure need it, judging from the looks of this place. Père Jorge earns golden stars for his celestial crown, and you'll earn golden écus for your pocketbook!"

Pierre just snorted.

"Come on, *mon ami!* Put on fresh robes and let us go among the people to spread the word about all the goods we've brought them. Big Jeannot can look after the pirogues and his savage oarsmen while we find that money-loving commandant who promised to have a house waiting. Then we can share a few rounds of rum with the local chaps and drum up trade."

"Étienne, you delude yourself," Pierre grumbled, half ashamed of his churlishness. He was never able to resist his friend's good cheer for long, but he was still in no mood to be mollified. "Even if *francs* grew like cherries out here, Étienne, we'd never sell our things. Who wants brandied pears that reek of the river, or silk from Marseilles that's been drenched by those muddy rapids? Or lace baked in the sun until it's as yellow as those hybrid *nègres* we saw on every street corner in New Orleans..."

"Frenchman!" Jeannot interjected curtly. Like all that breed of men who chose the life of *voyageur,* the burly boatman seldom spoke; but when he did, he plainly spoke his mind. "All goods w'at come t' Natchitoches smell like t'e river. An' you better b'lieve, Frenchman, out here in t'e colony yellow's not such a bad color at all."

Pierre laughed, in spite of himself. "*Touché,* my yellow boatman! I just proved your very point. I hired you for your reputation, in spite of your color. Then your talents so impressed me that I ceased to think of you in terms of any color at all. How else could I have said such a thing within your hearing?"

Big Jeannot did not reply, and a half-smile played around Pierre's rugged face, energized by the verbal joust. "We've both drawn blood in this little match, Jeannot. Shall we shake hands like gentlemen and call it a draw?"

"W'atever your pleasure, Frenchman," the big mulatto shrugged, settling upon a piece of driftwood as he lit his pipe.

Amid Étienne's enthusiastic chatter, Pierre freshened his wardrobe. Of course his friend was right. If they were going to be seen as purveyors of fine wares in this town, they could not arrive looking like river rats. The occasion demanded a silken shirt, with a handkerchief of Brussels lace tucked into one sleeve, and a pair of silver flasks filled with their best cognac to impress these woodsmen with the quality of their wares.

"You two dandies best watch your footin' as you climb t'at bank," Jeannot warned offhandedly from his driftwood perch. "One slip 'n your fancy pants'll be dyed red by t'is mud." He paused, drawing out his advisory for maximum effect. "'S matter o' fact, boys, you'd best watch your step wit' t'e locals, too. T'ey may look like peasants, but out on t'is frontier ever man's a lord, *sur ma foi!*"

Pierre shrugged indulgently. Sure footing was something he had never worried about in any company. Still, it took only seconds for him to realize the truth in the yellow man's words, at least as far as the river's bank was concerned. *Morbleu!* he muttered under his breath, wondering whether the half-caste bastard was prescient or whether he intentionally got them there right after a rain.

Étienne chuckled at his side. "Admit it, Pierre! We're greenhorns. Your ego may still be intact, but I lost mine at the sight of those tough Creoles downriver at Opelousas and Pointe Coupée."

"Pointe Coupée?" Pierre paused for breath as they crested the bank, resurveying the little town that awaited them, and he chortled as he recalled that last outpost on the Mississippi before they rowed their pirogues into the Red.

"*Bon Dieu!* Étienne. I'm not as tough as the *women* at that post, and I hope to God I never am. When I trade my goods for all the peltry and payroll of this *paradise* of yours, I'm out of here before I forget that Frenchmen aren't supposed to look or act like savages."

"Like those ruffians outside yon *Fleur de Lis?*" Étienne jibed, and Pierre's nose twitched as he followed the direction of Étienne's gaze. Another mud hut. Another mud hut in a street full of mud huts. *Excusez-moi!* Pierre mentally corrected himself. Sarcastically. *Bousillage—that fancy word makes mud sound better.* But a mud hut by any name was still a mud hut, and the only thing appealing Pierre could see at the rude tavern Étienne pointed to was the sign that named it. *Oui,* someone put effort into that, Pierre had to concede. Its scrolled board of royal blue, its golden fleur de lis, its white lettering, all were quite nicely executed. But had he been a betting man, he'd have wagered the place was named for all the lilies of France branded on its proprietor before they shipped him out from the Bastille. Even without the guttersnipes brawling in the doorway, the *Fleur de Lis* was hardly the type of place Pierre typically choose to frequent—though, from what he could see on this street, His Majesty's Poste St. Jean Baptiste des Natchitoches was not likely to offer any better.

"Pavie," he snorted. "I swear this is the last time I'll listen to one of your cock-eyed schemes. You got me drunk back home and plied me with pretty words, but right now what's ringing in my ears are the words of your friends in *la ville.*"

"Ah, forget those barmaids and their promises. There'll be girls here just as ready as those in New Orleans."

"Étienne, you know damned well I'm not talking about trollops. All I've remembered since I sobered up is the warning that factor of yours gave us about these frontiersmen having no respect for man, law, or God."

"*Ça,* Pierre," Étienne laughed. "The New Orleanians have no respect for God themselves, that old factor included. So I figure these peasants can't be too much worse. Cheer up, man. Look around you at the glory of the primitive state of nature, the breathtaking smells of the wilderness, the…"

✑ 2 ✑
At the Fleur de Lis, meanwhile

"Hey, Lecomte, look what's coming!"

"*Mon Dieu!* Lieutenant!" Private Jean Baptiste Lecomte gave a long, low whistle as his eyes followed the direction of his officer's nod. Hitching the faded breeches of his uniform, he grinned as he savored another swig from the leather flask they had been sharing.

"This wine is potent, Le Court. I swear I see two ghosts of the old commandant. *Ma foi!* Not since St. Denis prayed himself to death has this post been graced with so much finery. Those two fops make even you look like a peasant, and you wear a clean blouse every day."

The lieutenant laughed genially as he leaned against a gallery post and drew a pouch of tobacco from the cool, white muslin shirt he much preferred to the scratchy, regulation uniform of His Majesty's Marines.

"More officials, probably," a burly woodsman snorted behind them. "That's all we get out of New Orleans these days, more officials with their damned dos and don'ts."

"You need not worry this time, Baudouin," the lieutenant observed drily. "Those two lack the swagger we men of breeding learn in our dance classes, and the Crown does not waste its sinecures on bourgeois who can't strut properly. *Non*, I would say we have here two more merchants in search of a fortune."

"Perhaps we should do them a favor," Lecomte suggested. "Let's turn them around and kick their pirogues back toward New Orleans before they waste their fine youth in this place."

"Perhaps we should go ourselves, *mon ami,* before we waste our own," the lieutenant rejoined, an edge cutting through his crisp Norman accent.

"*Maudit!*" the woodsman snorted behind him, pausing to aim a stream of tobacco juice at a buzzing fly. "If you were honest with yourself, Lieutenant, you'd admit you're never going back to that fancy castle in France what your brother inherited along with the family title. You're married to this place just like the rest of us. Only, you'd be a lot happier if you'd face that fact and make an honest woman outa' that pretty li'l carpenter's daughter you moved down to the bluffs with."

Lecomte tensed. That carpenter's daughter was his own wife's sister, and her concubinage with the nobleman who thought she was good enough to bed but not to wed was a scandal even at this freewheeling outpost. Leastwise, it was among the priests and the womenfolk who had nothing more to do than gossip. That's why the lieutenant had moved down to the bluffs—although he claimed it was for the land—and Lecomte and his wife had gone with them.

Non. Truth was, Le Court could keep *two* women of his own down at the bluffs and none of his own men would fault him. Ensign, sergeant, or plain shirttail private like himself, the lieutenant treated them all as equals. That says something for a man, Lecomte told himself quite regularly. It's just the idea of *marriage* that reminds the lieutenant of all that class stuff inbred in him back home. Nobody can lay the blame, either, on his woman's mother being one of those girls shipped out here in the twenties to marry any soldier who'd have them. Their mother-in-law, to her credit, had been one of the orphans in that bunch, not one of the strumpets, and her daughters all made good wives. Lord knows, his was a jewel—and Louis Rachal felt the same about the one he married. But they were all, still, carpenter's daughters. Good enough for the likes of him and Rachal to wed, but not the lieutenant. Even in the colonies a carpenter was a carpenter, and no offspring of a carpenter could be allowed to inherit the fiefs and titles of France.

Le Court clearly read his thoughts. The lieutenant's hand was on Lecomte's arm before he could decide whether to try using it against the mouthy woodsman who never carried a weapon but had no trouble backing up his words whenever he shot from the lip.

"Let it pass, Lecomte, let it pass," Le Court responded tautly. "It's my place to deal with the remark. As for you, Baudouin, my personal life is none of your damned business. You'd best not forget that again or the next time you take off for the Arkansas without a trader's license, you'll find yourself brought back to the stockade in chains."

The rawboned Baudouin remained unchastened, as he mulled the consequences with which he had just been threatened. "Pardon me, Lieutenant." The apology, when it finally came, was a bit too smart and the bow that went with it was anything but repentant. "I forgot my manners. It's just a trifle hard for us humble Canadians to remember your fine station in life, sir, when you stand there in the same ticking breeches the rest of us wear."

"Satin breeches do not make a man, Baudouin. They only make him sweat."

The woodsman's scraggly eyebrows arched as he drew a fresh plug of Natchitoches périque from its well-stained pouch and drawled, "Does that mean my apology has saved me from the gallows?"

The officer's craggy face softened. "I said *stockade*, Baudouin, not the gallows. You're too valuable to hang." Le Court meant it. It was men like Baudouin who kept the Indians at peace and him out of war, and it had not escaped his notice that there had been no outbreak of trouble among the Arkansas tribes since the Canadian woodsman started trading there. It took a hell of a man to keep the Osage happy.

Baudouin grinned, his confidence restored, and Le Court smiled back indulgently at the crusty friend with whom he had been tilting. "I swear, Baudouin, if I were the king, I'd knight you today. Seigneur François Baudouin de las Arkansas, *diplomate extraordinaire.*"

"All it takes is loving the warriors, not the women," the trader retorted, staring pointedly at the lush who had just elbowed his way through the doorway. "It's damned fools like Dégoût here who paw every squaw what comes into the post who cause our troubles with the natives."

"*Hehn?* You jackass! You wanna say dat again?" the accused libertine shot back. From the folds of his blouse a blade appeared, as short and thick as the man who wielded it, but a strong hand wrenched his wrist behind him and he toppled into the dust. For a moment, the drunk stared stupidly, crouching at the feet of the giant who felled him. Then he wormed his way across the ground to retrieve the blade that had skittered beyond his reach.

"Go home, sculptor. You've had too much to drink already." The big man spoke genially as the drunk struggled to his feet, but—drunk or sober—Dégoût was the type to whom all kindness was patronizing. "Ah, M'sieur Crête," he slurred, his thumb flicking nervously across the tip of his chisel. "You not happy ownin' dis stinkin' place? You wanna own me, too?"

"Nobody owns anybody around here," Crête replied patiently. "Look, Dégoût. I'm a peaceable man, but you know I don't tolerate brawls. If you've got a gripe against somebody, take it elsewhere."

"My gripe's wit' de bot' of you—de big Canadian warthog and de Arkansas weasel! De two o' you make a pair. Somebody jes' needs t' carve *you* down t' de weasel's size."

"Yeah, yeah, Dégoût. And you are just the man to do it." The Jovian bar owner had long since learned to shrug off the Frenchman's drunken swagger. Whatever offense the lout perceived from whatever source, his answer was always a carving job. Yesterday, it was Anty's heart that was supposed to be fed to the crocodiles. The day before, it was Prudhomme's liver that would be staked to the palisades. If the lush ever found the guts to follow through on a threat, Crête figured, he'd run like a jackrabbit across the Tejas border, but like most bullies, the man lacked the guts for anything but bluster.

"You'll see, Pierre Crête! One day I'll pickle you like a prune 'n your own brandy!" the sculptor sneered. "I'll stuff you wit' your rotten rum 'til you're as fat as a Christmas pig! Den I'll stick you on a spike 'n watch you squeal." Dégoût's maudlin oaths continued to screech through the dank midday air, as he stumbled off the gallery and past the two strangers approaching in the street.

"Whew!" Étienne gasped, fanning a breeze with his handkerchief as he pivoted to avoid the drunk. "What's that I was saying about breathtaking smells…? Oh, *bonjour, mes amis,"* he quickly added as his pirouette brought him eye to eye with the trio on the gallery.

"*Bonjour,* yourself," Le Court replied offhandedly, casually rolling another smoke to replace the one Dégoût had knocked from him on his drunken sortie into the street. "And how many loaded pirogues have you gentlemen brought upriver?"

The directness of his question took Pierre aback. Étienne's contacts at *la ville* had warned them about the effrontery of these frontiersmen, but he had not expected the village loafers to demand his business. Even so, Pierre reminded himself, it would not do to antagonize future customers.

"Ah, M'sieur," he crooned, spreading his arms expansively, "a dozen loads of the finest wares Mother France has to offer, and more on the way." But then the gall that always seemed to bedevil him at the worst possible time creeped back into his tone and he pointedly added, "However, *mes amis,* our business is with the commandant. Perhaps one of you gentlemen is not too *busy* to direct us to him?"

Unruffled by the jibe, the lanky Norman met Metoyer's gaze and noted the condescension playing around the corner of his crooked mouth. "The commandant? You are out of luck, strangers. Perrier had business of his own to transact elsewhere today. Perhaps I can help?"

"We appreciate your concern, good fellow," Metoyer responded with a bit less civility than even he intended. "Possibly, you can—in a while. We'll need help in unloading our goods, but we have to settle our business with the commandant first. Can you tell us who runs the post when Monsieur Perrier is away?"

"Well, there is the *subdélégué,*" Le Court replied offhandedly, as he took another puff from his handrolled tobacco and tapped the ashes into the dust. "But he has no taste for problems. Besides, he is over at Los Adaës with Perrier. Then there is the lieutenant, but I think you would probably conclude that he is a very unlikely looking fellow. *Non,* my friend, I guess I would just have to say that the post more or less runs itself while the commandant is away."

"Hell, the post runs itself while Perrier is here," Baudouin growled, reinforcing his observation with another well-aimed stream of amber amid a chorus of guffaws from the tavern doorway.

Pierre smiled politely, feigning appreciation of the jest that was so blatantly disrespectful of authority, and again he thought of the factor's warning. Eventually, the sniggers subsided. "Perhaps, then," he asked, "you could direct us to the lieutenant you spoke of?"

"You've found him," the Norman replied casually. "First Lieutenant Louis Mathias le Court de Prelle, second and less-fortunate son of The Honorable Joseph le Court, Seigneur de Prelle of Camarette in Bretagne, at your service, sir."

The smile froze on Pierre's face. Le Court de Prelle? One of the oldest and noblest family names of Normandy? Here on this frontier? Clad like a peasant? Surely this tall, leathery blond must be a bastard son! Throughout the annals of France, Norman Le Courts had fought nobly in every major campaign Pierre could recall from his history classes at l'École de St. Sauveur. A Le Court de Prelle had ridden into battle at the side of Joan d'Arc. Another had handsomely ransomed Jean II, when a British king took him captive. One had even commanded the Order of the Maltese Cross. Surely, no scion of so illustrious a line, exiled bastard or no, would descend to the attire and company of ruffians, even in the colonies.

Pierre bristled. The man obviously jests! And takes me for a fool.

His gaze raked again over the lean man's frame, past the cut of his locks that was twenty years out of fashion, the open shirt that exposed a thick, bronzed mane against an even more deeply tanned chest, down to the coarse breeches, as long as a woodsman's leggings, not stylishly short and tight and worn over silk hose to emphasize the muscles of a comely pair of masculine calves. The gallery grew quiet before Metoyer's eyes came back to rest on the deep ruts in the Norman's face, prematurely aged from two decades of exposure to the tropical sun. Then the thin man's steel grey eyes locked Metoyer's, cold and unapologetic, and Pierre knew that the Norman did not jest.

"Forgive us, sir," Pavie interjected quickly. "My friend and I are new in the colony. We were naive to expect a King's Officer to be dressed in regulation uniform. That would be rather uncomfortable in this climate and unnecessary, I'm sure, outside of war or ceremony."

The officer acknowledged Étienne's concession with the barest of nods, as Pierre struggled to regain his aplomb. "My apologies, Lieutenant Le Court. The name is Claude Thomas Pierre Metoyer, son of the La Rochelle merchant, Nicolas François Metoyer."

"And you?" Le Court nodded toward Pavie.

"Étienne Pavie, also of La Rochelle." Pavie bowed deeply as he spoke, not so much out of courtesy as the need to hide his amusement over Pierre's discomfiture. His supercilious friend had earned a comeuppance once again.

"Pavie? I suppose, then, you're a brother of the merchant Louis Pavie? I've had a few dealings with him at *la ville*."

"*Hélas!* Even in the colonies my older brother's reputation precedes me! Cursed luck!"

"I will not hold it against you," Le Court rejoined dryly. "Out here, every man makes his own place. Now what can I do for you, gentlemen—in the commandant's absence, of course?"

Pierre drew a wrinkled letter from the embroidered purse that hung by a silver chain around his waist. "Sieur Perrier wrote that he had a house suitable for both living quarters and our shop. Is it possible you have been apprised of this, sir?"

"Somewhat. In fact, we have three empty buildings right now. I think the commandant had in mind to offer you the one I just vacated, but if you do not care for me as landlord, you may choose between Private Lecomte, here, or our brother-in-law, Rachal. The three of us have just moved our families down to our plantations upon the bluffs that you passed below here. Any of our town houses would accommodate your needs."

Private Lecomte? *Plantation? Town houses?* What was it Jeannot had said back there at the pier? Pierre asked himself. *Ma foi!* On this frontier, every man does think he's a lord!

The yellow man's warning resonated as Metoyer reassessed the men before him and reproved himself for not taking the boatman seriously. Still, a lifetime of class consciousness could not be shucked in just one afternoon; and Metoyer hastily made his selection between the three proffered choices.

"I'm sure your property, Lieutenant, will be quite acceptable."

"Bien!" Le Court tossed a ring of keys to his brother-in-law. "Lecomte, take those Indians I brought into town today and put them to work unloading the gentlemen's pirogues while I buy them a drink. Hey, Crête!" The lanky lieutenant slapped one arm around Pierre, the other around Étienne, and ushered them inside. "I've a couple of new customers for you, man."

"Customers or competitors?" the Canadian inquired jovially, as he wiped out three mugs with an already sodden rag and poured a round of rum.

"Competitors, frankly," Pierre replied. "The best liquors of France await you gentlemen. Delicate, racy, gustful! Whatever your taste, you're in for an experience you've never known before. No offense, Crête," he added broadly, as he tilted the mug and sampled it. "Your rum is far better than I expected to find out here, but..."

"And we should toast his fine taste," Étienne interjected more diplomatically. "But let me reassure you, Sieur Crête, we won't be your competitors in everything. Good liquor we'll have, *oui;* but we plan to open a mercantile establishment, not just a tavern. We've brought many fine goods and more will be arriving shortly."

"No offense to *you*, stranger," Crête rejoined, "but here at Natchitoches, there's no difference between one and the other. In polite company, I call myself a merchant, too. If you care to enter this humble establishment from the rear gallery, my new little wife will show you a nice assortment of wares to prove it." Calmly, the tavern's owner wiped the bar with the same towel he had used to clean their mugs, and slung it handily over his arm.

"Well, whaddawe have here now? Two peacocks!"

The voice and the smell were both familiar. Without turning to face the door, Pierre knew they belonged to the same drunk who had lurched past them in the street.

"Lemme guess," the voice continued. "The river musta washed you up alongside t'at uppity yellow down on the bank w'at t'inks he's too good t' sell a Frenchman his wine."

"Nobody's going to sell you any more to drink today," Crête replied matter-of-factly, as he straightened a round of chairs in one darkened corner. "Not in that condition. Go to bed, Dégoût, and sober up. Then tomorrow you can get gloriously drunk again."

"I'm not talkin' t' you, tavern man. I'm talkin' t' those two strangers. Hey, jack-a-dandys, turn 'round when I talk t' you."

Metoyer and Pavie turned slowly, appraising the source of the stench, the matted hair slicked down with grease, the nose that started off straight enough but veered precariously to the left before ending in a blob, the ruffled shirtfront stained with every shade of spirits available. Had the man been a silent drunk, Pierre thought, they could have amused themselves for an hour just cataloging those stains, from the orange-tinged apple brandy on the left to the brown Madeira on the right, aged now to the color of old blood. But, *hélas*, the sot was obviously in no mood to be analyzed.

"Two coxcombs from Paris, *hehn?* You bot' have t'e foppish look. You heard o' me, *non?* I'm Michel Dégoût, t'e sculptor, Toast o' Versailles."

"No, man," Pierre replied indifferently. "Can't say that I ever heard of you. But then, I'm from La Rochelle, not Paris. Perhaps your fame did not extend to the coast of France."

"Provincial popinjay! T'at explains it! No matter. Michel Dégoût's known t'rough all of France," he slurred. "T'at's why jealous rivals had me exiled to t'is pigsty wit' a fleur de lis branded o' me like some street whore from t'e Salpetrière. You!" The sculptor jabbed Pavie with a finger whose crooked bent hinted of another barroom fight. "You heard o' me? You heard fine men speak o' Michel Dégoût 'n his work, *non?*"

"*Non,*" Étienne replied, as he turned and poured himself another cup of rum.

"Uncultured rabble! Bot' o' you," Dégoût sneered. "Dirty salt smugglers exiled by t'e king, no doubt. Or bastids shipped out by some cuckold. Scum's all we ever get out 'ere."

Pierre's temper flared. It always did, and his own nose had suffered the consequences a time or two itself. No matter how many times Étienne pointed out to him afterwards the stupidity of responding to deliberate provocation, Pierre's temper still went right ahead and did its thing. "Would you care to repeat that outside, *sir?*" His left hand gripped the edge of the pine table before him as he sprang from his chair, his right hand hovering above the hilt of his saber.

"Outside? *Merde!* An' have you stick me 'fore I get out t'e door? No, M'sieur Fop, I can take care o' you ri't here!'"

A blade appeared in Dégoût's hand with more dexterity than Pierre would have thought possible from such a sodden source. For a moment he wavered, as better judgment cooled his anger. In a match of swords, or even pistols at five paces, he feared no man; but the knife fights of rabble were hardly to his taste—or talents.

To Pierre's mortification, the tavern crowd noticed his hesitancy. Chairs scraped quickly across rough plank flooring, as a pair of locals grabbed for the sculptor, but the barkeep had already wrestled Dégoût to the floor, leaving the others to pinion the flailing chisel. Then Crête hoisted the drunk, a dirty collar in one broad paw and beltless pants in the other, and heaved the man out the door.

"Well, Lieutenant," Pierre observed dryly, as order resumed and he regained some measure of composure. "Apparently, my friend and I have made our first enemy here already."

"You need not worry," Le Court reassured him, sauntering to the bar to refill his pitcher without breaking the stride of his speech. "The fellow is a sot and a boor, but he is no fool. His bravado emerges only when there's a crowd around to notice him and men he can count on to stop whatever trouble he starts."

"I hope you're right, Lieutenant…. No, save your liquor," Pierre protested magnanimously, as Le Court seated himself again and reached to refill their mugs. "I owe all of you, *mes amis.* This time, the drinks are on me, and I'll show you colonials how a fine quality cognac ought to taste!" From the waist of his satin breeches, Metoyer pulled his silver flask. "Étienne! Out with yours, too. We need to loosen up our new landlord before he decides what our rent will be…."

Pierre's words trailed off lamely as he watched his friend's face freeze, eyes transfixed on some point across Pierre's shoulder. Recalling the open window behind him, his back began to crawl. Slowly, he pivoted in his chair, and his gaze followed the line of Étienne's own across the room and out the widespread shutters.

Not more than a dozen feet lay between the tavern and the house that adjoined it, with its own window directly facing the one through which Pierre stared. On either side of the opening stood a woman as immobile as the Biblical pillars of salt, one white and one black, with a pile of neatly folded clothes on the table between them and more clutched to their breasts. Between them, a butcher's blade in hand, leered the sculptor.

"Crête, you cyclopic swine!" Dégoût trumpeted. "I wanna see you."

"What the hell, Dégoût?" the Canadian rumbled. "What are you doing in Derbanne's house? You know damned well when Pierre agreed to let you sleep on his porch, he told you never to set a foot inside."

"Dere you go ag'in, Crête. Tellin' me w'at t' do. If Derbanne don' wan' me in his house, he can come an' put me out. Meanw'ile, tavern man, I got a job t' do, an' de pretty woman here just give me w'at I need t' do it."

"What are you up to, Dégoût?" Crête asked, warily this time, as he eyed the carving knife lurching wildly in Dégoût's hand.

The sculptor squealed in reply. "I'm gonna get me a pig, Crête. Jes' like I said. I'm gonna spear me a pig." Dégoût's hand flashed then, and steel shot through the window in which he lurked. It whistled across the lean alleyway and zinged cleanly through the tavern window. The big Canadian gurgled and slipped to the floor, blood gushing from his throat where Mme. Derbanne's knife was firmly lodged.

Amid the screams of the women who flanked him, the sculptor's cackle pierced the heavy autumn heat. "*Nom de Dieu!* I got me a pig! See you 'n Tejas—or hell!"

A hue rose from the tavern crowd as it pushed and shoved its way out the broad front door, crying for vengeance. Calmly, the lieutenant rose to his feet, stepped across the fallen Crête, and nodded to Pierre and Étienne. "*Pardon,* gentlemen. Duty calls."

In a moment, the Norman was gone and the tavern emptied, except for the two newcomers staring across the cypress table at each other in a mixture of stupefaction, fear, and—to no small degree—intrigue. It was Étienne who broke the silence as he tipped his flask.

"Well, Pierre. I promised you excitement. It looks like we've found the right place!"

❧ 3 ☙

Spring 1767

Pierre did not even look up when she entered. He didn't have to. Were he blind and deaf, he would still know every time she walked through the doorway of their shop. Other women at this post smelled of garlic, but she smelled of gardenias—always—even through the long winter when no gardenias were in bloom. Again, Pierre felt that tightening in his loins that the scent of her always triggered, and again he deliberately ignored her. Étienne was almost through measuring the blue silk for Mme. Rachal. The slave girl could just wait her turn.

As he hunched furiously over the account ledger, Pierre could feel Étienne's smirk. Damn him! he silently cursed his friend. Étienne knows me all too well, every one of my weak spots; and he thoroughly enjoys exploiting them, just like a needling wife after too many years of marriage. Every time this black wench comes into the shop I suffer this same torment, and every time Étienne finds new humor in my agony.

Enfer! Pierre swore anew. Pavie's ribald jokes were funny enough in the taverns of La Rochelle, where lusty, peach-skinned barmaids are supposed to inspire ribaldry, but the man's verbal coupling of me with this ebony daughter of Africa has been insufferable.

Behind him, Pierre could hear his partner wrapping the blue silk, while Sieur Rachal's wife chattered endlessly about the Easter dress she planned to make and the gay dance planned for Easter night. After an eon, the woman's silk was wrapped and she was finally gone. Now Étienne can wait on *her*, Pierre sighed in relief—and send *her* on her way. Taut nerves screamed, as he re-added a column of figures for the third time.

"*Bon jour, M'sieur.*"

As always, the sound of her voice unnerved him. It was as soft and husky as he had remembered, with all the same suggestive nuances. Or was he only imagining those? Try as hard as he might, Pierre could find no trace of a guttural burr to betray her African ancestry. Instead, her French had a musical, tantalizing, Hispanic lilt. An affectation picked up from the De Sotos, Pierre told himself, deliberately picking fault with her. It's really too much, the way some of these blacks mimic their masters. Maybe that's why I like Jeannot so much. That yellow man doesn't try to be anybody but himself.

"Ah! The Black Gardenia of Natchitoches!" Étienne's flippant greeting to the slave girl broke Pierre's reverie. "It's been weeks since you have graced our humble establishment with your beauty, Coincoin. Has your mistress been ill again?"

Mon Dieu! Pierre jabbed his quill into the inkwell and swore again beneath his breath as black splatters flew across his ledger. Étienne is really going too far now, he told himself furiously. Undoubtedly, this bit of flirting with the sexy *négresse* is for my benefit. He's goading me again, in that sly way of his, the same way he goaded me into stowing away on that British frigate when we were twelve, the same way he conned me into sinking my inheritance into this Louisiana venture. Well, maybe that adolescent escapade was worth all the stripes the old man gave me when I got back home, and the gold sure is rolling in here at Natchitoches, but there is no way this *mésalliance* Étienne pushes so casually could come to any good.

"*Oui, M'sieur.*" Coincoin was murmuring in reply to Étienne's question, her low response polite but tantalizing.

That's the hell of it, Pierre thought. She mesmerizes without trying. Without even meaning to. It's no secret in this post that this woman of Mme. de Soto's has no interest now in men, but there are still a dozen jacks of all shades who would eagerly take the place of that Indian buck who ran off and left her.

"That strange paralysis again," the slave girl was explaining as Étienne gathered the items from her list. "It comes and goes, M'sieur. One day, Madame is quite well and active, and the next day her arm refuses to move at all, or her legs, or her back. Then it goes away as suddenly as it comes. Usually, the attack lasts only a day or two, but this time it has persisted almost four weeks."

"It's a shame. Your mistress is still so young," Étienne murmured sympathetically, although neither he nor Pierre felt any empathy toward the woman. This slave's mistress had aggravated them ever since they opened their shop. She was constantly faulting their goods or claiming errors on her account.

"*Oui,* M'sieur. It is a shame." Coincoin softly echoed. "But she has great determination and fortitude. In her own way, she is as strong a woman as they say her father was a man."

Fortitude, Pierre groaned. That's what I need to bear up under this strange affliction of my own. *Zut!* The fellows back home would laugh at me now. Me!

The Lothario of Rue des Dames, chasing every loose skirt in La Rochelle. How could I be immobilized now by a black nymph out here in the wilderness. *Mon Dieu!* I'm barely twenty-three. I'm too young to suffer from scruples. Maybe Étienne and Jeannot are right after all. Out here where there are so few people, especially women, what the hell does color matter?

"…three bolts of white linen, two spools of thread, four jugs of brandy, a pack of combs, three pair of silk stockings." Étienne was checking the pile of merchandise he had gathered on the counter against the list Coincoin had given him.

"*Hé*, Pierre! Isn't Jeannot supposed to be back by now? I knew we'd never tame that river rat. He doesn't know the meaning of time. There are too many goods here for this girl to carry. Somebody will have to deliver them, but who knows when Jeannot will show up."

There he goes again, Pierre thought. He dangles opportunity in front of me to see if I will yield and take it. Well, why not? As he pushed back impulsively from his desk, Pierre's chair leg stuck in the plush new rug he had added to his corner of the mercantile side of their Front Street shop, and he tumbled chest-first into the ink he had just splattered. *Blageur!* he swore anew. Now I'm not only bedeviled by the woman. She's made me as bumbling as a teenaged dolt.

"All right, Étienne, all right," he muttered, trying to recover his aplomb. "You've made your point. I'll take whatever the girl can't carry. God knows, you're too frail a fellow."

Pierre's jibe went unnoticed, and he regretted having made it. No man ever had a better friend than Étienne, Pierre rebuked himself. I'm the one who's acting like an ass. I've never taken his teasing seriously before. Why should I now? It's all this girl's fault. Her and those potions she's famous for. Her mistress may call them "medicine," but some voodoo brew's more likely. She's put a hex on me.

"Besides," Pierre continued aloud in a half-hearted effort to return his friend's jest in kind. "It's almost dark. What with that panther on the prowl every night, Mme. de Soto's favorite servant might not make it home unprotected. We wouldn't want that to happen, would we, my friend?

"By no means, *mon ami*," Étienne mocked Pierre's concern. "This young woman shows much promise. Who knows what the future holds for her? It would be tragic indeed if such a lovely creature were despoiled by some brute." Pierre ignored the remark, as he seized the first bundle Étienne had wrapped and slung it roughly across his shoulder.

"M'sieur, I'm quite capable of carrying in my head bundle whatever can't be loaded onto the mule."

"I'm sure you are, Coincoin. I'm sure you are. Undoubtedly, you are capable of many things. But women weren't meant to be pack animals."

"You are kind, M'sieur."

Pierre only grunted. He loaded the bundles onto the mule without a word, hoisted the remainder under his arm, and took the guide reins, leaving the slave woman to follow mutely in his steps.

The first faint glimmer of a moon flushed behind the clouds that had loosed intermittent showers upon the post all day. Past the long row of houses, Pierre tramped furiously, as his inner battle continued to rage between the desire he had stifled for too long and the prejudice he had nurtured even longer. Past the stockade with its still-rotting palisades, where an unseen soldier's long, low whistle reminded Metoyer that he was not the only white man tempted by the black nymph who swayed behind him.

"M'sieur," Coincoin finally called out to him, breathlessly. "I can go the rest of the way alone, M'sieur."

Pierre flushed, feeling a twinge of guilt for his thoughtlessness. Of course, the girl could not be expected to keep up with his angry stride. His problem was not her fault, anyway. Seeing the long rise of St. Denis Hill looming ahead, he seized upon the opportunity to pause—and apologize. Gruffly.

"That's quite all right, M'sieur," she reassured him. "I understand."

Like hell you do, Pierre thought to himself, although he could not utter the words aloud.

"I can go on from here, M'sieur. You are kind to help, but I'm used to the hill."

"Ah, but I insist, Coincoin." Pierre's voice was softer, huskier. Jeannot's right, he told himself again. Out here, what the hell *does* color matter? He cast a furtive glance at Coincoin as she stood beside the mule, perfectly composed, waiting only for him to proceed.

You could just take her when you get to that big clump of holly bushes halfway up the hill, his demons taunted. *She's just a slave.* Sure, his common sense shot back, and there'd be the Devil to pay afterwards. Everybody knows how soft that De Soto woman is toward this slave. I'd find my merchant's license revoked tomorrow.

Beside him, he could feel Coincoin's wordless gaze. Questioning? Knowing? Pierre stared at her then, appraising her openly by the distant glimmer of the post lights, with only the tensing and flexing of his fists betraying the tautness of his nerves. The muse stared back, her eyes narrowing perceptibly.

Damn it! Pierre swore to himself. I swear she *is* reading my mind. Well, why not? She's been propositioned before. The question now is what kind of proposition would do the trick. A pretty dress? Probably not. Mme. de Soto clothes her uncommonly well for a slave. Money? They say that's been tried, too. After that Indian buck ran off, a score of panting soldiers offered her their pay.

I wonder why the fellow left. Pierre's mind roamed as he mulled his options. Or why she didn't go with him? All slaves dream of freedom, or so I hear. Of course, though, it's not easy for a mother hen to run with a flock of chicks. How many did Étienne say she had? Three? Four?

An idea gnawed at his gut. A vague idea. A mad one, maybe, but it had promise. Again, he stared the girl in the face. Again, she returned his gaze. And there in the smoke of her eyes he saw his answer. There was the same deliberate, calculating determination that was keeping him at this post he so abhorred. Where there was profit to be gained, a lot could be tolerated—if the profit was big enough to justify the sacrifice. He had found the Natchitoches trade well worth the toll it had taken upon him; and in the eyes of the ebony goddess who stood before him, even by the faint light of early evening, he plainly saw the force that could entice but never conquer her own heart.

"Coincoin, I have a proposition to make." Pierre stated it plainly, eschewing all the delicate phrases with which he had wooed the lighter d'amselles of La Rochelle.

Her reply was as matter of fact as his approach had been. Yet, even cool and flat, her voice lost none of its seductiveness. "I assumed that, M'sieur."

"I've heard it said that your grandfather was a king in Africa. Is that so?"

"I've been told that, M'sieur."

"Then the life of a slave ill befits the granddaughter of a king, no?"

"Perhaps, M'sieur. Do you have something better to offer?"

"Possibly, Coincoin. Shall we be frank with each other?"

"Of course, M'sieur."

"I've been in this colony but a year, Coincoin. I have no wife, and I don't plan to take one. Not here. I have no intention of remaining in this wilderness; and when I return to France a richer man, I will wish to find a wife more suitable to my station than the women who are available here at Natchitoches."

"Of course, M'sieur," she repeated softly.

"In the meanwhile, the frontier is a lonely place for a man without a wife. Do you understand me, or should I put it more bluntly?"

"Your words are plain enough, M'sieur."

"I am considering the hire of a housekeeper, if the woman I have in mind is interested and if her mistress would rent her to me. Or sell her. I offer no pay to the woman herself, just kindness. But when I leave this post, I will see to it that the woman will be free. She and her children."

Coincoin's long sweep of lashes had not blinked, not even once.

"Do you think a young woman of much beauty would be interested in such a proposition?"

"I think she would, M'sieur," Coincoin answered calmly, with no trace of hesitation in her silky voice.

"Good. Tomorrow I shall see this woman's mistress. She has no love for me, but I hear she's quite fond of money. We should be able to work out an arrangement that will be rewarding to everyone concerned."

⌒ 4 ⌒

That same, long night

For the first time since the night Chatta left her, Coincoin could not sleep. Little Jean had sensed her restlessness and fretted fitfully, gnawing on his fist as he fought the itch of the tooth that was not yet ready to cut its gums. Just as she had seen Fanny do so many times before her—so long before, it seemed now—Coincoin took her newest babe into bed with her and crooned it gently to sleep with the age-old song of Christian mothers… *Ave Maria… ora pro nobis.* Holy Mary, Mother of God… pray for us. Coincoin had not consciously prayed to the Blessed Virgin since that autumn a year and a half before when Chatta suddenly announced that he could no longer endure the chains of slavery.

"Come with me, Coincoin. We can make it. I have friends among the Adaës, and they'll help us. It's only fifteen miles between this post and theirs. Other slaves have escaped. We can too. Once we're across the Spanish border, my friends will guide us through the Tuokani, the Ceni, the Caneci. Those nations hate the Spanish, and since we speak that tongue, we can convince them that we've fled from the Spanish, not the French. They will help us return to my people. Come, Coincoin…"

Chatta pleaded urgently, persuasively, with pretty words, a hungry mouth, gentle hands, and a forceful body that usually took away all her will. But he had no plan that could surmount the most insurmountable obstacle she faced, no painless way for her to cut the one agonizing tie that bound her to her slavery.

"Come run with me, Coincoin. You are not so far pregnant that you can't. Even if you lose that child you carry, it means just one less soul in slavery. You'll have more—all born free. As free as the panther that prowls the hills without fear. Free as the hawk that soars above us, preying instead of preyed upon."

"And as free as the mother lion who abandons her cubs," Coincoin cried. "You know I cannot run, Chatta. Not with three little girls who can barely walk and a babe in arms. And you know I cannot leave them. Don't torment me with talk of freedom. I cannot leave my children. And you cannot leave me!"

"We can make other babies, woman. You're young and fertile. Those children you grunted and sweated to bring into this world aren't really yours or mine. They belong to the De Sotos. They can sell them any time. They can whip them, if they want. They can order them to jump like a horse or sit like a dog or smile like a possum and we can't say no, that our children are not horses or dogs or possums, but *humans!*"

"We all belong to the De Sotos, Chatta. Fate meant it to be so. At least for now. One day we won't, but that time hasn't come yet. Until then, we can bide our time. Madame is not harsh. She has never whipped me or our children, and you know your charges about her selling us are not fair."

"She sold Mariotte, no?" Chatta demanded cruelly, knowing well the love Coincoin had for the young sister she had helped to raise; so he used that memory to press his point.

"*Oui,* but only to the Buards next door. That was different. Our parents were dead. Never has Madame sold a child away from its mother or father."

"She will!" Chatta swore, his voice cruel and cutting. "It's just a matter of time. Wait until she needs money."

"She won't!" Coincoin's voice rose in defense. "It is just not in her. People say she is mean, that she's cold and uncaring, but she is not. That is just her way of keeping others from hurting her the way she has been hurt."

"And the way you'll be hurt if you stay here."

Coincoin groped for words to make him understand, but he gave her no time to find them.

"You're content with your wretched lot! When I met you, you had spirit. I said to myself: 'There goes a woman no one will really own. They just think they do.' But I was wrong. You've become a dumb, mindless beast like all the rest of the blacks here. I shouldn't be surprised, though. You've never known freedom. How can you lust like me after a passion you've never known?"

"That's not fair," she had sobbed, as his words sliced through scars that had never healed. "You know me better. I've seen freedom. I saw it in my mama's eyes long before I knew what freedom meant. I felt it in my father's grip as he died, and I swore a sacred oath over his body that all of his and mama's dreams would live on in me."

"Then you violate your oath, woman!"

"No! Never! Those dreams are not dead! But a mama cannot leave her babies! That is not the price I intend to pay for freedom."

"Then you would rather cut me loose?"

"*Non!* I could never do that! Oh, Chatta! Don't hurt me this way! How can I choose between you and my children? They are the fruit of my womb. In them my father and mother live on; their ancestors live on. It's for them that mama's dream has to be fulfilled. But you, Chatta… my mahogany man… you are my heart. You are the blood that throbs in my veins. It is for you that I am a woman. How could I cut either of the bonds that tie me, *cher?*"

"Then it's up to me to cut the bonds myself. One of these mornings you'll wake, and I'll be gone."

Chatta had kept his promise. Within a week he had crept silently from the big four-poster François had carved for Fanny, and he had left Natchitoches while Coincoin, his infants, and the rest of the post still slept. As Chatta had predicted, leaving the slave camp had been no problem for him, since he and Coincoin shared the cabin her father built outside the camp's stockaded walls. Nor had there been a sentry for him to pass, since St. Denis Hill lay distant from the post. Silently, he had slipped down the back side of the hill, into the woods, into the night, into the forever.

114

Madame Marie had ranted, threatened, bullied, and coaxed. She swore that Coincoin and Chatta had betrayed her. She had *spoiled* them, and they had betrayed her goodness. Still, Coincoin would not admit that Chatta had discussed any plans with her. Instead, she prayed every prayer that the old Madame had taught her in her childhood. *Ave Maria. Pater Noster. Agnus Dei.* She prayed them all for two long days, just as she had prayed them day and night since Chatta had announced his intent. But her prayers had not kept him at the post, and her prayers did not bring him back.

On the third day, the new babe she carried within her punched her for the first time, and Coincoin knew she had her answer. Chatta was gone, but life would go on. She had known a man's love, reveled in his passion, and given her whole self to him, but that love had been faithless. The only love that had real meaning, that could never be betrayed, was the love of a mother for her child. Every time the new child stirred within her belly, she promised herself anew that no man would ever heat her veins again.

In truth, it had not been a hard vow for her to keep. There were no young and handsome *nègres* around St. Denis Hill to tempt her with their maleness—only the remains of Fanny and François's family whom Marie de Soto had bought from the other St. Denis heirs—and Madame's failing health placed endless demands upon Coincoin's time. So many responsibilities for the household had fallen to her that when she fell into bed each night, it was not the want of a man that kept Coincoin restless and awake. It was worry that Madame Marie's new baby would catch the measles from one of the older ones, or mental reminders to herself that Choera must begin the slaughter next Monday and Hyacinthe should be sent to the post before then for enough salt to cure the pork.

In her spare hours, Coincoin had tried to train her sisters in the healing mysteries of forest herbs, anticipating the day when she, herself, would leave the De Sotos. That day would come, Coincoin knew, but when fate called her she could not leave Madame with no nurse to care for her. As the months passed, Hyacinthe did show some aptitude, but it was far less than Coincoin hoped, and her exasperation often strained the bond that had grown between them since the death of their parents and the old Madame.

Coincoin's new babe had been born in March. A male child it was, long and lean with copper skin that would have made Chatta happy—a boy with straight, black silk instead of the nap Chatta had laughed at every time he looked at their chunky, black-skinned broad-faced Nicolas who looked so much like her own father. But Chatta would never know this son. De Soto's child, he had branded him—wrongly. As she sweated and grunted and screamed through the agonies of this child's birth, Coincoin *knew* he was not destined to be a De Soto slave, and that knowledge gave her all the courage she needed to endure his birth alone.

She had brought four children into the world before this. Always Chatta had been by her side, just as her father had helped her mother through eleven birthings of their own children. But François and Fanny were gone now, and Chatta, too, leaving no one for Coincoin but her little ones. They had become her strength, her purpose, and her life, and this new child she suckled that March of 1766 nourished her as much as she nourished him.

The year since Jean's birth had been a short one. The old sense of destiny again followed Coincoin as she dressed Madame Marie each morning, as she gathered her herbs from the backside of the hill, and often at night in her fitful dreams. When it would come, or how, she did not know. She only knew that whenever that destiny confronted her, she would know it; and she would accept whatever form it took.

Once, only once, had Coincoin tried to discuss her premonitions with her sisters, but Hyacinthe was still too young to understand and Mariotte had snipped back that all Coincoin needed was a man. Instead of scurrying away from Mass with her children, like a mother hen, she ought to stay and dally with the handsome bucks. Or, better yet, come along to the riverbank on Sunday evening for the *nègre* dances. Who knows? Mariotte had teased knowingly. She might even find somebody with more to offer than the slave boys could. *Well!* There really wasn't anything wrong with that, she had declared as Coincoin began to frown. The fates had ruled that they would always be poor slaves. They had a right to grab whatever pleasure or profit a poor slave could, did they not?

While Coincoin floundered in search of an appropriate answer, for the kind of guidance that Fanny would have given, young Mariotte drove home her point. What did it matter whether a generous fellow was black or white? Goodness knows, the other slave girls weren't nearly so persnickety and their white lovers were usually generous. That's what Coincoin needed, a man to give her pleasure and pay her for it, too!

Never again had Coincoin tried to reach into her sister's soul. When Mariotte looked at the world she saw only sensual pleasures. Men. Food. Pretty dresses to cover her plump curves. And when Coincoin looked at Mariotte, she saw nothing but complaisance. Nor could she find in any of her other siblings even a hint of the fire that once had burned in their parents' souls—not in Choera or Dgimby who lived with her there on the hill, or even Jeanne who had spent a more privileged life with the Sieur de Mézières ever since the St. Denis estate was divided.

In some ways, Coincoin blamed her faith—or the men who were supposed to nurture it. No sturdy oak had been sent to Natchitoches by the Church in half a dozen years, no one to shelter the seeds of religion, no one to produce new and fertile acorns from which a forest might grow. Instead, their latest Reverend Père had been a sapling willow who bowed and swayed under the gales of revelry and mutiny, and in the end he had allowed his flock to pack him aboard a pirogue and row him back to New Orleans. That was when Coincoin had lost her faith in the basic goodness of mankind, in the power of right to conquer all wrong. That was when she lost her faith in everything and everybody but herself and the destiny she knew awaited her.

Tonight she had met her fate. Just as she had expected, it came suddenly. Without warning. Just as she knew that she would do, she had faced it squarely, without doubt, without hesitation, without emotion. It would not be so bad a fate, she told herself. This Frenchman from La Rochelle was kind enough, and his flamboyance had mellowed in the year he had been at their post.

But he's haughty! A nagging demon began to taunt her, testing her steadfastness to the bargain she had made. *Oui,* that he is, her other self retorted. But then I've always respected pride.

He's too cocksure! He knew he could get you! True again, her determination argued back. He knows what he wants. Well, so do I. What's wrong with that?

But will he treat me well? Coincoin laughed cynically at that thought. Can any woman be sure of that in any man? Of course, she had been sure with Chatta, and he had never raised his hand to her, but their bond had been special. Never once, even, had she caught him flirting with any of the other serving girls—not even M'sieur Le Court's doe-eyed Thérèse whom half the men at the post had lusted over ever since the lieutenant brought her back from his trip to the Caneci. No, she thought, I'll take my chances with the tall M'sieur, with that cascade of mahogany curls and those knowing, grey-green eyes.

In truth, Coincoin worried little about the man's faithfulness—and the awful, blinding disease that too many faithless frontier men brought home to the women who shared their bed. Post gossip already had concluded that whatever the Sieur Metoyer might be, he was not a womanizer. Coincoin had listened often enough as Marie de Soto gossiped over the coquettes who chased him and lost their tempers when he failed to chase them back. If Madame was right, most would not have minded if he had caught them, with or without marriage. But girls who let themselves get caught get pregnant, and among the whites at this post marriage had to follow. *Non,* the man made it clear tonight that he was not looking for a wife and did not intend to let one trap him.

Indeed, the only thing that had surprised her until now about the handsome merchant with the crooked smile had been Mariotte's report that he would not even dally with willing slave girls. Not for pleasure or a price. Mariotte had tittered over that and suggested that he must have found himself a pretty boy instead. But then again, Coincoin reassured herself, the man had made it plain enough tonight that *that* was not his problem.

Whatever M'sieur's reasons, Coincoin concluded, it was not her place to ask. Nor did she really care. His proposition had been a business one. He did not expect love, nor could she offer any. He asked only for service and promised the same in return. That was enough.

Yet his eyes still haunted her as she flounced in her big bed, with only the infant Jean in her arms. Those deep, grey-green eyes had a warmth and softness that the M'sieur had tried to mask. Somewhere in her past, she had known and loved eyes like that before.

It was this vague memory of her past that brought a twinge of shame, as she contemplated the step she was about to take. Linked irrevocably to that memory was the image of her parents, of the warmth that François and Fanny shared and gave to everyone around them. She had never known that kind of warmth with Chatta, even when he fired her loins the hottest. Surely the kind of warmth that Fanny and François had was special.

Too, theirs had been a legal and sacred marriage, Coincoin now reminded herself. It had been sanctioned by the Church, as this relationship with the Sieur Metoyer could never be, as her love for Chatta never had been because he was not a baptized Christian and the priests had refused to wed them unless he accepted the Christ they preached.

So what? Coincoin now argued brutally. Fanny and François had been coupled without love at the order of their master. What was really wrong about this new coupling, when it would end the slavery that had destroyed her parents? It was a miracle that love had ever taken root in their marriage bed, much more so that it had grown and blossomed. She did not ask for miracles herself. Freedom would be enough.

Madame Marie would rant when M'sieur came tomorrow. Of that Coincoin was certain. She would insist that she could never do without her Coincoin. She would call M'sieur a selfish bastard for asking such sacrifice of a pitiful woman. She'd swear long and loudly that Hyacinthe could never take the place of her faithful Coincoin; and Coincoin knew, as Metoyer could never know, the truth with which Madame would swear that oath. She, Coincoin, did have a special place in the life and heart of the mistress who had long years before stood on tiny tiptoes to kiss away the fright of the helpless babe who had become her godchild. Between Marie de St. Denis de Soto and Marie Thérèse *dite* Coincoin there was a bond that neither time nor race nor rank could ever sever.

Oui, Coincoin assured herself. *Madame will make her usual scene. But when M'sieur leaves the hill tomorrow, I'll go with him.*

5

October 1777

Through the unshuttered window, Coincoin watched the new priest stride purposefully up the street. His was a walk no man could ever mimic. His steps were as short, cocky, and deliberate as the man himself; and they took him where he intended to go with incredible speed. Padre Luis de Quintanilla was a Spaniard who knew precisely where he was headed, and he never swerved one degree off course along his way. M'sieur called him a fiery jackanape, Coincoin recalled with a faint smile, and Madame Marie called him a meddling fool. The post surgeon actually had threatened to call him out after the crusading priest insisted the irreverent doctor be arrested for passing lewd picture cards during Sunday Mass.

Coincoin could not help but admire the man, as she admired all people who knew their own mind and lived true to themselves. But she could not rid herself of the fear that gripped her whenever he preached on immorality, cupidity, or the depravity of French men and slave women who openly violated the laws of God and man. Certainly, this new priest was no willow sapling. He was the strong, indomitable, spiritual leader their post needed—and she feared him as she had never feared any man before.

That same uneasiness overcame her now as Quintanilla strode confidently through their front gate. Anxiously, she called the twins from the shade of the pecan tree, where they had been gathering the fallen nuts. It was not easy to force calmness into her voice, but if her fears proved true, it would be better that the children not hear what might transpire. The twins were only nine, but both possessed a quick perception that was, all at once, a source of amazement, delight, and wretched frustration to the father who took great pride in them but could not bring himself to do so openly.

"Susanne, it is such a sticky afternoon and the little ones are restless. Take them to the shallows for a cool dip. But be careful not to take your eyes off them one moment, you hear?"

"*Oui, Maman.*"

"Augustin, go to the shop and tell M'sieur that Padre has come to see him. Be sure to stay there until M'sieur returns. You may be needed to help with the customers."

"*Oui,* Mama!" The boy's whoop left a trail behind him as he dashed off through the back garden, taking his favorite shortcut to the Front Street shop from which they and the Sieur Pavie had moved shortly after M'sieur rented her from Madame Marie.

The pastor's knock grew louder, more peremptory, as he waited for admittance.

"*Buenos días, padre. Está bien?*" Coolly, with no trace of the turmoil that churned inside her, Coincoin greeted the priest in his native Spanish. By now, she well knew how he felt about the "mulish souls" at the post who acted as though they still belonged to the King of France.

"Your master? Is he at home?" the Capuchin priest inquired peremptorily, giving no sign that he had noticed her courtesy.

"I am sorry, padre, but he has not yet returned from the shop. I have sent my son to tell him you are here."

As soon as she said those words, *my son,* Coincoin cringed within. It was such a normal thing for a mother to say, but not *here*. Not *now!* She could see Quintanilla's eyes harden as he looked around for the rest of her flock. She could hear—just as though she were sitting in the church itself—every one of the sermons in which he had railed about the *yellow bastards that the whole post winked at,* about the *scandalous example* they set and the *heinous sin* that was evident in the very color of their skin. In truth, she heard those exhortations of his night after night, after Pierre and the little ones had gone to bed and she lay sleepless, guilt-ridden, fearful of the consequences that awaited her—if not in hell, then in the months or years ahead as Quintanilla took firmer charge of the wayward souls at Natchitoches. *O, how long would a wrathful Lord tolerate such an abomination? How long would He let His people so openly defy his commandments?* That had been his refrain just this last Sunday. And now she asked herself *how long?* How long, dear God, would this new priest tolerate the family she and M'sieur had created?

Quintanilla's quick scan found no one but Coincoin, and from his probing stare that seemed to read every thought her face could not conceal, she knew *he knew* that she had shooed them from the house before she let him enter. As she gazed back, determined not to lower her eyes in shame, it occurred to her that he was much too calm. Nothing in the frail Capuchin hinted now of the nervous energy that always fired him. Instead, he had simply planted himself solidly in the center of Metoyer's carpet, as though bracing himself for a lengthy wait. Eventually, his eyes did lower to the floor, deliberately focusing on the Brussels import whose plushness seemed to offend his sandaled feet, and she could have sworn he was calculating the number of prayerbooks that carpet might have purchased.

Lost in their own separate thoughts, neither of them noticed the front door abruptly open and just as curtly close.

"Well, Reverend Père, to what do I owe this unexpected visit?" Metoyer's voice was cordial enough, as he entered his own salon and greeted his uninvited guest. But in his eyes, Coincoin could see a wariness that mirrored her own.

"Is it not a good padre's duty to visit his parishioners, Señor Metoyer? A good shepherd must keep close watch over his sheep lest they go astray." The priest seated himself then, unbidden and stiffly, on the delicately carved Louis Quinze chaise that Pierre had shipped out from Marseilles to the envy of less prosperous families at the post.

"Yes, so I've heard," Metoyer retorted dryly and pushed a thick mane of hair, prematurely graying, from off his neck, while Coincoin hastily appraised his mood. For October, it had been a miserably hot day. Tempers seemed short everywhere when she ventured out that afternoon for fresh produce, and now, from the flush of M'sieur's face, she feared his day had gone no better.

"May I offer you a glass of wine, Reverend?" Pierre's tone was civil. To anyone but Coincoin, it might have been deemed gracious. But she knew its every nuance. She knew when its timbre spoke of tiredness, or intrigue, or disgust, or want—and she knew now that their new priest could not have picked a worse day for trying to corral the strays in his flock. Or a worse stray.

"A cool drink of water from the cistern will suffice," Quintanilla replied. "I'm sure your servant does not mind fetching it."

Dutifully, Coincoin slipped from the room. Their ascetic pastor was not a man to ask for anything for himself. Clearly, his request was a mere ruse. Whatever he had to say would involve her, but she would not be party to the discussion. At least she'd had the foresight to send off the children! Whatever M'sieur and the priest had to say about her, she did not want her *enfants* to overhear.

"Señor Metoyer," the priest began as soon as Coincoin closed the heavy door behind her. "My son. I am well aware of the problems of frontier life, the hardships that sometime seem to make this existence unbearable, the difficulties of living by rules issued from the palaces of Madrid, the tempting examples set by the simple natives all around us who do not know the joy of Christ or the responsibilities of Christianity."

Pierre merely inclined his head in acknowledgment, drumming his fingers against his long, loose India breeches as he irreverently prayed that the cleric would get on with whatever he had come for.

"It is my own joy and love for Christ our Savior, and my responsibilities as His Shepherd, that brought me to this post, my son. Although the many pagan ways I have found here among baptized Christians have caused my heart much pain, I have still tried to be patient, for I know it is human nature to resist change."

Patient? *Zut!*

"There are some problems, my son, that compound themselves if decisive action is not taken to correct them. You know I have preached endless sermons, Sunday after Sunday, trying to bring home to my flock the dangers of certain sins."

Endless is right, Pierre mentally harumphed. Such long and violent harangues that most of your flock abandon you after an hour and a half and go home for dinner.

"Alas, my son…" Quintanilla let his pause hover in the air between them like the drone of a bee about to alight, until the clinching and flexing of Metoyer's fists assured him that this wayward soul clearly anticipated the sting.

"Alas, those to whom I have preached the most earnestly have ignored me consistently. That stubbornness has left me with no other choice."

From the drapes of his cassock, the padre pulled a folded square of parchment. "I have been forced, my son, to bring a certain problem to the attention of my superior, the Most Illustrious Señor, Bishop of Havana. Today, the porter from New Orleans, Señor Brosset, brought me his reply. Bear with me, son, while I read it—at least the first paragraph."

Without pausing for permission, the priest began to read. And it did not take long for his bee to home in on its target:

> To Fr. Luis de Quintanilla, Capucin and Curate of the Holy Parish of San Francisco, post of San Juan Bautista des Natchitoches, Colony of Luisiana.
>
> Your Reverence:
>
> The diligence you have shown in bringing before this office the problems of your ministry is commendable. By no means can the Holy Mother Church tolerate such open and heinous scandal between the Negro concubines of whom you write and their white paramours. These concubines must make use of the apostolic blessings. They must be persuaded to sanctify their sinful concubinage through the holy union of matrimony. But if in spite of your ministrations, they persist in their scandal, you must denounce them, Your Reverence, before the Royal Court of Justice so that they can be forced to right their wrongs and the scandal can be removed.

Metoyer made no reply. Quintanilla refolded the parchment and laid it ominously in his lap. Even in the shadows of early evening, he should have seen the fury rising in the merchant's face and the square jaw harden.

"Spaniard, you have lost your senses! Marriage? Between a Frenchman and a *négresse?* After you have been in this colony longer, Quintanilla, perhaps you'll come to understand its people and its law! Your Spanish peons and their *mestizo* sons over in the scraggly pueblos of Tejas may be too dull-witted to see any better life for themselves than hewing trees and grubbing the soil with a black wench forever at their side. But the Frenchman expects better things—and whiter wives!"

Pierre paused, his jawline eased, and a smile played at his crooked mouth as he called the Capuchin's bluff. "Besides, as you seem to have forgotten, padre, our Code Noir specifically forbids marriage between a Frenchman and a black!"

"My son, you seem to have forgotten yourself that this is now a Spanish colony, not a French one. It is *Las Sietas Partidas* of Alfonso the Wise, not the French Code Noir that must be obeyed now at this post."

Pierre tossed the point aside. "Spanish in name only, padre, and temporarily at that. Back in the sixties, when Louis Quinze gave this colony away, the Creoles warned him and your king. If Louisiana can't be French, it'll be *free.*" He could have elaborated. In fact, he was fleetingly tempted to do just that, but he suspected the warning would be lost on a zealot so blind to the passions of his own people. Whether the Spanish tyrants realized it or not, Pierre wanted to say, their days here were numbered. They had bloodily squelched the first Creole revolt, shortly after his arrival in the colony. But the thirst for freedom had spread now to the Anglo provinces to the east of them, and Quintanilla's cohorts would be well advised to watch out lest the spirit of freedom flare again in this colony they claim but will never *control.*

"Freedom is not the question at hand today, my son," the priest broke in. "We are discussing the sin of fornication that has become quite obvious at this post. Since I have arrived, I have baptized already one mulatto infant born to your black servant, and every Sunday she herds into Mass a whole flock of half-white children."

So? Metoyer silently challenged.

"Granted, Coincoin and her brood are not the only evidence of unholy lust at this post. Judging from the number of other mulattoes I have baptized since my arrival here, this sin is quite widespread. However, your *negra* is the only one who lives openly, without shame, with her partner in sin. I have no choice but to make an example of her."

"An example? Of Coincoin? Or me as well?"

"The choice is yours, my son. Whatever choice you make, I look forward to welcoming you back into the fold. Since I have been at this post, you have not once been to confession. Yet I understand you are from a pious family. I am told that your father's brother dedicated himself to our holy priesthood."

Pierre ceded not an inch of moral ground as he stared down his devil's advocate. In the man's thin brown face, hardly lighter than that of Pierre's own Susanne, he read no compassion. The pinched mouth itself was a sermon on *control.* The eyes, as black and hard as onyx, glinted with all the ambition that lay behind them. *Sur ma foi!* Pierre snorted to himself. When Quintanilla took his complaint to the bishop, he wasn't half as concerned with impressing a lesson upon his flock as he was with impressing his bishop with his zeal!

"Surely your heart is heavy with the sin it carries," the padre continued, attempting now to blunt the shepherd's rod with which he had been whipping this stray sheep into line. "Right your wrongs, my son, and let the Good Shepherd guide your life from this point on."

Guidance? Nothing the Capuchin could have argued would have had less effect on Claude Thomas Pierre Metoyer, who had allowed no father—real or otherwise—to dictate the terms of his life. "I need no guidance, priest! My life is planned, and it includes no marriage to a slave."

"Be that as it may, my son. You realize, though, that you leave me no choice but to report you to His Majesty's authorities at this post?"

"And you know blasted well that 'His Majesty's authorities at this post' take the sole form of Athanase de Mézières, in whose household there's a mulatto child born every other year—though the old man himself can't take the credit."

Before Quintanilla could respond, Pierre hammered on, driving his latest point as deeply as he dared. "Just what type of action do you think you'll get out of our commandant, padre? You obviously forget that his sister-in-law owns the woman you plan to use as your example. Let me warn you, Quintanilla, the de Soto–de Mézières–St. Denis clan has run this frontier for longer than there has been a post here, and they are not about to let the wailings of a cleric undermine their control."

The priest sighed. "My son, it pains me that you are taking this approach."

Pain was indeed evident in the careworn face that looked far older than his years. Even Pierre had to concede that. Luis de Quintanilla was an anachronism, a Christian martyr, a medieval crusader born into a Spain that was already dying from moral, cultural, and political decay. If the man's sermons had any base in truth, Pierre told himself in an effort to feel some jot of charity, when Quintanilla dedicated his life to Spain's colonial missions, he envisioned a life of sacrifice for God's glory, sowing the seeds of Christianity in the vast and virgin fields of the New World. Only, he had not expected his pagan flock to be men born in Spain itself, or even France; and that shock had been his greatest trial. Still, as he reminded them every Sunday and every holy day in between, Quintanilla knew his faith would conquer any test that God or man might put to him.

"De Mézières will do what he must," the Capuchin went on confidently. "He is morally bound to uphold the laws of His Catholic Majesty Carlos III. The law of Spain which now governs this post, whether you Frenchmen accept it or not, is the law that our commandant must enforce; and the letter of our illustrious bishop in Havana makes it clear what action both I and Señor de Mézières must take. The authority of our Holy Mother Church, is *supreme.* Will you not reconsider, my son?"

"You expect the impossible, padre," Metoyer muttered, weary of Quintanilla's persistence. Weary of the hellish, oppressive heat that had already lasted two weeks too long this year. Weary of his own inner conflict that had not abated even after his initial lust for Coincoin had been satisfied. Weary of the damned social conventions that required him to deny the children on whom he doted and the woman who supplied him every comfort and demanded nothing in return—other than the one never-repeated but never-forgotten promise he had made ten years before at the foot of St. Denis Hill.

"Then I shall do what I must," Quintanilla pronounced, rising abruptly. "God's will be done, and may he have mercy on both your souls."

Only at the door did he pause, momentarily. "I see that your servant has not returned from the cistern. No problem. I did not really need the drink anyway."

‍ 6 ‍

The night was a long one, for both Coincoin and Metoyer. He did not repeat to her the dire threats Quintanilla had made, but he did not have to. She had returned quickly enough with the drink, very quickly. But the scent of fear that had plagued her all summer had immobilized her from the moment that, on her return from the cistern, she had paused to open the heavy salon door and had heard him read the bishop's edict, *Denounce them to the Royal Court of Justice so they can be forced!*

What lay ahead? Never at this post had any public charges been made against the slave women who bore half-white children, or against the whites who fathered them. Was there a law against this, other than the sacred commandment she had tried to wipe from her memory these past ten years? Was there a punishment prescribed by law, other than the fires of hell that the padre promised every Sunday?

Afraid now, she reached across the darkness to seek comfort in Metoyer's strength, and again she was glad he had moved her permanently from her pallet to his bed, mocking her protests that appearances must be preserved although there was no one in their house to know except the Sieur Pavie and their own children. Again she felt the comfort that enveloped her every time his body touched her own, the warmth that pervaded her when she looked into his grey-green eyes. For ten years she had shared his life and his bed, but she still could not fathom why he made her feel like a small and trusting child, safe in the arms of a giant who understood her—and cared. Warmth and caring were not part of the bargain they had made.

Pierre caught and squeezed her hand, as her arm wrapped around him and her body snuggled closer. What could he say to her? For years, he had convinced himself that he had done the only thing he could do, that the course he had chosen was still the right one. The commandments of his faith, the rules of his society, were all admirable guidelines for men to live by; but man is only human, and man often fails to reach the ideals he sets for the rest of the world to follow.

Of course he had not married this woman he had enjoyed for a decade. He was not callous and he was not exploiting her. He cared as much for Coincoin as any Frenchman of good breeding could care for a woman of her race and station. He loved their children and did all for them a father could do in his position. He had badgered Marie de Soto for years and had at last worn down her stubborn refusal to let him buy his oldest four. Why, he even bought that half-Indian boy, Jean, that Coincoin had been nursing when she moved into his house.

Zut! He was willing, still, to buy those older girls Coincoin had borne her savage husband. He knew how it had seared her to the quick when De Soto sold her daughter Fanchon to the Lecomte Dupré plantations down at the Bluff, just

Fr. Luis de Quintanilla Religioso Capuchino, y Cura Par-
roco del sobredicho Puerto tiene el honor de representar a
V. m.d, que, hallandose obligado en virtud de su ministerio a
desarraigar los vicios, y cortar los escandalos que de ellos se
originan, no ha podido despues de muchas diligencias poner
freno al escandaloso amancebamiento de una Negra llama-
da Cuencuen esclava de Dn Manuel de Soto, alquilada muchos
años ha al nombrado Metoye, en cuia casa y compaña la
dicha Negra ha parido (no estando casada) cinco, ō seis
mulatos, y mulatas, sin comprehender en este numero
el, ō la, de que esta actualmente, embarazada, y como
esto no puede suceder en la casa de un soltero, y una Sol-
tera, sin que el Publico piense, y juzgue haber comercio
ilicito entre los dos mancebos, de que se sigue un grande
escandalo, y detrimento en las almas, y siendo le mandado
al Suplicante por su Superior el Ill.mo señor obispo de
Cuba, que en caso, que los amancebamientos no cesen despues de las amonestaciones apostolicas, los amancebados se en-
treguen a las Justicias Reales, para que los coerzan, y cas-
tiguen, cuio texto es el siguiente: Con los amancebados
use V.R. de los medios apostolicos: persuadalos, a que san-
tifiquen su mala amistad por la union del Matrimonio;
y si despues de todo insistieren, denuncielos V.R. a las Justicias Reales, para que los coerzan, y quiten el escandolo.
El Suplicante en atencion a esto a V.m.d denuncia la sobredicha
negra Cuencuen como publica, amancebada para que V.m.d
se sirva castigarla conforme a la Ley, prohibiendo bajo
graves penas de jamas bolver a entrar en casa del men-
cionado Metoye a fin de evitar el escando lo publico, man-
dando a su Dueño de ella de cuidar, que no incurra mas
en semejante pecado, porque de otra manera se expondra
a perder su Negra. Justicia, que espera de la equidad de
V.m.d. Natchitoches. octubre. 23. de 1777.
                    fr Luis de Quintanilla qui ut supra

Quintanilla's Bill of Complaint

23 October 1777

This document exists in multiple versions, with slight variations. The narrative within the text
summarizes the whole in order to present the essence of each version.

before the new Spanish governor arrested De Soto and sent him off to jail for his past treasons. That loss had been hard enough for Coincoin. She scarcely ate for weeks, until her rail-thin body and protruding belly reminded her that a new child was now at risk. At least the girls were just down at the bluff with the Widow Lecomte and her son-in-law—and the Lecomte-Dupré clan let Coincoin visit the girls whenever she pleased. It was the loss of her firstborn son, the one she called Nicolas Chiquito, that had torn her heart from her soul, when De Soto's creditors seized the boy and sold him off to Gil y Barbo in Spanish Tejas. Still, where Coincoin's other daughters were concerned, the De Soto woman's obstinacy would not yield, and—in his view at least—Coincoin herself was to blame for that. If she had not taught her Thérèse and Marie Louise all those esoteric secrets of African witch doctors, then the hypochondriac who owned them would not find them so indispensable!

Beside him, in that maddening way of hers, Coincoin seemed to read his mind. Her free hand began to caress him, softly, promisingly, as if to say, "I know you've tried and I appreciate it." For a moment his whole body, still muscular though thickening with years, tensed in protest against all the forces that had chained him to this colony and to this woman. Then, as always, his tenseness eased and he reached for Coincoin hungrily, and the two lovers silently consoled each other for what was left of their long and sleepless night.

The fears they calmed in each other's arms proved valid, even sooner than either of them expected. Before Metoyer dressed and left to open the Front Street shop, before the precocious Augustin had been dispatched to the riverfront warehouse to help Étienne begin their inventory, before Susanne or little Louis could finish breakfast and find their buckets to finish gathering the pecans in the backyard garden, the bailiff was at their door.

"M'sieur Metoyer," he began apologetically, twisting the paper in his hand. "This is none of my doing, sir, you understand. But De Mézières has issued an order, and I have to serve it. I'm sorry, M'sieur. It's an infernal infringement upon a man's personal life and an affront to his honor, and I hope you won't hold this against me."

"Whatever, Fournier. Do it and be done."

"Here, M'sieur, you can read it as well as I. But I will have to ask you to sign the back of the second copy, so I can return it as proof that the order has been served."

Metoyer took the papers roughly, marched to his desk, opened his inkwell, drew his quill, then signed the copy. Thrusting it into the bailiff's hands, he slammed the door and sank against it as he unfolded two sheets of paper.

Protest of Padre Luis de Quintanilla, Capuchin and Parish Curate—and Decree of His Honor Athanase de Mézières, Chevalier of the Royal and Military Order of St. Louis, Lieutenant Colonel, Lieutenant Governor, and Commandant of the Post of Natchitoches

Fr. Luis de Quintanilla… by virtue of his duty to eradicate the vices and relate the scandals as they occur, reports that after much diligence he has still been unable to end the scandalous concubinage of a Negress named Coincoin, slave of Dn. Manuel de Soto. She has been hired for many years to the man named Metoyer, in whose house and company this unmarried black woman has produced five or six mulatto children, not counting the one with which she is now pregnant.

Your honor, this cannot happen in the house of an unmarried man and an unmarried woman without the public thinking and judging there to be illicit intercourse between the two and this has resulted in a great scandal at the post and great damage to all its souls…

It is therefore prayed that the woman Coincoin be taken from Metoyer's house and returned to her rightful owner; that this owner be compelled, as she has heretofore refused to do, to control the behavior of her slave or else have the slave taken from her and sold for the public good. It is also demanded that the woman Coincoin be prohibited, under the supreme punishment, from ever again entering the house of the above-named Metoyer, in order to avoid future public scandal, and it is moreover demanded that she be castigated according to the law for her sins to date.

Padre Luis de Quintanilla—*Who is Supreme*

As Metoyer stared at the presumptuous signature, a sense of doom pervaded him. He had to force himself to turn the page and read the commandant's decree.

The only thing merciful about that was that it was brief.

> In consideration of the above, the aforesaid Negress Coincoin is denounced as a public concubine. The Sieur Metoyer is ordered to abandon her immediately. She is to return to her rightful owner, and that owner must deliver her to the Royal Court of Justice, so that she may be punished as prescribed.

> Athanase de Mézières, Commandant

✂ 7 ✂
Two days later

"Écoutez! Écoutez!" Fournier, the bailiff, intoned monotonously, as the teeming crowd jostled each other for a front row view. Every habitant in the district must have come into the post today, he mused as he surveyed the mob encircling him on the plaza. The padre may not be able to pack them into church on Sunday, but he's sure drawn his whole flock to this exhibition.

Forcing his voice to be impersonal, Fournier continued to drone the decree that De Mézières had given him only an hour before.

"The Negress Coincoin has been denounced as a public concubine and found guilty. It is the sentence of the court that the punishment prescribed by law be this day carried out as an example and a reminder to others who may be tempted to flaunt the commands of His Catholic Majesty and our Holy Mother the Church."

Coincoin stood impassively behind him, a tall, lissome Venus, her head shaved—denuded, as a badge of shame—but still held proudly. A symbolic sackcloth had been thrown loosely over the frame that eleven childbirths had ripened into voluptuousness. Her bare feet were firmly planted on the cart upon which she had been mounted, and she stared defiantly into the crowd as though she dared any of them to read aloud the word crudely emblazoned across that cart: FORNICATOR.

If the word bothered the bailiff, it was not evident, as he continued in the same staccato monotone he used to auction cattle or estates.

"It is the decree of the Court that the Negress Coincoin be driven through the streets of this post for all to see her guilt, that she then be taken to the door of the church, where she will kneel and beg forgiveness of our Holy Savior whom she has defied and defiled, that she ride the wooden horse in the center of this square until dusk sets upon her shame, and that she then be administered the twenty lashes the law prescribes."

A shocked silence hung over the public square, the curiosity of the crowd momentarily abated. For two days, the post had buzzed with rumors, as men and women, free and slave, had considered the outcome of their padre's latest challenge. Tippling bargoers had laid bets over whether their merchant friend would be fined or whether the commandant would ignore the little priest and wink on at harmless, male peccadillos.

Gossiping housewives had divided into battle camps between those who agreed that Reverend Père was a meddler and those with a flock of unmarried daughters who swore that the local men would be more interested in holy wedlock if the black girls were less available for sport.

As for the Negroes, more than a few had suffered the torment of their own questions. Would Coincoin's punishment—possibly their own one day—be the lash or the auction block?

Speculation was now settled. The sentence, but an anticlimax. Amid a few hooting catcalls from the young blades and snickers from more sanctimonious d'amselles or their mothers, Coincoin's cart squeaked out the gate and down the main street of town. Temporarily impressed, the *négresses* and their brothers, fathers, children, and husbands slowly followed, some mumbling beneath their breath, others agonizing over their own situations and the risks they now faced. The citizens of the district surged around them, laughing now, following the parade led by the public cart, and eagerly anticipating the festivities that always accompanied a court day.

Mutely, young Augustin Metoyer separated himself from the throng that towered over him—the jesting, uncaring masses that jostled past, oblivious of him and his shame. Fighting tears that scalded his soul more than his cheeks, the child turned his back upon the crowd as it elbowed its way toward town and followed a lonely, beaten path across the square.

Mud from a week of autumn rains oozed between his toes, but his usual recoil from dirt and grime that made him the frequent target of cruder playmates had been trumped today by a soil that stained *him*, not just his clothes. He was doubly glad that his chums had not seen him, that no one seemed to recognize him, and now he sought the one place of refuge where he knew no friends would look, the parish church.

For a moment, Augustin wished that he had obeyed M'sieur and stayed at home. "The crowd is too wild on court day," Metoyer had warned the children sternly, but the boy knew intuitively that this was not M'sieur's real reason, and for the first time ever he deliberately disobeyed the man who was both his master and his father.

As soon as the front door slammed behind Pierre that morning, Augustin had winked conspiratorially at the younger Louis, announced to his twin Susanne that he was off to groom the horses, and then left his sister to tend the babies while he slipped through the backwoods to the stockade that encircled the square, the government buildings, and the church.

He had arrived in time to see his mother mount the cart, to hear the bailiff's stinging words… *guilt… punishment… shame.* The nature of his mother's crime was still unclear. Such words as *concubine* and *fornicator* had never been explained to him. But their gravity was clear in those awful, searing words the bailiff finally said. *Twenty lashes!*

Augustin's heart had stopped. At least he had thought so, while the echo of those words fell upon him harder than the hailstorm he had been caught in a few weeks back. Never in all his years had the reality of slavery so touched him. Already he knew that he was privileged among other *nègres*, that he was well clothed and lived in a better house, that his master loved him because he was his father even though he dared not call him *père*. While he had seen, and heard, the flogging of both black and white miscreants, never had he or any of his family stood with bare back before a gaping crowd while a whip shredded their flesh. Fear, shame, and helplessness engulfed him now as he knelt in the pew he was never allowed to use on Sunday when the little church was full of masters, and he begged God to spare his mother the awful fate she faced when the sun set.

Outside the heavy door he had closed behind him, Augustin heard the surging crowd arrive and the creaking cart wheel to a stop. Again the throng grew still, as quiet as it had been while the bailiff read the court's decree. Only this time the bated breaths waited for Coincoin's forced confession before her Holy Mother the Church.

Her voice came through the door then, softly muffled by the thick walnut slab. Yet the firm, defiant pride Coincoin had shown as she stood astride the public cart was still there, unmistakable in the timbre of her words.

"My God, for whatever wrong I have done in this life you gave me, I do repent."

No trace of shame, no quiver of fear, betrayed Coincoin as she plunged on.

"I know, dear Jesus, that whatever punishment I must suffer, whatever cross may be laid upon my back, you will give me the strength to bear with the same dignity you showed at Calvary before your own tormentors."

Only then did the voice trail off. A last, soft "Amen" concluded his mother's affirmation of her faith and marked, Augustin knew, the resumption of her shame.

"Amen." The crowd automatically responded. Then, out of its murmur, there rose a wave of laughter as the frontier's wayward sheep realized that their herder had not yet corralled any strays. This one, for sure, would continue to go her own way.

On the dark side of the chapel door, Augustin heard their tittering but was much too young to understand the affinity that triggered it. Flushing anew, he plunged into a litany of prayers, thanking God that his mother's pride had not been conquered even when she was laughed at. Then he paled as he recalled the many sermons Padre had preached on the virtue of *humility.*

A fresh trail of tears began to weave its way down his nut-brown cheeks, and he yanked from his neck the chain of wooden beads Coincoin had carved for him, the Rosary that was just like the one her father had made for her that she still treasured. All the humiliation that churned inside him, he tried futilely to forget, as he recited aloud the rhythmic, soothing prayers of the Holy Mysteries Coincoin had taught him. Yet those litanies brought no comfort. Every Station of the Cross reminded him not of Christ's suffering but of his own, and between every Ave Maria and Pater Noster his mind chanted one solemn vow: *I'll never be shamed again! I'll grow up good if you'll make me free. Make us free. My mama, my brothers, my sisters. As free as papa is. We'll all be good and never offend you. I promise, God. Just make us* free!

The noisy mob dispersed outside, as the men returned to their taverns or the streets for a day of merrymaking and the women to their tittle-tattle on one gallery or another, where they would discuss the newest scandals not yet spied by Quintanilla's ever-vigilant eye.

Behind them Coincoin sat alone, quietly straddling the wooden horse that had been rolled into the center of the square. Her wrists roped firmly behind her, her form immobile and unbending, she stared into the rising sun and refused to think of the mortification that lay ahead, when the passage of hours would force her to soil herself while straddling her mockery of a mount. At least her back was to the chapel as Augustin slipped quietly out the door and fled for home, futilely praying to forget the sight he would always see.

⌐ § ⌐

At the other end of town, a jovial crowd soon thronged the tavern entrance of Metoyer and Pavie's Front Street shop and pushed its way inside.

"Hey, Pierre!"

A friendly hand slapped Metoyer across the shoulder and he cringed, cursing himself for opening the tavern that day at all. He had been damned determined, though, to act as if nothing was different, to deny that churlish priest the pleasure of knowing the pain he caused.

"Come on, Metoyer, buy us a drink and let's celebrate your victory."

"*Zut!* It's *his* victory," Étienne interjected good-naturedly. "*You* buy the drinks, Rouelle, and we'll all celebrate."

"*Sur ma foi, mes amis!*" the post surgeon cackled. "*Ah, ça,* Metoyer! I wish I could see Quintanilla right now. She sure showed him how much his meddling's worth!"

Again the surgeon slapped Pierre across his back, and *confrères* cheered. "Some men just never seem to learn," the man prattled on. "You'd have thought that priest would have gotten the message last week when he had me arrested for livening up his long dull sermons, and old de Mézières let me out with a token fine. *Merde!* There's no way our commandant's going to side with that priest against us. He's a man, no?"

Again Rouelle grinned knavishly, still oblivious to the fact that the object of his congratulations was in no mood to celebrate. "*Mon Dieu,* Metoyer! I'll bet the padre's back in his church now, crying blasphemy because you're not up there riding the wooden horse beside your pretty woman.*"

Like an alligator rearing up from the river below them, Pierre's thick arm snaked out with no warning, catching the surgeon squarely across his chin. Rouelle's jaw snapped backward and his knees folded as the stunned mob parted to let him fall.

"What the hell did you do that for, man?" a voice protested. "That's no way to treat friends who've come to toast your victory."

"There will be no toasting in this shop," Pierre retorted, and Étienne groaned at the thought of lost revenue. "Any bunch of men who want to make like gossiping hens can do it elsewhere."

"Now, Pierre," Étienne cajoled. "Nobody meant anything. There aren't any gossiping hens in this herd of bulls. It's just another court day, Pierre. Just another court day. Let's pour our friends a drink."

"You pour their drinks!" Pierre retorted as he stormed out the door. "I have better things to do."

He found Marie de St. Denis de Soto ensconced in a pile of pillows, all as white and plump as she had grown. Her coal black hair, generously streaked now with grey, was pushed carelessly into her ruffled bedcap, and coffee stains splotched the dressing gown that stretched taut across her bosom. Her pudgy fingers picked absentmindedly at the bowl of berries beside her, plopping them by two's into the round little mouth that now puckered more from age than pertness.

"Pardon the intrusion, Madame, but I have a proposition to make." Pierre spoke directly, even before Nanette could announce his presence. He had already wasted enough time convincing that fat, black guardian of her mistress's morals that he could not wait in the salon while the woman dressed.

"Well, I see you are your usual subtle self today, Metoyer," Marie responded dryly, heedless of the fact that she had unbuttoned the neck of her dressing gown as the morning had grown warmer. "No mind, I like forthrightness in a person; and so far as I've seen, that's your only virtue."

"Nanette!" she barked, and her old servant waddled in the general direction of Marie's bed. "Prop up my pillows so I can sit up in this damned bed."

"Yes, ma'am, I'll prop 'em up, ma'am. Yo better sit up 'cause it sho ain't proper for a lady t' entertain gent'men while she's lyin' down. Oh, but yo poor saintly mama would turn over 'n her grave, ma'am, if she could see t'is—or hear you talk t'e way you do. Profanity jes ain't for ladies, ma'am, much less 'n mixed comp'ny."

"Nanette, you know damned well I've never been a lady. *Ladies* don't survive on this frontier without a man to protect them, and I've had a deuced time keeping one of those. Now, if you're not too old and fat to make it out to the kitchen, I'm sure Señor Metoyer could use a cup of *tafia.* In fact, I could use one myself."

"What zat? Me go t' t'e kitchen an' leave you wit' t'e gent'man all by yo'self, ma'am? An' you in bed?"

"Woman, do you see anybody else around to play my dueña? It's a court day and you know it. Everybody's off at the post to watch that spectacle the priest has staged. Now get yourself out of here and get those drinks! Just because you suckled me when I was too little to care doesn't mean I won't sell you now if you don't do what I say!"

"Yo wouldn't dare," Nanette mumbled to herself. "Yo wouldn't dare."

"Cursed *nègres!*" Marie grumbled to Metoyer as Nanette sashayed slowly through the chamber door, deliberately pushing it wider instead of shutting it behind her. "The older they get the more they forget who owns whom. The only decent servant I ever had was Coincoin. Why in the devil I ever let you talk me out of her is beyond me."

"Well, behind that bluster of yours, Madame, I suspect there lurks a heart."

"You think me *soft? Sapristi!* I may be sick, Metoyer, but I'm not *soft.* I've run this family from this bed for eight years now."

Marie harumphed in obvious disgust. "Look around you, man! What other crippled-up woman do you see at this post with no husband and a flock of children who's kept her family together and off charity?" Only a fit of coughing spared Pierre, then, from the sermon she almost launched into, though she didn't have to bother. He'd heard it before. In fact, gossip was, she'd even written the governor to say how it just burned her up when that fool of a priest he'd sent upriver took her tithes and gave them to gutless wenches who wouldn't do whatever it took to support their own orphaned broods, because they were *gentle ladies.*

"Madame, you are definitely one of a kind," Pierre agreed, and his words were sincere. Marie de Soto was brusque and profane. In the years since he had come to this post, especially since she had taken to her bed, she had grown corpulent without any of the softness that usually accompanied such girth. No matter how he tried, he could not envision the coquette Coincoin said this woman was during their childhood here on St. Denis Hill. Still, he could not fault her either. Coincoin had told him of that love affair her brother had thwarted, and sometimes he wondered if that was why the woman had abetted his *mésalliance* with her godchild.

Oui, bluff and boisterous, imperious and intolerable—she was all of this. Still, he had felt pity for the woman when Spanish officials arrived to take over the post back in '69 and had promptly ordered the arrest of her husband for whatever crimes drove him out of Tejas in the first place. With her usual bluntness, Marie had ranted and threatened and written every official from New Orleans to Paris to Madrid, but the umbrella of French authority that her powerful family had held over Manuel de Soto for fifteen years was no protection after Louisiana was given to the Spanish crown.

Wisely, the Spaniards had left De Mézières in charge of this frontier, French though he was. They had no one else who could keep the Indians in line, and they knew it. From the time De Mézières had married into the St. Denis family, he had become more a St. Denis than the old man's sons. He had let the savages tattoo practically every inch of his body to prove his balls. He had made himself blood brother to every war chief within five hundred miles. After the passing of the old St. Denis, De Mézières *owned* the tribes, and the Spaniards were not fools enough to interfere. Even so, they drew the line between De Mézières and his brother-in-law. For De Soto's treachery against the Crown, he would rot for a decade in the vilest dungeon Mexico City had.

In all the years Metoyer had known Marie, her attempted salvation of her husband was the only challenge she had not beaten down, and that failure had brought out the worst in her. Only those who had loved her as a child, as Coincoin had, still insisted there was goodness inside the shrew Marie de St. Denis de Soto had become.

"Well, what about that meddling jackanape?" Marie inquired, after her coughing spell subsided. "I suppose he's gloating all over the post today."

"I've not seen him, Madame."

"I'll be hanged! I expected him to have another one of his sermons ready. It's not like the man to let a crowd gather without delivering another long harangue in his atrocious French."

Nanette waddled back into the room with a flask and a single cup, which Marie eyed irritably. "When you pour Señor's drink, woman, go back and get another cup."

"'Nother cup, ma'am? Yo only got one guest."

"You get another cup or I'll drink mine straight from the bottle. Now scat!"

"Yes, ma'am. Yes, ma'am," the old *négresse* muttered. "Yo shouldn't ax sech t'ings o' me, ma'am. Yo mama never taught me t' pour no lady nuttin' stronger t'an wine. I too old t' start learning new t'ings now."

"*Malédiction!*" Marie fumed behind the servant's slowly departing back. "Nanette's going to drive me to murder before Coincoin's girl gets back. Speaking of the post, I hear that things did not go too well at the trial." The change in Marie's voice was almost imperceptible, but Metoyer caught the note of worry that underlay her words.

"About what I assumed, Madame. Your brother-in-law could not afford to ignore the priest entirely. Quintanilla threatened to report him to the ministers in Madrid, and De Mézières still is being chastised by them for his efforts to open tobacco trade with Mexico. Another unfavorable report from Quintanilla to the Crown, and our post just might end up with a Spaniard for a commandant. No disrespect meant to your mother's people, of course."

"Of course," Marie retorted dryly. "Right now I've got no respect for Spanish bureaucrats either, and I'm losing it for my brother-in-law. You mean to tell me that Athanase compromised with the priest? He let you off, while they make a scapegoat of my woman?"

"That's one way of putting it, Madame."

"That's the only way of putting it! I thought he had more guts than that. Well, if that's the best he can do, I'll handle matters myself. Quintanilla wants more reports to Madrid? Fine, I'll send one. I owe him that for his blasted interference in my brother's estate. Because of him, Athanase and I had to fight Louis's will all the way to the Superior Council, when we could have settled things right here at the post. That bastard!"

Accustomed though he was by now to Marie's profanity, Pierre almost blanched. He had no love for the priest, but respect for the priesthood was the eleventh commandment of his childhood. Then he realized her bitterness had shifted from the priest entirely.

"Louis had no damned right to make a will leaving everything he had to that half-Indian doxy he married. Not after the way he treated Louise when Papa died!" She paused, lost in another battle that seemed, to her, to be part and parcel of this present affair; and Pierre recognized, intuitively, the wisdom of indulging her in her reminiscences.

"Of course, you don't know about that," she went on, "the Indian sister dear Louis barred from our house. 'No savage *métisse* will ever use the noble name of St. Denis,' he swore. Yet he gave that name himself to the half-breed Derbanne woman when he got to itching for her. How quickly he forgot…"

Marie's voice trailed off at last, cutting off the words she could not say: *How quickly he forgot his unfounded, baseless ravings against my swarthy lover….*

Instead, she snorted. "Anyway, that's not your problem, Metoyer. You have Quintanilla to deal with. *We* have Quintanilla to deal with. I do intend to write that letter! The man doesn't like scandal, does he? Well, he's going to have a hell of a time explaining to his superiors why he sent the brothers of St. Antoine to live, unchaperoned, under the same roof with Louis's widow."

Gloat was plain now, twitching at the corners of her mouth as a new thought struck her. So he threatens to sell my slave if we don't mind him? Well, maybe I will sell something, too: that oven I've been letting him use out of the goodness of my heart. He and the brothers will have a fine time then, trying to bake the wafers for Holy Eucharist. The ingrate forgets who supports the Order of St. Antoine on this frontier. If he thinks he is so *supreme,* just let him try surviving without my financial support!

"There is another way, Madame," Metoyer interjected. "There is another answer to his threat to have Coincoin sold off to New Orleans, for the benefit of the hospital…" Metoyer's voice went soft, cajoling, as he made his final point. "If you did not own her, Madame—if she were *my* slave legally—then I would have every right to keep her at my house.

"What? You scheming knave!" Marie screamed in reply. "So that's what you are after. *Malédiction,* man! I'll write my letter instead! You think I'd sell Coincoin? Consider yourself lucky that I've let you rent her all these years. Do you know the sacrifices I've made, while she's taken care of your needs instead of mine?"

"She did train her sister to take her place, and her daughters, too. Isn't that why you will not let me buy Thérèse or Marie Louise?"

"Those giddy girls are so useless I'm tempted to let you have them. No, Metoyer, if I get any worse, I'll need my Coincoin."

"If you get worse, Madame, you could always call for her. That would be understood."

"Promises!" Marie dismissed him impatiently. "I have no faith in the promises of men!"

"Shall we put it in writing, Madame?"

Marie sighed. "Look, Metoyer. You mean well. I'll concede that. And your solution isn't a bad one. But if I've told you once, I've told you a dozen times already: *never will I sell my Coincoin.*"

For the first time in Pierre's recollection, Marie's voice came close to being soft. "She's the playmate of my youth, Metoyer. She made me laugh when I had no one else. She knows when I hurt and why. Besides..." Her voice grew raspy again. "Besides, she's my godchild. No Christian woman should sell away her godchild."

"Even if it were for that godchild's good? If it were the best, the only recourse that she could take?"

"How do I know it's for her good? Just because you say so doesn't mean a damn to me."

"I know that, Madame." Metoyer hesitated. In ten years he had not put this into words for anyone else, but surely the time had come to do so now. He held no other card.

"Madame, has Coincoin told you of the bargain we made, before I asked you for her ten years ago?"

"Bargain? *Bon Dieu!* I thought she was in love! Every time she mentions you and her eyes start to smolder, I've reassured myself I did the right thing. I broke law and religion both for you two. And now you tell me there's nothing between you but a bargain?"

"There was a bargain, Madame. *Oui,*" he said softly. "It was an affair of convenience. At first. For all these years, Coincoin has kept her end of the bargain, and I intend to keep mine. I just did not plan for it to take so long."

"So what's the bargain, Metoyer?" Marie demanded.

"When I leave this post for France, I will leave Coincoin and her children free."

"You *what?* And how did you propose to do that, Metoyer, when you did not own any of them in the first place?"

"Ah, for that we are totally dependent upon you, Madame." Metoyer chose his words carefully. Candor ought to work now, he calculated. Candor, couched in terms that will flatter the image she wants the world to see. Candor followed by a challenge she cannot ignore.

"I underrated you, Madame. Ten years ago, I foolishly assumed you would sell her when I had enough to offer, but you have made it clear that Coincoin's tie to you cannot be bought. Now I'm desperate. Whatever price you set, I have to pay, but I think you will let me uphold our bargain—if you care as much as you say about the welfare of your godchild."

"Don't call my hand, Metoyer. The fact still remains that you had no right to promise freedom to *my* slave!"

"*Oui,* Madame, but when a young man sees a woman that he wants…," Pierre shrugged, acting the part of the knave she had accused him of being, playing deliberately upon the woman's memories of her own thwarted love.

"…he should do whatever it takes." Marie finished the sentence for him. "You win, Metoyer. You can have your *négresse* and your child she's carrying, if today's madness doesn't make her lose it. But it will cost you Metoyer. Fifteen hundred livres cash. As long as I'm making such a sacrifice, I might as well make it worth my while."

৶ 9 ৻
Twenty lashes later

Coincoin lay prone on the hard and unfamiliar pallet, unflinching, as Thérèse ripped off the remains of her robe and bathed the slices across her back and arms and buttocks.

The girl's touch is gentle, as gentle as Mama's was, Coincoin thought, and a surge of pride swept through her pain. Not the defiant kind of pride that had sustained her through this day, but soft, maternal, productive pride. I've trained this daughter well, she thought. Mama would be pleased.

"Mama…," Thérèse began, and even though Coincoin could not see her, she heard the tremor in her childish treble. Tears come so easily at that age, Coincoin remembered. The thirteen-year-old heart has not yet grown its shell.

"Mama…," Thérèse began anew, hesitating guiltily. "I was there! I saw, Mama! Oh, I know you told me not to come, so don't scold me. It's just that everyone was going, and I just had to go, too. I could not bear staying up here on the hill, not knowing what was happening to you."

"Madame needed you, Thérèse." Coincoin's admonishment was sharper than she had intended. "You should not have left her. You know she is having a bad spell, again."

"Well, she brought it upon herself," Thérèse shot back defensively, but her thin copper face brightened and she giggled. "If she had not screamed and ranted when padre marched you over here himself from M'sieur's house, then she would not have had another attack!"

"Madame just speaks her mind, child. Be glad of that. It means you will always know exactly where you stand with her."

"I know, Mama," Thérèse's voice went contrite. "The others were all leaving, except for old Nanette, who complained that she was too fat to waddle downhill, and I was moping. Well, just a little bit. Partly because you asked me not to go to the post, but mostly because I was worried about you. Madame could tell, I know, because she called me over to her bed and asked what was wrong. I insisted nothing was. I really did, Mama, but she sees through everything, and she told me I was better off not going. When I told her that *not going* wasn't bothering me nearly as much as not *knowing,* and that I would just die if I had to wait 'til the others came back before I knew what they had done to you, she just patted me on the hand and said, 'If you have to go, child, then go.'"

Coincoin could not bring herself to scold her daughter further. Still, she hated that Thérèse had seen and *heard* the things that had been said and done that day.

"Your sisters? Did they go, too?" Coincoin asked hoarsely.

"Marie Louise didn't. Her leg was bothering her again from that bullet. Besides, I don't think she'll ever go to the post again on a court day. Not after that drunk old Delago shot her last time for trying to run from him."

"And the little ones?" Coincoin was almost afraid to ask. Her older children, Chatta's children, might be grown enough to face the realities of slavery, and maybe she had been wrong to want to protect them from it, but the little ones were so innocent. How could she explain to them what had happened today, and why?

"No, Mama. They weren't there. I went by M'sieur's house while I was at the post, and they were all there shelling pecans. I don't think they even knew about it, Mama. Well, maybe Augustin did. He was a little strange over something. But then Gustin's always a little strange. He thinks he's special because he's half-white."

"Thérèse!"

"Well, it's true! It's true that he's half-white. That's what all this was about today, after all. And it's true he thinks he and all those yellow children are better than me and Marie Louise and Jean. Even Jean complains about him, and he's always been closer to you and those *other* children because he's always lived with you and *them*."

Her daughter's words cut into Coincoin deeper than any blow the whip had made. Painfully, she raised herself to look her daughter in the face, clutching the remains of her ragged robe in front of her. Thérèse, more than any of the five children she had borne Chatta, bore his mark—not just in the color of her skin but in her hawklike nose and her narrow eyes. But Thérèse showed little of the spirit that had driven Chatta back to his people. Or her into M'sieur's arms. Where had she failed with this child?

"Thérèse, we're all *family*. That includes *all* your brothers and sisters, not just the ones right here. All we have, as long as we are slaves, is *family!* and we have to hold that family close in our heart, no matter where we live."

"It's a trifle hard to hold you close, Mama, when you live in one house and we live in another!" Thérèse charged petulantly. Then she laughed, before Coincoin could respond, but it was a snigger more akin to revenge than joy.

"Looks like we're gonna be closer now, Mama, thanks to padre for making you move back here. Now it's Gustin's turn, him and the others, to do without a mother. Since M'sieur bought them last year, he's stuck with them, whether you're sleeping with him or not!"

Tears stung Coincoin for the first time that whole, long day. How could she make this child *understand* why she had chosen the course she had? How could she show her the *fire* that would forever fuel her actions? Thérèse knew nothing about love between a man and a woman. Or real rejection. Or the opportunities in the world beyond slavery for those who sought them hard enough. Coincoin struggled for the right words, but they just would not come.

"You still have not forgiven me for moving down to the post, have you?" That was all she could think of to say.

"Can you forgive *yourself,* Mama?" Thérèse shot back. "If you had been here with us, Madame would not have sold Chiquito!"

Ay-y-y-y. The child's words cut deeper with each new lash. *Chiquito. Nicolas Chiquito.* Her and Chatta's firstborn son.

"Thérèse, baby…"

"I'm no baby. Don't treat me like one!"

Coincoin flinched but held her tongue as she breathed deeply, trying to remind herself of her own adolescent struggles against the station life had assigned them.

"Thérèse," she began again, forcing her voice out slow and steady. "There was *nothing* I could have done to save Chiquito. After M'sieur went to jail and left Madame with so many debts, her creditors sued. Señor Barbo got a court order that let him take a slave equal to what Madame owed him. That just happened to be Chiquito."

"Just *happened?* They were supposed to take Dgimby's son! If you had been here…"

Coincoin snapped then, turning on her daughter with a harshness that nothing in their thirteen years had ever triggered—because nothing she had been through today compared to the pain her own daughter had inflicted now.

"Don't you chastise me, girl! It's high time you *listened!* Even if I had been here, Gil y Barbo could *still* have taken the wrong boy, and I could not have stopped him. Madame *did* try to get Chiquito back, but Barbo had already crossed the border into Tejas and the Spaniards there are still punishing Madame for whatever M'sieur did. You have no right to blame Madame—or me!"

Thérèse said nothing, ignoring all her mother's wounds now as she curled up inside herself, with long arms wrapped around drawn-up legs clutched tightly to her chest. Still Coincoin could see her nibbling at one lip. She was thinking. At least, the child was thinking.

"Thérèse, don't you see? What happened to Chiquito is exactly why I had to go with M'sieur when my *chance* came. Only if I'm *free*—only if I have the money to buy all of you free—only then can we be sure nothing like that happens again!"

She reached for her daughter's hand. Thérèse shrugged her off, but then the child unfolded herself from the shell in which she had taken refuge, pulled the wash rag out of the pan into which she had tossed it, and turned back to Coincoin. "Lie down, Mama. I've got to finish washing these wounds and dress them."

"What about your own wounds, *chien-chien?* Will they heal?"

"I don't know, Mama."

This time, when Coincoin reached for her daughter's hand, the child did not reject her. And so Coincoin pulled her down beside her on the pallet and drew Thérèse into her blood-streaked arms.

"Thérèse, I know it hurt you that I left you here ten years ago and went down to the post with M'sieur. I cannot undo that, but one day you will understand. One day, you will be grown yourself, and the time will come that *you* will have to leave *me.* You will *want* to leave me, because that is the way it should be."

"*Want* to? When does a slave get to do what she wants, Mama? You were lucky, so you forget. The rest of us have no choice about anything."

"Everyone has choices, child. We may be slaves, but we have minds and we have chances. We just cannot let our minds be blinded so that we cannot see—and *seize*—those opportunities, when they happen!"

Thérèse stared out into the darkness as Coincoin plunged on, driving home her lesson.

"Even the laws of the white man have laid down paths for slaves to walk right out of slavery. I don't mean *run,* not like your father did, so you will be a hunted animal. There are ways to leave slavery openly, to live in the white man's world, *freely,* even *richly!* I know, child. I've heard M'sieur and his friends talk of black men—and women too—in New Orleans and other places who not only are free, but *rich.* They own land and houses and businesses, even *slaves."*

"Slaves? Black men own slaves? White ones or black ones?"

"Don't be silly, child! White people are not slaves. At least not any longer. I did hear M'sieur say once that they used to be, many years ago in France. He says, too, that in the English colonies to the east of us, there are white servants who are *indentured,* which is another kind of slavery. Only it does not last for life, unless they marry black slaves. But all that is beside the point, Thérèse. Why can't black men own slaves? Or red men?"

Thérèse said nothing, so Coincoin ploughed on. "Among your father's people, there was slavery. In fact, they do make slaves of white people sometimes, especially the Spanish, whom they hate. Even in Africa, child, it is no different. My own papa told me on his deathbed that his father had slaves back there. And my mama's papa, too. In fact, he once had a white slave who had been brought into his village by a band of pirates."

"It's still not right, Mama! It's not right for black people to own other black people! Or for white men to own white ones."

"Thérèse, it is not the color of skin that makes slavery. It's *money*. As long as slaves make money for men, there always will be some kind of slavery—but it could not exist if there were not people willing to let themselves be owned. In this world, child, slaves do mean *money*. A lot of it. And money means respect. Those free *nègres* in New Orleans have learned that, and I can't blame them for living the way life is."

"That's why you left me, Mama?" Thérèse asked softly. "You think M'sieur will be your path to freedom and money and respect? Well, it hasn't worked! It hasn't brought you any of that."

"It will, child. From the time I was a little older than you, I knew what my destiny was. It has not happened yet, not all of it, but it will."

"Will it be worth it, Mama? Is it worth leaving your children?"

"It is *for you* that I want it, Thérèse! Do not act as though I am cruel and heartless, or that I chose M'sieur over you. Mother birds have to push their children from the nests. That is how they learn to fly."

"But we could barely walk, Mama. We needed your warmth and your love!"

"You've always had my love, child; and I've never been so far away that you could not come to me, nor I to you. We've had a lot of time together, while I trained you for Madame."

Coincoin cupped her hand under her daughter's chin and tilted her head upward so that Thérèse's eyes had to look straight into hers. Even by the flickering candlelight, she could see the uncertainty there, and it was Thérèse who finally turned her eyes away.

"You needed warmth, child?" Coincoin went on with deliberate harshness, telling herself that the child needed exposure to far more of the rawness of life than she had seen.

"We have to find our warmth within ourselves, girl! We cannot expect others to provide that. This is a cold, hard world! In France, M'sieur says, poor children are torn from their parents' arms when they can barely walk. They are loaded onto wagons and taken to big cities where they are kept in huts with no heat, and they have no mama close by to run to. All they have is a cruel master who makes them work in big factories, the kind of harsh, bone-weary work that neither you nor I have ever known."

Coincoin could see doubt still plain on the face of the grown child she was softly cradling. Desperately, she plunged on, trying to make her *see* and *understand* before her nature was too firmly bent in the wrong direction.

"You have no right to feel sorry for yourself, Thérèse. You are better off than any of those children, and you can be just as well off or as bad off as you set your mind to being. The choice is yours…."

A fresh pain seared across Coincoin's back, sucking her breath all the way down to her gut. By the time the spasm had past, her fury had wasted itself on the purely physical effort of *not giving in* to what had been done to her. Mustering her last reserves, she reached out one more time to the child she feared she had lost.

"Whatever you choose, I love you, Thérèse. You know that, don't you?" Coincoin said softly. And then it struck her that for the first time since Chatta left her she was actually pleading for someone's love and reassurance.

"Of course, I know that, Mama," her daughter replied contritely. "I do hurt when I think about your other children. I can't help but think you must love them more—and *him*—because you chose them instead of me and Marie Louise."

Thérèse's voice grew quiet, pensive. "*Do* you love *him*, Mama?

Coincoin's answer came quickly, perhaps too quickly. "M'sieur? He's a Frenchman. I have no right to love him. Surely that was made clear enough to everybody today."

"Mama, I didn't ask about what the *white man says* is right. I asked how *you feel.*"

The gate to the wall around Coincoin's heart slammed shut again. "Some things, Thérèse, even a child has no right to ask her mother. Here!" she added gruffly, thrusting the pungent rag into the girl's hand. "Finish with my back before I bleed to death. I cannot afford to die yet, child. My destiny is not fulfilled."

"Destiny, Coincoin?" It was Metoyer's voice that inquired softly from the doorway. "After today, you still believe in this destiny of yours?"

Coincoin did not even turn from her place on the pallet.

"After today, M'sieur, I'm more determined than ever."

"*Bien!* Faith deserves reward, Coincoin. Here," he tossed her a blanket. "As soon as Thérèse finishes with you, wrap yourself up—loosely, so it won't chafe your sores. Decency requires you to have some sort of covering when I take you home."

"Home, M'sieur?"

"Home, Coincoin. The good padre will undoubtedly rend his cassock when he hears the news, but he can no longer keep you out of our home. As of today, little woman, you belong to me."

⟋ 10 ⟍

In the year that followed

Quintanilla did not rend his cassock in frustration. He did not even hear the news, at least not for a while. Heady with success, the priest had packed his bags as soon as he heard the guilty verdict. While Coincoin rode the wooden horse, in defiance instead of the shame he had decreed, Quintanilla rode his mule westward to the Tejas nations. Convinced that he had set an example the post would long remember, he left it with a clear conscience for the journey he had long anticipated, taking the word of God to the "savage brothers" missionaries had not yet reached.

Eight uneventful months passed at the post he left behind. His parishioners reveled in the freedom his absence afforded but missed the controversy he had kept aboil. In January, Coincoin bore the child she had been carrying and named him Joseph, after the good man who had wed the blessed Virgin so she would not bear the Holy Child outside the sacred bonds of matrimony.

By February, she was her lissome self again; but Metoyer had found the pounds she lost.

"Watch it, Pierre!" Étienne teased. "You're going to be fat and complacent before you know it. When you get back to La Rochelle, the pretty young barmaids will tweak your nose and sit in your lap and call you *Gros Papa*. Are you sure you can handle the shock of leaving there a gay young blade and going back a pudgy old man?"

"At least I haven't given up hope of going back!" Pierre retorted. "You're selling us out, Étienne. It was not in our plans for you to marry a planter's daughter and settle here in the colonies; but if you aren't careful, that's exactly what you are about to do."

"The heart is fickle, *mon ami*," Pavie rejoined, with a quizzical look at his boyhood friend. "Are you sure you have not discovered that yourself?"

"Me? *Mon Dieu!* I'm still saving myself and my money for a poor nobleman's daughter back home. With my gold and her title, our children will have the best of everything. *Non,* Étienne, if I'm getting fat and complacent, it's because I can afford to be fat and I'm content with the future I've mapped out for myself."

"Whatever you say, old friend. Just be sure you don't lose that map or you might end up here forever."

Neither raised the point again. Two days later, Pavie broke the news that he was moving. The house he and Metoyer had shared was too small for all of them. Since he was contemplating marriage himself, Étienne pointed out, he needed more space.

Pierre protested, but just half-heartedly. Étienne was right. They both needed space. His own seven children, plus that half-Indian boy Jean, were far too many for the one room the young ones had been sharing—especially since they were as old as the twins now were. At ten, Susanne already had breasts. It was high time that she quit sleeping with her brothers.

Then, in June, Quintanilla returned, and the peace that had settled upon the household was shattered.

Dawn came gently on that twenty-ninth of June 1778, amid a balmy summer breeze. The mother robin that nested in the sweet gum tree outside Metoyer's window had satisfied her taste for worms and began to chirp contentedly on his sill. Still half-dozing, Pierre stretched his long, naked frame across the bed, the big four-poster François had carved for Fanny, and felt for Coincoin even though he did not expect to find her. She was always up by this time. As he nestled in the scent of gardenia she had left on the sheets behind her, the smell of frying ham tempted him to rise.

To hell with the shop! Pierre decided as he pulled on his breeches, a light cotton shirt, and the soft moccasins young Julien Rachal had brought back from the Caneci with his last load of deer hides. It's too fine a day to stay inside. Trade's been slow all week. Étienne and Jeannot can handle whatever comes in today. It's high time I kept my promise to Augustin and Louis and took the boys fishing down at the Point.

The back door slammed and across the yard there wafted the sound of his older son humming gently, the same song Augustin always hummed when he fed or groomed the horses. If it had a name or words, Pierre had never heard them, but it sure could charm that big stallion. Impulsively, he leaned out the window.

"Hey, Gustin!"

"*Oui,* M'sieur?"

"Come here, boy."

"*Oui,* M'sieur," Augustin repeated dutifully, as he set down the bucket of grain and tripped lightly through the gate into the little courtyard tucked outside Pierre's window.

He may have my brains, Pierre thought to himself as he watched the child approach, but he certainly doesn't look like me. If it were not for his coloring, no one would know from his broad nose and wooly hair that he had any French blood at all. A deuced shame! He has a quick head for figures and a knack for cutting straight to the core of every problem. If he had Susanne's or little Pierre's delicate Latin features and light complexion, I'd send him to Paris for a first-class education. That boy could make something of himself over there, if he didn't look so damned *African.*

"M'sieur?" Augustin prompted politely from beneath the window.

"Oh, yes, boy. Listen, when the horses get their fill, go dig some worms. Today we're going fishing."

"Fishing? *Oui,* M'sieur!" Excitement lit his deep brown face, and he took off for the stables to finish the feeding.

"Hey, Gustin!" Metoyer called again to the rapidly disappearing figure. "You'd better go over to the shop, too, and tell M'sieur Pavie that I won't be coming in."

Breakfast was waiting on the table when Pierre entered the salon. A generous platter of ham, fresh from the smokehouse, kept company with a plate of eggs swimming in the ham's own drippings, a pan of steaming cornbread, and bowls of strawberries surrounding a pitcher of cool cream.

Damn, but old Jeannot was right, he thought as he surveyed the feast. Here in this colony, every man *is* a lord! Why, slaves eat better than many of the craftsmen in La Rochelle. Sure, our housing's crude, but at least every man has his own and it sits on his own land, too. So what if our clothing is years out of style, it's a far sight more comfortable. Culture! That's all we need. Good schools for our children and some roads so we can bring up singers and acting troupes and painters from New Orleans. It will happen. If the fops in Paris don't lose their taste for furs, this colony ought to be doing pretty well in a few more years. Who knows? Even the fellows trying to clear and plant that land downriver might make a go at that, too.

"*Café,* M'sieur?"

"Of course, Susanne. Provided that you steeped it yourself. Nobody steeps coffee like you do, little one."

The girl beamed, doe eyes sparkling and a winsome smile flashing across a perfect row of pearls. How could two twins look so different? Pierre muttered to himself. Life's a ballbuster. Most folks would say it's better that the girl turned out comely instead of the boy, if there had to be a choice between the two of them. But the kind of life pretty young mulattresses live in this colony is not what I want for my daughter.

Morbleu! I've made a mess of things, Pierre swore, staring into his cup. Life looked so simple ten years ago. A nice little business arrangement with a comely slave. She'd warm my bed, and I'd free her and the children when I left. How in the hell could I have failed to consider that her children would be *mine,* too?

Furiously, Pierre jerked his flask off the sideboard and sloshed a generous measure into his half-empty cup.

Free is just not enough for one's own flesh and blood, he told himself again, as he had done daily ever since Coincoin informed him, offhandedly, two months before that Susanne had gotten her first period. Just as early as she, herself, had. *Curse it!* Two or three years from now, this girl will be attracting every buck at the post—of every color. And she'll choose one of them whether I like it or not. Then my own daughter will spend the rest of her life married to some black slave. Or warming the beds of one Frenchman after another who thinks she is good enough to sleep with but not to marry. That's a rotten life and there's not one blasted thing I can do about it. Intermarriage has been outlawed in France now, too. So I can't even send her back to La Rochelle and find an ambitious would-be merchant, willing to take a tawny wife in exchange for a financial stake.

Pierre's plate was empty before he realized that he was eating. Across the table, Coincoin was giving him a quizzical look, and even little Dominique's perpetual chatter had hushed.

"Sorry," Pierre mumbled. "I was thinking."

"We assumed that," Coincoin replied. "That's all right. None of us had anything important to say anyway. I was just wondering, though, where Augustin is. He should have fed the horses by now, and it is not like him to be late."

"Oh, I sent him to Pavie with a message. He's back now. I just heard the gate latch fall."

"What's the matter, child?" Pierre quizzed as Augustin entered slowly, his bushy brows almost crossing above eyes that always burned like coals. "You seemed happy enough when you left here. Now you look like it's the end of the world."

"I think it's the end of our fishing trip, M'sieur."

"Why? Did M'sieur Pavie tell you that I can't have the day off? The business is two-thirds mine, you know. I can out vote him any time."

"No, M'sieur Pavie didn't have much to say," the child replied soberly. "He just swore a couple of times and said he would not mind going fishing today himself. But on the way back, I passed the commandant, and he says he needs to see you, M'sieur. Now. He called it *urgent*. But he didn't never say what was *urgent* about it."

"He *didn't say*, Augustin. Not *didn't never*. In Spanish it is correct for you to use double negatives, but in French you cannot."

"Yes, M'sieur," the boy replied dutifully. "But does this mean we can't go fishing?"

"I don't know, child. We'll have to see. Get your bucket of worms ready. If I'm not back by mid-morning, you and Louis go on down to the river bank and see if you can scare up a few bream. I know you'd rather go after the catfish down at the Point, but we can do that another day."

Augustin's fears proved true. As soon as Pierre let himself into the commandant's office and saw Quintanilla pacing in the corner, he knew that the wrath of God personified was about to descend on him again.

"Shut the door, Metoyer," De Mézières greeted him perfunctorily. "Unless you want to give the post something more to gossip about."

"I suspect the padre's about to do that anyway," Metoyer retorted.

"Cankerous sores must be cauterized, Metoyer," Quintanilla intoned.

"Gentlemen! Gentlemen! Such exchanges will only make it more difficult for us to resolve this little problem."

"Little!" Quintanilla purpled. Pierre could have sworn that the hairs of the man's tonsured bob rose a good half-inch.

"This man's behavior is an abomination before our Lord! For sins like his, Sodom and Gomorrah were destroyed!"

"My good father," De Mézières cut short his sermon. "Your piety is commendable, but sin is your fight, not mine, and your battles are best fought in the House of the Lord. This is a government office, and my job is to keep the peace and the King's Law. Let's restrict our examination this morning to those aspects under the authority of the Crown, not the church."

The wiry priest, browned from his months on the plains of Tejas, raised himself to his full height and appeared oblivious to the fact that his stature still fell short of the pile of work on the commandant's desk.

"Señor de Mézières, I should not have to remind you that Carlos III styles himself Our *Catholic* Majesty, and that title clearly shows where the concern of our government lies. Our king wrestles with the spiritual welfare of his people as much as their temporal needs."

"Nevertheless," the commandant parried, "the fires of hell have not yet become a prescribed sentence for those who break His Majesty's laws. So we'll confine ourselves to the terms of that law. You said you have a complaint to lodge, Quintanilla. Make it and let's get this issue settled. I have far more important concerns than who's sleeping in whose bed."

"Señor! I am shocked that you take your responsibilities so lightly! This man has violated your own order of last October. You decreed then that the Negress Coincoin, whom you, yourself, judged to be a public concubine, must absent herself from the house of this man with whom she was living in open, scandalous, and unholy union!" Quintanilla paused, raking Metoyer with his gloat.

"I don't deny that," De Mézières prompted. "So?"

"I, myself, accompanied the woman from his house to be certain that the decree was carried out. I was assured by you, Señor, that she would never be permitted to enter his house and create further scandal; and it was clearly understood that you would compel your sister-in-law to fulfill her obligation as a Christian woman and supervise the behavior of her slave. Am I not correct?"

"More or less, Padre."

"Yesterday, I returned from my mission to the Tejas nations, a highly gratifying mission among a people most responsive to the word of God. Quite unlike many of the inhabitants of this post, I might add!" Again, Quintanilla shot his condemnation across the room to the doorway in which Pierre still stood.

"It's good to hear of your success, Father," De Mézières countered. "But do stick with the problem at hand, please."

"So what do I find on my return? This man and his *negra* have defied both your decree and the will of God! What's more, they have done so openly, and you have condoned their crime and their sin! I am shocked, Señor Commandant! Shocked."

The shock was palpable—and not just on the face of the priest, Pierre thought. The bulbous nose of the old commandant was now a deeper purple than the tattoos bulging from under the open front of his shirt. Only the priest seemed not to notice.

"In spite of our past differences, Señor Commandant, I still believed you to be a gentleman of honor and a conscientious servant of His Majesty's law. I was wrong. Your duplicity proves you unworthy of the office our Crown has entrusted to you as the civil and military commander of this…"

"Padre de Quintanilla!" De Mézières's voice was frigid. "You are far beyond the bounds of your rank or station. No one, I repeat, *no one* encroaches upon my administration of this post. I have ten thousand square miles to defend against a hundred Indian nations—many of whom have been far more hostile since you Spanish took over here. I have to keep this post solvent, and its inhabitants from starving. I have to make sure that the scum who come out here to escape the law do not kill the decent citizens—or each other, too often. I have no time, inclination, or obligation to spy into the privacy of bedchambers to be sure *your* commandments are enforced!"

Quintanilla remained unfazed.

"Not my commandments, Señor de Mézières. *God's law.* But that is not the sole issue here," he added, pausing, while his thin smile hinted ominously of more to come. "When you issued your decree in October, *you* made a law, señor. Therefore you are bound to enforce it. When the ministers in Madrid receive my report, you will have considerable difficulty explaining why you cannot implement what you order. Your only hope for retaining authority is prompt and decisive action, now that I have plainly brought to your attention this obvious violation of *your own* decree."

"Quintanilla," De Mézières rejoined wearily, "it may interest you to know that in your absence a resident of this post dispatched a complaint not only to your bishop in Havana but also to civil authorities in New Orleans and Madrid.

You, father, have been charged with mismanagement of parish funds, unfair taxation, encroachment into civil affairs that are not within your authority, and conduct that gives rise to scandal."

Not a muscle flinched inside the starched black cassock.

"Señor de Mézières, our Savior himself was accused falsely, but that did not destroy His ministry. God's word is supreme. As God's messenger to this post, *I am supreme*. I do not hide when the Devil's workers cast stones at me, because I have the Lord's assurance I shall prevail."

"We shall see, padre. And you, Metoyer? What do you have to say to all this?"

"Very little, de Mézières, but enough. Your decree stated that Coincoin was to return to the house of her rightful owner. She has done that, sir. However, the padre's complaint has reminded me that I forgot to file in your office a copy of a transaction I executed with Mme. de Soto some time ago. If you will call in your notary and have an official copy made, then it will become a matter of public record that the woman Coincoin is now my property and is legally obliged to reside wherever I say."

Metoyer nodded curtly toward the priest. "Have you any other complaint, father?"

A smile again played around the tight pinch that marked Quintanilla's mouth. "Yes, my son, I do. I recall your quoting to me from the Code Noir, which the French governor Bienville drafted in the early days of this colony. Since then I have taken the trouble to study the Code in detail."

Quintanilla paused for effect, as both Metoyer and the commandant eyed him warily.

"You are quite correct, Metoyer. It is still in force in Louisiana. Our own governor has incorporated it into our Spanish colonial law. So now I must quote to you one of its provisions: 'If any master take his slave for his concubine, then he will be assessed a fine. If there should be children born of their illicit connection, then those children and their mother will be confiscated and sold for the benefit of the hospital.' Article 10, if I recall correctly."

Pierre slowly lowered himself into the chair he had disdained until now. Damn! he swore under his breath. How could I have forgotten that?

"I am told, Metoyer," the priest continued unctuously, "that your *negra* bore yet another mulatto child during my absence, and I do not think there is anyone at this post so naive as to not know the identity of that child's father."

"You'd have a hard time proving that, Padre."

"I don't think so, son." The edge faded from Quintanilla's voice as the desperation on Metoyer's face told him he had won.

"Metoyer, I would hate to see the woman and her infant sold, because no child should be sold away from its father and no woman should be sold away from her children. Are you interested in a compromise, my son?"

"A compromise? You would compromise your principles, Father?" Pierre parried scornfully, still stalling, floundering for a way out.

"Not my principles, my son. One way or another, the woman has to leave your house. Permanently. We would only compromise on the mode by which that end is achieved."

"State your mind, padre," Pierre muttered.

"I'll give you three days, my son. Go back to Señora de Soto and see if she is willing to buy back her slave. I will not insist that she buy the children. They are yours, too, and you have a Christian obligation to rear them; but the woman must go. If Señora does not want her, then during those three days you must find another buyer at this post so the woman will not be moved far from her children. If you make this sale, you must also make a sworn oath, to file in this office, that you will never visit her or allow her in your house or otherwise have connection of any kind with her." His voice hung in the air, a whip still poised to strike.

"If you do not sell her, then I will ship her to New Orleans to be auctioned in accordance to the law, and the proceeds will go toward the support of the colony's hospital."

"Your compromise is as galling as your threats, priest!"

"I know, son. It is always painful for the sinner to cut the tie that binds him to his lusts. But it is a necessary pain. As Our Lord has told us, "If your right eye offend you, pluck it out.""

"I know the scripture, Quintanilla."

"Then think on it, my son. On Thursday, I will check back with this office to see what you have done. Good day, Pierre. God be with you."

Stiffly, the young priest then turned to De Mézières. "Señor Commandant, I will not post my report to Madrid until we see how this affair ends. Perhaps such drastic action on my part will not be necessary. Upon reflection, it seems to me that too many controversial reports from here might undermine the work all of us are trying to do. *Buenas días,* Señor."

"Well, Metoyer," De Mézières observed dryly as the priest gently closed the door behind himself. "At least, he gave you a choice."

"A hell of a choice!"

"Not the best ones in the world, admittedly. On the other hand, if you don't like them, there is another option he did not mention.

"No? What would you suggest, *mon ami?*"

"Manumission, Metoyer. Manumission. Quintanilla can't sell the woman if she's free."

ↄ 11 ↄ

The sun had not yet set behind the river when Pierre unlatched the gate, wound his way through the flock of chickens pecking at their evening corn, and whistled up the path to the gallery. He had scarcely opened the door before little Louis descended upon him, a hooked perch still wriggling in his hand, his pecan-colored face awash with eight-year-old eagerness to spill the details of how it had been caught. Pierre listened until Louis's excitement ran its course, then heaved the boy to his shoulders and went in search of Louis's mother.

"Coincoin? Where are you, woman? You think you don't have to greet me at the door any more with a mug of cool lemonade and a freshly filled pipe? You're getting damned independent, woman! Next thing I know, you'll be acting like you're free or something."

"I'm sorry, M'sieur." Coincoin came quickly, flushed and breathless. "Forgive me, M'sieur. I had ironing to do, so I made a fire in the backyard and set up my board under the big oak. I did not want the house hot when you came home, but I did not realize how late it was."

"Well, you can put away your iron and find your party dress, woman. We're celebrating tonight!" Pierre dumped the surprised Louis on the chaise, grabbed the boy's gaping mother, and swung into an impromptu waltz.

"Come, my African Queen, let's dance our way back into the grove!"

"M'sieur!" Flustered, she moved his hands from where they did not need to be, at least not while children's eyes were glued to the both of them. "M'sieur! You've had too much to drink!"

"Only a cup, Coincoin. Well, two. One to toast the good news I'm about to give you and one to forget the bad that's bound to follow."

"News? What news, M'sieur?"

"The best of news, the worst of news!" Pierre pulled from his shirt a crisp piece of paper, and bent down to the child who was watching him quizzically from behind the cistern. "Here, T'Pierre. Practice your reading. Let's see how much you've learned these past few months."

His namesake took the paper hesitantly. "M'sieur, there are too many words."

"Try, T'Pierre. You have to try, if you want to learn new things."

Six-year-old brows knitted across soft gray eyes. "An act... an act of... M'sieur, this next word's too big."

"Sound it out, T'Pierre. Break the big word into little pieces and sound each one all by itself."

"An act of... man... u... miss... man-u-mis..."

The child got no further. Long fingers that had lost none of their elegance to the heat of irons or the chafing of rub boards flew to Coincoin's mouth to stifle a scream of joy, a cry of pain. Her knees buckled, and she collapsed into Metoyer's arms.

"Scat, boy! Bring me the spirits of ammonia. Your mama's fainted!"

Gently, Metoyer lowered Coincoin to the ground under the cool spread of the grove that canopied their back garden, but the spirits weren't needed.

Before T'Pierre could scurry into the house and back, Coincoin's eyelids were fluttering in confusion, then embarrassment, as she sat up and straightened the skirts that had gone awry.

"I'm sorry, M'sieur! I don't know what overcame me."

"Joy, I hope," Pierre laughed.

"Joy? Of course, M'sieur. Joy."

"Obviously, you understand what this piece of paper is about, woman. But perhaps I'd better read it anyway."

Pierre read it, rapidly, anxious to finish what had to be done. The document was not long. It said little more than Coincoin had expected, but it said enough to end completely the life he had made for himself in the colony. Coincoin was free, immediately and irrevocably. When her children reached the age of twenty-one, or when they wed, whichever came first, they would be manumitted also.

"*Merci,* M'sieur."

The words almost choked in Coincoin's throat. Twenty years ago last April, she had made a solemn vow over the dead body of her father, and for twenty years she had lived with the expectation of this day. Her destiny had been fulfilled, at least this much of it, but the happiness she had thought it would bring just was not there.

Slowly she raised her eyes to meet Pierre's. As his gray-green pools locked her own eyes she knew, at last, where she had known those eyes before. They had been the eyes of that tall, olive-skinned man of her childhood, with the rugged face and the great mass of hair, so like M'sieur's, with the strong, broad shoulders just like M'sieur's, who had taken her own tiny hand in his powerful grip and had led her to find the golden egg. The man who had looked into her heart with those caring eyes and seen her longing had died soon after, without fulfilling the promise he had made to her papa. But he had been born again in that same year, half a world away, and he had come back. She was now free—*but would freedom be enough?*

Carefully now, so that her voice would not give her away, Coincoin enunciated the words she had to ask. "When do you leave, M'sieur?"

"Leave?"

"For your home. For France. You promised to free me before you left the colony, and now you have kept that promise. When do you leave?"

Does she really care? Metoyer wondered. Her voice is so calm, so perfectly modulated. It never reveals anything of what is going on inside that queenly brow of hers. Should I take the risk of telling her everything frankly, or play it cautious until she has had the time to make her own plans?

Pierre shrugged. "I promised you I would free you *before* I left, woman. I did not say how long before."

"Then you do not plan to go just yet?"

"Not just yet. There are still a few more things I want to do here, a few more things I'd like to try before I get too old."

"Oh?" Coincoin hastily dropped her eyes, afraid to say more, afraid for him to read her thoughts, at least until she knew what plans he had for her.

"What about you, Coincoin?" Pierre asked, with seeming indifference. "Now that our business arrangement is concluded, what plans do you have for yourself?"

"I don't know, M'sieur."

In that, she was not dissembling. She truly did not know. "I have never really thought beyond this point. Not seriously. Times and circumstances change. How could I make definite plans, not knowing when or how this day might come?"

"Of course." His reply was almost wooden. "I should add something more, Coincoin. This paper does not say so, but I will not set you free without a home or money. Would you like to go to New Orleans? There's opportunity there. I could buy you a small house on Rampart Street, where there are other women like yourself. You can take the children, and I'll give you a small annual stipend. With your talents, you would be the best nurse in all *la ville*.

Coincoin's throat burned. So it was, after all, nothing more than a business arrangement for him. Even after all these years. *He is not yet ready to leave this post, so he will send the children and me away, instead.*

"Whatever you think best, M'sieur."

"Whatever *I* think best? *Sacrebleu,* woman! You are now *free!* The choice is yours! No one has to make these decisions for you any more. If you want to go to New Orleans, all you have to do is walk into the commandant's office, ask for a permit like any of the rest of us, and take off. If you'd rather go west across the Sabine to look for your Chatta, you can do that, too. I'll even keep the children until you come back for them, or send for them."

"No, M'sieur," Coincoin whispered, resignation creeping into her voice. "Too many years have passed. Chatta may be dead. If not, he probably has another wife, and I could not share a man with anyone. I would rather..." She hesitated, afraid to say it, but then she could not hold back the question any longer.

"M'sieur, can I stay here? Do I have to leave this post? This is where I was born," she blurted. "My parents, my sisters, are buried on that hill behind the stockade. My..."

She couldn't say the rest. Steeling herself, she repeated with all the calm she could muster, "All my life is here, M'sieur. Do I have to leave?"

In spite of himself, Pierre laughed at her. "Woman, how many times do I have to tell you? Don't ask me what you *have* to do! What *I* want you to do no longer matters!"

"I'm sorry, M'sieur. It is habit. How can I suddenly change everything I have always done and said?"

Pierre scolded himself for laughing. That was cruel. Guiltily, he took her chin into his hand and tilted it toward him, probing deep into her eyes. A tear trickled slowly from the corner of one of them, the first tear he ever had seen her shed.

"You can't, Coincoin. I'm being unrealistic. It's just deuced hard for a man who has never been anything but free to understand what freedom must feel like for someone who's never known it! Maybe you would feel better if you stayed close for a while, here in this house if you want to, until you get accustomed to the idea of making your own choices."

Coincoin's breath scalded her as she struggled to dam the flood of words, tears, and fears. "Is that possible, M'sieur? I could stay? *Here?* I know our agreement is over and I'll ask nothing of you, but I have to work for someone, M'sieur. I'd rather work for you than for anyone else. I'll…"

Pierre's finger across her lips shushed her. His arms wrapped around her and his cheek tenderly nudged her head onto his shoulder. Never before had he held her like this. As an equal. Never in public, in fact, had he touched her in any way.

A dozen years of pretense! he cursed silently. Well, to hell with what people think! She's free now! They can't sell her away to New Orleans. They can't make her move out unless she wants to. They can't fine me until I lose everything I've worked for. She's *free!* Now I can say to hell with gossip! Color be damned!

"Woman, you can stay here on any basis you choose."

Coincoin pulled herself from his arms and stared him in the face. Openly, boldly, in a way she had never permitted herself to do since that night he had frankly propositioned her and she had just as frankly accepted. Since that night, she had been his lover. But she had still been his *servant,* and he had been the *master,* and no intimacy could have bridged that chasm.

"Pierre?" In spite of her inner bravado, the name still came out softly, timidly.

"Oui, ma chère?" Again, Pierre cupped her chin in the curve of his big palm and stared into her eyes. The tear was gone. It was radiance that glistened now in the moonlight that had fallen upon them.

"Pierre? If I have a choice, I would rather that *nothing* be different between us."

"Then we both have had our wishes fulfilled today, *chien-chien.* But there will be a difference. One for the better. Look here!"

One after another, he drew from the breast of his blouse a riff of papers.

"That little act of manumission is not the only document I've had drawn this day, Coincoin! You know that piece of land downriver that surrounds the Point where the boys love to fish? I checked with De Mézières, and no one has claimed it yet. It still belongs to the Crown, and it's mine for the asking. Eight hundred *arpents,* stretching across both sides of the river! I filed a claim."

"Land, M'sieur? What will you do with land? You'd only have to sell it when you go back to France."

"France be hanged, woman! *This* is where life is! Everything in life a man could want. Freedom. Room to breathe. Opportunity for riches. Barthelemy Rachal tells me he made five thousand livres last year from the tobacco he planted on that tract of his below the Point, and he's just getting started. Woman, that's more than the commandant himself makes!"

"But you're no farmer, Pierre. You're a merchant. What do you know about farming?"

"I don't need to know anything, not just yet. I can keep my shop and build my plantation, too."

"Here!" he waved more paper. "See this? This is a deed of sale for a dozen slaves. All strong, grown men who will clear that land for me. And this?" Pierre threw up another sheet. "This is a contract with M'sieur Barthelemy's brother Jacques. He's agreed to oversee the slaves and the planting. If this little venture works—and it *will* work, by God!—I'll build us a big fine house down at the Point and we can live the rest of our lives in peace. However we please!"

Suddenly Pierre halted, his eyes averted. "There is one problem, though, *t'chou.*"

"No problem could be a bad one now," Coincoin murmured, still dazed by all that her dreams had birthed this day.

"It shouldn't be, Coincoin. Not if all goes well. But there is always the possibility that things won't, and we have to face that squarely."

"What, M'sieur?"

"Pierre!"

Coincoin smiled contritely and nestled closer in his arms. *"Oui,* Pierre. What?"

"You remember my telling you last year that I had saved enough to buy Dominique and Eulalie from Madame de Soto, whenever that blasted woman finally agrees?"

Coincoin's heart lurched. *"Oui?"*

"That's what I used to buy you last fall, when Quintanilla forced my hand. I didn't want to tell you because I knew you would worry, and I figured that by the end of this summer, I would have enough spare cash again to buy the children."

Pierre paused, afraid to go on, yet knowing that he had to.

"Well, I did replace the money, Coincoin. Only, I had to use it today, for a down payment on those twelve hands. Then I had to mortgage everything else I own to secure the rest of the debt. If Jacques Rachal is as good a manager as I think he is, and if he makes us a decent crop the first year or two, we can clear what's due and we'll be on our way to riches. But if the crops don't make…" Pierre's voice trailed off. How could he tell her?

"If the crops don't make? Pierre?"

Abruptly he pushed her aside and leaned against the sweet gum tree, his face turned away from her so he could not see her eyes.

"If the crops don't make, then my creditors will get everything I own. The shop. This house. My rental houses. And all my slaves—not just the dozen men I bought on credit today. They'll get our children, too."

⟡ 12 ⟡
Summer 1779

The churchyard bell rang suddenly across the entire post. Housewives left their dinners on the open fires and merchants hastily locked their doors to scurry to the square. Not since the big fire swept through the lower part of town three years before had the bell pealed so insistently.

"Écoutez! Écoutez!" the bailiff intoned as the crowd assembled before him. "Listen, one and all! His honor, Monsieur Athanase de Mézières, Civil and Military Commander of this Royal Post of San Juan Bautista des Natchitoches, has a proclamation of grave importance to read to us this day."

De Mézières slowly raised his arm, signalling the crowd to silence. His uniform hung loosely on him, in testament to all the responsibilities that had worn away his spirit, his health, and his frame.

"My friends, my people. I have just now received a message from His Illustrious Señor, Don Bernardo de Gálvez, Colonel of His Majesty's Army and Acting Governor of the Colony of Louisiana…

> *To the commandants of the various and several military posts of the*
> *Province of Louisiana. Greetings—*
>
> Our Catholic Majesty Carlos III has declared war on the Kingdom of Great Britain. We have been fortunate to receive advance notice of this turn of events, and we understand that British officials here in the colonies are not yet apprised of the declaration.
>
> Since the Treaty of Paris in 1763, our enemy has held possession of the right bank of the Mississippi River and all territory east of it. Our French cousins who live within that domain have suffered great injustices under British rule, and their attempts to correct those injustices within the framework of law have been cruelly suppressed.
>
> For this reason, our French cousins on the upper Mississippi have joined forces with the revolutionists who seek freedom for all British colonies. It is regrettable that our kinsmen have resorted to anarchy, but the spirit that has driven them to rebel against British oppression is well understood. Freedom, justice, and right have always motivated the Frenchman and the Spaniard to action!
>
> Our Catholic Majesty Carlos III cannot condone anarchy. For this reason he has steadfastly refused to support the revolution in British America, and he predicts that the support given it by the ministers of France will result in great folly within that nation. It is not God's will that the righteous Spaniard or Frenchman should join hands with anarchists who seek to overthrow those whom our Lord has elevated to authority. Never can the servant raise his hand against the Master.
>
> However, it is the responsibility of the ruling class to police its own ranks, conscientiously and decisively. Our Mother Spain long has recognized the tyranny of English kings and their unholy lust for domination of the world. The godless, heretical British monarchy

has already forced its might upon the French territory in this New World. It has driven, like dumb cattle, a whole people from their homes on the Isle of Acadia. If it succeeds in quelling the protests of its American colonists, it will next turn its swords upon the last people who remain to oppose her in the new world—the colonists of Spain.

Therefore, in recognition of the rights of man to the kind of just and benevolent government that His Catholic Majesty provides, and in recognition of the threat to world peace that Great Britain now poses, His Majesty has declared open warfare upon the British Crown. It must be repeated, no alliance has been made with the American anarchists. Their approach to their problem is not the way of God and law. However, once our mother country has succeeded in slaying the British lion, she will see that all colonists of America enjoy the justice they deserve.

It is therefore ordered that all militia units within the colony mobilize immediately. Within two days, all units must leave to meet His Majesty's Army on the Mississippi, where we will then proceed to drive the unholy British from the American lands they have no moral right to possess.

A stunned silence hung in the July heat as De Mézières refolded the governor's proclamation and soberly faced his people. "My friends. Don Gálvez's words are clear enough. There is no need for me to say more. May God's will be done."

"Nom de Dieu!" a voice exploded behind Pierre as De Mézières turned from the crowd and marched back to the *casa real.*

"Behind all those fine words about French cousins and injustices, there's the same old chestnut. Old Carlos is back at war with England. *Enfer!* The Spanish have fought the English for centuries, and they'll keep on doing it long after all us Frenchmen are slit open by British bayonets. Why should we fight Spain's war? We're not Spaniards and never will be, no matter how long they claim to own this colony!"

A low murmur from the men and women who surrounded him echoed the man's protest. Poor, dumb fools, Pierre thought to himself. At last they have within their reach the opportunity they've wanted ever since Bloody O'Reilly and his Spanish fleet put down the Creole rebellion at New Orleans in '68. And they can't even see it!

The man's right in one respect, though, Pierre agreed as the crowd continued its mutterings. Beneath Gálvez's fine words, another message does come through: no matter how badly Carlos wants to conquer the British, he can't do it by joining forces with the rebels. That would be his surest bet, but he can't put his stamp of approval on any brand of revolution. That's all the excuse his Louisiana subjects would need to justify a rebellion of their own.

Morbleu! Carlos is playing with fire, no matter how he plays it. This war of his with George III will weaken the British Empire so badly that George will never put down the uprising. With luck, then, the Americans and our French cousins in Illinois will return the aid we're about to give them—and together we'll drive the Spanish Crown off this continent as well. *That,* my friends, is our one chance to become Frenchmen again, as we were born to be. But I damned well cannot drive that point home to you without inviting arrest for sedition!

"*Mes amis! Écoutez!* Listen a moment, friends!" Étienne entered the verbal fray that was now raging around them, and Pierre's spirits rose. Étienne, the diplomat. He always has a way of taking what cannot be said and making a way to say it.

In a leap, Étienne was on the platform that De Mézières had vacated in the center of the square, his arms thrown wide in a dramatic plea.

"*Mes amis!* You are right. We are Frenchmen. But Britain is our enemy, too. For as many centuries as our history and our legends can recall, we have fought the English on thousands of battlefields, in Europe and here in America. As Don Gálvez has so rightly pointed out, our French cousins in Illinois, in Québec and Mont Réal, and most of all in Acadie, have suffered terribly at British hands."

"You, Pierre Derbanne! You haven't said anything yet, but I heard you mention once that the noble family of Acadie, D'Amours de Chauffour, are your cousins. Are you not going to avenge the wrong done to them?"

"You, Louis Chauvin! Aren't you the nephew of old Joseph Chauvin de Charleville of Kaskaskia? A former commandant he was, and yet the British imprisoned him when he dared to protest their mistreatment of his people. His sons formed a militia company and marched off with George Rogers Clarke to drive the Red Coats out of Vincennes and Detroit and all the Northwest, and they are now leaders of the Revolutionary government in Illinois. Can you do less?"

"Can any of us do less, *mes amis?*" Étienne continued eloquently, tweaking the emotions of all those in his audience whose boasts and secrets and fears he knew so well from all the years in which they had drunk together, sung together, gambled together, and fought each other under the roisterous roof of his Front Street tavern.

"Our governor is right, my friends! Spanish Louisiana will be the next conquest of the British monster if we do not stop, right now, the insidious spread of its tentacles!"

"There's not a one of you who would hate more to leave this post and risk your life in war than I would. Padre de Quintanilla has already announced the first bann for my marriage. But ladies, I would readily ask my love to wait for my return. Can you not spare, for a while, the men you love? British persecution must be stopped!"

The crowd was still now, though here and there heads began to nod.

"My friends," Étienne's voice grew soft and persuasive, but soon crescendoed as he saw that the crowd was with him.

"We are all militiamen because it is our duty to be. Our two companies now wear the uniform of Spain, because the Lord has willed it. But it makes no difference whether we French march against the British under the Spanish flag or the French one. The urgency is the same. The results will be the same! We can make it happen, *mes amis!* The final, decisive end of England as a threat to world peace and a predator of humanity! Freedom! That will be our reward!"

"*Très bien! Bravo!*" someone bellowed from the crowd, and a chorus picked up the chant.

"Day after tomorrow," Étienne shouted, "I will greet the dawn right here on this square, my Charleville rifle in my hand, and my Spanish uniform on my back. I'll kiss my sweetheart good-bye amid the roll of drums that sends us off to war against the hated Redcoats. Who's coming with me?" he trumpeted. "Metoyer, *mon ami*, I know I can count on you!"

"*Oui,*" Pierre forced a grim laugh, "if I can kiss your sweetheart good-bye, myself!"

"Louis? Joseph? Ambroise?"

One by one, eagerly and reluctantly, the continental-born Frenchmen and their native-born neighbors committed themselves to war. Again, after a dormant decade, there arose in Louisiana the spirit that had compelled the Creoles to raise their arms against Spanish tyranny in '68, the same spirit that had resurged in that fateful year '76 in the British colonies to the east. Together, the French-Americans who had been rejected by their king and the Anglo-Americans who had boldly rejected theirs, would, with the help of the autocratic regime of Spain, make liberty the symbol of North America.

∽ 13 ∽

Three weeks later and three hundred miles away

On the 27th of August 1779, Colonel Bernardo de Gálvez put Don Pedro Piernas in charge of the city of New Orleans and prepared to leave the capital. No rumor of an impending British attack had complicated his plan. Indeed Gálvez's spies reported that British posts along the Mississippi and the Gulf were not yet aware of the declaration of war.

"*Bueno!*" Gálvez had declared, then mapped his strategy for an offensive.

"*Loco!*" his senior advisors then swore at him. "You leave here with all our men and a British fleet from Pensacola will sail through the Balize, up the Mississippi, and take this capital."

"*Yo, solo!*" Gálvez had shouted back. "*I, alone,* seem to grasp the fact that a quick, decisive attack on the British will bring the dogs to their knees before they can pounce on us! No battle will be fought in New Orleans, where my people will suffer. No! This war will be fought on British soil!"

And so at the end of August, in the wake of a hurricane that the timid saw as an omen, Gálvez marched northward with a meager band of five hundred men. His were recruits of every class, nationality, and color, and most of them raw recruits at that. *La ville's* militia stayed behind, but not just to maintain order until the town recovered from nature's tirade. Gálvez knew his advisors were at least partly right. The militia might be needed to defend the city, in case the British attack they predicted, and he privately feared, did materialize.

Meanwhile, upriver on the Mississippi's east bank at the British posts of Manchac, Baton Rouge, and Natchez, at least eight hundred seasoned soldiers awaited Gálvez's motley band. His only chance for success, he knew, lay in a complete surprise and the prompt arrival of the trained militias from Louisiana's country posts.

Within a week, they had marched only thirty leagues, through dense woods no road ever had penetrated, without tents to shelter them at night or sufficient provisions, amid the miasma of swamps and the torment of mosquitoes that plagued the Mississippi's lower delta. Ten leagues further, they were joined by jubilant contingencies from Opelousas and Pointe Coupée, all eager for the glory of battle. Twenty leagues up, there fell into the ranks the hoped-for units from the frontier post of Natchitoches. Victory was assured, and Britain's Fort Bute of Manchac fell before their charge like the hovels of *la ville* had fallen in the summer's gale.

Yet the victory was weakly celebrated. More than a third of Gálvez's troops were ill from hunger, fatigue, and exposure. "Six days thou shalt rest!" he commanded, "but on the seventh thou shalt march! Any longer delay and the British of Baton Rouge will be warned. We cannot afford to lose our element of surprise."

"Oh, Pierre," Étienne moaned from the corner of the dirt-floored barracks in which his friends had planted him on a confiscated blanket of scratchy wool. "I may never walk again, much less march."

"What, *mon ami?* You are disenchanted so soon with the glories of war? Our campaign has only begun! Far more glory awaits us. What we have enjoyed until now is only the first course of a splendid repast that Gálvez promises!"

Pierre forced his voice to be light, masking from his friend the worry that really gripped him. Pavie was indeed ill. Dysentery had hit him and countless others the day before their two companies fell in with Gálvez's forces, and Pavie had been retching violently ever since.

Together, Pierre and their two young friends, Ambroise Lecomte and Joseph Dupré, had carried Étienne the last ten leagues that stretched between them and Fort Bute. Since then, they had nursed him, spooning each meal down his raw throat, making endless trips to the river to empty the buckets of vomit that seemed to pour from him, and washing his crude bedclothes, as well as him, as fast as the hapless Étienne soiled everything.

"Ohhh, Metoyer," Étienne moaned anew. "Whatever you do, don't mention eating. I may never eat again either."

"*Bonhomme,* you talk as though you are ready to curl up and die. Now wouldn't that be a shame? Pretty Ma'mselle Buard would be a widow before she ever married. On second thought, I doubt she would suffer too severely. In a week's time, she should be able to find a dozen suitors to take your place."

"Well, at least I don't have to worry about that happening while I'm gone, since all the men from the post are here, except those who are too young to know what it's all about or too old to care."

"Not quite, Pavie. There's Ambroise's cousin, that hot-blooded Le Court boy. He may have gotten out of this war by shooting off his toe, but that should slow him down right handily when the lonely lasses start chasing him!"

"They'd have to be lonely to chase him," Étienne retorted with a weak grin. "He may be hot-blooded, but he sure didn't inherit his father's looks. Or his love for the military. Oh, but the old lieutenant did curse him roundly when he saw what Barthelemy did!"

"*Oui,*" Pierre agreed soberly. "That will be the death of our country yet— France, I mean. All the old and proud *noblesse de l'epée* have lost their taste for the sword that won them their nobility in the first place. They've sired a generation of rakes who buckle on the sabre only to uphold some foolish idea of honor. If France survives now, it will be up to us ambitious bourgeois of peasant stock to take up her standard."

Pierre's voice had grown grim, but then he forced himself to drop that subject. Light banter would do more for his friend's state of mind now than political philosophy.

"Of course," Pierre continued, "if all the *nouveaux riches* have stomachs as weak as yours, France might not stand a chance anyway. Just wait until we get home and Ma'mselle Buard hears how your bravado disintegrated into a pail of slop! If you don't perk up, Étienne, she's liable to toss you aside for a soldier who brings home battle scars on his chest, not his asshole."

"I have no worry, *mon ami.* The love my Marie Thérèse has for me is truer than that," Étienne rejoined good-naturedly. "Methinks you'd better worry about your own Marie Thérèse. If that African princess of yours gets lonely, she'll have no shortage of males around. Man, what ever possessed you to leave your woman down at the Point with a dozen bucks in the prime of their lives?"

Pierre's sympathy for his ailing friend melted amid a flare of temper. His auburn hair had lost much of its fire since the day they climbed Cane River's bank, but age had not cooled his quick temper one whit.

"Pavie, there are some things even friends shouldn't say to each other!"

"*Excusez-moi,* Pierre! I'll bow down and apologize if you want, but I'm likely to retch all over your fine boots."

"I won't take that chance, Pavie." Pierre retorted. "Just watch your tongue in the future."

Étienne reached out weakly and gripped his friend's hand, his drawn face turning uncharacteristically serious.

"*Mon ami,* we've come a long way together and I hope we go a long way further. I'm looking forward to bouncing your grandchildren on my knee alongside my own."

Pierre made no reply.

"Pierre, you know I meant nothing against Coincoin. You have one hell of a woman, and I'd be the first to say so. I thought she was one of a kind thirteen years ago, and I still think so. Only I never would have had the courage to challenge the world over her the way you have. I thumb my nose at people over little things, but when it comes to the big stuff in life, I'm a big chicken.

"*Poulet gros!*" Étienne went on mockingly. "*Oui,* that's me. But you, Pierre, have guts. Both of you have and I admire you for living true to yourselves."

Pierre nodded gruffly. Pavie was a talker. He could verbalize every thought that came from his mind or his heart. But never could Pierre comfortably share his inner self with any other soul. Whatever he had to do, he just *did.* No explanations given. His personal feelings were nobody's damned business.

Business, on the other hand, was a plane on which he and Pavie met quite well, and there were few men whose advice he valued more. Beneath his friend's cockiness, there lay brains that filed, cataloged, and analyzed everything around him. There had been few ventures Pierre ever entered into without first sounding out Étienne. Only two, in fact, since their arrival in the colony, and he was regretting his failure to do so in both instances.

The first hasty decision had been forced upon him. After Quintanilla threw down his gauntlet on the same day the old San Antonio trader arrived in town with a dozen prime bucks, Pierre had no choice but to move quickly before the slaves were grabbed by someone else and the opportunity lost. Still, there had been a belly full of fears since then, especially since this damned war erupted. If things go wrong back home and there's no crop this year, he reminded himself a dozen times a day, then *I've lost everything. We've* lost everything. The money, the shop, the houses, those would be bad enough. But if my slave property is seized for debt, how can I ever face Coincoin again? How could I live with myself? What kind of man am I to let someone take a mortgage against my own children?

It's up to Coincoin now! That thought was the other point that worried him, the other matter on which he had not asked Pavie's advice. He couldn't. Coincoin had made the decision and would tolerate no objection.

"How can you deny me this, Pierre?" she had demanded, both her hands propped indignantly on the hips of her sateen frock while Pierre's attention wandered over it. *Lime green's definitely her color,* he was thinking. *It's a good thing I pulled that bolt off the shelf before someone bought it.* But of course Coincoin had noticed his distraction and did not appreciate it one whit, even if she had been its object.

"Look in my eyes, Pierre, not at my body!"

Contritely, he complied, and she plunged on.

"For a year now, you've been telling me that I am free. I am on my own. I am accountable for my own actions. I owe no obedience or explanations to anyone. My future is in my hands. Well, my future is *my children.* Everything I have done in life has been for them... well..." He could have sworn her eyes danced impishly, for a moment. But then she had turned serious again, and her face took on a resoluteness he had never seen before.

"If this crop fails, Pierre, you lose your money. But I lose my *children!* As far as I'm concerned, I have a bigger stake in this now than you have."

"They're my children, too, you know," Pierre had reminded her softly.

"You should have thought about that before you mortgaged them!"

"Coincoin, don't you know I've told myself that a thousand times since? Every time little Eulalie crawls up in my lap and wraps those chubby little arms about my neck. Every time Susanne's saucy words remind me of my own headstrong youth...."

Pierre's voice had trailed off in memory, but the resolve in her face had soon brought him back to the present, to the frustrations that now tore him apart.

"You're right, Coincoin. They're your children in a way they can never be mine. I'm a father with no father's rights at all. I have no *paternal* right to give them the benefit of my experience and wisdom, and I have no *paternal* right to insist that they accept it. That's why I could not free them when I freed you. Only as long as I am their *master* and they are my *slaves,"* Pierre had winced at those words, "do I have any authority to guide them or teach them or control them."

She said nothing, so he ploughed on.

"Coincoin, I have no choice over their freedom and I had no choice about that mortgage. We needed those hands and all I had was a down payment. That damned old Spaniard kept insisting that the work I planned to have them do was too dangerous. They could catch malaria down in those cane brakes, or trees could fall on them as they cleared the land, and I could lose them all. Old Delago demanded security, damned unreasonable security, that he would get his money. I had no choice, Coincoin. It was either do as I did, or else not make this move at all."

"And you're a gambler," Coincoin's voice had turned soft and husky. It was still the same tantalizing, seductive contralto that had been his undoing in the first place.

"Pierre, I have accepted your gamble. Now it is your turn to accept mine. Will you?"

This time, he was quiet.

"Day after tomorrow, Jacques Rachal goes off to war with the rest of you. He has no choice, and we have no choice. If this year's crop is going to be made, someone has to do Rachal's job. Your slaves are not fools. There is no way they are going to stay down at the Point unsupervised. If no one is there to keep them, they will just walk off."

"We do have another option, Coincoin. Barthelemy Rachal has offered us his son to take Jacques's place."

"That's no option, Pierre! Baptiste-Barthelemy is a gangling boy. Too young for the militia even! No experience. No authority. All Sieur Jacques has to do is *look* at the men and they fall into line, but that boy would have to use the whip. Even if he has the stomach for that, I will not tolerate it."

"Then how would you control a dozen brutes, Coincoin?"

"With reason, Pierre. Don't laugh at me! I am serious! In the first place, I do not consider them *brutes,* and they know it. If their dignity is respected, if they have something to gain from their labor, they will work, whether Jacques Rachal or you or I are there to make them."

"*Gain,* Coincoin? What could they possibly have to *gain?*"

"Trust me, Pierre. Gamble with me, as I have done with you. Let me go down to the Point tomorrow and talk with them. If I think it will work, I will tell you when I get back. If I decide it will not work, we can forget the whole thing. That way, I will not have to listen to you scream unless it is necessary."

The challenge had intrigued him, although his fears were far from quelled. There was no doubt but that his hands liked her. She never had treated them with anything but respect and they never had shown her anything less in return—although he had no doubt, too, but that she would promptly scorch any one of them who ever showed a mite of familiarity or insubordination.

It must be in her blood, he mused. A legacy of that king from whom she claims descent. All these years, I've worried about her ability to handle freedom and she has amazed everyone. It's almost as if she were born to freedom, born into a different world from other blacks. The *nègres* sense it, too. Even mine. You'd think they know she was born to rule them.

As agreed, Coincoin had gone to the Point that next day, called the hands from their work, laid before them her proposition, and come away convinced her plan would work. As she predicted, too, Pierre had screamed.

"They will stay," Coincoin had announced matter-of-factly, when Pierre finally shooed the last customer from the shop and trudged home, dreading their last night together.

"The children and I will move tomorrow into the cabin Rachal threw up down there, and we will stay until he comes back. The hands will work for me. Together we will make that crop, Pierre. Together we will pay off the mortgage, and then we will share what is left."

"We will *what?*"

"You heard me plainly enough."

"What do you mean, *we'll share the profits?*"

"Exactly that. I explained our problem to them. I told them all about the mortgage, our children, and the war. Some of them have children, too. Did you know that? Children by women who had belonged to different masters at San Antonio, and they were sold away from their families by that old jackal who brought them here. They don't want that he should end up with my children, too."

"But what about the *profits?*" he had croaked.

"It is simple, Pierre. I have told them all that whatever we make off this year's crop will first go toward paying off the mortgage, and the cost of the seed, and the cost of feeding them, and the payment to Rachal for his time up to this point. Then, whatever is left, if anything is left, will be divided fourteen ways. That is one share for you, one share for me, and one share for each of them."

"You promised our *slaves* a share of the crop?"

"Precisely."

"*Morbleu!* How in the hell am I going to make money off slaves if I give them my profit?"

"This is not a permanent arrangement, Pierre. That is fully understood. I have told them plainly that it is a one-time offer, and that I have made it only because I need their help while you and Rachal are gone."

"But…"

"No *buts,* Pierre! This is to be *their chance!* All men must have a *chance.* The more committed they are to the work, the better crop we will make and the more profit we will all have. They can earn a nest egg for themselves. Maybe even buy themselves free so that those who want to, can go back to San Antonio, to their wives and their children."

"Buy themselves *free?* You're trying to get rid of my slaves before I even get them paid for? Woman, are you obsessed with this idea of freedom?"

"No. But every man, slave or free, should have the opportunity to be a *man.* If he is enough of one, he will seize that opportunity and make his own place in life. If he is too blind, or dumb, or lazy, then he was born to be somebody's beast of burden, and my conscience will never bother me over the fact that he is a slave. Ours or anyone else's."

"Woman, you're going to ruin me," Pierre groaned. Still, his gut told him that her damned scheme might actually work. It *had* to work.

Pavie would croak, Pierre thought now as he eyed the friend beside him. As ill as the man is, he'd cackle until he went into convulsions and that would only bring on the bloody vomit again. He decided it best not to tell him.

‿ 14 ⁀

Gálvez did not keep his own commandment. He gave his men just five days of rest and on the sixth his units marched. Many stayed behind, some with dysentery, some with malaria, and a few with measles, but Pavie insisted he was well and that his company was not about to leave without him. With Dupré propping up his left arm and young Lecomte supporting his right, Étienne trudged with his comrades to Baton Rouge.

"Blast it, Metoyer. We should have joined the cavalry. It's all my baby brother's fault. If the fool kid had not been afraid of horses, he'd have gotten himself an ensign's commission in something besides the infantry. Then when he wound up at Natchitoches and I felt duty bound to keep an eye on him, I wouldn't have ended up a foot soldier. *Mon Dieu!* A soldier looks more *dignified* on horseback."

"I can't imagine why you're worried about that," Pierre jested. "Nobody looks dignified with a case of loose bowels."

"Ah, your turn will come, false friend. Just wait until you need me to care for you. You won't be making fun of the situation then."

Jibe after jibe, league after league, their rag tag army marched upriver. On the thirteenth of September, they sighted Baton Rouge and spirits plummeted as they beheld the fort. Walls of rammed dirt stood nine feet high and eighteen feet thick, surrounded by palisades and a *chevreaux-de-frise* that mounted thirteen cannon. Outside those walls lay a monstrous ditch, as formidable as any medieval moat, and inside those walls, or so the officers at Fort Bute had told them, were five hundred men. All of them veterans. Gálvez's greenhorns now numbered barely half of that.

"*Yo soy invincible!*" Gálvez shouted defiantly when he surveyed the bastion they had come to take. "Odds be damned! I am unbeatable!" Yet the Spanish colonel was not vain enough to try to take the fort by direct assault as he had done to the weaker one at Bayou Manchac.

"A feint attack, men. A feint on one side to distract them and an unsuspected onslaught on the other. That's how we'll breach those walls. That's all it will take to bring this fort to its muddy knees. From that burned-out hill over there, the country militias will make the attack, led by Captain Bormé and his First Infantry Company of Natchitoches."

"*Merde!*" Étienne swore under his breath. "I told you we should have joined the cavalry." But before Pierre could think of a retort, Gálvez proceeded to outline his strategy.

"Meanwhile, the First New Orleans Regiment of Free Negroes will dig trenches along that ridge."

"On the other hand," Étienne reconsidered, "there could be worse units to be in right now."

"In front of those trenches," the colonel went on, "while the enemy is deployed on the other side by the country militias, the regulars shall erect a battery."

The ruse worked. Warned of the Spanish approach, the British commander already had ordered the burning of all homes, trees, and anything else that would provide cover to his attackers, but Gálvez still outfoxed him. From the scorched promontory on which they lay, the Natchitoches militiamen rained a steady shower of shot upon the fort and laughed at British bullets falling just short of their lines.

Under cover of the night, Louisiana's Choctaws arrived, eager to assault the fort, lusting for plunder, pillage, and the scalps the British in earlier years had encouraged them to take. Carlos III was now their ally, Spain had their service, but Gálvez held them in check. There would be no need for barbarity. The British were already at his mercy, even if they did not know it.

Then, while British frustrations focused on the militia that pestered them like mosquitoes too nimble to swat, the Spanish battery set itself up unnoticed on the opposite ridge and opened fire. Cannons exploded in unison. Four-pound balls plowed through the packed dirt and the palisaded walls, smothering the fort under a cloud of splintered wood and rich black mud that the Mississippi had spent an eon making. In three and a half hours, the artillery reduced the fort to chaos and rubbish.

"*Santa María!*" Gálvez swore as the British flag was lowered and the white flag of truce rose in its stead. Men shouted, danced, and hugged each other, while the country militia raised their cry, *Vive le français! Viva la español!* And beside the large Spanish banner that flew over their victorious battery, Pavie unfurled and planted his own, small, homemade rendition of the French fleur-de-lis.

"We've done it, men!" Gálvez trumpeted, when he at last quieted his jubilant forces. "The only question that remains now is the terms of surrender."

"*Caramba!* colonel, let's be greedy!" Étienne shouted from the rear ranks. "Go ahead and demand the surrender of Natchez, too. Let's save ourselves the fight!"

Gálvez's head spun toward the sound of Pavie's voice. "You!" he commanded. "Step forward, man!"

"Who, me?" Étienne queried innocently.

"You! What's your name, soldier?"

"Pavie of Natchitoches. But I'm no soldier, sir. At least not usually. I'm one of those damned French merchants you Spanish say we have too many of along the frontier."

"Shut up, Pavie," Pierre muttered from his side.

"A merchant, eh? Any relation to the young ensign whose commission I approved last year? I think Pavie was his name."

"Just brothers, sir. But I'll have to admit he proved to be a fair enough soldier in this campaign. I guess that's because he likes to fight. Me? I prefer talking. Don't get me wrong, colonel. I'm just as anxious as the next fellow to whip those Redcoats, but I'd much rather *talk* them into believing they've been whipped than to have to charge in and prove it."

"Señor Merchant," Gálvez panned. "I know a few generals who could take lessons from you. Incidentally, I like your idea about Natchez."

Having raised the flag of truce as his walls fell down, the English commander of Baton Rouge dispatched two envoys to the camp of the enemy, with his proposals for surrender. Gálvez sent them back with a curt refusal, a lengthy *papele* outlining his own demands, and a personal message to Colonel Dickson that the Redcoats had but twenty-four hours to agree to all his terms. Stalling as a point of honor, the British garrison made no reply. But on the stroke of the clock, twenty-four hours later, they marched from behind their crumbling walls, threw down their arms, and surrendered.

"You win, Gálvez," Dickson announced. "As one gentleman to another, I relinquish my sword to you personally, along with the order I have penned to the officers of Fort Panmure. I promise you, they and their grenadiers will turn over Natchez without a fight."

The campaign was over. Nothing remained but the routine dispatch of a small force upriver to remove the British garrison at the bluffs of Natchez. Colonel Bernardo Gálvez had left New Orleans with his calendar marked for two long and bloody months. He finished his work in just one, and without serious bloodshed. The Spaniard was jubilant with victory and swaggering with success, a success that had exceeded his boldest dreams.

"My men!" he threw his arms open into the breeze, as if to embrace them all. "*Yo no solo, todavia!* I am not alone, today, in this victory. It is as much yours as mine. Together, we Spaniards and Frenchmen, soldiers and—*sí*—even merchants, have subdued the English snake."

Cheers echoed through the lacerated walls of the fort, and Gálvez raised his arms again, soberly, to quiet his men.

"Still, the snake is not yet dead. We have driven the British serpent out of its last strongholds in the Mississippi Valley, but we have only cut off its rattlers. Its head still remains at the port of Pensacola and its heart lies on the Bay of Mobile. Not until we have taken those two British forts will we have rid North America of the Union Jack!"

The *joie de vivre* of his men went dead silent.

"Soldiers, I am heady with success now, but I am not drunk. The fact is, we lack the strength to do any further damage to the British. Today I ride back to New Orleans, where I will promptly post dispatches to Havana and Madrid. When I report the glorious successes that you few, brave men have accomplished, then the reinforcements, the money, the supplies, and all the artillery we need will surely be ours. Fort George of Pensacola and Fort Charlotte of Mobile will then fall before our onslaughts just as Bute and Baton Rouge have done."

"I do not promise you an easy victory," the governor went on. "The battles will be bloody. Some of you will be buried there along the Gulf. But *nombre de Díos,* men! If you fight like you've fought in this campaign, we'll own the Gulf!"

Silence still hung over the shelled fort, as each man weighed the personal implications of Gálvez's words.

"When I ride off, today, you men go home as well, except for Favrot's regulars. I am placing Don Pedro José Favrot in command of the new *Spanish* fort of Baton Rouge. When all is ready, men, I shall issue another call, and I know you will respond. Together, come winter, we will slay that British serpent."

Gálvez's grin was as broad as his plans as he continued. "The cold British don't enjoy our tropical winters anyway, much less the summers. We'll be doing them a favor to send those poor soldiers home, *verdad?*"

"*Verdad!*" The cry of support he had begun to fear he would not get rose at last from the ranks, as two hundred Frenchmen forgot their national differences and cheered their leader. Gálvez beamed, waiting for the accolade to subside.

"As your commander, I say 'thank you,' but such trite words are not enough for all you've done and all you've suffered. So I have found another way to say what is in my heart. When I left New Orleans, I planned a two-month campaign, and my disbursement officer brought a two-month payroll. You have completed our campaign in half that time, but you deserve full compensation. Therefore, I issue my last order to you on this campaign. Line up and collect your double pay!"

"*Bravo! Bravo! Vive el gobierno!*" The cheers did not subside until El Gobierno rode out of sight down the long, winding, muddy banks of the river that flowed southward to New Orleans.

The early winter rains had set in by the time the First Infantry Company wound its way back up Red River to the frontier. Pavie had sung their way home—every soldier's battle march, every sacred hymn, and every barroom ditty he had ever heard, until Pierre almost wished his friend would fall ill again.

"Why so glum, Metoyer?" Étienne laughed. "We're going home to our girl-friends, our wives, our lovers, and you act as though you wish yourself dead. Say, man, would you like for me to chant the *Diés Iræ*, so you can attend your own funeral while you're still here to enjoy it? Young Dupré, here, is a quarter Spanish. He can make like the padre and deliver the oration. Only he'd have to make it shorter than Quintanilla does or he wouldn't get done before we're back to Natchitoches."

"My son," Dupré intoned. "The Lord thy God shall not be mocked, neither He nor His Holy Servants."

"You're teaching this boy sacrilege, Étienne," Pierre countered. "You're leading this fine young man astray. Dupré's beginning to sound just like you."

The banter continued as they rowed their way upriver, past Le Court's Bluff, where the lieutenant's war-shy son hallooed enthusiastically from the grove in which they had caught him dallying with one of his father's Caneci maids, past the foot of the Isle of Canes where the dense brakes had not yet been penetrated by any habitation, and then up the old bed of Red River that wound gently into Natchitoches. Then their pirogues turned a familiar bend, and Pierre froze. Overland to the east meandered Bayou Brevelle, less than a half-mile away; and beyond that, just another mile or so, lay the big Point in the channel of Cane River that had now been taken over by the Red.

He could not wait. "Bormé!" Pierre called to his captain in the pirogue that followed. "*Mon ami,* you're no stickler for regulations. What say, I fall out of line here and you just mark me present when you dismiss these brave troops at Natchitoches?"

"You're asking special favors, Metoyer?" the old lieutenant retorted in feigned surprise. "What possible reason could you have for absenting yourself from our company out here in the middle of the wilderness. Why, there's not a soul around."

"Leastwise, no closer than the Point," Étienne drawled, amid the guffaws of the troops. "Let him go, Captain. He just wants to check on his *crops,* I'm sure." Again, a chorus of hoots echoed from the other pirogues.

"Believe it or not, Bormé, the man is right," Metoyer declared with more soberness than any of them realized. "While the rest of you get drunk tonight, I'll be counting *carottes* of tobacco, assuming that the hands didn't run off and let the crop go wild while we were fighting that damned war."

"Then hasten to your *crops,* Metoyer," his captain rejoined. "Pull the pirogue over, gentlemen, and let the man ashore; but be quick about it. We have a celebration waiting at the post tonight, and tomorrow, and maybe the next day, too, if Quintanilla doesn't herd us all into church."

Pierre's impatience was barely contained as he bade his *confrères* farewell, then struck overland for the Point, his boots dragging now with trepidation as much as the clayey mud left by autumn rains. By the time the sun fell this night behind the pine hills that reared westward of his land, Pierre would know the fate the gods had decreed for him and his unsanctioned family.

The gods! How loosely we use those words, he thought to himself as he plunged into the bayou and swam to the other bank with only one strong arm, the other holding his rifle and his ammunition high above the swollen stream. The gods... My God... God Almighty.... In a thousand ways, in the most casual speech, the unbeliever gives as much testimony to His existence as does any Christian. And in time of crisis, the worst of us is forced to reconsider.

Oh, *zut,* Lord! Pierre swore as he climbed ashore and an unseasonable chill cut through his sodden clothes. I'm no unbeliever. It's just that organized religion makes too many deuced demands on a person. It's *do this* and *don't do that* until sometimes it seems there's nothing left a fellow can do that he'd even want to. At least until he gets too old to enjoy life anyway. I'm not that old yet, Lord! Not quite.

An idea struck him as he plodded eastward. *Maybe we can reach a compromise, Lord?* You help me through this crisis, and I'll give more thought to going to Mass on Sundays. Maybe even confession... *Oh, maudit!* I can't go to confession.

There's just no way I'm going to give up what Quintanilla would demand. But at least I've settled down to just one woman, Lord. In thirteen years, I've never once been unfaithful. Surely that ought to merit some consideration, Lord?

The sky darkened and a sudden shower dumped its fury. Mud turned to a dull red soup as he sloshed the last mile across fields his Negroes had cleared but not yet planted. Pierre wrung the water out of his blanket and pulled it around him tighter to ward off the chill that gripped him.

In the distance, he could see the first faint lines of the field where he had left a promising stand of tobacco two months before. He had bought the best seed to be had. He and Rachal had ridden herd on those *nègres* from the day it was sowed in the beds. Not until each seedling had formed four leaves would he let it be transplanted into the fields, and then he had made sure that every shoot was checked daily for caterpillars. Each tender plant had been weeded by hand and pinched back after it grew exactly nine leaves, so the remainder would be thicker, longer, and juicier. Even the tobacco house was built and ready. But would the hangars now be full? Or was all that work for naught?

The rain slackened to a fine mist, as suddenly as it had begun, and Pierre could see scraggly stalks emerging through the drizzle—short, immature, and sparsely spaced. Oh, Lord! he moaned in desperation. Is this the neglected remains of what I planted? Or, merciful God, could this be the beginnings of the second or third cutting? Where in the devil are the hands? There's not a man-jack to be seen or heard! His pace quickened, fighting the mud that had accumulated on his once-fine Moroccan boots.

The slave camp and Rachal's cabin—Coincoin's cabin now—came into view and Pierre groaned. No smoke wafted above or around them, even though cook fires should already have been lit. To their left stood the tobacco house, optimistically large. Resigned, Pierre rounded its broadside and headed for the door. As he spied the chain that barred his entrance, his heart missed a beat entirely, before the thought struck him that there would be no need for a chain if there were nothing of value inside.

Frantically, he scoured the premises for something to climb upon, to peer through the foot-wide vent that crowned the walls of the shed. Behind the barn he found at last a sawhorse, dragged it through the mud, and climbed astride. Then, as his knees began to tremble, he sank back to the ground and let the reality of what he had seen rejuvenate his soul. Every hanger was loaded to capacity with leaves whose size suggested they were the second cutting. Along the walls, from earth to ceiling, stacked endlessly, were *carotte* after glorious *carotte* of tightly coiled, perfectly bound, rich, black, prime-cut leaves, already tagged and awaiting shipment.

Quickly, Pierre calculated. When he ordered that shed constructed, anticipating long-range needs, he had planned it to hold ten thousand rolls. Surely it held that now. At a minimum price of five livres a roll. Even after paying the fifteen thousand he owed for the hands, after all expenses of planting and shipping the crop, after feeding those Negroes for a year and paying off Rachal's contract, he should still have fifteen thousand left. Even dividing this fourteen ways, as Coincoin rashly promised, they would each clear more than a thousand—five times what free laborers make in this colony. *Morbleu!* Pierre swore. Those nègres have gotten rich off me this year!

Fifteen thousand livres profit. In one season!

Again Pierre calculated, quickly mapping strategy for years to come. Next year I'll have more land cleared and should do even better, and I won't have to give it all away to the hands. With that profit, I can enlarge my shop and find a bigger house. In a couple of years, I can buy a dozen fertile females. Then if they find my bucks attractive, I'll be set for life! Fifteen more years in this colony and I should have forty or fifty hands in the fields, even if I never buy another one. *Mon Dieu!* Old Jeannot was right, God rest his ornery soul. In this country, it is possible for any man to become a lord.

Pierre breathed the words again, very softly. *Mon Dieu!* And then he rolled his aching body over and fell to his knees. Slowly he crossed himself and began the prayer he had not said in so many years that he had all but forgotten it: Our Father who art in heaven, *hallowed be thy name...*

He was still on his knees outside his shed when Coincoin and the children turned the Point, the oars of their pirogues keeping perfect rhythm with their song, their faces still lit by the excitement of their visit with Françoise and Coincoin's Fanchon downriver at Lecomte's place. Had they not broken him from his spell, he would have been on his knees when his hands returned from the pass Coincoin had given them. For that, Pierre was thankful. It was too much already that Coincoin had promised them a share of his crop. How could he expect them to have any respect or awe left for him if they found him on his knees, somewhere other than church, when it was not even Sunday?

⌒ 16 ⌒
Winter 1780

Gálvez issued his second call in January, and again the Natchitoches militia wound its way down Red River to the Mississippi. This time, Pierre's leave-taking bore a different pain from the one that had eaten at his guts the previous summer. Already the first beds of his new crop had been planted, raked, trampled firm, and covered with cypress bark against the remaining winter frosts. Before Gálvez's troops reached Mobile, it would be time to transplant the tender seedlings. But this time, Pierre knew, he was leaving both his plantation and his family's future in capable hands.

Pierre's present worry was not for his family or his finances, but for himself. He could not define it, but somewhere, somehow, he felt a sense of crisis that did not stem from Gálvez's stirring speech about the British threat.

I'm getting old, he reminded himself. At twenty, a man sees war as adventure, a chance to prove his untried mettle. But I'm nigh onto forty. I've been where I want to go. I've seen what I want to see. I've more or less done what I want to do. I've found meaning in this life, and I love it too much to lose it—no matter how necessary this war may be.

Of course, he had not shared with Coincoin Gálvez's dire words about the coming campaign. Why should he? Women think only of home and family. It does not matter whether they be black or white, to women politics have no meaning. It had not mattered to Coincoin whether the colony belonged to France or Spain. Her life changed none at all when the reins of power shifted back in the sixties.

If the English were one day to march into Louisiana and take this colony, Pierre told himself, that would mean nothing to her either. But then, she did not know the English or their damned contempt for all other nations and races. No, if the English took the west bank of the Mississippi, as they had the east, there would be no hope for Coincoin or our children, no hope of their ever achieving the kind of lives they deserve.

So, Pierre had forced his leave-taking to be a light one, telling Coincoin that the capture of Mobile would be even more of a lark than their overrun of Manchac, Baton Rouge, and Natchez. This time, the spirited Pavie was left behind. Newly wed and still ill with recurring bouts of dysentery, he had been excused from active duty. The rigors that lay ahead, they all feared, would be more than many healthy men would endure.

On the fifth day of February 1780, Gálvez's force of two thousand men sailed out the mouth of the Mississippi. Regulars, militia, and glory-hungry volunteers. Black slaves eager for promised freedom. Swarthy freed men—cáfe-au-lait, tan, red, and ebony—anxious to prove their patriotism and their acceptance of the duties of citizenship. Creole French, proud and independent. And Spanish peninsulares, low of birth more often than not but still lording it haughtily, simply because they had been born on the Spanish peninsula itself rather than in the colony. Then into their midst there strode twenty-six raucous American auxiliaries, lending their flint to the double-edged sword the Spaniards were playing with in this international struggle for both power and freedom.

Forty-two leagues across the Gulf, due northeast, lay the heart of the British serpent, Fort Charlotte of Mobile. For two days, the Spanish fleet sailed in that direction: eleven frigates, transports, and brigantines riding a wave of exultation and the crest of confidence. The battle would be fierce. Gálvez had promised that. But they were prepared. In the wake of the Baton Rouge expedition, the colonel had been made a brigadier-general and the Crown rewarded his Creoles with the reinforcements, ships, and money they needed to launch their offensive against Mobile.

Now, amid clear skies, their fleet seemed to rule the Gulf. But the jealous God of the Sea resented the intrusion upon his domain and so, on the third day, Poseidon reared his head, shook his scepter, and roared. Overnight the breeze became unseasonably steamy. Its pace quickened. Violent gusts of heat churned from some unseen tropical furnace. Beneath the fleet, the sea began to bulge and boil, as the sky blackened.

"Lower those sails!" Gálvez bellowed from the full-rigged upper deck of the frigate *Corpus Christi,* as seasick landlubbers lurched for the bobbing rails to steady their footing.

On the lower deck, young Lecomte doubled over the railing, his face as green as the mold that clung to the bilge of his vessel; but before he could spill the bile that churned up from his innards, a lurch of the sea threw him backward into Pierre's arms.

"It sure is a good thing I don't go to war in search of glory," Pierre growled, as the lad's terrified fingers dug into his forearm. "All the devil I seem to do is play nursemaid. Haven't you ever been on a boat, boy?"

"Non," Ambroise groaned. "Nowhere but Red River, and pirogues don't go this fast. Ohhh, I'm ruined for life, M'sieur. The men will never let me live down this. The first storm that comes up, I retch like a pregnant woman."

"Well, if it's any consolation, Lecomte, you have plenty of male company." Pierre raked his eyes across the lower deck and found the misery in Ambroise's face reflected in a hundred others. "Look at it this way, boy. This old sea right now is just another untamed stallion. I've seen you ride a dozen of those. Give him his head, hold on tight, and sooner or later he'll wear himself out just like all the others you've broken."

A mist began to fall around them, but the drops grew rapidly bigger until they plunked on the old deck like giant legumes blown from some roof where they had been spread out to dry. Suddenly the sky cracked open, and from its darkened caverns there poured a fiery torrent.

"Batten those hatches, men! That powder in our hold is worth more to us than gold right now!"

All around Pierre and the sick bundle he still cradled, blinded crewmen stumbled to obey the general's order, their feet sliding across rain-slicked planking as the frigate careened with the gales. For an hour, two hours, they rode the inky waters in the pitch-blackness of mid-afternoon, rocking to the chaotic rhythm of the sea and crashing claps of thunder. Lightning crackled and flashed around them, like the endless zinging of a muleteer's whip. Then a fearsome bolt ripped the darkness and fired the whole sky with its brilliance. Pierre stared in horror as it unveiled a wall of white froth, soaring skyward for forty feet, gliding with unbelievable grace and speed toward the hapless fleet.

"Aport! *Por nombre de Díos!*" Pierre heard the general roar into his horn. "Hard aport! If that murderous wave catches us broadside, we'll all spill into Poseidon's belly!"

Pierre slid into another soldier, as a sudden list attested the helmsman's quick response. The frigate tilted sickeningly and arced a sharp ninety degrees leeward. Above him, on the top deck, he could hear frantic crewmen fighting to keep the ship afloat. Their curses pierced the thick oak flooring that separated the two decks, and the unseen soldier whom Pierre had toppled roughly translated their Hispanic oaths into the King's English.

Again Poseidon threw a bolt skyward. For an eternal moment, the sea, the heavens, and the fleet itself was bathed in a wash of white-hot fire, and then the granite wall of foam crashed upon them. Pressure sucked Pierre's breath from his guts, and he sickened as the water's force whipped him belly-forward across an upright, iron-laden barrel. His hand hit the sheath of cypress that encircled the staves, and its edge ripped his flesh as though it were a blade of steel. Yet, that barrel and his broad, bent back parted the descending wall of sea and left a slice of air for him to breathe as the wave crescendoed past.

In an eon, it was over. The squall subsided. The darkness lifted. Weakly, Pierre gripped the barrel he had so lately embraced and then he laughed, a raw prayer of thanks that Coincoin's cooking had reinforced his belly with a nice layer of padding. Then the horror of the scene engulfed him. All around, stalwart men had turned green and purple as they tried futilely to breathe air into their water-laden lungs. Broken bodies lay heaped against the hull. Beside him, the American soldier he had toppled now writhed blindly, his eyeball dangling where a flailing hand had gouged it. *Had it been his?* Pierre refused to hear himself think that thought. From the caverns of the sea there arose the screams of men who had been washed off board, and above him the general bellowed new commands.

"Ambroise!" Pierre cried. "God almighty, son, where are you?"

An interminable moment passed without an answer, and Pierre felt—really felt—the ultimate cost of war. In the Baton Rouge campaign there had been no casualties, just that gut-scalding, bile-raising, but miraculously nonfatal dysentery. Surely he knew from the beginning that this campaign would be different. Gálvez had promised that, and he had left Natchitoches after this second call fearing for his own life.

Of course, whatever vengeance the Lord might reap from him would be deserved, old sinner that he was—but this boy was different, Pierre cursed in that brief moment. Ambroise's life still lay before him. He was foolhardy and fun-loving, but he had a heart that loved everybody and everyone adored him in return. Why, God, should he be taken, even before the battle had begun? Oh, Mother of God, Pierre pleaded, how can I go home and face that boy's mama?

Pierre buried his face into his hands, heedless of the blood that flowed from his own trifling wound. Jean Baptiste Lecomte had been one of his first friends in this colony, and one of his best. Ambroise was the only son he left. The only offspring to carry on the family name. The only male to help his mama support that houseful of girls she had borne. How could he go home when all this was over and tell her that he had let the sea wash her only son right out of his arms?

That was when he heard the chuckle, soft and weak but still a chuckle, rolling all the way from Ambroise's lean belly. "M'sieur, don't look so happy. You're not rid of me yet."

"Ambroise! Where are you, you fool kid?"

"Here, M'sieur." Frantically, Pierre followed the laugh and found him. There, on the back side of the barrels, was the young private, calmly straddling the largest of the cannons they had loaded aboard their frigate at the Balize. "I think, M'sieur, I've just broken in another horse."

Relief flushed him, but with the bluster of all men who shackle their emotions, Pierre's voice turned gruff. "Well, get the hell off there. Some man you're going to grow up to be, sitting on your ass while there's work to be done."

"Ah, but it's not an ass, M'sieur," Ambroise rejoined, patting the cold belly of the howitzer. "This is a fiery stallion, and I've much respect for worthy steeds."

"There are only two kinds of horses, boy—beasts of burden to help the poor man labor and toys for the rich to play with. You can't afford the luxury of a horse that can't do your work, and the kind of work that iron horse does is of no use to us right now." Pierre thrust a bucket into his young friend's hand. "Now get your butt off its mount, and let's bail water overboard before the whole deuced ship sinks."

"Yes, *sir!*" Ambroise snapped to attention, still mounted, his bucket pointed to ready; but his salute was lost in a cacophony of screams that rose from the transport beside them. Both men turned starboard, just as that vessel gave another shudder; and they froze, knowing what was about to happen while utterly powerless to do anything about it.

The pitiless gale had driven the transport backward, and then sideways, into the port of the frigate that sailed behind it. The far ship was almost buried in the sea, the tips of its bow and stern rearing above the water like twin peaks above a low, drifting cloud. In front of them, the transport heaved once more, an empty, splintered, cavernous tunnel where its stern once had been. Another violent belch and it dived backward into the same bottomless sea that now swallowed the hapless frigate.

Crewmen and soldiers tumbled into the turgid water, clutching at whatever debris floated past, cursing and wailing for ropes to be thrown. Then at a distance, they saw the other menace for which the Gulf was famed. Long, slender, and silvery grey, moving swiftly through the choppy waves toward floating pools of blood: the incredibly beautiful, wickedly ugly, serpents of the sea.

"My God, M'sieur! What is that?"

"Sharks," Pierre breathed, almost inaudibly, as much to himself as in answer to his young friend's awestruck question. "Sharks."

Screaming men were yanked then from the waves and hauled aboard with a fury Pierre never had seen before. Great lines of men on every ship that still floated, battered and bruised already by the stony wall of the sea that had collapsed upon the fleet, heaved on the ropes they had thrown to their *compadres.* Flailing men dangled in the air, bounced brutally against the hulls, and were dragged, scraping and screaming, over the railings. Again the ropes descended into the waters, but the gaping jaws already had reached the eddies that circled where the two ill-fated ships had been.

It was then that blackness, mercifully and mercilessly, closed again upon the scene, shielding from their eyes the horror that followed. Cool, chilled air spiraled into humid heat, whirling splintered debris and helpless men against the hulls, the masts, the goffs and booms of the ships that had survived.

The placid eye of the hurricane had passed, and now the murderous force of its backwinds caught the crippled fleet and pushed it inland. Thirty-five, sixty, ninety knots an hour, they slid over the pitch-black surface of the Gulf, reeling drunkenly under a starless sky as gut-sick men lay on the sodden flooring of each deck, hugging each other for both physical and moral support, swearing, praying, believing that none would live to see the morning.

At some point in the late hours of their dark infinity, the sea calmed, the winds spent themselves, the torrents slackened and then fizzled to a steady, soul-soothing mist, and the weary survivors slept. Within hours—or was it only minutes?—the first faint pink glimmers of a new day washed over them. Amid its promise restless men, soul-battered and bone-crushed, stirred from their fitful sleep.

Pierre awoke to find himself propped against the hull. A fine specimen of the New Orleans First Black Militia, now bedraggled and beaten, lay nestled in his lap; and against his broad shoulder there leaned the soft, angelic face of Ambroise. As his salt-swollen eyes batted painfully in an effort to focus, they fell upon the eternal symbol of the Louisiana colony, a bold pelican perched on their lower foredeck.

"Land, ho!" an unseen voice bellowed in the unmistakable accent of a New York Yonker, and the indomitable Gálvez, weary yet wide awake in spite of his sleepless night, corrected the cry in words his own men could better understand. *"Una isla, mis hombres, sola una isla."*

The island lay less than five hundred yards away, as whiplashed as the Spanish flotilla and the men it carried. In disbelief, Pierre stared at a majestic palm that towered above its fallen brothers. Yet even this citadel of nature had not survived unscathed. Its trunk was pieced by a plank of solid oak that still protruded, fore and aft, as the tree stood ethereally rooted to the ground like a stalwart, disbelieving man who had been totally run through by a rapier.

Mooring his fleet beside the isle, Gálvez assessed his losses, and with the skill that had made him both a governor and a general, he rallied his forces. They had lost two of their eleven ships, together with the supplies each carried. What remained would have to be rationed somewhat, but not severely since the number of their men had been reduced as well.

By mid-morning, the wounded had been crudely cared for, and Gálvez turned his attention to their most pressing problem. Amid the endless hours of the night, thanks to the fierce, immeasurable winds that had shoved them backwards, sideways, and forward at frightening speed, the general and his navigators had lost their bearing. Did they lie now off the coast of Cuba, behind the horn of Tejas or, God willing, at some point in between?

By mid-afternoon, Gálvez had his answer. As limping men, soldiers and sailors alike, mopped the decks, repaired the last of the masts, and ran up the sails anew, a ship appeared on the southeast horizon. For minutes, it seemed to hover questioningly, then slowly its bow turned aport and it began to inch away, but not before Gálvez had raked its length with his spyglass. Across its side he read the legend *Brownhall,* and above it he had seen the superimposed, tricolored crosses that had long fired Spanish generals to action.

"The Union Jack!" he bellowed. "Abeam, men! Right and full sail!"

His fleet sprang to life. For an interminable moment, the *Brownhall* faded into the horizon as it sped, forewarned, away from its pursuers, but then the Spanish fleet gained its wind and the ponderous British victualer of sixteen guns was no match for the lighter Spanish vessels.

Gálvez's flotilla closed upon the prize, nine eagles fanning out to encircle, then descend upon, its prey. The *Brownhall* opened fire from all sides, and the

Corpus Christi shivered as a cannon ball tunnelled through its upper gunwale and another ripped its mizzin-royal. Before any serious damage could be done to his own fleet, Gálvez ordered the fire returned, and the outcome was predestined. The lone *Brownhall,* its course originally chartered for Mobile, its hold heavily laden with presents the British hoped would buy the aid of Southern Indians, could neither outrun nor outfight its enemy.

Gloating over their first confrontation, their course now corrected by the captured British mariners, Gálvez's fleet turned northward toward Mobile Bay. Yet the British had some small revenge. The bearings that King George's navigators gave Gálvez took the fleet off its intended course. Even though the Spanish commander had anticipated deception, and had adjusted his calculations accordingly, it was not Mobile but the Bayo de Perdido—Lost Bay—at which his fleet landed. He had overshot his mark.

With no outward sign of the fear that now gripped him, Gálvez reassessed his situation. Fort Charlotte of Mobile lay to the west of him, at least fifty miles overland and more than twice that distance by water route around the Punta de la Mobila. To the east, a quarter of that distance away, lay Fort George of Pensacola. The Spanish war eagle was, in truth, a crippled pigeon, trapped within the coil of the serpent, not knowing the direction from which the fangs would strike.

The prudent course, the only course his advisors would have recommended had he consulted them, would be to turn his fleet out of the bay and retreat to New Orleans. But Bernardo de Gálvez had never stood accused of being a prudent man. It was not prudence that had earned him the rank of captain at the age of seventeen, in recognition of his valor in the Portuguese Campaign of '62. It was not prudence that had won for him the Baton Rouge campaign and earned him the generalship he now held.

If any attack were still to be made on Fort Charlotte, Gálvez knew, it had to be immediate. The heart of the serpent had to be pierced before the Indians or British spies reported their presence to either fort. On the one hand, his mangled force, no longer wanting for supplies but seriously short of ammunition, was in no shape for battle. On the other hand, somewhere in the Gulf that stretched between them and Havana, there should be another fleet sailing toward Mobile, manned by the fearless officer who had fought beside Gálvez in that Portuguese Campaign, José de Ezpeleta. With reinforcements to augment his losses, Gálvez gambled, victory still was possible.

He gave the order. Within an hour, they abandoned Perdido and charted a course westward. By the next morning they skirted the Punta, then sailed boldly into Mobile Bay itself—past Massacre Island, past Fish River, past Dog River, and up to Choctaw Point. There, Gálvez's fleet weighed anchor in the broad light of day, within sight of Fort Charlotte itself.

Frightened Tories fled their homes, seeking refuge within Charlotte's walls. Winter rains resumed, fierce and unrelenting, as Gálvez's men went into action. Sodden and chilled, Pierre worked feverishly beside two thousand other troops, unloading the last supplies from their moored ships. Under cover of the night, they erected barriers both west and north of the British town, and then dusk fell again on their completed earthwork. The moon failed to rise, or at least to pierce the dense cover of nocturnal fog, and Gálvez gave the final order that thrilled the young Lecomte but corroded Metoyer's guts.

An ensemble of three- and four-pound cannon boomed in unison. Fire exploded through the night, hissing, seething, soaring balls of fire that the British promptly returned. Everything that lay along the murderous path of their crossfire was leveled—homes, stables, and storehouses; even the church. The cannonade went on relentlessly, with every boom exploding Pierre's lungs as he and other infantrymen lay in the dubious safety of their trenches. Days rolled by in numbing procession. Yet, miraculously, no stray cannonball felled any of Gálvez's troops. God truly was on their side.

On the first of March, the Spanish general pushed further his test of British mettle, dispatching a memorandum, couched in diplomacy and phrased in the French that Britain's Colonel Elias Durnford was said to understand. Fort Charlotte should surrender to the Spanish siege. By dark, Charlotte's commander returned his reply: The lady would not give up her honor. For the first time in the course of his campaign, the imperturbable Gálvez cursed when he read Durnford's reply:

> I have the honor to acknowledge the receipt of your Excellency's summons to surrender immediately to your Superior forces. The differences of numbers, I am convinced, are greatly in your favor, Sir, but my strength is much beyond your Excellency's conception. Were I to give up this Fort, on your demand, I should be regarded as a traitor to my king and country. My love for both and my own

> honor direct my heart to refuse surrendering this Fort until I am
> under conviction that resistance is in vain.

The cannonade resumed its furor as each enemy held off the other. With each day that passed, Gálvez grew more fearful that Durnford's courage sprang from a certainty that reinforcements were on their way from Pensacola. His hunch was right. On the fifth of March, Fort George's colonel, John Campbell, dispatched his Sixtieth Regiment, then his famed German Waldecks; and in their wake he followed with his best Pennsylvania regulars and artillery. Theirs would be a march of seventy-two miles, overland through uninhabited, inhospitable swampland, but Campbell had every expectation that his 552 men would arrive in time.

By the ninth of March, Gálvez's spies still had reported no British advance upon their rear. Then, as the general's tension mounted to bottled fury, there sailed into the bay four transports flying the tricolor of Carlos III. José de Ezpeleta had arrived with his 567 Cubans. Working furiously through the night, the fresh forces unloaded the Cuban transports and erected new emplacements.

At dawn on the tenth, Colonel Campbell and his British arrived at the mouth of the Tensas River and prepared to cross the bay into Mobile, but the cautious British and their methodical German cousins lost too much time in the mundane work of felling trees and building rafts, while the Spanish cannons continued to sing in unison and kept the sky afire.

On the fourteenth of March 1780, as Campbell's forces marched their last miles upon the rear of Mobile, the Union Jack inched its way downward inside the smoking remains of Fort Charlotte, and the white banner of truce was slowly raised.

"Gawdamighty!" a lanky Carolinian exclaimed profanely beside Pierre, as the British troops, all 278 of them, filed slowly through their breached walls. "For this, we brought fifteen ships and twenty-five hundred men! Hell's bells, man! When you Romans throw a party you do things on a right grand scale!"

The compliment was wasted. French and Spanish, even Latin and a fair amount of Greek, Pierre had studied all of those at L'École de St. Sauveur, but Yanqui English was not among his repertoire of languages. Yet, curiously, the same reckoning, in more melodious French, flashed through Pierre's thoughts.

The battle that had been feared so greatly, prepared for so carefully, might have been the lark he had told Coincoin it would be. Fort Charlotte had been taken without any direct combat, and it could have been done with a quarter of their number. Aside from the cold and sodden trenches, aside from the deafening roar that still reverberated in his ear drums, aside from the savage, homicidal hurricane—which really had been an act of nature, a thing apart from the war itself—aside from the damned *nuisance* of it all, this campaign had gone quite well. All that remained was Pensacola itself; and considering the ease with which Mobile had been taken and the fright with which Campbell and his Pensacolians had fled, Gálvez probably would not need the help of his country militia in lopping off the head of the British snake.

Still, that thought did little to assuage the worry that now ate at Pierre's gut. There on board the *Corpus Christi,* in the brief, eternal moment that the murderous wave had engulfed them, in the fear that had gripped him when he thought the sea had snatched up young Lecomte, he had seen the infinitesimal line that lay between life and death. Not just in battle but at any moment, in any place, life could pass into nothingness without warning. A hurricane, a tornado, a bolt of lightning, or the bite of a snake. Any of these could be that line.

For almost forty years, Claude Thomas Pierre Metoyer had stared life in the face, scoffing at its restraints, forcing his way toward whatever goal enticed him, charting out his own course with total disregard for the lanes of passage society laid down for different men. But in the end, no man ever has absolute control of his own life, and this realization wounded Pierre gravely, although he had survived the war unscathed.

At any time, under any circumstance, the thread of life by which that fearsome, omnipotent God dangled all men could snap. What would happen then? The fiery pits of hell for his own soul, surely. But worse, what of the woman he would leave behind? She would be free but penniless. Since he had refused to marry her, since he still could not or would not marry her, she would have no legal rights to the estate she had helped him build.

What of that estate? His family in France had no use for it, although by law it would be their inheritance. They would only sell it—the land, his shop, his houses, his slaves, *his children.* All would go on the auction block and the money shipped abroad to the family who, even though he loved them dearly, had not lifted one finger to earn a single *sou* of it.

He had run out of choices, and he knew it.

◌ 17 ◌

La Ville, three weeks later

It has not changed, not really, Pierre reflected as he and Ambroise turned left off Calle Conti onto the notorious Calle de Bourbon. A little Spanish grillwork here and there on the newer buildings, a few older landmarks blown away by one hurricane or another. The streets now have Spanish names instead of the French ones Étienne and I learned so well when we first came to this colony. Still, New Orleans is basically the same. Certainly the same as it was when we left here this winter. Yet it is different. Or is it me that's changed?

His gaze swept past the street loafers, unabashedly dishevelled and cheerfully oblivious of their own stench, past the little *négrillons* who hung on every corner, ready to dance and grin for any passerby looking prosperous enough to throw down a *centavo* or two, past the open tavern doors where tawdry wenches hung onto the arms of drunken soldiers, fresh from war and freshly paid.

Tawdry. That was the difference. The Vieux Carré might look the same, but he felt it differently. Everything about it. The *joie de vivre* that danced coquettishly in every giggle, that boomed from the raucous jokes, that sang in the never-ending cries of the street vendors with their crevettes fresh from the Gulf and their piping hot calas and their cigarillos of aromatic perique, that jutted from the proud stride of the loin-clothed Indians with their baskets and colorful blankets. Somehow, in the space of one season, it all had turned tawdry.

Two handsome quadroons slithered past, their smooth curls of ebony bound high and cascading from an artful arrangement of soft plumes that perfectly matched the colors of their silk frocks. Both smiled winsomely as they passed the pair of handsome soldiers, appreciatively assessing the rugged maturity of the one and the pretty innocence of the other. Predictably, Ambroise bowed and tipped his tricorn, his eyes sliding past their ripe smiles down to the tawny shoulders that rose above the décolletage of their gowns. Wordlessly, Pierre nudged him forward.

"Ah, M'sieur," Ambroise protested as the two *criollas* winked and continued on their way. "Did you ever see such lovely specimens of God's creation, with those dark limpid eyes, those lips of ruby, those figures that would make Venus herself jealous? Surely man was meant to bow down before such handiwork of God and pay his homage!"

"It wasn't the God of Creation you were thinking of paying homage to. It was the Goddess of Love," Pierre grunted.

"Well?" Ambroise replied with a shrug and a mischievous grin. "The God of Creation did make man and woman, no? He designed us quite well for *l'amour.* Who am I to scorn the pleasures He created for us, especially when they come packaged like that!"

"With those two, son, you'd be taking on more pleasure than you can handle."

"Ah, let me try, M'sieur, let me try!"

"No way, Ambroise. I promised your mother I'd watch after you, and that's exactly what I'm doing. If you want to tumble every wench at Natchitoches when we get back, that's between you and Padre Quintanilla, but…"

"Miséricorde!" Ambroise butted in woefully. "That's the problem! Where do I find such exquisite beauties at Natchitoches, such pearls of nature, such deliciously tempting daughters of Eve holding out their apples?" Ambroise drooled, as Pierre laughed.

"Of course, Coincoin's Fanchon would be a nice consolation," he continued blithely. "That satiny skin, those wickedly exotic eyes, that queenly stature…." Ambroise groaned in recollection. "Ah, I have suffered the agonies of the damned ever since my sister bought her from the De Sotos. But, *hélas!* that mahogany goddess is off-limits. If I ever bowed down before her font of Venus, my mama would skin me with the nearest rawhide."

"I suppose there's no point in my asking you whether Fanchon herself is amenable?"

"Look at me, M'sieur. Could any female behold this fair face, so gentle, so innocent, and fail to melt right into my arms?"

"I wouldn't be much of a judge of that, lad," Pierre laughed. "Angelic male countenances never did appeal to me."

"Hey, Metoyer! Lecomte! Haven't you foot soldiers had enough marching? It's time for celebrating!"

The call came from the doorway of Juan Ortiz's El Gato. It was not one of the taverns Pierre frequented on his business trips to *la ville,* and he had passed it by without noticing the friend who loitered in the doorway. He had learned early that Ortiz's tavern catered to a roisterous crowd, and he had shied away lest a loaded drink find its way into his stomach and a steel blade into his throat while some *ladron* made off with the gold he always carried to New Orleans to purchase his merchandise.

"Dupré! You tomcat!" Metoyer retorted as he slapped his fellow infantryman on the shoulders and eyed the baggage on his arm. "Now, what are you doing here wenching? I thought you had promised yourself to Ambroise's sister. Poor girl, languishing at home, praying her Rosary every day in hopes you'll hurry back to marry her. And here you are on Calle de Bourbon sampling sweet tarts."

"I'm not wed yet, *mon amigo*. I'm not wed yet! Hey, brother-in-law-to-be!" Dupré disengaged himself from a golden-haired nymph almost as tall as his own five feet and six inches, and wrapped his arm around Ambroise. "What say you to a celebration? My last one, I swear! Tomorrow, we all go back to Natchitoches, and the good padre will read my banns, and then I'll turn overnight into a church-going, God-fearing married man. Tonight, *hombres,* I want to get drunk!"

"Splendid, brother!" Ambroise retorted. "Of course I'm duty-bound to my little sister to keep an eye on you. I shouldn't let you get into any trouble—alone! Hey, Conchita!" He slapped a dark-haired barmaid on her thinly clad rump. "Bring the bridegroom a fresh mug of whatever he's drinking, and brandy for my friend and me."

"It's not Conchita," she pouted. *"Se llama Rosa!"*

"Sí, Rosa, sí. Just bring the drinks and I'll call you anything you want. *La flora! La bonita! Mi cara!"* The girl's oily face brightened and her grin exposed a gaping hole where two teeth once had been. Ambroise groaned, cursing his luck under his breath as he followed Pierre and Joseph to a darkened table.

Suddenly Pierre stopped short in front of him, so short that Ambroise all but collided with him. On the far side of the table to which Dupré was steering them, three strangers sat, arguing excitedly over a game of *troucs.* But Pierre's stare hinted that the men weren't strangers. Not all of them. Ambroise's eyes followed Pierre's gaze and centered upon the middle man. Tall, husky, mahogany hair, a cigar clamped in his square, youthful jaw. There was something familiar. Surely he'd never seen the man before, Ambroise told himself, but he sure looked like someone he ought to know.

"Franc!" Pierre exclaimed beside him. "You tadpole! You've grown into a full-fledged bullfrog."

The cigar dropped, and then the younger man's eyes lit in recognition.

"Pierre? Is that you underneath that grey *perruque?* No! Don't tell me that's your own hair! *Mon frère,* what has this colony done to you? You have more furrows in your mean-looking face than Papa ever had."

In a second Pierre had pushed behind the table and locked the stranger in a bear hug. "What the devil are you doing over here, boy?"

"Come to seek my fortune, Pierre. What else? Word's gotten back to La Rochelle that there's money to be made in Louisiana. Certain merchants, I hear, have done quite well, especially out on the frontier. Don't worry, though. I won't give you any competition. Big cities are more to my taste. I'll take New Orleans, and you can have your Natchitoches."

"As far as I'm concerned, you can have all of *la ville* you want. This city's too wild for an old man like me, brother. Speaking of wild, meet my young friends. Two of the finest untamed bucks the frontier ever produced, Ambroise Lecomte and Joseph Dupré. Boys, meet my brother, Franc."

The party fizzled. The barmaids wiggled everything their frocks already revealed and hinted at more to come, but Pierre and Franc never noticed. The two young brothers-in-law-to-be were restless for action, but Pierre and Franc were too busy talking to bother drinking. The younger Metoyer had swept his older brother, in spirit if not in heart, back to France, back to the Bay of Biscay, and back to the parish of Notre-Dame. New Orleans, El Gato, and the party were forgotten.

Eventually, Franc noticed. "Hey, Pierre! We've forgotten our manners. These friends of yours are not interested in who Tante Euphrosine married last year. Let's either join their party or leave them to their sport. I have a room upstairs. Do you want to go up and talk or stay here and get drunk?"

"Let's go talk." Pierre flipped a couple of *reales* on the table in payment of the drinks he had forgotten. "I'm too old to keep up with these wild ones. I guess it wouldn't do any good to tell you two to behave yourselves. Eh, Ambroise."

"No good at all, M'sieur. None whatsoever." Young Lecomte grinned. "You two old men go enjoy yourselves upstairs, and I promise you we'll do the same."

"I'm sure you will," Pierre retorted, and wrapped his arm around his younger brother. "Lead on, *mon frère.*"

Alone in the bare quarters Franc had taken, the brothers talked. Childhood memories revived tears and laughter. Fifteen years of separation were relived, to the extent each felt comfortable in sharing the personal directions his own life had taken. Still, as the night passed into dawn and Calle de Bourbon began to fall asleep outside, Pierre had the distinct feeling they had been talking around each other, while the real things that had to be said remained unspoken.

"Okay, boy," Pierre said suddenly, wearily. A long pause hung in the air around them. "Out with it!"

"With what, Pierre?" Franc countered innocently.

"With whatever you came over here for. You've already told me that you're helping brother Jorge run Papa's old shop and that it is comfortably supporting both your and Jorge's families, as well as Mère Susanne. Obviously, you're not here to settle as you first intimated. So, what's your reason?"

"It's true, Pierre," Franc protested. "I really am thinking of opening an outlet here in the colony. Jorge can supply first-rate goods, and I can add the usual colonial markup. We should do quite well."

"Probably. But I have a gut feeling there's more to it."

"Well, of course, the family's anxious to hear some news of you, too. You never were much at writing, you know."

"I've written enough to let you know I'm still alive and doing well. What else is there to be said?" Pierre countered.

"Plenty—about you. You never mention yourself, Pierre, only your work. You've been over here fifteen years, and you've not once mentioned any woman, much less a wife or family. You haven't married have you, Pierre?" A sharp edge crept into Franc's voice.

"If I had, my family would know of it."

"No plans? The frontier's a lonely place for a man, so far from those who care about him."

"I think your care is getting too damned personal!"

Franc laughed. "Simmer down, Pierre. You see, Jorge is a bit concerned about all this property you are amassing here. If you have no wife or *children*..." The undercurrent in Franc's voice was still there, despite his attempt to hide it behind a smile. "...then what's to happen to your fortune if you should succumb to some tropical disease? You know Jorge. He would hate to see some greedy colonial official get his hands on it."

"You may assure Jorge there is slim possibility of that. Our commandant is honest enough. If anything happens to me, you and Jorge and the others will be notified to claim everything the law gives you. And if I don't marry, you can rest assured that colonial law would give you everything." Pierre paused for deliberate emphasis, smiling blandly. "Unless, of course, I leave a will directing that a portion of it be disposed of otherwise, in which case colonial law would still insist that my dear siblings get two-thirds of my estate. Assuredly, *mon frère,* Jorge need have no worry."

Franc returned the smile. "Pierre, you are free to dispose of all of it in any way you wish, as far as I'm concerned. What you do with what you've worked for is no business of mine."

Somehow, Pierre found that hard to believe.

"Of course, Jorge always was a trifle greedy, but he doesn't need the fruits of your labor. Seriously, Pierre, it really is you and your welfare that concern us."

"Oh?"

Franc continued smoothly. "It would be far better, Pierre, if you had a wife and children to carry on, to build your business into a family empire, to perpetuate the proud old name of Metoyer. *Zut!* Pierre. It just is not natural for a man not to want children, not to leave a part of himself behind!"

"I am well aware of that." Pierre's eyes grew cold. Of all the children his stepmother had borne his father, Franc always had been his favorite, but there were limits to affection. Intrusions upon his personal life were affronts he had never tolerated.

"Get to the point, boy. You've come to say something, and you still haven't said it."

Discomfiture was plain on Franc's face, even by the thin light of early dawn. "All right, Pierre. I had hoped it would not be necessary for me to have to say it. The whole family voted, and I was elected to the chore. It's what I came for, but I still wasn't prepared when you walked up to me tonight like the ghost of Lucifer himself."

"On with it, Franc."

For a long moment, the younger brother stalled. Pensively, he pulled a slim case from his ruffled blouse and carefully removed one cigar.

"Smoke?"

"No, thanks," Pierre grunted impatiently.

"You're not making this any easier for me, Pierre."

"Why should I?"

"Perhaps you're right. We're meddling in your life, Pierre; but we have a right to. We're family. We always have been. Not just *half*-family. The fact that we have different mothers never has made any difference."

"Nor will it ever," Pierre replied gruffly, his eyes watering in spite of his anger and frustration. "Your mother raised me when my own died. Mère Susanne has been the only mother I remember, and I love her dearly. So much, in fact, that I…" His voice cut off abruptly.

"That you what?"

"Nothing. Nothing important." He had been about to say *that I named my first daughter for her.* But he could not very well say that.

"I have the feeling, Pierre, you were about to bring up the very matter we need to discuss." Franc's eyes were cool, appraising, but Pierre stared them down without flinching.

"If you won't open up to me, Pierre, I'll have to pry it out."

"As you wish."

"Very well, then. Two weeks before I left, we had a visit from Oncle Jorge. He has retired now from active ministry, you know."

"I had not heard."

"Yes. Of course his visit had a superficial purpose," Franc laughed nervously. "One as thinly veiled as my own. It was not long before our uncle felt moved to share with us a letter he had received."

"A letter?"

"Yes, one from a fellow servant of Christ. A Spanish Capuchin here in the colony."

That figures! Pierre swore to himself, the fury of past combats raging anew. *The man has not been able to whip me into line behind him any other way, so he tries this.* But his voice was flat as he muttered aloud, "Padre Luis de Quintanilla, The Supreme."

"Yes."

"Even if I merited sainthood, that man would be my devil's advocate." The bitterness in Pierre's voice chilled even him.

"On the contrary, he seems to have your best interest at heart."

"And so?"

"Eh?"

"What did you all decide? You and Jorge and Oncle Jorge and the rest? You held your family council. What's the verdict? Am I disowned? No, I doubt that.

You can't afford to disown me. I've already received my inheritance. The only inheritance at stake now is the one I leave to all of you."

"You're not being fair, Pierre. I have no interest in your deuced money. It's you we care about. Mama is crushed, you know. She blames herself for not preparing your innocent soul for the temptations of life."

"Don't say that, Franc," Pierre muttered hoarsely.

"I have to say it, Pierre, because it's what she said." Franc's voice turned soft, as he gripped Pierre's hand across the table and pleaded.

"Pierre, if you care about Mama, about us, about the family's pride—about your own pride—for God's sake straighten out your life! We want to see our family live on here in the colonies, where you have taken it, if that is your wish. But it is only fair sons of France we can claim, proud offspring of Charlemagne, not dusky hybrids that belong to no race and no people."

"You've no right to say that," Pierre protested thickly. "You know nothing about life here."

"I know enough, brother, and we do have a right. We're your family. What we do reflects upon you, and what you do reflects upon us."

"But things are different here!"

"Christianity and decency are the same everywhere, Pierre. You've made a mockery out of everything Oncle Jorge has stood for in his life, out of the virtue of your own mother and mine, out of the honor that always guided everything our father did."

"And you're making a mockery out of the affection I always had for you!" Pierre shot back savagely. Shoving away from the table, he stormed to the door. "Never have I tolerated any man telling me how to live my life. If you weren't my brother…."

Pierre did not finish. He could not. He slammed the door behind him as he stalked out, shaking the flimsy walls of El Gato as if to shuck off everything in life that ever had tried to box him in. Oblivious to the din, the stench, and the smoke that exuded from the barroom, he stormed into the dawn, laughing uglily at himself. Now he knew how a British murderer felt on his day of retribution, already drawn and now being quartered as a beast of burden was tied to each limb and driven in opposing directions to tear him asunder.

Race. Frustration. Remorse. Love. Those were the four beasts that ripped him, heart from soul from guts from loins, as he stormed through the early morning streets of the Vieux Carré. Muttering savagely, he sidestepped a tavern fracas that had spilled into Calle Bienville and clenched his fists as he fought down the desire to join the senseless, primitive, hate-cleansing brawl.

Calle Dauphine. Calle San Carlos. The streets blurred one into the other until he found himself at the very edge of the Carré. The fog was lifting and childish laughter tinkled through the early morning air.

Without thinking, Pierre turned toward the sound. Fresh pain gripped him as he beheld a pair of tawny children, as beautiful as his own Susanne and T'Pierre, running hand-in-hand to meet the vendor with his basket of hot calas at the corner of Rampart Norte and Iberville.

What had Franc called such children? Hybrids that belong to no race, no people? He was right, but he was wrong. They are a race apart, a people all their own. Strong, beautiful, and intelligent. Sensitive and proud. But most of all a vital link to bridge the chasm of suspicion and prejudice that stood between the white man and the black.

Yet those angelic children, his own children, were unmistakably the symbols of shame that Franc saw in them, symbols of the unholy, unbridled lusts that led man and woman both to defy the laws of church and state.

Morbleu! Pierre cursed the point for the thousandth time. Such symbols are meaningless here in the colonies! We have to make our own rules to survive, and barriers of race are as senseless as barriers of class. Still, the laws of Europe do prevail, Pierre reminded himself bitterly, and we are forced to live outside those laws. I should have made Franc see that. I should at least have tried, even though I know damned well he and Jorge and Mère Susanne are too steeped in the rules that govern their little world to accept the realities that exist out here.

Maybe if I took the children to La Rochelle, gave the family a chance to know them? With a cynical laugh, Pierre discarded that idea almost as soon as it came to him. Never would they be able to look into Augustin's eyes and see the intelligence that burned there. No, their stare would never make it past the lad's burry head before they lowered their eyes in shame.

They were Pierre's children, his flesh, the sparks that fired his paternal pride, but never would his family accept them and never would they forgive him if he flaunted them in their faces. In a sense, too, they were right. For centuries their family had stood for honesty and integrity; no matter how humble the origin of their name, his family had made it proud. Mère Susanne had raised him in virtue, just as Franc said. He had donned an acolyte's robe almost as soon as he graduated into pants, and he had even felt holy standing there at the altar, beside the priests, holding *La Sainte Bible,* lighting the tapers that symbolized the flames of faith. It had been a long time, a *long* time, since he had felt holy.

It was then that he gave in to the inevitable and turned his steps back toward the heart of the Vieux Carré. Resignation steeled him as he veered again onto Calle San Carlos, but still he faltered, momentarily, as he faced the door he sought. Slowly, deliberately, he read the sign he had seen a hundred times before: *Leonardo Mazange, Notario Publico.* Resolutely, he pushed open the door and stepped inside.

It was early. Pierre had lost all track of time, but the sight of the notary, still dressed informally in his shirt sleeves and blowing the steam from a cup of *café noir,* told him that Mazange had not yet expected his first *cliente.*

"Perdón, Señor," Pierre began apologetically for his intrusion. Still, he was glad he had arrived before the notary's office filled with the usual nosy assortment of townspeople.

"Esta bien, Señor. Como está? What can I do for you?"

"I need to make a will, Señor."

"Sí. Life is uncertain, *verdad?* We should all be prepared."

The notary settled at his desk and extracted an ivory sheet of parchment from his bottom drawer. Then, casually, he turned and reappraised his *cliente.* His eyes raked Metoyer from his crumpled tricorn hat to his dirty boots, but he did not miss the aristocratic bearing, the gold rings, the tooled Moroccan leather of those boots that belied the militiaman's uniform. Quietly, he withdrew several more sheaves, refilled his inkwell, and settled down to what would, undoubtedly, be a lengthy document.

"You may begin, Señor."

For an interminable moment, Metoyer made no reply. Then, slowly, he began to dictate the testament that would forever guarantee his children and their mother a life of freedom and a share of his estate, as well as the solemn oath by which he made the expected public denial that would permit the family of his birth to keep their pride while he would live forever with the guilt of betraying his own progeny.

IN THE NAME OF GOD ALMIGHTY, I, Claude Thomas Pierre Metoyer, being of sound mind and believing as I firmly believe in the mystery of the Holy Trinity and all other articles that our Holy Mother, the Catholic and Apostolic Church does teach. Fearing death, which is natural to all creatures, I do hereby make my will and pray that the solemn Queen of Heaven, Mother of God, will intercede for me with her precious son to pardon the gravity of my sins and place my soul on the road to salvation.

FIRST. I commend my soul to the same God and Master who gave it to me. I bequeath my body to the earth from which it was formed, requesting that I be shrouded in the most humble manner possible and that three masses be said for the repose of my soul.

SECOND. I declare that I am a bachelor—and therefore have no children.

Pierre's voice betrayed none of the pain that almost choked him as he went on resolutely:

THIRD. I order that the private paper I made in presence of the witnesses Joseph Pavie and Jean Baptiste Trichel in the year 1778, by which I declared free the *negra* named Marie Thérèse (called Coincoin), should have its entire and due effect as if it had been drawn before the notary public, and I beg my executors not to obstruct her freedom in any way.

FOURTH. I order that after my death has been verified, the mulattoes Nicolas Augustin, Marie Susanne, Louis, Pierre, Dominique, and Eulalie, all children of the *negra* Marie Thérèse shall be freed, as they were sold to me by Doña María des Nieves de St. Denis on that condition.

FIFTH. I bequeath to the above-said mulattoes, together with their mother, their brothers Antoine Joseph and Pierre Toussaint who were born free, in order to help them support the burdens of liberty, five *arpents* frontage land on both sides of the Red River, located at the

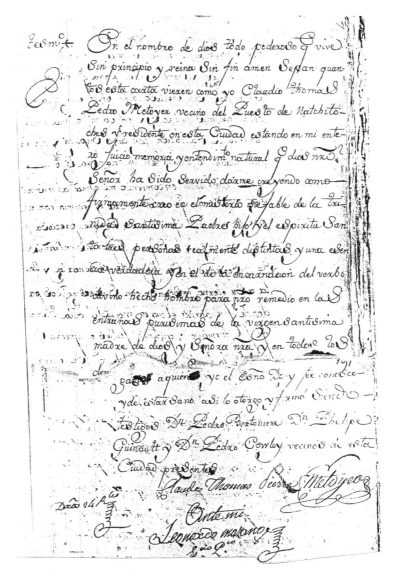

New Orleans Will of Claude Thomas Pierre Metoyer

The above illustration depicts the opening and closing of Metoyer's seven-page will, which is summarized in the facing narrative. He left the document with the New Orleans notary Leonardo Mazange, so that its provisions for Coincoin and their offspring would not become fodder for post gossip at Natchitoches. Because he made two subsequent wills, the last of which was probated at his death in 1816, the New Orleans document remained buried, unknown, in Mazange's records until research on this story began in 1972.

207

post of Natchitoches. This land is to be taken from the twenty that have been give me by the government of this province.

SIXTH. I command that after all my debts are satisfied, any goods that remain shall be liquidated and divided as follows: two-thirds part to my closest relatives, as the law decrees, and the other third part to the eight mulattoes under the express condition that their mother is to have the enjoyment and use of it for the rest of her life.

SEVENTH. I appoint as my executors my friends Étienne Pavie, Jean Baptiste Prudhomme, and Paul Marcollay, knowing that they will carry out the trust I hereby place in them.

MAY all inherit with God's blessing, and with understanding, for such is my wish.

{signed} Claude Thomas Pierre Metoyer

PART THREE

1788–1816

The Planting

Manumision of Marie Louise
by Marie Thérèse Coinquin

"29 January 1795, before me, Don Louis Charles DeBlanc, …Civil and Military Commander of the Post of Natchitoches… there has appeared Marie Thérèse Coinquin, free Negress, resident of this Post, who declares and confesses having by these presents, of her pure and entire wish, given liberty to Marie Louise, her slave and her daughter, whom she purchased of the Sieur Pierre Dolet…"

Coincoin's 1795 manumission of this daughter reflects the long years that it took her to pay off the debt she contracted in 1786, when Pierre Dolet first agreed to the purchase and manumission of Marie Louise.

210

∽ 1 ∾
13 October 1788

The yowls of the bear pierced the early morning fog, awakening Coincoin inside the cabin a few hundred yards away. She cringed. She always cringed. After five years, she had not accustomed herself to that brutal sound of pain.

Bracing herself, she rose in the predawn haze and slipped from the big four-poster she shared with Marie Louise—the same majestic, intricately carved bed that had filled François and Fanny's cabin as incongruously as it now filled her own. Gently, so as not to wake the grown, crippled daughter who would be of no use to her in the task ahead, she propped her back against the bedpost to pull on her cotton hose, worn and yellowed with age but skillfully darned by Marie Louise's nimble fingers. From the peg beside her, she pulled a heavy skirt and blouse and hastily donned them, her tension yielding briefly to the soft comfort of the homespun, tightly woven cottonnade. With her head wrapped in a linsey scarf and a burlap shawl around her thin shoulders, she unbolted the door and braced herself against the early morning chill and the job that lay ahead.

The frenzy of her quarry showed no sign of easing as Coincoin slipped quietly across the clearing. The moon had waned, but the faint rays of the early morning sun had not yet driven away the fog. Even without seeing the animal's hulk, she knew it was massive from the force of its bellows, and each of them cut into her as savagely as the cat o' nine had done all those years before. She could almost feel the bite of the long iron teeth on the trap she had set the night before.

Silently, Coincoin prayed that the brute's energy would soon spend itself enough that she could approach it without fear that, in one last spurt of fury, it might rip the chain that lashed its trap to the mammoth oak and lunge upon her. A rifle ball, she knew, would quickly end the creature's agony, but she also knew that her powder keg was almost empty and long winter months lay ahead before she would see any cash from this year's tobacco crop. No, powder could not be wasted on an animal already trapped.

Like a tigress stalking her prey, Coincoin prowled at the edge of the clearing and waited. The hours passed but the grey fog had barely thinned by the time the bellows faded into moans. Quickly, she closed upon her quarry, anxious to end its pain. One rapid thrust of her knife into the cleavage of its throat brought a sickening gurgle, and the eyes of the beast rolled into the final wrench of death.

Coincoin had been right. The bear was a behemoth. With a practiced hand, she slid the sharp blade between fleece and flesh, peeling skin from rippling sinews. This one's fur would make the winter robe Dominique badly needed. At fourteen, the boy was himself a bear of a man, and her godsend at times like this when the demands of life exceeded her strength. By noon, Dom should be back from the bluffs with the woman Coincoin was getting from the Lecomtes. By then, she would have the carcass waiting, cleanly stripped and gutted. With Joseph's help, Dom could haul it to the smokehouse.

Five hundred pounds minimum, Coincoin calculated. At least five jars of grease to be rendered for market, and enough cured meat to feed the family for three months. No, four, she corrected herself with a twinge. Now that Pierre had taken T'Pierre back with him to keep his ledgers, she did not have to fill her cookpot so full at each meal. With Susanne in town, too, and Augustin, Jean, and Louis at work on Pierre's place across the river, that left only one bottomless appetite to fill, Dom's. The rest of her flock were still children; and frail Marie Louise and her child, the good Lord knows, ate no more than sparrows.

Marie Louise. Coincoin smiled softly; and again, as they always did when she thought of that gentle daughter, her shoulders squared and she felt good. Really good. Reborn. Inspired. Of all she had done in her forty-six years, it was the down payment she had made toward her daughter's purchase that made her the proudest. Her own gift of freedom, when Pierre gave it to her, she took as her due. That was God's righting of past wrongs done her family. This tract of land, where she had helped to harvest their first crop, this too had been accepted from Pierre as payment for her decade and a half of service.

But her purchase of Marie from the Sieur Dolet was different, truly her first accomplishment in life. It was her proof that she valued the very meaning of freedom—her testimony, to a world that really didn't care, that she would forever use the privileges and opportunities of citizenship to restore her family to the respect and honor that was its right.

Marie Louise's purchase had been no small accomplishment, either. For six years after Marie de Soto moved off to Opelousas, taking the crippled Marie Louise and Thérèse with her, she had saved every centavo she could earn toward the day she might buy those daughters. Six long, bone-weary years in which she had asked Pierre for nothing—in truth, she would not have taken anything more from him even had he offered, not after he came home from war and painfully suggested that Coincoin stay in the cabin on the Point while he returned to their old dwelling at the post. It had been Susanne who Pierre had taken back to the post to tend his house, cook his meals, and keep his fine clothes washed and pressed. Coincoin had spent her days, then, as she had while he was away at war, overseeing their slaves and crops. But when dusk set in and she was left to face the lonely nights that stretched between Pierre's visits, she turned to her mother's art in search of solace, brewing medicines for the neighbors now settling around the Point, too far from the post to avail themselves of an officially licensed doctor. And she had hoarded every coin they paid her.

Night after night, Coincoin labored by the faint light of her bear oil lamps, her bones aching from weariness, her flesh aching from want, but that labor was her salvation. It consoled her when little Rosalie was born two months premature and died shortly after. It diverted her distraught mind when Pierre's visits grew fewer and farther between.

Still, the centavos that seemed to come in regularly did not rapidly grow into pesos. First, word came from Opelousas that Thérèse had almost died in childbirth, and Coincoin dipped into her hoard and went southward to nurse her daughter back to health. Then in her absence, young Eulalie succumbed to fever and Coincoin returned in time to bury another daughter, borrowing again from her savings to give her child the fine burial Pierre always called vainglorious.

Then her sister Mariotte had come pleading for help. The neighbor to whom de Soto had sold her had died, and the property division among all the Buard heirs had left his widow strapped for cash. Mariotte feared she would be sold again, and her little Adelaïde, as well—who knows where! She had already lost her son in the plague of '79, and her other daughter had been given to the Buard girl who married Étienne Pavie. If Coincoin would lend her the money to pay down on herself and Adelaïde, the Widow Buard would let her work off the debt. Of course Coincoin had helped her. Mariotte was the baby sister for

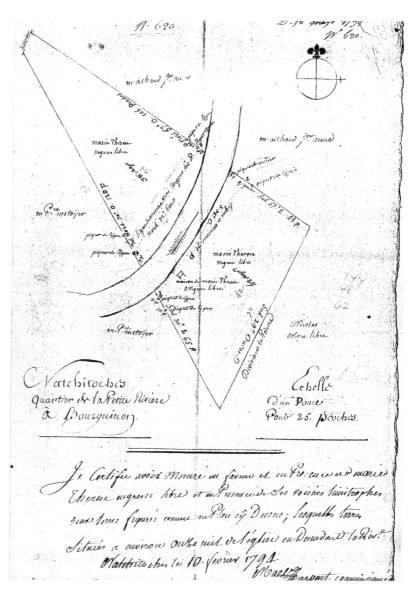

Spanish Survey
Homestead of Marie Therese, Negresse Libre

This survey of the Northern sliver of Pierre's plantation, given to Coincoin at their parting, marks the site of the rude "maison" where she would spend the rest of her days. The surveyor in 1794 found a square little cabin with a front gallery. With time she would enlarge it, but modestly.

214

whom she had named her own first born, her Marie Louise. How could she turn down her sister's plea?

Finally, in the spring of 1786, Coincoin had counted her small hoard and jubilantly declared she had enough to make the long-awaited down payment on her poor, maimed, firstborn daughter. But Marie Louise herself thwarted those hopes by producing a healthy baby that raised her value considerably in the eyes of her master.

Then came the night Pierre rode out from the post, down the new river road, sodden from both rain and rum. Sitting stiffly in the straight-backed chair that she had carved to match her father's bed, he had watched her croon to sleep their youngest, the little François who he had named for his brother Franc, and then he had announced, just as stiffly as he sat, that the time had come for each of them to live their own lives.

Coincoin had accepted the edict with a coolness that matched his own. She had known the day would come. Theirs had been as much a business relationship as his partnership with the Sieur Pavie had been, and that brief, wild, interlude between her manumission and the war that had turned her lover into a stranger had been nothing more than that—an interlude, a wayside pause, as each continued down the separate paths fate already had laid out for them.

The break had been inevitable. Coincoin told herself of that repeatedly throughout his perfunctory discussion of the financial details that would conclude their arrangement. Eventually, Pierre had finished and rose quickly, muttering that he was due back at the post, but in his eyes Coincoin had read the naked pain his voice had clothed. Impulsively, she rose on tiptoe to kiss him farewell and tell him that she understood; and that kiss had not been their last one. Her light, loving gesture had melted his resolve, and he crushed her in his arms for one long, final night.

A thousand times, between a thousand kisses, he told her then that there was no other way. He was too old to keep on fighting the pressures of his family or the weight of his own conscience. And a thousand times she reassured him that she understood, although she didn't. When Coincoin finally dozed in the last quiet hour before dawn, Pierre slipped her head gently from his shoulder, dressed in the dark, and mounted the horse that he had neglected to unsaddle during the passion of the night. Coincoin heard him go, but pride kept her in their bed—her bed now—while Pierre rode off, back to Natchitoches.

At last she rose and bathed her swollen eyes, but then she froze before the lavish mirror Pierre had jauntily hung on the plain mud walls of her cabin. Like Eve, as she tasted the bittersweet fruit of knowledge and saw her nakedness, Coincoin knew then why Pierre was gone. She stared at the face before her, noting cruelly how her almond eyes had sunk above the chiseled bones of her cheeks, how the crepe of age was already wrapping itself around her long neck, how the years had turned the black velvet of her close-cropped hair into tweed. Then she understood why Pierre no longer found the strength and passion to combat the forces that always had opposed them.

On the mantel, he had left behind the paper he had read to her the night before. She could not read it for herself, but she did not need to. For the rest of her life, Coincoin would hear the echo of his cold, flat voice as he read to her the terms of their parting.

The little corner of Pierre's land where Rachal had erected their crude cabin, that sixty-eight-arpent slice that Pierre's first slaves had cleared, was now hers. Once his hands had stripped the fields of his present crop, she could begin to plant her own. But, of course, she lacked the labor to farm it on the scale Pierre had done.

Two each of every specie of animals that he owned were also hers. Their children remained his property, her son Jean as well as the first five she had borne Pierre before Quintanilla's meddling had won her freedom. As before, Susanne would tend his home, Augustin, with Louis's help, would oversee the plantation Pierre had begun across the river, but the younger T'Pierre and Dominique could remain with her to help her make her start.

Finally, for the remainder of her life or until Pierre freed the last of their children, whichever occurred first, she would receive an annual stipend of 120 livres to help support her and their three freeborn infants. When the day came that he manumitted their older sons, they must then assume the responsibility of supporting their younger siblings and their mother if she needed it.

Beside that paper on the mantel lay the first of those promised payments, 120 livres. Within the hour, Coincoin dressed, fed the little ones and left them to the care of T'Pierre and Dom. Straddling Le Roi, she turned her big roan furiously into the north wind, driving him all the way past Natchitoches to Bayou Pierre and the house of the Sieur Dolet. The next day she returned with Marie Louise and the infant behind her, a conditional bill of sale tucked into the bosom of her dress.

In the months that followed, she had quailed more than once at the magnitude of the debt she owed. Coincoin had given Marie Louise's master the entire stipend Pierre left to support their children for the next twelve months, and she had recklessly promised the man several years' worth of her annuities to come. Marie Louise and her babe were as good as free, but Coincoin had to scratch, like chickens in an abandoned barnyard, to find food for her family and seed for her crops.

It had been a lean two years since then. A poverty-plagued, hand-to-mouth eternity it seemed. But she never told Pierre of their plight or of the use she had made of his money. Her children never once complained of the bear meat they had grown sick of, or begged her for a taste of ham or bacon from the hogs she now slaughtered for sale. As the river became more thickly settled, the demand for both her medicine and her nursing increased as well, and the lame Marie Louise had taken charge of the house and children. Ingeniously, Louis rigged another trap, this one to catch the turkeys that ranged the woods, and then Coincoin began to market that delicacy at the post.

Oui, freedom had been hard, Coincoin reminded herself now as she cut away the big bear's heart, his livers, his sweetbreads, and took them to the cistern and bailed out the water to wash them for lunch and supper. Yet the want and deprivation would soon be behind them. Pierre had sent her third annuity payment this past week, and Dolet had agreed to postpone the due date of her debt to him. She had planned to use Pierre's stipend to pay down on her Fanchon and bring that daughter home as well, but the Widow Lecomte's daughter had refused to sell her. Instead, she offered to rent to her—for the same sum—a stout, hardworking woman to labor at her side.

So Coincoin had accepted the counter offer and sent Dominique to the bluffs to fetch the woman, confident that her year's crop, even though the market was depressed, would finance that arrangement for years to come. With another hand to help, productivity should expand, and the next time she made that trip to Opelousas, she should have the silver to bring Thérèse home as well—that is, if the ailing Marie de Soto could be persuaded to part with Thérèse's care.

For a moment, just a moment, Coincoin's resolve had almost stumbled as she approached the precipice of becoming what all slaves feared and all free men respected: *the master.* No, she was not yet an *owner,* but she was no stranger to the path that linked slave and free and she knew that it ran in both directions.

Her noble mother had lived and died in poverty and was buried in ignominy, but Coincoin was now Marie Thérèse Coincoin, *Négresse Libre,* woman of property. Her children, God willing, would have the respect that freedom and property could bring.

As she heaved the first basketload of bear meat to her waist and headed toward the smokehouse, the immensity of her new life dumbstruck her, but then she laughed—exultantly, joyously, like the child her parents had known. Dropping the basket and thrusting her fists heavenward in triumph, she shouted to the winds.

"Oui! I did it, Papa! Mama's dream has happened! Your child is free! Your grandchildren shall be free! We will be rich! We will walk with our heads proud and poor folks, white folks, will bow to us! *Oui, Mama, the vanquished is now the victor.* That warrior-king who fathered you has been avenged the enslavement of his daughter... *You are avenged!"*

The last remnants of the October fog had lifted and the breeze had stilled. Through the quiet grey morn now there wafted a distant toll of bells from the parish church, and then the song flew from her heart and plummeted, like a wounded bird, and she, too, sank into the lingering dew.

She had almost forgotten. It was the thirteenth of October, and it was, truly, the day that one life ended for her and a new one began. As the peal of bells went on relentlessly, Coincoin buried her face in the wet, rotting leaves around her and she cried. For the rest of her life, she would not remember this as the day she entered the master class, but as the day that Pierre and Étienne Pavie's widow pledged the sacred vows of marriage. Tonight, a white Marie Thérèse would sleep in Pierre's arms.

∽ **2** ∽

September 1790

Ah! Ça ira! Ça ira! Ça ira!
Celui qui s'élevé, on l'abaissera
Celui que s'abaisse, on l'évera.

The little army of Creole peasants tramped down the dirt street that wound through the center of Poste St. Landry des Opelousas, armed with their flasks of *eau de vie* and fired to song by the latest tavern reports of the People's Revolution in France.

"*Liberté!*" their leader shouted between each verse, and his mock battalion of barefooted and moccasined youth echoed his battle cry. *Egalité! Fraternité! Vive la Révolution!*

Coincoin wound her way through the curious crowds that had gathered to watch the show. These street scenes are becoming shamefully common, she muttered. Grown boys parading like children in idle play. In those dirty, tattered rags they are too lazy to wash and mend! Led by indolent, unappreciative sons of planters who have worked all their lives to better their families' lot. If all those young sluggards would spend their time in honest work instead of revelry, they could earn the equality they cry for. And the Lord knows they have freedom already. Too much of it. Freedom not to work. Freedom to start trouble.

"*Vive la France!*" a familiar voice cried from the crowd. Coincoin drew up short and stared.

Père Delvaux! The rotund, black-garbed figure of the new Natchitoches curate was unmistakable. Augustin had warned her that Quintanilla's replacement was a revolutionary. The last time he and Louis had gone to Nacogdoches to deliver Pierre's goods, Père Delvaux had been there, too; and Augustin had unhappily recounted for her the riot their priest had incited there in Tejas. Never had Delvaux been so open in his home parish, but there had been rumors enough at Natchitoches that his frequent trips away from the post were more political than religious.

"*Vive la liberté!*" Delvaux shouted again as he pushed through the crowd to join the demonstrators. Following his lead, other spectators took up the hue and the march, as Coincoin continued to gape in disbelief, struggling to reconcile in her own mind the difference between the last two priests on their frontier. Padre de Quintanilla had preached total, unquestioning obedience to the laws of both God and the King. But this new priest, if rumor could be believed, would do away with kings altogether.

A man of the people. That's what he had called himself the first Sunday he said Mass at Natchitoches, and the people had cheered him. After years of chafing under Quintanilla's rein, the frontier flock fell in love with the big, jovial pastor who promised to take their hands and walk with them through life's trials instead of driving them as they had been driven. She had grown to love him, too, for the goodness he inspired and the brotherhood he preached. But revolution? She could not help it now. She felt betrayed.

The motley crowd began to surge past Coincoin, following in the wake of the impromptu demonstration, and she stared at the emptied streets again, this time in pure frustration. A whole row of shops confronted her, all with the same sagging, louvered shutters and open doors, and all temporarily abandoned. Each had a sign out front that identified its owner or his business, and she could read none of them. She should have asked directions from someone in the crowd before it passed her by, but she had been so startled!

"Madame? Pardon my effrontery, but you look a bit lost. May I help?"

The voice was low, well-modulated. The grammar was perfect, but beneath it there lay a curious undertone, a burr that suddenly reminded Coincoin of her long-dead mother. She turned, and the sight of the man who greeted her disconcerted her still more. This, surely was one of those men Pierre had spoken of, she thought to herself as she struggled to regain her composure. One of those wealthy *hommes de couleur libres* for which the south of Louisiana was already famed. The man who stood before her was a model of fashion, and Coincoin's hand flew unconsciously to smooth the wrinkles from her plain, blue skirt.

For years now, she had scoffed at women she called *clotheshorses*. What one wore was not important, so long as it was clean, ironed, and mended. For a decade, as she hoarded every *real* toward the day she could buy the last of her enslaved children, she had spun her own cloth and dyed it with the remnants of the indigo she processed for market. But now, as she stood before this handsome, swarthy gentleman in his biscuit-colored frock coat, its shawl collar elegantly piped in chocolate velvet, and in his skintight coffee breeches and riding boots of the finest leather—now, the vanity Coincoin thought she had buried the morning Pierre left her flared anew, and she struggled against a sense of shame.

It is a wonder he even called me Madame. There is nothing to distinguish me from a slave. Nothing at all.

Coincoin need not have worried. Martin Baptiste had watched her from the moment she tied her pirogue to the foot of the bridge and jumped ashore with the youthful grace that was still her nature. It was her face, though, that had arrested him, a face exquisitely carved by nature, as ageless as silk, with the same flare of nostrils his own beautiful mother had worn. And her head had the same queenly cast, beneath the turban that left him wondering whether her hair might be black or grey. From the maturity of her composure, he guessed rightly that she was close to his own age.

A stranger, surely, Baptiste had told himself. He had spent his life in the Opelousas district, but never had he seen that face or that form before. Of that he was certain. Nor could she be a slave. It was a traveling bag she carried, not a basket of produce for sale. A former *courtesan* from New Orleans? His eyes reappraised her common garb and decided not. If she were indeed from Rampart Street, she definitely had not arranged a proper settlement at the end of her last plaçage.

Out of curiosity, he had followed her, until he spotted the opening he had hoped for. The crowds had passed on down the street and left her standing there alone, looking as helpless as he, himself, had felt the first time his father sent him to *la ville*.

"Madame?" he repeated, taking one of her calloused hands in his own slender tan ones to graze her fingers lightly with his lips. "Permit to introduce myself. Martin Baptiste, *homme de couleur libre,* and a planter of this district. You are new to Opelousas, *n'est-ce pas?* If I may help in any way, you have only to ask."

"Merci, M'sieur," Coincoin murmured, resisting the impulse to lower her eyes as his gaze lingered questioningly, appreciatively, upon her face.

This will not do! she thought, directing that reprimand entirely to herself, and she willed her eyes to stare directly into his.

"I'm from Natchitoches, M'sieur. Marie Thérèse Coincoin, *Négresse libre.* Yes, I have been here in the Opelousas district before, but just once and never within the village itself. I'm looking for the merchant Le Haut, but…"

Her voice trailed off in embarrassment at the confession she had to make. Then she scolded herself anew. *Never* had she allowed herself to suffer shame for the limitations of her life, and this was no time to start. "I cannot read the signs, M'sieur," she added bluntly. "Would you be kind enough to show me the way?"

"Certainement, Madame." Taking Coincoin's elbow, seemingly heedless of the incongruity of her homespun against his linen, he led her a short way down the street.

"Hélas! M'sieur Le Haut's shop appears to be closed, Madame."

Indeed the shop was closed, not just temporarily vacated as the others were around it. The latched shutters and bolted door attested that its proprietor had gone considerably farther than the other storekeepers at this moment. Coincoin's heart sank, and her disappointment was so visible that Baptiste tried to lighten her mood with a smile and a jest.

"There you are once more, Madame, with that lost-sheep look on your face! Is there anything else I can do?"

"No, M'sieur. You are kind, but…"

"But still I have not helped. If there is *anything* I can do…" His graying brows bristled seriously over his soft brown eyes, calculating how to string out the moment. "Could your business be transacted elsewhere, Madame?"

Coincoin hesitated, feeling helpless in spite of her resolve. And thoroughly vexed with herself for letting her weakness show. "*Possible,* M'sieur. I'll ask around the post. You see, my son has been corresponding with M'sieur Le Haut, and he had assured us that he would have four *vaches* to sell me when I arrived."

"Cows, Madame? You made a trip for *cows?*"

Coincoin's temper flared, but then she saw the twinkle in Baptiste's eyes and bit back the retort she had almost uttered.

"*Pardonnez-moi,*" he apologized softly. "I was merely jesting. It just seemed strange that you would come so far just to buy four cows. But, of course, your reasons are none of my affair."

This is all ridiculous. Utterly ridiculous! Coincoin muttered to herself. Woman, you are forty-eight years old. This man cannot be any younger! Yet here the both of you stand like gawky adolescents at their first fais-do-do. Make your explanation. Excuse yourself. And move on with what you came for!

"No apology is needed, M'sieur. Your concern has been very gracious. But, no, I did not come just to purchase livestock. That is only a secondary matter, but it is one I need to settle. If you will excuse me, M'sieur…"

His eyes did not release her. For an awkward moment, each struggled to find the words that should come next. It was Baptiste who spoke first.

"Madame, my plantation is close down river, and I have cattle to spare. I would be happy to sell you whatever you need."

Coincoin could not decide whether to murmur the expected thanks or mutter them. "Your kindness is appreciated, M'sieur Baptiste, but I would not want to impose. Perhaps M'sieur Le Haut will be back soon."

"Madame, Le Haut is a man of some years and considerable wealth. He travels frequently, and it is quite possible that he may not be back for weeks.

Did he know that you were coming today?"

"*Non,* not today." Coincoin was trapped. What other option did she have? Had she been the swearing type, she would have taken great satisfaction now in borrowing a few of Marie de Soto's choice expletives.

"Then it is settled, Madame. You will buy your stock from me. What's more, so no one can accuse me of taking financial advantage of a woman in distress, you may not only name your price, but you may take your pick of my herd."

"M'sieur, you are too kind," Coincoin murmured in resignation.

"*Bien! Bien!* Then shall we take my carriage out to my place? A servant can row your pirogue down."

Carriage? That *was* too much! "No!" she responded, a bit more tartly than even she intended. "Just give me directions, and I'll find my way." But then, seeing the cock of his eyebrow, she smiled wryly and apologized.

"M'sieur, forgive me. I'm not myself today... It's been a long trip... I..."

Ma foi, woman! What's come over you? You are as flustered as a giddy girl!

"M'sieur," she began again. "I really am grateful for your offer. Still, I have another matter to attend. Would it be possible for me to wait until tomorrow to call for the cows?"

"Of course, but I shall count the hours, Madame Coincoin. And not because I am anxious to sell my stock."

The man's tone was light, still teasing, but his eyes said far more and her exasperation turned to panic. *Non! Never again!* she swore furiously. Maybe I *should* wait until M'sieur Le Haut returns and buy the stock from him as planned. That way, I can tell this aging cavalier goodbye right here. Only he may be right. I have no way of knowing when the merchant will be back, and I *must* have those cows.

Then the other thought struck her, the nagging fear that she had refused to let herself acknowledge although the possibility was very real. In truth, Coincoin now admitted to herself as she stood in the dusty street that wound through Opelousas and pondered the business she had come to transact, in truth *I might not have to buy any cows at all—if Madame Marie is not amenable.*

223

◦ 3 ◦

Marie was amenable, only it was not her nature to make that fact too obvious. She greeted Coincoin profusely, before she knew the purpose of the visit, wrapping her gargantuan arms around her godchild's slender frame with such exuberance that Coincoin almost fell across the sick woman's bed.

"Coincoin! What have you done to yourself? You're as thin as a willow!"

Coincoin winced, but knew her one-time mistress spoke the truth. So she simply parried, "We cannot all be pleasingly plump, Madame!"

"Ah, but you would be if you had my problems. It's been so long since I've been out of this damned bed! When were you here last? Eight years ago? *Oui,* and in all that time, I've not been up at all. I can't even turn myself over any more. I feel absolutely nothing from my waist down. Nothing at all—and I mean *nothing.*"

Coincoin groped for words, but Marie did not wait for her to find them.

"Your sweet Thérèse does everything for me now," Marie continued. "Everything but eat! That's all the accursed pleasure I have left in life and I do enjoy that, as you can see."

"I'm sorry, Madame." It was all Coincoin could think of to say, and she was indeed sorry. Yet, for a moment after the words slipped out, she expected Marie to explode. Pity was one thing the woman never brooked. Curiously, Marie made no protest.

The old mistress could not have known it, but in the silence that hovered between them at that moment, Coincoin's compassion battled with her resolve. She shuddered unexpectedly at the thought of asking so helpless a woman the favor she had come to ask—but she was a mother also, and a mother's first concern is always her own children. Whatever sympathy nagged at Coincoin now was not one she could afford to entertain. She would do what she had come to do, regardless of how ill Marie might be.

"Madame," she began resolutely, but Marie de Soto wanted chatter, not resolve.

"Come, Coincoin. Sit here on the bed and let's talk. Tell me everything that has gone on at the post these past eight years. I hear Quintanilla's been transferred to the bishop's office to keep his books. A fitting assignment for a nitpicker, *hehn?* What about yourself, Coincoin? How is old Metoyer? The children?"

Coincoin answered all her questions, painfully but honestly. Pierre's new wife, the *other* Marie Thérèse, had borne him a child already and was expecting another. Yes, he was quite the doting father, as he always had been, only now he could be one openly.

Oui, Coincoin continued, Pierre had become quite a prosperous planter, the largest slaveholder along the river. He had even become a *syndic* for the new settlement around the Point, and dispensed justice quite fairly. In fact, he was now a pillar of the *church*, believe it or not. The new priest had appointed him chief warden!

"Well, I'll be damned!" Marie chortled after Coincoin relayed all this news. "Maybe Quintanilla's prayers had some power after all. But what about you, Coincoin? You've not said one word about yourself. How are you and your family?"

"Quite well, Madame." Coincoin's voice lowered perceptibly, but then she braced herself. "We've had no more than the usual fortunes of life. There was another spell of the fever last fall."

"So I heard."

"My sister Hyacinthe and brother François both fell ill," Coincoin continued stoically. "Hyacinthe died." Coincoin said it simply, asking no sympathy, and Marie was not the type to give it.

"And little Fanchon? Does the Widow Lecomte still own her?" Marie's voice was clearly unapologetic for having sold Coincoin's child in the first place. "I suppose she's found herself a handsome *nègre* and has a flock of children now."

"Yes and no, Madame." The terseness of Coincoin's response said far more than the words she carefully chose. "The widow's daughter—the one who married Dupré—owns Fanchon now, and my daughter does have children. But she has not married the man. She cannot."

Marie cackled knowingly. "Don't tell me! Little Fanchon's lover is white!"

"Oui."

"Anyone I know?" Marie's eyes danced, roused by the whiff of scandal.

"Her children use the name Lecomte."

"Aha! And the widow has but one son, as I recall! Well, look at it this way, Coincoin, he may free her."

"She doesn't need him for that!" Coincoin exploded. "I'd buy her freedom. If only the Duprés would sell her to me!"

"Oui, oui," Marie agreed soothingly. "I'm sure you would. Well, what about

the twins? They're grown, I imagine."

"Quite so, Madame. They are twenty-two now."

"And married?"

"No, neither of them." Coincoin's tenseness eased briefly, and a smile began to play around her lips. "In fact, Pierre keeps a closer eye on Susanne than your brother did on you."

"More effectively, I hope!" Marie chuckled.

"Definitely! On the other hand, he urges Augustin to marry."

"Eh? Any prospects?"

"Perhaps. There was a girl at New Orleans." Coincoin dismissed that subject quickly, "but she wasn't for him. It is the little Agnes he seems to be serious about..." Coincoin's voice trailed off lamely.

"Oh, the Poissot *mulâtresse?* Of course, I remember her."

Of course, Coincoin echoed silently, though you could hardly be blamed for the way your daughter treated that child. When your Manuela married young Poissot, she knew about Agnes. Athanase and his father already had bought the child from Pierre Derbanne so they could free her, and they had taken Agnes into the family home. The whole post knew why, and your daughter had to know. But then, she's not half the woman you are. You never would have looked upon that poor child as an insult to yourself, or treated her the way your daughter has treated Agnes.

"Tell me, Coincoin," Marie's voice was almost soft, as if she read Coincoin's thoughts and was asking her to understand. "How did the case come out? Some gossiping busybody told me that Agnes filed charges against my daughter for mistreatment, but no one has told me of the outcome."

"Nor me," Coincoin replied quietly. "It just seems to have been forgotten, and neither Augustin nor Agnes has ever mentioned it."

"C'est la vie, Coincoin," Marie replied cynically, *"n'est-ce pas?* But I do wish them the best. You know that. They were both good children. Together they should do well in life."

"Merci, Madame. I hope so."

Marie's adipose jowls suddenly grew quite firm, as if they had found new reason for being, a fresh direction in which to shape themselves. "Coincoin! If Augustin's getting married, he needs land. Have you ever thought of petitioning the Crown for a grant? You and Augustin, both?"

"A *grant*, Madame?"

"Of course. There's unclaimed land everywhere, and the Crown's almost begging people to take it. They want settlers to farm this country so badly they're even inviting *Américains—Protestants,* no less!—into Louisiana and giving them land every day."

That explains it, Coincoin thought to herself—all the freckled faces and sunburned skin she saw on the streets of Opelousas. Not at all like Natchitoches where the only Anglos were a privileged few who had come straight from England with enough money to marry into the best Creole families. *Oui,* it also explains all those hotheads in the street. The *Américains* obviously have brought in their revolutionary ideas as well!

"I'll have to say that for the Spanish king," Marie prattled on. "He has enough horse sense to see that the future of this province depends upon agriculture, not gold or Indian trade."

Coincoin nodded her assent, partial at least. Certainly Pierre and the Buards and the Prudhommes were proving the future of agriculture there on the Cane. But land could not till itself. Somehow one first had to make the money to buy labor, and at Natchitoches, as far as she had seen, those who made that money—every one of them, from M'sieur de Mézières to the old lieutenants Le Court and Poissot, to the peasant soldiers like the Lecomtes and Rachals—had made their fortune first in pelts and trade. Even Pierre and M'sieur Pavie and the other Front Street merchants. They all owed their start to the skins brought back from Arkansas and Tejas, to be swapped for goods. *Skins.* In spite of herself, Coincoin cringed as a realization hit her then—a thought she'd never had and never heard before: all fortunes along the Cane were made on *skin.* The animal skins brought there simply paid for the human skin brought up from New Orleans and San Antonio.

She shivered. Even though it was just September and fall had not yet set in. Marie noticed. "Are you all right, Coincoin? That's twice you've shivered. I guess you managed to find a breeze! Anyway, as I was saying, there are some conditions you'd have to meet, but the land still would be free."

Coincoin forced herself back into the present, knowing she dared not offend Madame just now. "*Oui,* Madame. Pierre applied for a grant and had no trouble getting it, but…"

"But what, then?"

"I'm a *négresse!*"

"Well, that's obvious. So what?"

"No *nègres* ever have gotten a grant, at least not at Natchitoches."

"Then you can be the first, you and Augustin."

Coincoin frowned. "I'm not sure, Madame. I applied for title to the sixty-seven acres Pierre gave me. But when it comes to asking for free land, perhaps it would be better if only Augustin did that. I would not want to jeopardize his chances with a petition of my own. The governor might think us too greedy."

"Coincoin!" Marie cackled. "The governor has nothing against greed, so long as it doesn't interfere with his own. There's no reason your whole family can't apply, once they are all free and of age. I assure you, the Crown won't hold your color against you. Look at that man Baptiste here at Opelousas. He's become quite a prosperous planter, wealthier than most whites."

"Martin Baptiste?" Coincoin had not intended to mention him. The words just popped out when Marie brought up that name.

Marie's brows cocked quizzically and the old mischievous grin played around her puckered little mouth. "How curious. I didn't think you had been down here to Opelousas but once, and I hear Baptiste is not a traveling man. Apparently, though, one of you gets around more than I assumed."

"Oh, no," Coincoin hastily interjected. "I just happened to meet him, this afternoon in fact. There was this demonstration at the post..."

"*Sacrebleu!*" Marie snorted, Baptiste forgotten. "Not another one?"

"*Oui.*"

"They're going to wreck this colony, Coincoin. They ruined France with that damned revolution, and they'll do the same here. But then France was ruined already by all those noblemen who taxed the peasants until children died of swollen bellies from living off nothing but mash and water. De Mézières's nephew, too, has been just as guilty as the rest of the nobility, although he thinks he can usurp the throne now by fooling the rabble into forgetting he's the Duc d'Orléans. I swear! That name he's adopted is absolutely ridiculous. *Philipe Égalité!*"

Coincoin said nothing. She had her own feelings about all the talk of war, but this Duc d'Orléans or Philipe Whoever was not anyone she knew anything about.

"We don't have that problem here, though," Marie went on. "Nobility never has been worth a tinker's damn in Louisiana, and rightly so. We have enough égalité and liberté to satisfy everybody but fools. You! Why you, Coincoin, are proof of that!"

"*Oui,* Madame," Coincoin agreed, and meant it. She had told Chatta that when he wanted her to run away like a criminal. She had told young Thérèse that, the night the child had nursed her wounds. The laws of Louisiana did allow for freedom and equality, at least for people with enough gumption to go for it, and anybody who would not—well, they hardly deserved either one. It was not freedom and equality their frontier needed, but *stability.*

"It seems to me this revolution is dangerous," Coincoin agreed. "If people can arm themselves and destroy authority, then who is going to keep the law? What law can there be? What would protect the good people from the bad?"

"Precisely! That's what's happening now in France, and it could happen here if somebody doesn't squelch the fools and the rabble." Marie paused, a glimmer of amusement softening the seriousness that had washed over her gray face when Coincoin first mentioned the demonstration.

"Of course, when one thinks about it, it would be quite natural for *you* to oppose any revolution that threatened a monarchy, since your grandfather was a *king.*" A hint of the impish girl Coincoin had adored danced now around Marie's eyes, and Coincoin smiled.

"That really has nothing to do with it, Madame. It just seems to me that changes have to happen gradually. People need time to get used to new ways of doing things. The old ways have been around so long that a lot of the problems have been worked out of them. New laws mean new problems. The world will never agree on anything anyway. If we tolerate revolution just because some people do not like the current laws, what's to stop more violence by those who don't like the new ones? It seems to me that once something like that gets started, it would have no end."

"Exactly!" Marie interjected, and then resisted her usual temptation to take over the conversation. This new side of Coincoin was intriguing. Of course, she always knew that her godchild was intelligent, but....

"That's what I keep telling Louis," Coincoin went on without a pause, mother-worry creeping across her face. "Every time Pierre sends him and Augustin to New Orleans, Louis comes home filled with wild ideas about revolts and spouting all this nonsense about *liberté* and *fraternité.* Augustin and I tell him that he will have his liberty soon enough, if he has enough sense not to make trouble."

"Then Pierre's freeing him?"

Coincoin nodded, concern evident on her face. "Pierre has promised all of them freedom in a year or so, but lately he has begun to doubt whether Louis is mature enough to live on his own. Goodness knows, the boy has given him enough cause for doubt. If the soldiers had caught him in that demonstration at Nacogdoches—armed, no less!—and him legally a slave…"

Coincoin could not finish putting that thought into words. She did not have to. Marie knew as well as she did the penalty for slaves who armed themselves for any insurrection.

"It sounds as though Metoyer gives the boy too much freedom," Marie snorted.

Coincoin smiled wanly. *"Oui,* Madame. Half the post thinks he is free already. They even tried to make him pay taxes last year!"

"Quintanilla must have been behind that," Marie jested

This time Coincoin did not join her laughter. The lengthening shadows in the sickroom reminded her that this day's visit already had stretched on longer than she had planned. There had been enough amenities. They had shared the news and commiserated over each other's woes. They had even ventured into politics, which Pierre always said was not a woman's business anyway. The only thing left to talk about was the weather, and Coincoin never had wasted time on that.

Clearly, the moment had come to say what she had to say. So Coincoin said it, bluntly, with a resolution that forestalled any interruption from Marie.

"Madame, I'm getting to be an old woman. The dear Lord already has given me more years than he gave my Mama. But the day my Mama and Papa died, from the fever they took while trying to save *your* mother, they charged me with a responsibility I am bound to fulfill."

Marie's head cocked quizzically, and Coincoin plunged on. "Everything I have tried to do since then has been done with that in mind, and I have done most of it. I have fought every obstacle in my way. You have helped me, too. I would be the first to admit that. But now I have to do the hardest thing of all."

Coincoin paused deliberately, playing the game of cat and mouse she knew Marie liked to play.

"What's your obstacle this time, Coincoin?" her old mistress parried, feigning innocence.

"You, Madame."

"Me? Why, whatever could I have that you would want?"

"My daughter."

"What! Thérèse?" The shock was real. Marie flushed red. "You would take from a sick old woman her only comfort in life? *Merde*, woman! She's the only person who cares enough for me to empty my bed pans and wipe my ass without grumbling! She's the only one who knows how to treat the pains that all the doctors laugh at! How could you make such a demand? Of *me*, of all people?"

Coincoin smiled sweetly, confidently, without attempting to reply to Marie's outburst. She had only to wait, she knew. She should bide her time and let the woman rave until she had spent herself, and *rave* was exactly what Marie did.

"What right do you have to come and demand a slave from me, Coincoin? Your daughter is *my property! Mine*, for me to do with as I please! Have you forgotten that? I've been too good to you all these years, woman. I've let you take advantage of me anytime you pleased, and you've just plain forgotten the natural order of things. *Nobody* comes to me and demands my property. I do not dispose of anything until I'm ready!"

The face grew redder, the chest heaved excitedly, the breath came in spurts and gulps, but eventually Marie spent her fury. Coincoin said nothing in the meanwhile, letting the tirade wane on its accord—at least until Marie announced with blunt finality, "I'll never part with Thérèse until the day I die."

"That's good enough," Coincoin replied quietly. "I do not have enough money to pay for her outright anyway. I only have fifty pesos."

"What!" Marie exploded anew. "This is an insult, Coincoin! You come to me with only fifty pesos in your purse, and you expect me to sell you my best slave?"

"Not just her, Madame. I want Thérèse's son, too."

"By the sweet blue eyes of Jesus! You have cheek, Coincoin!" Marie's jaw clamped shut, but then she snorted—more in exasperation than anger. "On the other hand, you've always had cheek, so I shouldn't be surprised at this."

Coincoin's smile was unperturbed. The question was settled already, and they both knew it. All that remained was the haggling over details.

"Madame, I have made arrangements to buy four head of cattle from Sieur

Baptiste, and one of your neighbors has agreed to the run of her pasture, at a reasonable fee. With your permission, I want to give the cows to Thérèse, for her and her son to start a herd. I'll pay you the fifty pesos now. As I get more, I'll pay you that, whatever price you set. Thérèse and José can sell milk and butter in the neighborhood to help with the payments. We will agree, though, that she will stay and nurse you as long as you need her."

"*Ma foi!* If all you can pay now is fifty pesos, I won't live long enough to collect all my money. Metoyer paid me fifteen hundred for you and your Joseph, and the child was just a babe inside your belly. Thérèse's son is at least eight years old. The two of them are worth far more than you were. They'd cost you a fortune!"

"To me, they would be worth whatever price you set. But you know that already."

Marie did not answer, not directly. Instead she bellowed, loudly enough to be heard throughout the length of her commodious home.

"José! I know you're out there! I hear you carrying on with Thérèse. Get in here and let the woman do her work!"

The door opened quickly behind Coincoin.

"*Sí*, Señora?"

"I have a paper for you to draft, José."

"Of course, Señora." The Spaniard hastened to Marie's rosewood desk to procure a quill and parchment.

"My business manager," Marie remarked offhandedly to Coincoin as though the young man were not even in the room. "At least, he calls himself that, and I indulge his ego."

Coincoin made no answer. It had not been necessary for Marie to explain the young Spaniard's presence. She had recognized José Gutierrez instantly. It was his own name that Thérèse had given eight years before to the *pardo* son she bore, the child whose father she would not identify even for her own mother, and that had pained Coincoin considerably. If it was Gutierrez, she could accept the fact. From all reports, he was a good man. Still, if Thérèse was going to pick a *poor* man, she'd have done better to pick one of her own race and married him.

"Are you ready, Señora?"

"Not at all. But it looks as though I don't have a choice in the matter. I don't know why I let this woman badger me into things!"

Coincoin wanted to laugh, but she wisely kept her silence as Marie began, peremptorily, to dictate the document:

> I, Doña Marie des Neiges de St. Denis de Soto, out of the goodness
> of my heart, have agreed to sell my *négresse* Thérèse and her child
> Joseph Maurice, to Thérèse's mother Coincoin for the paltry sum
> of 650 *livres*...

⌘ 4 ⌘

August 1792

Coincoin was silent as they rode down the long avenue that led to the Big House. The poplars that lined either side are only saplings, she thought to herself, but in a few years they should be as majestic as Pierre's new home.

Every day for the past six months, Coincoin had looked across the way from her own cabin and watched that Big House rise imperiously out of the raw earth where virgin forest had stood a few years before. To her own surprise, she could find neither envy nor jealousy in her heart. Pierre was prospering, but God had been good to her, too. She was doing every bit as well as she had hoped, and her children would do even better. One day they would have their own Big Houses in this new raised West Indian style with those wide verandas and tall pillars that had become the rage of late.

Their buggy drew to a halt on the drive that circled in front of Pierre's manor. Deliberately, Coincoin remained in her seat and waited for Augustin to lay down the reins, walk around, and help her to the ground. She had no way of knowing whether someone might be watching from the Big House, but that little gesture still made her feel good—as good as the new dress that Augustin had talked her into having Marie Louise make for her. He had even designed it, copying the modish fashions he had observed on the stylish ladies who promenaded the banquettes of *la ville*.

Coincoin had laughed at the new straight skirts, and scowled at the prices they were being charged for simple cotton, now that silks and satins were falling out of favor. But at just this moment, she took uncharacteristic pleasure in the fact that she could approach Pierre's new home *and* his wife with some semblance of prosperity herself. Self-consciously, she readjusted her chic *chapeau de paille* as Augustin tied the buggy's reins to his father's new hitching post and paused to stroke the mustang he had roped and tamed on his last trip to Tejas.

The man who answered their knock on the paned front door was a stranger to Coincoin, although obviously not to Augustin. His greeting was civil, but decidedly cool.

"Good day, Figaro," Augustin responded. "Is M'sieur at home?"

The black was slow in answering. His round face was as starched as the cravat of his full livery, and Coincoin could read the hostility in his eyes. Figaro, obviously, was that new English Negro Pierre had bought from the Carolinas, the one who had been trained by Huguenots in Charleston. It was just as obvious to Coincoin, too, that he resented the license with which she and Augustin used Pierre's front door instead of the servants' entry.

"*Non,*" the butler retorted shortly in Augustin's direction, his eyes ignoring Coincoin entirely. "He rode out t' Mister Prudhomme's place. He'll be back by noon."

For an English *nègre*, Coincoin thought, the man's French was not bad. He did have that same haughtiness, though, that Pierre said all the English had.

"Who is it, Figaro?" a thin voice called from somewhere beyond Coincoin's path of vision, but she recognized the voice. Coincoin would know that voice anywhere.

"*C'est Augustin, Madame.* Him an' his mother, I b'lieve."

"Oh, yes, Figaro. M'sieur sent for them."

Marie Thérèse Eugenie Buard Pavie Metoyer appeared at last behind him, tall and big of bone—a solidness so mismatched to the frailty of her pitch that she disconcerted everyone at first meeting—and pale to the extreme. While her Gallic neighbors chalked up her color to her Swiss ancestry, outsiders read on her face the same drawn and weary look that so many frontier women bore.

Coincoin, herself, was momentarily startled. She had expected the woman's garb to reflect the luxury of her new surroundings, but Mme. Metoyer's frock was a simple housedress, covered with a limp white apron, no less. And her hair! The straight threads that were now more grey than blonde were pulled back even more severely than they were at Sunday Mass.

"Well, show them in, Figaro," Mme. Metoyer ordered impatiently, but the houseman paused perceptibly.

"I think they was leavin', Madame. I tol' 'em M'sieur is out."

Not once, yet, had any of them addressed Coincoin, and the pride of which she had drunk great draughts before responding to Pierre's summons had begun to waver. She was acutely out of place. As always, her response to unease was to confront it, so she spoke now, without waiting to be addressed, and her voice revealed no trace of her discomfiture.

"You are quite right, Figaro. We are leaving. If you expect M'sieur by noon, my son and I will wait for him in our buggy."

"Why, you'll do nothing of the sort!" Pierre's wife was genuinely shocked. "My husband sent for you, and you have both taken the morning off from your business to come. He would expect you to wait in his office until he returns." Pleasantly enough, she nodded toward the chamber that stood at the end of the long salon. "Figaro, show them to M'sieur's study. Coincoin? Would you like for me to call Susanne? She's just reading to little Elisabeth."

"Oh, no! That's not necessary," Coincoin demurred, struggling to find an air of courtesy that would not hint of servility as well.

"Well, of course it is! She can fix you a pitcher of cool lemonade, and the three of you can visit while you wait for my husband to return." Mme. Metoyer smiled as she said that, with a casualness in which Coincoin could detect no spite. Then she went on without a pause. "I can manage the babies by myself for an hour or so. M'sieur should be back by then."

With a brief *bon matin,* Pierre's new wife absented herself, and Coincoin noted with uncharacteristic pettiness that the sound following the woman as she walked was not the seductive swish of silken petticoats but the jangling of her household keys.

With brusqueness bordering now on incivility, Figaro ushered them into the study. Coincoin remained standing, stiffly, in the center of the room that was almost as big as her entire cabin, taking in every detail from the wainscotting to the panelled walls, and Augustin smiled to himself as he settled into an overstuffed leather chair. He had been in his father's study many times, both during and after its construction. He was as much at ease in Pierre's Big House as he was everywhere he went, but he keenly felt his mother's disconcertment. He tried small talk to set her at ease, but he could think of nothing they had not already discussed that morning. It was his twin who rescued them.

"*Maman!*" Susanne squealed as she ran lightly into the room and hugged her mother. Her eyes twinkling, Coincoin responded with the same ritual they had followed for the dozen years since Pierre had taken their daughter back to the village to keep his house. Even though Susanne long since had matured, even though she and the family had been at the Big House across the river from Coincoin for over a month now, and Susanne had come to see her weekly, they still began each visit with the same ritual.

"Susanne!" Coincoin held her child at arms' length. "My! How you have grown!"

As always, Susanne smiled back playfully. And, as always, Coincoin's eyes lingered upon the beauty of the woman she and Pierre had created. The years had molded Susanne into art. Smooth, coal-black hair, lustrous almond eyes sculptured into the delicate, high-rising curve of finely chiseled cheekbones. An upturned nose attested all her sauciness and a full, ripe mouth hinted at the passion waiting to be loosed. Her frock was as simple as ever, but it had far more flair than the drab housedress of her mistress, and beneath its thin, gay fabric, delicately sprigged with yellow rosebuds that set off perfectly the golden highlights in her skin, her body curved enticingly.

Still, there's something different, Coincoin thought suddenly to herself and studied her daughter more intently, from the soft slippers that shod her tiny feet to the shiny locks that she always coaxed into fashionable ringlets.

That was it! Today, there was no sign of those curls, with gay little bows tucked here or there. Instead, the fine auburn silk that was Susanne's pride was almost hidden under a lacy handkerchief, tied bandana-style, around her head. Impulsively, Coincoin smiled, but Susanne did not share her mother's humor.

"What are you smiling about, *Maman?* It's not funny. It's hot, and it's a mean order, and I hate it!"

"An order? Whatever do you mean, child?"

"You haven't heard, Maman? All colored women in this colony now have to wrap their heads in a *tignon*. A *handkerchief!* No more pretty ribbons! No more fancy feathers! Those are just for the *white* ladies now. All those ugly shrews down in *la ville* who couldn't get a man to look at them if they paraded around naked have been complaining to the governor because their men like to look at *us!* So now we have to wrap our hair up as though it were something shameful, and we aren't supposed to wear pretty clothes any more, or anything nice!"

"Well, I guess I'll have to find some poor white woman who can use this new hat of mine," Coincoin retorted dryly.

"Maman! How can you say that so lightly?"

"Child, some things are worth getting upset over and some aren't. Rules like that aren't new. In France, they say, only the nobles used to wear bright colors. The merchants and peasants had to wear drab ones."

"And they rebelled in France, too!"

"If that is why they are rebelling, then their reasons are as senseless as their killings. Clothes are not that important, child! Even as she said it, Coincoin knew that argument would not work. She knew because, an eon ago, she had been twenty-five herself, and so she began again.

"Susanne, *cherie,* I know how you feel. Yet, in a way, we have brought it upon ourselves. Too many *nègre* women, especially the free ones down at *la ville,* use their looks to keep from working. They would rather make fancy sporting ladies of themselves and find white men to support them than…"

She floundered, unsure of how to extricate herself from the subject she had plunged into. God knows, she was not without fault herself. She had been Pierre's concubine, one of those *placées* as they delicately called themselves now, for which the Louisiana colony was notorious. But, then, whatever she did she had not done to avoid *work.* She had never tried to shirk honest labor. And so she plunged on.

"If we are free, Susanne, we have an obligation to ourselves, to everyone, to be good citizens. To *contribute* to society. If most free *négresses* would do that, then we could earn respect, and there would be no need for laws like this one you are talking about."

Susanne did not answer. Of all the directions this conversation could have taken, this was absolutely the worst. Now she was worried. Her mother would never agree to what she and her Papa—though she dared not call him that aloud—had to propose! Desperately, Susanne was about to suggest that her mother go home, that M'sieur would probably be gone all day and it might be best for them to come another time. But the thought came too late. Pierre was there.

As Coincoin watched him enter, in his new white linen riding habit with black, patent-leather jockey boots gleaming so brightly they mirrored the florals of his new carpet, as he seated himself so easily behind his new mahogany desk that was almost as large as the bed they once had shared, Coincoin felt none of the old tenderness that once hurt her.

Oui, Pierre was a different man now, just as she was a different woman. Try as she might, she could not recall now the feel of this man's arms around her, his urgent lips devouring her. It was as though the two grown children who flanked them, with their telltale skin of brown and tan, were conceived as immaculately as Jesus himself. Then a smile overcame Coincoin. A sense of liberation. And for the first time since she entered this house she was now at ease, as completely as though she were in New Orleans discussing business with her factor.

"Augustin said you wanted to see me, Pierre."

"Yes, Coincoin. We have two items of business we need to attend. Well, actually, only one item of *business*. The other...." His voice trailed off as he glanced at Susanne. "Well, let's take them one at a time, shall we?"

"As you wish, Pierre."

"Besides, there's no rush," he continued pleasantly. "Gustin! I know you'd prefer something stronger than lemonade. That's refreshment for ladies!" Pierre rose and crossed to the short *bibliothèque* that matched his desk, then filled two glasses of claret from a decanter of Bohemian crystal.

"You're looking well, Coincoin."

"Merci," she replied quietly, noncommittally.

"I hear you made an excellent crop this past year. Commandant De Blanc tells me he issued a passport for your barge to ship 10,000 carottes to market."

"Nine thousand and nine hundred," Coincoin corrected. "Also three hundred hides and two barrels of grease."

Pierre laughed. "That's what I said. An excellent year. I trained you well."

"Pardonnez-moi," she retorted. "But my father taught me to grow tobacco long before I ever met you."

"Touché! All right, Coincoin, I'll admit it. Whatever I taught you, that wasn't it."

Coincoin could feel the blood rush to her face and again she thanked her fates that she was black. Were she as sallow as Pierre's wife, her blush would have been even more embarrassing than Pierre's remark.

Metoyer did not notice her disconcertment. "Coincoin," he began softly. "The time has come for me to keep another promise to you. Augustin has asked my permission to marry Agnes."

"Oui." That was all she could think of to say.

"I've given it, and I understand you have no objection."

"Non."

"Bien. I'll tell Père Delvaux to announce the banns." Pierre turned to his son. "When do you want to marry, boy?"

"The twenty-second, M'sieur."

Pierre frowned, ever so slightly. "That's mighty close. There won't be time for announcing three banns."

"I know, M'sieur, but Père Delvaux's no stickler for banns and that date is special to me."

His father cocked a quizzical eye, but Augustin did not elaborate. Shrugging, Pierre went on with more serious issues. "Of course, marriage entails responsibilities, but I think you are well-prepared. At least you will be when I give you this little paper."

What Pierre passed to Augustin was no small scrap, but a lengthy document, very legal looking, although Augustin could not read it. "That, my boy, is my wedding gift to you," Pierre went on softly. "You're free, Gustin. I have no more control over you. There are only two conditions outlined in that paper, and I have no worry about your fulfilling either of them. First, I expect you always to look after your mother's needs." Pierre smiled broadly. "Though from the look of her attire and that buggy outside, she doesn't seem to be in serious want."

Coincoin smiled back blandly, but as quickly as Pierre's grin had come, it dissolved.

"Still, reverses do happen, and that's the reason for the other stipulation, Gustin. If my chil... if my *young* children should ever be in need, at any time in their lives, I expect you to help them to whatever extent you are able. That's the law of manumission in this colony, but I expect it of you also. I'm sure you will honor it."

"Yes, sir."

"What do you plan to do with yourself, boy, now that you are free?" Pierre asked the question offhandedly, and from his mien no one could have guessed the pain he felt at cutting this tie to his eldest son. "Do you plan to help your mother farm, or would you prefer to stay on as my overseer?"

"If I have a choice, M'sieur...," Augustin's voice was polite, but it was clear he already had ideas of his own. He hesitated, hoping for some clue to his father's

Manumision of Nicolas Augustin, Mulâtre
by Claude Thomas Pierre Metoyer

In accordance with the rights he reserved in his marriage contract with Marie Thérèse Buard, Widow Pavie, Metoyer manumits "for faithful services," his "mulatto slave named Nicolas Augustin, about twenty-five years of age."

reception of the idea he was about to propose.

"Of course you do, boy," Pierre retorted gruffly, and Augustin rushed on.

"M'sieur, downriver at Yucca Bend in the bottom part of the Isle, there is this tract of land. I've been down to look at it several times. No one has claimed it yet, and it's covered in cane brakes. But that land is *rich*. The soil oozes with life when you roll it between your fingers. It's just a small piece, but I'd like to farm it if the governor will let me have it."

"So. I was right. I feared you'd leave me. I have to admit you're the best damned overseer I've ever had, and just as fine a blacksmith as they say your grandfather was."

"It's not that I want to leave you, sir," Augustin interjected hastily.

"I know, boy." Pierre forced himself to laugh. He'd had his own ideas, too, when his father wanted him to stay there in La Rochelle and help with the family's shop. "Tell you what, Gustin. First thing in the morning, I'll go with you into the post to see the commandant. We'll file your petition and get his permission for you to start clearing that land. You have a long, backbreaking job ahead of you. Do you want to borrow a couple of my hands to help?"

"Thank you, M'sieur, but I'd rather do this on my own. You can help me file the petition, but I won't need any help on my land save what my brothers can give me. Even François is big enough now to clear away the brush after Joseph and Toussaint and I hack it down."

"I see you have your future well planned," Pierre retorted wryly.

"Yes, sir. I do."

The confidence in Augustin's voice brought back memories to Pierre of his own youth, and again he was proud of the son life would not let him acknowledge. Again, too, he felt a keen sense of loss. He would have liked to help this son plan his life.

Augustin read the hurt in his father's hooded eyes. "M'sieur, there is something else you could do for us, if you would be so kind."

"What, boy?"

"Mama has not mentioned it, but she wants to apply for a concession of her own. Would you help us file her petition?"

"Well!" Pierre retorted with some surprise. "I knew you were doing well, Coincoin, but I did not expect you to start enlarging your operation. Do you have a specific tract in mind? One near Gustin's, perhaps?"

"Yes, I have a tract in mind, Pierre, but not down on the Isle. I already have more farm land than my woman and I can handle, and Augustin will need his brothers. But if I had grazing land over in the pine hills past Old River, I could enlarge my herd. Since cattle run wild and feed themselves and reproduce naturally, I could start a nice *vacherie* with little expense. In fact, I've already found a Spaniard to oversee it for me."

Pierre nodded appreciatively, more impressed than ever with the business acumen Coincoin was developing. "The matter's settled then. We'll all ride into town tomorrow, including Susanne. Since the governor's decree is now being enforced here at Natchitoches, she'll need some pretty fabric to make those tignons she'll be wearing."

Pierre laughed, but Susanne's rosy mouth was puckered into a pout. She had sat here for an hour, discussing everyone's plans but her own, and she was clearly wishing her papa would tell Mama what he had agreed to.

Pierre read her mind, and his voice softened as he turned back to Coincoin. She did not fail to catch the wariness in his eyes.

"There's one other matter, Coincoin."

"Oh?" Somehow, deep inside her, Coincoin felt what was about to happen, and her whole being protested violently, even though she knew neither Pierre nor their daughter would understand her protest.

"Coincoin, Susanne is now a young woman. She has been for quite some time."

"*Oui?*"

"And all young women think of love—of a man to care for them."

"Of course, Pierre," Coincoin began shortly, "but Susanne has not found anyone who interests her."

"She has now, Coincoin. He lives close by, so she won't be far from either of us. She would still help my wife run this household. The only difference would be that she would have a home of her own, to go to at night, and someone to give meaning to her life."

"She does not need a man for that!" Coincoin protested irrationally.

"Everyone needs love," Pierre rejoined, and Coincoin forced herself to ignore the insistence in his voice.

"Coincoin, have you met the new doctor who moved up from *la ville*? Joseph Conant?"

The doctor? "No!" Coincoin cried. "No, and a thousand times, no!! He's *white!*"

Pierre did not answer. No one in the room spoke at all, and the echo of Coincoin's words bounced off the walls that were closing in on her.

"Pierre… Susanne…," she croaked. How could she make them realize what she was trying to say? How could she sit here in front of Pierre and tell Susanne it was better not to have loved at all than to be hurt the way she would be hurt if she started this affair with a man she could not marry—if she had not started it already. Coincoin eyed Susanne warily, searching for reassurance that it still was not too late.

"Maman, M'sieur has given me his permission. Please give me yours," Susanne entreated. "Really, Maman, I don't have to have your permission. You don't *own* me. But I do want your blessing."

"I cannot give it Susanne. I just can not!" Coincoin breathed, her words almost choking amid the memories, the heartaches, the fears that engulfed her.

Pierre interceded again. "Coincoin, Susanne is a woman now. She's almost twenty-five, even though it is hard for us to realize it. We have been fortunate, we still are, that she cares enough to seek our blessing."

His voice was insistent, begging Coincoin to understand. How could she say *no?* She knew it pained him as much as it did her. She knew he would rather, a thousand times over, that his daughter picked a man she could wed, legally and sacredly, as Augustin was about to do—a man of her own class and race, neither white nor black. She *knew* how many times in the nights they had spent together, he had cursed in his sleep, battling dreams—nay, nightmares—of a possibility he refused to face: his golden daughter in the arms of a *nègre*. But she also knew he battled his demons for naught. There were so few free men here of Susanne's caste, and she was much too proud to respect any man who was not his own master. *Non,* truth is, they always knew what path Susanne would take in life: plaçage with a Frenchman of wealth and status. Pierre was just the first to admit it.

"Maman?"

"Coincoin?"

They pressed her for an answer. Only Augustin did not say a word. Helplessly, Coincoin searched her son's face for guidance, and his eyes told her that he understood exactly how she felt. Still, his lips would not say no to his own father. She knew, then, that she had lost this battle, that she never had stood a chance in the first place. The urgency of youth, that crazy and inexplicable need for becoming one with another human being, which was so much a part of being young, was just too much for one old woman to withstand.

She had lost. Yet she understood why. She had fought this same battle with herself after that unexpected, heart-lurching meeting at Opelousas with the widowed Martin Baptiste, after the glorious, carefree day she had spent on his plantation when she went to call for those four cows.

Oui. Coincoin had won that battle with herself, but it had not been half as hard to deny herself as to deny Susanne. When her own heart was lonely, she could laugh at it, taunting herself that she was too old and withered for physical love. Besides, she had her children and her grandchildren to live for. But none of these arguments would work now on Susanne. The girl was young. So beautiful. So ripe for love. She had no children, and without a man she never would. How could she deny her daughter what was meant to be?

"*Oui,*" she announced wearily, ignoring the disappointment she thought she saw in Augustin's piercing eyes. "You win."

Coincoin's shoulders squared, and she sat even straighter in her chair. Only Augustin could see, in that one defeat, his mother become the old woman she believed herself to be.

⁂ 5 ⁂
22 August 1792

The wedding was a simple one. At daybreak that Wednesday morning, the small bell François had cast a half-century before rang melodiously through the post, calling all to daily Mass. As always, on a busy weekday morning, the faithful were few, but on this day their numbers doubled as the small wedding party from downriver slipped quietly into the congregation. Midway through the Mass, Père Delvaux paused, opened his arms in invitation, and the betrothed pair came forward, hand in hand, to exchange their vows and receive the nuptial blessing.

Augustin's voice did not falter as he recited the ritual words with Agnes, and he purposefully raised his voice so his mother could hear his pledge distinctly.

Not since his grandparents had married in the old chapel fifty-seven years before had any of their family been joined in holy wedlock. This day was part of his mother's dream that God would steer her family back to the path the Mother Church would have them follow. That was why he had chosen this day to make that dream happen—a present to his mother on her fiftieth birthday.

There was no blessing of the rings. Augustin could not afford one for his betrothed, and he would not let his mother buy it for him. The day would come, he knew, that he would adorn every finger on Agnes's fair hands, but until then no outward symbol of his love was needed to prove to her that his devotion would be eternal.

Augustin stood raptly through all the prayers, his gaze never leaving the delicate face of his young bride. Not until Père Delvaux placed his outstretched hands above their heads and began the final blessing did Augustin become aware of the actual words the priest intoned, and then a sense of gratitude, a spirit of dedication, enveloped him as he accepted trustingly the promise he read into that holy blessing.

May the peace of Christ dwell always in your hearts and in your home. May you have true friends to stand by you, both in joy and in sorrow. May you be ready with help and consolation for all those who come to you in need. And may the blessings promised to the compassionate descend in abundance on your dwelling.

"Amen," Augustin answered firmly; and for him that one word was not the same prayer of hope that brought comfort to the poor and desperate. It was a prayer of thanks for the blessings he *knew* his God would give them in the years ahead.

May you be blessed in your work and enjoy its fruits. May cares never cause you distress, nor the desire for earthly possessions lead you astray. But may your heart's concern be always for the treasures laid up for you in the life of Heaven.

"Amen," he repeated, recognizing in Père Delvaux's words the Lord's affirmation that his faith would be well rewarded, along with His warning that the treasures he would amass on this earth should not blind him to the charity he owed all who were less fortunate.

May the Lord grant you fullness of years, so that you may reap the harvest of a good life and, after you have served him with loyalty in His kingdom on earth, may He take you up into His eternal dominions in heaven.

May the Lord grant *both* of us a fullness of years, Augustin echoed silently, as the priest continued the ritual and his own gaze returned to the flawless face of his tiny bride. He had been slow to accept the fact that he loved Agnes. But he knew now he could never fulfill his mission without this patient, understanding, but enigmatic helpmate at his side.

It had been a blessing that Desirée had rejected him, Augustin thought suddenly. It was Providence that she had refused to leave *la ville,* refused his honorable proposal of marriage, and became instead the *placée* of that wealthy Anglo merchant. His love for the tall and willowy Desirée had brought him nothing but torment, but Agnes consoled him when he was troubled, inspired him when his faith wavered, and warmed his loins in a gentle and loving way that he knew could last forever without burning out his soul.

Père Delvaux's benedictions flowed once more into the ritual of the Mass, but Augustin scarcely noticed. Together, he and Agnes tasted the Body and Blood of the one Eternal Savior, and together they led the congregation from the sanctuary as the *chanteur* raised the lilting Latin strains of the Recessional. A few brief well-wishes from friends who had stood as sponsors to their union, and all was over. An hour before, Augustin had been a free man, totally unfettered by any tie of bondage to another mortal. Now he had forfeited a great measure of his freedom. Yet never, in the long and fruitful life that lay ahead, would he regret his bondage to Agnes Poissot.

Gaily, the small wedding party wound its way downriver, with the bridal pair ensconced in the seat of honor atop Coincoin's new buggy, flanked by the stallions of the solemn Dominique and the flippant Louis, whose litany of suggestive jests embarrassed the bridegroom more than it did the bride. Coincoin followed quietly, smiling, straddling Le Roi as she always had before Augustin persuaded her to waste her money on that *cabriolet.* And beside her, Susanne perched modestly upon one side of the gentle thoroughbred Joseph Conant had given her the morning after she moved into his bed.

In their wake the others followed, Pierre and T'Pierre, young Joseph, Toussaint, and François—all cackling appreciatively at Louis's jests—together with Agnes's preadolescent sister Marguerite, already making eyes at François, and their stout and boisterous mother who cooked for Pierre Derbanne's family and laughed now just as heartily as the menfolk at Louis's double-entendres.

At the Point, Augustin left his family behind. With a bridegroom's typical impatience, he declined their offer to stay a spell. Beyond the Point, River

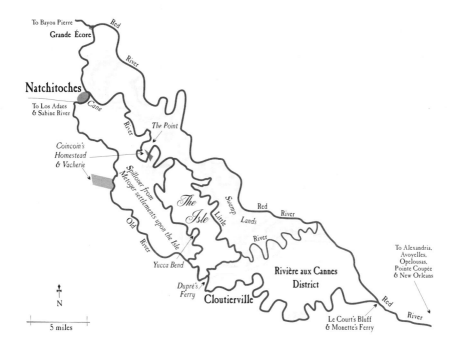

Map labels:
To Bayou Pierre
Grande Écore
Red River
Natchitoches
To Los Adaes & Sabine River
Cane River
The Point
Coincoin's Homestead & Vacherie
Spillover from Metoyer settlements upon the Isle
The Isle
Old River
Swamp Link
Lands
Red River
River
Yucca Bend
Dupré's Ferry
Cloutierville
Rivière aux Cannes District
To Alexandria, Avoyelles, Opelousas, Pointe Coupée & New Orleans
Red River
Le Court's Bluff & Monette's Ferry
N
5 miles

Isle of Canes and Cane River
from Grande Ecore to Le Court's Bluff

From time primeval, a massive raft of logs dammed Red River above Grand Ecore, making the land of the Natchitoches the uppermost limits of travel or settlement. From there, tribal trade created the footpath that became El Camino Real, linking the Natchitoches to Los Adaës and Mexico City. Meanwhile, spring thaws in the western mountains, at the headwaters of the Red, sent great floods that spilled over the lands. Below the post, a catastrophic surge in the 1760s caused the river to jump its course from Old River to the stream known as the Cane, carving a navigable waterway through the richest loam in the region. It was then that the Le Courts and the Lecomtes and the Rachals, the Duprés and the Derbannes, and then the Metoyers and Prudhommes began to hack out their plantations from the canebrakes of the Isle and the district that stretched from there all the way down to Le Court's Bluff. Then, in the 1830s, the clearing of the great Red River Raft by the U.S. Army Engineers, caused the Red to leap once more to the channel it now occupies—leaving the Cane a bucolic stream winding lazily through a rich and storied countryside.

Road wound into the forest, so the bridal pair left the buggy and climbed into Augustin's well-worn pirogue. By dusk, they had reached Yucca Bend and the small, crude cabin he had thrown up in the restless, hungering weeks he had waited for Agnes to become his bride.

The pale glow of the lantern softened the barren room as Agnes surveyed the home he had readied for them. A bare bench stood lonesomely in the neatly swept dirt at the fireplace end, facing the wall that held a simple rope-slung bed. On unshuttered shelves across another side, Augustin had carefully stocked a small store of food: dried, peppery *tasso* from the cow he had just helped his mother slaughter, coarse homeground meal, some cheese, a small crock of lard, corn for the chickens Coincoin had given them, dried fruit from her storehouse, and a small basket of fresh wild peaches from the tree he had found on the backside of his land.

Agnes chatted gaily, teasingly, as she dipped lightly into the stores and spread the quick repast Augustin could have done without. The gnaw in his gut was not a hunger for fresh fruit and dried meat. But with the calm that dominated everything he did, Augustin checked his own desire and let his bride savor the pleasure of preparing their first meal.

In the night that followed, they sampled much more—and shared much pain, although Augustin had not foreseen the latter. Their stomachs satiated, they tumbled laughingly onto the moss-filled mattress and drew the gauze netting quickly to shut out the swarm of mosquitoes that the smoke pot on the table did not seem to faze. Agnes insisted that the lantern not be snuffed, and Augustin eagerly agreed. In his own joy that her beauty would not be hidden by the darkness, he did not realize that a far darker reason underlay his bride's request.

Softly, Augustin loosed the thin cotton frock that clung enticingly to Agnes's tiny fame, letting the gown fall slowly from her tawny shoulder, baring her full round breasts, her delicately sloping waist. But the soft light also fell mercilessly upon a maze of ragged scars that crisscrossed her chest, her ribs, her back, and he stared in unwilling horror.

It was Agnes who spoke first, softly. "I should have shown you sooner, Gustin, but I was afraid you would not want to spend your life making love to such ugliness."

"Ugliness?" Augustin almost choked on the word. "Oh, Agnes, my lovely little angel. You will always be beautiful to me, no matter what anyone does to you. Oh, Agnes."

Gently, protectively, Augustin wrapped her fragile shoulders in a pair of arms made massive by the bellows and hammers of his father's blacksmith shop. For a moment he had a wild impulse to feel that maze of scars as if he needed to be convinced that they were real. How could anyone do *this* to someone as gentle as his Agnes?

"Why?" he blurted out at last, without meaning to ask. "Why would she do this? It was *her,* wasn't it?" Fury hoarsened him, bass-deep though his voice always was. Not since that day he had hidden in the church and listened to the distant crack of the whip across his mother's back in the *place d'armes* had he felt such helpless rage at the cruelty of fellow humans.

"It's not important now, Gustin. It's all behind us," Agnes answered with a fire that hinted of hatred as well as want. Her lips sought Augustin's eagerly, demandingly.

"Love me, Gustin! Love me so I will know I'm still a woman, still desirable, in spite of... this..."

Urgently her hands caressed the full length of his body, exploring him as she had never been free to do in the furtive minutes they had spent alone together in the past, as Augustin dared not let himself do to her just now for fear that curiosity would override his passion.

"Don't be gentle, Gustin. I'm not used to gentleness," she cried. And so Augustin forgot himself. Forgot the patience that was forever a part of his nature. Forgot the horror that had unconsciously repulsed him. Forgot the pity that had made him almost afraid to touch this woman lying now in his arms. Forgot everything but the hungry, crazy want that had made him into only half a person. And he crushed unto him the other, newer, half of his heart, his soul, and himself.

Agnes told him, eventually, after their passion had spent itself and the lantern on the bench had burned itself out and she had risen to relight it. That was when he realized that her need for light was not prompted by an eagerness to feast her eyes, her hands, her body upon his nakedness, but by a deep and terrifying fear of darkness itself.

"Agnes?" His voice was soft, but insistent. "There should be no secrets between us, *ma petite.* I have to know the woman I'm married to in more than just the Biblical sense of the word."

She was silent as she slid the lid back on the chamber pot, slipped back into bed, and fastened the netting behind her. For an eon she did not speak at all. Augustin waited.

Ten years had passed since the post first gossiped over the suit the young Poissot *mulâtresse* had filed against Athanase Poissot's wife. Not once in those ten years had any gossip been able to report the nature of those charges or the outcome of the suit. The case had closed as abruptly as it opened, and in all the years Augustin had courted, off and on, the girl who filed those charges, she never had allowed that subject to be broached.

Now he gave her no choice. They were one. Her pain had become his pain. Her fears, his fears.

"The memories hurt, Gustin," Agnes said at last.

"Then I'll hurt with you, and we'll cleanse ourselves of those bitter memories and begin a fresh life together. Just you and me, with no ghosts from your past to haunt us."

Slowly, Agnes took his broad hand into her tiny one and stiffened his forefinger into a probe. Softly, she traced it under her armpits, across her chest, following one broad whelp that completely encircled her upper torso.

"That, Gustin, is a rope burn from the time she hung me naked from the ceiling and left me dangling there, my feet just off the floor, all day and all that night to make me apologize for burning her. I didn't hurt her on purpose, Gustin. She had tried to hit me, for no fair reason, and my hand flew up instinctively to protect my face, but I was ironing and the iron was in that hand. I didn't mean to do it to her, Gustin. It was her fault and I would not apologize. I never would have, not even if she had left me there a week, as she said she would."

"Then who cut you down?" Augustin asked softly.

"Her mother-in-law. The old lieutenant's wife. She had gone down to the bluffs to visit her Dupré son. When she came home she found me there, naked and filthy where I messed all over myself and the floor when I could not go to the latrine."

For once in his life, Augustin could think of nothing to say, nothing that would heal the wounds she carried inside her.

"You wonder why I need the light?" Agnes went on with a harshness he never had heard from her before. "Has anyone ever locked you in the darkness in a trunk scarcely bigger than your own body? Or in the latrine so that you cannot escape the stench? Or in the storehouse with just rats to keep you company, only it is so black you cannot see them even though you feel them crawling all over you, nuzzling you? Have you…"

"No! Stop it!" Augustin cried at last, as he wrenched himself from her and flung back the netting, heedless of the drove of mosquitoes that descended upon him once he left the shelter of the bed.

"I can't take any more of it, Agnes. I should not have asked!" Augustin stared into the wall of darkness outside of the frail cabin light.

"But it *is* a cleansing, as you said, Gustin," she cried back. "I still hate the woman. I think I always will, but…"

Agnes's voice grew quiet, barely audible. "But I cannot hate my papa. M'sieur Athanase was just so mesmerized by her! That's why he would not stop her, no matter what she did to me."

"He permitted this? He knew about it and let her do it?"

"Oui," Agnes replied so softly that he had to return to the bed to hear her. "Sometimes he tried to protest, but then she would accuse him of caring more for me than for her, of siding with *the bastard* instead of his own wife. That always stopped him, because he worshipped her completely. If it had not been for his parents—only the old lieutenant wasn't there so much of the time."

"Then why did you stay with them so long?" Augustin asked, desperate to understand the woman he had married and the inexplicable way she could slip so quickly from mirth to moodiness for reasons only she could see somewhere in the recesses of her mind.

"You were free, weren't you, Agnes?"

"Oui, but what can a child do? They bought me from Mama's master when I was only six. The old M'sieur freed me, and took me into their home. Where could I go? If I had left him, who would have fed and sheltered me and kept me clothed? I don't fault Papa's parents, Gustin. They loved me as though I were their own and I loved them, too. They just didn't know what went on behind their backs, and in their goodness they never could have believed the half of it."

"But you said she found you herself, the time your father's wife hung you by the rope?" Augustin protested.

"That's when I left, Gustin. The old M'sieur got me that job then, keeping house for the Rachals, and made arrangements for me to live with them." Agnes's voice grew husky. "That's why he died, I know. It wasn't only his eyes that were almost blind. His heart was, too. The shock of seeing such meanness in his own family was just more than he could bear."

Gently, Augustin took her into his arms again and began to kiss away all the hurt she had kept bottled up inside her for so long.

"He's gone to his reward, *ma petite*. But he left his goodness here behind, packed into one tiny, beautiful bouquet."

Agnes smiled wanly, then winsomely as the mischief danced back into her ebony eyes.

"But I don't want to be good now, *mon cher*. I want to be naughty and wicked! I want to taste all those forbidden fruits that were a sin for us until this morning."

"Whatever you want, *chien-chien*," Augustin murmured as he laid her back again onto the soft, yielding mattress. "I'm your slave, Agnes, what would you have me do?"

ᘡ 6 ᘠ

August 1795

The last decade of the eighteenth century rolled on productively for Coincoin's family. Within months, both Augustin and his mother had tentative titles to the land they sought. On the broad expanse of her eight hundred arpents, rolling gently through the pine hills past Old River, Coincoin established the vacherie she had planned and hired the Spaniard to oversee her herd. Augustin's grant was far less generous, less than half of the size of his mother's concession, but the tract he had chosen in the uninhabited lower reaches of the Isle of Canes—straddling both banks of the river—was dark, rich, virgin loam. There, with the help of his three free brothers, Joseph, Toussaint, and François, Augustin began to clear the cane brakes. Within a year, both his land and his bride had borne fruit.

At the post he had left behind, there seethed violence and intrigue that threatened the success of both Augustin's and Coincoin's dreams. The Spanish king had gone to war against the rabble who had beheaded his Bourbon cousins, and the French Creoles of the Spanish province of Louisiana were caught up in the conflict. As Pierre had predicted a decade and a half before, the Anglo allies they had made across the Mississippi were eager now to help the Creoles who had supported their own fight for freedom. And so, agents of the American general George Rogers Clarke stood ready to recruit an army from the new United States to liberate the colony of Louisiana.

Perhaps nowhere within this colony did the spirit of *liberté* burn as fiercely as it did at the outpost of Natchitoches, whose inhabitants had long angered Spanish officials with their independence and disdain for royal authority. Led by their firebrand of a priest, the young men of Natchitoches, and the not-so-young as well, formed the secret brotherhood of *Les Revenants,* and those "Ghosts" soon spread throughout the hinterlands of Louisiana and Tejas.

From the barrooms of San Antonio to the parish sanctuary of Avoyelles way down in the ankle of Louisiana's boot they raised their tankards to the inspiring strains of *La Marseillaise* and preached sedition against the Spanish tyrant. By 1795, *Aux armes, citoyens! Formez vos bataillons! Marchons, marchons!* had become as familiar an anthem along the borderlands as on the streets of Paris.

While Clark and his French conspirator, Gênet, argued passionately for President Washington to approve their revolutionary plot, while the Spanish governor Carondelet tried futilely to remove the insurrectionary priest from his frontier stronghold, Les Revenants of Natchitoches took matters into their own hands. Like phantoms under cover of night, and in the clear light of day as well, they attacked all symbols of Spanish domination, including fellow Frenchmen who supported the Spanish Crown. Families were torn asunder as staid members such as Augustin preached the virtues of moderation and hotheads like his brother Louis argued for action.

In the heat of August 1795, Les Revenants struck more reckless blows, and this time the official they felled was the post surgeon, Conant. The patriotic furor of the Ghosts who attacked him got out of hand and only chance spared his life. The hapless doctor was already senseless when another Revenant, one who had not been apprised of the attack for reasons that were purely personal, happened upon the scene. The attackers fled and left their victim to the care of that *confrère* who happened by, Pierre Metoyer's new overseer—his son Louis.

Louis carried home the bloodied body of his sister's lover, and Susanne tended Conant's wounds. Tenderly, she spooned broth between his lips as he slipped in and out of consciousness for two long days, all the while shushing the baby-cries of their firstborn son, Florentin, lest he disturb his father's fitful sleep. On the third day, Conant rose, weakly but adamantly insisting that he had business at the post, and he rode into Natchitoches at the side of Susanne's father to file charges with a commandant who did not want to press them.

"*Merde*, De Blanc!" Pierre swore in disgust. "Are you our leader or a gutless coward? As syndic of my district, I demand that you do your duty to maintain peace at this post, to protect the decent citizens, and uphold authority. You've bowed to the rabble much too long!"

Not a muscle moved across the bland face of Louis Charles de Blanc, in the wake of Metoyer's insult. He just demurred. "As a wise old sage has put it, Pierre, discretion is sometimes the better part of valor. In this matter, I am confident the present unrest will wear itself out if we ignore it. These men crave martyrdom. That's what feeds the lifeblood of such causes. If we deny them that, Les Revenants will die a natural death."

"Meanwhile, how many people of this post must die also, as Conant almost did? I tell you, De Blanc, this insurrection demands prompt, decisive action that will crush it, the kind of action your uncle would have taken. Never would De Mézières have tolerated such open disrespect for his authority. Nor would your father, when he held the command of Natchitoches. Nor your grandfather! If the stories I've heard about old St. Denis are true, he'd have had the heads of every one of them lined up on spikes outside the stockade. But there you sit in your chair, the scion of a long line of powerful commandants, quaking at the threats of rabble-rousers!"

"Is that really what you want me to do, Metoyer?" De Blanc parried. "If I order my guardsmen to decorate the walls of this post with the severed heads of our friends and neighbors, then I would be more guilty of bloodlust than Les Revenants themselves, as guilty as the barbaric mobs that have taken over France. I will not descend to that level."

"Then you can at least arrest the hoodlums who terrorize out district!"

"Those who attacked Conant?" the commandant parried.

"The whole worthless lot of troublemakers!" Pierre shot back.

"You forget, Pierre. They mask themselves."

"Masks? *Mon Dieu!* Everyone at this post knows who the Ghosts are, masks or no."

"Pierre, perhaps the commandant is right," the doctor interjected. "Perhaps I should let the matter drop."

"If you fear reprisals, then go on home, Conant. I'll press the suit for you. Just name those cowards who jumped you, and I'll charge them all with disturbance of public peace and safety. Then with a little persuasion," Pierre smiled crookedly, "They'll implicate their whole bunch, down to the last cowardly *ghost*."

"Pierre," the doctor began again hesitantly, but De Blanc cut him off. "Never mind, Conant. It's my politics that Metoyer disagrees with, not yours. I'll handle this."

With his customary leisure that Pierre mistook for lassitude, the commandant opened the drawer of the Regency desk he had ordered from Marseilles in more settled times and removed a cigar. Not the crudely rolled périque that served most Natchitochians, Pierre observed with a snort, but a thinly tapered *cigarillo*, the best Havana sold. Then, from a richly carved box of ancient rosewood atop his desk—one with striking resemblance to the chest Coincoin had inherited from her father, Pierre could not help but notice—De Blanc carefully extracted a match and lit his smoke, letting Pierre fume while he leaned back into the butter-soft leather of his chair.

"Pierre," De Blanc finally began, "despite our occasional differences in politics, I've always considered you a friend. I like you and respect you, and that is why I'm saying what I'm about to say."

"You are quite right," he continued, deliberately turning his drags and puffs into pregnant pauses. "Almost any man here at the post could name a dozen or so members of Les Revenants. Putting their lists together, I could draw up an indictment that would be quite complete. In fact, I don't doubt but that I could sit down right now and draw up that list alone. But quite a few of my good, law-abiding friends would suffer when they saw the names on that list."

Pierre snorted, unimpressed.

"Quite frankly, Pierre, I'm reluctant to arrest as traitors the impetuous and misguided sons of my friends and supporters."

"Then you would let personal relationships override the welfare of this post?"

"Would you have me do otherwise?" De Blanc countered quietly. "What if your own brother, or son, were involved?"

"That's a pointless question, since I have no brothers at this post and my two sons are still in dresses."

For a long moment the commandant made no reply. Idly, he strolled to the window and eyed the restless, youthful crowd that always seemed to loiter these days outside the *casa real.* The faces changed from day to day, but this troublesome core of discontent was small enough. He need only watch—and keep his spies well paid.

"Metoyer, Conant has made his complaint in your presence, but he omitted one significant detail. From what my own informers tell me, I'd say he did so for your own sake."

De Blanc could see surprise flicker across Metoyer's craggy face, and he smiled. He had found Pierre to be an excellent syndic, definitely a man of character. Still, he preferred the less moralistic Metoyer in whose dram shop he had spent much of his youth.

"As you recall," De Blanc went on, "Conant's attackers fled when another man approached, one of their own whom they respected. But that compatriot was not privy to their plans because he had a certain attachment to the doctor. When he happened upon them, by chance, they fled lest he discover the identities of those who had betrayed his friendship."

"*Hehn?* What are you getting at, De Blanc?"

"The identity of the man who saved Conant's life. Conant avoided saying so, but that man was your, ah, overseer. Your Louis."

Pierre's guts knotted. "Well, what if Louis did happen by and stopped the assault? That scarcely incriminates him," he protested irrationally, refusing to acknowledge the blind spot he had sheltered for months now.

"As you said yourself, Pierre, the whole post knows who the members of this society are."

De Blanc was right. The whole post knew. Pierre knew. He had heard familiar voices among the hooded marchers who paraded through the post. He had heard a very familiar voice. At other times, too, he had heard young Louis expound openly like Philipe Égalité himself, and that was why he had refused to manumit this son. Louis was still too impetuous, too hotheaded, too irresponsible. He was not yet ready for the *liberté* he cried for.

"Pierre, the matter is even more serious when all aspects are considered." De Blanc's voice was now grave indeed. "Louis has long lived as free at this post. You've permitted him liberties no slave enjoys. But there are rumors that he is, indeed, a slave."

Metoyer was silent, his face stubborn and immobile. Les Revenants, of course, risked their heads when they preached sedition, but when a slave did so the public danger was far greater. In that case parental influence could not be counted on to buy a pardon.

"I have attempted to investigate the rumor, Metoyer, but it has been the damnedest situation. I can't find a record of the boy's manumission among the civil papers in my charge. For that matter, I can't find one for his mother either. When I asked the priest for a record of Louis's baptism to ascertain whether he was born free, that rascal just smiled and said certain portions of the baptismal registers have been lost."

A glimmer of hope arose in Pierre's eyes, as he began to realize the implications underlying De Blanc's words. The commandant was, indeed, a friend.

"Since I lack official proof of Louis's status, Pierre, I must ask you for your oath on the matter. Can you swear to me that this young fellow is indeed a free man?"

"Of course," Pierre lied without a moment's thought.

"Then the matter is settled," De Blanc replied blandly. "However, I do suggest that you keep the fellow down at the Point and out of mischief."

An idea came to Pierre then, a totally illegal proposition in view of the fact that Louis was indeed a slave. Eventually, that little matter would have to be straightened out, when the boy matured enough that he could cut him loose, but in the meanwhile…

"De Blanc?" Pierre began aloud. "Louis's basic problem is an excess of drive and energy. He's chomping to carve his own niche in life. It's not enough for him to just drive my slaves. What he needs is a piece of land to call his own, something worthwhile into which he can channel his energies and ambition."

Pierre hesitated, assessing the commandant's reaction thus far. It was hardly a feasible time to approach the man, in view of the way he had just attacked him, but if De Blanc was sincere about conciliating all factions at this post, then he should be agreeable.

"If you would be so kind as to recommend Louis to the governor, De Blanc, I would like to enter a petition in his name for a concession."

"Oh? Do you have a specific tract in mind?"

"Yes, next door to my… to Louis's brother Augustin, there is a tract that has been abandoned for several years now. Silvestre Bossier claimed it back in the eighties. I think he even sent a couple of hands on it to begin clearing; but he soon pulled them out, swearing that the land was not worth the labor it would cost him to comply with the terms of the grant."

De Blanc nodded. "He said as much to me when he returned his Order of Survey and Settlement. But you think the land is good?"

"Perhaps." Pierre shrugged offhandedly, knowing damned well that it was as fertile a tract as Augustin's land and a half-dozen times larger. De Blanc read his mind.

"If I recall, Metoyer, that's a very sizable chunk of land. In fact, it's more than the eight hundred arpents the law sets."

"Perhaps," Pierre replied casually. "But even double concessions are allowed sometimes. I'm sure those conditions could be met. Besides," Pierre smiled conspiratorially. "The larger the tract the longer we keep the boy out of trouble, *non?* I think we could justify this by saying it is in the best interests of your administration."

"Possibly, Metoyer, possibly." De Blanc's chuckle was promising, but his eyes were cold. "However, all this still leaves us with our original problem. Shall we get back to the complaint Conant filed?"

Neither Pierre nor the doctor replied as they waited for the commandant's decision.

"What do you say to a compromise, gentlemen? I'll arrest the man Conant identifies as the ringleader of his attack. This will be a simple assault charge, with the usual fine, to serve as an example to his conspirators, but we will not implicate the Ghosts in any way. I still believe their ardor will dissipate if we ignore them."

For a long, soul-searing moment, Pierre's conscience taunted him. This whole affair ran counter to all his principles. In saving Louis, he betrayed his own sense of right and wrong, but what choice did he have? Without waiting for the doctor to answer, without even glancing in Conant's direction to read his intent, Pierre agreed. Then, for the sake of Susanne's brother, Conant did also.

1803

Louis moved immediately to Yucca Bend. With the help of a strapping young black Augustin had bought from François Davion, he threw up a temporary cabin and began to clear his eleven hundred arpents. In time, he took a wife, the half-French, half-Cancci Thérèse Lecomte, whose mother had belonged to the old Lieutenant Le Court in the days when Indian slavery had been legal in the colony. As the seasons passed, the family's hold upon the Isle of Canes grew steadily. One by one, Pierre freed the other children Coincoin had borne him. The only heartbreak Coincoin could not live with now was the thought of her Chiquito. Thirty-two years after her firstborn son was seized by Gil y Barbo and taken to Tejas, Augustin had found him at Nacogdoches. They had bought his freedom back in '93, but Chiquito still refused to leave the Spanish and join the world they were carving out of the Isle of Canes.

Acre by acre now, cane brakes gave way to tobacco fields, which produced pounds of gold the young freedmen would not let themselves enjoy. With money, the ambitious man could buy more slaves to help him clear more cane brakes, *non?* Larger fields meant larger harvests and more profits with which the young Metoyers could also buy up neighboring tracts that white friends had received as grants but had not cared to develop. By the time Augustin celebrated his tenth year of freedom, over five thousand acres of the Isle of Canes bore the name *Metoyer, h.c.l.—homme de couleur libre, free man of color*—on parish maps and more than a dozen slaves called them "master."

The people, as Augustin had begun to call his community, swelled in number, as he joined his mother's benevolent raid on the slave households of fellow planters. The Widow Lecomte and her son Ambroise, whose *nègres* long had been friends of Coincoin's family, were favorite targets, and one after another of the Lecomte slaves moved to the Isle with their manumission papers in hand. One after another, too, the golden-skinned and newly freed Lecomte girls, themselves a mixture of French, Indian, and African, began to marry Augustin's brothers, and proved themselves as fertile as the land.

At the post they left behind, turmoil and intrigue did fade away, as Commandant de Blanc had known it would. America's president rejected the Clarke-Gênet scheme for an invasion of Spanish Louisiana, and the rebellious Creoles

Manumission of Marguerite
by Widow Lecomte

Marguerite Leroy, the carpenter's daughter who had wed the soldier-planter, Jean Baptiste Lecomte, agreed to the manumission of several of her slaves by Coincoin and her sons. In the above document she manumits the fourteen-year-old mulâttresse Marguerite, daughter of Joseph Trichel's négresse, Marie. An accompanying document states that freedom was purchased by Coincoin's son Augustin. Within a year, Marguerite would wed Augustin's brother Dominique Metoyer.

were left to fight their cause alone. Older rebels recalled the disaster of the '68 revolt, when so few challenged the might of the Spanish Crown, and the new rebellion fizzled. As another century dawned on a troubled world, however, fate promised to reward the faithfulness of Louisiana's Creoles to the French *fleur de lis*. His Catholic Majesty, the King of Spain, staved off war with the imperialistic, Revolutionary government of France by giving it a handsome gift, the now-prosperous colony of Louisiana.

Within that war-torn nation itself, Napoleon Bonaparte had come to power. A man who believed in religion only for its expediency, Napoleon arbitrated differences between the revolutionary government and the Catholic Church to the benefit of both. His Code Napoléon, a model for modern legal justice, became the law of France and peace descended, albeit temporarily, upon the people who had been torn by civil strife for more than a decade.

In that historic year 1803, Pierre Metoyer returned to the land of his birth. He, too, had been torn by inner strife far too long. Like the old Bourbon dynasty that controlled the France of his youth, the *ancien régime* of the family he left behind was also gone. Mère Suzanne, Père Jorge, God rest their souls, were but a painful memory from his past.

The old Pierre, like archaic France, had suffered the agonies of rebirth. In that re-creation, his attempts to expunge the guilt of his affair with Coincoin had brought him no more inner peace than had the countless decapitations committed by the mobs of Paris in the name of reform. The memories of Pierre's youth were still specters he had to put to rest, and his pride in the new caste he had created was a positive good, too long neglected, that he had to nourish before his numbered days ran out.

So, the aging Pierre did not go to France alone. Sailing from New Orleans amidst luxurious accommodations he never imagined amid his first crude crossing, he stood beside the railing and watched the New World fade from sight, one patriarchal arm slung fondly across the husky shoulders of his firstborn and the other wrapped proudly around the slender, Latin frame of his fair T'Pierre.

Metoyer's homecoming was an enlightenment for all of them. In the égalité and fraternité of the new French regime, all men were of equal worth. Senseless laws against interracial marriage had been renounced. Even the Marquise de Beauharnais, kinswoman to Napoleon's Josephine, had taken as her new husband a *mulâtre* widower of considerable wealth and character.

In almost every city and village they visited, Pierre's modishly attired sons enjoyed the kind of respect, indeed égalité, that both their parents had dreamed of for them. Born in the wilderness, exposed to no more culture than the bars of *la ville* could offer, their whirlwind tour was a fantasy that fired their imagination toward even more daring goals. Upon the Continent they found a world they never knew existed, and a long-sought understanding of their father's old reluctance to yield himself to the colonies. As a result of the six short months they spent abroad, young T'Pierre would live out his years in restless discontent with his lot in Louisiana, and Augustin would be forever challenged to transplant and nurture the culture of France upon the Isle of Canes.

In the banquet of wonders Pierre spread before them on the Continent, Paris was the pièce de résistence.

The Louvre, with its wealth of art like nothing either of the young Creoles had seen before. There, in amazement, Augustin and young Pierre found splendid reenactments of the Biblical events they had envisioned so ineptly during the sermons of one priest or another. There they came face to face with one portrayal of their faith they never had conceived: a rare, ancient painting from early Christendom that portrayed the Holy Madonna, not with the fair and Florentine features popularized by painters of the Renaissance but as a dusky beauty.

The Sorbonne, founded by the Church as a theological school five hundred years before. Provincial and untutored as he was, Augustin still recognized that boundless knowledge existed beyond his imagination. One day, he swore, with God's help and continued profits from his plantation, he would hire a teacher from that institution to bring all its knowledge to the Isle.

L'Arc de Triomphe... la Colonne de Vendôme... the cafés that buzzed with the talk of Voltaire, Chateaubriand, and Saint Simon. Three months before, Augustin had never heard their names. Now he strained to hear every scrap of conversation that explored, vilified, or proselytized their ideas.

In Paris, too, Augustin met a little man, no taller than himself, who showed him that physical stature was no measure of a real man's worth, that race did not have to be an eternal barrier, that even men of second-class caste could become *first citizen.* If an obscure Corsican, bold of dream and sage of mind, could bridge the river of blood that had divided France, then there was hope for Augustin, hope for his Isle and his people; hope for bridging the chasms of suspicion, fear, envy, and even hostility that divided the races in Louisiana.

It was at Mme. de Montesson's maison on Rue de Bon Coeur that Augustin met that Corsican.

"*Madame?*" T'Pierre had quipped when their father waved down a hack outside the Maison d'une Bonne Nuit, where they had lodged for three glorious weeks, and ordered the driver to her house. The man had cocked the unruly brow above his one good eye and sized up the provincial trio, from Pierre's leathery face to the brown ones of his sons, and T'Pierre, with his usual bent of mind, misread the churl's long stare.

"The *celebrated Madame* de Montesson?" T'Pierre arched his own slender brows. "M'sieur, should I ask what kind of *madame* this is, or what she is celebrated for?"

"Not for what you have in mind!" his father chortled before Augustin could mutter the same thought.

"*Hélas!*" T'Pierre rejoined. "You promised to show us *all* of France, M'sieur. You promised us *experiences* like none we've had before. Now tell me, what naive young lad from the colonies would not have had a palpitating heart to hear you mention a *celebrated* Parisian *madame?*"

"At the sight of this one, you'd be cured quick," Pierre retorted. "I've never laid eyes on the lady, but I suspect she was rocking a cradle before I ever laid in one."

"Mme. de Montesson?" Augustin interjected suddenly, more to himself than to the others. "Mme. de Montesson? *Hé,* M'sieur, wasn't she the old commandant's sister? M'sieur de Mézières's sister?"

"She was."

Now Augustin knew where he had heard the name. "She's a writer, is she not? The one Ma'mselle Elisabeth's been reading?" A half-smile flickered across his broad face. "Isn't there another essayist in that family?"

Pierre missed the humor. All he felt was the irony, and the guilt that it had been the illiterate Gustin just now, not the educated T'Pierre, who recognized the woman's name. Again he cursed himself and his own prejudices. He should have taught Gustin as he did T'Pierre. Education had been wasted on the younger boy. Ah, *oui,* the lad was handsome. He and Susanne had *class.* They had elegance. If only Augustin had looked more like them, if he had not been so damned *brown* and broad of nose, if his hair had been floss instead of wool, Pierre would have developed his potential. *If only I had not been so damned prejudiced,* Pierre admitted to himself, I'd have done it anyway!

"*Oui,*" he echoed aloud, at last. "Madame de Genlis. The lady is Madame's niece and an even-more celebrated writer."

"That's the one!" Augustin chuckled. "I should have remembered her name myself, as many times as I've heard Susanne take it in vain!"

Pierre smiled at last. "Your sister definitely is not an admirer of Mme. de Genlis. That's for certain. Sometimes I could swear that Elisabeth reads Genlis's *Lettres sur education* to Susanne just to watch your sister's temper flare. 'The minds of women should never be aroused," he parroted. "'Women were born for dependency. For their duties, they need training in mildness and method, patience and prudence…' "

"No lessons in *l'amour?*" T'Pierre interjected roguishly.

Metoyer's answer was lost as their carriage careened wildly, veering into an ancient street no wider than an alleyway. Grimy stone walls rose on either side of them, almost within arm's reach. Dirty urchins infested almost every doorway, some in rags that barely covered their nakedness, and Augustin thought suddenly of all the *négrillons* back home. Even in the abjectness of their slavery, they did not live in squalor such as this. Nor did such filth spew from their lips.

Above them, from an overhanging room, a slovenly wench dumped the contents of her chamber pot into the street, and T'Pierre wrinkled his nose in disgust.

"If this is the neighborhood the old dame lives in, M'sieur, she's safe from me. I like my women a little classier."

Pierre stopped him rather curtly. "I can assure you that wherever Mme. de Montesson lives, you'll find there more class than you've ever seen. She's had her share of suffering these past ten years. She's lucky to be alive. There weren't too many duchesses in France who came through this revolution with a head still on their shoulders."

"A *duchess?*" T'Pierre's long, low whistle faded into the din of Rue des Mendiants, but Pierre could see that his blasé son was impressed.

"Not just a duchess, *mon frère,*" Augustin corrected. "This one is *the* duchess of France. Widow of the Duc d'Orleans himself—who fortunately did not live to see the shortening of his cousin Louis XVI, am I not right, M'sieur?"

Pierre nodded.

"And stepmother to none other than Philippe Egalité. I'm sure you recall him," Augustin jibed. "You and Louis sang enough rabble-rousing songs in his honor back in the early days of the Revolution."

T'Pierre had recovered his aplomb. "Ah, big brother, of course I recall; but then I lost my respect for the man when he lost his head. A leader must always keep his wits, *n'est-ce pas?*"

The hack veered suddenly again, and the street broadened into a languorous thoroughfare, bathed in a warm June sun that the alleyway behind them must never have seen.

In spite of himself, Pierre felt relief at the change of neighborhood. He had promised the old Demoiselle de Mézières before he left Natchitoches that he would take care of this silly piece of family business for her, but he was not a man who enjoyed the company of strangers. Certainly not old ladies who had fallen on hard times and subsisted on grandiose memories. Elisabeth-Marie-Felicité-Nepomucene Mauguet de Mézières, the only offspring of old Athanase's short marriage to St. Denis's daughter, was more than enough for Metoyer to endure. Of course she had assured him that her aunt would welcome him graciously; but, after all, the Demoiselle de Mézières had not heard from the old duchess in years. Who knows what may have happened to her in the meanwhile?

"M'sieur Pierre," she had pleaded. "You *must* take this brooch to my aunt! You see, M'sieur, it has inside a likeness of my grandmother, Madame's own mother. When my dear papa sent me to France for my education back in the fifties, Mme. de Montesson gave me this to pass on to my own children, so that the Mézières in the New World would never forget the people from which they came."

The old maid's eyes had clouded then, and Pierre swore roundly to himself as the predictable tears came. Not a flood of them. The Demoiselle de Mézières was too delicate a lady for that. Her kind wept softly, but they made their point just the same.

"You know, M'sieur Pierre, that I have no children. How could I marry here in Louisiana? You are a Frenchman, not a Creole. You understand that I could not mingle such a pure and noble blood line as mine with the commoners in this colony."

Pierre almost scoffed then, at the thought of how freely her libidinous brothers mingled that bloodline with every variety of wench that crossed their paths. But, of course, the memory of his own past had silenced him, a guilty memory of the superciliousness and condescension with which he had taken Coincoin into his bed.

"Your brother in L'Abadie?" Pierre did venture to ask. "Does not he and his wife have children there in Tejas who would someday treasure your grandmother's brooch?"

She chattered on, as though she had not heard him, but he knew she had. The look that clouded her steel grey eyes told him that, and he did not need to wonder why. That brother had married his *mestizo* lover. In Tejas, both the Church and the State recognized their union. But his sister could not and Pierre understood, even though it pained his own soul to admit it.

So he had taken the broach, in its small velvet-lined case permeated with all the mold and must that infested all antiquities along the steamy banks of Cane River.

The hack screeched abruptly to a halt, jolting Pierre from his reverie. Beside him, T'Pierre whistled appreciatively again, and Pierre followed his gaze to the tall Georgian mansion flanked by an expanse of formal gardens. Mademoiselle de Mézières had said that her aunt's name was on Bonaparte's civil list, but even Pierre had not expected a pensioner to live so royally, with a trio of guards stationed outside her door, no less!

"*Tiens!*" T'Pierre drawled. "It looks as though the old dame came through the Revolution with more than just her head intact. I thought only Richelieu's mistresses survived in such style!"

"*Mon frère,*" Augustin chided, "there are more ways for women to achieve wealth than by prostituting themselves."

T'Pierre grinned. "Maybe so, big brother, but that's the best way I know of, for all concerned."

Guilt stabbed at Pierre again, and he interrupted his younger son's banter more curtly than he intended.

"Come on, boys, let's not sit out here gawking like provincial popinjays. We need to get this over with. Tomorrow we'll take a coach to L'Orient to sail for home."

᥀ 8 ᥀

The guards eyed them warily but made no challenge to their approach. As they mounted the broad expanse of steps, they could feel the trio silently ring itself behind them and their discomfiture mounted, not to mention Pierre's annoyance with Demoiselle de Mézières for sending them here in the first place.

The butler who answered their ring was curt. Madame was entertaining. Madame was not expecting them. If M'sieurs would like to leave their cards, perhaps they might be asked to call back another day. The butler's demeanor, however, drastically improved when Pierre slipped a franc, as well as his card, into the man's palm. In view of how far they had come, the servant then conceded, the least he could do would be to tell his mistress they were here. Madame could decide for herself whether the intrusion was worth an interruption in her little game of cards, *n'est-ce pas?*

Madame decided that it was. It was not in her nature to turn anyone away, even when she had important guests. When Charlotte-Jeanne Bérard de la Haie de Riou, Marquise de Montesson, had first met Louis-Philippe, Duc d'Orleans, at the royal court of Louis XV so many years before, the old duc had been captivated as much by the young widow's goodness as her beauty. In the years since, the bloom of her youth had died, as had the old Duc, but the genuineness of her character still won over all who met her. Even the few critics who failed to appreciate her literary talents found themselves praising her sense of *égalité*. Madame de Montesson, as she now styled herself in the new democratic manner, was a product of the old regime, of the nobility and artificial class divisions the Revolution had overthrown. In the Reign of Terror, her titles had brought her imprisonment instead of privilege, but she had survived. Despite her lofty birth, Madame was a woman for all people, affable to her inferiors, polite but never subservient to her rulers, obliging to all.

If she had not been all this and more, she would never have left her game of cards or left the young companion whose calls had become less frequent these past three years but were a nourishment to both of them. She would never have taken the risk, at this moment, of answering a stranger's intrusive call.

Madame was cordial, but Pierre and his sons were still ill at ease. The presence of those guards behind them was an ominous reminder that the headiness of France in 1803 was still a superficial air, and beneath Madame's pleasant greeting lay a wellspring of wariness born of ten years of utter lawlessness. Briefly, Pierre stated his mission and a ray of curiosity broke through the caution that clouded her eyes. When he produced the timeworn box Mademoiselle had entrusted to him, those eyes teared as she slowly opened the lid and beheld her mother's brooch.

"Messieurs," the old woman began at last, her face as gray as the plain day-dress she wore. "Messieurs, I am forever in your debt." Her voice began to shake and she swallowed, visibly, then tried again.

"Ten years ago this month, the Great Reign of Terror erupted here in my beloved Paris. I was imprisoned. My home, my treasures, everything my family left me were wantonly pillaged by those who abused the ideals of our Revolution. After 9 Thermidor, I was released, but the mobs had destroyed everything dear to me."

Her eyes lowered again to the brooch. Slowly, she pressed the little latch upon its side and raised its cover, then fresh tears welled as she gazed upon the faded miniature of her mother.

"Until now—until you brought me this, messieurs—I had no keepsake left to treasure, no hope of ever again seeing the dear face of my mother until God calls me home."

Pierre and his sons shifted their weight self-consciously, almost in unison.

The old duchess's gravelly alto was barely audible. "Messieurs, what can I do for you in return?"

"No return is needed, Madame," Pierre reassured her gruffly. "Your late brother was my friend. I could never repay the debts I owe him. Your charming niece," he went on hastily and with somewhat less sincerity, "is my wife's friend. It is a pleasure to be able to do for her this one small favor while I am in France."

"Where are you staying, Messieurs?" the duchess persisted. "Jacquitte will dismiss your hack and send a carriage for your baggage. You must spend the remainder of your visit here."

"You are kind, Madame," Pierre protested. "But we leave Paris tomor-row."

"Then you will at least spend this night."

"*Merci,* Madame, but…"

"There can be no buts, Messieurs!"

"*Sapristi,* Charlotte!" a voice swore good-naturedly behind her. "You, a lone female, inviting three male guests to spend the night? All of Paris will wag their tongues tomorrow."

Again, they could feel the guards tense behind them as Madame's guest strolled into the hall; yet the uniforms remained frozen in their posts.

"General!" the old lady snapped back fondly at the guest she had all but forgotten since Jacquitte had interrupted them with the report that three colonials were at her door. "When did you and Rose-Josephe begin to worry about gossip? Besides, all the wagging tongues of France had their fill of me long before either of you was born."

T'Pierre's brows cocked again. It was almost a habit with him. But they quickly lowered under the weight of his older brother's glare.

The general just smiled. "You win, as usual, Charlotte. At least with me. I'm not sure where you stand right now with the guests here on your stoop."

"They will stay, of course," the old dame retorted. "The Messieurs Metoyer are cavaliers, you can see. They are much too gentlemanly to refuse an old lady's hospitality."

Obviously, they had no choice—despite the fact that each of them had keen anticipations for his final night in Paris. For Pierre it was to be the opera, for Augustin another evening lecture at the Sorbonne. For T'Pierre, well, whatever T'Pierre had planned, he had assured them with a grin, they really would not care to tag along. Fate had now changed those plans. To a large measure, it would change Augustin's life as well.

The general was an enigma. Curiously, to Pierre and his sons, the duchess seemed not to notice that no introductions had been made. While Jacquitte sent the coachman for their baggage, while the guards were summarily waved back to their station before the portico, the little party retired to the duchess's salon. Yet another soldier stood mutely before a garden window, ostensibly engrossed in the antics of a pair of squirrels. In one corner of the room, two hands of tarot cards were fanned face down on opposing sides of a small table, mute testimony to the game their visit had interrupted. Pierre politely suggested that it continue, but the duchess declined. Still, the general seemed in no hurry to take his leave.

"You are a Creole, Messieur Metoyer?" he directed his inquiry to Pierre.

"No, I was born at La Rochelle, but emigrated shortly before the Spaniards took over Louisiana. My sons were born in the colony."

The little general nodded. "I thought as much. My wife is Creole also."

"Oh?" Pierre inquired politely, "from Louisiana?"

"No." The general laughed shortly. "She was born on Martinique, though it makes little difference. She has scant interest now in any of the colonies."

Madame de Montesson smiled fondly at her friend. "Our Rose-Josephe is a true daughter of France, General. She would be happy no where but here."

"How well I know!" the general rejoined. "Not even you could persuade her to join me in Egypt."

Small talk continued, while Augustin discreetly studied his surroundings. The old dame's salon had furnishings for which he did not even know a name, but there was one thing of which he was certain. Everything about her reflected her gentility, her aristocracy. These furnishings, whatever they were, were elegant and luxurious but in no way ostentatious. The architecture, from the winding staircase to the wainscotting, was magnificent without pomp, ornamental yet not ornate. One day, God willing, he'd have this kind of home himself.

Meanwhile, Pierre just as discreetly inquired about the general's career. Never yet had he met an officer who did not enjoy retelling his battles and reliving his glory, but this little general was different. He seemed to prefer politics to war, reform to battle tactics. Even more exasperating, there was something deucedly familiar about him.

"This is your first visit to France?" The general clearly was directing his question now to Augustin.

"*Oui,* Monsieur-General."

"Well, what do you think of our Revolution, our reforms?" the officer asked bluntly.

Augustin began cautiously. "There is much that impresses me, Monsieur-General. The school reforms are encouraging. This new Code Napoléon is surely the most progressive and judicious law of any in the world."

The little general nodded vigorously. He seemed almost pleased and so Augustin continued.

"I was particularly gratified last year to learn of the Concordat between France and the Church. This is one of the things that had disturbed me the most about the Revolutionary reports we received in Louisiana—the treatment of your holy leaders, the seeming loss of faith among so many people."

Again, the little man nodded, his thin locks falling across a high and bony forehead. "I'm a skeptic, myself, but I'd be the first to acknowledge there never has existed a more effective control over the baser instincts of mankind than the Church. A simple, unquestioning belief in God and his commandments prevents more crime and injustice than any law man can devise. No country can afford to put policemen on every street corner, but as long as people believe in God and fear His retribution, society can get by with a lot fewer guards."

This time it was Augustin who nodded.

"That is where our revolution really went wrong, was it not?" The young general continued, as much to himself as to the other guests. "We murdered our king and drove away our priests. That left no figure of authority to control those baser instincts. Every society has to have a strong, central authority. All people have to have discipline. Without discipline, without *self*-discipline, there is no real liberty."

Before Augustin could interject his assent, the general changed the subject. "Were you born free?"

"I beg your pardon, Monsieur-General?"

"You two," the question embraced both Augustin and T'Pierre, "were you born free or slave?"

Never before had any man asked Augustin so painful a question, so bluntly, or with such seeming unawareness of the pain it could cause. To Augustin's surprise, he did not really mind now. It seemed a natural question for this man to ask, and so he answered it.

"Our mother was a slave, Monsieur-General, until our father freed her. I was manumitted at my marriage ten years ago, and Pierre two years ago, just before his own wedding."

"Do you own slaves?"

"A few."

"Then what do you think of our problems in St. Domingue?" the general persisted, and Augustin could see now why this question had been prefaced by the others. He laughed.

"Monsieur-General, if you are asking me, you will get one answer. If you are asking my brother, you will get quite another. I'm a staid old man before my time."

"You've always been a staid old man," T'Pierre interjected.

271

Augustin smiled tolerantly and went on. "I am not a revolutionist. T'Pierre could easily be one. Obviously, we are not abolitionists or we would not own slaves. We believe in treating our servants humanely. We believe in encouraging the more ambitious to work for themselves in their spare hours, to accumulate savings and buy their freedom. But we cannot condone revolt, murder, or any of the other atrocities that are said to have occurred in St. Domingue in the name of liberty."

The little French general sat pensively. Not a wrinkle moved on the face of the old duchess as she fought back her own memories of atrocities Augustin never could imagine. Amid the silence that loomed between them, Augustin could not resist adding one further thought.

"At the same time, it hurts me to hear the St. Domingue rebels referred to as *savages*. To be very blunt, Monsieur-General—Madame—I see little difference between the way the black slaves of St. Domingue have treated their former masters and the way the white mobs of Paris have treated France's aristocrats. Or the way in which some of the Anglo-Americans and the British treated each other in that fight for freedom."

The general's face was as sober as that of his companion. "You are quite right, Messieur Augustin. But what about the slaves in Louisiana? With the hordes of refugees from St. Domingue that are pouring into New Orleans, the Louisiana slaves surely are aware of events in the Caribbean. Will there be repercussions in your colony, in your opinion? Would your colored population support such a revolt?"

Augustin did not answer quickly. Once again, the general had forced him to face issues he had preferred to skirt even in the privacy of his own thoughts; and so he paused before he answered, to quickly sort his emotions from his common sense.

"Monsieur-General, I am no longer qualified to speak for the slave. However, it is my opinion that the free man of color in Louisiana would have nothing to gain by encouraging a slave rebellion. He now has almost all the privileges he could ask for and stands a good chance of winning the rest of them. An overthrow of the system by the ignorant masses of slaves, or a wholesale emancipation, would have only one result. The free man of color, who has won his freedom with his initiative and ambition, would then be submerged into the black masses. No, the *homme de couleur libre* in Louisiana never would support a slave revolt."

"He has in Anglo-America, or so I've heard."

"We've heard those same reports," the old Pierre interjected. "But Louisiana—*grâce à Dieu!*—is not subject to the Anglo-Americans!"

"What if it were?" the general persisted. "What would happen, let us say, if France were to sell Louisiana to those United States?"

"I'll tell you what would happen," Pierre broke in again. "Every hope I've had for these boys would be gone forever! Everything they have worked for would be lost. These sons of mine are well on their way to becoming respected gentlemen in Louisiana. They deserve to be!"

"Of course," the general interposed quickly.

"In Anglo-America, they never would be! *Never* could they hope to be full citizens, successful businessmen, contributors to society. Never could they dream of becoming *leaders* in that regime. Not them nor any of the hundreds of other young men of their class we now have in Louisiana. Never!"

"Corsicans were second-class citizens of France when I was born. Now, a Corsican is First Consul of France," the general argued, just as intensely. "Society does change."

The colonials did not return his argument. Suddenly they knew why this little general had seemed so deucedly familiar. The ivory bust of Bonaparte the Corsican that stood in the Louvre, the two-dimensional image of the First Consul on those rare coins they had seen once or twice since arriving in Paris, both were too stylized. The real man was bonier, lankier. Less ethereal and more intense. The real Bonaparte was far smaller than anyone might guess from that bust or those coins. But there could be no doubt, this was he.

Pierre glanced quickly at the duchess, and in her quiet smile he saw his confirmation. That was why she had been so wary when the three of them appeared unannounced and unidentified at her stoop. The city was thick with rumors, rife with plots. Her concern over the strangers had not been for herself, but for her old friend who had, of late, assumed such importance to their nation.

Suddenly there flashed before Pierre a vivid memory of his first day in Natchitoches, when he had failed to recognize the superior rank of a new acquaintance. Then, as now, he had been at a loss for words. Old Étienne, glib Étienne, had carried him through that embarrassment. He sure as hell missed Pavie!

It was Augustin now who broke the long silence that discomfited the three colonials but seemed to amuse the First Consul. Stiffly, Augustin rose and bowed before the little Corsican. Never before had Pierre seen Augustin bow to any man, not during his son's twenty-five years of slavery nor in the ten years of second-class citizenship he had endured since then. Obviously, Augustin bowed now only because he felt the man deserved it.

"My apologies, Monsieur-General," Augustin said gruffly, "and my respects. We are honored that you have shared with us your company and your concerns."

"On the contrary," Bonaparte smiled. "I've appreciated your candid thoughts. Perhaps I should have introduced myself, but it is seldom I have the privilege now of asking people for their opinions and getting honest answers. When I saw that you did not recognize me, I could not pass up the opportunity to elicit your views."

Augustin still stood before him, riveted to the Turkish carpet. Bonaparte flexed one short leg after the other and pushed himself up from whatever kind of chair it was that enveloped him. It vexed Augustin that he did not know such things. There was so much he did not know!

The old dame rose, too, as T'Pierre and his not-so-agile father hastened to their feet.

"Charlotte, I've dallied longer than I should have," Bonaparte said gruffly. "If I dally any longer, my wife will accuse me of finding someone younger than you to share my dalliance!"

The duchess laughed as he kissed her cheek a fond goodbye, but his face turned somber. "Thanks for the sage counsel. I've said it before, Charlotte, and I mean it. You've never misguided me."

"At least you pretend to listen," she rejoined.

"Which is more than we can say for Josephine, *n'est-ce pas?*"

"*Ah,* General! When are you going to forgive little Rose-Josephe for not joining you in Egypt?"

Bonaparte grinned again. "Not until she tells you she is sorry for ignoring your advice while I was gone!"

He turned, then, to take his leave of the three subjects from out in his colonial empire. His face was marble now, every inch the mien of the First Consul, and Pierre could see that the bust in the Louvre was exactly the way Bonaparte looked when the man gave way to the demigod he would soon become.

With a worrisome sense of business left unfinished, Pierre watched him follow the old Madame to the doorway, trailed by his silent guard. There was something peculiar about the little Corsican's gait, Pierre thought. The man had carried France smoothly from its chaos, and yet his own carriage was almost clumsy. Half the world acclaimed him as a man who knew his own destiny and his country's as well. Yet his steps seemed downright uncertain.

For years to come, when Pierre recalled his native France, he would see that troubled gait of the Corsican general, that face of marble neither T'Pierre nor Augustin had glimpsed. Pierre had returned to his homeland in search of solace, but he would leave it now with a heart more troubled than the one he had sailed with from *la ville*.

Still, the trip was not in vain. Augustin had found his birthright and his inspiration, his commitment and his confidence in what the future held and in what he could do, must do. At his mother's knees, he had been taught the story of her past, the legend of that distant king whose daughter had been captured into slavery and brought across the waters to the post of Natchitoches, where she had wed a young Ewe artisan who had, himself, been kidnapped from the markets of Dakar. As a child, Augustin had been thrilled by that oft-repeated story, but it never had seemed to be any more a part of *him* than the story of Joseph's sale to slavers by those older brothers who envied his coat of many colors. In truth, Pierre's own accounts of France had also lacked the essence of reality, that elusive, tangible quality with which Augustin could identify; at least until now. While Augustin never would see the land his mother spoke of in awe as *Africa,* his father's France now became a seething, glorious, inspiring reality that permeated his every fiber, every pore.

As he sailed homeward, Augustin mentally mapped the Gallic world he would build on the primitive, primeval Isle of Canes....

There would be a *church*, he vowed solemnly. In every community they visited in France, despite the faithlessness of the Revolution, there was still a church within walking distance. But for Augustin's family, it was a full day's ride to l'Église de St. François at Natchitoches. Monsieur-General was right. So far removed from God's presence, it would be too easy for his family, *his people,* to lose their faith in God, their respect for the love of brother and neighbor. A church would not be an easy goal, *certainement.* Oh, he could build the sanctuary easily enough, he and his brothers. But a sanctuary was not a church without a pastor, and colonial priests were in short supply. Yet, with prayer and devotion, the colonists could overcome that want. He and his people could overcome that want.

Schools, with teachers, and a host of tradesmen, artists, and artisans—it would take all of these to make the Isle a thriving, pulsing community like those he had found in France. But all were possible. Fine homes like Madame's, elegant but not ostentatious, would replace their rude log cabins and huts of *bousillage.* They would import their furniture from France itself—some of those fashionable pieces Madame had that he had never seen before. There would be sterling silver, clocks, a library with books, a *pigeonnière* like the one in the far corner of her gardens, a race track. Ah, even Ambroise Lecomte would envy him his race track!

Justice. Above all, there must be law and justice on his Isle, Augustin knew. All people needed law, and a strong authority to enforce it, as the General himself agreed. Augustin was the eldest brother. He must be that leader. It was his sacred duty, especially if the governor continued to ignore the needs of the settlements that were everywhere springing up at points far distant from the central posts. He would be fair and impartial, Augustin vowed to himself, but he would still be firm. He would be knowledgeable, too. Even though he could not read the laws, he already knew many of Bonaparte's codes by heart, and he would learn the rest.

That was when Augustin recalled the little general's last question, *What if France should sell Louisiana to the United States?* The law would then change, surely. Louisiana would change. His Isle would have to change, if his father's frequent denouncements of the Anglos had any basis in fact—and Augustin was not a man to doubt his father's words. The privileges he and his family had won through manumission and hard work, the rights of man that the French revolutionists had fought for and bestowed upon their colonial cousins when they reclaimed Louisiana, the respect that Augustin and T'Pierre had enjoyed for three exhilarating months on the continent and hoped one day to know at home, all these would surely be threatened if the Anglos took their colony. But, then, Augustin remembered the Corsican, whose isle had been overrun by France in the very year of his birth. Now a little Corsican was the First Consul. There *was* hope, under any regime. The little general proved that.

⟨⟩ 9 ⟨⟩
Fall 1804

Pierre's fears came true. In the winter following their return from France, Louisiana's prefect, Pierre Clément de Laussat, handed over his citizens to the United States in return for President Thomas Jefferson's promise to pay Bonaparte eleven million dollars. The upper reaches of this vast colony became the new American territory of Louisiana, with its capital at St. Louis, while the lower reaches of old Louisiana were now the Territory of Orleans, its capital still at *la ville*. Within months, the French commandant of Natchitoches was replaced by an American commander, and Poste St. Jean Baptiste was renamed Fort Claiborne by the new, blue-coated, English-speaking professional army that replaced the militia in which Augustin and his free brothers had proudly served.

The long-standing hostility that plagued the Louisiana-Tejas frontier, the traditional rivalry of Frenchmen and Spaniards along the borderlands, continued to fester under the new American regime. Napoleon had sold the colony without defining its limits. American officials claimed that the western boundary of their territory was the Sabine River, while Spain insisted rightly that it had always lain eastward along the Red and the Cane. Since much of the new civil parish of Natchitoches, by this time, lay within the contested area, its people were again caught in the international struggle for power, and the French planters in the valley of the Cane became the victims of political leaders who tried to break each other's hold on that disputed frontier.

By the fall of 1804, the Isle of Canes and the Rivière aux Cannes district that stretched placidly southward from the lower reaches of the Isle were an armed camp. Rumor had it that the commandant of Nacogdoches offered freedom to all Louisiana slaves who sought refuge in Spanish Tejas and that his agents were traveling the length and breadth of northwest Louisiana, enticing blacks with the lure of liberty. In the new county of Natchitoches, the great plantations and the great masses of the enslaved centered upon the fertile Isle and the Rivière aux Cannes.

Singly and in swarms, those slaves fled their masters under cover of the night and patrols doubled. By day, Augustin and his brothers worked their fields. By night they rode, well-armed and wary of the slightest unrest or unusual actions.

Unlike most of their friends and fellow planters, they could boast that none of their blacks had yet absconded, but Augustin harbored no illusions. Their *nègres* were not bound to them by any tie of race or blood. He treated his servants kindly, clothed and fed and housed them well, but they were still his *slaves,* and Augustin well knew the hunger for freedom that could drive the enslaved to desperation.

The fifteenth of October was the feast day of Ste. Thérèse, his mother's patron saint. Within their household it always had been a Holy Day, and Augustin brought that custom with him to the Isle. For want of a priest to say Mass for them that morning, he had called together his people and their *nègres,* led them in prayer, exhorted them on the virtues of love, cooperation, and industry, and then announced that the rest of the day would be a holiday.

Amid the cheers of his hands, he left his brother François, twenty now and a bull of a man, to oversee their celebration, and he rode off downriver to Louis Derbanne's place.

For some time now, ever since the death of Agnes's mother, he had promised her that he would buy her brother Remy, but the slave troubles had caused him to procrastinate. Tomorrow was Agnes's birthday, and he knew no present would mean as much to her as would her brother. Five years before, he had gifted her with the manumission papers of Marguerite, the little sister who still made eyes at François, and it was long since time for him to bring Remy to the Isle as well.

True, young Remy was a much different matter than his sister. The boy was slow in speech and thought, simple of heart and totally trusting, and Augustin frankly doubted his ability to survive in the free man's world. Agnes would care for him, though, and she would be far happier if she, instead of the Derbannes, held his title.

An eerie stillness greeted Augustin as he left the river road and turned down the path that led to Louis Derbanne's Big House. A notary as well as a planter, Derbanne was doing exceedingly well, and his spacious new house of *brique entre poteaux* was now the envy of area planters. Although Augustin would not allow himself to share their covetousness, he did admire the beauty of the setting Derbanne had chosen, the broad expanse of gallery that swept around all sides, the clean and sparkling whitewash and brilliant shutters as green as the woods in the first flush of spring. Yet it came to Augustin as Bonhomme clipped up the lane that his friend's estate was also as quiet as the forest becomes when its inhabitants sense the smell of danger.

Warily, he dismounted and tied his horse to the new hitching rail, with its handsome pair of brass horseheads. The yard around the broad front steps was bare, somber. No watchdog announced his presence, and a solitary rooster screeched in fright and scurried into hiding as he approached. No bashful, tittering *enfants* greeted him in the yard. His friends were childless. But there should have been the sound of children at play in the slave camp behind the Big House, and his apprehension mounted. As Augustin stepped upon the gallery, he spotted the half-open door.

"Louis!" he cried in alarm, knowing that if his friends were gone, they never would have left their home open. "*Mon vieux!* Are you there?"

Silence answered him. Pushing the door full wide, Augustin stepped cautiously inside and drew up short in horror.

"*Mon Dieu!*" he whispered as he surveyed the Derbannes' new salon. A fine, upholstered canapé and chaise stood slashed, tables overturned. The cut-glass chandelier that had cost Louis a whole bale of cotton lay in a smashed heap on the mud-smeared carpet. Doors sagged, gaping open, on the tall pair of matching armoires. Drawers hung precariously from the *escritoire* and the buffet, and brocaded drapes dangled in shreds from the rods on which they had been hung.

His anxiety mounting, Augustin checked every chamber, and the same chaos greeted him. From the front gallery to the rear, his friend's home was ravaged, plundered, and devoid of any sign of life, save that lone rooster.

"Louis! Mme. Derbanne!"

Still no answer. Fear gripped Augustin as he ventured onto the back gallery and surveyed the empty camp, the broken doors of the smoke house, the storehouse, the stables. For a moment he just stood there, fury raging beneath the calm into which his face habitually was molded.

A cricket chirped somewhere, breaking the deadly silence. Then, below his feet, from under the floorboards of the gallery, he heard the unmistakable sound of low but frenzied breathing, the frightened whimpers of a trapped animal—or a terrified man. Cautiously, Augustin descended the long, broad sweep of steps that sloped downward from the gallery of Derbanne's raised West Indian cottage and there he found, behind a keg of spilled rum, his wife's young brother.

Remy crawled slowly from his shelter, his eyes as round as goose eggs, his face as blank as an unused ledger. Gently, Augustin took his hand, led him to the lower step, and sat him down.

"What happened, Remy?"

The boy's mouth quivered, but no sound came out, and Augustin could have sworn in desperation.

"Out with it, boy!" His voice was harsh, deliberately cutting, as he tried to break through the wall behind which Remy's mind had taken refuge.

"M-m-m'sieur?" It was all the boy could stutter, and his gangly arms twitched in uncontrollable agitation.

"M'sieur Derbanne? Where is he, Remy?" Augustin shook the boy's shoulders and Remy winced in pain from the force of the stubby fingers that dug into his thin flesh.

"Spr-spr-spring house…," he eventually stammered, and Augustin waited to hear no more. With the boy scrambling to keep astride, he loped past the empty *nègre* camp and down to the bank of the river. There, under the cool shade of a grove of hackberries, he found the new spring house. Inside, bound and gagged, lay Louis and his wife.

"Bless you, Gustin, and the Lord that brought you here," Louis murmured through swollen lips as Augustin cut him and his wife loose. Then, with tears in his eyes, the slender Frenchman wrapped his arms around his burly friend and, for a moment, clung to him for support.

Wordlessly, Augustin turned his gaze to his friend's young wife. Her hair was disheveled, her clothing ripped, shock glazed her blue eyes. He could not ask the question he wanted most to ask. Marie Françoise Derbanne was not only Louis's wife, but also Baptiste-Barthelemy Rachal's sister. Both her husband and her brother were dear friends, and he could not find a delicate way to voice what her *déshabillé* implied. But Derbanne saw the question in his eyes and clasped his hand again upon Augustin's shoulder as he wrapped the other arm around his wife.

"No, Gustin. We're all right. She's all right. Roughed up a bit but nothing more."

"*Bien!*" Augustin acknowledged gruffly, embarrassment darkening his already swarthy face. "What happened, Louis?"

Tersely, Derbanne told him, and the details were even worse than Augustin had feared. Shortly before daybreak, a rider had passed the news of four slaves absconding from the nearby plantations of Lecomte and his brother-in-law, Alexis Cloutier. Cautiously, Louis had loaded his rifle and set it beside the *escritoire* when he began his day's work, but he had not expected trouble from his own *nègres*. The firebrands in his camp had left more than a month ago. The rest, or so he thought, could be trusted. He had been wrong.

"Jean Baptiste?" Augustin asked, inquiring about the overseer who had run the Derbanne plantation since Louis had taken office.

"He and his wife went down to see his mother. She's ill."

The break had come just after breakfast, Derbanne reported. Marie Françoise had gone out to the kitchen behind the house. A couple of their hired *négresses* had overpowered her. Louis had heard her scream but before he could reach the rear door with his gun, the men had taken over the house itself.

They ransacked everything, inside and out, Louis related bitterly, in their search for guns, powder, and provisions. The women had raided Marie Françoise's wardrobe, piling layers of her delicate chemises atop their own field clothes. One of the hired ones had even dropped her skirts and changed into Marie Françoise's dainty, lace-trimmed pantalettes—right before their eyes, as unashamed of her nakedness as of the lice that forced her to scratch at the tuft of hair she exposed. That one had always been a hussy, Louis quickly added. He was not surprised at her. But *his own* people were *good* people—or so he had always thought. *Why? How* could they have done all *this?*

Augustin could only shake his head—not knowing how to explain to this freeborn friend the snarl of emotions that, like a heap of tangled fishhooks, pricks and punctures the mental state of every slave who tries to sort good from bad, right from wrong. Derbanne's *grandmère,* like his own, had been stolen from her tribe in childhood and sold into slavery. For Louis's grandmother, like Gustin's mother, that slavery had meant sexual servitude. Eventually, each of them had won the heart of the man who took her to bed, along with freedom for her children. But Louis Derbanne was a generation removed from that degradation—never had he been forced to call any man his master—and his grandmother had been red, not black. That fact alone had allowed the Derbannes, in their borderland society along Cane River, to cross over the color line and call themselves *white.*

No, Augustin decided, his friend would never understand why "his people" had done what they did that day. In truth, Augustin knew that he himself would never sort out that tangle of fishhooks. All he could offer his distraught friend was more emotion, not an answer.

281

"Louis, it's one thing for *nègres* to steal away into the night, quietly and peacefully," he said at last. "I can't find it in my heart to fault those who do. But wanton destruction cannot be condoned. Once men turn violent, murder happens next. Or worse," he added, delicately avoiding Mme. Derbanne's eyes.

"We'd best warn the neighbors, Augustin. If we're not too late!"

"I'll do it, Louis. You stay with your wife. She needs you. Besides, you have no horses left. I'll pass the warning. Within an hour, *mon ami,* we'll have a posse on its way."

Augustin kept his promise. As the sun began its downward drift behind the Red River, a mounted army of thirty planters, armed and angry, pounded furiously through the pine hills that rolled between the Cane and the Sabine. Even without their pack of yelping hounds, they could have followed the runaways easily, for the *marrons* left behind a trail littered with spoils they already had tired of and abandoned horses that had grown lame or weary and had been discarded in favor of fresher mounts from the herd they had stolen.

Night came early, but Augustin and his men did not stop. They could not stop. The Sabine lay just west of them, and America's claimed jurisdiction ended at that river. If the *marrons* were not seized before they crossed the water, they would be harbored by the *alcaldes* of Spanish Tejas.

Blackness descended upon the forest and their hard-pressed mounts slowed to a canter, shying at the screech of owls, whimpering at the scrape of brush and bramble they could not see. A mile. Two miles more. Then a sudden clearing appeared, devoid of life. As the weary posse drew up short on the muddy banks of the Sabine, the moon wandered out from a drifting cloud and sprayed its light upon the western slope. There were the *marrons*, dancing gaily around the Spaniard who had led them to freedom, chanting *Viva Ferdinando Septimo!* Long live Ferdinand the Seventh!

Spring 1805

"I tell you, men, this lawlessness has to stop! If those American cowards at the fort will not protect us, then we have no choice but to take things into our own hands!"

Alexis Cloutier had planted himself firmly on his veranda. One clenched fist pounded the brick pillar beside him, as he addressed the carefully chosen friends he had called to this meeting. The hairs of his short, black goatee bristled and anger contorted his lean face.

"We've had all we can tolerate, *mes braves!* If these insurrections continue, there will not be a slave left in this parish by year's end. We will be ruined, I tell you! We've spent our lives trying to make something of this wilderness, but there won't be a manjack of a Negro left to work this land!"

"What do you suggest, Alexis?" Ambroise Lecomte asked quietly through the cigar that was habitually clamped between his teeth. His now-pudgy face was placid, and his rotund frame leaned casually against the facing pillar. His air belied it, but beneath his nonchalance, Ambroise was concerned. He had always considered this brother-in-law of his to be an impetuous hothead, but this time he was in complete agreement with Cloutier's fears.

"Action!" Alexis hissed. "The kind of action that pantywaist in charge of Ft. Claiborne will not take. It was a sad day for Natchitoches when Felix Trudeau was forced to yield command to Edward Turner and those *Américains!*"

"Have you tried to reason with Turner?" Ambroise persisted.

"The man won't listen! All he can think of is the damage his career might suffer if war breaks out with the Spaniards. He'd let our whole economy collapse before he'd risk hurting his damned career."

"It seems to me Spain's the one who's inviting trouble," Barthelemy Le Court interjected as the crowd around him nodded its assent. Le Court packed his pipe and waited for the hubbub to subside before going on.

"It wouldn't be us who started the war. Those Spaniards already have. Just last month, I took Ursulle back to Tejas to visit the tribe her mother came from, and for the first time in my life I feared for my scalp every minute I was there. Those Indians were openly hostile, and her uncle finally told me why. Spanish bastards from Nacogdoches have gone among all the Tejas nations, trying to rile them up against the French and Americans. For a hundred years, the western tribes have been our friends, but they aren't friendly now."

"I've heard the same thing from my wife's people—and others," Louis Metoyer agreed, his face uncharacteristically sober. "Thérèse's half-Caneci, you know, but some of the Caddoes have told me the same."

"We've all heard rumors of this!" Cloutier shouted angrily. "Turner insists we have no proof. I say we have all the blasted proof we need!"

Grimacing, he drove on, his voice rising sharply as he sought a commitment from the men he had assembled. "I know you all agree. Let's hear it if you do. Let's see how many of you agree that something's got to be done!"

"*Oui! Certainement!*" From the brick pathway to the cistern, almost every man who crowded Cloutier's yard vowed agreement.

"One moment, Cloutier," Lecomte interjected. "Before we all blindly agree to another one of your schemes, suppose you tell us exactly what you have in mind."

"Just what I said, brother-in-law," Alexis retorted. "Action! I propose that the whole lot of us, mounted and armed, descend upon Nacogdoches and teach that pack of Spanish devils to stay out of our lives."

"*À bas les diables!*" an eager youth cried in assent, and several others took up the chant. Cloutier smirked and the scar that ran downward into his goatee, a relic of one duel or another, puckered in satisfaction.

"But, *cousin,*" Barthelemy interjected, "attacking civilians would be an act of crime, not war."

"Little difference," Cloutier snapped. "After all, civilians do make up the militia." A hint of a smile played around his lips as he added a taunt, "Are you still afraid to fight? I thought you had become a man since Gálvez's campaign."

"*Mes amis, mes amis!*" Augustin stepped in congenially from Ambroise's side. He had not yet entered the debate. It was his nature to study all sides of a matter before committing himself to any course, but it seemed to him that the most feasible approach had not yet been suggested. "Gentleman, in past years I've dealt with the man who is now commandant at Nacogdoches. In fact, many of you have. We've all drank and gamed and hunted with many Nacogdochians, *n'est-ce pas?*"

"*Oui,*" several voices admitted.

"Before we condemn our friends there and goad them into a war they probably don't want any more than we do, I suggest we talk with them. Surely, we ought to make some attempt to find out whether these slave problems are the design of Spanish officials or the handiwork of a few troublemakers. If it should be official policy, then Louisiana might be justified in taking military action, but if not…"

"Talk!" Cloutier snorted. "Metoyer, you sound now like that Anglo captain at the post. We can all see how pudgy your belly's gotten. Obviously, your guts have turned to English pudding."

"Be quiet, Alexis," Lecomte interjected. "Augustin makes sense. It would not take long to send a delegation across the Sabine. We could meet with the commandant, quietly ask questions among our friends, and report back within a week."

"I agree," Le Court enjoined. "What about you, Athanase?"

His brother nodded.

"Dupré?"

"Oui."

"Baptiste-Louis? Julien?" The two Rachal cousins agreed also.

One by one the others voted to support the compromise Augustin had suggested and then chose three men to represent them, men of steady temperament and sound judgment, fluent in the Spanish tongue. Men with contacts among those Nacogdochians who valued the friendship of the French. Augustin was the first named; the delegation had been his idea. The second chosen was his old friend Jean Prudhomme and the third, Remy Perot, Dupré's cousin.

It had been ten years since Augustin had ridden into the dirt-poor village of Nacogdoches, settled by the families driven from their Los Adaës homes when the Spanish closed that post back in the seventies. Now, he was pleasantly surprised at the progress the Tejas frontier had made during the decade he had buried himself in the cane brakes of his own plantation.

The adobe buildings that hugged the streets seemed brighter, newer. Cows still ambled undisturbed down Calle del Pilar, and chickens still pecked for worms in its muddied potholes, but the people who wove in and out between the animals were better dressed, their faces less pinched by hunger and less worn by care. Señora Brazos's decrepit old tavern, where he used to stay, was now abandoned and Perot guided them to a newer, whitewashed *cantina* on the opposite end of town.

"Mama Catarina!" Perot exclaimed as they stepped into the smoke-filled din and an old woman, as wide as the doorway, with long earrings dangling far below the dyed braids that coiled around her head, flashed them a broad grin.

"Señor Remigio!" she cried, waddling in their direction, her generous bosom heaving in and out of the low cut of her bodice.

"*Mi amigo francés!* For why have you stayed away so long, Remigio Perot?"

"*Mi labor, mi familia.* They keep me busy, Mama Catarina," Remy replied as contritely as a neglectful son, while she enveloped him in a hug.

"*Sí, sí!*" The grin stayed plastered in its place as her voice boomed across to the far reaches of the room. "Chatta! Come here, old man! Look who's come back for to see us!"

Augustin froze as he saw the old Indian slowly rise from the back table where he had been entertaining two *patrons* with some sleight-of-hand. From forgotten recesses of his childhood, Augustin recalled that name, but it was impossible for him to make this stooped, timeworn man fit the mental image of the proud young Chatta he had heard his mother describe to Jean in their childhood. This was not the image of the man, the father, whom his half-brother had left home to find years before.

The old man limped his way across the cantina, his gaunt shoulders hunched beneath the silver mane that flowed across his loose, sleeveless shirt. His eyes squinted in recognition, and he gruffly stretched out both his gnarled hands to grasp Perot. Not a word passed between them, but Augustin could see the deep affection that flashed in both their eyes.

"Remigio? These are your friends, *verdad?*" Catarina's cackle pierced the maze of questions that whorled in Augustin's mind. "How do they call themselves, these handsome hidalgoes?"

"*Caramba!*" Remy laughed back. "My manners are now as bad as your curiosity, Mamacito! This fair young *hombre* is Jean Prudhomme, and the quiet one behind him is Augustin Metoyer."

Prudhomme nodded politely, but Augustin stepped slightly forward, bowed to the old proprietors of Cantina Catarina, and gallantly kissed the woman's hand.

"Ay-y-y!" she moaned, and her big black eyes rolled. "Dear Jesus, give it back to me, my youth! Send him back to his plains, this old *indio mío*, this bag of bones I wed, and let my arms hold again *un hombre macho!*"

The aged Indian gave no sign that he heard his wife's faithless prayer. He had not yet said one word, but for a second—just the briefest moment—when he had turned his stony gaze upon Augustin, a flicker of surprise seemed to dart through his enigmatic eyes. Augustin did not have to wonder why. He knew how much he looked like the menfolk of his mother's family.

Within the hour, Catarina's Apache servant had spread before them three sizzling beefsteaks, each as large as the platter that held it. The fried cakes of bread, from coarsely ground *maíz*, were too greasy for Augustin's taste. Since his introduction to the cuisine of France, he had spurned the frontier custom of smothering everything in lard. But the pungent chili peppers had been picked at the moment of perfection, and Augustin downed them with gusto.

While the Frenchmen cleaned their plates, Catarina chattered incessantly, totally unaware that Remy's brief interjections were skillfully channeling her gossip to the subject they had come to investigate. By the time the servant reemerged from the kitchen with bowls of wild berries in pools of cream, the Creoles had learned that their runaways were being welcomed royally by the Spanish commandant, Ugarte. Most, to date, had been escorted safely to the Río Grande, where livelihood had been promised them, but a few had stayed behind.

"*Sí,*" Catarina assured them. She knew every one of those and who they worked for. "*Primero,* there's the one what calls herself Victoria. She work the fields for Nepomuceno de la Cerda. *Segunda,* there's Lisa. The Ruíz brothers, they take her for a maid. *Tercero...*"

The Creoles recognized them all. This one had fled from Cloutier. That one from the Le Courts. Mentally, they made their lists. When they met with Ugarte, they would demand the return of all of them.

"But how do the people feel?" Perot asked offhandedly. "Is it true they are against slavery now?"

"*Tal vez,*" Catarina shrugged. "*Los vecinos,* we no can afford *esclavons* anyway. Not most of us. Young Gil y Barbo, Flores, de la Vega—those men are rich. They have *dinero* for to buy many *esclavons,* but we no have it. All *los esclavons* could be freed and it would make us no matter."

"*Sí,*" Perot agreed casually. "But *los Americanos?* We French have heard rumors, Mamacito, that Spanish Tejas intends to drive the Americans from Louisiana."

This question struck a much dearer chord. Catarina's hands, her arms, and her bosom all responded. "*Sí, el comandante, el gobierno, sí.* They sit at this same table, and they argue with Flores. They want it back, all *la Luisiana,* and they try to make Flores promise to fight, because they know what Flores do the rest of Nacogdoches will do, *tambien. Pero,* Flores, he say no. *Los hombres* at Natchitoches are his friends. Our friends. We no want to fight *amigos.*"

"Flores, *sí,* he's a good man," Prudhomme agreed politely.

"*Sí, sí. Muy bueno.* You know him, Señor?"

"Slightly, Señora. We have business from time to time." With some effort, Prudhomme suppressed a grin as he recalled past attempts to best the Spaniard in those business dealings. Flores was a damned hard man to best.

Augustin remained silent, picking absentmindedly at the berries that were too tart for his taste. Ever since he put in the sugar mill on his upper plantation, he had grown accustomed to sweeter food. And his stomach had grown rounder.

Across the table, Chatta had remained just as quiet, sitting like a granite mountain whose peaks had begun to slide. His lids drooped, and Augustin could not decide whether the old man was dozing or was lost in another world.

The chatter drifted on to less consequential matters. Perot had picked from his old friend what they had come to learn, and now Catarina was passionately recalling memories of a younger Perot and her sweet Rosa and the wild *charivari* the town would have given them after their wedding—if only her Rosa had not worn that red dress to the bull run down the main street of town, if only the bull had not been nicked by one of those bullets the drunken rowdies kept shooting into the air, if only the bull had not been passing right by her own sweet Rosa right when he was angered…

Once, amid this litany, the old Indian stirred, and Augustin nerved himself to ask the man a seemingly innocuous question about his past. But then Chatta's head fell abruptly again upon his chest, and he drew a long sonorous snore that shook Catarina from her painful memories and let her laugh again.

"*Mi viejo!*" she cackled. "He go to sleep now with the chickens! Drink your tequila, *amigos.* I go help the old man to his bed." Despite all the verbal jibes she had directed his way that night, her touch was tender as she took his shriveled arm and moved to help him from his chair. "*Vamos,* Chatta."

The ancient Indian stared blankly for a second, as if startled. Then he turned, jabbed a long, stiff finger toward Augustin, and for the first time that night he spoke.

"You! Metoyer! You help an old man up the stairs?"

I was right! Augustin thought to himself, with a curious mix of exultance and dread. I did see recognition in his face! Still, Augustin masked his interest behind a pleasant smile, rose politely, and followed the stooped form as it hobbled across the room.

"There!" Chatta commanded brusquely when they reached the top landing, and Augustin led him into the indicated room. Suddenly, he wondered just what there was to say to this old man. How much dare he say? He need not have worried. The words came quite naturally. Indeed, it was the taciturn Chatta who had the questions to ask. All Augustin had to do was respond.

"Sit!"

Augustin sat.

"You from Natchitoches?"

"*Sí,* Señor."

"Your father be the merchant?"

"He was, until a few years ago."

For a while the old Indian said nothing more. Then he spoke quietly. "You be the brother of the boy Jean, the one who calls himself Jeannot Metoyer?"

So Jean did find his father! Augustin thought to himself. How else could the old man know about him?

"*Sí,* Señor—and Chiquito," Augustin replied again and Chatta went silent, his face hardened. The room grew so still Augustin could hear the breaths of both of them, his own slow and deep, the old man's quick and sharp. He let the point rest. Whatever Chatta's relationship with the son who had stayed on in Tejas with his slave wife and children, even after Augustin had come here with Coincoin's money to buy his brother's freedom back in '93, it was obviously not something Chatta wanted to share.

"Your mother be Coincoin." It was not a question, just a statement. Chatta already knew the answer.

"*Sí,*" Augustin answered softly.

"You know me? You ever hear my name?"

"Yes, Chatta."

"Good." Pleasure was evident in the old man's eyes.

"She well, your mother?"

"She's well." Old now, thought Augustin. Just as you are. She's getting deaf, and her hair is silver. But he could not say any of this aloud. The old man had his own visions of the Coincoin he had left behind, and Augustin could not shatter them.

"She still pretty?"

"*Sí,* Chatta, *muy bonita,*" and Augustin meant that. To him his mother always would be beautiful. A silver crown was as majestic on her as the black velvet of her youth had been, and age had not stooped one inch her proud carriage.

"*Sí,*" the old man echoed, smiling softly to himself as he remembered things that Augustin could never know.

"I hear she free now."

"For almost thirty years, Señor."

"She have money?" The old man spoke sharply, and Augustin smiled.

"*Mucho dinero,* Chatta. She has a dozen *esclavons* of her own now, and nearly a thousand acres."

"*Bueno!*" He nodded ever so slightly as he spoke the word.

He really means it! Augustin thought to himself. He's really glad to hear that she's done well.

"She good woman, Coincoin. Stubborn, but good. All the time she tell me she be free one day, and rich too. Always she mean what she say!"

"*Sí,*" Augustin agreed with a broad grin.

"I be free, too." Chatta said quietly. "I told her I find freedom, and I find it."

"And happiness, too, I hope?"

"*Mas o menos,*" he shrugged. "*Mía* Catarina, she good woman, for an *Española.* She marry me at San Antonio. She bear me sons, and Rosa."

Augustin opened his mouth to ask about Jeannot, the other son his mother had borne Chatta, but before he could frame his question the old man began to slump again.

"You go now, Metoyer. I old man. I get weary."

"*Sí,* Chatta." Augustin rose and impulsively embraced the drooping shoulders. "*Vaya con Díos, amigo.*"

The Indian did not answer. He had already sunk into his dreams, and Augustin was lost in his for the remainder of the night. Perot and Prudhomme had downed their bottle of tequila by the time he rejoined them, and he declined their offer to break open another. He needed sleep, but they could stay and toast each other's health with the locals.

Augustin did not sleep, though. Every time he closed his eyes, there floated into the darkness the memory of the Chatta his mother had long ago painted for him and Jeannot—a Chatta who was tall and erect, with a strong face and many muscles. That was when Augustin knew he would not tell Coincoin about this meeting. He could not destroy her dreams. It would serve no good. She would be pleased that Chatta had asked about her, that he had spoken softly of her, if he told her. But Chatta had a wife, a white Spanish one. A wife he had married in the church. For Chatta and Coincoin there could be nothing now but their separate memories.

The rest of the mission went almost as smoothly as their visit with Mama Catarina. Augustin rose at daybreak, breakfasted lightly, and walked over to the office of Don José de la Vega, ostensibly on business for his father. But their conversation wandered to other subjects, and Vega more or less echoed the observations Catarina had more colorfully expressed.

Meanwhile, Prudhomme sought out his old acquaintance, Antonio Baca, on the pretext that he was looking to buy a skilled hunter. As he hoped, Baca invited him and his friends for their midday repast. Again, this Spaniard and his other guests revealed nothing but affection for their old friends at Natchitoches, and all inquired solicitously over this or that one.

Only the commandant marred the picture all were drawing of the relationship between Natchitoches and Nacogdoches. Ugarte was urbane, cordial but far from candid. He remembered Augustin well and inquired after the rather impetuous young brother who had accompanied Augustin on his business trips to Tejas. His voice was too smooth, though. His manner cagey. His every statement ran counter grain to the reports everyone else had made.

Sí, the commandant agreed blandly. He was aware that a few planters at Natchitoches had a bit of a problem with runaways. There would always be that problem wherever slavery existed, no?

No. He did not know of any fugitives from Louisiana who had come into Nacogdoches. *Sí,* there was a woman by the name of Victoria who worked for de la Cerda. Perhaps she was born at Natchitoches. He could not be expected to know such things. In any case, she was a *mulata libra.* He had heard some one or another say that she was born free.

No! Of course, he could not let them take back the woman, or any others they mistakenly thought to be runaways from the Natchitoches district. He had an obligation to all his people, black as well as white. He could not let the free Negroes of his town be taken up as slaves by anyone who wanted them.

Pero, no! By no means was it the wish of Spain to drive out the Americans. *"Mi amigo,"* Ugarte gestured broadly. "Look around you in this town, all through this jurisdiction. You will find countless *Americanos* among us, Davenport, the Wallace brothers, Edmund Quirk, Quinelty. *Los Americanos* are our friends, just as you have been."

Then God help the Americans! Augustin thought to himself and politely ended their conversation.

By noon that same day, their third in Tejas, the three Creole planters had again mounted and were headed east toward home. Not one had found the courage yet to speak what was in his heart, but each knew the recommendation he would have to make when they reported to their friends and neighbors.

Beyond any doubt, it was the official policy of Spanish Tejas to create turmoil in American Louisiana. Yet there was no way that the Frenchmen along the Natchitoches frontier could raise arms against their sister settlement on the other side of the Sabine because the *people* there were still their friends.

There was no other course for them to follow, save to let the American commander and his superiors at New Orleans and Washington City continue their diplomatic negotiations of this problem with Spanish ministers in Madrid. That would take years. In the meanwhile, the settlers of Natchitoches would continue to suffer as they had already. There would be much more financial loss, possibly ruination, as slaves that were worth the life's work of their masters continued to abscond. Worse still, they would continue to go to bed each night with fear, the ever-present terror of all masters whose rebellious slaves outnumber them. The fear of open revolt, rapine, and murder.

11

Advent 1812

For Augustin and his colony on the Isle of Canes, problems were just beginning. The changes Pierre had predicted, should America absorb the colony of Louisiana, came as quickly as he feared they would. Their language remained French, as it had even throughout the long Spanish era, but one by one, in numerous ways, the Creole customs gave way to Anglo ways.

The lands that always had belonged to the Crown, and had been given freely to industrious settlers, were now federal lands that must be bought. This one change mattered little to Augustin and his people. The foundations of their fortunes were laid already. But the hordes of poor and pinched-face Anglos who rolled hopefully into the territory in their canvas-covered wagons were frustrated by their own government's restrictions and sorely envious of the wealthy men of color who greeted them.

At first, Augustin and his people welcomed the swarm of newcomers with the same friendliness they had shown to the trickle of Englishmen who had in past years been attracted to the frontier by the generosity of the Spanish Crown. But *en masse* the new arrivals proved far less amicable and far more suspicious, intolerant, and offensive.

They came uninvited into the territory, then complained that they feared for their lives among so many *free niggers* who were dangerously allowed to own firearms. They spoke neither French nor Spanish and then complained about the *illiterate foreigners* who could not understand plain English. Their strength multiplied each year by the thousands, and they promptly elected their own men to the legislature. There, almost as their first act, they challenged the *ancien régime's* staunch defense of free Negro rights.

Some battles the Creole statesmen won. A *nègre,* free or slave, must still be treated equally in any court of law, and a free *nègre's* word was every bit as good as that of a white. But when the question of the ballot box arose, the Anglos won their argument that not even free Negroes with money and learning could be trusted to select moral and able public leaders.

Among the *ancien* population, too, there were a few men willing to adopt the new Anglo interpretations of *laissez-faire* and quick to recognize that American authorities would support their actions. Sylvestre Bossier was such a man.

The Territory of Orleans was three years old when the Anglo government opened land offices in the towns of Natchitoches and Opelousas and posted notice that all who claimed property under French or Spanish titles must file their proofs of ownership. Their *claims* for land, as the new government called them, would have to be evaluated by the general land office in Washington City. So Augustin and his people had gathered their papers in that year 1806, rode into the town of Natchitoches, and filed their titles, justly expecting a routine approval.

The years passed, and the Metoyer brothers steadily improved their plantations. The uncertainty of the slave situation discouraged them from investing further in Negro property, but the ones they already had were reproducing prolifically. Each time the priest came up from Opelousas to serve the Natchitoches parishioners who were again without a pastor, the Metoyers presented for baptism a host of healthy Negro infants alongside their own tawny-colored babes. The back reaches of their lands reverberated with the sound of falling trees, and new earth was plowed and put to crops. Yet American titles to the plantations they had acquired by Spanish grant and purchase were slow in coming.

In the winter of 1812, after his crops were laid by, his fences mended, and his *nègres* has settled into the pre-Christmas lull, Louis packed his brocade carpetbag, saddled his new blooded stallion, and rode over to see his elder brother.

"Mon frère! Are you building a house or a replica of *le palais Versailles?"*

Augustin laughed. "It's no palace, but I'll admit I'm straining my resources to give Agnes the best I can afford."

"If you ask me, Gustin, it looks like an imitation of Alexis Cloutier's house!"

"Eh, bien! All these raised cottages look much the same. Just wait, though. You see that arch above the central doorway? There will be a fanlight window there. I've already ordered it from New Orleans. Above it, on either side, will be twin dormers. And you see that wing they are adding on the west? That will be the chapel. If I can afford to build a house, I can at least afford to add one room for devotions, seeing that it will probably be years before we get our church here. If the new American bishop cannot spare a priest to serve the whole ten thousand square miles of Natchitoches Parish, we don't have much hope of getting a priest here on the…"

"Gustin?" Louis interrupted with obvious impatience. He was far more concerned with their economic plight than their spiritual one.

"Oui?"

"Don't you think you're taking too much of a chance, building this house before you get clear title to the land?"

"The titles are coming, Louis. You are too impatient. These things take time. As our American lawyer keeps telling us, the wheels of government crank slowly."

"Then I think it's time we used some of our own grease instead of depending entirely upon Murray's."

"Now, that is exactly what I mean, Louis," Augustin laughed fondly. "You are too impatient. William Murray is honest. He will get our titles for us."

"Maybe. But he's too damned slow about it. *Zut,* Gustin! I've just got this gut feeling that all's not right. I don't know whether it's Murray's fault or somebody else's, but something's wrong."

"Obviously, you're going to find out what," Augustin observed dryly, eyeing the carpetbag tied behind Louis on the broad black rump of his stallion. "Even though they have closed our land office and you have to go to Opelousas to ask your questions?"

"You're damned right. The way I feel right now, I'd go all the way to Washington City. Provided, of course, that you approve."

Augustin smiled tolerantly. Whenever Louis asked his approval for anything, it was mere formality. Over the years his other brothers and sisters, even his mother now, had fallen into the habit of asking his advice on everything from money to marriage, but Louis was not the type to want or countenance any man's advice. At forty-two, Louis's jowls were sagging and his stomach had begun to paunch—too much wine and women, Augustin kept telling him—but he was still the same Louis of his youth, impetuous and hotheaded.

"You are headed out now?"

"In the morning. Tonight, I'm riding up to Mama's. The old man sent Ben down earlier today with news that a Virginia trader is on his way to Opelousas with a fresh lot of hands. I need another blacksmith. I've put off buying one in hopes all this slave unrest would settle down; but I can't put it off any longer. Ben says father is looking to buy several more hands himself. So in the morning, we'll go down together from the Point."

"Then give my love to Mama. I'd like to hope that Brother Ben would keep you out of trouble. But putting him in charge of you is not much different from giving the Devil the keys to hell."

Louis grinned. "Well at least he's white. If any evil *Yanque* tries to claim me as a slave, Ben will be there to protect me."

"If anyone tried to jail you as a runaway, I suspect he would get what he deserved!" Augustin retorted, but his eyes were serious. "Take care, brother."

"Have I ever, Gustin?" Louis teased. "Care takes all the fun out of life!"

His riding crop slapped sharply across the stallion's rump, and Augustin was left standing in a cloud of dust, as Louis rode at his usual breakneck speed up River Road.

As always now, Louis found Coincoin's cabin painfully empty. One by one, her children had married and built their own homes on their own places. Except for Toussaint, who showed no haste to take a wife. He had been born too late to benefit from the liberal land grants of the Spanish and, like the young Louis, he had floundered restlessly until Coincoin bought for him a small and undeveloped farm near her own. During the day, Toussaint cleared and tilled his soil, with the help of half of Coincoin's hands, and by night he returned to the cozy comfort of his childhood home and the lonely company of his guitar.

It was still daylight when Louis arrived, and Toussaint was out. He found his mother in her tobacco house, supervising the repair of her drying racks. Past seventy now, Coincoin could easily have retired to a life of comfort, but age had diminished neither her boundless energy nor her stubborn will, and she refused to yield to any of her children the reins of control over the small homestead Pierre had given her.

As always, Louis's brief visit was a sedative to his restless soul, a trip back into the placid world of childhood. But, as usual, the palliative wore off by morning, and the restless Louis rose at the first low of stirring cattle in Coincoin's shed, anxious to be on his way. Crossing the river, he wound down the lane of poplars that led to Pierre's Big House. His father slept late now, but Ben was up and waiting; and Louis greeted him warmly. Despite the vast difference in their ages, as well as the other never-mentioned barrier that stood between Pierre's dusky children and his white ones, Louis still felt a close affinity with the young Ben.

Sometimes, even, he forgot that Ben was white—that he was Mme. Metoyer's son and not Susanne's. The old Madame had borne him, but she had been sickly ever since. It had been Susanne who had nursed Ben at one breast while she nursed her own Florentin at the other. And it had been the frail Ben, needing care and love so badly, who had helped Susanne survive the desolation that followed Conant's abandonment of her and Florentin to take a wealthy wife in *la ville*. Even after the widowed Baptiste Anty offered to fill the void the doctor left, and Susanne had accepted him, little Ben had remained as special to her as the flock of girls she proceeded to bear for Anty. In truth, Ben was special to all of them.

In many ways, Louis often thought, he and Ben were more alike than any other pair of Pierre's children by either of his two Marie Thérèses. Ben was impetuous and temperamental, but he had a solid head on his shoulders for a young man still short of his majority. Ben was popular, too, a friend of everyone. He never met a stranger—white, black, red, Creole, or Anglo—who stayed a stranger for long. The boy would go far in life. Louis could see that. Much further than any of his older, colored brothers could hope to go.

Leisurely they breakfasted, laced their coffee with brandy to store warmth for the road, and within the hour were on their way. Two days later, they rode into Opelousas just behind the Virginia slaver, whose platform was being erected in the center of the square. As the coffle of Negroes lined up, a curious crowd of buyers clustered about the blacks. The trader moved rapidly among his wares, snapping his cane occasionally across a shin as he urged, "Look lively now, boy. Perk up there."

Louis and Ben dismounted and moved among them, with some advantage. The Virginian's lot was mostly one of English Negroes, but the buyers assembled this morning were almost entirely Creole. Few, if any, would have been schooled abroad, as Ben had, or otherwise motivated to learn the English tongue.

Rapidly Ben questioned each slave in the square, this one's age or that one's skill. If a woman seemed likely, he inquired whether she had children in this lot who should be purchased with her. When a brawny blacksmith impressed him, he asked pointedly whether the man had a wife somewhere whose haunting memory might tempt him to run away. While Ben queried the Negroes, the practiced Louis, well-trained by Coincoin, made his own medical examination of those Ben deemed likely.

"You! Nigger! Whaddaya up to? Git 'way from there. You got some idea 'bout cuttin' my stock loose or sump'n?"

Louis heard the voice behind him distinctly. Although he recognized few of the Anglo's words, he clearly understood the tone. Calmly, he turned and stared the Anglo in the eye, sizing up the man who had approached him. The trader was dressed decently enough, albeit a bit too loudly for Louis's taste. The man's striped waistcoat almost matched the purple of his close-fitting trousers, and his wildly flowered silk cravat was tolerably clean. The parchment colored tailcoat could have used a pressing. All things considered, Louis decided, the trader would have been more comfortable in linsey-woolsey and brogans.

"Boy! Hasn't anyone taught you manners? You're s'posed to take off your hat when a white man talks to you!"

Louis continued to stare the man down, and the deep-wine colored top hat that he had ordered that summer from La Rochelle, a perfect match to the contrasting lapels of his black woolen riding jacket, stayed at the same cocky angle on his head.

"Hell!" The Virginian swore to no one in particular. "Another one of those uppity yellers who can't speak English. This territory'd be a decent place for white folks, if we could clean out the whole damn passel of these hybrids."

"Mr. Bell!" Ben interjected quietly from Louis's side. Seldom did Ben meet a man he did not like, but this was definitely one.

"I can assure you, Mr. Bell, that Louisiana has always been a decent place to live, at least until lately. Unfortunately, we have now been invaded by certain classes of people who have no respect for their fellow man and no breeding to temper their intolerance or their ignorance."

"Well whaddaya know," the slaver sneered. "We have a matched pair, here. An uppity nigger and a smart-mouthed kid. Didn't nobody ever teach you better'n to insult your elders?"

"My comment, sir, should insult you only if you consider yourself one of the lowlifes to whom I referred."

The Virginian's eyes narrowed and his tongue rolled broadly behind his underlip, as he transferred his plug of tobacco from one cheek to the other.

"Seems like your breedin' ain't so good itself, boy."

"To the contrary, Mr. Bell. I've been taught to show respect to anyone who merits it, regardless of age or color. Of course, if you think I need a lesson in deportment, I would be happy to meet you later, anywhere you choose, and let you try to teach me—with the weapon of your choice."

The trader's jowls attacked his plug furiously, and a nervous finger tugged at his too-tight collar.

"Now that would hardly be sportin' of me, seein' as how I prefer a healthy bout of fisticuffs t' those sissy li'l pistols you French fops like, an' seein' as how a frail li'l dandy like you wouldn't have a spittin' chance against a real man."

"I assure you, Mr. Bell, even at fisticuffs the odds would not be what you expect."

The Anglo wavered. "Besides, I've never soiled my hands on no *nigger lover,* an' I ain't about to start now. Your kind ain't worth the trouble."

"I hope you also feel *my kind* is not worth the financial loss you have just incurred. I came prepared to pay you top price for at least six prime hands. And this gentleman with me, whom you have inexcusably insulted, could buy your whole lot and pay you cash."

Nervous eyes blinked, and Bell quickly reassessed the situation. "Well, now, seems t' me grown men ought not let li'l pers'nal diff'rences get in the way of bus'ness. Here, take a look at this strappin' fellow I got here."

Throughout the encounter, Louis had stood quietly. The words that both men flung into the crisp autumn air were unintelligible, but there was no mistaking the gist of their conversation or the slaver's present effort at reconciliation. Louis raised his cane and lightly tapped the Virginian on the arm. Bell turned, and Louis bowed in his most cavalier manner.

"Non, M'sieur. Adieu!"

Quietly, he took his younger brother by the elbow and steered Ben toward the street, leaving the Anglo and his Negroes gaping at their back.

"Sacrebleu! Quel salaud!" Louis swore furiously as soon as they were out of hearing. "Another two minutes and I'd have fed that *cochon* my card!"

"No, Louis," Ben replied soberly. "This is the United States now, not a colony of France. The Anglos fought their revolution for liberté but not égalité. If you had even threatened Bell, you'd have been thrown in the stockade and you know it."

"Hell, boy! It would have been worth it."

"No, it would not."

"Morbleu! What kind of a man, as husky as a work-ox and in the prime of life, would let his kid b...," Louis caught himself in time before he actually said the word that still remained unspoken between them. "...let a kid do his fighting for him?"

"There are all kinds of ways of proving oneself to be a man, Louis," Ben shot back, and Louis almost smiled as he heard in Ben an echo of staid old Augustin.

"Louis, the approach you took back there proved you to be a far better man, a *gentleman*, which is one thing that Anglo *canaille* could never be no matter how much money he makes off the black flesh he peddles."

"Zut, Ben!" Louis retorted. "Whatever I think of the man, I'll not fault him

for his occupation. We're making a fair amount of money ourselves off the labor of our blacks."

"Louis, that's absurd! The hands we buy become a part of our family, a part of our lives. We don't buy them one month, fatten them up like swine for slaughter, and then sell them as soon as they are plump enough for us to turn a quick dollar. We nurse them when they are sick, feed them when they are too old to work, take them to church whenever we go ourselves. *Hé!*" Ben drew up short. "Here's the land office. You still want to check in with them here?"

"I certainly do!" Louis replied emphatically. "That was my main reason for coming."

The pair stepped quickly across the long gallery that was shared by a fresh row of storefronts, and Ben steered Louis toward the door with the proper sign.

"Bonjour, M'sieur," Louis politely addressed the clerk in the shiny black suit and uncomfortably starched collar who sat alone inside. *"Je suis M'sieur Louis Metoyer de Natchitoches."*

"I'm sorry, but you will have to speak English. It is the official language now."

"Of course," Ben interjected smoothly. "My companion does not speak it fluently, but I will be happy to translate for him. Your name, sir?"

"Thomas Culley," the clerk looked pointedly at Ben. "And what may I do for you, young man?"

"Mr. Culley, my name is Metoyer. Ben Metoyer. My companion is M'sieur Louis Metoyer. We have come from Natchitoches to check on the status of his landholdings."

Culley peered cautiously through his spectacles. This had been the damnedest situation he'd encountered since crossing the Mississippi. Too often he had taken a swarthy Latin for a light-skinned Negro and then treated a high-yellow as a white. The tic of his eye gave away his disconcertment as he continued to assess the pair, before he finally convinced himself that the younger one was indeed white although the older one certainly was not. He continued to address the younger one.

"His *land*? Don't you mean his *claim*?"

"No," Ben responded evenly. "I mean his *lands*. Plural. The ones he *owned* before your government ever *claimed* title to them."

The clerk appeared not to notice Ben's point. "I believe you said his name is

Louis? Are you also saying that this Louis has several claims on file here?"

"*Monsieur Metoyer* has several *plantations,*" Ben replied, a bit more forcefully. "And none of them are small. However, paperwork has been filed with you for only two of them. Titles to the others were purchased after your government took over Louisiana and proceeded to *claim* the land."

"Hmmh, let us see," the clerk continued blandly, still ignoring Ben's rebuke. "Ahem!" His face crinkled. "Apparently there is some problem here. Excuse me, please. I must confer with the registrar."

Ben rapidly translated for Louis as the clerk disappeared into an adjoining office.

"*Oui,*" Louis nodded seriously. "I thought as much. Somehow, I..."

"*Messieurs,*" a voice interrupted in a tone that was adequately nasal although it was still more English than French.

"The Messieurs Metoyer from Natchitoches! Of course. *Je suis Levin Wailes,* Registrar of Lands for the Opelousas Land District. You wish to inquire about your claims?"

"*Oui,*" Louis responded, grateful to find a man in charge with whom he could speak directly. Ben was helpful, in situations like this, but it was deucedly awkward trying to speak through somebody else's mouth. He simply must find time to learn this language.

"M'sieur Wailes. I have filed paperwork on two tracts that I hold by Spanish grant, numbers R&R 39 and B1953. These were filed immediately after the Natchitoches office opened in '06, but I have not heard any word regarding them since the office there was closed."

"*Un moment,* M'sieurs," Wailes purred, as he shuffled the same pile of papers. "Aha! Here we are." Then he frowned, just briefly, before his face recovered its bureaucratic smile. "No problem, M'sieurs, none at all with R&R 39. It should be approved soon. The title appears clear enough."

"And the other one, M'sieur?" Louis inquired. R&R 39 was the smaller of the two tracts for which he had filed his titles, only 450 arpents. It was the Yucca Bend place, more than twice that size, which most concerned him. That was the one he had fertilized with his blood and his sweat.

"Ah, my good man," Wailes went on congenially. "There we do have a problem. It seems that paperwork has been submitted also by another gentleman, and his file includes proof of ownership."

"M'sieur Wailes! That is impossible!" Ben interjected. "This gentleman here has been in sole possession of that plantation since the year I was born!"

"It's all right, Ben," Louis cautioned, with a tight rein on his own concern. "I'm sure there is a mistake we can straighten out easily enough."

"His name?" Louis asked the registrar levelly. "Can you give me the name of the mistaken claimant?"

"Of course, M'sieur Metoyer. The man who has submitted his proof of ownership is Sylvestre Bossier. Perhaps you know him, sir? He's married to the daughter of our esteemed citizen, Luke Collins."

Louis knew him. And Bossier's Anglo in-laws.

"That is impossible, M'sieur," Louis insisted, politely but firmly. "Bossier was given an Order of Survey and Settlement to that property in '89 by the man who was then our commandant, Louis Charles de Blanc. Less than a year later, he returned that order to De Blanc, swearing that the land was not worth the trouble and expense involved in clearing it and building the necessary roads and the bridge across Bayou Platte. His petition for a concession was then cancelled and returned from the governor's office. Have you taken a deposition yet from De Blanc?"

"Well, no," Wailes conceded.

"May I suggest that this be done, sir? As you undoubtedly know, De Blanc is now a justice of the peace down at Attakapas. He will confirm what I have told you. He will also attest that five years after Bossier forfeited the land it was still vacant. That is when I applied for it. De Blanc issued a new Order of Survey and Settlement to me, and I have been in possession of the land ever since."

"Obviously something is wrong, M'sieur, with one claim or the other. As I see it, though, from the papers that have been filed, M'sieur Bossier's claim is as valid as yours."

Both Louis and Ben stared in disbelief. Wailes went on. "You say that Bossier returned his Order of Survey and Settlement to the commandant? But Messieurs, the gentleman has submitted that very order with his claim, as proof of his ownership."

"Then his paper is a forgery!" Louis snapped coldly, all patience lost. "Either that or else he stole his forfeited papers from the commandant's office at Natchitoches. I repeat, M'sieur Wailes. He gave up his papers in 1790. I was shown them by De Blanc in '95. There is no way that Sylvestre Bossier could claim title to that land!"

"M'sieur Metoyer, I notice that you, too, filed an Order of Survey and Settlement, but I do not see a patent from the Crown giving you final title."

Louis shrugged, his temper rising. "Most of us on the frontier never received a *patent,* as you call it. You know that, if you've studied all the papers that have been filed. The old surveyor went blind shortly after he got there."

"And you made no effort to find another?"

"M'sieur Wailes, there was no question of *finding* one. Either the government had a surveyor to send or it didn't. For those of us on the frontier, it didn't."

"Yet if you did not have that survey made, then you did not comply with the terms of the grant. In that case, your Order of Survey and Settlement would carry no more weight than the one submitted by M'sieur Bossier, *n'est-ce pas?"*

"Non! N'est-ce pas! Morbleu, Wailes! That land is mine. I chopped trees while my blisters bled so badly the ax handle would slip out of my hands. For three hellish years, those blisters never had a chance to heal. I hacked through cane swamps only mosquitoes would live in, and they welcomed me by the millions. What blood I had left, they took. They ate on my face until it was as swollen as a drowned corpse. I lived and worked with a handkerchief across my nose and mouth to keep from breathing the damned things into my lungs. But, by God, after seventeen years I have 250 acres of it under cultivation and a good sturdy house. That land is *mine,* Wailes, and neither Bossier nor anybody else is going to take it away from me!"

"M'sieur, M'sieur," the Registrar resumed unctuously after Louis's tirade had spent itself. "There is still the law, and if M'sieur Bossier's original title is as valid as yours, then under American law…"

Ben interrupted him. "Mr. Wailes, I do know something about American law, and I am aware that ten years of uncontested possession constitutes legal possession. M'sieur Metoyer will have no trouble proving his possession."

"Perhaps not, sir. However, I must advise you that M'sieur Bossier also claims to have had men residing on that place."

"That's a cursed lie!" Ben knew the minute he said it that it wouldn't help their cause, and he could see Wailes's eyes turn cold.

"There is no way *we* can determine that, sir. It is the duty of this office only to rule on the validity of titles presented to us. Therefore, the report we submitted to Washington City said plainly that, in our opinion, one set of paperwork for this property is as valid as the other."

Louis sat down for the first time since he entered the office. Seventeen years of the kind of labor he had done at Yucca Bend had made a hard man of him. He had fought off panthers and pulled oxen out of quicksand. But he was now gut sick.

The registrar continued. "Gentlemen, I am confident that the national office will agree with my judgment. In that event, it will be necessary for one or the other of you to take the matter to court and let a jury of your peers decide the rightful owner."

"Then I'll see him in court!" Louis exploded. "No matter how many other ways you Anglos have changed our ways of doing things, I'll still get fair treatment in a Louisiana court of law. My peers at Natchitoches know and respect me. They'll give me my title."

Without another word, without waiting to see if Ben was still beside him, Louis stormed out of the U. S. Land Office, bounded over the rump of his stallion and pummeled the dust out of Opelousas.

Ben caught up with him just north of town, where the dirt road to Rapides and Natchitoches wound back into the woods.

"*Sacrebleu,* Louis! Wait up!"

Louis reined furiously, and Ben's overtaxed mare panted to a stop beside him.

"*Mon Dieu,* Ben, there's a limit to how much a man can take and still call himself a man!"

"I know, Louis, but you were right back there. You will win your case in court. There is no doubt about that."

"You're damned right there's not."

"So, there's no reason to get upset, *non?*" Ben said soothingly.

"There's a hell of a reason! That bastard Bossier has gone too far. I never would have thought this of him!"

"We still don't know what his reasons are, Louis."

"Damn his reasons! I'll show him. I'll beat him in every court in the territory, if I have to. I'll win at Natchitoches, and he can file his appeals all the way to *la ville.* But I'll still beat him."

"A court fight could be costly, Louis. If he hires a good lawyer, you will have to have a better one."

"I can afford it. But I'd fight him even if I couldn't. I'd mortgage every acre and every hand I've worked for before I'd let a lying thief take what's mine."

"Speaking of hands…" Ben saw his opening to divert the subject. "Since we thumbed our nose at the offerings of that Virginia trader, we'll be going home without any."

Louis sobered. The Bossier matter had riled him so that he had stormed off without thought to his other reason for the trip.

"You're right, Ben. I do need that blacksmith. Maybe we ought to ride on down to *la ville,* since we're this far already."

"Or Natchez? I don't know if you heard it or not, but some of the buyers back at the square were talking about a flatboat of *nègres* that's on its way to Natchez." Ben grinned. "I've never been to Natchez, Louis, but I hear it is *wild!*"

Louis grinned back broadly then, Bossier ignored for the moment.

"It's certainly no place for an innocent young lad to go alone. If you're bound and determined to head for Natchez, boy, then I'm obliged to go, too. Just to keep you out of trouble, of course."

ꙮ 12 ꙮ

Natchez was wild, indeed. And there had, indeed, been a fine lot of Negroes delivered to the slave pen of Micajah Pratt. The ferry operator confirmed both facts as he carried them across the Mississippi.

"First things first, my boy," Louis cautioned when they rode off the ferry and surveyed the two-hundred-foot bluff that soared above them. A broad common, verdant and lush, crowned the top of the slope; and behind the green stood a sprinkling of tall mansions. But at the foot of the hill, there sprawled the most notorious little town in all the 2,340-mile length of the river that sawed America in half.

Natchez proper was far from *proper.* It was squalid and dirty, congested and noisy. Half-naked Indians lurched down Silver Street past half-naked strumpets, and every other building seemed to be a saloon. Louis reined up short beside a slender, swarthy man who appeared to be a cut above most of the rabble. From the coloring of the man's skin and the delicacy of his features, Louis guessed, rightly, that he was a Canary Islander—a local farmer, probably, who had settled this Mississippi town under the Old Regime.

"*Habla Español, Señor?*"

"*Sí.*"

"*Dónde está el corral de esclavons?*"

The farmer pointed southward to a wooden building near the edge of town, with an adjacent stockade.

"*Gracias, Señor.*" Politely, Louis tipped his hat as the man nodded in acknowledgment, and then wheeled his stallion in the direction the man had indicated.

The slave yard was empty, but the day was balmy for December and the door to Pratt's pens had been left open to advertise his wares. From the doorway, Louis and Ben could see that the Negroes already were being groomed for sale. They stood quietly, just inside the open door, while Pratt continued his instructions on what he deemed good and proper behavior. On either side of the bare showroom, small doors led into adjacent pens where men and women were separately quartered when they were not being exercised, groomed, or displayed. Today, Louis noted, the holding pens were empty. The Negroes lined up here before them would, apparently, be the whole lot offered for sale.

For a fleeting moment, his conscience nagged him. It always did, every time he approached a lot of Negroes on the block or in the pen. On his own land, working bareback beside his hands, sweating from the same heat, drinking from the same gourd, and eating the same food they had grown together, he felt no guilt. It was only at these public sales that a persistent, unbidden voice told him men and women weren't meant to be auctioned like swine and cattle.

Louis brusquely pushed those thoughts aside. These Negroes were certainly a better lot than the ones Bell had shown at Opelousas, and better treated, too. Each had a new outfit of clothes, quite adequate for the chill of early December. The men were freshly shaven, and all were obviously bathed. They were lined up now in perfect order according to their heights, not by age or by their color, which ranged from the deepest black to almost white.

Quickly, Louis scanned the lot of men, noting several likely prospects, but as his eyes swept a second time down the row of females, a tall girl boldly caught his eye and he stared back.

She was the lightest of the lot. Indeed, in any other place, she could have passed for white. Her curls were the color of wheat, her eyes the blue of Lake Pontchartrain on a summer day. She could be no more than seventeen, but the gaze that returned his stare was knowing. Suddenly Louis felt uncomfortably warm, and he knew that, whatever the price, he was buying this one. Even so, he fought back a rush of fury that such a woman could be bought without her own consent. It wasn't *right,* he argued with himself for want of anybody else to argue with.

The girl spoke. In English. Louis could not understand the light trill of her words, but he could see the taunting laughter in her eyes, and Ben chuckled.

"Shall I translate for you, Louis?"

"*Oui,*" he grunted, again cursing himself for not having bothered yet to learn this new language. Aside from a few profanities picked up here and there, he knew even less of English than he did of Latin.

"*Bien, mon vieux,* it seems she has noticed your interest and assumes you might want to buy her. She asks if you would like to examine her in the back room to be sure that she has no hidden sores."

Louis grunted again, negatively, as he struggled to keep his eyes off the curves the loose fit of her cheap dress could not hide. He did not need to strip her. He could already envision what every inch of her must look like, as soft and blonde and downy as a new spring chick.

"You know, Louis, it might be a good idea," Ben teased. "Who knows, she might have a back full of scars. You would not want a slave who has already proved to be surly and recalcitrant."

"I'll take the trader's guarantee for that," Louis retorted.

"Gentlemen! What might your needs be today?" Micajah Pratt had not noticed their presence until the white girl spoke, but then he welcomed them affably.

"You are both in luck, gentlemen," he went on without waiting for their reply. "The best Negroes of the lot are still here. Indeed, I did not plan to offer any for sale until tomorrow morning, but since you have come, what can I show you?"

For a moment, Ben hesitated in his reply. The crisp Yankee accent, so different from the drawl of most migrants into Natchitoches, had taken him by surprise, and he had been forced to concentrate intently to follow the man's staccato flow of words.

"Thank you," Ben replied at last. "I'm looking for a half-dozen or so field hands experienced with cotton, and my companion needs a blacksmith."

The trader eyed Louis with some amusement. "A blacksmith? Then he is looking at the wrong lot, my friend. He won't find a smithy among the wenches. Perhaps, sir, your companion has other needs as well?"

Louis nodded toward the girl. "How much?"

Ben translated, and the Yankee's smile grew broader.

"Babe? Ah, but Babe's the pick of my lot. The best house wench I've ever had the pleasure of offering. I could easily get a thousand dollars for Babe."

"Bien!" Louis replied without waiting this time for Ben's translation.

"What!" Ben exclaimed. "Louis are you mad? Thérèse doesn't need house help and you don't need another female hand. Even if you did, you could get one anywhere for far less than a thousand dollars."

"I'll take her," Louis repeated stubbornly. "Now ask about the blacksmiths."

Ben shrugged his resignation and translated Louis's request.

"Ah, of course," Pratt beamed, delighted at the prospect of a buyer who spent so freely and asked so few questions before he bought.

"Here we are, gentlemen. This is Primus, and no finer smith ever stoked the coals. He can shoe a horse faster than four men working together. He can take a piece of iron and make it sing. He can…"

While the slaver continued to praise the many talents of Primus, Louis examined the man carefully. His stomach was hard, with no hint of fat. He had a full set of teeth that exuded no odor of decay. His nails were short, but firm and pliable; not a single one cracked as Louis bent them and he nodded his approval. The man's health appeared sound.

Only the eyes troubled Louis, but not that much. There was a hint of something in the man's intense stare, and for a moment Louis almost asked to take him to the back room in hopes they could question Primus out of hearing of the slaver. But then he dismissed the idea. He had bought a recalcitrant slave or two before. They had come around with the right kind of treatment.

This time, to Pratt's surprise, Louis haggled. The price was too high. Didn't he have another blacksmith to offer?

Well, yes, but…. The slaver began to worry. Clearly this buyer was not the easy mark he had thought. He might not be able to get rid of the big yellow buck so promptly after all. Skillfully, Pratt edged Louis back toward Primus, but this time his price was lower.

"*Seis cents,*" Louis stated shortly.

"Six hundred!" Pratt exclaimed when Ben translated for him. "He's worth far more than the yellow girl!"

"I agree," Ben replied without waiting for Louis's own response, "but that's the offer. If you don't like it, you don't have to take it."

Pratt took it. He had hoped for more out of this prime specimen of a man, but six hundred was still a handsome profit. Indeed, almost all profit. Quickly, he took the bills Louis counted from the fat roll he wore under his belt, and he continued his unctuous spiel, praising for Ben's benefit now the exceptional qualities each of his Negroes offered.

If Ben protested that a man was too old, the slaver promptly ordered the hapless fellow to do cartwheels across the room or sprint across the exercise yard to convince his prospective buyer that he was, indeed, in fine shape. Unlike Louis, Ben did insist upon taking the likely ones to the back room; but he checked only the backs and shoulders of the females, scrupulously avoiding the lasciviousness with which some buyers were known to ogle, prod, or paw the women while their dress tops were down. At last he found seven hands that pleased him, and he drove a fair bargain for a youth of limited experience.

"No chains, Mr. Pratt!" Ben ordered as the slaver began to manacle their choices. The Yankee stared at him incredulously.

"Mister, take an old man's advice. They will overpower you before you are a block away and, on these streets, you won't find a public-minded citizen to come to your aid."

"Then rope them together lightly," Ben insisted. "Nothing more."

Pratt shrugged. "It's your risk. You've paid for them now. I guarantee my wares to be in good health, but nothing more."

"We will take the risk."

Business done, the two Metoyers then let their minds roam to the other things Natchez had to offer. Leading their small coffle down Silver Street, Ben eyed the saloons, cautiously checking for the cleanest-looking one whose sign advertised rooms as well as whiskey. Alone, he would have gone to Michie's Tavern up on Main, where the Prudhomme boys said they always stayed. But that famed establishment would probably decline to rent a room to Louis. At last, Ben made his choice from the options Silver Street had to offer, stepped inside, and wound through a thin assortment of fairly respectable-looking men.

"What'll ya have, Mister?" the weary-eyed proprietor asked indifferently.

"A large room, M'sieur."

"A *large* one?"

"My traveling companion and I have just purchased nine slaves. They can sleep on the floor, if the room is large enough."

"It will be. They don't need much space. That'll be six bits for you and your friend and four bits apiece for the hands. Supper's included, but breakfast ain't."

"Very well." Ben removed six golden eagles from his purse and laid them on the bar. Quickly, the saloon-keeper's paw raked them into the pocket of his apron.

"Second door on the right, sir."

"Thank you."

Ben wound his way back to the door and nodded for Louis to bring the coffle inside.

"Hold up one minute there, boy!" The Anglo's voice had lost its monotone.

Politely, Ben turned and inquired, *"Oui,* M'sieur?"

"Where does that man of yours think he's going?"

"To our room, M'sieur."

"Well, you can take your hands upstairs and bed 'em on the floor alright, but we don't cater to high yellows."

"I beg your pardon, sir?"

"You heard me, Frenchie. Niggers can sleep on the floor, but from the looks of the fancy duds your friend's wearing, he 'spects to sleep on a bed. No niggers sleep in my beds."

"I paid you for our room, sir. Six dollars in hard specie."

"But you didn't tell me your *traveling companion* was this yellow man. This here's a respectable place, boy. Your friend will have to go down to the Crow's Nest or one of those places."

"Then I'll have to ask for my money back." Ben's voice was dangerously calm. The tavern-keeper sullenly reached into the pocket of his apron and withdrew six bits. Ben let the coins lie on the counter where the man had plunked them.

"Not just my companion's fare, but the whole six dollars."

"Like hell! You paid for lodging for you and your slaves, and you got lodging for you and your slaves. That part of our bargain holds, Frenchie."

"I bought a package of accommodations, sir. You have now broken the bargain. I insist upon my money."

The bartender's eyes never left Ben's face, but his hand was inching slowly under the counter toward one of the pistols that were never out of his reach.

"Freez, bastid!"

The Anglo froze. He had completely ignored Louis throughout his exchange with Ben, and it had been a mistake. Louis's rendition of one of the few English expressions at his command was more comic than threatening, but the bartender had no doubt about the seriousness of the long, slender-barreled pistol that had sprung from Louis's waistcoat and was now pointing at his own belly.

"Both hands on the countertop, M'sieur," Ben quickly commanded, as Louis edged backward against the wall beside the door, sheltering his back in case any of the tavern crowd happened to be the keeper's friend.

The Anglo's adam's apple bobbed as Ben swung himself lightly across the bar and dipped into the man's dirty apron.

"You see, sir? My six eagles, no more." Again, Ben loped back over the counter, then bowed deeply. "It has been interesting doing business with you, sir—even if it has not been a pleasure. *Au 'voir!*"

Louis's pistol stayed in his hand all the way down Silver Street, but none of the tavern crowd bothered to follow. The Crow's Nest, as the Anglo had said, was less selective in its patrons. The fact was obvious from the fetid odor that greeted them at the doorway. It was the kind of place that Ben had, on one or two occasions, visited on a lark with wilder friends in *la ville,* but he never had cared to stay in one. Still, he hesitated now to risk an inquiry at any other tavern, lest Louis meet rejection again. Silently cursing the damned attitude of the Anglo who would let a dirty white man sleep on his bed before he would a clean, colored man, Ben plunked down the three eagles demanded by the slattern who ran the Crow's Nest and led Louis and their coffle up the stairs.

"*Nom de nom!*" they swore in unison as they surveyed the accommodations.

"There's not even a lock on the door, Louis. We can't leave the *nègres* to go down for a drink, much less a card game!"

Louis loosened the ropes that cuffed them and sternly pointed them to the floor, then checked the rumpled bed for lice before settling gingerly upon it.

"You go on out, Ben. I'll stay here with the hands. I probably wouldn't find a friendly game of cards in this town anyway."

Louis's anger was carefully controlled, his voice completely flat. But Ben knew the undercurrents of rage and frustration Louis was feeling, and he could not help but share his older brother's pain.

"I'll tell you what, old man," he retorted, forcing gaiety into his voice. "I'll go out and get a bottle and bring it back up here. And maybe a loaf of bread and some cheese. I'd rather sup with you here than that rabble downstairs, for sure."

"*Merde,* boy! Natchez has far more to offer than vittles and rum. This is your first night in Sodom, and you're going to stay up here and go to bed with *me?*"

Ben laughed. "That would undoubtedly be safer than going to bed with the likes of what we saw downstairs! Now settle down and try to keep your hands off that pretty little wench of yours while I find us a bottle and some food."

It wasn't Louis's creamy, golden-haired Babe who kept him occupied, though, while Ben was gone. It was the blacksmith. For an hour the slaves had followed them mutely, not uttering one word as long as he and Ben kept up their banter. But the moment Ben left, Primus started jabbering, and for the life of him Louis couldn't understand one word of the man's English.

As the other Negroes began to laugh, Louis's frustration mounted and he rued their decision to buy English slaves. The one he had already, he had bought down at Pointe Coupée. With *him,* it was the black man who was out of place, the only one who could not speak French. Now *Louis* was the goat in a corral full of mustangs, and his handicap made it damned hard for him to maintain any air of authority. Fortunately, Ben did not tarry long.

"Boy, can you tell me what this man I bought is jabbering about?" Louis greeted his young brother as Ben came through the door.

"Eh?"

The Negro began again. His big eyes rolled expressively, his arms waved, and his voice bounced up and down in obvious agitation. Ben listened until he was through, and his face clouded; but then he laughed as he saw one bit of humor in his brother's problem.

"Louis, old boy, it looks as though you have bought yourself one ripe plum and one bad apple. Fortunately, you did not pay as much for the apple."

"*Hehn?*"

"Your big man claims he's freeborn, not a slave."

312

Again the agitated Negro erupted into a torrent, but Ben shushed him.

"No, Ben," Louis interjected. "Let him talk. What's he saying?"

Ben shrugged, then nodded to the Negro to begin again. As the slave trader had said, Primus was indeed a blacksmith; but if his story had any merit, he never had been a slave and the Yankee trader had kidnapped him in the port of Charleston. Thirty-five years before, in the colony of South Carolina, Primus swore, his father had joined the Continental Army to fight the British, alongside his master. At the close of the war the master had given the father his freedom. Two years later, he had married a white girl named Nancy Baker...

"Married?" Louis interrupted incredulously. Until now, he had been inclined to believe the Negro's story and had been cursing himself for not heeding his first impression about the man. But this last claim was preposterous.

"*Zut*, Ben! Anglos don't let their women marry blacks."

"He says they do. According to him, there's no law against it in South Carolina."

"Ask him if there's a record of that marriage, if he has proof that he is free."

Ben translated, listened through another flood of words, then turned back to Louis.

"He says that South Carolina does not require couples to create marriage records, but that there are sworn testaments on file about the marriage, and about his free birth, and his own marriage as well."

"He has a wife?" Louis asked quietly.

"So he says. A wife and a house full of little ones."

"That settles it, Ben. Tell the man that as soon as we get back home, you'll write whomever he says. If he's playing me for a fool, I'll stripe his hide. He can count on that. But if he's really free, then I'll pay his way back home."

Ben told him, and the blacksmith grew suddenly still. Before all of them, a tear began to trickle down his face, and from the look in the eyes of the other eight slaves they had bought that morning, Ben and Louis knew they had won the grudging acceptance of all of them.

The next morning they crossed the Mississippi and headed home. As Louis promised, when they reached the Isle of Canes, he had Ben write that letter. By early February, the Clerk of Court for Orangeburg District, South Carolina, had sent his response.

Everything Primus had claimed was confirmed by the clerk's letter. Quietly, Louis accepted the loss, had new free papers drafted for Primus, gave him a horse and directions home, then paid him fair wages—not only for the two months he had labored for Louis, but for six weeks, too, that Primus had lost from his life while the slaver shipped him from Charleston to what he thought would be a gullible market on the Mississippi.

Louis had been taken. The fair Babe had more than lived up to his expectations, but the Yankee trader had deliberately sold him a worthless title to the blacksmith. The man had knowingly wronged both Primus and Louis, and Louis was not a man to forget, much less forgive, any wrong.

∽ 13 ∾

Spring 1813

As Augustin had hoped, his new house was finished in time for spring planting. It was not so fine a "Big House" as he would have liked to give his Agnes; but, as she kept telling him, there was no hurry. He was not old yet. If his mother was any example of what he could expect, he had another thirty good years left before age would begin to slow him.

Sometimes Augustin could not help but wonder if those thirty years would be enough. Already he was forty-five and so much remained undone. Things that *had* to be done, if all the hopes and dreams he had for his people were to materialize.

"Gustin!" Agnes chided, "You expect the impossible! It's only been twenty years since your papa freed you. Look what you've done already! Man, you were born with the odds against you. You came into this world enslaved and illegitimate"—Augustin winced at that word—"and you grew up illiterate and poor. Despite your papa's money, *you* were poor, and you've taken nothing from him. Everything we have today has come from your work and your brains!"

She was right, and Augustin knew it, though his modesty would never have let him say those things himself. Well, she was almost right.

"You left out the most important thing, Agnes. I've had God's help."

"Of course, Gustin," she agreed softly, but then an impish grin wiped away the age lines that now creased her face between her generous mouth and the apples of her cheeks. "You worked for that, too, you know. You've prayed harder than any ten men."

Laughing, Augustin tumbled her across him. Her round little *derrière* had grown plumper with each baby Agnes bore, but she still fit comfortably onto his lap.

"I've also had your help, *chien-chien.*"

Agnes shifted her generous bosom before it smothered him. "Ah, and what demands you have made upon me, in the field, in the kitchen, day and night, night and day! But, don't worry. I haven't minded a one of them."

"Especially the ones at night, *n'est-ce pas?*" Augustin teased.

"Especially!" She nuzzled her nose softly in his side-whiskers as the tied ends of the gay tignon she had donned for the day's festivities tickled at the corners of his eyes. Augustin bounced her off his lap.

"If you don't scat, woman, I'm liable to make another demand, and we won't get to the races."

"You mean you'd rather spend a Sunday afternoon riding horses than me?" she sniffed in mock offense.

"I'll let you wonder about that..."

"Papa?"

For a moment Augustin was startled. He had not heard Baptiste-Augustin come into the room, and his first reaction was to wonder how much his son had overheard. Then he smiled at his own foolishness. At fifteen, Baptiste-Augustin was no child. There was no harm in the boy knowing that desire was a part of marriage, too. That was far better than having him grow up thinking physical love was just for hot-blooded youth in somebody's hayloft.

"Yes, son?"

The boy's embarrassed grin told Augustin that he had heard enough. "There's a strange gentleman outside asking for you." His voice lowered. "A white one."

"Eh? Show him in, son. It's not gracious to leave a guest standing alone on the stoop."

"Yes, Papa."

The man was indeed a stranger. As Augustin watched him slowly mount the stairs, he concluded that he had never seen the man anywhere before. He was short, slender, and pale to the point of haggardness, with strands of gray already streaking his thinning hair.

"Bonjour, M'sieur," Augustin greeted his guest cordially. His bow, though, was stiffly formal, and he did not offer his hand. That was a custom he had abandoned some years past, ever since the Anglos had come into the territory. Too often his hand of friendship had been rejected, and some of those to whom he had extended it had recoiled openly from the idea of his touch. This time, though, Augustin's reserve was hardly necessary. His guest responded in Augustin's own tongue and offered his hand.

"Bonjour, M'sieur Metoyer. Please accept my apologies for intruding upon the privacy of your home." The voice was not strong, but the man's French had a pure Parisian accent that was seldom heard on the frontier.

"You are not intruding, M'sieur. You are a welcome guest. Please be seated."

The man accepted the proffered sofa, but sat stiffly on the edge of its cushions.

"Brandy, M'sieur?… M'sieur…?"

"Chevalier. Louis Chevalier. And, *oui,* I could use a bit of brandy. It has been a rather long trip, and I have to admit that I am ill accustomed to this climate."

Augustin had assumed as much. It was still early spring, but the pale-faced man was perspiring quite profusely. It was also obvious from his rumpled clothes and the drawn look in his eyes that he had been through some exhausting days. In fact, Augustin thought suddenly, this M'sieur Chevalier does not look well at all.

Checking his curiosity, he filled for his guest a small mug, one of the six matching lead-crystal cups he had splurged on his last morning in Paris. The design was exquisite, the weight perfectly balanced; but it had been the ivory bust of Napoleon imbedded upon the side of each mug that had compelled Augustin to buy the set he really could not afford.

"Merci," Chevalier murmured as he took the cup. In one gulp, he downed the brandy. Then he blanched and slumped onto the sofa.

"Agnes!" Augustin shouted, and in an instant she was at his side, taking charge of the strange M'sieur Chevalier.

"Take his feet, Gustin! Help me stretch him out. Here, put these pillows under his feet! Raise them high so the blood will run down to his head."

Deftly, Agnes loosened the man's ill-fitting collar and unbuttoned his sticky shirt. From some mysterious cache, a fan appeared in her hand, fluttering briskly, and in a minute Chevalier's translucent eyelids were fluttering also.

Agnes stared at him bluntly. "M'sieur, are you hungry?"

"Agnes!" The directness of her question shocked even Augustin. "My apologies, M'sieur. My wife is rather plain-spoken."

The gratitude in Chevalier's eyes was clear to see. "She is good, sir. And quite right," he whispered. "I've not eaten in three days."

"*Ma foi!* Help me get this poor man to the table, Gustin! Famie!"

"Yes, ma'am?" Their cook waddled through the doorway, where she and her curiosity had been lurking ever since M'sieur Chevalier was ushered into the salon.

"Get out to the kitchen and get some of those meat pies you fried for the races. And some cool lemonade. And a loaf of fresh bread, with butter."

"Yes, ma'am."

Famie wasn't happy. The feast she had prepared for their Sunday outing was not just for the family. She'd also planned "leftovers" for Big John, the Lecomte's driver whose appetite was as legendary as his *amour*. It was Big John, not some mealy-faced stranger, who was supposed to be wooed by her cooking. Still, her resentment eased a trifle as she watched the man down her offerings and the color creep back into his pallid cheeks.

One by one, Augustin's flock of children drifted in, as curious about the newcomer as Famie had been, at least before she had to forfeit Big John's meat pies. Like Famie, they were more than a little anxious to be off to the races. Impatiently, Agnes began to shoo them out.

"Oh, no!" Chevalier protested. "Let them stay, Madame. I like children about me..." His voice faded. "I've never had any of my own, you see."

The Frenchman's hand went out to the nearest child. "Come here, son."

The child wavered. Chevalier winked and crossed himself. "I promise I won't eat you. I'm already full."

The little boy grinned, yielding a little.

"I'll bet your name is Thomas."

"No, M'sieur. Joseph."

"Ah, Joseph, of course. You even look like a Joseph. And I'll bet you are six years old if you are a day."

"Almost, M'sieur."

"And you can ride a horse already, *n'est-ce pas?*"

"*Oui,* M'sieur. A *big* one." Joseph stood on his tiptoes and stretched his hand as far as his arm could take it to show how tall his horse stood. Then he reassessed the level of his hand and balefully lowered it a bit for honesty's sake.

Chevalier laughed and tousled the boy's soft hair. "Ah! A little saint in the making!"

One by one, he singled out all the others—Baptiste-Augustin, Marie-Louise, Maxille, Auguste, Pompose, and Susette. Even the little François-Gassion, still a babe, did not escape his notice. Eventually, though, Chevalier grew quiet, his face sobered, and he stared Augustin straight in the face.

"*Merci,* M'sieur," he said simply. "I am indebted to you, although I am much embarrassed."

In truth, Augustin was as embarrassed as his guest, but he gruffly protested. "There's no need to be, M'sieur. Life doles out difficulties to all of us from time to time."

"*Oui,*" the Frenchmen agreed. "I call them The Lord's Examinations, little tests to see how well we have learned our lessons in humility and fortitude."

"You are a philosopher, M'sieur Chevalier?"

"Only a teacher, M'sieur. Which reminds me of the purpose of my visit."

Augustin waited quietly for the man to continue, but a small flame of hope began to glimmer. Had this needy stranger at his door been a test for him as well? Perhaps, a reward from God in case he passed his own test?

For a moment, Chevalier said nothing more, as he toyed with the little mug that held his lemonade, a match to the one in which his brandy had been served. Then he ventured to ask, "You are an admirer of our Emperor, M'sieur? Napoleon of France?"

"*Oui.*"

"I was, too. Once. I cheered him when he was named First Consul. After the misrule of the Directorate, France badly needed a decisive leader who could restore our confidence in government. Then when the Peace of Amiens was announced and ten years of war ended on the Continent, I gave thanks to God for having sent us such a leader."

Augustin nodded. "*Oui,* I was there in '03 and heard many men say the same."

318

"I know," Chevalier replied and went on, ignoring the quizzical look that Augustin now gave him.

"Unfortunately, the man was not content to rule a peaceful France. No one could have imagined the measure of ambition that seethed inside our little emperor! In the name of liberté, he has overrun most of Europe, but he has made a mockery out of the liberté our Revolution won for man. Since he crowned himself l'Empereur, he has become a despot. He has stifled intellectual thought and crushed political freedom!"

Augustin again nodded, pensively, somewhat taken aback by the passion with which the stranger spoke his mind. "I have heard as much, but then so much of what passes for foreign news here in Louisiana carries the flavor of our Anglo presses." Augustin smiled. "Naturally, we French are prone to add a grain of salt when we sample their offerings."

"That's unfortunate," Chevalier declared. "I cannot know what you have heard, but on my solemn oath I swear I have nothing good now to say about the man."

Augustin was silent as he contemplated the implications of Chevalier's words. It was the France of 1803 he had absorbed, a France that rode exultantly on the crests of peace. A France heady with the success of its revolution, cheering the man who had lifted it above the sordidness of the lawless mobs. Chevalier had now smashed for him that idyll.

The stranger seemed to sense his thoughts. "There is still much good in France, M'sieur. Despite Napoleon's efforts to crush all who oppose him, there are many who work to keep alive the good our Revolution has produced. Among my colleagues at the Sorbonne..."

"The Sorbonne!" Augustin interrupted, breaking one of his own cardinal rules. "You are from the Sorbonne?"

"I was," Chevalier replied, and Augustin detected an edge of bitterness in that unfinished statement.

"Until the Emperor demanded my dismissal. My exile. That is why I have come to see you M'sieur Metoyer. Abbé Durand recalled a visit you made to the university during your tour of France, and the passion with which you vowed that one day you would bring a teacher from the Sorbonne to your Isle."

But then Chevalier hesitated, uncertain of how to go on, framing his words as politely as he could. "Of course, Monsieur Abbé has heard nothing of you since and, quite frankly, he did not know whether you would be, ummh, *ready* yet to employ a tutor for your children. But since I had no other prospects outside France…" His explanation broke off into a shrug.

Augustin rose abruptly and stalked to the window, waiting before he spoke to be sure his voice was steady.

"M'sieur Chevalier, you are an answer to my prayers. I've had tutors. Several of them. Each soon left when he found… employment elsewhere." Augustin had almost said *when he found whites willing to match my generous pay,* but he could not say that aloud. Slowly, he braced himself and turned to face his visitor again.

"You see, M'sieur, there are too few teachers in this state, at least good ones. Our children have learned to read and write from those who have come and gone, but I want more than that for them. They need an *education.* They need the classics, mathematics, the English language, and law. Most especially now, law."

His face hardened, almost imperceptibly. Chevalier could see the inner battle he was fighting as he went on.

"We need a permanent academy on this Isle, M'sieur. I have seven children. My brothers and our sister have thirty-five more. We have friends, as well, who are not of African descent although their children are. These men can well afford to pay tuition for their children's education, but they cannot find a school that will accept them. I intend to build that school here on the Isle. But we need teachers."

Chevalier rose and extended his hand in pledge. "M'sieur Metoyer, *mon ami,* you have one now."

Augustin stared deeply into the Frenchman's eyes, gauging the depth of his sincerity, and this time he saw the tutor that would not desert them. Wordlessly, he dropped the man's hand and wrapped him in his arms.

∽ 14 ∾
Winter 1814–15

Napoleon was indeed forced to abdicate, but it was a British-financed invasion of Paris which wrote that epic moment into history. Having thereby rid herself of her greatest menace, Great Britain then unleashed her force, full-strength, upon the new American nation that had declared war on her two years before. By summer, Redcoats descended upon the Atlantic Coast. Savannah and Charleston were bombarded. Washington City was burned.

Then winter came, so cold and harsh that the Crown abandoned its Atlantic Campaign and sailed into the sunny Gulf of Mexico. While English-incited Indians threatened the safety of the Louisiana interior, British boats invaded the new state from the sea. The month of December 1814 marked not only another advent of Christ's birthday but also the advent of the English Navy upon the city of New Orleans.

Andy Jackson, fresh from his military victories in West Florida, hastened to the defense of *la ville*—Crescent City, as the Anglos now called it. From the capitol there, Governor William C. C. Claiborne called out the militia. On the Isle of Canes, Nicolas Augustin Metoyer called together his people.

L'Académie de l'Isle, which had become their meetinghouse as well, was packed. Augustin's call was answered not only by his brothers and their families but by all the worthy free men of color and their fathers whom Augustin called his friends. Here were the Le Court boys, Valery and Athanasite, sons of Barthelemy by his handsome Indian, Ursulle. And Baptiste-Louis Rachal's strong quadroon lads, Espallier and Pierre, born of Françoise Lecomte, whom he had bought from the widow's heirs and freed. Here were Seraphin and Manuel Llorens, whose Spanish father Francisco had moved of late into the parish with the boys' mother, Francesca Nivette. And Augustin's own nephew, François Nicolas Monet, whom Alexis Cloutier's half-brother Louis Monet, had fathered after he married the Widow Dupré and added Coincoin's Fanchon to his harem. Then from the upper reaches of the parish there had come the Mézières, the quadroon grandchildren of the old commandant, and the Grappes, the ruddy tri-racial sons and grandsons of the old French sergeant Alexis, whose alliances with the Indians had kept peace on the frontier for fifty years.

"Ma famille, mes amis," Augustin began, then smiled and waited for the impetuous cheers of the youth to subside.

"Mes braves," he began again. "As all of you know, our country is now at war with Great Britain. Yes, we have been for the past two years, but until now the conflict has been far distant and has little concerned us here on the Isle. Now the enemy is beating at our door. If the Redcoats are not stopped, we'll celebrate this Christmas in obeyance to the Church of England, not the Church of Rome."

The tumult rose anew, and Augustin lifted his hands for silence.

"Over the past ten years, my people, there have been many changes in Louisiana. We free men of color, men of property, have been denied some of the most basic rights of man. Those who do not know us argue that our African and Indian ancestry makes us unfit for citizenship, that nature did not endow us with the intellect or humanity that worthy citizens must show."

An angry undercurrent buzzed the length of the long hall, and Augustin pressed on. These remarks were necessary, but they were not the points he wanted to dwell upon.

"Our governor is an Anglo, but he is still a good man. In many ways, he has stood firm in our support. When he organized the territorial militia, the free men of color at *la ville* volunteered for duty, just as they always have, but the Anglos did not want them. It was Claiborne who reminded the newcomers to our state that Louisiana's *hommes de couleur libres* fought for Anglo freedom in the last war with England. With Claiborne's support, our friends in *la ville* were allowed to form two units made up entirely of free people of color.

"But our present emergency is worse than even Claiborne foresaw," Augustin went on. "Not only has he mobilized the New Orleans militia, but he has found it necessary to call all militia in the state to the defense of our capital against the British. The governor also has issued a plea for more volunteers."

Cheers roared back in response and Augustin smiled.

"I knew my people would not disappoint their governor."

"Gustin!"

"*Oui,* François?"

All heads turned toward Augustin's younger brother and had no trouble finding him. François always stood a head above any crowd.

"This morning I was up at Ben's place. Before I left, Colonel Bludworth came by to tell Ben about the call up. Seeing as how Bludworth is head of the militia, I figured he would sign me on."

François's face, already swarthier than those of his other brothers, darkened still with the maze of hurt and incomprehension that Augustin knew so well. *Big Little Brother* they all called him. Physically, François was a giant, but at heart he was a child who had never learned to handle rejection.

"He stalled. He told me that my poor, motherless children might end up without a father, too. I told him I was as ready to fight for my country as the next fellow. That's when he said it. He told me plainly that the territory won't allow no *mixing* among its troops!"

A furious outburst greeted François's report, and this time Augustin had far more difficulty quieting the din. The fact that he shared their indignation did not make his task any easier.

"Bludworth's statement was correct, François. That has been the policy ever since the new government arrived in Louisiana. Free men of color may serve but only in their own companies and only if they are officered by whites."

"Then we'll form our own company," Baptiste-Augustin shouted impetuously, and the other boys took up his hue.

"Yeah, Ben will be our captain!"

"What about Chevalier?"

"Jean Prudhomme?"

"Baptiste Lecomte?"

Augustin quieted the hubbub once again. "You are right. We would have no problem finding white friends to serve with us. However, no company can be formed without the legislature's approval, and they have not given the governor any special authorization for us. Anyone from the Isle who decides to fight will have to go down to *la ville* and join the free *mulâtres* there."

"Those companies won't hold us all, Gustin!"

"Again, you're right, Louis," Augustin replied quietly. "Obviously, our legislature has seriously underestimated the patriotism of Louisiana's free men of color. Well, this is our chance to show them! We will turn out in such numbers that the existing companies cannot accommodate us, and because they need men so badly, they will have to authorize new companies."

Augustin paused, as his face grew more determined. "If enough of us from this parish respond, we should be authorized to form companies of our own. It is not inconceivable that when this war is over, we may be able to keep our companies, to have a permanent militia here on the Isle. Once these Anglos realize we are sincere, that Louisiana is *our home,* and that we *are* worthy citizens, then by all that is holy, they cannot continue to deny us our rights! Not if they are the Christians they claim to be."

"By God, Gustin, you're right!"

"*Mais oui!*" another echoed.

To a man, Augustin's people agreed, as they usually did with his decisions.

At times, the more hotheaded of them chafed when he called for patience and the more irreverent joked about his piety. But when they had a problem, when they needed advice, when differences among them called for arbitration, it was always Augustin to whom they turned.

On occasion, the milder problems were still taken to their mother, lest Coincoin feel she had outlived her usefulness. Augustin had cautioned them and they all agreed, their mother was now aged and she had already done so much. Her last years should be tranquil, unburdened by their cares and worries. So, gradually, Augustin had assumed responsibility for the welfare of their family, and as the family grew into a community, he had become its figurehead. Today, as always, they acknowledged his leadership.

"Two things more, my people," he continued when their clamor had run its course. "There are two other requirements the governor has set. The first puts age limits upon the volunteers. No man can be over forty-five; but since I'm the only old man in the crowd, this regulation won't affect the rest of you."

Augustin smiled then as he anticipated the effect his next words would have. "And no free man of color can volunteer if he is under the age of eighteen."

"Morbleu!"

"Zut!"

"Nom de nom!"

The reaction from the young blades was about what he had expected. Calling for silence, he went on.

"There is also a property qualification. To make sure that only those colored men with community interest at heart will take up arms, we are acceptable only if we have landed property worth at least three hundred dollars. Some of our sons may not meet that qualification. Therefore, I suggest that if any of you have not already given a portion of your land to your older sons, you should do so immediately. Not only will this enable them to serve but it will help them make their own start in life. The way the political climate is in Louisiana, they can't afford to wait until we die before they get their inheritance."

A murmur of approval rumbled among the men assembled, but here and there Augustin still saw worried faces.

"*Mes amis,* I know, too, that some of you will have no inheritance at all from your fathers under the present laws of the state. Come see me tomorrow. My brothers and I will deed enough to each of you, on credit. The only security you need is your word that, if you return from this war, you will repay us as soon as you can."

Silence fell then upon the assembly. For some, it was born of the gravity of war that Augustin had underscored with his *if you return*. Even the youth who had swaggered in and shouted the loudest in their bravura had been reminded of the reality they faced. But others were simply dumbstruck at the offer M'sieur Augustin had laid at their feet. Young Monet, whose father had never acknowledged him and never would. Augustin Cloutier, his cousin, whose white father claimed none of his own mixed-race offspring. So many times, in their hearts, those boys had envied their other cousins—the Lecomtes whose father accepted responsibility for the fruits of his dalliances, and the Le Courts and Grappes whose sires were true fathers in every sense of the word.

And so, it was then and there, in this gathering, that Augustin Metoyer became the patriarch of all on the Isle of Canes—not just a moral leader to his siblings but a father for all those who otherwise had none to claim.

"One thing more!" he went on now, attending to the last of the practical concerns that war had forced upon them. "I know, too, the hardship posed by the timing of this war. Those of us who plant cotton are trying to find shippers, and after the first of the year the tobacco market opens. The present problems at New Orleans may delay things, but the market will be buying before you can return. Since I'm too old to fight, I'm volunteering for duty as business agent for those of you who need one."

"Go now, *ma famille, mes amis.* Our country needs you. But first, let us ask God's blessing upon this mission and His mercy upon your lives."

Their prayers were answered. The war was short, the casualties few. At least on the American side.

On the fourteenth of December, the British Navy captured the American fleet of gunboats that had been sent to stop the Redcoat advance. By the twenty-third of December, His Majesty's General, Sir Edward Pakenham, had reached Bayou Bienvenu, where Andy Jackson swore he'd stop them. But the Americans lost that battle, and British reinforcements drove them back to the very doorsteps of *la ville*.

There on the plains of Chalmette, the gallant defenders threw up a crude but formidable earthwork, in a desperate attempt to keep the Union Jack from waving over the city of New Orleans. Both armies swelled in size, in anticipation of the coming clash. Sir Pakenham raked his spyglasses over his sea of Redcoats and counted ten thousand men, while Andy drawled salty greetings to new arrivals from Kaintuck who raised his force of rawboned, greenhorned, multi-hued recruits to seven thousand.

On the twenty-seventh of December, their Christmas celebration done, the British attacked, but the Americans would not be routed. On the eighth of January, his patience completely spent, Sir Edward ordered a direct assault. By sheer force, he would shove aside the motley militias that stood in his way.

Andy ordered his men to hold their fire. Not until the Redcoats stood two hundred yards away did the French muskets and the Tennessee squirrel guns crack alongside the boom of the artillery. Before that bloody battle of New Orleans was over, Sir Edward lay dead on the field of Chalmette beside two thousand of his men. In their trenches, Andrew Jackson's militia counted only thirteen dead and fifty-eight wounded.

The war was over. In fact, it had been for a fortnight, although neither army knew it. The feisty Jackson thanked his own troops lustily. And then that irascible, opinionated Anglo, whose distaste for the darker races of America was already legend, shocked the world with his boundless praise for the *hommes de couleur libres* who had fought with him on the plains outside New Orleans.

⁓ 15 ⁓

On the ninth of January 1815, seven thousand raucous soldiers descended upon *la ville* and seized the bars, the taverns, the ballrooms, and the bawdy houses. Inspiring strains of the *Star Spangled Banner* mingled indiscriminately with the lyrics of *La Marseillaise,* as Anglos from a dozen states and Creoles of all hues celebrated their victory arm-in-arm in an esprit de corps that Louisiana had never known before and never would again.

The love affair between New Orleans and its victorious army still blazed when Augustin and his string of barges arrived two days later with the produce of the Isle. Effervescent buyers offered top rates for their twists of tobacco, and an ecstatic factor reported unheard of prices for their cotton. The markets were ravenous, and Augustin had shrewdly timed his arrival. While other planters sat cautiously at home, fearful that the city would fall into enemy hands, Augustin had confidently loaded their barges, manned them with his ablest hands, and poled his way downriver. If the reported stalemate were not broken by the time he reached Orleans Parish, he would wait it out on the plantation of his old friend, De Lisle Sarpy. Then, when the British were finally routed and their blockade broken along the Gulf, his goods would be ready to supply the war-starved world.

There had been no wait. As he tied his barges at Sarpy's Landing, Augustin heard the news of peace and declined the overseer's invitation to spend the night. Sarpy was already at his town house in New Orleans. By morning, Augustin was there also, although he found the city far from peaceful.

It was there that his brothers found him. Weary from a month of war and two days of revelry, they had followed their young *compatriot* Jerome Sarpy to his home on Rue de Rampart to recoup their strength and regroup for another assault on New Orleans's taverns. There, when they finally awoke, Jerome's mother broke the news that Augustin had arrived at the town house of M'sieur Sarpy the day before.

"Damn!" Louis swore in mock regret. "There goes our fun!" In truth, he was not so disappointed as relieved. At four that morning, at the dark end of the quay where they were settling inconsequential differences with militiamen from Avoyelles, he had admitted to himself that he was too old for both war and the kind of carousing on which young blades spent their manhood.

"Smile, Louis!" T'Pierre jibed. "If Augustin is here, then our crops are, too. If our crops have been sold, that means money. With money we can have a hell of a better time than we can without!"

"Speak for yourself, brother. I'm trying to remember that I'm a married man."

"That never bothered you before!" T'Pierre shot back. "Are you feeling your age, big brother?"

"My age? *Zut!* I'm just two years older than you."

"*Oui,* but then some of us have kept ourselves in better shape."

"*Touché! Touché!*" Louis grinned. "Come on, Pierre, it's time we looked for Augustin. François? Dom? Are you two coming?"

"Whenever François completes his *toilette,*" Dominique retorted. "Judging by the preening he's been doing ever since he shimmied into that new suit, I think the grieving widower plans to replace his Marguerite at that ball tonight."

François's walnut face took on a mahogany hue as he flushed. "Aw, hush, Dom!"

Dominique laughed. "I'm just jealous of your wardrobe, lad. With a dozen children to feed and clothe, I might not ever get one of those shirts with that fancy upturned collar."

"Well, maybe you oughta spend more time drinking and playing cards and less time in Maggie's bed."

"Ah! But whiskey and cards aren't half the fun! Come on, my boy, let's go before Louis gets impatient and leaves without us. If he collects our money from Gustin, we won't ever see it. Jerome? You coming with us?"

"If you have money to spend tonight," young Sarpy chirped, "there's no way you'll leave me behind!"

As they hoped, Augustin had indeed sold their crops, settled their accounts with the factor, and collected their proceeds. In spite of the war that had taken them from their farms—indeed, because of it—they had done better than they had hoped. As Louis also had suspected, Augustin had no plans to stay in *la ville* and had assumed that his brothers would be returning home with him.

François was crestfallen. In fact, he was adamant. "I ain't going back now, Gustin. You go if you wanna, but I ain't going!"

"You *aren't?*" Augustin asked pointedly.

"There you go again, correcting my grammar. I aren't going. I ain't going. You can put it any way you wanna, but it means the same. I'm *staying.*"

Augustin smiled tolerantly. When François got in one of his bullheaded moods, there was no arguing with him. Obviously, he had found something in the city that the Isle could not offer.

"Any special reason, François?"

François just shook his head.

"Come on, François!" Louis jibed. "You're not being honest with Gustin. Gustin *always* expects us to be honest with him."

"I just ain't got nothin' to tell."

"Maybe not, but you sure have plans, boy! I've seen it in your eyes ever since Émile Dupart took you home with him. What was the name of that pretty little sister of his who asked you to the ball tonight? Arthemise?"

Louis was laughing, but Augustin's face turned ashen.

"The ball? François, is Louis talking about the kind of ball I think he is?"

François shrugged evasively. "Hmmph, that depends upon what kind you're thinkin' about."

"François, you know what kind I mean. Those quadroon balls are not for us. The Rampart Street mothers take their daughters there to meet rich *white* men. They are not looking for colored husbands, and any one of us who sets foot inside the door is asking for trouble."

"I've been invited!" François insisted stubbornly.

"By whom? Nobody can invite us to one of those."

"Oh, it's alright, Gustin," Louis interjected. "Right now he actually could walk into a quadroon ball, or just about anywhere else here, and no one would object. We're heroes in this crazy city, Gustin! We're the men of the hour! Even *l'Abeille* praises us daily and on its English pages, no less!" Louis's arms flung wide. "The whole city embraces its valiant *hommes de couleur libres* who saved her from the British!"

"It's not just the city's embraces that concern me. It is those of this girl." Augustin retorted, outdone with Louis's interference as he struggled to reason with their gullible younger brother.

"François, these girls do not marry our kind. Even if this Arthemise likes you, her mother will reject you. These mothers raise their daughters carefully. They train them in all the graces that a wealthy and cultured *white* man would appreciate. They do not do all this so their daughters can end up on some country farm, married to somebody colored, and raising another flock of children who could never hope to pass for white!"

Augustin's voice was urgent, but deep inside him he knew that all his warnings would be ignored. A long-forgotten pain reminded him of his Desirée, who had led him on for fun and then laughed in his face when she had a *real* offer from that Anglo merchant—the one who had later strangled her when their first child was born a few shades darker than he expected.

"François, I don't want you to be hurt." Augustin plunged on, furiously. "If you don't think I know what I'm talking about, just ask Jerome! He grew up on Rampart. Go on, Jerome. Tell this big fool."

Young Sarpy unrolled his lissome frame from the window alcove where he had been sitting. "You're right, of course, M'sieur Gustin. I'm twenty-five and I don't have a prospect of a wife. In fact, I'm not sure I would even want one from here. Not that there aren't plenty of good girls around, Arthemise Dupart included, but as you say, they are reared to expect more than the world allows us to give them."

Jerome had said nothing he had not expected him to say, but his assessment gave Augustin pause. Jerome was right; *la ville* not only offered little to its *hommes de couleur libres* in the way of wives, but little economic opportunity as well. Many of these young men like Jerome, like Émile Dupart, were well educated, but there was no worthy way for them to use that education. Barred now from the professions, they could only take up a trade and then compete with the hordes of poor immigrants who would work for almost nothing just to live in America.

But on the Isle, *oui!* On the Isle, Augustin's people needed tradesmen, too. Skilled craftsmen. Then they would not have to take their work upriver to Natchitoches to have it done by outsiders. He and his brothers already had begun to groom their sons to fill these needs, but why should they have to wait until a new generation had matured?

With financial backing, these young men from New Orleans could open shops on the Isle, and goods could be shipped to them more cheaply than all the way to Natchitoches. Merchandise would cost less for all the community, and their money would stay there on the Isle, among themselves, instead of going to the shopkeepers in the town. They could use another teacher, too. The academy had far too many students for Chevalier to teach alone.

"Jerome?" He abruptly changed the subject. "What are you doing now? Your livelihood, I mean."

"This and that, M'sieur Gustin," he countered, his face flushing.

"Your father sent you to France for study, didn't he?"

"Oui."

"Are you interested in a teaching post?"

"On the Isle?" Sarpy's eyes narrowed as he considered the possibility.

"Oui." Augustin repeated aloud the thoughts, the plans, the opportunities that had just presented themselves to him, and as he spoke he scrutinized the young man carefully. Before he was through, he knew that Jerome would agree but he could not help adding one last *pièce de résistance*.

"Besides, Jerome, I have three daughters, and their mother's been raising them to cook and sew and keep a country gentleman's home. There's not a *courtesan* in the lot!"

Jerome laughed, his green eyes twinkling above high, soft-tan cheeks. "M'sieur Gustin, you have found yourself another teacher. Mind you, though, I will not teach forever. When I save the money, I aim to be a planter—and a businessman. I am a man of much ambition despite my present pecuniary embarrassment."

"Then we welcome you to the Isle, Jerome."

"Speaking of the Isle, Gustin," Louis interrupted. "When do you plan to leave?"

"At daybreak."

"Then I'll meet you at the landing. But tonight I'm going to kiss this city farewell in style! I have money in my pocket again, and my liver has rested long enough. I don't guess you want to come along to look after my soul?"

"Louis, I have given up on your soul, but do be careful with that money. Your pocketbook should always be greener than your liver."

⁓ 16 ⌒

Day had not yet dawned when Louis roused his older brother from his sleep. Augustin had taken in a performance of Gluck's *Iphigénie et Aulide* at the Maison de Opéra with De Lisle Sarpy, in his old friend's personal booth where their mixed company would be a private matter. After sharing a warm toddy and a postmortem of the plot, Augustin had bid Sarpy good night and left instructions with the butler to wake him an hour before dawn. He had scarcely dozed, however, when he felt a rough hand shake him and heard Louis's muttering.

"Gustin!"

"Hehn?"

"Wake up, old man. We've got problems!"

"Louis? How did you get in here?"

"I banged on the door. How else? The old butler finally let me in. Gustin, you'd better sit up and listen, 'cause I'm not sure I've got the guts to admit this to you more than once."

Augustin swung out of bed, intuitively shucking his nightshirt and slipping into the street clothes he had carefully folded across the *chaise*. For Louis to wake him in the middle of the night, contrite and reasonably sober, something was wrong.

Elizabeth Shown Mills

It was. François had gone to his ball, Louis reported, and not one person had challenged his presence. But when he spoke to Arthemise's mother, the woman had laughed in his face. Hurt and angry, Big Little Brother had stormed out into the night, and Louis and Dom had found him drowning his disappointment at Les Trois Filles.

"And?" Augustin prompted curtly.

"Well, naturally we had to keep him company. I mean, he was in no frame of mind to be left alone. If he'd kept on drinking, the mood he was in, he'd have ripped the place apart."

"So, to keep him from drinking, the two of you get him involved in a friendly little game of cards, *n'est-ce pas?*"

Louis grimaced. "Ah, brother, you know me too well. But I swear, it wasn't our fault."

"Blame's not important right now, Louis. Go on."

"Well, our luck was going real good, Gustin. I swear. We were raking it in, but the stakes were small. Then someone mentioned a game going on in the back room where the pot was bigger and I figured, what the hell! I mean, I had some money to spare. You got a real good price for our crops!"

"And you also had a few drinks too many in your blood."

Louis halfway grinned. *"Oui, oui.* That's always my downfall."

"So you took the men's offer for a *friendly* game in the back room, and Dom and François dutifully followed their older brother."

Louis's remorse was beginning to seem genuine. "Well, at first Dom didn't want to go, but the men began to make remarks about chicken-livered yellows who had no guts for a *real* game of cards, and, well, you can figure out the rest."

"All of you lost your money."

Louis nodded ruefully.

"All of it?"

Louis nodded again. "Dammit, Gustin, I can take my loss. And I don't feel too badly about François. As drunk as he was when we found him, he'd have ended up losing his money and a lot more if we hadn't come along. But Dom just can't afford it. He made a helluva crop this year, but he's got more children to support than you and I and François all put together!"

"Where are the others now?"

"In the alley behind Les Trois Filles. At least, they were when I left them."
Augustin still made no move to go.

"If you'll forgive my impatience, Gustin, I think we'd better hurry a bit."

"For what? You have already lost your money."

"I know it, damn it! But François is pretty riled. He won't leave, and I'm not
sure how long Dom can keep him under control. He almost tore into those men
in the tavern, armed guards and all, when he realized we'd been taken. We got
him out of there, but the more he fumed about it, the madder he got. When I
left he was right ready to go back and take them all on."

"That figures. All right. Let's go. You can tell me the rest on the way."

François was still in the alleyway, muleskinner drunk and bull mad. Augustin
could hear his curses a block up the street. T'Pierre had heard them, too, from
whatever nearby bawdy house he had been visiting, and he leaned now, nonchalantly, against a lamp post at the end of the alleyway, laughing at Dominique's
futile efforts to calm their younger brother. Quietly, Augustin sidled up beside
T'Pierre, paused, and appraised the situation.

"Well, are you going in or not, Gustin?"

"*Oui,* and you'll be right behind me, Louis. Whatever I do, just *follow
suit.*"

"Ah, Gustin!" Louis winced. "That's a low blow, brother."

"Appropriately aimed," Augustin retorted, as he strolled into the alley. "*Nom
de nom,* François! I never would have believed this! As many times as you've been
to *la ville,* you let yourself get suckered in by a couple of tarts and con men?"

François sputtered, nonplussed to see the pious brother who never savored
the nightlife of any city. Still, he was neither too drunk nor too mad to deduce
who had gone for Augustin; and he glared at both brothers as they approached
him.

"Yeah, Gustin!" Louis rejoined. "I wish you could have seen the hussy that
had hold of him when I found him tonight. She was leading Big Little Brother
around like an ox pulls a plow."

Augustin returned the laugh. "Maybe I ought to hire the woman before next
planting. I'd have the straightest rows of cotton in all Louisiana."

François winced, his anger shaken. He was twice the size of this brother who
ruled them all but he knew he would never be half the man, and he had spent

thirty-one years torn between a need to be himself and the hope of living up to Gustin's expectations.

Augustin recognized his conflict and never had exploited it, until now. Now he had no choice. Nothing short of shame would sober François enough for him to see that he needed more than brute strength to take the armed guards of Les Trois Filles. François would have his revenge, but it would have to come another way.

So he plunged on. "I sure wish I'd have been there tonight to see the mess you three got into. It might have been even better than the opera."

T'Pierre chuckled from his stand across the alley. "Maybe you'd like to chip in your own money, Gustin, and let them do it all over again, with us as spectators this time."

"*Oui,*" Augustin agreed with mock seriousness. "Why don't we stage a show and sell tickets? At least we'd get back *some* of our losses."

"*Hé!* I like that idea, Gustin," Louis chimed in, "I can think of a few good names for it, too. Like 'Three Fools and Their Money' or 'Dim Wits and Big Tits.'"

Dominique and François still were not laughing. Characteristic behavior for Dominique, Augustin thought, even when Dom hadn't lost a year's income. But in François's eyes, he could see the hurt and he knew their banter had hit home.

As he watched the muscles slacken now on the big giant before him, he almost regretted the tactic he had used. Stripped of anger, remorseful at last, and remembering again the rejection his offer of love had met that night, François looked like nothing else so much as an overgrown child. Augustin had a sudden impulse to take him in his arms and rock him as he had when François was a baby. *Mama was right,* he thought. *God knew what he was doing when he put the sense of a child into the heart of this man.* Without softness and with so much power, François could have been dangerous.

T'Pierre and Louis were still tossing jibes at each other across the alleyway when Augustin's reverie was broken by a reminder of the job they still had left to do.

"Come on, boys. We have to find the rats who cheated you before they crawl off. Louis, Dom, give me every detail you can remember about Les Trois Filles."

"Well," Louis quipped, "the first one's tall, she's the one with the big tits, and the other two…"

Augustin stared at him frigidly. "The fun's over, Louis."

"*Oui,*" his brother conceded contritely, then roughly sketched for Augustin a verbal picture of the tavern. What details he forgot, the sober Dom well remembered. Augustin hesitated for only a moment, then outlined his plan. Since he and T'Pierre were the only ones unknown to the crowd of that particular tavern, they would play the marks. François, Dom, and Louis were assigned the backup work.

Appropriating the bottle from which T'Pierre had been swigging, Augustin tossed back a mouthful, swished it around a few seconds and spat it out, deliberately spraying it on his suit so he would reek convincingly. Then, arm in arm with T'Pierre, guffawing boisterously, he staggered out of the alley and around to the front of Les Trois Filles. As they paused inside the doorway, blinking at the lights, a flock of floozies gathered around them like crows watching a farmer plant corn.

"Buy me a drink, *cher?*" A blonde-wigged mulatto with a crepe-skinned bosom heaving over her low-slung bodice purred hoarsely in T'Pierre's ear. Her long cat-nails idled across his slender belly as she assessed the quality of his suit with a practiced eye.

"If I wanted a woman as old as my mother, I'd have stayed at home," Pierre snapped.

"*Mon ami!*" Augustin recoiled, before the crow could do the same. "T'ere's no need to be unkind to t'e lady." Wrapping an unsteady arm around her, he cozied up and pretended to use her as a prop.

"Y'see, ma'am, our hearts are jes' set a'ready on two ot'er girls. We he'rd all t'e way upriver about t'ese *jumeaus*. A real matched pair. T'e most beauteous in all t'e city, we're tol'."

"Bullshit!" she spat with a Tennessee accent. "Spindly twits. They ain't got ha'f the know-how. They just cost more. 'Specially for yellow men. They's white."

Augustin leered. "T'ey'll be worth it."

Her heavily lidded eyes narrowed to a slit. "Sure yo' can 'ford 'em?"

Augustin pulled from his pocket a large enough roll to make his point, then slid it back before somebody else got ideas that might interfere with his own.

This time, the rouged lips stretched into a grin that clearly was not fake. "Grab yo'selves a table, honey buns, 'n have a drink on t'e house. I'll send 'em out when they's free."

As Augustin shuffled over to the nearest table, with T'Pierre as his latest prop, the orange-skinned doxy headed directly for the back room Louis had described. Through the door, as it opened and shut, they saw the same two guards, their chairs reclining against the back wall, their guns across their laps. Two men sat talking at the table. Both were armed and neither looked like a pigeon. Sprawling back in his own chair, Augustin rolled his eyes around the barroom for a quick assessment and concluded that if a showdown came, the crowd would definitely side against them. His plan *had* to work.

The door reopened and the same tart sashayed across the room, her bosom heaving even more rapidly. Again she disappeared, briefly this time through a dirty curtain. When she reappeared, the twins were on her arms.

As the blonde had said, *pretty* did not describe the pair. Even under the flickers of a scattering of oil lamps, Augustin could tell their skin was as blue-white and thin as mother's milk—sickly, in his estimation. Both heads of hair were as bright as apricots, the same shade as their freckles. He had never cared for apricots. But, oh, those curves! *Faced with curves like that,* he grinned, *lechery's definitely not hard to fake.* One look at his brother's face told him T'Pierre was thinking seriously of doubling his own pleasure.

"Hello, honey," each of them crooned, in perfect unison, as they wrapped long arms around them.

T'Pierre was mesmerized, and even Augustin marvelled at the smoothness with which the twins operated. In less than two minutes, they had steered the conversation from their charms to cards, and in another two they had invited an idler to join them. The snappy cut of the man's garb, the glibness of his tongue, the nervous twitch of his fingers, everything about the man hinted of his occupation.

Still Augustin could understand how his brothers had been taken. These tantalizing Irish colleens and the Ohioan with his perfectly polished manners were treating the two *hommes de couleur libres* as though they were ambassadors from Bombay. The drinks seemed to replenish themselves. The jokes, the laughter, the flirtatious glances, the promising smiles, the soft thighs pressing under the table, the winning cards…

Holy Mary, pray for me! Augustin thought to himself in disgust. I know exactly what is going on, and I'm still enjoying it! A sharp glance across the table told him that T'Pierre was even more entranced. He dare not let this drag on.

Augustin crowed and raked in another pile of winnings. "Wit' t'is streak o' luck, maybe we oughta be playin' f'r higher stakes, P'erre!"

His brother came to, right on cue. "I dunno, Gustin. T'is crowd's real rowdy-like. Somebody starts a fight, and one o' t'ese ruffians 'd be all over us 'n our money."

"Ah, that's no problem, lover," his chippy purred. "Les Trois Filles has all sorts of private rooms."

"Oh?" T'Pierre purred back.

"Sure and begorrah! Even if you're just interested in a little game of cards, we have a room for *that,* too!" She laughed softly, leaning over him, her voluptuous breasts rubbing slowly, tantalizingly, across his arm as she whispered confidentially. "Behind that little door at the back, that's where the big games are. There's even armed guards to protect all your hard-earned money."

The Ohioan clearly heard her stage whisper, and he raised his black brows smoothly. "Well, gentlemen, that sounds good to me. Are you interested?"

"Shertainly!" Augustin slurred, stumbling as he rose to lead the charge.

The two men Dom had described still sat at the table in the back room as they tripped through the doorway, and Augustin drew up short in feigned surprise.

"Sh'pologies, m'sieurs," he lisped. "Didn't know t'is room was taken."

"That's quite alright, sir." The taller man rose politely. "As a matter of fact, we're two hands short of a game. John Ferguson's the name, sir. I'm down from New York lookin' to see a bit of the city. This here's Jean Toulouse. He tells me he was bred 'n born right here."

Smooth, Augustin thought to himself as he leaned unsteadily against the door.

The Ohioan shrugged. "Fine with me."

"Shertainly, shertainly, *mes amis.*" Augustin boomed, groping drunkenly for the nearest chair. As the New York Anglo eyed Toulouse, Augustin suppressed a smile. Obviously the gamblers assumed he was too drunk to stand, but he had very expediently appropriated the chair nearest the doorway, and T'Pierre had plopped down quickly at his side. Their adversaries were lined up now, directly in front of their own guards, like turkeys on the limb of a winter-bare tree.

Augustin leaned forward in his chair and slapped out a nice stack of bills. "C'mon, men. Th' biggerdepot, th' biggermywinnin's."

The men complied. The cards flew and the game moved rapidly, much as it had outside. Only the stakes were now higher, far higher. Soon, the Ohioan pulled his lace-edged handkerchief and began to dab his brow.

"Gentlemen, this game is getting too nerve-wracking for me. When it comes to cards, I just don't have the constitution you Creoles have. What do you say to playing table limit and getting this game over with one way or the other?"

"Shure, shure," Augustin agreed, amicably elbowing Pierre. "Whaddabou' you, *mon ami?*"

Pierre cackled. "Well, now, I always hate t' take a man's money 'n a hurry, but if t'e man insists…"

"No objection." The New Yorker seemed unperturbed.

"Whatever your pleasure," Toulouse agreed.

The game went on. This time, though, the pot began to grow in front of the lean Ohioan. Within half an hour, he had used every trick Augustin had ever seen and many that he hadn't, but he had expected as much. In fact, with a few unorthodox aces up his own sleeves, he could afford the luxury of admiring the man's dexterity.

The pile in front of the Ohioan continued to grow, and Augustin pulled one bill after another of his roll. It was getting close to time.

Three more hands, and T'Pierre's nervousness was showing. Augustin's own palms began to sweat. His roll was getting uncomfortably small. If François did not hurry…

"My friends, it looks like Dame Fortune has turned against you," the Ohioan purred as he raked another pile into his pot. "Are you sure you want to go on?"

Augustin stiffened in his chair. "Shertainly! Shuffle!"

The Ohioan shuffled. The New Yorker pulled a long, black cigar from the pocket of his waistcoat and began to coax a flame along its tip. His Creole companion leaned back languidly in his chair and yawned, and from the floor beneath his feet, Augustin felt a bump. Pierre slowly shifted to the front of his chair and, in perfect unison, the two brothers sprang tall, pistols drawn.

The Ohioan calmly stared. "Nice try, yellow boys. But it won't work. Even if you kill the five of us, which isn't likely, there's only one way out of here, and you won't make it through that saloon out yonder."

"But you are wrong, M'sieur," Augustin corrected. On cue, three wide boards between them began to creak and then slowly rise, wrenching themselves from their pegs. The breach was wide, as wide as François's back, and from the floor's yawning pit, the barrels of two shotguns edged upward.

This time the Ohioan dabbed at real sweat on his forehead, but he still blustered. "Even that way, you won't make it halfway down the street. My friends out there'll be on your tails like hounds after poontang."

Augustin smiled. "Perhaps. But then they might be too busy to bother. Rope, François?"

"Right here, brother." François's mammoth arm ascended through the hole and the rest of him followed, pushing the planking from his path. The cigar fell from the New Yorker's mouth, and the Ohioan's face lost the last of its color.

"Gawddam!"

François grinned, his broad white teeth glistening in the lantern light. "Well," he drawled. "It shore is nice t' be remembered!"

"Then get the hell out of there and leave them to their memories," Louis snapped from the black depths below the floor, and Augustin laughed.

"Patience, brother. We have to be sure they are tied well. How much did you say they owe you?"

"Twenty-five hundred each for Dom and François and three thousand for me."

"All right, T'Pierre," Augustin ordered genially. "You're our family bookkeeper. Settle up our accounts."

T'Pierre complied. From the pile on the table he carefully counted out each brother's share, then his own. The drawstring of his pouch was halfway tied before temptation overcame him, and he reached into the pile and added a premium for their troubles. Quickly he passed the pouch down to Louis and then scooped the rest into another bag and passed it down as well.

"That's the insurance money, Louis. You'd better be ready to invest it!"

"I'm on my way, *frère!*"

"Then we're right behind you."

The crawl space was as rank as unwashed chitterlings, Augustin thought, groping his way out behind his brothers. As they surfaced, momentarily blinded by the moonlight, they could hear pandemonium break loose in Les Trois Filles, where Louis had tossed the *insurance* money into the barroom by the handfuls. The floozies squealed and shoved, while drunks crawled out from under tables like cockroaches. While the trussed Ohioan and his cronies writhed behind the bolted backroom door, Augustin, Louis, Pierre, Dom, and François calmly mounted the horses Dom had held in readiness and rode off into the night.

Within an hour they were aboard their flatboats. Augustin, Louis, Pierre, and Dom, at least. Somewhere between Les Trois Filles and the bank of the Mississippi, François had managed to disappear. Their *nègres* were at the poles, ready to heave off for Natchitoches, yet Augustin refused to go. If François did not appear by daybreak, he was going back to find him.

The moon waned. The pelicans began to stir from their nests and waft out across the Mississippi in search of breakfast. The peach-tinged rays of dawn bounced off the blackness of the water and sprayed across the bank. Then came François, bounding furiously toward the barges and, scrambling willy-nilly at his side, a hastily tied bundle in her hand, was the prettiest but skinniest little woman Augustin had seen since he arrived in *la ville*.

"Augustin, meet Arthemise," François grunted as they clambered aboard and he yanked loose the rope that tied them to the pier. "Now we'd better get outa here!"

⌘ 17 ⌘
September 1815

François married his Arthemise, but Augustin insisted that he do so honorably. When their barges docked at Yucca Landing, Mademoiselle Dupart went home with Augustin, not with François, and Agnes welcomed the unexpected addition to her own flock of girls. Not once did it occur to her to resent the woman François obviously adored, even though the dead wife he was replacing was Agnes's own sister.

When the next mail left for New Orleans, it carried Augustin's letter to Mme. Dupart. Her daughter was well, he informed her, and her virtue was intact. But Arthemise's will was obvious. He and his family had accepted her into their home and their hearts, and they would give their blessing to the marriage, if

Mme. Dupart gave hers as well. Within three weeks the lady and her baggage had arrived at Yucca Landing, where she disdainfully announced that she had come to *investigate* the people her daughter was *involved* with. She stayed for the wedding, of course.

Having settled his family's love problems, or so he thought, Augustin turned his attention to more pressing matters. That spring he had shocked his family and his fellow planters of the parish with the announcement that he would grow no more tobacco. The future of their country lay in cotton. Now that the war with England had been settled and Napoleon was ousted from the throne of France, the world was at peace and its demand for that fibre was insatiable.

Augustin had made more from the cotton he planted this past year than off the tobacco grown on twice the acreage. In the coming year, all his cleared land would be put to cotton, and he was building one of those new gins with teeth to clean the lint. If any of his neighbors were tired of doing theirs by hand and wanted ginning done, he would be happy to take their contracts, when his own people did not need the gin.

Augustin's real worry in that summer of 1815 had been his mother. Coincoin was now three-quarters of a century old. Her hearing was almost gone, and her eyes had dimmed, but she was still as peppery as she had been at twenty. She bathed daily in the river and scoffed at her son's warnings that she might slip on the muddy bank or be caught up in an eddy when there was no one to help her. The resolution that had always driven her now bordered on cantankerousness, and she turned aside all suggestions that she leave the old homeplace and live with him.

"Go on, Gustin!" she scolded. "I have no use for those Big Houses, sitting up high and sassy on those brick stilts, just daring a storm to come along and blow them down. *Non!* When I lay my old bones down at night, I want to smell the raw earth close beneath me."

Augustin tried to argue that the new West Indian homes had long since proven themselves safe, even in Louisiana, but she cut him off.

"Besides, I have the best of two worlds right here, Gustin. I have the satisfaction of knowing I could build my own Big House if I wanted it, and I have the pleasure of my memories within these walls."

Augustin could not argue with that. It was the memories that kept her there, and he knew it. She spent most of her nights alone now, since Toussaint had built his own little place on the land she gave him, but those nights were never lonely. She would lie, so small and shriveled, in the broad expanse of that four-poster bed and pray herself to sleep with her fingers entwined in the Rosary her father had carved for her in that long-ago childhood. Then she would dream her own private, secret dreams of a proud, young Chatta or a virile Pierre.

When sleep eluded her, she took to the rocker where she had nursed and cuddled so many babes, and crooned her own self to sleep on the same soft songs. At mealtime, her table was never empty. There was always a flock of chattering, happy children to share it with her. Sometimes there was the little Eulalie, as plump and gay as she had been before she succumbed to that fatal fever. Or Rose or Catiche or one of the other sad-eyed, sweet-souled little children she had bought and freed and raised after her own babies turned overnight into grown men and women.

That was why, Augustin knew, she had let the servants go. She had insisted that her children needed them more than she did, even though they all knew that her children could well afford their own.

"Take them on!" she had argued. "You need another woman, Susanne, to help you look after all those girls of yours. And you, Louis, you never have gotten another blacksmith to replace that free fellow you wasted your money on. Go on and take them home. I've found a neighbor to rent my land now. What use do I have for hands?"

So her children had taken them, and Coincoin had been left alone with no one to interrupt her, to drag her from her memories into the cruelness of an old woman's world where one's children no longer needed her and men no longer wanted her.

She was happy. Happier, Augustin knew, than she would be if she were living with any of her children. But she was still *alone*. If she took ill, her memories could not cure her and no ghosts of the past could tend her. She would die helplessly, harshly, instead of softly in the bosom of the children she had borne and suckled.

It was T'Pierre and Toussaint, and the urgent needs of the young and virile, that finally took his mind off Coincoin in the late heat of that long summer. First Toussaint had come to him, tears streaming down the cheeks that grew plumper with each season. Then Augustin had been forced to seek out T'Pierre,

Coincoin's Cabin

Time has decayed the little cabin in which Coincoin began her life as Marie Thérèse, negresse libre.
Only a surveyor's markings hint at its size and style. But it was a style that followed function and
rarely varied. A pair of rooms, each with a front door and a window, might serve as a duplex—one
side for the family of an unpretentious master, the other side for the family's slaves—and a small
gallery typically wrapped around the house. Eventually, in Creole fashion, one end of that gallery
might be enclosed to accommodate a growing family or another slave or two. In the nineteenth
century, as the original bousillage began to crumble, such homes were often sheathed in boards,
American-style.

who had suffered his own grief and rebounded into the first comforting arms he found.

The crux of the problem—the crux of all men's problems, Augustin sometimes swore—was a woman. Too short, too fat, and too lonely, Toussaint had fallen hopelessly in love with a girl too young and far too pretty. To Augustin's younger brother, who saw life in simple terms, there was no problem. His "little woman" was still enslaved, so he would buy her free. In gratitude, then, his Henriette would become his wife.

But Henriette Cloutier had her own ideas, and Toussaint bore no resemblance to the dashing man who filled her thoughts. In the spring of 1810, Toussaint had taken the proceeds from his first crop and paid a call on the Widow Lecomte's daughter who owned "his Henriette." Gladly, he mortgaged everything but his soul to secure the balance of the debt, and when he left he took with him the object of his adoration.

But she spurned him. The more he wooed her, the more she shrugged him off. He serenaded her with every love song he could coax from his guitar, and she laughed. In pique, the rejected lover took her back to the plantation she was born on and forfeited his down payment, but his ache for Henriette had never waned.

The years had passed and the starry-eyed child had grown into a woman, but she took no husband and no lover, and so Toussaint continued to nurse his dreams. Henriette was a good woman, and good women appreciated faithfulness in a man. In time she would realize that his love was true.

That was before the torrid summer of 1815, when Toussaint's brother T'Pierre became a widower. He had hardly returned from war when his Perine fell ill and, as the heat grew more unbearable, she withered away. The sensitive T'Pierre was inconsolable, and when his grieving children cried, he tried to be their mother also.

"You have to find a woman," Augustin counseled him. "You need someone to tend those children. You can't keep on dragging babies around the fields while you oversee your hands. Don't you have a serving woman who can keep house and cook and look after babies?"

"No," T'Pierre had admitted vaguely. "Perine always insisted upon doing her own work. She said servants were too much bother. All I have are field hands."

"Well, go hire a housekeeper!" Augustin ordered.

That was when Pierre had remembered Henriette, the sweet young woman who took such an interest in his little ones whenever they chanced to meet somewhere. Especially of late. So he hired her from the widow and she moved upriver into his home. And that was where Toussaint found her. Only it was not T'Pierre's motherless children whom she was comforting that night. It was not T'Pierre's *enfants* she was cradling in her soft arms.

It had been a hot and sultry evening, the kind of night that makes men itchy, and the lonely Toussaint had walked across the fields to sit a spell in the coziness of his brother's little family. In his pocket he carried a new whistle he had carved for the youngest Pierre, a clothespin doll for the sweet Susie and a basket of fresh figs for his Henriette.

But it was later than he realized. Pierre's house was dark. The shutters were open, begging for even the smallest breeze; and the moon rose languidly as he approached the clearing where his brother's cottage stood. That was when he saw the lonely T'Pierre, lost in the comforting world of *his—Toussaint's*—Henriette, and she was lovelier than even Toussaint had imagined. Before his eyes, the moonlight turned the full length of her body into pure, shining gold; and Toussaint sat down beneath the spreading arms of a moss-draped oak and cried.

By dawn, his hurt had turned to anger and he took his complaint to Augustin. Their pious, righteous brother had always counselled them to live decent lives. Augustin, he knew, would right this dreadful wrong! But Augustin's reaction was not what he had expected.

"By damn, she's *mine*, Gustin! She always has been, and she'd have come to realize that right soon if T'Pierre had left her alone!" Toussaint swore irrationally, and Augustin's heart ached for his plump, melancholy brother whom no women seemed to want.

"T'Pierre's a monster!" Toussaint raged. "He's hid it all these years behind those soft, soulful eyes and that delicate face that's been blessed by the Devil himself. God didn't mean for anybody to look like a boy forever! But the badness in him has come out at last! My Henriette went to him and tried to help him care for those poor children. Then he *used* her. He *abused* her!"

"Did you hear her screaming, Toussaint?" Augustin asked quietly. "Was she begging him for mercy? Fighting for her honor?"

"No, but he's still to blame! There's too much goodness in Henriette. She's young and innocent and felt sorry for him. So he tricked her just to satisfy his own lust. And that poor wife of his dead no time at all!"

"Toussaint, T'Pierre's lonely, too," Augustin said softly. "A lonely man is a vulnerable man. You know that, yourself. But T'Pierre has another pain. When a man's had a woman lying in his arms for a dozen years and suddenly those arms are empty, well, the ache can just get to be more than a man can bear. Even a good man."

"You're taking T'Pierre's side!" Toussaint raged.

"No, Toussaint. You are both my brothers. I love you both the same. Love does not take sides. But a brother's love can look at life more objectively than a man does when he wants a woman."

Toussaint's round face was as hard and flat as a millstone, but Augustin could see that he was beginning to accept the inevitable, and Augustin relented. The boy has shouldered the weight of that fruitless love for far too long, he thought. This has to be settled.

"All right, Toussaint. I will see what I can do. I will talk to T'Pierre and Henriette. But mind you, brother, it was you who came and asked for my counsel. You are the one who demands that I straighten out this mess with your brother and the girl. So whatever I decide, whatever *they* decide, I insist upon your promise that you'll abide by that decision."

Toussaint nodded. "You got it, Gustin."

When the sun went down and the evening breeze blew in cooler off the river, Augustin took Toussaint's grievance to their brother and the woman that one wanted and the other had. As Augustin expected, his efforts were in vain. It had been T'Pierre's soulful eyes that Henriette had dreamed of all those years while she rejected Toussaint and every other would-be lover. As long as Perine lived, she had kept her want for T'Pierre locked inside her. But Perine was gone now; and if T'Pierre would have her, then she was *his*. Pierre, himself, torn between his loneliness and his need, his grief and his vulnerability, found it far less painful to accept the girl's decision than to make one of his own.

Augustin issued his edict as gently as he knew how. The misery on Toussaint's face, as he accepted the pronouncement, was as plain as his approach to life; but Augustin made it clear that he had no other choice. Henriette had chosen for herself. When a decent period of mourning had passed, she would marry their brother and no man could lust after his brother's wife.

Toussaint nodded, accepting both Augustin's commandment and the Lord's. As long as Henriette was T'Pierre's wife, his heart would obey; but he'd still love her. No lust. Just a simple, chaste, undying worship.

✍ 18 ✌

A week later, on the thirtieth of September 1815, Claude Thomas Pierre Metoyer gave up his struggles also. The heat of that summer had brought the fever to the whole length of Cane River. Perine had been one of the first to succumb, the aging Pierre the last. Neither of the women who had shared the old Frenchman's life was there to share his death. His pale wife had died two years before, and never would his lover have been called.

In the waning hours of Pierre's life, it was not the capable Susanne who nursed him but the wispy-faced, strong-willed Elisabeth—his *other* daughter who insisted even to herself that she was his *only* one. Never had she accepted or understood the life her father had lived before he married her own saintly mother, and even less could she comprehend her mother's acceptance of her father's past.

Susanne had cared for Elisabeth from her infancy, and at some long-forgotten point in those childish years, Elisabeth had adored her beguiling nursemaid. But as she grew and lost her innocence, as she came to understand the meaning of Susanne's presence, her love for her tawny sister was replaced by the thorns of embarrassment, resentment, and denial.

Susanne had stayed with her father and his second family until Madame herself had died. She had promised Pierre, years before, that she would tend his ailing wife as long as she was needed, and she kept that promise. After death came for Mme. Metoyer in the winter of 1813, Susanne had turned over the household to Pierre's young and newly married daughter, and she had bought a plantation on the Isle to be near the widowed Frenchman, Baptiste Anty, who had shared her life ever since the doctor left her.

Ben and Victorin had married, too, and each began their separate lives. Their frequent visits to and from their older, darker brothers had continued; but at the Big House on the Point, Elisabeth made it clear *les mulâtres* were not welcome. Her young husband, Jean Prudhomme's brother Narcisse—being genial and in love—supported her. Old Pierre did not argue either. Weary and yearning for the peace he had never found, he simply saw his older children elsewhere.

Twice before, once when he returned from war and again when the old century gave way to the new, Pierre had felt the frightening, unrelenting march of time, the uncontrollability of earthly life, and he had set his affairs in order. He had no premonition, though, when the end finally came.

On Thursday, he had supped with Jean Prudhomme, on his friend's plantation. That night, a cold sweat had seized him, and by daybreak he was delirious. The doctor promptly leeched him. By the next nightfall, he was beyond all hope. Dutifully, Elisabeth sent for Padre Magnes, but the priest did not arrive in time. Alone, Pierre Metoyer made his own accounting for his life, on his own terms.

The burial was a simple one, as he had wanted. Mortified, Elisabeth let her brothers order from the blacksmith a plain iron cross, after both refused to entertain her plea that a stately marble monument be ordered from New Orleans. The funeral mass was private, the burial attended only by their family: Elisabeth, Ben, Victorin, the spouses they had married, and the half-sister whom Mme. Metoyer had borne in earlier years to Étienne Pavie.

By nightfall, Pierre had been laid to rest beside the woman he chose to be his wife. But, as the few symbolic grains were sprinkled across his coffin, another woman and her children watched quietly from the lengthening shadows up on St. Denis Hill. After Padre Magnes and the mourners closed behind them the big iron gate to the parish cemetery and rode off toward their homes, after the sexton had filled the grave and carefully replaced the chunks of clover that had carpeted the ground before that day's disturbance, Pierre's other family rode down the hill to say their own farewells.

With the moon rising behind them, the old woman knelt—not to pray, but to plant, amid the clover, one small bush. Pierre would sleep throughout eternity with his white wife at his side, but into the soil that he would soon become, the roots of that bush would twine. And above his grave, for all the world to see, those branches would grow and spread and shed upon his grave an endless shower of gardenias.

That night, Coincoin packed her meager wardrobe in the now-faded carpetbag she had sported when Martin Baptiste spotted her at Opelousas. The elegant four-poster was loaded on the practical wagon that had long since replaced the *cabriolet* she never liked, and she closed the little cabin on the Point. Augustin and Agnes gave up their cozy chamber with its marble fireplace and its *trompe-l'oeil,* and they moved into the Stranger's Room that every gracious Creole *maison* had.

As Coincoin had argued in the past, these "Big Houses" with their ground-floor basements and their raised living quarters were not for her. Her knees soon grew too stiff to climb the soaring sweep of steps that anchored the upper gallery to solid ground, and as the winter set in she stayed inside. Too weak and too slow to be of use to Agnes in the household, she spent increasing hours in the small wing on the west where Augustin had built his family's chapel. By day she prayed, lost in her own world somewhere between this one and the next. By night, as her family clustered in the bosom of their home, she came to life again and regaled the young ones with tales of that distant king in Africa.

By spring, her strength was almost gone. The small walk from her chamber to the chapel greatly taxed her, so young Baptiste-Augustin built for her a little altar in her room. *Make it plain,* she said. *Just big enough to kneel before.* Still, he added a shelf and a small glass door, so she could store her father's Rosary and the holy water Padre Magnes always blessed for her when he came down to the Isle.

Easter dawned gloriously, and Coincoin seemed reborn. Young Pompose helped her into her treasured frock of soft sateen, lime-green, and into the silken hose, the white kid gloves, and the feathered hat that Susanne had ordered for her from *la ville.* Then, sitting imperiously between Augustin and Agnes on the seat of her son's fringed surrey, Coincoin led the family's processional into the post.

In all her years, Coincoin never had missed an Easter Mass, but where she found the strength for this one, Augustin could only marvel. Her head sagged through the Benediction, and Agnes urged him to forego the celebration in the cemetery, but Coincoin would not hear of missing any of the day's festivities.

As she had done every Easter since she was seventeen, she placed a spray of snow-white lilies on the mound of stones that marked her parents' common grave. Easter had been their time of dying, but for Coincoin it was never a day of mourning. For nearly sixty years, the ritual passage in that day's Mass, *Dying, he gave new life,* had been as much a tribute to her father as to her Savior, and the renewal of life and hope they celebrated each Easter morn was as personal to her as it was holy.

That duty done, she climbed the slope of St. Denis Hill, as she had for all those Easters, with her flock in tow. Pride would not let her notice that the little hand she took to guide up that long hill, was supporting her instead. For sixty years she had boiled their eggs, dyed them yellow with ayac wood and red with achechy juice, and hid them in this meadow while little fingers pretended to cover eager faces. Knowingly, as always, she rewarded the expected peeks with a dramatic show of hiding those eggs behind every generous clump of greenery. And then, as always, she took the hand of the smallest child and led it to the special spot where the biggest egg of all had been tucked away from sight.

Today's hunt took far longer, but no child showed impatience as she hobbled through her ritual. The sun was already bowing westward, toward Los Adaës, before she signaled Agnes to retrieve her baskets from the buggy for their picnic amid the clover. Then, as toddlers napped in grownup laps, Coincoin called their older siblings for one last game of Nip 'n Tuck.

The mothers gossiped and the men smoked, whiling away the debt of time they owed their Mère Coincoin. All except Augustin. No one offered to join him as he wandered now across the hill and over to its crest, and he was glad. Gazing down upon the spot where the old *place d'armes* had been, he could hear what none of them had heard, or at least remembered: the echoes of the bailiff, the tumult of the crowd, the whisper of his childish prayers, and those soul-searing cracks of the cat-o'-nine.

Inevitably, his gaze wandered past that abandoned square to the spot where the old *casa real* had stood. He could not help but smile, recalling the pride with which his mother had marched into the office of the commandant and filed the papers that freed her oldest daughter. She had seized the *plume de Blanc* held out to her, and unwaveringly made her cross below the line where the commandant had written her own name with those all-important afterwords, *négresse libre.*

After that, Coincoin had gone back often to the *casa real*, as well as the office of the judge who now recorded their transactions. Curiously, as that thought came to him, much of the anguish that had plagued him this day melted in the sunset. His mother had, indeed, come a long way from the day she had ridden that wooden horse in the public square and refused to acknowledge the shame that had been heaped upon her. In four decades, she had become not just a woman of property but one of the wealthiest in the parish, even though she had chosen to live out her life in the simplicity with which she had been raised.

The frolic behind him continued on, and so he wandered back to the parish cemetery, to the umbrella of the live oak that shaded the grave of his own firstborn daughter, just past the mound where Coincoin's parents lay. *Mais oui!* he thought, as he stood between them. The old granddaughter of that king has avenged the injustice done her family! And *that* is the greatest legacy she will leave us. The land, the slaves—one day, those will be gone if these Anglos have their way. The life we have always known will be destroyed in spite of my efforts to insulate our Isle. But the pride Maman has taught us, the respect for all our heritage, for all the people who made us what we are—*that* no one can ever take away.

Still, the foreboding that plagued him that Paschal Sunday, as his mother sought to recapture in one last day the essence of her lifetime, could not be shaken. It clung to him like the evening fog off Red River, as Coincoin hobbled down from St. Denis Hill and announced that the day was done. It followed him, as she led their processional back down River Road to the Isle. And he nursed it in the moonlight that sprayed across the gallery of his Big House while, inside, Coincoin refused to let Susanne undress her and hang up her treasured frock. "Pierre *likes* lime green!" she scolded, and Susanne did not argue.

One by one, the children and the grandchildren, a stream four-dozen long, filed in to say good night as she held court in her old rocker. Then, Gustin's youngest, the little François-Gassion, stayed on to recite for his Mère Coincoin the Pater Noster he had just learned. Painfully, she raised herself from the creaking rocker and knelt beside the big four-poster to share his prayer, and when he finished she wrapped his little fingers around the Rosary her father had once carved.

"For you," she whispered. "From one François to another." Then she kissed his puzzled brow goodnight and shooed him out the door.

Easter Monday dawned gray and hazy, and Agnes shushed her family so Mère Coincoin could get her rest. By nine, the fog had lifted, but no sound came from Coincoin's chamber. Still unalarmed, Agnes put down her mending and went to check on her old *belle-mère*. Coincoin lay across the still-made bed, smiling softly, small and wrinkled in her lime green frock. Her soul had gone to find her parents and her Pierre.

351

PART FOUR

1816–1856

The Reaping

"There are also, in the vicinity, a large number of free-colored planters. In going down Cane River, the Dalmau called at several of their plantations, to take on cotton, and the captain told me that... beginning ten miles below Natchitoches, he did not know but one pure-blooded white man. The plantations appeared in no way different from the generality of those of the white Creoles; on some of them were large, handsome, and comfortable houses...

"They were honest, and industrious, and paid their debts quite as punctually as the white planters, and were... good citizens in all respects. One of them had lately spent $40,000 in a law suit, and it was believed that they were increasing in wealth.

"If you have occasion to call at their houses, I was told, you will be received in a gentlemanly manner, and find they live in the same style with white people of the same wealth. They speak French among themselves, but all are able to converse in English also, and many of them are well educated."

—Frederick Law Olmsted
A Journey in the
Seaboard Slave States

✣ 1 ✣
September 1816

The soft flush of a hundred lanterns bathed the dancers in a golden glow as satin skirts swayed and tight knee breeches pirouetted in perfect waltz time. Past the pavilion, sweethearts slipped in and out of the gardens, vainly hoping to escape the ever-present eye of staid old maids and watchful mothers, and a host of males who had rather drink than dance clustered here and there to discuss the price of *nègres* and the speed of their thoroughbreds. At the end of the lane that wound past the Big House, cook fires crackled under vast iron cauldrons, and the steamy aroma of gumbo filé wafted through the night, tempting the children from their play and the old ladies from their gossip.

Augustin stood quietly on the upper gallery, a patriarch surveying his domain, the attentive host checking the smooth execution of his *soirée*.

"Una fiesta magnifica, Señor Metoyer! The wedding feast of Cana pales in comparison, I fear."

"Ah, Padre Magnes. You are kind, in many ways. I have not yet thanked you for coming out to the Isle tonight, but your indulgence is very much appreciated."

"No problem, Señor. You have the bishop's indulgence to thank, not mine."

"Sí, that too. But without your recommendation to the bishop—most certainly without your willingness to make the trip out from town—he would never have granted us the dispensation to hold the ceremony in my private chapel instead of the parish church."

"Señor, it is no trouble, these trips to the Isle. They are my pleasure, spiritual nourishment for my tired soul, *verdad!* This enchanting land of so much flora and fauna is a paradise, *mi amigo.* To set foot upon your Isle is to enter another Eden."

Augustin smiled wryly. *"Sí,* but like the other Eden, Father, this land is not without its temptations."

"Tal vez. But it is an excellent job you have done of curbing those tempta-

tions among your people. Not once in the three years since I came here from Nacogdoches have I seen one of your family drunk, or heard of any charged with brawling or any public offenses of any kind. I've written as much to the bishop. Even tonight, I have stood here and thought about this, my friend. Your women are lovely, and their attire is quite modish. But it is *modest* as well. Not one gown have I seen cut so low as those some women now wear in town. Such fashions are nothing but the design of the Devil himself! It shames me when I am forced to look upon their nakedness!"

The graying brows of the Spanish padre knitted under his balding pate. "There is only one thing that troubles me, Augustin. That is the dispensation I obtained for your son and his bride. I know that past priests here have ignored our Church's prohibition of marriage within close kinship. At least, those regulations have not been applied to parishioners of African and Indian ancestry. But your people are neither slaves nor savages. You are worthy members of society, and you should avoid such a dangerous practice."

For a long moment, Augustin made no reply. What could he say? The priest was right, and he and Susanne had adamantly opposed this marriage of their children. But their opposition came too late. This day had been long in coming, and they should have seen it sooner. When Baptiste-Augustin had first begun to squire the little Marie-Suzette Anty to one party or another, he and Susanne had smiled approvingly upon the boy's concern for his cousin who did not yet have a beau. But as the years passed and neither of the youth showed any sign of finding other interests, Augustin and his twin had realized too late the folly of their parental indulgence.

Still, the young lovers were right in every defense they had made. Who else did they have to choose from, except their own people? There were only three classes in this parish—whites, slaves, and *themselves*. Never could they marry the first, not legally and sacredly, and never could Augustin consent now for his children to marry the second. Too many years had passed, too wide a chasm had grown between them and the slave ranks they had left behind. Too many changes had been wrought in the larger society whose mores they had to respect if they were to *be* respected.

For a man or woman of *nègre* ancestry, neither freedom nor money could be enough now. Culture, reputation, and *birth* were far more important in the new Louisiana. His children, his brothers' children, had been born free. A great measure of French and Spanish blood flowed through their veins. Indeed, they were the offspring of the best families in the parish. But any child of theirs who now wed a *nègre* or a slave would not uplift their spouse's lot as Dom and T'Pierre and François had done in decades past when their first wives were bought and freed before their weddings. *Non!* The way things stood now in this new Louisiana, if any of his people married a *nègre* or a bondsman, society would treat them as a black or a slave.

That could never be permitted. For the good of his people, Augustin had already forbidden it. To this new breed who had taken over their land—these *Américains*—a *nègre* was a *nigger;* but his own family was neither black nor white, not in color or in culture. For them to escape the degradation of the black man and the slave—whom these Anglos treated as one and the same—their people had to be a race apart from any other.

Non. Baptiste-Augustin and little Suzette had little choice.

"Of course, I do realize that your children's options are limited," Padre Magnes continued, and Augustin was startled by the echo of his own thoughts. He already knew that Magnes's disapproval of this marriage was not a chastisement of him personally. Clearly their pastor understood why they had to seek dispensation for a union their Church forbade. Still, Augustin reminded himself, there were other ways he could have forestalled any such situation as this between his son and his twin sister's daughter.

"That is the only reason, Augustin, that I agreed to petition the bishop for a dispensation."

Augustin nodded soberly, and his voice was heavy as he replied. "I am not without blame, Father. I should have brought in more youth from New Orleans or Opelousas."

"Then do that, son. There are many young men and women now among your people. We can look out across this crowd right now and see matches in the making. As things stand, these youth have no other choice. You and your brothers already have married into almost every free family of color at this post and heaven forbid that my parishioners should spawn any new ones for you, although I'm sure some of them will. Yet even that will not solve the need of those who are looking now for love."

"Yes, Father," Augustin agreed, and the priest smiled at the gravity of his voice.

"Forgive me, *mi amigo*. I have done the unpardonable. I have chastised a host. This little lecture should have waited until another time."

"Not at all, Father."

"Then the subject is closed. Just do what you can, Augustin. With whatever you cannot prevent, I will always help."

"*Gracias,*" Augustin murmured, then sprang forward as the old priest paused before the long sweep of lavishly garlanded steps that stretched downward from the gallery.

"*Un momento, Padre!* I am going down, too. Let me help you with the stairs. Agnes has bedecked those rails with every flower for miles around. There's no spot left a man can hold onto for safety. Here, take my arm, and then I'll see if I can find you a fresh glass of something."

Freshening the pastor's drink was no problem. For tonight's *fête,* Augustin had ordered five kegs of burgundy, three of Madeira, four each of rum and brandy, and even one of bourbon for the few Anglos whose acceptance he felt he could expect. And, unlike the host who threw the wedding feast at Cana, he had not skimped on quality.

Augustin had, in fact, planned this affair to be the most memorable any of the Islanders, white or colored, could ever recall; and he had planned well. Toussaint's band was the best in the whole north half of the state, and the bows of their violins danced through the most fashionable music of Europe between haunting renditions of old frontier favorites to which only a guitar could do justice.

The new pavilion that stretched between the Big House and the riverbank sported a canopy large enough to shelter guests in the event of unwelcome weather. Beside the vast cauldrons of gumbo there were steaming pots of hot tamales, red beans and rice, and the mouth-watering, peppery meat pies for which Natchitoches was already famed. Large crocks of lemonade and anisette, fresh and cool from the springhouse, covered one whole table, and coffee another. There *had* to be coffee, not only for those who did not drink but also for those who had drunk too much.

It was one of the latter who caught Augustin's eye as he handed Padre Magnes a fresh glass of burgundy. Politely, he excused himself and ambled casually in the man's direction, chastising himself anew for having included Valerin de Rossier on his guest list at all. Had he followed his own inclination, he would have omitted the man completely, but that would have created ill will with Tante Mariotte and her Adelaïde. On such a joyous occasion as the sacred marriage of his firstborn son, Augustin wished nothing but goodwill among all his people.

De Rossier might be French, Augustin mused as he steered himself through clusters of friends and well-wishers, but the man was surely one of the most despicable whites he ever had the displeasure of knowing, and he had been sorely disappointed when his aunt's daughter had moved into De Rossier's home. Adelaïde's earlier unions—illicit, both of them—had been scandalous, but at least the men had been decent Creoles. In fact, young Joseph Dupré would probably have married the girl if the laws of the territory had let him. Dupré had loved Adelaïde blindly. Before he died, he had legally acknowledged their children as his own—the little Manuel, Valsin, and Doralise. He even left his estate to those children and their mother.

But then Adelaïde had proved herself unworthy of his bequest. Within months of Dupré's death, rumor had it that she was trying out replacements, and she had confirmed that fact herself in no uncertain terms. When talk of her conduct reached Augustin and he had called her in, she answered his summons sullenly, listened defiantly to his gentle but unasked-for counsel, and then exploded.

"Gustin, you're my cousin, not my father! And you don't own me either! I'm living my life by *my* rules, not yours. You may be content with your lot in life and you may think it's good enough for your children, but your ideals and your standards are full of shit!"

Her ugliness had cut as deep as she intended, but she was not done.

"Let me tell you about the *real* world, Gustin! Being *white* is all that matters. Money don't matter. Poor whites can still vote. Your kind of morals don't matter. If they did, then all your fine friends who run this parish wouldn't be leaving their wives' beds in hope they can jump into mine."

"You'll never make yourself white, Adelaïde," Augustin interjected quietly. "No matter how you debase yourself."

"No, but the men I have my children by will *all* be white! I intend to have as many children as your God will give me and every one's going to be whiter than I am. I'll see that my daughters do the same until we breed our line white enough that my family can leave this place for somewhere they aren't known. Then my offspring will *marry* those hoity-toity bastards who think colored women are fit only to fornicate with!"

Four years had passed since that failure to steer Adelaïde onto the path of respectability, and in those four years she had lived true to her own ideals. Within months she was pregnant again, and when that child was born she boasted of his blue eyes and straight brown hair. She never bothered to name his father. Augustin feared that she could not.

His soul pained to the quick, Augustin had prayed that the Lord would change her heart as he, himself, had not been able to do. When Tante Mariotte told him that Adelaïde had settled down again he thought his prayer was answered. But Valerin de Rossier was no answer to any prayer. It wasn't just that the man was white and could not marry Adelaïde. He was also crude and intolerably profane. He drank too much and worked too little, and more than once since then Augustin had suspected that Adelaïde's rash of bruises and swollen eyes were no accidents at all. The man did acknowledge the twins she bore him a few months back, but not once had he shown any fatherly concern for them; and the drunken lechery he was now directing toward Adelaïde's oldest daughter palled this celebration for Augustin far more than had Padre Magnes's lecture.

"M'sieur de Rossier." Augustin's voice was civil but taut as he caught up with the Frenchman on the fringe of the crowd. "I see you are enjoying our family's celebration tonight."

"Oui-ee!" De Rossier hiccupped, squeezing the girl to him more familiarly than propriety permitted. "Ze weddin's, zey always did 'cite me." His free hand began to crawl up and down Manon's slight arm and she shivered, inexperienced and afraid. Her big green eyes turned pleadingly upon her older cousin.

"Why, Manon!" Augustin casually chided. "Did you not bring a shawl? September evenings do turn chilly, child. Run up to the house and ask Cousin Agnes to get you one."

De Rossier's squeeze tightened, as he purred. "Ah, ça! If ze filly's cold, I'll keep 'er warm. Ze truth it is, I cou'd use a l'il of ze warmin' too."

Augustin tried a different approach. "Then perhaps you'd like a cup of hot coffee, De Rossier?"

"Café? Sur ma foi, bonhomme! I like ze café ze way I like ze women. Hot 'n fresh 'n creamy."

While his words were directed to Augustin, the man's eyes were sliding the length of Manon's budding body, mentally tasting her, and Augustin's fury mounted. Never had he permitted a brawl on his premises, much less initiated one, but this man's behavior was intolerable. Seething beneath his self-imposed restraint, Augustin made one last attempt to resolve the matter civilly.

"Manon will be happy to get your coffee, or to ask a servant to bring it while she fetches her shawl."

Again the child responded quickly to Augustin's suggestion and attempted to extricate herself from the roaming fingers of her mother's lover, but De Rossier's grip tightened.

"*Merde,* Metoyer!" the man cackled, but there was no laughter in the eyes that stared Augustin down, silently daring him to use the fists he knew Augustin was clenching. "S'pose *you* fetch ze café, Metoyer, 'n I'll take care of l'il Manon…"

His mouth gaped mid-slur, as he felt the unmistakable prick of a knife blade in his ribs and a herculean arm clamped around him much too jovially. His eyes flickered nervously now, from Augustin to the pair of men who suddenly flanked him.

"*Tiens!* M'sieur François… M'sieur Louis… Ze party, it is nice, *non?*"

"*Mais oui!*" Louis responded, his wide smile frozen into place. "And we plan to keep it that way. Why just yesterday Big Little Brother here was telling me that there was something he'd like to do for you, M'sieur de Rossier."

"*Mais oui!*" François agreed. "This does seem like a fine time to do it." Beneath his vice-like grip, De Rossier began to squirm, but wavered again as another prick of Louis's carefully concealed blade pierced his waistcoat.

Augustin smiled genially, and even the closest onlooker could not have suspected anything was remiss. "I am sorry you are coming down with a chill, M'sieur, but François will be glad to see you home. Your road back into the hills is not one I would take alone at night. *Bon soir.*"

If De Rossier responded, his answer was lost as the band struck up a lively mazurka and he marched into the night, pinioned in François's close embrace.

"Thanks, Louis," Augustin's voice turned grim.

"Think nothing of it, brother. We're glad to oblige. Incidentally, where did the child go?"

"To the house, probably. From the looks of things tonight, I had better keep her there. If she goes back home with her mother—with *him*—she will not be safe. Damn that Adelaïde and the mess she has created."

"Whoa, Gustin! I don't believe it. Was that a cuss word you said?"

Augustin ignored his jibe. The fury De Rossier had sparked had been simmering far too long. "Believe me, Louis," he said tightly, "in another moment, I would have…"

"No, you wouldn't have, Gustin," Louis interrupted. "You never would have broken up your son's wedding party with a *mêlée*. Besides you know what the consequences would have been. There'd have been the Devil to pay!"

"Then the Devil take the consequences!"

"I'm serious, Gustin. For once. Cowards like De Rossier don't fight back like a man. If you had forcibly removed his arm, he'd have screamed assault. In the morning he'd file charges against you, and there would be no lack of white witnesses."

"And all of them my friends."

"*Sapristi!* Be realistic, Gustin! Friends or no, they'd have to admit in a court of law that they saw a colored man lay hands on a white one. Whatever the reason, that admission would be all De Rossier would need to send you to jail. That's what happens to good guys like you who try to do things honorably."

Louis was right. Augustin knew it. The truth was as bitter as vetch and he could hear the echo of Adelaïde's mocking laugh.

"*Malédiction!*" Augustin swore again. "Adelaïde is still the crux of the problem. I must have another talk with her. Maybe if we both talk to her."

Louis shook his head firmly. "Nothing doing, Gustin. If she tries to take Manon back home with her, back to *his* house, then I'll back you up on that. But Laïde's life is not my business. If De Rossier's what she wants, she deserves him."

"*Parbleu,* Louis! She cannot see past the color of his skin!"

"His color's not so bad, Gustin."

"I did not say it was. It is her obsession with *white* that is the problem. We are only as good as we make ourselves and she is not bettering things for any of us. When she flouts decency, it is harder for the rest of us to command respect—and no matter how white her children are, they'll never *be* white."

"Leastwise, not here. But that's not their only option," Louis reminded his brother bluntly.

"Ah, *oui.*" Augustin's voice softened noticeably. "That's why you freed Babe—and sent her and the boy north?"

"Well, why not?" Louis countered. "*Mon Dieu!* It just wasn't right for her to be a slave, or be treated like a *nègre*. She's white. She's beautiful. Intelligent.

Good, too, in spite of that tough shell she had to grow to survive her lot."

Augustin suppressed the retort there was no point now in saying. His brother was only partly right. No woman should have been forced into the situation Babe had endured before Louis bought her—or after. Truth was, Louis should never have bought her for the reason he did, and no matter how much he blamed society for her plight, he had to share that blame.

"Her neighbors in Illinois accept her as white, Gustin," Louis went on, oblivious to his brother's silent indictment. "Antoine, too. Or Anthony as she calls him. The boy didn't inherit much from me in the way of looks anyhow. Growing up where he is, where nobody knows his origin, he can be what he wants to be—as long as he has money and a good education. I'll see that he has both. So what's wrong with that?"

"Nothing, Louis. Except for the obvious fact that you had no moral right to father him in the first place. Still, whatever there was between you and his mother, at least you didn't turn yourself into a breeding animal out of a blind desire to be something you can't and a cold denial of everything you are."

"Well, in the end it may be the Adelaïdes among us who come out ahead." Louis's voice grew quieter as he chomped on his cigar.

"Look, Gustin. I respect your judgment. Everything you've done so far has worked out for us. You're one hell of a businessman, and you're well on the road to earning the respect you want so badly."

Louis could tell from Augustin's clamped jaw that his flattery was not working, but he stubbornly plowed on. "Gustin, none of us are pie-eyed youth any more, but you're still strong and healthy and you just might live long enough to do all you plan. Me? I'm still not convinced that money, education, culture, piety, or anything else is going to earn us the *equality* you think it will. On that score, Adelaïde is likely right. We're just not *white*."

Augustin shook his head slowly, his jawline hard beneath the bushy pair of mutton chops that were almost completely silver now.

"Equality can be earned, Louis. Blacks have been despised in America because they are the symbol of slavery, but every slave like Babe who's put on the auction block makes a lie out of that symbol."

The skepticism was plain on Louis's face, even in the moonlight. Augustin did not yield—would not yield. Could not yield.

"Louis, most Americans, and I'm talking about Creoles as well as Anglos, have not known enough *nègres* outside the framework of slavery to accept us as people just like themselves. There have not been enough of us who are their equals. As our numbers increase, we can prove we are just as intelligent and can be just as successful, just as refined, and just as pious as the best of them. Then people will realize that all races are equal and that slavery should not be based upon the color of skin but upon natural differences in abilities and ambition."

"Gustin, I take it back. *You* are still a pie-eyed dreamer! You'll never live to see that day!"

"And you're a pessimist. A man of little faith." Augustin smiled fondly.

"No, brother. I'm a realist. Look around you, Gustin! How many of your white friends do you see? Plenty. Almost every other man out there is white. They know you; they respect you. You've proved to them that you're intelligent and industrious. And your piety, God knows, has never been in doubt! These men even accept and respect the rest of us. Sinners though we are, we're no worse than any of them."

Augustin did not protest. Louis's assessment here was fair enough.

"They still don't consider us their equal, Gustin. How do I know? Look again—at the women this time. They're all tan. They're all our women. Not a one of our white friends brought their wives and daughters, and you can mark my words, brother: *they never will.* That, Gustin, is the real measure of equality, and *that* you'll never live to see."

2

Fall 1818

When the bargeload of Negroes pulled up at Yucca Bend, Louis recognized Micajah Pratt immediately. The man was older, his clothes seedier, but there was still the same codfish face, gaunt frame, and clipped Yankee accent as he hallooed his oarsmen to a stop. Nonchalantly, Louis continued tagging the cotton he and François were moving from the gin to the landing, in expectation of that afternoon's steamboat run. As he secured each tag, his brother casually hoisted the bale and toted it to the dock like Atlas carrying the heavens above him.

The slaver came ashore uninvited. As Louis and François continued their work, the man found a tree to lean against and openly gawked at François, chewing away the whole while on a stem of Johnson grass he'd obviously picked up somewhere downriver. Louis fumed at the thought of the seeds the man was carelessly scattering. He'd spent years stripping his place of that rogue weed and now he'd likely have a fresh crop of it taking over his fields and ditch banks come next spring. Still, he held his temper. Pratt was the kind of man who would likely ignore him, if he called his hand, and Louis was the kind of man who could bide his time, knowing that a reckoning day was coming. In fact, it was not far off, Louis decided, as he took in the stupefaction and greed that was plain on Pratt's face while he watched François work.

The man finally approached them, affably, when the last of the bales were tagged and loaded. "Pratt's the name. Micajah Pratt from New Orleans, and I'm a trader by calling."

To Louis's relief, not a flicker of recognition seemed to pass across Pratt's face as his gaze raked Louis from head to toe, obviously appraising the cut of his clothes that was better than most people expected on a farmer of Louis's color, and the girth that a man like Pratt would probably interpret as a lack of self-control. Casually then, almost too casually, the slaver's gaze went back to the barefooted giant by Louis's side, naked save for dark green breeches, above which a mass of muscles, as browned as coffee beans, glistened under the autumn sun.

"Yes, Pratt? What can I do for you?" Louis replied civilly, with only a trace of a Gallic accent marring his now well-practiced English.

"I'm looking for the owner of this place."

"You found him, Mister."

The man paused only a second, then went back to chewing at his twig of Johnson grass, obviously reassessing his approach to whatever business he had planned to propose.

Louis returned the slaver's stare in kind. After Yucca Bend became a popular landing for river traffic, he had quickly learned that the best way to deal with these Anglos who stopped and gawked at the "colored Islanders" as though they were sideshow freaks was to simply stare them down. Truth was, he'd overheard enough of their idle chatter to know what Micajah Pratt was likely ruminating on right then. The likes of Pratt usually considered the likes of Louis to be "the damnedest thing they ever saw," and that left them downright perplexed as to how to "keep those coloreds in their place" when the colored's "place" they were standing on was a far sight better than what they had at home. On good days, Louis could even laugh at their debates over what kind of *masters* these "coloreds" were. While some of them swore that "yellow Frenchies" were all soft and lazy and tolerated all kinds of vices in their quarters, others declared no masters were meaner than the ones who had been slaves themselves, and that these mixed-breed Islanders were as bad as the worst. In the end, Louis had long-since observed, most ended up deciding it didn't really matter anyway, since business was business.

Louis also decided just now that he had wasted enough of his time. "Is there something I can do for you, Pratt?" he prompted, a bit more shortly than he had intended.

"Yes, sir," the slaver chirped back, pocketing his Johnson grass as he obviously concluded that business was business and all the rest didn't really matter. "Who might you be, sir? I always feel more comfortable talking to a man when I can call him by his name."

"Louis Metoyer. This is Yucca Bend you're at."

"Yes, of course, Mister Metoyer. You're just the man I'm looking for. As you can see, I deal in slaves. The best available. I've brought a bargeload up from the city and plan to take them overland from here to Texas, but business acquaintances tell me that you and your brothers might be in the market. I'd be happy to give you your pick of my lot."

"We might be interested," Louis replied noncommittally. "It's almost noontime, though, and you must be exhausted from the heat. I wouldn't feel right doing business with a tired and hungry man. Come on up to the house, and we'll talk about it over a good meal."

The Yankee trader wavered. "Well, I've never been one to socialize with my customers, sir," he laughed nervously. "My good father, God rest his soul, always taught me to keep my business and my pleasure separate."

"That's an admirable policy, Pratt," Louis retorted dryly, "particularly for a man of your trade."

Pratt colored, and the Johnson grass came back out of his shirt pocket while he ruminated a bit further. Probably wondering—Louis told himself—whether his natural aversion to dining with a colored man might cost him a sizable chunk of business. Again, the slaver obviously decided that business was business.

"Well, under the circumstances, Mister Metoyer, I suppose it would be ungracious of me to refuse a man's hospitality."

"Good," Louis declared. "François, when you go to the quarters to eat, take the man's *nègres* and his guard and see that they're all fed."

"Huhn?" his brother responded blankly.

"You heard me. You may be a free boy, but as long as you work for me, you take my orders. Now get moving!"

François stared at his older brother, confounded for a moment. Then a broad grin lit his face and Louis relaxed. Sometimes François did not catch on fast, but Louis had counted on his cooperation even if he did not understand.

"Yassuh, Mista Louis! Whutever you say, Mista Louis!"

"Damned fool," Louis mumbled as he led Pratt from the dock. "I've just about reached the limit of my patience with that boy. He's not only dumb, he's a troublemaker."

"He's free, you said?"

"Yeah. If he wasn't, I'd have sold him off long ago."

"Then why do you keep him on here?"

"I can't get rid of him," Louis grumbled. "He's been hanging around ever since he took up with one of my wenches. I figured as long as he's under foot, I might as well put him to work. God knows, he's big enough to do the work of four men."

"Your generosity has not worked out so well, I gather," Pratt sympathized.

"Not one damned bit. Since he's come here the other hands have started getting uppity, and I know he's putting them up to something. It just doesn't do to have free laborers mixing with the slaves. It gives them ideas."

"How right you are, sir!" Pratt agreed smoothly. "So why don't you run him off?"

"Oh, I've tried, a half-dozen times. He keeps coming back. He hides down in the woods for a while and sneaks into the quarters at night to see his woman. After a while he's coming back openly again. What can I do? It's not against the law for him to visit his wife and as long as I don't catch him breaking any law, I can't call the sheriff out to get him."

Louis drew up short before the long, rambling gallery of the whitewashed bousillage cabin that had been his home, and Thérèse's, for more than twenty years.

"Here we are, Pratt. It's not all that much. I've wanted to build a Big House for ten years now, but I've had a string of problems getting the government to

Yucca House

Yucca House, built in the first decade of the 1800s by Louis Metoyer on the plantation now known as Melrose. After his widow and son moved into their Big House in 1833, this rambling cabin of bousillage, shingled with cypress, was put to use as a slave hospital for the planters of the Isle. During reconstruction, it served briefly as a community school. In the twentieth century, when the mistress of Melrose became a patroness of the arts, Yucca became the home of one writer-in-residence, François Mignon, who encouraged Melrose's cook to try her hand at painting the plantation life she saw around her. Thus was born the career of the world-class primitive painter, Clementine Hunter.

confirm my title to this piece of land. As long as my case is still in the courts, I can't see fit to build a fine house for somebody else to claim. Besides, we have just the one son, so this is adequate."

"Of course, Metoyer. You're a prudent man."

"If it's all right with you, Pratt, we usually eat out on the back gallery on warm days, to catch the breeze."

"Beggars can't be choosers, Metoyer," Pratt retorted, laughing heartily at his own wit, and then added ingratiatingly, "I can't see where you owe anyone apologies for this house, though. Yes, sir, it's fine. It's clean and neat and spacious, and there's none of the usual clutter of farm tools—not even back here. Yes, sir, I always did think these country houses would be quite handsome without all the clutter that's usually around."

"That's what storehouses are for," Louis retorted bluntly.

"Yes, yes. I agree. Ah, and this is your wife, sir?" Pratt beamed broadly as he extended his hand to the hefty *négresse* who was briskly wiping the gallery table. The woman gaped in surprise, and Louis suppressed a smile.

"No, Mr. Pratt. Frosine's our cook, and the best one on the Isle, I promise."

Pratt hastily withdrew his hand, obviously nonplussed.

"My wife is in town today, Pratt. The Ladies' Society at the Church is having its monthly meeting to embroider altar cloths or whatever. At least, that's what they claim to do, but I'm sure they do more gossiping than anything else."

Pratt smiled nervously at Louis's last remark and took the chair offered him. The table was spread sumptuously, and a shirt-tailed lad with a belly that bulged as prominently as his eyes briskly pulled the rope to the large ceiling punkah that fanned the flies from the table.

"What type of hands do you have in this lot, Mr. Pratt?" Louis inquired with seeming interest as the man picked sparingly at his ham and biscuits and ignored the squash and greens altogether.

"Most any kind you'd be interested in, Metoyer. Clearly, you don't need a cook, but there are two or three fine seamstresses, a midwife, a first-class carpenter, and a couple of dozen prime field hands."

"No blacksmith?" Louis could not resist asking.

"No. No blacksmith in this lot. Everything but a blacksmith," Pratt replied innocently. "Good smithies are hard to come by."

"I know," Louis snapped. "I've been needing one for years."

"Oh?" Pratt responded blandly enough, while Louis reprimanded himself. The pleasure of baiting this man was not worth the risk of a premature exposure. If nothing triggered the man's recall before he left the Isle, Louis would have all the revenge he'd craved these past six years.

"You don't think I could interest you in anything else?"

"No, Pratt. My other needs are pretty well taken care of for the time being, but next trip you make upriver, stop by again and maybe we can do business."

"Of course, Mister Metoyer." The trader paused. "What about your brothers? You think any of them might be in the market just now? I'd be happy to look them up."

"Tell you what, Pratt. You don't even have to do that. Just pull up a rocker and take a snooze. In this climate, a man shouldn't go back to work on a full stomach anyway. I'll send that boy François out to my brothers' places. If any of them are interested, they can come over here and you won't have to drag your stock all up and down the Isle."

"Now that's right kind of you, sir."

"Think nothing of it, Pratt. I'm always willing to oblige a good man."

"Incidentally, Mister Metoyer—about this big free boy, that François?" Pratt's tone was offhanded, just as Louis expected. "Did you mean what you said about him being a troublemaker, or might you have been just a trifle put out with him at the moment?"

"I'm always put out with that boy," Louis muttered.

"Well, there are ways of getting rid of troublemakers, you know, and getting a little reimbursement for past troubles while you're at it."

"Oh?" Louis's interest was definitely not a pretense.

"Especially with these free-niggers. Don't get me wrong, Mister Metoyer. I mean no offense. There are hardworking, upstanding free men of color like yourself who are a blessing to society. Then there are those poor, trifling, no-account free-niggers. I'm sure you understand the difference."

"Of course," Louis simpered.

"That's pretty much the same difference as there is among my people. There are hardworking industrious whites and there's poor, shiftless white-trash."

"Of course, of course."

"The only difference is that where no-account free-niggers are concerned, there are ways of ridding society of them, if someone is public-spirited enough."

Or unscrupulous enough, Louis could have added; but he leaned back in his chair and waited attentively for the slaver to continue.

"What that boy François needs, for his own good, mind you, is to be put into a situation where he'll have to work and learn to take orders. That just might develop some character in the boy."

"Think so, Pratt?"

"I know so. Seen it happen time and again. Tell you what, sir. Since I'm on my way to Texas, this seems like an opportune time to do that boy a favor and get rid of your own problem. If I were to take him over there, it wouldn't be so easy for him to slip back here again to stir up trouble among your hands. Don't you agree, Mister Metoyer?"

"Well, let's say I'm interested, Pratt."

"Of course, you understand that I'd be taking some risk."

Anyone who tries to abscond with François will risk more than he expects, Louis thought, and quickly suppressed his grin.

"On the other hand, Pratt, if you're successful, your risk would be highly profitable, would it not?"

"Profitable enough."

"Naturally," Pratt continued, "you would deserve a certain consideration, sir, for past troubles the boy has caused you, and his wench would probably mope around for a while until she found some other buck. That little decrease in productiveness ought to have some value placed on it as well."

"All total, then, just what kind of a value would you place on this boy—for me?"

"Hmmh. An even one-fifty, shall we say?"

Louis pondered the offer. "Nahn, Pratt, I couldn't consider it. I'd be taking my share of risk, too. Not that I wouldn't trust you to keep a closed mouth, should you have any trouble, but when two strangers go to bed together they both run the same risk of walking away with lice."

"Very colorfully put, sir." Pratt was stalling, waiting for the counteroffer.

"I have my own reputation to think about, Pratt. If I'm going to risk that, then I'd at least have to get enough out of this to hire a good lawyer, should this little matter come to light."

"How much do you figure that would cost you?"

"Five hundred, Pratt. No less."

"Five hundred! I'd hardly get more than that for the boy in Texas."

"You'd get much more. Eight hundred minimum, Pratt, and probably a thousand for a man like him. I know the price of hands, too. And if I know traders, I think you'd be happy to make three to five hundred clear profit off any one of them."

Pratt smiled genially. "Wouldn't any man? All right, Mister Metoyer. You have a bargain. All we need do now is to arrange the proper circumstances. Naturally, we'll need somewhere to conduct our business unobserved, but since I don't know this neck of the river I'll have to trust your judgment."

"Taking the boy's the least of your problems, Pratt. He's as strong as a mule, but he's as dumb as one and he has three vices. He drinks too much, he likes to gamble, and he's plumb lazy. Sober, you'd never take him with ten men to help you. Get him drunk and you can lead him around like a fancy puppy on some fine lady's leash."

"Sounds good to me. When and where do we get him drunk?"

"Not we, you. He's supposed to run the gin for a while tonight to help us catch up. If you happen by with a deck of cards and a jug of whiskey, he'll forget all about the gin. I'll be waiting for you at the barge to collect my due."

"It's as good as done, friend." Pratt extended a twiggy hand and Louis gripped it jovially, squeezing far more pleasure than necessary from their shake.

"So, Pratt, just pull up a chair and snooze. I'll go find that boy and send him over to my brothers."

"Thanks, sir, but if it's all the same, I'll take my hands on back to the barge. I've never been one to waste the daylight hours napping, and I wouldn't want them catching such habits. I'll exercise them again for a while. Got to keep them healthy, you know. Then I'll check out your mercantile houses here on the Isle. I need to swap my barge for a wagon and round up a few things to head out overland."

"As you wish, Pratt." Louis shook his hand again. Enthusiastically. "It will certainly be a pleasure doing business with you tonight."

As Louis expected, none of his brothers, or Susanne either, were interested in Pratt's Negroes, but they were more than willing to help Louis with his planned revenge. While Pratt drilled his stock, Louis drilled François; and then Susanne's son Florentin rode over with Dom to make a show of checking out Pratt's offerings.

When the sun set on the river that night, François was at his post, singing lustily but working little. With eight wagonloads of cotton waiting under the shed, it was a hell of a time to sit on his butt, he had grumbled to Louis, but if Pratt was expecting a lazy son-of-a-bitch, then he could be the best damned lazy son-of-a-bitch the man ever saw.

François was doing just that, sitting on his haunches and tinkering with a row of clogged-up gin teeth, when Pratt's wagon came to a rough halt in the road and the man descended, mumbling a string of impious oaths.

"Hey, boy!" Pratt curtly interrupted François's song.

"Yassuh?"

"I just bought a wagon and some supplies at Sarpy's store down the road, but it turned dark before I could make it back to the landing. I think I hit a pothole. I need help to push the wagon out."

"Yassuh. Jes a moment, Mista, an' I'll see whut I ken do." Lackadaisically, François poked again a few times at the clogged up teeth, fished around in his pocket for a fresh plug of chewing tobacco, and finally ambled over to the wagon.

"Yassuh, Mista, ya rolled ri't into de middle o' dat hole. You musta bought yo'self a blind horse, too. It ain't so dark he couldn't a seen his way 'round it."

"There's nothing wrong with the horse I bought, boy," Pratt shot back. "It's your roads. If you can call these cowpaths *roads*. It's hard to believe this river's been settled for a hundred years and there are no better roads than these."

"Dey gits us whar we wanna go, Mista Pratt. Heah, ya take dose reins an' when I lif' dis wagon ya lead dat ol' hoss off gently."

"When you *lift* this wagon? Boy, it's loaded! There's a keg of whiskey, another of meal, a batch of…"

"Mista, I ain't no store-clerk an' I don't need yo shoppin' list. Jes' git ready t' move dat hoss."

Dutifully, Pratt took the reins and then stood gaping as François effortlessly lifted the wheel, the wagon, and its load.

"Mista, yo wagon ain't a woman I can hol' all night. Is ya gonna move yo horse or ain't ya?"

Pratt moved it. The wagon rolled out of the puddle he had deliberately driven into, and the slaver extended his hand to François in a show of appreciation. "Boy, you do beat all I ever saw."

"Den ya got a lot lef' t' see, Mista."

"Oh, I've seen it all, boy. People are my business. As a trader, I'll have to say it's almost too bad you are free. You'd be worth a nice sum to somebody."

"Mista," François grinned. "I's worth eva bit dat much t' me."

"I expect you are, boy. Look, I owe you something. How about a drink before I roll on, and then you can get back to your work?"

The grin grew wider. "Well, I's not in that big a hurry, Mista, an' I do make it my practice t' neva turn down a drink!"

"You're a forthright man, too, François. I can see that. I like that in a man." Pratt rummaged through the gunny sack of supplies he had just purchased. "Here, I ought to have a cup somewhere."

"Oh, I don't need no cup, Mista," François laughed, and hopped into the wagon. In one deft move, he had the bung-hole unstopped and had lifted the barrel to his lips. It stayed there long enough for a long, deep draught—without a drop spilled—before François set it back in the buckboard.

"Yo' wanna drink, too, Mista?"

"Eh? Oh, no." Pratt replied, awestruck in spite of himself. "As a matter of fact, I'm not a drinking man. But you go right ahead, boy. Have another. That was some feat there!"

"Aw, 's nothin'," François mumbled modestly and heaved the barrel's bung-hole to his lips again, knowing the slaver could never tell that his tongue made a real good stopper.

"I'm serious, boy. I'm a man with a good eye for opportunity, and you've just given me a business idea." Pratt's voice was purring now, and he leaned back leisurely against his wagon.

"You are wasting yourself out here on this farm, François. Why don't you come along with me? I hit all the big towns, and together we could do right well. Folks pay good money to see exhibitions of strength like yours, and you could give them a show the likes of which they've never seen. We can call ourselves partners, boy. I'll handle all the arrangements, you put on the show, and we'll split the money. How about it?"

François pondered the offer, visibly wavering. "Mista, dat's ri't kind o' ya, but I dunno. My woman's heah."

"Well now, François, I travel this river quite a bit. You can still see a lot of her. Besides, she'll want you more if you're not around so much. That way, she won't get to taking you for granted like women do."

François puzzled over the prospect some more. "I dunno…"

"I'm in no hurry, boy. I'm pulling out in a few hours, but I won't pressure you to make up your mind right now. Have another drink, and I'll wait until you've decided."

"Thankee, Mista. Don't mind if'n I do," and the slaver laughed at the haste with which François accepted that offer.

"Tell you what, boy… you play cards?"

"Yassuh," François grinned again.

"Then why don't we just visit a spell and have a friendly game and you can ask me more questions about our business arrangement and have a few drinks more while you think it over."

"Well, I dunno, Mista. 'Bout de cards, dat is. If I's don't git dis gin a runnin', Mista Louis'll have *me* runnin'."

"Then I'll take you anywhere you want to go, boy."

François snapped his head sharply a time or two, making a show of shaking off the buzz that Pratt would be expecting by now.

"Massuh?" his slur seemed just about right. "Won't ya jes' sit dere an' wait till I get dis ole iron a crankin' again. Den maybe we's talk 'bout it s'more."

"Fine, boy, fine. Why don't you bring that keg in with you, though? If a man has to work at night, he at least ought to have something to keep his wits sharp."

François teeth gleamed in the moonlight as he grinned his appreciation. "Yassuh, Massuh, ya sounds like a ri't nice feller t' do bus'ness wid."

The rest of the night proceeded just as Pratt, Louis, and François planned— each in his own way. Within an hour, François was grinning nonstop and promising to follow Micajah Pratt anywhere. Within an hour and a half, he was in the buckboard, manacled, and Louis was collecting his $500. Within two hours, Pratt's wagon was rolling off toward Texas with the slaver and his guard comfortably ensconced in the driver's seat and the Negroes stepping smartly in front of the horses. Behind them in the night, though, Louis's son kept watch, following with all the silent stealth he'd learned from his mother's people on the western plains, while Louis himself hied into the post of Natchitoches to report a kidnapping.

By noon the next day, young Baptiste-Louis was back at Yucca Bend with the hoped-for news. Sheriff Bullitt's posse had taken the slaver and his coffle into custody. But on the lad's heels there came the sheriff's deputy also, with a summons made out in the name of Monsieur Louis Metoyer.

"My brother? You found him?" Louis inquired calmly of the deputy.

"Oh, he's in town, sir. Mr. Bullitt's got to hold him a while. Just for questioning, sir. There's some sort of complication, I think. That's why the sheriff sent for you."

The complication was about what Louis expected. The slaver was not the kind of man to take his punishment alone. Caught with a well-known *homme de couleur libre* shackled to the rest of his slaves, Pratt had calmly produced a bill-of-sale, made out in his name, and signed by one Louis Metoyer, who therein acknowledged receipt of $500 "for my boy, François."

"Well, Metoyer?" Benjamin B. Bullitt asked quietly after he fished the paper from a pile on his desk and passed it to Louis.

"Hell, B.B. First you have to tell me what it says, because I never learned to read—French or English."

"Or write?"

"No."

"Not even enough to sign your name?"

"I let my son do that for me."

"And that signature on the bottom is not your son's?"

"B.B., if Baptiste-Louis couldn't write any better than that after all the years I paid a tutor, then I wasted my money."

Bullitt laughed and leaned back casually in his chair. "I figured as much, Louis, although I also figure there's more to this story than I've been told."

"Now, B.B. it's all pretty obvious to me. Your men caught a slaver with a free man chained to his coffle. So he produces a fake bill of sale to cover the kidnapping. What else is there to tell?"

"I'm waiting to hear it, Louis."

"Well," he shrugged innocently. "There's not much more I can add, except

376

that this isn't the first time Pratt's tried to rob a free fellow of his liberty and a buyer of his money."

"Then you can testify in court that he's pulled this before?"

"If need be."

"Where was this?"

"Natchez. He sold a free fellow over there that he had stolen out of Carolina."

"You were a witness?"

"You might say that," Louis replied evasively.

"You testified against him there?"

"Come now, B.B. You may be married into the Rachals, but you're still an Anglo, and you sure weren't raised in Louisiana. You're telling me you don't know that outside this state, white juries don't want to hear a colored man testify against a white one?"

A long slow grin spread across the sheriff's face. "So Pratt got by with his trick over in Mississippi because you couldn't testify against him? Well, now, isn't it a coincidence that he tried the same thing here in Louisiana, and to your own brother, no less."

"The Lord works in mysterious ways, sheriff," Louis drawled back.

"And this unlucky fellow who bought the free man over in Natchez, this wouldn't have been you by any chance?"

Louis grinned, sheepishly. "Well, B.B., if I'm going to testify against Pratt here in a court of law, I'll have to tell the whole truth, I guess. So I might as well go ahead and admit it now. Yeah, I was the fool who gave Pratt eight hundred dollars for one hell of a blacksmith and a no-good bill of sale."

"And Pratt has given you five hundred for another no-good bill. That still leaves you three hundred dollars short, Louis."

"Now, sheriff, I thought we'd already settled the fact that my signature's not on Pratt's bill of sale. But you can figure it any way you want. As long as Pratt serves his time for kidnapping a free man into slavery, I'll take my losses without too many regrets."

"Then you can write off that account as paid in full. I promise you, Louis, that man will get what he deserves here in my parish."

∞ **3** ∞
1826

Sheriff Bullitt lived up to his word. But elsewhere in Louisiana, seeds of intolerance and suspicion between white and black, Anglo and Creole, slave and free, continued to grow; and the free men of color who had so recently risen from the ranks of slavery reaped the worst harvests. Whites who feared the growing number of black slaves swore free Negroes gave them dangerous ideas, and they screamed for legislation to outlaw all contact between the two. In turn, the proud *hommes de couleur libres* who hoped to survive in the more oppressive climate found it far less galling to voluntarily cut all ties with their slave origins than to submit to laws forcing them to do so.

Other Anglos nervously eyed the mushrooming ranks of free Negroes and feared the day their wealth, abilities, and numbers might earn social equality as well. Publicly, men championed the cause of racial purity and condemned unholy amalgamation. But privately the ageless urges of mankind continued to spawn new children who would not find acceptance in the black world or the white. In retaliation, white wives then lashed out at all women of color, calling them "Heaven's last worst gift to man."

True to the age-old adage about politics and strange bedfellows, the free *nègre* was turned into Louisiana's political prostitute. The same men who condemned them by light of day courted them under cover of the night, and those who wooed them to satisfy their own passion for power crossed all lines of class, religion, and national origins.

The Islanders fared no better, in spite of the self-sufficiency Augustin had planned for them. Indeed, their growing fame made them prime pawns in the Latin-Anglo struggle for control of the state. Those who hoped for their support first courted their patriarch, but Augustin's own hopes of equality did not blind him to flattery or deceit. Those who failed to ally him to their dubious causes then burrowed stealthily among his people, using the young and more gullible to spread their propaganda.

Alexis Cloutier was such a man, and the political bonfire he built in the 1820s flared throughout the state, singeing the political careers of his colleagues and burning out his own bold dreams.

In the gray, lackluster days of dying winter in 1826, politics was the least welcome of Augustin's concerns. His little Susette, who had wed one of the city youth he brought to the Isle, was now a widow, left with a mortgaged store to operate, two *enfants* to raise, and a stubborn determination to do it all herself. The cotton market was sorely depressed, speculators refused to buy, and rumor had it that business houses in Liverpool and Manchester would soon close. Across the Sabine, in the trouble-plagued district of Nacogdoches, the clash between Anglos and Latins threatened to become a war, and the restless François-Gassion, craving glory and excitement as only a seventeen-year-old imagines it, pleaded with his papa to let him join the rebels who sought to turn Spanish Tejas into an American Texas.

It was in the midst of these worries that Ben Metoyer appeared at Yucca Bend waving a copy of the *Commercial Review*. "Gustin! It's finally happened. That kettle of fish Cloutier's been trying to fry is splattering grease over all of us."

Augustin smiled at his half-brother tolerantly. "Ben, you're too educated. Forget the metaphors or similes or whatever they're called and say what you mean in plain words."

"Ah, Gustin! I'm just practicing my oratory. If I do run for a seat in the House, I have to be able to match metaphors with all my verbose colleagues."

"If you run for the Legislature," Augustin retorted bluntly, "you would do better to stick to plain language that says exactly what it means instead of leaving people to guess. The voters are tired of double-talking, double-dealing politicians."

"You're right again, Gustin. That's exactly why I want to run. There's only one thing that worries me—this lean and hungry look of mine. Folks are apt to think I'm looking to fatten myself up at the public trough."

"It may be they'd prefer you to an incumbent who's already grown fat and prosperous in office."

"Maybe, maybe so. Speaking of incumbents, Gustin, our senator has been cooking Cloutier's fish at a pretty high temperature, and using the damnedest fuel, too. Have you seen this copy of the *Review?*"

"Apparently not," Augustin retorted dryly. "I have to wait until my sons read it to me, you know. I assume that is the issue the steamer dropped off at noon?"

"It is. Let me read you this one, Gustin. It can't wait."

"It can wait long enough for us to go into the library, boy. My arthritis is getting too bad for me to stand out here on the gallery in the cold when I don't have to."

"*Oui,* Gustin," Ben agreed sheepishly. "Lead the way."

Ben's spectacles were on and the journal folded to the proper page even before he settled into the chair across from Augustin's desk. "It's right here, on the second page, under the heading—listen to this now!—*Uppity* Free Negroes."

Augustin felt the first sting from the "hot grease" Ben had mentioned and decided the boy's metaphor made sense after all.

"It's an editorial, mind you. And the editor has outdone himself this time."

"So what did he write, Ben?"

"Tripe. Pure tripe. Listen to this…"

> A lively debate has been occurring in the legislative halls of this state since the introduction of a petition by our senator from Natchitoches, Placide Bossier. The signers of this highly disrespectful and menacing paper…

"Disrespectful and menacing?" Augustin echoed incredulously.

"That's what it says, Gustin, although I thought I worded it in quite respectful terms. But, wait, let me finish this…"

> …signers of this highly disrespectful and menacing paper are all residents of a worthless strip of marshland known as the Isle of Canes…

"A *worthless* strip of *marshland?*"

"I swear, Gustin, that's what it says."

"I gave the *Review* credit for checking its facts better than that. A state journal certainly ought to."

"Hold on, Gustin, there's more…

> Moreover, our good Senator has informed us that the twenty-odd persons who signed this inflammatory petition are all free men of color and others who have no political rights whatsoever.

This time, Augustin checked his growing rage and let Ben go on without interruption. The matter was indeed serious.

Our trusted Senator, like the statesman that he is, has presented the petition without making any commentary on the disrespectful terms with which these people have addressed the first body politic of this state; and his committee has given it all the weight that could have been attached to a prayer from our constituents drafted in the proper language. But the very absurdity of this paper's demands has caused it to be rejected.

"I feared as much," Augustin declared soberly.

"Well, damn, Gustin, they've not heard the last of us! Bossier deliberately sabotaged our petition and he did it with outright lies!"

"Apparently, the Bossiers are still smarting from Louis's defeat of Sylvestre in Louisiana's Superior Court," Augustin observed tautly.

"Well, it was Louis's land. But even if it wasn't, that would still be no justification for Placide's action. How dare he dismiss that petition by telling the other senators it was signed by 'twenty-odd free men of color and other persons having no political rights'! By Jupiter, you got *forty* names on that petition, and half of those signers were white planters. Bossier knows that. He knows every one of them."

"But the *Review* doesn't."

"So it has relied upon our *trusted* senator's words. But that hardly matters anyway. Judging from the tone of this article, the *Review* would believe anybody who called a *nègre* a *nigger*. Listen to the rest of this, Gustin."

> It is a sad day for Louisiana when uppity high yellows and mixed breeds become bold enough to *address demands* to the good citizens of this state. It is obvious that the handful of Negro-lovers in our legislature has been allowed to control us for too long. Unless we insist that our legislators put these impudent blacks back in their place, they will soon be demanding not just an equal right to vote but an equal right to our women as well!

"I don't recall demanding either, Ben!"

"Of course, we didn't. All we asked for was a fair hearing to our views on Cloutier's plan to divide this parish. And it doesn't matter that I'm white or you're colored or what race any of the signers are. All that matters is that we are taxpayers—the heaviest taxpayers in all the ten thousand square miles of this parish, and we said so in that petition. Sure, this parish needs dividing. But we're not the people who ought to be cut away. I live just ten miles from Natchitoches. You're only eighteen. Let them cut away Bayou Pierre or the Allen settlement. Some of those people have to ride eighty miles to get to our courthouse."

"But, of course, Cloutier's not interested in Bayou Pierre or the Allen Settlement."

"He's not interested in a damn thing but Alexis Cloutier. He's been planning this for years, Gustin, and we should have seen it coming. First he takes a chunk of his land and carves it up into lots, then packs down some dirt and calls it streets. Well, he can draw a map and add all the fancy names he wants, but his so-called town of Cloutierville is still a cotton field in the middle of nowhere."

"A cotton field with a chapel," Augustin interjected, still chafing over the fact that the bishop had agreed to accept the new St. Jean Baptiste des Cloutierville as a mission while rejecting the Isle's request for a mission of its own. Cloutier's donation to the diocese had not been a small one.

"Gustin, it's obvious that he's had this in mind all long. Lay out a town, build a church, and then get his political cronies to create a new parish so he can make his town the parish seat."

"That is exactly why I refused to have anything to do with the scheme when he and Bossier brought me their petition for the division last year. A new parish would not do anything for the people of this region except increase our taxes, and I told them that. We have already put a lot of money into that new courthouse and jail at Natchitoches. The last thing we need is a new parish that would then have to purchase more land for public buildings."

"Cloutier's land—at Cloutier's prices!"

"Precisely. Then we would have to pay the salaries of another sheriff, another judge, another court, and more legislators."

"I wonder, Gustin..." Ben mused.

"You wonder what?"

"How the *Commercial Review* would react if it knew that our esteemed senator and his friend begged for your signature last year on their own petition to divide this parish. I'll bet he didn't tell that to the *Review* or the Senate when he foully discredited us and our own petition."

"Of course not," Augustin muttered. "Nor would he point out how many of the signatures on his and Cloutier's petition belong to the same colored men they now discredit."

"Or the chicanery they used behind your back to get those signatures from some of your people."

"I'm still disappointed over that, Ben. Not with Cloutier. I expected as much of him. But I didn't expect my own family to fall for his tricks."

"He's a persuasive man, Gustin. The same arguments he used on our white neighbors would be just as effective on your people. When heavy taxpayers are promised a reduction in taxes, they listen. But he had an even better approach to use on your family. What *homme de couleur libre* today would not be enticed by the promise of a new government for Louisiana that would be run by cooperative Creoles instead of arrogant Anglos?"

"That's no promise, it's a baldfaced lie. That is why Cloutier made the rounds here on the Isle, gathering signatures, while I was down at *la ville...*" Augustin's voice waned wearily. "So what are you proposing now, Ben?"

"I honestly don't know, Gustin. I thought that a second petition from us, signed by all the inhabitants of this region in united opposition to the division, would convince the legislature, but Bossier bested us. Now he's put through a motion appointing commissioners to lay out a dividing line."

"Ben, it seems to me that there are only two things that can be done. Our right to petition may be disputed now, in spite of what the law guarantees us, but we can still speak our minds in the *Natchitoches Courier*. If we can create enough controversy, enough doubt, over the legality of Bossier's action, then maybe we can stall the legislature's final decision until after the election."

"At the same time, a *Courier* campaign just might discredit Bossier enough that we can oust him!"

"Precisely. You always did have a way with words, Ben. I'm glad you volunteered to do the writing."

"Volunteered? You've given me no choice, Gustin! Oh, well, it will be good publicity for my campaign."

The strategy worked. In the steamy months that followed, every other issue of the *Courier* carried an eloquent plea for justice from "The Inhabitants of the Isle of Canes" or a blunt exposé of political ramrodding by their incumbent senator. Occasionally, that politician deigned to reply, like a horse flicking its tail at a pesky fly buzzing around its rump, but his rhetoric was less than convincing. When the ballots were counted at the end of that tempestuous summer, Senator Placide Bossier was unseated by a planter friendly to the Isle; and Ben Metoyer had won the House seat.

But Cloutier and Bossier did not concede defeat. When the first session of the Eighth Legislature convened at New Orleans after Christmas, the new senator from Natchitoches was not recognized, pending Bossier's challenge of the election. In the meanwhile, his legislative cronies tried to force the passage of his bill in both chambers. On the second of January, Representative Morris of Rapides reintroduced the act in Louisiana's House; and the freshman legislator from Cane River popped to his feet.

"Mr. Speaker—Ben Metoyer from the parish of Natchitoches."

"Mr. Metoyer!" the speaker said shortly. "If you wish to debate this bill, you're out of order. This is merely a routine procedure for reintroduction of pending business. Recognition denied, Mr. Metoyer. I order the bill to be referred to the Standing Committee of Recital and Unfinished Business. Next!"

Ben sank to his seat. One by one, the old bills left from the Seventh Legislature were reintroduced and assigned to the same committee. Once that formality was done, the speaker opened the floor for consideration of the individual bills and, again, Congressman Morris promptly requested the floor. Again, he was acknowledged.

"Thank you, Mr. Speaker," Morris simpered, as he stared pointedly in Ben's direction. "I hereby move that the petition of sundry inhabitants of the interior part of the Parish of Natchitoches, who pray for a favorable division of that parish, be taken under consideration by this body."

"So moved, do we have a second?"

"I second it," a crony interjected.

"All in favor?"

"Aye," the body echoed.

"The motion stands approved, Mr. Morris. Do you have any further argument to present in its favor?"

Morris presented his case smoothly, reminding his colleagues that the petition already had been accepted by their body in its previous session, that a committee had been appointed to study the division and had ruled favorably upon it, that a second committee had been appointed to lay out the boundary line, and that the line now had been drawn. All that remained was routine approval of their recommendation.

Again, Ben was on his feet. "Mr. Speaker!"

"Yes, Mr. Metoyer?"

"With due respect to my colleague, Mr. Morris, the issue in question is not a routine one. This body remains unaware of several crucial points. It has been subjected to fraudulent reports based upon the misrepresentation of facts and the mishandling of assigned responsibilities, and the routine passage which my colleague urges would be detrimental not only to the residents of my parish but to the state as a whole."

"These are serious charges, Mr. Metoyer." The Speaker's voice was grave as he turned to the veteran legislator who had reintroduced the bill. "Does Mr. Morris wish to rejoin?"

The bow Morris made in Ben's direction was as patronizing as his tactic.

"Mr. Speaker, my young colleague is to be commended for desiring to participate so promptly in the proceedings of this august body. However, he has not been privy to past proceedings, nor has he been a member of this House long enough to be adequately informed. The petition of his constituents who pray for the division was presented in due form, and it has been appropriately studied. This body can ill afford to repeat all past proceedings for the personal benefit of our new colleague. I would suggest he bow to the integrity of this body and accept the decisions it made prior to his coming down here to share with us all the wisdom he has accumulated in his few short years."

"Mr. Speaker, may I reply?"

"Of course, Mr. Metoyer."

"That petition for a division of our parish does not represent the wishes of a majority of my constituents, only that of a few men with selfish interests. In fact, it is far short of the required number of signatures of registered voters, and if my colleague denies that fact, then I challenge him to submit the petition for your personal examination alongside a roster of our qualified voters."

This time, it was Ben who bowed confidently toward his adversary.

"At the same time, Mr. Speaker," Ben continued, "this body should take note of another fact. Twenty-three of those signers are free men of color whose signatures were obtained by fraud. Their names were presented to this body, illegally and deliberately, as being the signatures of qualified voters."

"May I remind this body that when these same men, who are all honest, industrious citizens and heavy taxpayers even though they are denied the franchise"—Ben strongly emphasized that point—"when they learned of the fraud that had been perpetrated, they conscientiously submitted a legitimate petition to you, in which they were joined by seventeen of our area's leading white planters, to inform this body of the deception. But the sponsors of this bill deliberately denigrated the citizenship of those white planters—*my* citizenship, gentlemen, because I authored that petition. Our protest was rejected by this body after my esteemed colleague swore to you that all of us—myself included!—were *uppity Negroes* who had no rights."

Ben's voice turned cold as he stared Morris directly in the eye. "As the author of that second petition, by which we seek to rectify the earlier fraud, I request that our statement be reintroduced to this body. And, by God! I challenge any of my colleagues here to repeat the charge that I am a Negro and that I have no legal rights!"

"Now, now, Mr. Metoyer," Morris began, ingratiatingly, without waiting for the permission of the Speaker. "I assure you, no such claim is being made. Sounds to me like there was just a misunderstanding."

"You're damned right there was!" Ben exploded, ignoring the furious rap of the Speaker's gavel.

"Gentlemen, gentlemen! Personal exchanges are inappropriate on the floor of this chamber."

"My apologies to *you,* Mr. Speaker," Ben replied politely, his anger masked behind a grim smile. "If I may continue, sir?"

"You may, so long as your remarks are civil and are addressed to this body as a whole."

"Mes amis..." Ben turned and opened his arms to all his colleagues. "It cannot be denied that the parish of Natchitoches, by far the biggest in this state, imposes inconvenience upon some of its inhabitants. My sympathies go out to the settlers who have to ride eighty miles through dense forests and swampy bogs to get a license to marry their sweethearts or to settle the estates of their loved ones. But the men who petitioned this body for a new parish are not motivated by such a need, only by greed. There is no hardship in their region and I speak from personal knowledge because I live among them."

"My friends and colleagues," Ben went on persuasively, his voice ringing throughout the chamber. "The new parish that has been proposed would contain just ninety voters. Yet the representative and the senator they would send to this body would have a vote equal to your own. Would this be fair to any of you, who represent many times that number?"

That got their attention. As a rumble of interest turned into a hubbub, the Speaker's gavel sounded. Ben raised his hands for silence and then continued.

"Gentlemen. I may be an inexperienced legislator as my colleague has pointed out, but I know this state well. I was born and raised here, while Mr. Morris was not. I have business associates and friends in every parish. I honestly believe that your constituents as well as mine feel the division of present parishes can be justified only when there is evidence of *necessity*."

Heads bobbed in agreement, encouraging Ben to go on. "The creation of a new parish would increase the expenses of this state as a whole. That means additional taxes on your own constituents, does it not? My friends, as the new representative of all the people of Natchitoches, I cannot with clear conscience ask that the rest of this state support the personal designs of one or two residents of my own district. Thank you."

Ben had made his case. A chorus of agreement drowned out Morris's objection, and the proposed bill was remanded to yet another committee for study. Morris demanded the chairmanship and got it, but the new legislator from Natchitoches was given a seat as well. For five weeks Morris wrangled unsuccessfully for a majority vote. Seeing defeat at hand, he declared a deadlock and demanded a House vote without submission of his committee's report. The Speaker overruled his motion. Three days later, when Chairman Morris read his committee's report, his bitterness was clear to all his colleagues:

> The majority concludes that the proposed division would be equally injurious to those who petition for and those who oppose it. Therefore, this committee recommends its rejection. Signed: P. Le Bourgeois, Jacques Lastrapes, and Benjamin Metoyer.

Morris's voice was tight as he threw the report on his table and added his personal objection.

"Mr. Speaker. We were originally presented with a petition by leading citizens of Natchitoches, men who conduct a large percentage of the affairs of that parish.

They have asked respectfully for this body's consideration of their difficulties. Even though the more unstable and indecisive elements of the parish"—Morris stared scathingly at Ben—"have withdrawn their inconsequential support, the original petition still stands. The original need still stands. Therefore, I beseech my colleagues to reject this committee's report, to reject again the opposition's petition that is signed predominantly by Negroes, and to approve the division that is prayed for."

The debate was short. Within an hour, Ben was back in his rented hotel room, penning his own report to the parish constituents whose interests he recognized even though the state denied them his representation.

> Monsieur Augustin Metoyer
> The Isle of Canes
> Parish of Natchitoches
>
> *Mon cher Gustin*—
>
> We have won! The good *homme de couleur libre* of this state may not yet have the vote, but his right to obtain redress for injustices by means of legislative petition has been upheld by this body. The petition of the inhabitants of the Isle of Canes has been accepted! The House has approved our Committee's report to reject the proposed division. I am confident that the Senate, now that P. A. Rost has been confirmed as Bossier's replacement, will soon vote as the House has voted.
>
> Gustin, I know these are trying times for you and all your people. You feel used. Abused. I know it is tempting to conclude that society cares nothing for the *nègre* other than what it can get out of him. Your tax money is freely accepted—nay, demanded—and yet some try to say that you have no right to any voice in deciding how it will be spent. On the one hand, some call you "uppity" for daring to use the rights the state does give you, while the unscrupulous tempt you with promises of more rights they can't give, just to further their own causes.
>
> I make you no outright promises myself, Gustin. I am one man

alone, and it is nigh impossible for one man to change the world. Nonetheless, as long as I'm in the legislature, I'll continue to do all I can. Don't despair, Gustin. Remember, you've won a victory today. Indeed, we have proven more than even you hoped. We've shown not only that the *homme de couleur libre* still has rights in this state but also the importance of his role in the delicate balance of power that reigns. Not only is your support courted by those in need, but it was your opposition to Cloutier, your spearheading of the second petition, that successfully broke his scheme.

With or without the vote, Gustin, your people are still important to the welfare of our parish, and your feelings are still respected. We've proven that today.

Give my regards to all and tell them that I will report again when Cloutier's unholy bill is rejected by the Senate as well.

Your servant, your friend, and more,

François Benjamin Metoyer

Lent 1829

It was bitterly cold for late February and Augustin's knees ached. His fingers stiffened as the chill bored through the cowhide of his gloves, and he dropped the ball of twine he had been using to check the plumb line on the framework of the dividing wall.

"What you need is a good hearty drink, Gustin! Here, take a swig and warm your bones."

"Thanks, Louis. I had almost decided you and the hands were not going to show up this morning."

"We damned near didn't," Louis swore furiously, stamping his boots to force blood down into his toes. "If I hadn't promised the men a liberal supply of liquor, I think I'd have had an uprising on my hands when I ordered them out this morning."

"A *liberal* supply?"

Louis grinned. "Don't worry, Gustin, it won't be all that liberal. I'm paying for it. But I wouldn't ask any man to work out in weather like this without something to warm his innards. *Ma foi!* This cold spell is a rotten break. If those three days of sunshine had held a while longer, we might have finished this church before plowing time."

"We will finish," Augustin declared grimly. "Frankly, I am more worried about the altar getting here on schedule. Did Agnes tell you that Baptiste-Augustin and Suzette wrote from Rheims? They have found a man there who will carve us a replica of the altar from our family's old church, but he cannot guarantee it will be here by July."

"That's when the Bishop is coming?"

"Late July or early August, according to the new priest. Père Blanc thinks Natchitoches will have its own church in perfect order by then. I wish I could be as optimistic about ours. As long as I've dreamed about this day, it grieves me to think we may have to dedicate an empty shell."

"It won't be quite empty. We'll have the pews in."

"Yes, but the paintings of St. Augustin and St. Louis, and the Stations of the Cross, and the statues of the Madonna and St. Joseph—these have all been delayed. Maybe I should have ordered them from New Orleans instead of having Baptiste-Augustin commission them in France. The timing of his trip was just too late… What's so funny, Louis?"

"I was just thinking."

"*Hé?*"

"About those new Baptists who've moved in. Imagine what they must be saying about us Romans. Here we are building our church with Demon Rum and the folks up in Natchitoches financed theirs with the Devil's Lottery! Lord have mercy on all our souls, Gustin. We'll have two churches in this parish now, and both will be stained with the hand of Lucifer himself!"

"I see no shame, Louis. Our rum and brandy is not half as destructive as those corn-squeezings the Anglos claim to use for medicine, and sooner or later they will learn that cognac and wine are far more healthy than our drinking water. Especially when the fever hits the river. *Non,* they can rail all they want against us 'Popish heathens,' but a man who imbibes in moderation is following the example of our Lord Jesus."

"And gambling, Gustin?" Louis teased. "You can quote scripture on the holiness of wine, but I don't recall anything among His miracles about laying bets and buying chances."

"Well, it worked a miracle at Natchitoches, didn't it? How else could the people have raised twenty-five thousand dollars to build that fine, brick, twin-towered edifice? And don't tell me the *Américains* didn't buy their share of lottery tickets!"

"And pocketed their share of the winnings, too. *Zut,* Gustin! You know me. I enjoy a bit of chance as much as the next fellow. Maybe more. Still, it just doesn't set right with me that a *church* be built that way. They could have done with a less pretentious building and put their own labor into it as we're doing. Ah, forget it, Gustin. Pay me no mind. I'm just getting old and sanctimonious."

"There's no greater reformer than an old sinner," Augustin quipped.

"Then may the Lord spare me from myself! *Ga ça!* Look at that, Gustin! That boy's making a mess of those joints! Hey, Scipio, hold up there!"

"Yassuh, Mista Louis?"

The lecture on the craft of carpentering that followed was punctuated by Louis's colorful expletives, and Augustin smiled tolerantly as he turned and made his way stiffly to the lumber shed. The stock was getting low, so he began a mental inventory of the planks and beams on hand and the number of new ones that must be hewn. Engrossed in that task, amid the hammering and sawing that Louis's hands were now deep into, he missed the arrival of a visitor. In truth, he might have missed it anyway. Tobe Bradshaw was one of those men who shuffled through life, rarely attracting the notice of those who crossed his path.

"Mista Metoyer?" he hallooed. "Good day, sir. It's a fine buildin' you're throwin' up there, sir."

Augustin checked his irritation at the unexpected interruption of his calculations and nodded politely to his visitor. "Good morning, Mr. Bradshaw. What brings you out on a cold day like this?"

The question was not an idle one. Augustin actually was curious. In the several years since Bradshaw moved to the parish and found himself a place back up in the pine hills near Coincoin's old *vacherie,* Augustin had observed that the man rarely bestirred himself even when the weather was fine. Not in the daylight hours, at least, and certainly not this early in the morning.

A grin split the man's pock-marked face as he hastily doffed his hat. "A bizness man's gotta tend his affairs, come rain or shine. Right, Mista Metoyer?" The dog-eared hat inched nervously around in hands that were bare but shaking from more than the cold, Augustin suspected.

"Certainly, Bradshaw. Then it is business that has brought you to Yucca Bend?"

"'S matter of fact, yes, Mista Metoyer. Yestidy, since the weather looked lak it was fixin' to be plumb nasty, I stayed in an' went over my affairs, an' I sez to myself, 'Bradshaw, the best thing you ken do right now is to go see Mista Metoyer. He's a good, honest man who 'preciates a good bizness opportunity, an' he's allus willin' to help a good man out.' Yessir, that's whut I said to myself, an' I tol' the missus that, too."

"Thank you, Bradshaw," Augustin said noncommittally, waiting for the *Américain* to continue.

"That's 'zactly whut I come fer, Mista Metoyer. I got a li'l bizness deal that I know you'll be r'it int'rested in. You see, I got this nice l'il piece of land back up in the hills…"

Thirty acres of red clay, Augustin thought to himself, recalling the tract behind De Rossier's place. Thirty acres that weren't too bad when they were first cleared, but the topsoil wore off fast, and you've spent your days lolling on your porch instead of pulling cocoa weeds.

"…an' I plan to put in 'nother crop o' cotton this spring. But you know, these been purty hard times, Mista Metoyer. It rained all las' fall an' the cotton lay in the fields…"

While you lay around drinking, Augustin added to himself.

"…an' the factors down at New Orleans, well, you know better'n I, sir, they ain't int'rested in li'l planters lak me. They don't try so hard t' get a good price fer the bales we send 'em. Not lak they do fer you, sir."

Augustin still stood quietly, his back turned against the sharp North wind as he waited for the man to go on with his proposition.

"Yessir, Mista Metoyer. It wuz purty bad las' year. But this one'll be better. I ken feel it in my bones. The onliest problem, sir, is that once you have a bad year, it don't leave cash fer the nex' year's crop. You know whut I mean, sir?"

"Of course."

"So I thought t' myself, 'Mista Metoyer! Now there's a good man wit' cash to spare who's willin' t' put it out at int'rest t' a good risk!'"

"The Louisiana Planter's Bank makes that type of loan quite regularly, Bradshaw. Have you been to see M'sieur Rachal, their Natchitoches agent?"

The man's eyes drifted, but not before Augustin noted their bloodshot threads. "Well, I never care t' have much dealin's with banks, sir. I seen too many poor friends lose whut they had by gittin' mix't up wit' banks. No sir, I'd ruther do bizness wit' friends... you know how planters help each other out when one gets in a pickle...?"

The words just hung there in the air between them. Clearly, Bradshaw hoped Augustin would catch their drift and spare him the rest of what he had come to ask. Augustin simply waited, so Bradshaw plowed on.

"Jes las' week down at the tavern, sir, I overheerd Mista Prudhomme tellin' Mista Lambre that he'd borrowed a thousand off you t' keep from cashin' in his bonds 'fore they matured. An' I think, 'Now there's my man. Mista Metoyer'll lend me five hund'ed dollars t' make my crop an' tide me over 'til that big harvest comes.'"

"Your tract has thirty acres, Bradshaw?"

"Yessir. All cleared, too."

Except for the cocoa weeds, Augustin thought grimly. Still, he could not help but feel a twinge of sympathy for the man, at least for the family that had to depend upon him for support. His voice was gentle when he spoke again.

"Mr. Bradshaw, I do appreciate the delicacy of the situation you are in right now, and I know you are looking to better things this fall. But lending money is a business proposition even among friends, and investments have to be made in the way that will do the most good. Do you mind if I make a suggestion, Bradshaw?"

"No sir, not at all, sir."

"I have ridden by your place a time or two lately; and, frankly, I cannot agree that it would be a good business proposition for you to invest in seed, bagging, roping, and everything else it would take to make a cotton crop. Those cocoa weeds on your place have gotten out of hand. They would choke out your crop before midsummer."

Bradshaw smiled deprecatingly as he tucked his hat under his arm, fished a joint of sugar cane from his pocket, and bit off a plug. "Well, like mos' planters, sir, I got a few weeds here an' there, but the wife an' chillun'll chop 'em out when the cotton plants start comin' up."

"Mr. Bradshaw, cocoa weeds do not chop out. There are just two ways of getting rid of that problem once it gets as bad as yours. One is to move off and leave them, and heaven knows there are enough people who do that, but I do not advise anyone to give up so easily."

"You got 'nother suggestion, Mista Metoyer?"

"Yes, Bradshaw. Let your land lie fallow this year and invest a few dollars in a herd of hogs. Put up some fencing and confine them to the area where your problem is the worst. Let them root out the weeds, cocoa grass, and everything. Then next year you can plant a crop there."

"Well, I dunno, Mista Metoyer. A good planter jes can't lie 'round an' not even try t' make a crop fer a whole year. No sir, I'd ruther take my chances on hoein' the cocoa outa the cotton."

"It was just a suggestion, Bradshaw. But it's my best advice."

The man stood planted in the winter mud outside Augustin's woodyard. "I'd still lak to make that loan, Mista Metoyer, an' put in a cotton crop. I'd pay you goin' int'rest an' put my land on the line as c'latteral."

"I'm sorry, Bradshaw." Augustin shook his head gently. "That hill land, the best of it, is only worth two dollars an acre right now, and you'd never get that for yours unless you get the cocoa out. Your thirty acres are only worth fifty dollars tops. It is just not good business for anyone to lend five hundred dollars on fifty dollars worth of security. If your crop does not make—and, frankly, I do not see how it could—then you would lose your land and I would lose most of my money."

Bradshaw shriveled. "That's your decision, sir?"

"Yes," Augustin replied quietly.

"Well, thank you kindly, sir. I 'preciate your consid'ration anyhow, Mista Metoyer."

"Bradshaw!" Augustin called as the skinny Anglo trudged despondently away. "If you change your mind about a herd of hogs, let me know. I would advance you for that."

"Thank you, sir, but I don' think so." For a moment, Bradshaw wavered, then studied the structure that Augustin's hands were erecting.

"Mista Metoyer, there's one other thing, if'n I may be bold 'nough t' ask."

"Yes, Bradshaw?"

"I hear tell you're buildin' a church house there?"

"Yes?"

"Fer your family?"

"Yes."

"Well, I know this is mi'ty forward o' me, sir. But you know, my missus is a Roman, too?"

"Yes," Augustin replied again, with a vague recollection of a swarthy little Spanish girl, old far beyond her years, with a flock of ragged children pulling on her skirt tails.

"I've never gotten too enthused over 'ligion myself, an' there's no real preacher 'round here anyhow, 'ceptin' Romans, an' that's not my style... no offense, Mista Metoyer."

"Of course not," Augustin replied patiently.

"But the l'il woman's real devout. Yessir! The onliest problem is that since the ol' church burned in Natchitoches we sorta got outa the habit o' ridin' so far come Sunday, so she moved her membership or whutever y'all call it, down to Cloutierville. But now that church's closed—you heard that, sir?"

"Yes."

Bradshaw grinned again, fatuously, exposing a crooked row of sugar-rotted teeth. "Yessir-ree! Y'all really bested ol' Cloutier on that one. Hot damn! He jes' gave up completely an' sold his whole town an' moved downriver!"

"So I've heard," Augustin replied noncommittally.

"Well, some o' the stores are closin' now, an' somebody killed ol' Doc Carles whut was livin' wid that pretty li'l yallow girl, an'... well, the town's jes' sorta dyin' down an' I don't have much hopes they'll open that church agin real soon."

"I'm afraid of that, too, Bradshaw."

"That's whut I wanted to ask you about, Mista Metoyer. I know it's ri't forward o' me t' ast this, but would it be too pushy if'n I brought my wife an' chillun over here, when y'all's preacher comes out, I mean?"

"Of course not, Bradshaw. The Church of St. Augustin may sit on my land, and my family may be building it, but it will still be a house of God. Its doors will be open to everyone. A number of our white friends have already expressed an interest in attending."

Tobe Bradshaw extended his hand then and pumped Augustin's own enthusiastically. "Yessir, Mista Metoyer. Like I said, you're a good man. I'm ri't sorry we couldn't do bizness, sir. But it'll be nice seein' you onc'n a while on Sundays, sir."

Sieur Nicolas Augustin Metoyer, f.m.c.
and his Church of St. Augustin

Portrait painters have traditionally posed their subjects with objects and backdrops meaning-ful to their character. For Augustin, it was not a book or a bust or a fox hound that he chose to symbolize himself, but the Church of St. Augustin that he had built across from the front gallery of Augustin Manor.

∽ 5 ∾
February 1832

Young Gassion had shucked his coat, rolled up his shirt sleeves, and was fanning another pile of cornstalks into a blaze when Augustin reined up quietly on the turnroad. Unnoticed, he sat there, ramrod straight, silently appraising his son and the progress of the task at hand. The field was almost cleared, he noted approvingly as three *négresses* scurried to the edge of the field with more armloads of brush for his son to fire. By noon, Augustin calculated, the plowing crew should be at work, and by Monday they should be planting the corn.

At last his son paused, impatiently brushing away the sweat that rolled into his eyes, and Augustin called with mock severity, "Hey, boy!"

Surprised, Gassion looked up quickly, then grinned.

"Youse talkin' to me, suh?" he rejoined, as he caught the deprecating tone in his father's voice.

"You are out here working like a field hand, *non?* You had better expect to be taken for one."

Gassion smiled again. Placidly. But his step was brisk as he closed the distance between himself and his father's horse.

A smile of his own softened Augustin's weathered face, crinkling the corners of a set of eyes that could drill right through a son whose actions seriously displeased him. Still he was not done with this one. "You are supposed to be *driving* our hands, son, not helping them do their work. The overseers of this parish are likely to take offense at your egalitarianism."

"What a man does on his own land ought to be his own business," Gassion declared. "Besides, you worked alongside our hands when you were young and itching to get things done in a hurry."

"Things were different then, son." Until now, Augustin's voice had been light, teasing. It had been years since he had found serious fault with this youngest son of his. Not once had cross words passed between them since the boy got over his Texas fever. But Augustin's voice took on a note of soberness now, as he continued.

"François-Gassion…?"

"Sir?"

Augustin thought a bit longer about the point he needed to make and how best to make it. "I have not raised you to be the kind of *gentleman* who spends his days gaming and his nights wenching, but there is no longer any reason for a son of mine to actually labor in the field. Our hands will respect you more, and our neighbors as well, if you are mindful of the vast difference between you and field hands."

"*Oui*, Papa. I'm duly chastised." Gassion's tone clearly belied his words. "Have you finished your rounds?"

"Just about. There's still a little piece across the river I must check. By the way, I spotted a section of fencing that is almost down on the backside of the field behind the church."

"I've already ordered Philippe over there with a couple of helpers, sir."

"Good." Augustin nodded approvingly and again counted his blessings for the way this boy had turned out. Five years before, he had been seriously worried.

"Son, are you serious about Flavie Mézières?"

"*Sir?*" Gassion stammered momentarily, taken aback by the suddenness of the question. Then his eyes lowered, and his toe began to kick intently at a clod of dirt. He was almost a bashful adolescent again, and Augustin could not hold back a smile.

"I do not mean to pry, boy; but, if you are thinking about marriage don't be expecting me to give you a plantation all your own like I did for your brothers and sisters."

Gassion was visibly surprised. The look of worry that clouded his face was unmistakable. Of course, he had expected something. Augustin knew he would. All of his other children had gotten the same start in life on the day they married, two hundred acres of land—*uncleared* acres—so each would have to work just as he and Agnes did to build their own fortunes. The problem was, he had no uncleared land left and all the good land on the Isle had been taken.

Augustin smiled. "I'm making you a different offer, son. Marry your Flavie. Bring her here. Your Mama's lonesome all day by herself with no little ones around her. Start your family here, Gassion, and stay with me as my overseer."

He paused then, searching for a hint of acceptance, a reaction of any type, in his son's face. At last Gassion spoke, carefully framing his words so as not to hurt his aging father's feelings.

"Papa, there is nothing I'd like better than to stay close to you and Mama as… as long as the Good Lord's willing. But that just wouldn't be right, Papa. A man has to be his own man and make his own place, if he's a man at all."

"You have already proven your manhood, son," Augustin replied gruffly. "Five years ago, I would not have made you this offer, but you're not the boy you were then. Truth is, I need you. I'm just too old now to run this place alone."

"You have grandsons as old as I am, Papa. Why not one of them?"

"Mais non!" Augustin grimaced in mock horror. "Why should I start all over again training somebody else when I have done such a good job with you?" Gassion still wavered. Augustin understood. "I know, I know. No lad with gumption wants an old father telling him what to do once he's a grown and married man. In fact, I would think less of you if you were content to take my orders for the rest of your life."

"But…"

"That is why I am retiring, son. The day you marry is the day I will put this place under your control. Then, when the Good Lord takes me, it will be yours completely. House. Land. Negroes. Everything."

Gassion said nothing. He would accept. Augustin knew that. Gassion was just not a man who made snap decisions, and so it was Augustin who broke the silence. "Of course, I will probably give you advice now and then. I give all my people advice, whether they want it or not." His eyes twinkled, a maze of smile lines crinkling their corners. Still, the jesting elicited no answer, prompting Augustin to try another tack.

"Son, you know I have more than I can handle. Dealing with all our people's problems is a full-time job, not to mention the church, the school, and my investments."

Gassion's brows were knitting now. He was clearly on the verge of relenting. Assured of victory, Augustin decided he could afford to soft-pedal. "Of course, I do not want to pressure you, boy," he added. "Take your time deciding. You can mull over it today and let me know tonight. Tomorrow. Next week."

Gassion's slow grin gave away his answer. "Sorry, Papa! I won't be home tonight for supper. I'm riding into town to have Père Blanc announce banns for Flavie and me. Now you'd better let me get back to work. If this place is going to be mine, I can't let the hands go lazy."

"Better yet, boy, you go see your Flavie tonight, and I'll ride into the post to make your arrangements with the priest, *non?"*

"Oui," Gassion threw over his shoulder as he loped back to the field and snatched a pitchfork from the hand who had been leaning on it.

Shaking his head fondly, Augustin wheeled his mount and headed back northward, up the long meandering isle, toward the now-sprawling town of Natchitoches. Spring rains had not yet set in, and River Road was hard and dry. The steady clip-clop of his stallion's shoes almost mesmerized him, easing somewhat the ache that now seemed to keep him company wherever he went. Agnes had noticed the stoop that was beginning to set in and the occasional flinch that he was not able to hide, and—bless her!—she had held back the fluffiest cotton from their last crop and personally stitched and stuffed a new mattress for the massive bed they had inherited from his mama. That had helped. At least it made his mornings much less stiff, but the daily ride he still insisted upon had become, some days, a trial other men would have shucked.

Mile after mile of cleared fields now passed him by. An occasional live oak still stood, silent relics of the forests and canebrakes that once had lined this river. But beneath their spreading arms the small cottonwood and rosebud seedlings had given way to neat, whitewashed slave cabins, or a handsome home, or a store, a tannery, or a tailor shop. Store-porch crowds doffed their hats as he passed, and Negroes called in greeting from the field.

"Mornin', Massa Gustin."

"Good morning, Paul... Rosetta... Prince..." Augustin knew them all. He made it his business to know them all. Between them, his people now held title to more than three hundred slaves, but he could call each by name, and he had stood as godfather to scores of their children.

Humming softly to himself the old, wordless tune that always charmed his stallion, he rounded the next bend, passed a long row of cotton sheds, and then drew up short as a spirited little pony came dashing down the lane from the grove where Baptiste-Augustin and Suzette were building their own Big House.

"Whoa, Vulcan!" Augustin reined his big stallion, waved, then waited patiently for the pony and its little rider to approach. Of all his grandchildren, Baptiste-Augustin's little Barbe was the one on which he doted, so much so that even Agnes had been moved to warn him Barbe should not be spoiled. He just could not help it. She had saucy ringlets like her grandmother Susanne once had, the same olive skin that her mother had inherited from the French Antys, and the teasing ways of his own Agnes.

"Grandpère! Grandpère Gustin!"

Tenderly, Augustin leaned down to the pony that whinnied to a halt beside him, and Barbe kissed the tip of his broad nose. "Is that a new pony, *ma petite?*"

"*Oui,* Grandpère. Papa got him from Cousin Louis Monette when he went down to Cloutierville yesterday. I've been waiting for him for *months!* Ever since Christmas, at least!"

Augustin nodded in mock seriousness. "That is a long time for a little girl to want for anything."

"Oh, I know," she retorted petulantly. "But Papa kept saying *wait...* wait 'til next Christmas... *wait* 'til my birthday. That's what Papa always says about everything."

"Patience is a good habit to cultivate, *chérie.* So what did you do to wangle it from him?"

"I had to promise I'd help embroider all the new linens Maman planned to make this spring. Six pair of pillow cases, eight sheets, and a tester, too!"

"I hope he made you promise to take care of the filly as well."

"Oh, he did!" Barbe's green eyes danced. "I have to feed her, and groom her, and exercise her every morning! That's the best part! It gets me out of the stuffy sewing room! I'd just go absolutely crazy if I had to sit all day with that embroidery hoop, while the whole world *happened* outside. Come on, Grandpère! I'll race you!"

"No way, child!" Augustin laughed. "That filly looks too fast for my old stallion. I have never lost a race yet, and I do not intend to let you be the first to best me. Go on, *chérie.* Let your horse have his wind. I plan to visit a spell with your papa. When you get back you can ride into town with me. Where is your papa, by the way?"

"In the Big House, giving directions all over the place. 'This molding's too wide! That molding's too narrow!' "

Augustin chortled. That did sound like her papa! Leaning down again from his big stallion to her pony, he lightly kissed her good-bye with his usual, *"Au revoir, ma petite."* He had to bite back a grimace, then, as he swung upright into his saddle and his back protested mightily. Yet that was not the sole reason he sat and watched that granddaughter disappear down River Road amid a cloud of dust and a melodic trill of *eeeei-yaiii, eeee-yaiii* that only Barbe could leave behind her.

Eventually, his joints eased themselves back into place. By the time he wound up the lane to the new house Barbe's father was building, his son was no longer where she had left him. Baptiste-Augustin had, in fact, lost his patience with the interior carpenters and was now directing the crew in laying the brick walkway that would circle around the gallery.

"Calm down, son," Augustin cautioned in greeting as he dismounted. "The house will be done before it's time to plant the cotton."

"Eh? Papa!" Baptiste-Augustin's lean face relaxed, and he wrapped a lanky arm affectionately around his father. "Actually, it's not the cotton planting I'm worried about. It's the progress Oncle Louis is making on his own house."

"Oh?"

"He cornered me into a bet." Baptiste-Augustin was clearly chagrined. "If I move into my house before he moves into his, Oncle Louis foots the bill for my housewarming party—as many guests as I care to invite. But if he gets moved in first, I not only have to foot the bill for mine, but for his, too."

"Sounds fair enough."

"Oh, it's fair, but I don't aim to lose. The furniture and carpets I ordered from Europe have arrived at *la ville*. I got a letter from Auguste yesterday."

"Oh?" Augustin could not help it. He still chafed every time that son of his was mentioned. As badly as the Isle needed merchants, Auguste had set up his shop down in New Orleans, where he and some white partner had attracted the "exclusive" clientele Auguste preferred. Sometimes, Augustin muttered—and not always to himself—nothing about the Isle seemed good enough for that son.

"Auguste is sending my furnishings up next week by steamer. This place has to be ready to move everything in when it arrives. But at the rate those carpenters are working… "

Augustin sighed, settled himself onto the nearest sawhorse, and lit his pipe while Baptiste-Augustin continued on with his litany of things to fret about. "You do surprise me sometimes," he remarked offhandedly when his son had finally spent the last of his frustrations.

"How's that, Papa?"

"As big a dither as you are in right now, how did Barbe persuade you to take yesterday off to go to Cloutierville?"

Baptiste-Augustin's face turned dark. "It wasn't Barbe. It was a summons from the *syndic.*"

"Eh?"

"Adelaïde's got herself into another mess. I swear, if I ever see Valerin de Rossier again, I'll kill him!"

"I thought she had ended that affair with him years ago."

"Oh, she did—*her* affair with him. But once the likes of De Rossier gets hooks into something, they never let go. This time, that bastard really outdid himself. He came by Adelaïde's the other night, hoping to hop back into her bed just as though she had never kicked him out, but for once she wasn't in her bed. In fact, she wasn't even home. There was nobody there but Marie, so he decided she'd do just as well."

"Marie? My god! The girl's his daughter!"

Baptiste-Augustin's face twisted into a look of pure hatred. "Apparently that makes little difference to that wretched *cochon!*"

"Did he...?" Augustin simply could not put it into words. There were few foibles of mankind he had not encountered in his sixty-four years, but such utter vileness as this was unspeakable.

"No. She put up a pretty good struggle for such a little thing. Bashed him over the head with a lamp and knocked him out for a short while—long enough for her to run downriver to Dupré's store. Only the fool kid was too ashamed to tell Manuel what happened. That was for the best, I guess. Manuel would have killed him. After so many years of protecting all his mama's kids against De Rossier, he hates that man deep. But even he never thought the bastard would try anything on his own daughter."

"So, how did you two find out?"

"De Rossier tried again night before last."

"May God have mercy!"

"Adelaïde came home just barely in time. He had already ripped the poor girl's clothes off. Beat her senseless first. He was shucking his trousers when Adelaïde came sashaying in. I'll say that much for the old girl. She hasn't lost her spunk. Her riding crop was still in her hand, and she almost cut De Rossier to shreds before he sobered up enough to get out of there—leaving his pants behind, of course."

Baptiste-Augustin smiled grimly. "In fact, Laïde cut him up so badly in one certain spot that it will probably be a long time before he bothers anybody else, woman or child."

"Then he filed charges, I gather. That's why you were at Cloutierville?"

"Yes, but Adelaïde and Marie filed a counter-suit, and had me called to testify—along with Manuel, Émile Dupart, and half a dozen others who know De Rossier and his past brutalities."

"So, how did it all come out?"

"Charges against Adelaïde were dropped, and the *syndic* put De Rossier under a peace bond prohibiting him from going near Marie. Not that he acknowledges her as his daughter any longer. In fact, that was his whole defense. Considering Adelaïde's reputation, he swore Marie could be any man's daughter and as far as he was concerned, she was fair game for anybody!"

"Then he picked the wrong *syndic* to use that argument on," Augustin declared. "There's no more honorable man than Jean Pierre Marie Dubois. He does not treat any woman as *fair game,* be she yellow, white, black, or red." Augustin could have said more. Much more. Not even Baptiste-Augustin probably knew just how many times, of late, the widowed mamas and distraught fathers among his people had gone to one notary or another along the Cane for those peace bonds—the only means they had now to stop one white male or another from stalking, importuning, and molesting their young daughters.

"I wish we could say we've seen the last of that dog, Papa," Baptiste-Augustin continued on. "But we haven't. De Rossier will be cowed for a while, at least until Laïde's cuts heal, but nothing will ever change him."

"Then let us hope that someone shoots him before one of us has to!" Augustin declared, as Barbe heeled her pony to a halt in the lane beside them, and he hastily changed the subject to one more appropriate for her ears. Impatiently, she waited for them to finish talking, trotting her little filly around in circles until she could no longer contain herself.

"Grandpère?" she pleaded.

"I'm coming, *ma petite*—with a pocketbook full of change, too. What will be our treat this time, your licorice or my taffy?"

"Licorice!" she squealed, wrinkling her nose. "I can make us the taffy!"

"See you, Papa." Baptiste-Augustin lightly embraced his old father again. "Give Maman a kiss for me."

"I'll give it to her, but she'll still collect another one at the races Sunday."

"I'm sure she will," Baptiste-Augustin laughed as he waved good-bye. "There's never been a race yet without Maman there giving away her meat pies and collecting kisses in return. Sometimes I wonder if all your old friends go to the races to bet or to help themselves to mama's cooking and kissing!"

"It's her cooking, boy," Augustin called over his shoulder as he and Barbe clipped off toward town. "Just the cooking."

∽ 6 ∾
That Saturday

"Gustin! *Mon ami!*"

Augustin had no sooner helped Agnes from their carriage at the end of the lane that led to Jean Prudhomme's race track, than a strong hand clasped his shoulder familiarly.

"*Hé*, Jean, old friend! You are not down at the stables yet, haranguing your jockey?"

"I've said all I have to say so many times that he's sick of hearing me. *Bienvenu*, Gustin. I had just about decided you weren't coming. Last week's big hunt must have been too much for an old sport like you!"

"Old? Speak for yourself, Jean. Anytime you can stay on a horse for three days and follow a pack of hounds, I'll be right there beside you."

"Speaking of horses, we are in for a dandy race this afternoon. There's a new kid here from down at Alexandria. He can't be more than sixteen or seventeen, but he's racing his own horse and it looks like a good one. He's just liable to nose my Pericles."

"Perhaps, but he won't touch my Dauphin Noir!"

Jean chuckled. "He's just liable to do that, Gustin. You'd better warn that grandson who rides for you to give this new kid a wide berth."

"Thanks for the caution, Jean. Not that it is needed, of course. So who is this fellow?"

"Jones is the name. Carroll Jones. From Tennessee originally, I hear. He's a chestnut-colored kid whose father moved him to Louisiana and freed him. I tell you, Gustin, he rides as lightly as a summer breeze, but that mare of his is a Gulf gale. In fact, that's what he calls her, Hurricane. I'll give you two to one, Gustin, Jones beats you."

"Sight unseen, I don't bet on any horse, *mon ami,*" Augustin laughed, "but I'll lay you the same odds that I beat you!"

Neither Augustin nor Jean had cause to worry about the new competition. Young Jones was entered only in the mile beat, while the old Cane River pair preferred to race in the two- and three-mile runs. Still, Hurricane seemed to be everything Jean had said she was, and Augustin's brief appraisal of her as she stood on the sidelines whinnying under Jones's softly rubbing hands convinced him to risk a few small bets on the unknown mare.

Louis, he soon found out, was more reckless. Of course, Louis had been riled.

The Isle races were generally a Creole sport. Still, they always drew a few area Anglos who liked to race, gamble, drink, or all three. It was one of those who had Ben cornered when Louis approached him at the track, and Louis recognized the voice even before he saw the face that went with it. Joe Haney was a newcomer to the area, but his reputation had spread quickly and Louis never crossed paths with him without recalling the quip Jim Bowie made down at the billiard hall at Cloutierville—that you could always spot a Tennesseean because he walked around with tobacco in his pocket, a bottle in one hand, and his prick in the other. Haney fit that description right well.

"I tell you, Mista Metoyer," Haney was whining to Ben as Louis approached, "somebody oughta stop that new boy from racin'. These coloreds are taking over this track. It's bad enough the way y'all's Creole yellows butt their way into this gentleman's sport, but this new nigger is just too much. The boy wouldn't be so uppity if we wuz back in Tennessee, I'll tell you."

"Mr. Haney," Louis interjected tartly, "you're not in Tennessee now. We don't go to your state and tell your people they need to change their ways. We expect the same of Tennessee gentlemen who come here… Good afternoon, Ben."

"Hello, Louis," Ben replied, slapping his brother cordially on the back as they both attempted to ignore Haney's sputtering response to Louis's dress-down.

"I tell ya," the Tennessean persisted, "it's an insult for that boy to bring his half-breed horse onto the track."

Ben raised one eyebrow, considered the remark, and then smiled pleasantly enough as he brushed off the man's crassness yet again. "Not really, Haney. We don't bar men or horses here on the sole basis of their breeding."

The barb wasn't wasted. Louis could tell. Haney's eyes narrowed into cracks above ruddy cheekbones so high Louis was tempted to wonder whether the man's name-calling wasn't an effort to divert suspicion from his own origins—and he wasn't the least bit surprised when Haney decided to ignore Ben's observation and take another tack.

"Then I'll make either one of ya a little bet. I'll give ya odds that colored boy's pony'll eat the dust of every horse on that track."

"It's a bet," Louis retorted. "And I put fifty dollars on the pony's head."

Haney paled. "Well, now, I din't 'zactly have that much in mind, Metoyer. I wouldn't honor no darkie's horse by bettin' that much fer or agin' him."

"Take the bet or leave it, Haney."

Haney took it, grudgingly, and he lost. Jones's spotted filly, mixed-breed though she was, stood placidly throughout the afternoon, showing no sign of impatience as the simple two-mile beat and the three-mile beat, and then the two-out-of-three two-mile beats were run. When the mile beat was finally announced, Hurricane cantered to the starting line; but the minute the pistol roared, the dappled roan was a length ahead of her closest competitor, and before the sprint was over she widened that distance considerably.

The crowd surged upon the young jockey from Alexandria with congratulations and envious offers to buy his horse. As Jones parried their propositions and accepted their goodwill, Joe Haney sidled backward through the crowd, edging slowly closer to its fringe.

"Why, Mr. Haney," Ben hallooed unexpected at his side, and his hand closed firmly upon the man's arm. "Leaving us so soon?"

"Oh, no, sir," Haney mumbled. "Just lookin' fer my brother-in-law, sir. You know Tom Matson?"

"Indeed, I do," Ben said smoothly. "A fine fellow. But I do believe you are looking for him in the wrong direction, Haney. Matson's up at the track talking with Louis Metoyer. You remember M'sieur Louis?" Ben added pointedly. "The gentleman with whom you placed your bet?"

Haney's eyes darted nervously as Ben's grip swiveled him back toward the track. "Bet, sir? Oh, yeah. That's right. We did make a little bet. Fancy that," he laughed edgily. "I almost forgot."

"I thought as much," Ben retorted. "Ah, here they are, Haney. Good evening, Tom. It's nice to see you again, sir."

"Evening, Ben," Matson replied warmly. "I hope you weren't foolish enough to place any bets against that new horse like I did. Augustin just beat me out of five dollars, and Louis tells me he took my brother-in-law here for fifty. I swear, Haney! What ever possessed you to make a bet that size?"

Joe Haney bristled, not at his wife's brother, with whom no love was lost anyway, but at the fresh reminder of his situation. To the man he had bet against, Haney knew, fifty dollars was little more than pocket money. For *him,* that was his profit off four bales of cotton, and he had only shipped twelve to market that winter. But now Haney's bravado was bolstered by the presence of menfolk from his own family and he turned belligerent, confident that all the past differences between himself and this brother-in-law would not amount to a hill of beans stacked up against outsiders.

"I wuz tricked, that's whut I wuz," Haney whined.

"Tricked?" Matson's skepticism was obvious.

"Yeah. From beginnin' to end. This yeller friend of yours cornered me into makin' that bet. Then he paid off the other racers so the nigger's horse could win. Any fool could see that. Not one of those riders even tried to catch up with that little jockey. They just set back an' let him steal the race. But I'll tell you one thing, this big yeller here's not gonna take my money."

"Joe, a bet's a bet," Matson declared, his face coloring from embarrassment at his inlaw's behavior. Again he rued the day his little sister eloped with the churl.

"Among *gentlemen* it is; but among a bunch of bastids it ain't. An' that's exactly what these yellers are. Right, big man?" Haney sneered, for once staring Louis in the eye.

"I say you throw around words too freely, Haney. I hope you are just as eager to back them up."

"Oh, you're cunnin', ain't you?" Haney taunted. "You think you're gonna goad me into fightin' you like you goaded me into makin' that bet ag'inst my better judgment. You musta inherited that cunnin' from your white trash pappy—whoever he was. Well, I never stopped to friggin' with niggers like he did, an' I don't fight 'em either."

"Then perhaps you'll accept my challenge?" Ben interposed quietly.

Haney wavered. "Now look, Mista Metoyer. I got no quarrel with you, an' you got no quarrel with me. No, sir. None whatsoever. Just because your family wuz nice enough to free these folks an' let 'em use your name, don't make you responsible for 'em forever. No, sir."

"I *am* responsible for upholding the good name of my father," Ben shot back through a jaw that had hardened instantly into the square visage of the old Pierre. "Here is my card, sir. You may now name the time, the place, and the weapons—unless you choose to apologize to Monsieur Louis."

Haney's eyes spat venom. "I don't apologize to his kind."

"For God's sake, Joe, reconsider!" his brother-in-law pleaded. "I won't let you do this. If you don't care anything about my sister and the children she bore you, I do."

"If you care anything about their honor," Haney retorted, "you'll be my second. The whole family's honor is at stake here, Matson. Those yellers tried to cheat me."

"Joe, dueling's against the law!" Tom insisted.

"Oh, that don't bother Mista Metoyer none," Haney retorted. "If Mista Lawmaker hisself don't have no respect for the law, a body can't 'spect us poor folks to have none."

"Then where do we meet, Haney?" Ben demanded tersely.

"Daybreak in the mornin's good 'nough fer me. Down at the buryin' grounds by Shallow Lake," Haney snickered. "That'll make it easy for your family to bury you."

"Then the fates are against you already, Haney," Ben retorted. "My family does not use that cemetery."

"Well, hell, they can haul your dead ass all the way back to Natchitoches, fer all I care. You jes' be there with your pistil an' your second."

"We'll be there," Louis interjected, defiantly glaring down Augustin's reproving gaze.

"Nobody said anything about *you*," Haney shot back, with a jerk of his head toward Ben. "I'm fightin' *him.*"

"Most certainly!" Ben vowed through clenched teeth. "But I have the privilege of choosing my own second. You chose your brother-in-law. I choose my brother."

◌ 7 ◌

The holy day of Sunday, 11 March 1832

The long-overdue spring rain set in that night. By the small hours of the morning, its fury had waned but a steady, unrelenting drizzle taunted Ben, Augustin, and Louis as they rode soberly down River Road toward Shallow Lake. An occasional screech owl mocked them from the pitch-black recesses of a stretch of woods, but otherwise there was no relief from the grim, foreboding silence that pursued them.

No man deserves to die this kind of death, Augustin thought savagely to himself. Ben had joked the night before about dying honorably with his boots on. If Haney's bullet is lucky, Ben would die wallowing in the mud, and there is no honor in that. *Non,* a man who has lived in peace as Ben has done should go in peace, quietly, in his own bed, leaving behind only memories of the good he had done in his life, not the murder he had died trying to commit.

"Well, well," Ben drawled suddenly as they rounded a bend and approached another clearing. "The party is awaiting us already. Cheer up, fellows! If you go in there looking like there has already been a death in the family my *honorable* adversary will conclude you have no faith in me."

"I have no faith in this kind of hellishness," Augustin retorted.

"Ease up, Gustin. Ben knows by now how you feel."

"All right, Louis. But I am praying for you both and you know it."

For thirty years, Augustin had found solace in this little cemetery, nestled languorously along a fingerlake on Ambroise Lecomte's plantation. He had stood at that friend's side when Père Delvaux consecrated these holy grounds on one of his pastoral trips downriver from Natchitoches, back in Spanish times. Since then, he had come here more times than he could remember, for the burials of friends and inlaws, and in between he had come back to pay his respects and soak in the peace that always seemed to fill his soul in this grove of trees. Now, this morning, he had come to defile the place.

"Good morning, gentlemen," Tom Matson greeted them stiffly as they dismounted and tied their horses to a nearby tree.

"Good morning, Matson," Ben responded, nodding curtly in Haney's direction. Then his face brightened as he spied the slender, silver-haired Frenchman who stood beyond. "Jean! Thanks for offering to arbitrate our little *affaire d'honneur.*"

"I didn't offer, Ben," Prudhomme declared. "I insisted upon it. Your disagreement took place on my land. I'm honor-bound to make certain that it is settled fairly. Not that I expect otherwise. Both the Metoyers and the Matsons are my friends. So, I'll start by asking: will any of you reconsider?"

"Hell, no!" Haney spat.

"Non," Ben echoed tersely. "This matter must be settled with an apology or a pistol."

"As you wish. Seconds, are you ready?" Jean called quietly.

"As ready as I'll ever be," Matson muttered, his eyes seeking out Louis's own as though begging him to understand that his support of his sister's husband was a thing apart from his friendship with Louis.

Louis understood. *"Oui,"* he responded, just as gravely.

"So be it," Jean proclaimed. "Haney… Ben… shake hands and take your stances."

Stiffly, Ben extended his hand, but Haney ignored it. "I don't shoot my friends 'n I don't shake with my enemies."

"Joe," Matson begged. "It's ritual."

"Well, I never cared for rigmarole." Haney smiled crookedly, shifted his plug of tobacco from one cheek to the other, then spat a wad of juice in Ben's direction. "'Course, if Mista Metoyer don't like it, he can always refuse to fight."

"Mais, jamais! Never!"

"Then turn your backs, gentlemen," Jean ordered with grim finality, and Augustin steeled himself as the men solemnly stepped off their paces. It was he who had taught Ben to shoot, but he had never expected this diabolic test of his tutelage. He had promised their father that he would always be this brother's keeper. Today he was failing that charge. *For God's sake, Ben,* Augustin pleaded silently, let the fool shoot first! Let him fire off wildly. He's bound to. Then take your time and aim right where you want to hit him.

Ben seemed to hear his bidding. He turned slowly, deliberately, his arm extended and poised. True to Augustin's prediction, Haney fired recklessly, but with the luck of those whom the Devil has blessed, his wild shot ripped through Ben's extended forearm. The fine ivory-handled pistol Ben had inherited from old Pierre dropped to the mud, its load unintentionally discharged by the jolt of Haney's bullet. Still, Ben himself remained planted upright, his sheet-white face masking his pain, as his free hand tried to stanch the flow of blood from an arm that hung limply at his side.

"Hot damn!" Haney cackled. "An' the next shot's mine!"

Nothing but the drizzle broke the silence that followed that cackle. The referee's voice, when it finally came, was frigid. "M'sieur Haney! You may not shoot an unarmed man. At this point, since each of you have fired, you have the option of declaring the matter settled."

"Joe?" Matson pleaded softly.

"Hell's bells, man! My luck's goin' right. You expect me to chicken out now?"

Augustin could plainly see the disgust on his old friend's face, as Prudhomme struggled to maintain some semblance of civility. To his knowledge, Jean had never raised his pistol to another man, but he had refereed far too many of these senseless duals that were, in both of their estimations, the least civilized contribution France ever made to the *civilization* of *savage* America. Jean, he knew, would brook no infringements upon the unwritten code that governed this hellish custom.

"Then would you consider a continuation of this affair with M'sieur Metoyer's second?" Prudhomme interposed, again offering the man an alternative. "Your opponent is wounded, M'sieur Haney. I doubt that he could hold a gun in that hand, much less fire one, and I know you are too much of a gentleman to take pleasure in an uneven match."

"Well, I ain't never yet shot a cripple." Haney fished a while in the pocket of his baggy pants for a fresh wad of tobacco and eventually poked it through a reasonably complete set of discolored teeth. Whether he was stalling for time or deliberately squeezing from the moment all the attention he could get, Augustin could not decide. The man's bottom lip bulged where he had tucked the wad, and he worked furiously at it for a while to extract its juice, before his eyes narrowed again above those cheekbones Augustin had rarely seen on the Anglos who had moved into the parish of Natchitoches. *Ma foi! Louis is right!* Augustin thought suddenly, as the darkening mist cast Haney's ruddy face in shadow, and despite himself he felt a twinge of pity. Nor could he help but wonder just how far removed the man actually was from the Redbone past he tried to bury by heaping epithets on others.

"And I ain't never stooped to fightin' a yeller," Haney finally continued. "But what the hell. If I can beat the best the *honorable* Metoyers can offer, I can dam' well do their bastids!"

The drizzle quickened, and the early morning sky turned inky as Jean positioned the adversaries back to back for their new match. Louis squared his shoulders against Haney's and felt the Tennessean flinch at the touch.

"For God's sake, get this over with!" Matson pleaded again. With all these trees around us, if lightning sets in, we'll all leave widows today!"

"Then count us off, Jean."

One. Two. Three. The slow, fatal, march of time echoed across the little clearing and the lake, mocking Augustin again as he stood helplessly by and watched another brother challenge the fates.

Nine. Ten. Turn. *Fire!*

The blast from Haney's pistol lit up the torrents around them and crescendoed to a thud when his bullet hit the weeping willow behind Louis's back. For a moment the man stood agape, but only for a moment, as the reality of his situation hit him. As Louis hesitated, fleetingly wondering whether he should fire or call the matter settled, Haney seized the opportunity. Leaping to the side of his second, he yanked the pistol from Matson's belt and turned to fire again.

Louis did not allow him the chance to commit that final dishonor. Calmly, deliberately, he raised his pistol, sighted down its slender barrel, and fired, dead-center, into the inch-wide valley between Haney's eyes.

It was Matson who moved first. "Well, that's that," he announced simply. Retrieving his pistol from where it had fallen, he lifted his brother-in-law's crumpled form across his shoulders and carried it to his horse, heedless of the blood that poured onto his own back. Louis followed him helplessly, floundering for words.

"Tom…"

"There's nothing to say, Louis. We both did what we had to do. You've been my friend ever since I came here. If I ever leave, I hope you'll be my friend still."

"You know I will, Tom," Louis said miserably. "Always. Look, Tom, if your sister needs anything…"

"We'll be all right, Louis. Our family can take care of our own."

"I know you can, Tom. I just mean, if there is ever *anything* I can do…"

Matson leaned from his mount and thrust his hand out to Louis. "We're friends, that's enough," he mumbled, then yanked the guide rope to Haney's horse and led it away.

For the first five miles back up River Road, Louis sat in total silence, his reins as slack as his face, while his mount dumbly followed behind Augustin and the hastily bandaged Ben. Then for the next five miles Louis talked nonstop, cleansing his soul of the guilt and remorse that threatened to wrench him apart—as well as the fear that the news of his deed might turn the public against his people. For four decades they had lived peacefully on the Isle, helping their neighbors. Still, there were those who envied them for their prosperity or despised them for their color, those who would seize upon any infringement of the law by them as an excuse to take away what was left of their rights. And now he had committed murder. *He had killed a white man.*

"You had no choice, Louis," Ben told him gruffly, unnecessarily. "If there is any trouble, I'll take full blame."

"That won't do any good, Ben. I'm the one who put the bullet in Haney."

"Nom de Dieu, Louis! He proved the kind of cur he was when he grabbed Matson's pistol to fire at you again without waiting his turn. A mad dog is a menace to society. You had to shoot him down."

"That's what I keep telling myself," Louis replied miserably. "It's just no comfort."

"It should be. Hey, Louis! What do you say to racing me home?"

"You? Race? Ben, you're in no shape!"

"Zut, Louis. I could hold these reins in my teeth, and my horse knows every turn in the road. Besides, we're just a mile from your house."

It was just a ruse. Augustin knew it. Ben's arm had to hurt like hell, despite the mud poultice he had applied before they mounted. But there never had been anything like a race to turn Louis's mind from trouble, and if Louis ever needed to forget his problems, this time was it.

"On your mark... go!" Ben cried, like the adolescent kid Louis used to race up and down the Point, and Louis could not resist the challenge.

"Hey, no fair," he shouted in his younger brother's wake. "You started too soon, but I'll catch you kid, I'll... "

He never finished his jibe. Startled by the sudden prod, his horse surged forward blindly, and one forefoot found a muddy pothole that her eye missed.

The mare's leg twisted, and she flung her low-crouched rider across her head and into the grove of cottonwood they were approaching.

Augustin heard the crunch, the sickening, fatal, crush of bone, as Louis catapulted head first into the trunk of the nearest tree. Before Ben could rein to a halt, Augustin had leaped from his horse with an agility long forgotten; but the blood that spewed from Louis's mouth told them there was nothing they could do, short of summoning the priest.

As Ben pounded furiously upriver, heedless of his own pain, Augustin slowly lowered himself into the mud beside his brother and cradled Louis's head in his lap, using his gnarled fingers and the soft mist of raindrops to wash the mud and blood trickling from Louis's mouth.

"Gustin?"

"Oui, mon frère?"

"That was a dumb fool thing I did this time, *non?*"

"It was an accident, Louis."

"Or justice."

"Non!" Augustin cried savagely, fighting the tears that were stinging him more fiercely than the rain. "It was *not* justice!"

"Gustin?"

"Oui?"

"Tell Baptiste-Louis to finish the house. I promised his mother we'd be in it by Easter."

"Oui, Louis."

"And tell Thérèse to hold that housewarming anyway—for us and for your Baptiste-Augustin when his is built. I want laughter in our new homes, Gustin. No tears."

"Mais oui, Louis," Augustin repeated the words yet again, numbly, for want of anything else that he could say.

"She gets it all, Gustin. And Baptiste-Louis. Tell him to make our hands toe the line, and not to let his little Théophile-Louis grow up indolent. I won't rest easy if my son and grandson fritter away everything I've worked for."

"They won't, Louis. You've raised your son better than that."

Louis's hand gripped Augustin's leg in a painful wrench. "One thing more, Gustin! You have to promise!"

"What, Louis?"

Louis Metoyer's "African House"

Melrose Plantation

Not a single nail holds together this little cabin, two stories high, where Louis hid his legacy to the woman and son he could not claim, lest he destroy for them the future that would free them from their past. The mushroom roof of the building still hides its own secret—an upper story—and shelters the lower floor from the most-torrential rains. Horizontal posts, wedged between the roof's edge and the upper walls, have held its weight since the eighteen-teens. Its builder was likely the adult male "African Negro" whom Augustin Metoyer purchased on 2 June 1809. Over nearly two centuries of use, it is said to have also seen service as a storehouse and a jail for slaves who committed one infraction or another. The lives of all the African-Americans who tilled the plantation's soil were commemorated in the mid-twentieth century by the plantation cook and primitive artist who used the four walls of the upper story of the African House as murals to depict a myriad of aspects of black rural life.

"See that Babe and Anthony get it, Gustin... *promise!*"

"Louis, I promise, but *what?*"

"Under the floorboards of Babe's old house... the one the African built... third board from the right side of the door. There's a box, Gustin. It's for Anthony."

"They'll get it, Louis. I promise."

"It's his money, Gustin," Louis said urgently, clutching at Augustin's arm. "It's for him to finish his schooling. He's going to college in the East... even if I won't see him graduate. Even if I lived, I couldn't see him graduate."

Pain gripped Louis again—the pain of dying, the pain of living, the pain of senseless laws and hate-ridden people. But the pain passed, and an ethereal smile washed over his face.

"This old sinner's met his Day of Reckoning, Gustin. You'd better pray for me one last time..."

Ꮪ 8 Ꮪ

Into the 1830s

Both Louis's Big House and Baptiste-Augustin's were built by Easter. Around them on the Isle a score of two-storied, white-columned mansion houses rose majestically as the thirties brought a fresh wave of prosperity. Even Auguste, the second-born son of Augustin and Agnes, who always had an ambitious finger in every promising pie, recognized the boundless possibilities that cotton now offered; and he left his New Orleans firm in the management of his white partner to buy a plantation on the Isle.

It was not a raw plantation either, the kind his brothers began with, the kind his father had given him when he married and he had promptly rented out. Nor the kind of small tract he had been buying for rental to one poor farmer or another. *Non,* the Baptiste Adlé place that Auguste now acquired was a fifteen-hand half-section, and its mansion-house came well stocked with fashionable furniture and elegant drapes that the Adlés had recently ordered through Auguste's New Orleans firm. As usual, Auguste had little ready cash to make his purchase. As fast as he took in a dollar, he always turned it back out again into one enterprise

417

Melrose,
Louis Metoyer's "Big House"

Construction was in progress when Louis died on 11 March 1832. The son who finished it, Baptiste-Louis, did not long survive him. Amid the depression that followed, it would be lost for debt by Louis's free-spending grandson, Théophile-Louis. In the wake of the Civil War, a new owner, a Scotch-Irish immigrant named Joseph Henry, gave the name "Melrose" to the plantation in tribute to the abbey where the heart of the warrior Robert Bruce lies buried. In 1975 Melrose was declared a National Historic Landmark.

or another. But in the new economy of the 1830s, he confidently signed his notes to Adlé for the entire fifty thousand dollars, payable sixteen thousand each spring through 1839.

Auguste and his modish wife then moved into their mansion in grand style. Only Augustin was not impressed.

"Son, everyone trusts your judgment. I know you have administered a dozen estates in this parish for planters of all colors. But what you have done now just plain worries me."

"What's different, Papa?" Auguste inquired offhandedly as he poured his father a glass of imported cognac from an exquisitely cut decanter, and drew up a plump *tabouret* for Augustin's feet. "I've bought land before."

"At reasonable prices and on reasonable terms." His father's tone was sober.

"By today's prices, this plantation was quite reasonable."

"That's the problem, son. Today's prices," Augustin retorted grimly. The real estate bubble that threatened their economy was, he knew, no bogey man. Speculators had gone wild. Andy Jackson had tried to curtail credit through a presidential order that government lands be paid for only in gold or silver. Yet, lunatics were paying insane prices for worthless, scrubby pine land—prices he, Augustin, used to pay for prime river-bottom tracts! America was headed for a crash, he was certain of that, and now was no time to go in debt for the kind of place Auguste had just acquired.

"Now, Papa," Auguste replied indulgently. "Land becomes more valuable when there's less of it to go around."

"And credit becomes more risky when too much of it goes around!"

Auguste laughed and swished his cognac unconcernedly around the rim of his glass. "Everything's done on credit, Papa. That's just the way business operates today."

"Then heaven help our country, because we're in for a fall! And those of you who are overextended will fall the hardest."

"Overextended?" Auguste parried, and Augustin could see his impatience mounting. "Look, Papa, you said it yourself. Every one else respects my judgment. Believe me, I have figured this out carefully. Counting my lands, my interest in the firm, my hands, and other investments, I have an accumulated worth in excess of seventy thousand dollars. Not counting this new place. That is a fortune in

Auguste Metoyer

Born 1800
to
Nicolas Augustin Metoyer
and
Marie Agnes Poissot

Marie Carmelite "Melite" Anty
(Mme. Auguste Metoyer)

Born 1807
to
Sieur Jean Baptiste Anty
and
Marie Susanne Metoyer

an economy in which labor costs a dollar and twenty-five cents a day."

"And aside from this place, you owe for nothing?"

"Oh, I have a few notes out here and there, like everyone else, but they are nothing to worry about."

"How much of that seventy thousand dollar figure of yours did your wife bring into the marriage, Auguste? I know Susanne and Anty both gave Melite a sizable dowry when she married you."

"Ah, yes, it was sizable enough, but it's in no danger. Look, Papa, as I said, I have—or Melite and I have—capital investments worth more than seventy thousand. I can well afford to sign a note for fifty. Besides, I did not have to put up collateral anyway. All it took was my signature and that of one surety."

"Who signed for you?" Augustin asked warily.

"Baptiste-Louis."

Augustin groaned. "Son, that grieves me even more. Not only your life's work is on the line now, but the plantation that Louis worked for, too. Young Baptiste-Louis will lose that if you fail."

"Papa!" Auguste's voice rose in exasperation. "I assure you, no estates are on the line. If worse comes and I can't make the payments on this place, I'll just let it go back to the Adlés. Since I haven't paid anything on it anyway, I will have lost nothing."

"If worse comes," Augustin retorted grimly, "the economy of this nation is going to collapse and prices are going to fall with it. You have never lived through hard times, boy; but I tell you, you're going to be left owing fifty thousand on a plantation that would sell for no more than ten!"

Auguste sat confidently across the broad room from his father, flexing his fingers as he always did when he was annoyed, his face a study in controlled impatience and filial tolerance. It was Augustin who lost his temper completely as he read his son's thoughts. His gnarled fist slammed onto a dainty mahogany table beside him, and a Dresden statuette shattered from the vibration.

"*Parbleu!* Auguste! How can I make you understand? This country is headed for a crash—and you along with it. If prices fall, not only will the value of this place drop, but everything else you have. That seventy thousand dollar you figure on paper will not be worth a fifth of that. You will drag Baptiste-Louis under with you. The land my dead brother fought to tame and fought to keep, you and his son will end up losing on an auction block!"

"No, Papa… "

"Don't you 'no Papa' me, as though I am a doddering old fool!" Augustin flung at his son as he stomped from the salon. "I am going home. For once I intend to try to forget my family's problems. This is just too much!"

The first of Auguste's payments came due that May, but he could not make it. The world's economy collapsed that spring, 1837, critically ill from speculative fever, overextended credit, and a weak financial pulse. Banking houses toppled and the government ordered all public monies into its hands. Merchants failed around the globe. Northern factories closed. Stored crops were worthless, and Southern planters who routinely relied upon Northern capital to finance each year's planting and harvest found themselves without seed money. Planters worth a hundred thousand dollars suddenly had no means to feed and clothe their families or their slaves.

In the parish of Natchitoches, where the planter owed the merchant, who owed the schoolmaster, who was himself indebted to the baker, who had built his own shop with a loan from the planter, frightened men took desperate action. Friends sued friends and brothers sued brothers, dispossessing them from their lands and homes, only to find that there were no buyers for the vacated property and they were left to pay additional taxes they could not afford. So, the victors of these court suits found themselves dispossessed in turn. Weak-hearted men gave up the struggle altogether and left widows and orphans to solve the crisis alone.

On the Isle of Canes, the insulated, self-sufficient *créoles de couleur* survived most of the nation's illness without serious suffering. As Augustin had constantly advised, most of them had avoided needless credit and ostentation. They lived well, but only as well as each man could afford. Their hands—or their menfolk in the young families that did not yet own slaves—raised their foodstuff, and their women preserved it. Children were reared in expectation of a good life, but most were taught that wealth was earned and kept by thrift. In the wake of the Crash of '37, like winter squirrels, the Islanders fell back upon their reserves. All except Auguste. He had none to fall upon. As his father had predicted, he dragged Baptiste-Louis into his disaster.

In the city of New Orleans, the firm of Metoyer, Jonau & Co. went bankrupt. Hundreds of its customers could not pay their long-standing accounts, and the firm, in turn, could not pay its own suppliers. To stave off demanding creditors, Auguste gave his own personal notes to cover his share of the debts. When those notes fell due, he still had no funds because the men who leased his lands could not pay their rent. There simply was no market now for the new crops they had produced. The series of "small and inconsequential" notes Auguste had dismissed so casually to his father, ranging from nine hundred to nine thousand dollars each, fell due as well. Then Baptiste Adlé filed suit against Auguste and Baptiste-Louis for repayment of the $50,000 debt.

"Papa, I need help," a contrite Auguste confessed at last in the summer of 1839. Two years of deprivation as he never had known before had left him gaunt and haggard, only half the man his father had been at forty. Two endless years of sidestepping loans and making promises he knew he could never keep—to himself as well as to his wife and creditors—had broken the self-assurance with which he had always met the world.

"How much, son?" Augustin asked quietly, without censure or reminders of his past advice.

"To clear all my debts? Sixty thousand."

"Auguste, you know I cannot lay my hands on that kind of cash right now! No one can." Still, the old man's voice was gentle. "What do you have left, son?"

"Not much, Papa," he confessed. "There's the small plantation south of here, with the Big House on it that I have been renting out, and a couple of partially cleared three-hundred-acre tracts across Little River. Narcisse Prudhomme has offered me three hundred and seventy-five dollars for one of them, but I can't let that land go for a dollar or so an acre!"

Augustin winced. Narcisse Prudhomme. Jean's brother—but also the husband of his own half-sister Elisabeth, who still denied their kinship. Squaring his old shoulders, he reprimanded himself for that thought as soon as he indulged himself in it. "Son," he finally said, sticking to the issue at hand, "even if you did give it away to Narcisse, it would still make no difference in your debt. In fact, it would not even pay a year's *interest* on your debt."

"I know, Papa," Auguste said despondently.

"What about Melite's dowry, and her inheritance from Susanne?" Augustin asked painfully. Of all the ways in which his accumulated years now taunted him, this was the worse: the steady, relentless beckonings of the Grim Reaper to those he loved.

de feue Susanne Metoyer

Passif

Dû à Florentin Conant

Pour un cheval à lui appartenant à la succession $ 110.—

la moitié sur le produit de la vente à
une charrette & de 3 reins   10.—

divers comptés par lui pour l'Ct de
la succession sur Bordeaux &c   2,637.85

sa commission comme administrateur
de la succession de 2½% $ 61,600.15½ 1,540.—   4,297.85

Répartition :

à Florentin Conant
Pour la part qui lui revient
comme héritier   11,460.46½

à Emanuel Florens
Pour sa part comme tuteur des en-
fans mineurs de feu Mde Arsène
Metoyer son épouse   11,460.46½

à Jn Bapte Metoyer fils d'Augustin
Pour la part de son épouse Mde
Suette Metoyer comme héritière   11,460.46½

à Henri Octave Dérouce
Pour la part de son épouse Mde
Aspasie Metoyer comme héritière   11,460.46½

à Auguste Metoyer
Pour la part de son épouse Mde
Emilie Metoyer comme héritière 11,460.46½ 57,302.30½

                               F Conant
                                 admr $ 61,600.15½

Distribution of Proceeds among Heirs of
Marie Susanne Metoyer

At her death in 1838, despite the worldwide financial crash that occurred the year before, the twin sister of Augustin Metoyer left an estate valued at $61,600.15½—the equivalent of $1,183,382 in modern currency. As a point of contemporary comparison, when the federal government in 1850 began to record property valuations on its censuses, the average farm in the parish of Natchitoches—one of the richest parishes in a state whose economy had already rebounded—was valued at $1,664. Susanne's principal plantation, land alone, went for $20,000, but her household inventory shows that she lived frugally. The only luxuries in which she indulged herself were a set of sterling silver flatware and a bicycle.

First there had been Louis, in that senseless spring of '32. Then the gay T'Pierre in '33. For four years, then, there had been a lull, a temporary respite, in which the Angel of Death seemed to have forgotten the Isle of Canes. But in the last long and terrible season of heat, He had reached out greedily, sowed the fever up and down Cane River, and reaped Augustin's beloved twin, their brother Joseph, his own son Maxille, and his daughter Marie-Louise who had wed Susanne's only son Florentin Conant. Then he took Victorin, the eldest of the three white siblings whose care his dead father had charged to him. Finally, that dreadful plague had felled the young Baptiste-Louis, who was already stressed from worry over the fifty thousand Adlé was attempting to collect from him, given that Auguste could not pay.

Still, the pain had not ended there. In the Holy Season of this spring, Dominique had slipped quietly into the night, as their own mother had done two decades before, leaving Augustin with no companions of his youth except Toussaint and François, the baby brothers he had rocked, fed, and spanked. Except Ben, whom Susanne had nursed with her own mother's milk, and Elizabeth, that sister who still disclaimed him. Now, his own beloved Agnes lay at death's door.

His Agnes. By this point, Augustin had totally forgotten the question he had asked his son, and a flicker of a smile lit his face as he recalled the curvy, tempting bride who had fired his blood, then the plump matron who had been his helpmate for almost a half-century. But the smile faded before it could catch hold. His Agnes now tossed feverishly in the same big four-poster bed in which his mother had died. She had not eaten in so long that her robust flesh had withered into great folds of flab. His Agnes no longer knew him when he wiped the sweat from her graying face or kissed the fingers he had adorned with all the rings he had promised her.

"Papa?"

Augustin started, shaken abruptly from his reverie. Wearily, he squared his shoulders and forced his mind back into the world of his son and the urgent problems of the living. "Forgive me, Auguste. My mind drifted away for a moment. What did you say about Melite's inheritance?"

His son's face reddened from its usual shade of light pecan to the flush of mahogany. "Well, Papa. Melite insisted that we use it to repay the debts. Some of the debts at least."

"You mean she has nothing left? Not even dotal interests from her father and mother?" Augustin's voice was as hard now as flint, as he began to calculate the course his son must take.

"No, sir."

"What about this year's crop?"

"It's still clear of mortgage, sir. The drought has been pretty bad, but even if the crop makes, there's no cash for bagging or roping or shipping it to market."

Augustin paced the length of his office, the same path he always paced, where the vivid floral pattern of his carpet now was worn and faded. Auguste sweated profusely as he waited, and he reached for the latest copy of *The North American Review* on his father's desk to press it into service as a fan.

"All right, son." Augustin at last made his pronouncement. Bending painfully, he retrieved a metal lockbox from the heavy iron safe behind his desk.

"I'll lend you as much as I can spare right now, which is twenty-three thousand and thirty-one dollars. You will make out a note to me in that amount, payable upon demand. You know I will not demand it, at least not until your present situation has improved, but if you have not repaid it by the time I, " his voice trembled slightly as memories overwhelmed him again, "go to meet my brothers, then this will be deducted from your share of whatever I leave behind."

"Yes, sir." Auguste said humbly.

"Now this is what I expect of you in return." Patiently but in excruciating detail—excruciating for both of them—he outlined the steps Auguste must take. Even this much money would not save Auguste and Melite from creditors unless their affairs were managed carefully in every regard. Therefore, first, Auguste must draw up a deed giving Melite full title to the plantation with the Big House, as well as one of the smaller tracts, and that document must make it clear that both are due to her for her dowry and her parental inheritance. "Which it is, *ma foi!*" Augustin added, visibly piqued. "By law, her money is *hers*. It should not go to settle *your* debts, and your creditors have no right to touch it."

"Yes, papa."

"To be doubly safe, I suggest that you have Melite file for a separation of property and the right to administer her own affairs, free from your control. She could not do any worse than you have done with it."

"No, sir," Auguste admitted ruefully, although he cringed at the thought of the humiliation that step would bring. Although Louisiana's new *Américain* laws had encouraged some wives in the parish to sue their husbands, demanding to manage their own property, it was unheard of among *their* people on the Isle!

"This will insure that she and your children will always have a roof to sleep under and land to till," Augustin continued bluntly. "In fact, I suspect Melite is enough like her mother to manage her estate quite well."

"You really think all this will work, Papa? We both know Adlé will try to get a judicial mortgage on that land on the basis that it has always been mine."

"Probably, but he will still lose. Louisiana law gives a man control over his wife's property, but it still guards her dotal and paraphernal rights." Augustin stared pointedly at his son. "It does so in order to protect her against a husband who might gamble or mortgage her money away."

Auguste attempted a halfhearted laugh. "Well, you have to say that much for me, Papa. I'm no gambler."

"There is a lot of good I could say about you," Augustin muttered gruffly, "but none of it would solve your problems. Now, about this loan…" Unsparingly, he laid out the rest of the steps Auguste would have to take. Ten thousand—he calculated quickly in his head—would pay all the outstanding debts, excluding Adlé. Those should be taken care of immediately. Thirteen hundred should then be set aside to finance the harvest, ship the crops, and support the plantation until the crop was sold. The rest, he should take to Adlé.

"The way the economy is now, son," Augustin predicted, "the man will be happy to get eleven or twelve thousand cash. Adlé is not unreasonable, and I dare say he would give you an extension, once he sees you are trying to pay. That would be far cheaper for both of you than more court battles, and if you can persuade him to drop that suit against Baptiste-Louis's heirs, they might have a chance to survive this depression themselves."

"They'd have stood a better chance if Baptiste-Louis had taught his wife a little about business," Auguste muttered. "Instead, he left a naive widow with an elderly mother-in-law and an adolescent boy to support."

"True enough. Everyone makes mistakes. But Baptiste-Louis never had a chance to correct his."

Auguste smiled wryly. "That feels like the prick of a barb, with just enough paternal padding to make it tolerable."

"The same old one I always use," Augustin smiled back, but his son's haggard face tightened as he rose. Auguste was halfway to the door when he impulsively turned back, closed the distance between himself and his father, and wrapped the old man in his arms.

"I'm not good at eating crow pie, Papa. I've always had a taste for strawberries. But thanks. I'll make it now. This looks to be a fair crop year for me in spite of the drought, and Pierre La Cour promises to pay three thousand dollars of what he owes me on the addition I sold him to his plantation. It might be years before I clear the last of what I owe Adlé, but I'll do it.

"I know you will, son," Augustin said quietly. "You're honest and you always did have spunk. Are you going up to see your Mama?"

"Yes, Papa."

"Kiss her for me. She won't know the difference, but do it anyway."

ᐁ 9 ᐃ

January 1841

The bells of St. Augustin pealed from the belfry tower and the winding river carried its echo up and down the length of the Isle, calling the faithful to worship. As always when Père Guistiniani made his monthly trip out from Natchitoches to say Mass, he had come the evening before and supped with the widowed Augustin and Gassion's growing family. Then the two men had sat into the small hours of the morning—one old and one less-so, one white and one less-so—savoring their pipes and discussing the problems of the ministry.

As always, too, the pair stood regally this Sunday morning in the doorway of the chapel, welcoming their parishioners, Père Guistiniani on the left and Augustin on the right, wrapped warmly against the winter cold in a black topcoat and muffler of soft wool, with furlined gloves and boots of the finest leather. Only his head was bare. It was never so cold that Augustin would not remove his top hat before he stepped onto the sacred grounds of the church.

"*Bon matin*, Grandpère, Père Guistiniani."

"*Mais oui*, Manuel. That's a fine filly pulling your carriage this morning. I don't believe I have seen her before."

"No, sir," Emanuel Dupré beamed. His square, flushed face was a masculine replica of the now-aging Adelaïde; but Manuel's countenance was a happy one that always brightened Augustin's heart. Try as hard as he might, Augustin never could find in this lad a trace of Adelaïde's cynicism that long had been his despair. The lad's a Dupré, thank the Lord! Augustin thought to himself this blustery morning as he cocked one eyebrow questioningly and waited for Manuel to continue.

"I won her in a poker game last night, sir."

"I figured as much," Augustin retorted, masking his own smile as Manuel belatedly remembered to remove his own top hat and then sauntered inside.

"Good morning, Mr. Metoyer, Father Guistiniani. It's good to see you again, both of you."

"And you also, Widow Thompson." Augustin flashed a cavalier smile in response. "My, but your little flock of daughters gets prettier every time I see them."

"Thank you, Mr. Metoyer. I'm right proud of them myself, if I may say so."

"Of course you may, Widow Thompson. You have every right."

"*Holà!* Gustin. Père. It's good of you to come out to the Isle again, Père."

"It's always my pleasure, Sieur Prudhomme," the jovial priest replied.

"By the way, Gustin," Prudhomme paused to add, "will you be at the cock fights this afternoon?"

"No, Jean, I think I'll sit them out today."

"Good," Prudhomme nodded. "I have a little matter I need to discuss with you sometime, and today should be as good a day as any."

"Two o'clock then?"

"*Bien, bien.* I'll be there."

Jean was punctual. It was his nature to be. Augustin and Père Guistiniani had dined leisurely after Mass with Gassion's family, and then the good father had tarried to drill young Gus on his catechism. He had bounced the younger babes genially on his knee, and paid Gassion's wife the usual litany of compliments on her hospitality. At last, he asked for his horse to be saddled and was barely astride before Jean rode into the yard.

"You're leaving so soon, Père," Jean asked politely.

"*Oui,*" Sieur Prudhomme. I should have left sooner. I am likely to be late for Rosary and Benediction at Natchitoches tonight, but I was having such a happy time in the bosom of M'sieur Metoyer's family."

429

Père Guistiniani turned warmly to Augustin. "Again, thank you for your hospitality, Augustin, and for the job you are doing here on the Isle. Never before have I had parishioners quite like your family."

"I do not doubt that!" Augustin chortled. "Have a nice ride back. We will all look forward to your next trip out."

"Merci. Au revoir."

"Au revoir, Père."

"Zut!" Jean sighed, tweaking the long, upturned ends of his graying mustache, as the priest rode out of sight. "I had a moment's worry, Gustin, when I came up the lane and saw him still here. The little matter I need to discuss with you this afternoon is hardly one to bring up in his presence!"

"Eh?" Augustin cocked his head in curiosity.

"No hurry, though. No hurry. Let's get in out of this damned cold and you can pour me a drink. If you can still stand out and talk in weather like this, you're holding up better than I am."

As Jean said, he was in no hurry. For the first hour, he talked about everything else except the "little matter" he had come to discuss. Together, he and Augustin worried over the price of cotton, which was down to nine cents a pound and still falling, and the fresh wave of business failures throughout the world. Clearly, they both agreed, the depression was getting worse, not better.

"I'll survive, though," Prudhomme predicted confidently. "If I live long enough. My main concern is the children."

"Both sons inherited your sound judgment, Jean. They will come through this."

"I expect so. But it's the young ones I'm thinking about now—er, Pompose's children."

Augustin did not need an explanation. Everyone along the river knew that after the frail Mme. Prudhomme died so young back in '18, leaving those two little boys, Jean swore he would never marry again. Instead, he had turned to the boys' nanny; and the life they had shared since then had added another two sons and a daughter to the children Jean generously supported.

"As you may have heard, Gustin, I gave my little Aspasie her freedom some time back—she and her brothers, as well as their mother."

"Oui?"

"Well, Aspasie worries me now, Gustin. The boys seem to be doing all right, but lately I've seen Aspasie out walking with some of the slave boys she grew up with. Gustin, I can't have my girl going with the blacks! I just can't!"

"I know," Augustin said simply. From the recesses of his mind there rang the echoes of that long-ago conversation in his father's study, when old Pierre had said more or less the same thing to Coincoin about Susanne.

In the century past, Augustin knew, when Louisiana was so young, it was quite possible for a white or a freeman to "go with" the blacks openly and still be accepted in society. His father had. But times had changed so much. The difference had been serious enough when he and Susanne were young and looking for love, but since then…. *Non,* young Aspasie Prudhomme was mostly white. If she socialized in the black world, she would earn for herself the same degradation all blacks suffered.

"That's why I'm asking for your help, Gustin. The child's mother tells me that one of your grandsons, Florival, I believe, has squired Aspasie to a few dances."

"*Oui.* In fact, he brought her out a couple of Sundays ago to see me."

"Do you think Florival might be ready for marriage? There's a lot to be said, Gustin, for such a union. Obviously they like each other, and our families always have been friends. Naturally, I want Aspasie to have the best in life that she possibly can have, and she could do no better, as far as I'm concerned, than a grandson of yours. By the same token, she's been raised well, and she'll make the boy a good, virtuous wife."

"I'm sure she will, Jean."

"There's one other consideration, too, Gustin. You need to know that I've already promised Aspasie's mother a thousand for the girl's dowry. I'm willing to add another fifteen hundred donation to that. Combined with what Florival will undoubtedly get as a wedding present from Baptiste-Augustin and Suzette, the young folks should start off quite comfortably. It would behoove both of them to consolidate their nest eggs. In times like this, it's the only chance young people have."

"True," Augustin said slowly. "Jean, you know I'm agreeable. I even think Florival will be, too, judging from the looks he was giving her the other day. Still, it is totally up to them. I will call Florival in and talk to him, but I will not put any pressure to bear on the boy. He is the one who has to spend his lifetime with whomever he marries, and I will not force him into a union he will not be happy in. No amount of money is worth that."

"Of course not, Gustin."

"What about Aspasie? Have you mentioned this to her?"

"No, not yet. But what do young girls really know about love? They moon over a different young blade every week, depending upon who brought them the biggest bouquet of wild roses or asked for the most dances at the last ball."

"Perhaps," Augustin smiled. "But if Aspasie is like the rest of the Prudhommes, she will know her own mind. I have not known one yet who did not know exactly what he or she wanted and how to get it!"

Jean laughed. "A point well made, Gustin. I can't argue with it."

"Then it is completely up to the young ones?"

"Completely. Still, I suspect they will both follow our advice. By the way, speaking of lovers, has Toussaint married T'Pierre's widow yet?"

"No, and I doubt that he will, although I would never say that to his face." Augustin sighed wearily at the very thought of that long standing problem. Toussaint was now a fifty-eight-year-old boy, as blindly in love as he was when he tried to buy Henriette's freedom thirty years before. To Henriette, though, he was still a friend, a brother, and everything else but a lover. It was Émile Colson she had been seeing lately, and it was likely to be Émile Colson she would marry. He just wished she would hurry up and do it. T'Pierre had been dead for eight years now, and the longer she remained a widow, the more hopeful Toussaint has gotten.

"Grandpère! I have the most fabulous news!" Lost in his thoughts, Augustin had not heard his granddaughter as Barbe bounded up the stairs and scooted in from the gallery. Lost in the excitement of her own world, she had not noticed that he had company.

"Oh! I'm sorry, sir!"

"That's all right, Barbe," Augustin greeted her fondly, smiling at the sight of her in the beaver-trimmed coat and mittens he had given her last Christmas, pertly blowing little puffs of breath upward to warm her reddened nose.

"Forgive me, M'sieur Prudhomme! I didn't see your horse outside. Well, I really didn't look," she added lamely.

"There's no need to apologize, Ma'mselle. I was just leaving anyway." Jean bowed politely, though a bit stiff with years, as he rose.

"By the way, Jean, you do remember my granddaughter Barbe? Florival's sister?"

Prudhomme's surprise—and interest—was visible. *"This* is Barbe? The child who used to follow you around worshipfully at the races?"

"Until she grew up and discovered boys!" Augustin laughed.

"I am sure they have discovered her, as well!" his old friend replied appreciatively, as he studied her soft, bouncy brown curls and dancing green eyes, the finely chiseled, upturned nose and the slender form—and especially the creamy olive of her complexion. Again, he told himself that the marriage of his Aspasie to this girl's brother would be an ideal match.

"Do talk to your grandson, Gustin. I will be anxiously awaiting his decision. Good day, M'amselle. Please give my regards to your family."

"Oui, M'sieur." Barbe curtsied graciously, but the heavily paned door between the salon and the gallery had barely closed behind the departing guest before Barbe shucked her winter wear, bounced onto the warm spot he left on the sofa, tucked her daintily shod feet, boots and all, up under her, and hugged her knees ecstatically.

"Oh, Grandpère, you'll never guess what!"

"You're in love," Augustin teased.

"Oh! You spoiled my surprise! How did you know?"

"This just seems to be the day for it."

"Hehn? I mean *sir?"*

"Nothing, child." Augustin sank back onto the sofa beside her and propped his own feet up on the tabouret. To his dismay, they seemed to swell now whenever he stood for any time at all, and those once-a-month Sunday mornings at the chapel door had become a painful trial of his faith.

"Who's the lucky fellow, *ma petite?* If I recall correctly, you danced with twenty-three of them at the Christmas Ball, and as far as I could tell every one of them adored you."

"Oh, Grandpère," she giggled. "That's why I love you. You make me feel *special.* Bernard does too," she added dreamily.

"Bernard? Sieur Dauphine's son?"

"Oui. Oh, I've had the wildest fantasies about him ever since he came to teach in l'Académie, but I never dreamed he'd feel the same about me. Isn't he the most *divine* man, Grandpère?"

"Well, I have never been one to think of other men as divine, at least not the way you mean it," Augustin countered lightly, but the news did not sit well upon his heart. Dauphine was well educated, probably more so than any *Créole de couleur* in Louisiana, and it had been quite a coup when Augustin had attracted the young man to l'Académie de l'Isle after his return from Europe. Still, Dauphine worried him. The lad's admirers called him poetic, but when Augustin looked into the brooding pools of Dauphine's eyes, he saw trouble.

"Has Dauphine said anything to you yet, child?"

"*Oui!* But I wish you wouldn't call me a *child!* I'm a woman now!"

"I know, Barbe," he smiled. "Forgive an old man for his habits."

"He asked me this morning. In *church*," Barbe giggled. "Right when Père Guistiniani intoned *To you I lift up my soul!* Oh, don't look like a fuddy-duddy, Grandpère. I know you don't like whispering during Mass. But it's not every day a girl gets proposed to by the most magnificent man in the whole world."

"Has he spoken with your father?"

"He will tonight. But I just had to tell you first. I know Papa will say yes. He *must!*"

"Barbe?" Augustin's voice was grave, but his granddaughter was so mesmerized that she did not notice. He began again. "There is no gentle way to say what you need to hear; but please believe me, I say it because I love you and I care about your happiness and your future."

This time she caught the anxiety in his voice. "Oh, Grandpère, you sound positively foreboding!"

"Old men worry, Barbe. By the time a man's past seventy, he's seen so much of the world. Too much, maybe. Was it not Dauphine who showed that little fit of jealousy at the ball when you turned him down to dance with Antoine Rachal?"

"Well, I'd already promised Antoine. I couldn't break a promise!"

"That's not my point."

"Oh, you're worried because he gets jealous." Barbe's eyes danced impishly. "Really, I don't mind a beau being jealous. I think it's romantic! It means he *cares* about me."

"It might mean he cares too much, *chérie*—too much about *possessing,* and not enough about *loving.* Love does not try to imprison a person, or bind too tightly."

"Oh, Grandpère, really! Bernard's not tried to do *anything* such as *that!*"

"There are many ways of doing it, *ma petite.* Most are hard to see when one is blinded by love. Promise me you will give it your serious thought?"

"Oh, I promise," Barbe laughed. "I think about Bernard all the time. *Coo-lee!* It's almost dark. I must dash home and put on a fresh dress before he comes courting tonight. Mama agreed for me to invite him over for supper!" She jumped lightly on her feet and bent to kiss the tip of his big broad nose a fond good-bye, as she always did.

"Oh, by the way, if Papa says yes, can you arrange for Père to marry us on the next trip out? I know that won't give Mama much time to plan a wedding, but Bernard doesn't want to wait. He's afraid he might lose me! Fancy that!"

Augustin forced himself to smile. "If your father says yes, I'll talk to Père. Perhaps we'll make a double-wedding of it."

"Oh?"

"Sieur Prudhomme thinks there might be a match in the making between Florival and Aspasie."

"Oh, there is," Barbe squealed, "but…"

"But what?"

"Well, I'm not sure we should make it a double wedding. I mean, Sieur Prudhomme would come, wouldn't he?"

"I am sure he would. Is there some reason you do not like him, Barbe?"

"Oh, no. It's not him… and not me… I mean, well, it's Bernard. He saw me talking to one of M'sieur's sons before church this morning, and it was all so innocent. He just asked me about the new filly papa bought from him because he knew it was a present for me. Only, Bernard was a little bit upset. I mean, he more or less told me that he did not ever want to see me talking to a Prudhomme again. Or any *white* man."

Worry stabbed at Augustin again.

"Oh, I don't really blame him," Barbe went on hurriedly. "You see, he loved this girl once in New Orleans, but she turned him down to *placer* with someone white. Oh, don't look so shocked, Grandpère! Of course, I know about such things! What's important is that Bernard told me all about this disastrous affair of his. See? He's totally honest, and this explains why he's jealous. He's afraid of being hurt again. But I'll never hurt him, and so he will soon get over his jealousy. Just wait and you'll see."

"I hope so, child."

"Only, in the meanwhile," Barbe added hesitantly, "I think I should avoid the Prudhommes."

"Whatever you say, *chérie*. I only want your happiness," Augustin said quietly.

Despite himself, memories of the long-forgotten Desirée flitted back to taunt him, and for a moment his heart went out to young Barbe's Dauphine. But then an ache overwhelmed him, and it was not the vise of past wrongs but a clutch of worries over those to come. Masking it all, he kissed her good-bye, closed the door behind her as she skipped gaily down the outside staircase, and sank into his chaise in the shadows of his salon—alone now, with the bittersweet memories of his past and his premonitions of all he saw ahead.

✂ 10 ✂

Barbe's papa agreed to the marriage, as she knew he would, and she scheduled hers for Sunday morning so she could leave with Dauphine on her honeymoon to St. Louis and points north before her brother wed Aspasie Prudhomme that same evening. Old Chevalier, who had long since retired from l'Académie to the plantation he had saved for years to buy, had agreed to teach Dauphine's classes in his absence. Three months elapsed, then, before the honeymooners returned to the Isle of Canes.

A week more passed, then ten days, and Barbe did not come again to Yucca Bend to see her old Grandpère, even though she and Dauphine had taken a residence just a mile upriver. At first Augustin reminded himself that she was now a married woman and he could not expect her to be as close to him as she had been before. She had a home and a husband to care for now, and he would be selfish to expect her to come tripping gaily up his steps every other day to share her secrets. Still, he missed her, and so one morning after breakfast, he called his houseman to bring his buggy around and he rode up River Road.

Dauphine had just left, as Augustin had hoped, and Barbe greeted him warmly. She was already dressed. Beautifully so. Obviously Dauphine had outfitted her with the latest fashions in St. Louis. Her curls were artfully arranged and her cheeks hinted of just the slightest brush of rouge, but her eyes were hollow. She chattered on, describing everything they had seen, everywhere they had gone, but her laughter had none of the lilt that made Barbe *Barbe*.

"What is the matter, *chérie?*" Augustin asked abruptly, interrupting her long description of their train ride from St. Louis to Chicago.

"Why, Grandpère! Whatever do you mean?"

"Do not fence with me, child. You are not happy. I can see it in your eyes. In your voice. In the way you move. Everything you do and say seems to be calculated to hide your real self. You never were like this before."

"Before what, Grandpère?"

Augustin did not bother to answer. His eyes looked deep into hers, searching for the truth, until her eyelids dropped and she turned her face aside.

"I'm just not a child any more, Grandpère."

"We have already agreed on that."

For a moment she hesitated, coloring ever so slightly. "I'm *enceinte*," she said softly.

"I am not surprised. That goes along with marriage. But that is not your problem, Barbe. I have seen enough pregnant women in my lifetime to know they do not wither. They bloom. If they are happy."

"You think I'm not happy, Grandpère?" she countered again.

"That's obvious, child."

Barbe was silent, and her silence was a clear admission.

"Can I help, *chérie?*"

"Oh, Grandpère!" she wailed, throwing herself into Augustin's arms as though she were a child again.

"Now you are beginning to act like a pregnant woman, crying on a moment's notice," Augustin tried to tease, softly patting the fluff of curls upon his chest. "Tears are normal, only your grandmother usually shed hers when there was absolutely nothing to cry over."

"Well, there isn't really," she sniffed. "It's just me. I just don't know what to do."

"About what?" he asked quietly.

"About Bernard's jealousy. Oh, Grandpère. I wish you had tried harder to make me understand. I thought it was sweet that he *cared* so much. But you were right! It does make me feel like I'm imprisoned inside someone else's world!"

Augustin said nothing. What Barbe needed, he knew, was to think through the frustrations pent inside her.

"Grandpère, I've never done *anything*. I'd never be unfaithful to Bernard. I would not even want to. I'm just not that kind of person. But he gets the wildest fears, every time another man even looks at me. Once a bellboy brought a pitcher of cool water when I rang for it, and he asked if there was anything else he could do for me. It was all totally innocent, but Bernard flew into a rage! Oh, Grandpère, what do I do?"

Augustin's voice was heavy. "There is not much you can do now, child. He is your husband. For always. Whatever his faults may be. All you can do now is what you say you are doing. Be sure your own behavior is above reproach. Always. Then pray for him and for yourself." Although he could not bring himself to say so plainly, in his own heart Augustin doubted the man would ever change. This news of hers, which was no news at all to him, pained him so much that he rued the day he had invited that troubled scholar to the Isle. The only comfort he could find, or give, now was the surety that if she prayed for it, she would find the grace to continue loving the good in Bernard and to accept the rest.

So, Barbe tried. For a while her prayers seemed to be answered. As her pregnancy began to show, she stayed in even more than she had before, embroidering the chest of dainty cottons and linens the baby would need, and her husband glowed at the domesticity that greeted him each evening. Anxious to convince him of her commitment to home and marriage, she sought out the company of the one companion she knew he would approve, her cousin Perine—the most domestic, *plainest,* and least coquettish spinster that surely ever existed on the Isle of Canes! From Perine, she even learned to cook.

"*Ma foi!*" she found herself muttering under her breath one day, elbow-deep in flour and nauseous from the smell of the peppery mix that simmered on the cookstove, waiting to be assembled into meat pies. "*Ma foi!* I can't even *eat* the damn things now! Why in the bejibbers am I making them?"

It was during Christmas week that little Augustin Dominique was born, and Dauphine became the most enraptured father in the world. As soon as Manuel Dupré reopened his store after the holidays, Bernard ordered an elegant, leather-bound and gold-tooled little book, its pages blank; and he filled it with loving poems to his new son. Too soon, as Barbe regained her lithesomeness, as she grew bored of Perine's talk of *recipes* instead of Cousin Elise's *outré* new frock, and she began to leave the house with Augie to show him off to all her friends after her housework was done, Dauphine's jealousy returned. By spring he was even moodier, more chameleonic than ever.

That was when they began to fight. The tempestuous Barbe had curbed her nature past endurance. She had meant it when she told her Grandpère she was not the kind of wife to dally with another man. When she pledged her troth, she had given up all the coy but meaningless flirtations that come so naturally to pert and pretty girls. Yet neither her faithfulness nor her prayers had cured her husband's unreasonable, unbearable jealousy.

So they fought. If Antoine Rachal doffed his hat at her outside church, even with his own sweet bride on his elbow, or if Tranquilin Lecomte stopped to twit little Augie's nose, Bernard read something more into their actions. Especially those of Tranquilin. Although young Lecomte's Indian aunt was the old widow of Barbe's Oncle Louis, his own mother had been white, and Tranquilin moved freely in white society. That, Bernard could never forgive.

After every argument there always was a week or so in which Bernard really seemed to change. He would lavish Barbe with presents, a matching vanity set from Manuel's store, perhaps, or an ivory comb to hold her curls. He would stand over her for an hour at night, brushing her long, unfurled locks. When little Augie cried in hunger and Barbe went to nurse him, Bernard would while away the interval caressing the silk stockings Barbe had carelessly flung on the boudoir chaise, or pensively fondling the bottles of creams, lotions, and perfumes he was always buying her. He would sit up through long and sleepless nights and compose sonnets of love to his sweet Barbe. Sooner or later, though, his inner torment would overwhelm him and there would come another senseless clash.

By the next Christmas, Barbe was once more *enceinte* and again, as she stayed modestly at home, Bernard's jealousy abated. Three weeks before their third anniversary, she presented him with another son, and then the old cycle of their lives began again. She donned a new gown for the infant's christening, and his eyes devoured her hungrily. Yet by the time they returned from the chapel, he was in another rage over her warm greetings to the Monette cousins who had attended.

That fit of fury soon faded into remorse, as usual. As the long summer waned in '44, Barbe had begun to hope again. She even said as much to Perine, who had by this time become her sole companion—and that, itself, gave testimony to how desperate Barbe had become. Born to privilege, sheltered from want, and indulged by all for her saucy charm, she once had fancied herself *princess* of the Isle. In those childish games that had lasted way too long into her adolescence, it had been Perine, two years younger and infinitely plainer, who she had relegated to the role of lady-in-waiting. Those roles had stuck. Now, as the adult Barbe struggled with the consequences of her vanity, it was the illusion she had created of herself as *princess* of a perfect world that kept her from admitting—to anyone but her Grandpère—that the world she had created for herself was disastrously *imperfect.*

Trapped by her pride, she simply lived her charade, until the morning Perine walked over with yet another smock she had made for Barbe's new babe. Touched at that moment by her cousin's utter *goodness,* Barbe had spilled her grief, her hopes that Bernard had begun to mellow, her fears that he never would, and her desperation to escape the mess she had made of what was supposed to be her *perfect* world as Mme. Bernard Dauphine.

The no-nonsense Perine, as Barbe should have known she would, counseled her to pray for the best, but prepare for the worst. If Barbe expected her looks to support her in happiness and high style, then she might as well give up on Bernard now, move down to *la ville,* and find somebody more to her liking to set her up on Rampart Street. But if she was as virtuous as she claimed, then she'd better fill her pretty head with something practical that she could make a living at. Otherwise, the princess would one day be a pauper.

As the shadows of the morning began to shorten, Perine had left her with a sudden, "Oh, my goodness! It's almost noon, and I promised Grandpère I'd clean the church today!" Then, in her wake, there had come the young M'sieur Prudhomme, in search of Barbe's brother Florival.

"I'm sorry, M'sieur," Barbe told him. "I've not seen him for several days."

"*Zut!*" he swore mildly. "I've got this horse he's been wanting to buy, and since I was on my way down to Cloutierville, I thought I'd drop it off, but no one was at home when I passed by his place."

"You're welcome to leave it here, M'sieur. I'll see that he gets it."

"*Merci,* Madame. I really appreciate that. It will save me another trip. Say, I hate to impose still more, but I'm hellishly thirsty. Can I beg a drink of water?"

"Of course. Come on in," she smiled, and went to fetch the pitcher and a glass from the buffet.

That was when Bernard came home for lunch, and the scene that followed was one Barbe knew would haunt her forever. His delicate face turned as white as he longed for it to be when he walked through the doorway. The sensitive flare of nostrils that once had excited Barbe began to quiver, and the limpid green eyes hardened into a hatred she had never seen before on any man. As Prudhomme extended his hand in greeting, Dauphine drew back his riding crop and its whip snapped across the shoulders of his guest. By the time Prudhomme recovered from his shock and succeeded in wresting the crop from his attacker, a half-dozen more blows had fallen.

Denuded of his weapon, Dauphine stood defiantly, glaring wordlessly, as if he dared the Frenchman to use the crop on him in return. Prudhomme threw it aside. For a moment he started to explain the innocence of his presence there, but then he saw the futility of any explanation and he left with a simple, expressive, "Oh, hell!"

Barbe did try to explain; but the queerest, almost ethereal, look possessed Bernard's face and he walked out their door without his lunch. By the supper hour, his classes at l'Académie had long since ended, but Dauphine still did not come home. Her eyes reddened from a day of crying that had upset the little Augie as much as it had her, Barbe went to bed alone for the first time in three years of marriage, but she lay sleepless. Another day dawned, and a warm sun began a game of peek-a-boo through clouds dancing on a breeze. That was when she heard the hooves of an approaching horse.

Barbe's heart leaped, momentarily, but then she heard buggy wheels rolling amid the hoofbeats and knew it was not Bernard. Desolately, as the wheels stopped outside, she opened the door and collapsed into her grandfather's arms.

"There now, child. It's all right, *chérie.*" Over and over, Augustin whispered soft words of comfort until her sobbing eased. "Things always work out, *ma petite.*"

"Oh, Grandpère!" she wailed.

Augustin gently wiped a pool of tears from the deep sockets of her eyes. "I presume Bernard's not here."

"*Non,* Grandpère," she sobbed. "Not since yesterday noon."

His face was grim. "I hate to tell you, child, but Bernard was not at school when the students arrived for class this morning."

Barbe's swollen eyes widened in surprise and fear. Bernard had never missed a class, not one, since he arrived on the Isle, except for that period of their honeymoon. "But where?"

"We do not know, *chérie,* but Dubreuil, the new math teacher, found this on Bernard's desk. It was on top of everything else, on the first sheet of a fresh pad. Oscar told me what it says, more or less, but it is something you should read for yourself."

Her eyes glazed with fear, sleeplessness, and a thousand questions and regrets; she all but snatched the paper from her grandfather, sank into her chaise, and unfolded it.

*Adieux**

Dearest one, why have you
So soon dispelled the transports of my love?
Do you remember the days when you were so enamored
And you promised me a happiness without regret?
Adieu, good-bye, pardon if my faithful heart
Cannot detach itself from you.
I am going to pay today with my life
For the happy day when I received your trust.

> *Good-bye, from the celestial vault of heaven*
> *I will watch over your destiny.*
> *There will end the unhappiness of life,*
> *Which already approaches its end.*

When tormented by a secret pain,
Your fickle heart will recognize the sorrow.
Come, pray to God at my tomb, please,
For there you will be reborn to happiness.
And the Eternal One hearing your prayer,
In memory of our past love,
Will place a flower on the marble tomb
Which will cover my dried remains;

> *Good-bye from the celestial vault of heaven,*
> *I will watch over your destiny.*
> *There will end the unhappiness of life,*
> *Which already approaches its end.*

---

*Published posthumously in *Les Cennelles* (New Orleans, 1845).

Barbe did not cry as Augustin had thought she would. Instead, she fainted. Drawing on a strength he did not know he still had, he gathered her into his arms and put her into his carriage, then her babes, and he took his little Barbe back home with him.

They did not find Dauphine that day, but as dusk fell Jean Prudhomme rode out to see his old friend. Painfully, he related how Bernard had appeared on his son's gallery the night before, card in hand, to demand a duel. Reluctantly, young Prudhomme had agreed to meet the schoolmaster at daybreak, on the opposite side of Bayou Brevelle at the point where the stream was usually forded. But Dauphine had not kept that appointment. At first, Jean's son had assumed the man had changed his mind, but the more he recalled the hate in Dauphine's face, the more convinced he became that nothing short of death itself would have kept him from that rendezvous.

As the sun rose again on the east side of the river, a search party fanned the banks of old Bayou Brevelle, the muddy stream that sliced the Isle in two. In one of the clumps of brush that lined the stream, a half-mile from the rain-swollen shallows where he was to have rendezvoused with Prudhomme, they found him.

Frail and ascetic, Dauphine had always scoffed at all things physical and had turned lovingly to his books. The scholar had never learned to swim. At his end, possessed by jealousy, blinded to caution, and driven to keep his assignation with a man whose expertise with pistols was well known, he had attempted to ford the swollen stream alone. There, in the pitch black hours of predawn, he had lost his footing and had been swept away. Dauphine still had kept his appointment with death.

11

September 1845

"Mr. Metoyer, you just gotta understand my position!" The burly captain was twice the size and breadth of Augustin as he stood before him, barring the entrance to the steamboat's gangplank. A wild mop of carroty hair tumbled from beneath his cap, and his ruddy complexion was flushed with more than the autumn heat. His right eye twitched nervously as he stared at the withered old *Créole de couleur* who confronted him, dressed to the nines, and his face was plastered in exasperation.

"The way I see it, Mr. Metoyer, I'm doing you a pretty big favor just stoppin' here at Yucca Landing to drop off your newspapers. I mean, back in the days when this was the main loadin' point for the Isle, it wasn't such an inconvenience to the boats to do you a little favor such as this, but my company's rule book says I don't have to stop this steamer anywhere on the Isle 'cept down at Dupré's Ferry."

"Captain Callahan?" Augustin's inflection suggested that he was about to ask a question, but his tone was imperial. "It was in June that you took over this Cane River run, wasn't it?"

"Yessir, 'bout that time."

"By June our family had already shipped its produce to market, so I cannot expect you to be acquainted with the full extent of the business we do with your company."

Augustin's voice was as taut as his face, now, but it stayed well under control.

"Mr. Callahan, last year we loaded onto this one steamboat one thousand one hundred and sixty-seven bales of cotton, upon which your company collected from us over four thousand dollars in shipping fees. This is exclusive of the other produce we ship from here and the goods we bring in. My people now amount to one hundred and twelve families. We operate five mercantile establishments and other shops that serve farmers for ten miles in every direction. Your company, until now, has shipped all the goods we order from New Orleans or from Europe. Would you not say that puts us among your best customers?"

The captain's distress was visible in the bobbing of his adam's apple. "Yessir, Mr. Metoyer. I've not done any checkin' of back figures yet, but assumin' what you say is true…"

"If it were not so, I would not have said it," Augustin interrupted curtly. "I will overlook everything you have said up to this point, since you are new on this run. But I'll tell you this plainly, Callahan: when you empty your boat at Shreveport and come back by here on your way downriver, I expect a stateroom to be reserved for me and my son. We ship first class, and we travel first class."

"But Mr. Metoyer! I read the company rule book through an' through. It's just against policy. Colored people sleep on the deck. The staterooms are for… for…"

"For whites, Mr. Callahan?"

"Yessir."

"Then you had better look at me and see nothing but my white blood, Mr. Callahan—or green, which is the color of my money. My people do not sleep atop the freight on deck, among slaves and white trash. When we take this boat to New Orleans, we take a stateroom, and we will have one this time or else the one hundred and twelve families of this Isle will do their shipping with the *River Queen* from now on."

"Now, Mr. Metoyer. I'm sure we can work out a compromise or somethin'. Maybe a couple of special cots tucked off somewhere?"

"Callahan, when you get to Natchitoches, you take a few minutes and go see some of those merchants who patronize your boat there. You ask them two things. First, you ask them whether I have misrepresented to you the volume of shipping my people do. Second, you ask them if I am not a man of my word."

"Now, I don't doubt that, Mr. Metoyer."

"Then you think on it before you get back here. I am confident that in three days you will pull up here at Yucca Landing and your crew will carry our baggage to our stateroom. *Au revoir,* sir!"

Seventy-two hours later, the *Neptune* sounded its whistle at the juncture of Bayou Platte on the boat's return trip downriver. Within ten minutes it had pulled up at Yucca Landing, and its captain stood attentively by the gangplank as Augustin, Gassion, and a pair of servants strode to the dock, where a ready crew relieved the servants of the luggage.

"Right this way, Mr. Metoyer," the captain boomed. "This is your son, sir? Good to know you, too, sir. By the way, I picked up another passenger a bit upriver who says he's a good friend of yours, a Mr. Prudhomme. I'm glad you'll have genial company to while away the trip with, sir."

"I'll bet you are, Captain Callahan. Thank you. We have always enjoyed our excursions aboard the *Neptune*. I am sure we shall this time also."

"Gustin, you old fox!" Jean greeted him warmly as the double-decker built up a head of steam and wheezed on down toward Le Court's Bluff and Monette's Ferry, where it would then head back into Red River for its descent to *la ville*. "I hear you gave Callahan a hard time the other day!"

"Eh? Do folks along this river have anything else to do but gossip?"

"Nothing more pleasurable! I rode into Natchitoches yesterday, and everybody was laying bets on the new captain and what he was going to do with you."

"I hope you put your money on the right odds."

"Oh, I did, Gustin! Say, there's a friendly game of bourrée going on in the back of the dining room. I don't know a couple of the fellows, but I recognized James Wallace from Caddo Lake and old Cornelius Cargill's son, Derostus. You two interested?"

"What else does an old man have to do for fun, Jean?" Augustin chuckled. "Gassion?"

"You go ahead, Papa. I'll sit this game out. I'm behind on my reading, and if I don't catch up this trip I likely won't have another chance until winter."

"Well, for once I'm glad I never learned to read!" Augustin chortled again. "Go on and bury yourself down in the stateroom. I'll see you at supper."

At a quarter past four, the card game broke up, and the men left the dining hall as waiters began to set up the tables for the evening meal. By five before five, long lines were forming in eager anticipation of the bell that would ring promptly on the hour. Freshened for supper, Augustin and Gassion rejoined their old friend on deck and took their places in line, but when their platters were served they turned abruptly and headed away from the long rows of tables. Jean followed them and discreetly caught Augustin's elbow.

"Gustin! You're not going to eat out on the deck, are you?" he asked quietly.

"Of course not. We always take our plates to our stateroom."

"Well, I won't hear of it, Gustin! You paid for first-class passage, and you'll eat with first-class passengers!"

"Jean, there are things a man can do and things he cannot. There are points to push, and there are those not worth bothering over. When I travel, I expect a good bed to sleep in and privacy to do it. I expect to be fed just as well as any other man. Beyond that, if they do not want me to sit down at their dining table, then I do not care for their company either."

"To hell with *their* company, whoever *they* are. You are in my company, too, and I insist, Gustin."

"Jean," Augustin patiently explained the obvious. "Every table over there accommodates far more than just the three of us."

"Then, by Jove, we'll find a smaller table. Waiter! Where's that little table we used for our card game?"

"Jean, for goodness sake! Don't start a scene," Augustin muttered.

"Oh, hush, Gustin! Waiter! There's space for that little table by the railing where we'll have a prime view of everything that passes by. Set it up there."

"But Mista… "

"Young man, I'll call your captain if I have to, but I'd prefer to eat before my food is cold. I want that small table set with fresh linen and three sets of flatware, and I want it done promptly."

"Yassuh, Mista."

"Jean," Gassion murmured amid the bustle of setting up the table. "We really wish you would not do this. Papa and I would much prefer the privacy of our stateroom."

"Well, I much prefer your company to some of the rabble I see around here. But if you don't sit down and start eating, we're not going to finish before they clear the place and bring in sleeping cots for the second-class passengers. Gassion, how did your reading go? Find anything worth discussing?"

"Most of it depressing," Gassion replied resignedly. "Every newspaper I picked up had nothing but reports of bad crops, caterpillars, and budworms, or last year's flood and this year's drought."

"The situation is getting desperate. There's no doubt about that. It has been seven years since the crash, and we haven't had a decent crop year yet. I swear, I don't know how much longer people can survive. The children have been wanting me to bring a painter up from New Orleans to do more family portraits, but that's a luxury nobody can afford right now."

"Didn't Feuille do a couple for you when he was up here in '36?" Augustin asked.

"*Oui*, but the family has grown so much since then."

"I know how you feel. He did oils of Agnes and myself, and Auguste and Melite gave him a commission for theirs, but then the fever season ended and he was in a hurry to get back to *la ville*; so the rest of my people didn't get theirs done before the crash. It's beginning to look as though they never will."

"Frankly, Papa," Gassion interjected, "your words may be more true than you realize. The way things are shaping up on the race issue, we may never again find an artist to take our commissions . The white ones will no longer do it, and the colored ones won't stay in America because there aren't enough well-to-do colored Creoles to keep them in business."

"I'm ashamed to admit it," Jean agreed quietly, "but you may be right. The newspapers praise America for being the 'great melting pot,' or something equally silly; but the races and the nations haven't come together. There's more intolerance now than there ever was."

"Especially toward colored Creoles," Gassion said with a bitter edge cutting through his low voice.

"Especially," Jean agreed soberly. "Catholics everywhere in this country are treated like foreigners, at least outside of Louisiana, but colored Catholics are pariahs twice over."

"I'll tell you both," Gassion muttered, attacking his duckling with considerably more vehemence than warranted, given how well the chef had braised the fowl before smothering it in mirlitons and Bordeaux, "it makes me seethe every time someone mentions the African Colonization Society. 'Ship them all back to Africa,' they say. Well, why not ship all the English back to the British Isles? This wasn't their country to start with, either!"

"Ah, but Gassion! The British say they came voluntarily while the Africans were forced," Jean reminded him.

"Nonsense! They conveniently forget all the poor debtors, and the hungry boys who stole bread, and the starving women who sold the only thing they had to sell and ended up being shipped over here as criminals. Those people didn't come voluntarily. It would make just as much sense to hunt down all their descendants and ship them back to England as to take every colored man and herd him onto a boat to Liberia."

"You're right, of course, Gassion, but I doubt if the Anglos in Washington would care for it. To hear them tell it, *they* built North America."

"That's why I don't listen to Anglos, Jean. By God! My Papa did his share. I've done my share. Our family took land nobody else had the guts to tackle—just like yours did—and we made it into something. We've been in America for more than a century, damn it, and its ours! Africa has no meaning for us, though I can imagine how far I'd get telling that to the men who run our parish now."

"The majority of whom are immigrants themselves."

"You're damned right, Jean. As far back as I can remember, the so-called *Américains* who have run Natchitoches have been immigrants from the British Isles—old Judge Carr, Henry Boyce, Chichester Chaplin, William Long, Joseph Robinson, John Payne, Lawyer Tuomey! Well, as far as I'm concerned, I have more of a stake in this country than any of them have. A hundred years more."

"Yet your rights are getting fewer with every legislative session."

"I know, Jean," Gassion said despondently. "Ever since my wife died, I've thought about taking the children away from here and relocating in Mexico."

"Mexico?" Augustin interjected.

"*Oui,* Papa. You know one of the Chevalier boys went down last year, and his letters back have been encouraging. And just this afternoon, I read an article on the subject in July's *U.S. Magazine and Democratic Review.* It says the same thing that Chevalier's been writing."

"Which is?" Augustin asked skeptically.

"That the Negro is a free man there, socially as well as politically. That nine-tenths of the population there belongs to the colored races."

"They are Indians for the most part, son, or Indio-Spaniards. You know as well as I that Indians are far more acceptable in society."

"Sure, Papa, but this article says there are plenty with Negro ancestry as well."

"Oh, I don't doubt that," Augustin retorted, remembering their border runaway problems forty years before, but Gassion's enthusiasm was not to be dampened.

"It says that many of the generals, the congressmen, even the presidents, are of mixed blood."

"I don't know, son," Augustin continued pensively. "What you have said is true enough. But there's still the white element to consider, and in Mexico that element is Spanish. I have never trusted the Spanish and I don't think I ever will."

"Given a choice between Spanish or Anglo domination, which would you choose?"

Augustin was silent as he pondered that one. "Truthfully, I cannot say. I grew up under the Spanish Crown, among a people who fervently believed they would one day be French again. Well, we were; but it did not last. We were sold out a second time." Wearily he sighed and laid down his cutlery, his appetite completely gone. "I guess I am one of those old reactionaries who persist in hoping that sooner or later we will bounce back into the arms of France."

"Papa! Don't tell me you've joined Louisiana's Society of French Sympathizers!"

"No," the old man replied soberly. "I have not gone that far, but it is nice to dream. Sometimes, I think if I could relive my life, I would settle in France instead of staying here."

"Then your children would have all been poor, money-grubbing bourgeois, no different from the Yankee shopkeepers you scorn, Papa. A man who owns his own land has a certain independence."

"Independence?" Augustin snorted as he thought of how chained he had been to that land for the past half-century, and in his heart he knew it was his slaves who had chained him there. Not just him but all his people, because all of them had followed his own lead. Five hundred men, women, and children now depended upon them for their meat and bread three times a day. Regardless of whether the weather was good or bad or whether the crops made or not, their slaves still had to be fed and clothed. Doctors had to be paid, as well as the priest who came out regularly to baptize and bury them.

"Oui!" he sighed at last. "Sometimes I honestly think we would have been better off if we had become shopkeepers and never bought the first slave."

"Really, Gustin!" Jean interjected. "Am I hearing abolitionist leanings from you? Don't tell me that you are going to free all your slaves in your will?"

Augustin smiled. "No, Jean. Well, yes and no." His voice lowered, lest the other diners who had finished their supper and had begun to filter past them might overhear his remarks. "Before Agnes died, Jean, we began freeing most of the newborns. By the time her estate was settled, we had scarcely a slave child left under the age of ten. Sure, they were still *there,* with their parents, so no one has ever suspected—but they are growing up free."

Across the table, above the small bouquet of hedge roses the waiter had set between them, Augustin caught his son's eye and observed the brow that had tensed above them. He knew Gassion had not been pleased, none of their children were, when he and Agnes told them what they were doing, and he had tried to make it up to them after she died. Gassion could, in fact, use a reminder of that just now, and so he went on blandly, "After Agnes passed on, Jean, I divided up just about everything I had—land and slaves—between my children, except for a few servants I have promised to leave free. What my children do with their inheritance is up to them, but, yes, Agnes and I did consider manumitting all our slaves."

A forkful of cornbread dressing plopped back onto Gassion's duckling as he struggled to digest what he had just heard. "Are you serious, Papa?"

"Quite serious. The only reason your mama and I decided not to free the adults as well as the children was the shape our economy was in after the crash. We could not just turn them out and watch them starve, and the debacle Auguste made of his finances and the help we had to give him did not leave us with cash to hire our slaves back as free labor."

"Why free them at all, Papa? You invested a quarter of a million dollars in our hands!"

"And we are losing money on that investment every day this depression continues. Besides, the older I get the less convinced I am of the morality of slavery."

"Then you'd better lower your voice again, Gustin," Jean cautioned, "before you're overheard."

The old man winced, reminded of the precariousness of their position in the *new* Louisiana and the extent to which he had let the changing political climate compromise what he once considered to be unwavering integrity.

"*Ça!*" he grunted. "At my age, Jean, if anybody wants to throw me off this boat right into the middle of Red River, for speaking my mind, it would not make much difference. The Good Lord won't give me too many more years anyway. I have already lived longer than my mama and papa both."

"But, Papa," Gassion began again hesitantly. "I've heard you defend slavery too many times. From my earliest childhood, I remember your arguing that it was no betrayal of one's own people for a colored man to own a colored man."

"Or for a white to own a white, which they used to do. Or for a black man to have slaves as they still do in parts of Africa as you should know from your own reading. Race is not the issue. We are all God's children. That's what I've always taught you. The only difference is that when I was young and full of steam, it was easy enough to fault people for *letting* themselves be kept in slavery. I could tell myself I was only following the natural order of things when I bought them. Only…" Augustin's voice trailed off wearily.

"Only what, Papa?"

"Only, I'm old now, and a man's conscience bothers him in his dotage. I cannot convince myself that I am any less evil just because I did what society let me do."

"*Mon vieux!*" Jean jested, or tried to. "If you sound any more like a Quaker, our church is likely to excommunicate you!"

451

"No, Jean. The Church is moving away from slavery, too. My old mama told me that when she was young all the priests had slaves. In fact, I remember it myself. Now, very few of them do. Slavery's dying, *mon ami*. People still do not want to admit it—not the Southerners who own them nor the Northerners who finance our operations—but the institution of slavery is in its last days. This depression is nothing but the leech that drains the last of the lifeblood from the dying."

"Then we'll never recover. Is that what you are saying, Papa?"

"Oh, we will recover. One way or the other. There might even be a few more good years again after the economy and the weather straighten out. Still, you mark my words, son. Within your lifetime, slavery will end." Augustin pondered that for a moment, as he toyed absentmindedly with his glass of tea—sweet tea, which, strangely enough, he had also lost his taste for since the time, back when he and the state both were young, he had put in the sugar mill. *Mais oui!* he thought soberly. In the end, all desires are the same. *What we don't have, we crave. What we do have, we no longer want!* But, of course, that was not what Gassion needed to hear just now.

"*Oui,* son," he finally concluded, aloud. "You will survive. But it will be under a far different order of things."

"Then maybe I should think seriously about taking the children to Mexico."

"*Non!*" Augustin's sudden fury surprised even him. "It is too late for that. I could have left sixty years ago, but you cannot leave now. This is your heritage, Gassion! Regardless of how Louisiana changes, this is *our place*. We Creoles built this state, and we will not forfeit it!"

In the thrall of his agitation, Augustin had not realized how loud his voice had risen until the stricken look on his son's face caused him to glance around them. Most of their fellow diners had left, but the dropped jaws, the staring eyes, and the furrowed brows of those who remained cautioned him that he was creating ill will for the white friend at his side, as well as his son. Taking a deep breath to calm himself, he finished what he had to say.

"*Non,* Gassion. You may lose your hands, but Cane River is in your blood, and our Isle is your home. We took a primordial forest and we created a civilization. This is where we are rooted, this is where we *belong,* and this is where we shall stay!"

৩ 12 ৩
March 1847

"Hear ye, hear ye, hear ye!" Sheriff Théophile E. Tauzin intoned impassively from the broad doorway of the parish courthouse. "By virtue of a writ of seizure and sale issued by the honorable District Court of the said Parish of Natchitoches in the suit of *Phanor Prudhomme et al.* vs. *Théophile-Louis Metoyer,* there has been seized all property in the possession of the said defendant."

A hundred times before, Augustin had stood amid courthouse crowds while other parish sheriffs spieled similar words in the same vacuous monotone that never seemed to vary from one official to the other. A hundred times before, Augustin had bid impersonally upon the property that one man or another had lost to his creditors. Never before, however, had he stood helplessly by and watched any of *his* people's land—their home, their heritage!—go on the auction block.

"In accordance with the law," Sheriff Tauzin continued dispassionately, "I have advertised for sale in the official paper of this parish the following seized property: first, the tract of land whereupon the said Théophile-Louis Metoyer now resides..."

"The heart of Yucca Bend," Augustin murmured miserably, as the sheriff continued with his long recital of the property's legal description.

"I know, Papa." Baptiste-Augustin wrapped a lean arm around Augustin's shrunken frame, his heart aching more for his father than for his young cousin who had gone so foolishly into debt.

"Son, that was Louis's Spanish grant. Oh, if you could have seen how he worked to make a plantation out of those canebrakes. Now, it's gone. And that little old hut where he first lived—that will be gone, too. And that rambling cabin he built when he and Thérèse married. And the Big House he was building her when he died..."

"I know, Papa," Baptiste-Augustin repeated foolishly. Of course he knew all this. His papa *knew* that he knew all this. But that really did not matter. The old man was talking more to himself than to anyone else.

"Tonight, that grandson of Louis's will walk out of his Big House, with his carpetbags filled with all those fine clothes he bought on credit, and he will shut that door behind our family forever. Tomorrow, someone else will move into those walls Louis wanted to be filled with laughter."

"I know, Papa."

"Next, we have a certain tract of land on the right bank of the Old River," the sheriff continued, "being an undivided one-tenth part of the old Spanish grant issued to the free Negress, Marie-Thérèse Coincoin, and more accurately described as…"

"That's my mama's vacherie! You remember right before she died, she called all her living children in and divided it among us?"

"Yes, Papa."

"We have used it as common grazing ground ever since, but now some stranger will own Louis's center part and slice our land in two."

"Also a certain tract of land on the south bank of Bayou Platte, containing four hundred arpents.…"

"That was *my* land," Augustin muttered furiously. "One of the first pieces I bought with my own money. But since it bordered Louis, I swapped it to him for a piece he bought downriver, to help him consolidate his operations."

"Papa," Baptiste-Augustin said hesitantly. "I haven't said anything about this before now, because I did not want to build up hopes that may be dashed, but I'm going to bid on that tract myself, if the price doesn't go too high. Because it was yours, I do want to keep that in the family."

Augustin's gaunt hand gripped his son's and squeezed it in wordless thanks.

"Also a certain tract across Rivière Brosset or Little River, known as Lot 6 of Section…"

"You know, Papa, it was a sad day when Baptiste-Louis's widow let that young whelp of theirs talk her into giving him the legal right to handle his own inheritance. This depression has broken thousands of good men. A nineteen-year-old pup like Théophile-Louis didn't stand a chance. Even if he didn't have the sense to realize that, his mother should have."

"She was a mother, son. Mothers can be blind to their children's shortcomings. Besides, Marie was always naive and inexperienced herself."

"She did well enough fighting that court suit against Adlé, when he tried to collect the rest of Auguste's debt from Baptiste-Louis's estate. *Ma foi,* Papa! Life is ironical. Last spring we celebrated when the Louisiana Supreme Court threw out Adlé's suit against her and Théophile-Louis, and now we stand here and watch creditors take the place anyway."

"You did what you could, son. You lent him all you could spare, to stave off the banks."

"And Barbe's new husband was even more generous. Old Nerestan Rocques would pour all his money down a sinkhole if Barbe rolled her eyes at him."

"Truth is," he went on disgustedly before his old father could murmur something in her defense, "we were all pouring our money down a sinkhole. Four years ago, when Théophile's mama had the courts declare him an adult and he celebrated his manhood by getting married, I witnessed his marriage contract. That boy had over a thousand acres, a fine, well-furnished mansion-house, and thirty-three slaves. His father and grandfather had made him the wealthiest nineteen-year-old *man* in the whole parish of Natchitoches!"

"And in four years, he has frittered it all away. Forty years of work gone in just four!"

"That's the truth, Papa," Baptiste-Augustin muttered. "We can't blame it all on the depression, either. The rest of us have survived. He could have, too, especially with the three thousand dollars in silver that Oncle Louis's widow gave him when he married. He not only went through that, he went thirty-six thousand dollars in debt! How could anyone who had everything he needed already have spent so much money in so short a time?"

"Almost everything he needed, son," Augustin corrected. "He still lacked *discipline*. Marie should have remarried. A boy needs a firm hand to guide him, not a couple of lonely widow-women to pamper him."

Baptiste-Augustin winced at that, reminded of his own shortcomings as a parent. Boy or girl, they all needed discipline—not indulgence. He was just as guilty, where his Barbe was concerned. Had that fortune been hers, he knew, she would have spent it just as fast.

"Six thousand dollars! We have a bid from the Hertzog brothers for six thousand even. Do I hear another?"

"Sixty-two!"

"Sixty-two hundred it is now. Folks, that's a pitiful sum for a top-notch plantation and a big, fine mansion-house! Do I hear seven?"

"Seven thousand!" Henry Hertzog bid again from his front-row stand.

"Seven thousand!" Augustin sputtered furiously. "Even after the crash, that plantation was appraised at forty thousand!"

"It's still worth that, Papa. Only no one has that kind of cash left."

"You would have, if you had not already lent most of it to the boy. Or Ben would have, God rest his soul. I would have, if I had not given all of you your inheritance in advance to help you through the depression."

"Is that my final bid, gentlemen? Then eight thousand three hundred and forty dollars, it is. To the Messieurs Henry and Hypolite Hertzog. Now, we have here the lot of fine hands from off this same plantation…"

By noon, the ordeal was over. Baptiste-Augustin had bid successfully on the Bayou Platte land, and others in the family had redeemed a few of the *nègres* to keep families from being divided. But the heart of Yucca Bend was gone forever from the family that had nurtured it to life, and Yucca Bend had always been the heart of the Isle.

For fifty years, Augustin and his people had spread upward, downward, and outward from the Bend, bringing into their grip every tract of land that could be bought, the new land that each new generation had to have if their society was to grow and prosper. Around their land, they had built a wall of self-sufficiency to protect them from the increasing opposition and decreasing opportunities of the nineteenth-century South. That wall had now been breached. An outsider now owned their heart.

"Papa, it could be worse. Much worse," the ever-practical Baptiste-Augustin pointed out reassuringly. "Of all the people who bid on that property today, we could not have hoped for better neighbors than the Hertzog brothers."

"*Oui,*" Augustin conceded. "But this is just the beginning, son. Mark my words. Henry and Hypolite are good men, but they are both prone to rely too much upon credit themselves. One of these days, they are going to end up just like Théophile-Louis. What will happen then to Yucca Bend? Or to you, son, and the rest of our people? God spare me! I hope I will not live to see it!"

❧ 13 ❧

Augustin's despondency persisted all through the summer and the fall, and that Christmas was the lowest one he had ever spent. Père Guistiniani came out every week during Advent to say Mass, but Augustin no longer greeted his people at the door. He was still early to every Mass—that habit was too ingrained for him to break—but now he hobbled directly into the chapel and lowered himself painfully into his pew. The front pew on the right. The one that had been set aside for him when St. Augustin's was built. Now, when Mass was over, the parishioners surged forward, to pay their respects, before filing out the door. Not until the church was emptied would Augustin hobble back to his house and, with more pain than he would admit, pull himself up that long sweep of stairs between the ground and the gallery that his mama had warned him, thirty years before, was utterly impractical.

On Christmas Eve, to cheer Gassion's motherless boys, Augustin pushed himself from his mama's rocker and went with them to cut the biggest fir they could find on what used to be her vacherie. Before they could load their tree onto the wagon, he was wheezing. By the time they had hauled it home, his eyes were feverish.

"Papa! You shouldn't have!" Gassion chided as he helped his father up the stairs and into the salon. "Here, wrap this shawl around you and go sit in front of the fire while I warm you some brandy."

Dutifully, Augustin obeyed.

"Whatever possessed you to go out in weather like this, Papa? You'll be eighty years old next month! You have no business exposing yourself. I could have gone with the boys. Or one of the hands could have."

"I always took them," Augustin protested weakly.

"You've always spoiled them, that's what. Ever since their mama died—no, it goes all the way back to *my* mama's death! You've not been content to be their grandpère, you've tried to be their mother and grandmother as well."

"An old man has to be good for something, son."

"Ah, Papa," Gassion countered affectionately. "You've done more than enough for all of us, for too many years."

"I have not done half of what I should have done!"

"Hehn? Whatever could be left that you haven't?"

"I could have saved Louis's land."

"No, you could not have!" Gassion retorted with more exasperation than he meant to show. "We've been over and over that, Papa. It's just one of those things that was not meant to be and has to be let go of! This year's crop was a good one for all of us, and I really believe the depression is over. It just didn't happen soon enough to save Oncle Louis's land."

"I should have had a real church here, too," Augustin went on as quietly as though his son had never interrupted him.

"A church? We have one, Papa."

"No, I mean a *real* church. A *parish*. There are over six hundred of us now and nearly as many *nègres*. We need a priest here among us all the time, not just one day a month."

Gassion shook his head again, but smiled and the patience in his voice carried not a hint of the number of times they had already gone over that sore point. "We'll never have our own priest as long as they are in short supply in the diocese. The way North Louisiana is growing, priests are needed everywhere. We're lucky, Papa, even to be a mission of Natchitoches."

"Oui," Augustin murmured, more to himself than to his son, "and nuns, too. We need nuns to teach our girls the things young ladies need to learn."

"Ah, Papa. Now you *are* dreaming! Come on, I'll put you to bed."

Christmas morning dawned, cold and clear, but Augustin did not appear at Mass. The chills had gripped him during the night, and his tissue-thin, nut-brown skin had turned as hot and pink as the pokers he used to heat on his father's forge. By breakfast more than fifty of his people had already called, bearing the gifts that each of them had carefully chosen for their Grandpère, as he was called now by all his nieces, grandnephews, and second cousins twice removed. But the teenaged Gus, Gassion's eldest son, turned them away at the door with the grim news that their Grandpère was too ill for visitors. That is, he turned them all away but the one who refused to go.

"Who's tending him?" Perine Metoyer demanded, pushing her way through the broad, double doorway into the salon with an assertiveness that few twenty-something spinsters could pull off.

"Papa is, and Alphonse is helping."

"Your papa and that child? For mercy's sake!" Perine's plump face, already plain enough that Gus would not have been interested in her anyway, screwed itself into agonies of worry and dismay.

"Here!" she ordered, thrusting a gaily wrapped box into her cousin's hands. "That's the lap robe I knitted him, but he won't need it if we don't get him well. You put it somewhere, and *I'll* go take care of Grandpère."

"But Cousin Per…"

"And here! You might as well take my coat, too, since I'll be here a while."

"Yes, Cousin."

Perine was, indeed, there for quite a while. Doctor Scruggs rushed in as soon as Mass was over, to check the old man thoroughly. It was a severe case of the grippe, he pronounced—a fact Perine had already deduced. Then he proceeded to leave directions for treatment, all of which Perine had been doing.

"I don't know why you bothered calling me," he concluded, and Perine smiled back placidly in reply. "I didn't."

"Eh? Well, somebody did. No matter. I always feel better knowing I can leave a patient of mine in good hands."

"Thank you," she acknowledged.

"Apparently you've had a pretty good teacher, girl."

"The best. My mama taught me nursing, and she learned it as a child from the best there ever was around here—her African grandmother."

"You don't say! That wouldn't be the old Coincoin, would it?"

"*Oui.*"

"Well, I'll be hanged! I've heard tales about that woman ever since I came to this parish. Her spectre has all but haunted me, you might say. I don't believe I've treated an old-timer yet who didn't compare me to her."

"I'm sorry, sir. You have a hard example to follow."

"Eh?" Samuel Oglesby Scruggs peered down at Perine over the top of his rimless glasses, with a look that would have withered most of his patients, even if they did not already know his reputation as Cloutierville's finest. "I trained at one of the best medical institutions in this country."

Perine just smiled.

"So that doesn't mean much in comparison?" Scruggs observed, drily. "No mortal can compete with a legend. I shouldn't even try. All right, ma'mselle, keep up the good work, and I'll check in once in a while."

The physician's idea of "once in a while" proved to be a daily visitation. Punctually at 7:30 every morning, before his daily rounds began, he appeared at the door of the Big House with the casual announcement that he "just happened to be in the neighborhood"—and more than once Perine was tempted to retort that she had never known a Cloutierville doctor to have so many patients on the Isle.

Although she never would have admitted it, she was secretly glad to have

Scruggs there to approve her daily ministrations, or else she could never have borne the worry. Despite both their care, Augustin hovered at the edge of death. Pneumonia settled into both his lungs, and then his dropsy flared anew. By the end of January his stomach was ominously swollen, his face bloated almost beyond recognition, and his eightieth birthday came and went as abysmally for him and his people as did their Christmas.

As Perine had promised, she stayed. Her parents did not need her. 'T Pierre's son—the third Pierre in his line—and his cousin-wife Desneiges, Joseph's daughter, had plenty of other children at home to take over her chores. It was Augustin and his somber household who needed help. Badly. Perine waited attentively upon the old man who was her great-uncle twice over, feeding him and sponging away his fever, changing his soiled linens and cleaning him tenderly. In between she brought order to the home that a houseful of men had let lapse into a state she considered chaos.

"Sukie!" she beckoned sternly one morning to a presence she had eyed, unimpressed, for several days. "Aren't you supposed to be the housemaid?"

"Yas'm, Miz Perine," the Virginian puffed up proudly, counting the inches between her fine height and that of the little woman she considered a pasty Creole dumpling.

"Well, it's a clear day outside. Get all these carpets out on the line and beat them until you can't get another speck of dust out of them."

"Laws! Miz Perine! I's too old for dat kind of work!"

"Then we can get another housemaid, *non?*" Perine replied evenly enough, although her eyes held no patience. "How long has it been since those draperies were taken down and washed?"

"I's don't ri'tly know, Miz Perine. I can't 'member dat far back."

"I thought as much," Perine retorted. "That's obvious from looking at them. It's no wonder the old man has trouble breathing, with all the dust in this place."

"Yas'm, Miz Perine," Sukie intoned, her raisin-colored face clearly showing her resentment. Still, she remained glued to her spot while she reassessed her situation in light of the trials that had brought her to where she stood. When her old master's land had worn out and he had decided to move West, it had just about killed her to think of leaving the old homeplace where she had grown up and birthed her children. When she'd heard that she'd be leaving her daughters there in Virginia, with their own babies, she had almost paid the hoodoo man to put a hex on the whole venture; but then her master promised to make her Bruno his new overseer. Only, Bruno had caught the fever just two months after they got here, and her white folks had decided to move on to Texas.

That was when someone had told Augustin about her grief at leaving Bruno buried in his unmarked grave at Shallow Lake, and he had talked her master into selling her so she could stay. Even then, she'd still had her doubts about belonging to a colored man. No real *black* person, as far as she could see, cared for these *nothings* who weren't either black or white, and she'd heard no end of stories about how mean they could be as masters. So far, she conceded, not one dire tale had proved true and she had thanked her Jesus every Sunday for her good luck of ending up with a Metoyer. At least she had, until lately. *Dis Miz Perine*, she had muttered to herself for a week now, *was jes' sumpin' else.*

"By the time the sun goes down today, Sukie, I want every carpet and every drape cleaned, and I don't care how many girls you have to pull out of the quarters to get it done. They aren't doing anything out there anyway, except sitting around dreading for the weather to warm up and planting time to come. On any other place, the mistress would have them spend their winters sewing or spinning or helping out in the Big House."

"I's always dun all dat, Miz Perine," Sukie replied resentfully. "Evuh since the ol' missus died, the young missus always let me run the Big House m'self."

"And when the young missus died you obviously quit work," Perine retorted. "As long as I'm in this house, Sukie, it will be *clean*. If that's asking too much of you to do alone, then you bring in whatever help it takes. I am not unreasonable, Sukie, but I will not tolerate dust or dirt."

"Yas'm." The broad face turned as bland as an eggplant. "Miz Perine? How long's you plan t' stay heah?"

"*Hehn?*" The question took Perine completely by surprise. She had never given a thought to that, not in the long daylight hours when she bustled through the Big House as though it were hers already, nor at night when she dozed beside Augustin's big four-poster on the little cot to which she had grown quite accustomed. Nor did she give any thought to the question now.

"How long?" Perine answered matter-of-factly, when Sukie boldly repeated her question. "For as long as I'm needed. From the looks of this place, that's liable to be a while!"

As the days began to lengthen and the sun shone more warmly through the window panes, the glow seeped back into Augustin's ashen face, and under Perine's control of his diet, his swelling gradually abated.

"Child, what's today?" Augustin asked weakly one morning as she propped him up against his pillows and sat beside him with his breakfast tray.

"March the fifteenth, Grandpère."

"Ah, the Ides of March," he smiled wanly.

"*Oui.*"

"Wasn't that the day Julius Caesar made his speech about somebody or other's lean and hungry look? I still remember when Chevalier gave that book of Shakespearean plays to Baptiste-Augustin, and the boy read me the one about Caesar."

"*Oui,* Grandpère. You know, you're going to have a lean and hungry look, yourself, if you don't eat your breakfast."

"What kind of appetite do you expect a man to have when he's done nothing for ten weeks but lie in bed? Tomorrow's Sunday?"

"Yes, Grandpère."

"The first race of the season?"

"*Oui.*"

"Will they open the season at my track this year or at young Lecomte's?"

"He drew the long straw this year, Grandpère."

"Well, tell my son not to plan on going. If the weather is still good, I want him to help me out to the porch. I'm ready to sit out a spell and breathe God's fresh air."

Gassion was quite content to miss the races. For better than a week now, he had been hoping more anxiously than usual that his father would soon be up and about, and well enough for the two of them to have a long, private talk.

"You go, instead, Perine," he insisted. "Gus will take you. You've been cooped up in this house since Christmas. You need an afternoon off."

Perine protested, as Gassion knew she would, so he frowned and made dire remarks about this still being *his* house; and she capitulated in good spirit. By mid-morning, she had completed the ministrations her Grandpère needed and had readied a picnic basket full of meat pies and roasted sweet potatoes and ham biscuits and pepper jelly and fresh lemonade and fig cakes and pralines that would see her and Gassion's sons—and likely a dozen of their friends as well—through the day's festivities.

"Fine girl. Yes, sir, that's one fine woman," Augustin nodded approvingly as they sat on the gallery and watched Perine, Gus, and the younger boys ride out of sight.

"I hoped you would feel that way, Papa."

"*Eh?*" Augustin's eyes came alive under the mass of folds that now hooded them. "Is there something I don't know? Don't tell me that boy of yours is thinking about marrying her. Gus's too young. He's not even eighteen yet, is he?"

"Not quite," Gassion laughed nervously. "And no, he's not thinking about marriage. I am."

Augustin weakly raised his hand to another set of young folks who passed by and called to him in greeting, but his attention did not stray. "It's about time, son. Your wife's been dead five years now. But if you have Perine in mind, then I'm against it."

That was not the response Gassion wanted to hear. "But, Papa, you said you liked her."

"I do. She's a fine niece, and she'll make some man a good wife, if she can find one who realizes that beautiful pearls come inside plain old oysters."

"I've already realized that, where Perine is concerned," Gassion said softly.

Augustin's voice was curt, unusually so. "She's still not for you, son."

"Why not?"

"She's your cousin, boy. Not just once, but twice over. Her papa's papa was my brother and her mama's papa was my brother. I was dead set against her parents marrying each other, and I'd be even more set against your adding to the mistake."

"Look, Papa. I know how you feel about us marrying our cousins, and I'm likely to have a hard time getting a dispensation now that Père Guistiniani's being replaced... "

"He's leaving?" Augustin interrupted.

"Yes, I'm sorry. I forgot to tell you."

"It looks as though I slept through a lot this winter... *Hé!* Did you see that?" Augustin cackled suddenly.

"What, Papa?"

"The Sarpy boy. He was dashing down the road there at a breakneck speed until he saw me sitting out here on the porch!" Augustin crowed. "Then he reined up that horse of his real short-like and pranced by here so slowly, tilting his hat all nice and respectable-like; but the minute he rounded that bend where he thought I couldn't see him, he kicked that horse back into action. Listen to those hooves!"

"Yes, Papa," Gassion smiled dutifully, determined not to be distracted from his argument.

"As I was saying, Papa. I just don't have that much of a choice in wives, and I hope the new priest can see that. I hope *you* can see that. Things have not changed at all, Papa. There are a lot more free colored Creoles in the parish now, but we are all related by blood or by marriage. At least the ones who are worth anything, and I know you wouldn't want me to marry some lazy wench who doesn't do any work unless it's on her back."

"Then at least pick one of us who is not such close kin!"

"Who, Papa? I'm almost forty years old and never was much to look at. I'm a lousy dancer. I can't sweep a woman off her feet or charm her either. What's more, I have a ready-made family for her to tend."

"You managed to find two wives before."

"When I was younger, and I buried them both. As far as women are concerned now, I'm a jinx. I'd consider myself lucky if Perine would have me."

"You haven't asked her?"

"No, sir. I wanted to talk to you first. Still, I can't help hoping, Papa. She seems to like it here and, you know, hard times have plagued her parents since the Big Crash. I can offer her a lot more than she would have at home. The children like her, too, Papa. She'll be a good mother for them."

"I can't argue with that. It's the children the two of you will have together that worry me, son. You are just too closely related."

"The bishop may feel that way, too, Papa. Still, if Perine will have me, and the bishop will approve, do I have your blessing?"

"*Oui,*" Augustin said at last. "If the bishop approves."

The bishop did. Reluctantly. As for Perine, she accepted Gassion's proposal quite matter-of-factly. So she stayed on at Augustin's Big House where, for all his stated opposition, she cheered his soul, and not a day went by that he did not ask himself how, during all the years of this girl's childhood, he could have doted so on Barbe and missed the real pearl in his family.

By the time Gassion and Perine held their simple wedding at St. Augustin, she had brought back into the Big House the kind of order that Agnes always had insisted upon. The new household staff she trained to replace the too-old Sukie were all hard workers, carefully chosen for that fact. They also were young, lighthearted, and appreciative enough of being brought in from the field that they obeyed her orders without a question or a sulk.

By Christmas, Perine was *enceinte*. Although given to plumpness, her bone structure was quite frail, and this first pregnancy left her with a weakness that warred against her lifetime habit of work, work, work.

"Come sit, child," Augustin constantly urged. "The house girls can handle things now, and you have to take care of yourself and the little one."

"But what do I *do,* Grandpère? I have already knitted everything to be knitted, embroidered everything to be embroidered, and read every book in this house!"

"Then sit down here with me, child, and I'll tell you a story—a story your great-grandmother told me when I was younger than little Alphonse. Let me tell you about her own grandfather who was a king."

✍ 14 ☙

December 1856

The wiry priest rose hastily from his chair as Perine entered to announce that breakfast was being served downstairs. "Go on down, Père," she urged. "I'll sit with Grandpère. If he wakes, I'll call you."

The young cleric's face was haggard from a sleepless night, his hair as rumpled as his cassock. Still he declined her offer. "You're thoughtful, Perine, but no. If he stirs, I must be here. He will want to make his last confession, and I cannot deny him that solace."

"Then let me bring you something, Père. I'll fill a plate for you."

Wearily, he brushed back the thin, unruly locks that were just beginning to grey. "I don't eat much, Perine. Just coffee and maybe a roll, but we could use some fresh firewood. I put the last on a while ago. I don't ask for myself," he added hastily. "I don't mind a little chill, but the M'sieur deserves to be comfortable."

"You both do, Père," Perine said softly. "Now sit back down and try to rest. I won't be long."

Father François Martin sank gratefully into the chaise, flexing for a moment his cramped legs and knotted back. After twenty-three hours by Augustin's bed, his every muscle cried for release. In the long night that was now behind him, he had said the Rosary to himself until his fingers were numb. He had prayed every prayer he ever learned in the seminary and recited the litany of saints until the repetition almost lulled him into the sleep he had been fighting. Then when his mind screamed for rest, he had paced the floor to stay awake, until his pacing roused Gassion who dozed fitfully in the chair on the backside of the bed. By one means or another, Père Martin had made it through that night, but Augustin did not stir.

It had been at dawn the day before that young Gus had come for him, just as he was leaving his little cabin for the half-mile walk he made every morning to the church. That dawn, for the first time in the nine months he had been on the Isle, the bells did not peal the Angelus, and there was no daily Mass at St. Augustin. Instead, Père Martin had knelt beside the bed of the stricken Augustin and administered the last rites of the Church.

"You might as well go on to Mass now, Father," Dr. Scruggs had then declared. "There's nothing more you can do here. His stroke was massive."

But Père Martin had planted himself resolutely beside the big four-poster and refused to go. "I'll say Mass here this morning."

"Here?"

"Here. M'sieur has not missed a daily Mass since St. Augustin was declared a parish and I became its priest. He will not miss this one either."

The service had been brief. Only Perine, Gassion, and their children clustered around the bed, as Père Martin consecrated the Body and Blood of their Savior before the little altar that a teenaged Baptiste-Augustin had made for his Mère Coincoin when she occupied that same room so many years before. By the close of the Mass, Augustin still had not stirred, but the prayers had soothed the souls of those who attended him and left them all with an inner peace that could sustain them even if, as they feared, he did not rally long enough to receive the last rites of his church.

"Père, your breakfast?" Lost in his own reflections, his gaze fixed on the withered form that lay so still under the heavy satin tester, Père Martin had not heard Perine return.

"Oh, thank you, daughter." His eyes smiled softly as he took in the two trays she carried. "You're joining me?"

"*Oui,* Père." For a while, they sipped their coffee in troubled silence. The crevettes were piping hot and lavishly sugared, and Perine had filled the plate with more than the mere one he had asked for. From the sideboard, the aroma of ham, peppered eggs, and warm pear preserves chased the scent of death from the sickroom and mingled pleasantly with the lingering fragrance of the incense Père Martin had used at Mass. Yet neither of them felt like eating. Eventually, it was he who broke the stillness of their worries.

"Perine, how old is he—the old M'sieur?"

"He'll be eighty-nine next month." Her voice broke, and she corrected herself. "He would have been eighty-nine."

"He's an indomitable man, Perine. He just might fool you and celebrate that birthday after all."

"*Non,* Père. Not this time. Once before he did, but I think now he's just plain tired. He's done almost everything he ever wanted to do in life. When you came last spring, that was the culmination of just about every dream."

"It really meant that much to him?"

"It meant everything. For sixty years that's the one thing he wanted most of all, to see his Isle made into a parish with a full-time priest."

"Then I wish I had come sooner."

"You're here now, Père. That's enough."

Their small talk faded as each sank back into private thoughts. Perine knew she had not said enough, yet she feared that if she spoke she would say too much. It was not just Grandpère who had been grateful for all the bishop had done that past year. In every way, it seemed of late, the new Louisiana—*Anglo* Louisiana—challenged every article of faith, custom, language, and law upon which their society had been built; and for *Créoles de couleur* on the Isle of Canes, their very day-to-day existence had become the running of a gauntlet. To the *public servants* sent by Washington to *serve* them, all Creoles—white, black, or colored—were an inferior caste. Census takers who owed their jobs to patronage labeled them illiterate, despite their years of education, if they were not fluent in both oral and written *English.* But the worst ignominies were reserved for those whose complexions were browner than clam chowder or ruddier than a

Georgia peach. Anglo officials, when the Islanders had to consult them, rudely called them by their first names and then bestowed *Mr.* and *Mrs.* upon whites whose homes were hovels in comparison to their own.

Only their faith sustained them, and that faith had not forsaken them. When, three years before, North Louisiana was made into a separate diocese and a bishop was sent to Natchitoches, they had prayed that God would move the bishop to give them a parish of their own. He did indeed consecrate the chapel of St. Augustin as a full-fledged church, the seat of the new Parish of St. Augustin that would serve the Isle. Then he raised the eyebrows of the Protestants in their midst by creating a mission for white Catholics along Old River and assigning that new chapel to the authority of the *colored* church of St. Augustin. Unfazed by that public outrage, he had blessed St. Augustin's parishioners with an even greater favor: the new pastor who Bishop Auguste Martin sent to serve their daily needs was his own brother. And now, on his last trip to the Isle, he had lifted their hearts higher than anyone's but Grandpère had dared to soar, and Perine still feared that something would kill those dreams.

"Did the bishop tell you," she ventured to say at last, "that he may send us nuns next year? That the Daughters of the Cross from Avoyelles might open a mission school for us?"

"*Oui.* Day before yesterday, when he rode out."

Perine nodded. "That's when he told Grandpère, and he was so excited. Too excited," she added painfully, as her gaze fell once more on the bed where he had not stirred for hours.

"I'm afraid he was," Père Martin agreed slowly. "M'sieur rode over in his buggy to see me as soon as the Bishop left. He was full of ideas and suggestions, as though he had been planning this for years."

"He had, Père."

"I should have known."

Fighting back the tears she knew her Grandpère would not want, Perine rose to set their emptied mugs on the sideboard and then busied herself in straightening the bedcovers for the dozenth time. Her voice was harsh, almost savage, when she spoke again.

"God forgive me, father, but I hope he goes now! Amid the joy of this good news. We all know what's coming. I hope God takes him, so he will not live to see the ruin of everything he worked for!"

God granted her wish. Within the hour, Sieur Nicolas Augustin Metoyer, *homme de couleur libre*, passed from the world in which he had made for himself and his people a place their changing world could not tolerate. When Perine took their trays downstairs, and Père Martin turned briefly to stoke the fire, the old man's soul slipped quietly away.

All day and all that night, his body lay in state on his bier—the great mahogany four-poster François had carved for his princess more than a hundred years before. All day and all that night, the Islanders came to pay their homage, not only his people but the countless whites who called him *friend* and the slaves who mourned the passing of a man who daily showed his care for them. When the evening Angelus tolled somberly across the river from the belfry of St. Augustin, almost a thousand Islanders filled his Big House, its galleries, and its yard as Père Martin, barely refreshed from an hour's nap, led them in Rosary and Benediction. When they reassembled at the appointed hour on the morrow, it was the bishop himself, in black stole and cope, who led the Psalms that began the mournful ritual.

Out of the depths I cry to you, O Lord, Lord hear my voice....
Have mercy on me, O God, in your goodness; in the greatness of your
   compassion, wipe out my offense....
Indeed, in guilt was I born, and in sin my mother conceived me....
Cast me not out from your presence, and your holy spirit take not
   from me.
Give me back the joy of your salvation.... I will teach transgressors your
   ways, and sinners shall return to us....
My sacrifice, O God, is a contrite heart.

Tenderly, the corpse was shrouded in white silk and lifted into the waiting casket, a cradle as black as ebony, painted and polished until it shined like glass, then lined in the richest velvet and studded with gold tacks. Amid the wails of the blacks who had served him and the sobs of his own people, Augustin's casket was shouldered by the pair of sons who survived him, and their own firstborns, and the throngs parted in his salon, across his gallery, down his sweeping bank of stairs, and across his broad lawn as he was carried high and nobly to the waiting hearse.

Somberly, Gassion mounted Augustin's big stallion, raised before him a silver cross, and signalled the mournful cortège to begin. The procession stretched for a mile or more behind him—an endless line of carriages and buggies, surreys and cabriolets, mourners on horseback with arm bows of wide black lace and ebony bands of ribbon woven through the combed manes of their mounts—as they made for Augustin one final circle around his Isle. An army of slaves followed on foot, old men supported by the young ones, mothers with babes in arms, some crying from grief, others singing with a new freedom that had been Augustin's last gift to them.

The Church of St. Augustin could not hold their number. Mourners spilled over into the balcony, the nave, the east gallery, and the west one. All its symbols of joy, all its glorious reproductions, the crucifix, the splendid painting of St. Augustin—the humble physician who was the patron of the parish—the poignant statuette of the Virgin Mary and her Holy Infant, all were shrouded in mournful crepe.

Before the altar, with bent heads, there stood the largest concourse of priests ever assembled in the diocese. Bishop Auguste Martin, with Père Dicharry and his assistant pastor from the parish of Natchitoches. The young Père Beaulieu who had been called from France to the reorganized congregation of St. Jean Baptiste de Cloutierville. And Père Martin, the stalwart pastor of St. Augustin, who still had found no more than three hours of sleep in the past three days. Together, the august concelebrants led the mourners through the plaintive and triumphant prayers of the Réquiem et Kyrie, the Diés Iræ, the Tuba Mirum, and the Recordare.

Flanked by a pair of sad-faced acolytes, shadows from their lighted candlesticks dancing upon their chasubles, the priests ringed the coffin and cleansed it symbolically with the holy sprinkler and thurible, then bowed their heads for the prayers of absolution. Then the throng of a thousand mourners, white and black, free and slave, lifted their voices in the age-old song of all mankind, *Libera Me.*

"Requiéscant in pace."

"Amen," the mournful crowd intoned.

"Dómine, exáudi oratiónem meam..."

"Et clamor meus ad te véniat."

The concelebrants raised their arms in holy blessing, *"Dóminus vobíscum."*

"Et cum spíritu tuo."

The doleful prayers drew to a close, and the congregation rose from its knees, bracing for its last ordeal—the irrevocable, consummate yielding of their loved one to the vault that would forever after hold his bones, but not his soul.

"My children!" The bishop's hand stayed them. "My children, there remains yet one tribute to the beloved soul who has been called from us. In the night that has passed since our Christ and Lord reached out His loving arms and drew Nicolas Augustin Metoyer unto His glorious bosom, amid the tears and sadness that he has left behind him, each of you has paid to him your own tribute, in your own way."

The bishop paused, his voice heavy.

"Today, I have paid my own unworthy homage to a man whom I have come to love as dearly as my own brother. A man I have respected as much as I honor and respect the parents who gave me life, taught me values, and sacrificed themselves a thousand times that I might have the blessings I enjoy today…"

The quiet sobs that the prayers had stilled began anew as the Bishop's words brought fresh reminders to each man and woman of the countless debts of love and guidance they owed their Grandpère and now could never repay.

"My children, there has been paid to Nicolas Augustin Metoyer a still higher tribute. One I wish a thousand times over I could have read to him a week ago. I know that such earthly honors as this one pales in comparison to the glory that now envelops him. Still, for those of us he left behind, it still has great meaning and should bring a sorely needed comfort.

"My children," the bishop continued softly. "There arrived yesterday at Natchitoches a letter addressed to 'Monsieur Nicolas Augustin Metoyer, Patriarch of the Isle of Canes.' With the permission of his sons Auguste and Gassion, I would like to read it to you now."

23 September 1856

My Dearly Beloved Son in Christ,

Your Bishop, the Most Reverend August Martin, has reported to me the creation of the Parish of St. Augustin de l'Isle. I wish to extend to the souls of this parish my personal love and blessings, but most of all I want to send to you, my son, my sincerest appreciation for all you have done to make this new parish a reality.

I have been informed of the many trials to which Our Faith has been subjected on the frontier of Louisiana. I am aware of the godless elements that even now test that faith. But I have also been informed that you have stood for sixty years as a bulwark against all who would destroy the Word of God in your midst.

My son, I know—I can at least imagine—the countless trials you have faced yourself, the challenges that have confronted you, not only for your unwavering faith but for your color also; and so your faithfulness has twice the meaning. I say to you, Son, that you stand today in the very shadow of the ancient Job, an example to all men of Goodness, Love, Charity, and undying Perseverance.

And so, my son, I extend to you across the waters that separate us physically but could never separate our hearts, my hand in love, appreciation, and admiration. May God bless you and all the people that you lead.

Your Holy Father and Your Friend in Christ

Pius IX

PART FIVE

1859–1876

The Reaving

"I took no part in war-time politics because I had no right to do so. Though free men of color, we were no more considered than if we were slaves."

—Deposition of Gassion "Gus" Metoyer Jr.
Gassion Metoyer v. The United States
Southern Claims Commission
File 20895, RG 56
National Archives

"Our services were offered to the Confederate States Government, but were refused because our company was composed of free men of color. We disbanded.

"On the evening of the night Dr. Burdin was killed, I was going to the church to the funeral of my aunt. He stopped me and ordered me to meet him at the church that night, he said there were some jayhawkers a few miles above there and he wanted us to go capture them & those who refused to go, he would have their houses burnt and their families killed."

—Deposition of Joseph E. Dupré Jr.
Widow Jean Napoleon Burdin v. The United States
French & American Claims Commission
File 209, RG 76
National Archives

∽ 1 ∾

October 1859

As war clouds loomed

On 16 October 1859, a fanatic Ohioan with the innocuous name of John Brown launched his infamous attack at the little Southern town of Harper's Ferry. In those curiously targeted mountains of western Virginia, Brown found few slaves to liberate and even fewer willing to be aroused. Within two days, his ragtag force had surrendered to the U.S. army under the young colonel Robert E. Lee and Lee's lieutenant, J. E. B. Stuart. Come December he would be hanged. Tactically, Brown's raid had been a fiasco; but—prophetically—the first casualty of that first skirmish of what would become America's Civil War was a free Negro.

Across the nation, lines were being drawn in preparation for that bigger conflict. Harper's Ferry was but a bugle cry urging both sides into formation. On the Isles of Canes, as elsewhere North and South, houses divided in their response to that bugle's call. Thinkers and worriers, such as Gassion Metoyer, who had reluctantly assumed his father's responsibility for the welfare of "their people," battled the doers, the hot-blooded youth who were already singing *Aux armes, citoyens! Formez vos bataillons!* The unresolved issue was *which side should they join?* Some passionately argued for support of their Creole homeland; others just as passionately embraced the seductive promises of equality that they heard from the Anglo North. Then there were the dreamers, such as Manuel Dupré, who frustrated Gassion most of all with expectations that the looming conflict would actually bring together Louisiana's deeply divided cultures—not just black and white, but also Anglo and Creole.

"*Zut,* Manuel!" Gassion's pique was obvious as he sparred a few days later with the cousin who had been his lifelong friend. "You are illustrating my very point right now."

"*Hehn?* How's that?" Manuel Dupré asked offhandedly while he made last-minute preparations for the evening's invited guests. Having refilled his decanter with fresh Scotch, he checked the supply of Havanas in his cigar case and paused, as always, to admire the exquisitely rendered hunting scene inside its lid. It was a gift he treasured, sent to him by a cigar-chomping, fox-hunting, poker-loving crony of his younger years who had fled to Cuba. Yet, as always, lifting that lid was for Manuel a painful reminder of the cultural rift that pitted traditional French ways against the ideology of the Anglos who had taken control of their state.

Manuel's grief had still been raw over the death of his cousin Louis—and the official hubbub over the Metoyer-Haney duel still had not subsided—when troubles had flared again. An Anglo newcomer, in the broad light of day at Lecomte's racetrack, had opened fire from a sniper's hole and killed Manuel's friend, Breuville Perot. Rumor had it that the bullet was intended for the man who stood at Perot's side: Manuel's in-law through the Rachals, the French-born doctor François-Marie Normand. The assassin himself accused his employer, the young general François Gaiennié, who had wed a legal granddaughter of the old Pierre Metoyer. Friends and family had taken sides, and tempers had escalated until they were settled by a duel on Sompayrac's Savannah outside Cloutierville. Gaiennié had ridden home that day, prone across the back of a black horse whose color announced to his widow the outcome of the match. Normand had sought refuge in Havana.

In the New Regime that, by then, had a solid chokehold on Louisiana's Creole culture, such *affaires d'honeur* were prosecuted as murder—even when, unlike the old Metoyer-Haney affair, all parties involved were white. Never mind that it had, again, been one of those *redneckaméricains* who had sparked the incident. Surprise ambushes were a time-honored way of settling scores in hotheaded, rambunctious, nineteenth-century America; but regulated, premeditated duels, *by Jove!* smacked of the *Romish* rituals that Protestant America abhorred.

Protestant *vs.* Catholic. Anglo *vs.* Creole. Cultured wealth *vs.* envious poverty. White *vs.* brown *vs.* black. Though Manuel never would have admitted it—if Gassion had suggested it—the cigar box Normand had sent was, for Manuel, a Pandora's box of troubles he tried to forget in ways that nurtured his roots, such as tonight's little *fête.* Yet Gassion, to Manuel's chagrin, was not content to nurture. He much preferred to prod and prickle.

"You really don't want to hear this, do you Manuel?" Gassion persisted, pressing his cousin into another of the debates Dupré detested. "I'm talking about this little dinner party of yours. When my father entertained the old Ambroise

Lecomte, he did so in his home, amidst his family. Not in the rear room of a mercantile house."

"Ah, now, cousin," Manuel forced himself to grin good-naturedly, as he made his last-minute scan of the little chamber, checking every detail. The pillows were plumped on the sofa and chaise of lustrous chocolate corduroy. The draperies of ivory linen hung crisply from their tailored, French-pleated valance. The game table with its matching chairs upholstered in soft leather was now elegantly set for supper, an aromatic Havana by each of the four plates. On the buffet that stood beside it, there waited a fresh deck of cards, still wrapped. And on his linen shirtfront, the ruffles that rippled down each side from collar to belt were a curious contrast to the burly, light-copper face that attested Manuel's Indian heritage.

"As you can see, *mon vieux,*" Manuel went on smoothly, "this is no ordinary 'back room of a store.' This is my retreat, where the babel of my brood never disturbs me."

Gassion relented, momentarily. "You mean, where Margie never opens the windows to let out the smoke of your cigar!" Manuel chortled at the jibe; but Gassion homed in again on the question Manuel had ignored.

"I'm serious and I want you to answer me honestly, Manuel. If you invited Ambroise to dine with you at home, would he accept?"

"Well… " Manuel was clearly reluctant to say what the question demanded. "Gassion, why do you always put things so negatively? Ambroise likes my family, and he's always acknowledged that Margie and I are his cousins."

"Just not the kind of cousins that he brings his wife to visit," Gassion insisted. He really did not mean to be cruel to the friend with whom he had hunted squirrel as a boy, courted sweethearts as a young lover, and sparred with ever since the two of them realized that their philosophies were poles apart. Still, it was long since time for all of them to be honest with themselves. Dupré's kind of blindness would be the death of them in Louisiana's increasingly hostile political climate.

The clench of Manuel's broad jaw suggested to Gassion that his point had struck home, so he moved on to address the broader issue that was at stake. "Manuel, the truth is that neither our money, our culture, or our religious leadership in this parish has earned us any equality at all, and all the rights we once had will be stolen from us, if we don't do something to change the direction in which the South is headed."

"Such as?" Manuel asked quietly. "We can't speak out publicly now without being called uppity or accused of fomenting trouble. After that so-called plan for a slave revolt down in St. Martin Parish, our whole caste is condemned."

"That's exactly what I am talking about," Gassion pushed, "and it was a white man who concocted that plot. Where *race* is concerned now, few people act logically."

Gassion drew a long, slow sip from his cognac, giving Manuel time to reflect upon that thought before he continued the argument his cousin did not want to hear. "This world has gone crazy, Manuel. The word *Negro* is now a synonym for every ill in society. Something has to be done to bring Southerners to their senses!"

"It's not just the South, cousin," Manuel protested. "Our caste still has more opportunity here than anywhere else. I hear Ohio is trying to drive us out completely, and California won't let one of us testify against a white at all, even if we're the injured party! At least we still enjoy those rights in Louisiana's courts."

"For how long, Manuel? Haven't you heard about the new petition before our legislature? They're already trying to make it illegal for us to testify in a case involving whites."

"It won't pass," Dupré argued stubbornly.

"Maybe not this year, but it shows the changing mood. Next time, it very well might pass. That's just one example. What about next year's election, Manuel? Do you think any of us will be welcome at the polls?"

Dupré was silent. His Jersey bull of a face was sober and pensive.

"We won't!" Gassion declared. "Politicians here at Natchitoches have winked at our color before, when they hoped our vote would help them. That won't happen again, not after the scandal down in Rapides Parish over voting by Carroll Jones's Ten Mile Creek community."

"I suspect you're right, cousin," Manuel admitted slowly.

"I know I am! One by one, every one of our rights is being taken from us. Do you take the newspapers from Opelousas?"

"*Non.*"

"Antoine Meuillion sends me his when he's done with them. I wish I had brought you the last issue of the *Patriot*. White planters down there sent a resolution to the legislature that exceeds any attempt at oppression ever made in this state!"

The bell tinkled at the shop's front door, rescuing Manuel from the sermon that was obviously coming. "'Scuse me, cousin," he interjected, "that must be Ambroise and Louis." He rested his drink on the marble top of his rosewood serving table, traipsed through the storefront he had left lighted until after the arrival of his friends, and then muttered when he saw it was a late customer instead. While Gassion nursed his own drink, along with his worries, Manuel gathered the quinine and the bitters Mrs. Spillman said she was running low on, agreed with her that nobody could afford to run out of either with malaria still on the river, politely inquired about her husband—*George? was that his name, Gassion wondered offhandedly as he listened to their prattle*—who had come there as Lecomte's new overseer, escorted her to the door with some words of worry about her walking home alone at night, and then headed back to his salon, hoping that Gassion had turned his mind to other things. He should have known better.

"Would you believe," Gassion went on, "those Opelousas *Américains* are actually protesting our right to own slaves? Never, ever, has anyone tried to deny us the right to own *any* kind of property!"

"Cousin," Manuel muttered, more gruffly than he intended, "you've done a helluva job of spoiling my party mood tonight, and the party hasn't even started."

"Good. I hope I have. It's time we concerned ourselves less with dinner parties and horse races and more with the serious situation we face."

"*Zut!*" Manuel swore. "No one will take those Opelousas folks seriously."

"Don't bank on it. The same measures are being introduced into legislatures all across the South. They are saying the same things elsewhere that the Opelousas paper says."

"Which is?"

"That our ownership of slaves is the worst of the *evils* we represent! They actually claim it is 'repugnant to the laws of good society, good government, Nature, and God' for us to own 'beings of our own color, flesh, and blood'."

Hehn! Manuel snorted to himself at the ridiculousness of that argument. There were too many slaves now, in every state from Delaware to Texas, whose flesh was every bit as white as their masters', and far more who carried the blood of white men in their veins. "*Non,* cousin," he reasoned aloud. "If it's repugnant to hold people of the same blood in bondage, then there are a million slaves with white blood whose owners would have to free them."

"You are making my point again, Manuel. It's not the ownership of slaves by a man of shared blood that is opposed. It's *our* ownership of slaves. It's the free colored man's growing wealth that's repugnant, because whites know that equal wealth and equal culture deserve equal political and social rights."

Gassion's voice had turned cold, his face twisted into the same bitterness that often contorted it of late. "Let me quote you another line from that same article, Manuel. One of the resolutions passed down there starts out by declaring, 'Whereas the free colored population of this state is *principally* composed of individuals too lazy to work, and numbers of them live by stealing and other malpractices…'"

"Lazy?" Manuel protested. "I haven't missed a day of work since I turned ten, and there has not been one of us convicted of theft in this parish for as far back as I can recall."

"There never has been, Manuel. I know because I spent a whole day at the courthouse checking that as soon as I read the *Patriot's* diatribe. The point is that our enemies use lies like that to inflame the ignorant masses against us. Their purpose, and they've said so, is to justify a special set of laws for any free Negro accused of crime."

"Such as?" Manuel asked, a wary note creeping into his voice at last.

"How about *enslavement for life* if we are convicted of anything?"

"My God, Gassion! That would be open license to enslave every free colored person in existence. Anyone can trump up charges, and there will always be crooked judges who can be bribed!"

"That's exactly what I'm talking about. Eventual extinction of our class."

"*Non!*" Manuel stubbornly shook his head. "The good people of this state would never let such a measure pass."

"I wish I had your confidence. In fact, the Opelousas men are demanding that the justices of the peace try colored Creoles by the same rules that apply to slaves."

"*Hehn?* Then we couldn't testify in our own defense if someone did try to force us into slavery!"

Gassion's laugh held no humor. "You're concerned now, Manuel? Shall I tell you about the latest resolution introduced into our state legislature?"

"You must spend all your time reading," Manuel grumbled back, as he stooped again to check the pots warming on the coals, reassuring himself that the roasted leg of deer was not drying out or the rice dressing getting soggy. "Damn! I wish Lecomte and Monette would hurry. My man brought this stuff over from the kitchen a half-hour ago."

Gassion pointedly ignored Manuel's distraction. "It pays to be informed. Would you believe that certain people of this state are so concerned with our welfare as to propose a law giving us the 'privilege' of 'voluntarily' returning to slavery?"

"Mais non! You jest!"

"I do not jest, Manuel. I have never been more serious. The plight of the free colored man in this state is very serious. Our only salvation, so far as I can see, is the election of Abraham Lincoln."

"Absurde!" Dupré's concern at last reached a pitch that satisfied his cousin. "All right, Gassion. You may be right on some things, but the election of that white-trash would ruin us completely. If the Republicans nominate him and he's elected, the South will crumble. Slavery will crumble!"

"Nonsense, Manuel. Lincoln's not for freeing the slaves. Not *en masse.* He's no abolitionist, but he does seem to believe in the rights of men."

"A different set of rights for different men, according to what I hear," Dupré muttered. "Not even your Lincoln believes in equality."

"Perhaps not, but he is the best hope we have."

"Then we have no hope at all. If Lincoln is elected, the South will pull out of the Union. We're against everything the Republican Party stands for—free-soil, tariffs, internal improvements at federal expense. All those things would benefit the North and the West, but they would cripple us economically."

"That's no justification for withdrawing from the Union, Manuel. All parts of a Union must support the good of the whole."

"Sur ma foi! That conviction is all that has kept us together this long."

For a while the both of them fell silent as they pondered the gravity of the threat faced by the Union that Creole Louisiana had not asked to join but had nonetheless embraced. Argue though they might over the cause of that threat, they both knew the threat was real, and they both knew the results would be cataclysmic for the world they had created on the Isle of Canes.

Amid the silence of their thoughts, from beyond the clearing occupied by Dupré's Store there at the juncture of Cane River and Bayou Derbanne, the distant whinny of a pair of horses, the long slow rumble of a chain, and the hallooeing of the hands who manned Dupré's Ferry around the clock, announced the approach of riders across the river.

Anxious to rebut Gassion's heresy before his friends arrived, Dupré plunged back into his argument. "Lincoln's election would be the final blow, cousin. If that happens, the abolitionists will gain control. We'll have to secede to survive."

"*We*, Manuel?" Gassion picked at him. "Who is this *we* you speak of? The South of the white Anglo or the South of the colored Creole? Do you really think free men of color would have a chance anywhere in the South if the slave states form a separate government?"

"Of course," Manuel argued back, yielding not an inch. "Right now, we're scapegoats, but secession would eliminate the need for scapegoats. It's all the fault of those abolitionists, Gassion. They just won't let slaveowners alone. Slavery wasn't profitable up North, so now they play holier-than-thou—or else they come South and start plantations of their own, like all those New Yorkers in the Mississippi Delta."

"I'll grant that, but how does that make us scapegoats?"

"Because the more Northerners butt into Southern business, the more defensive Southerners become. White Southerners," he added, unnecessarily.

"Of course," Gassion interjected, but Manuel ignored his sarcasm as he continued his line of reasoning. "When a man's livelihood is threatened, he gets damned defensive. So, the more abolitionists rail against slavery, the more Southerners argue it's a positive good."

"Then white Southerners should not object to our ownership of slaves. We're helping the positive good, *non?*"

"*Non*, cousin," Manuel sighed. "We're the flaw in that logic. It's not enough any more to argue that slavery is permissible because it's always existed. Now the argument has to be that slavery is *beneficial* to society because blacks and coloreds aren't capable of caring for themselves."

"Aha, and we...," Gassion broke in, understanding at last the point of Manuel's argument, but his cousin yielded no turf.

"Exactly! That theory won't wash as long as we exist and prosper. So the pro-slavery devotees, like your men at Opelousas, see no course but to legislate us out of existence. I still say that most people in this state would never go that far."

"I wish I had your confidence," Gassion sighed.

"Then look around you, cousin! Our neighbors are still our friends. White

Creoles and colored ones have always been friends. I'm living proof of that. When old Alexis Cloutier tried to steal the inheritance papa left me and I was too young to fight him, our white friends took him to court and stopped him cold."

That was a point Gassion could not argue with. Time and again it had happened throughout the parish of Natchitoches, from the Coindets of Cane River to the Perots of Bayou Pierre. The courts had consistently upheld the right of white fathers to leave the fruits of their labor to their offspring by women the law would not let them marry. So, too, he had to remind himself, the appeals court of just about every Southern state was full of similar cases. It had shocked him when Sam Scruggs made that point one day, but then Scruggs had taken him down to the newspaper office at Alexandria, where there was a full run of Southern court reporters, and the facts he saw could not be argued with.

"So, Gassion," Manuel proposed, "what stand will you take on the issue? Will you join me in supporting secession or no?"

"*Malédiction,* man!" Gassion exploded. "The South could not survive on its own. Independence requires self-sufficiency. Remember the principles my papa used to preach?"

"Self-sufficiency. Self sufficiency!" Manuel couldn't help grinning.

"That's the South's problem, Manuel. Right there. No self-sufficiency. Southerners who have money plough it right back into land and slaves, into showplace homes they can't afford, and other trappings of the good life. Then they borrow Northern capital to finance each year's crop. Like Auguste did. When we felt the first financial pinch during the Crash of '37, he took a tumble. That's what the whole South would do."

"I'll concede that," Manuel nodded.

"We're totally dependent upon Northern goods because we love the earth and scorn the factory," Gassion declared. "Still, what worries me the most, should the South secede, would be the Northern reaction."

"You think they'd try to stop us?"

"You can bet your sweet cigar on that. There would be war, and the South does not have the resources to win it."

"We might surprise you, cousin."

"*We?* You'd fight?" Gassion's incredulity was obvious. Manuel just turned his back and squatted before the fireplace, checking the leg of the deer yet again.

"Manuel?" Gassion prodded.

"Oui, cousin," Manuel replied at last. "If it comes to secession and war, I'll go the way Louisiana goes. This is our home. Our families were Creoles long before we were *Américains."*

"But…"

"No more buts, cousin," Manuel declared with finality. "I do not want to hear another word about politics tonight. I planned this little dinner party to forget all these troubles, and I hear Ambroise and Louis out front now. If you don't feel up to being pleasant, you don't have to stay."

Gassion stayed, as Manuel knew he would, but the subject of politics was not dropped. In the year that followed, wherever and whenever Southern men gathered—white or colored, Anglo or Creole, Protestant or Catholic, at the dinner table or the bar stool, at the races or the front porch of the country store—slavery, secession, abolition, and war were all their constant companions.

∽ 2 ∽

Spring 1861

The Year of Decision—1860—had lived up to the hopes of many and the fears of most. In Louisiana, Creole moderates under Pierre Soulée lost to the "Southern Rights" faction under John Slidell who, ironically, was not a *real* Southerner but a transplant from New York. As the presidential election drew near that fall, secessionists brought in the Northern-reared and educated "Southern fire-eater" William L. Yancey, to argue their cause. When the ballots were finally tallied, their candidate had carried thirty-six out of the forty-eight Louisiana parishes, while Abraham Lincoln's name did not even appear on the ballot. As a secession convention met in the Baton Rouge statehouse during a frigid January of 1861, a coalition of Cane River's Anglos and Creoles, led by Dr. Samuel Oglesby Scruggs and Victor Rachal, argued passionately for the Union's preservation. They argued in vain. William Tecumseh Sherman, Superintendent of Louisiana's military academy, then resigned his commission and returned to his native Ohio, while P. G. T. Beauregard, Superintendent of the U.S. Military Academy at West Point, resigned his own commission and returned to his native Louisiana. The pawns of war were moving into place on America's chessboard.

By February, Louisiana's North Carolina-born governor had issued a decree declaring that all persons residing in the state for twelve months would become citizens of the state—all *white* persons. The Creoles of color, whose families had nurtured Louisiana's growth for a century before Governor Thomas Moore's arrival, did not merit citizenship in the new Confederate state of Louisiana. In *la ville,* free men of color volunteered for active Confederate service but were rejected, while politicians in the city tightened controls over that caste—arresting many on unsubstantiated charges of spreading "incendiary sentiments" among slaves. Then a new decree forbade colored churches to hold services, unless a white slaveowner and a peace officer were present.

All that, and more, were the subjects that Gassion and his son Gus had argued about all that Sunday morning after Mass, even after Perine had called them to the dinner table.

"Politics!" she sputtered in exasperation as they finally seated themselves and she set a heaping platter of fried rabbit in front of them. "I sure wish you had brought that wife of yours with you, Gus, so we could have a decent conversation."

Her menfolk ignored her, but she was not about to yield her ground and retreat to the kitchen. So she rearranged the steaming bowls of mustard greens, field peas, butter beans, creamed corn, and fried okra that already burdened the broad mahogany table Augustin had imported from Marseilles. As they heaped their plates, she sent her little Rosine and Flavie to retrieve the baskets of corn muffins from the warming oven.

"Isn't there anything else the two of you can talk about at Sunday dinner?"

Gassion smiled indulgently, crossed himself, and bowed his head to ask the Lord's blessing upon the bounty He had provided. Perine's question went unanswered.

"Papa, I don't understand you any more," Gus plunged back into their topic before his father's final *amen* faded into the chill that blew in off the gallery. "A year ago, you argued that Lincoln was our only hope. Now when you mention his name you all but spit it out."

"That's because Lincoln has failed us. Manuel was right about him. It's plain now that Lincoln will do nothing to help the colored planter."

"Perhaps that's because Lincoln's ideals are not limited to special interest groups, Papa. Maybe he's interested in what's best for *all* Americans. He does want peace."

"That's exactly what I want!" Perine interjected testily, but then her voice turned soft and pleading as she locked her husband's gaze with her own. "Please, *cher*? Just one Sunday dinner with no talk of war and hatred?"

This time, Gassion relented. He always did when Perine's pleading eyes probed into his own. The sturdy little cousin he had married had been everything he had hoped for in a wife. Even more. Motherhood had slimmed her plumpness, brightened her plainness. Each of the six children she had borne him over the past twelve years had added a new sparkle to her eyes, new laugh lines around the lips she used to purse habitually in her spinsterhood. *Oui,* motherhood had added fire and spirit to her once-staid soul.

"*Oui, chien-chien,*" he echoed aloud, his mouth twisting into the crooked smile that had been his legacy from the Gallic grandfather he barely could remember. "We men keep forgetting that women don't care for politics."

"Being a woman has nothing to do with it. It's being *Christian* that counts. The Lord tells us to love our neighbor, but when people talk politics these days, they all talk hate and war, not Christian peace and cooperation."

"We didn't start that, Cousin Perine," Gus butted in. "It is the rest of the world who hates us! That means we have to be prepared for whatever direction politics takes. Otherwise the free colored Creole won't survive in America."

"Well, I've done my share of preparation," Perine retorted. Indeed, she had, Gassion thought. She had listened to him and Gus argue so much about a future in which they'd lose all their slaves that, in a fit of pique six months back, she had let all her houseservants go. Since then, she and the children had survived quite well. Not only were their daughters learning new skills and more discipline, which Gassion had expected, but even their young sons were starting to take responsibility for their own personal needs, instead of expecting to have someone wait on them hand and foot. "So what have I learned?" Perine challenged the both of them. "Number one, whatever course America takes, we will survive. Number two, there is nothing either of you can do to change the direction of politics no matter how much you fume and mutter!"

Gassion forced himself to chuckle at their exchange, to ease the tension that always seemed to exist now between them and this older son Flavie Mézières had borne him. Always passionate and quick-tempered—a legacy, his papa had said, from the old commandant who had ruled the whole borderlands back in the Spanish days—Gus had thrust himself demandingly upon a world he did not understand, a world his father could no longer understand, and a world that would never give the boy a chance to live up to his heritage. Gassion worried. Gassion argued. But Gus *hated!*

Gassion sighed, yielding to another of those attacks of weariness that came too frequently of late—weariness of the worrying and the arguing and particularly the hating. Things were so much simpler, he thought, back in Papa's time. Or maybe it just seemed so because we had Papa to sort out life's confusions. *Ma foi!* how I miss the old man. He would know the best course for us right now. He should have been here running for president! *Hé!* Gassion snorted at that thought. *A colored man as president?* God's world would never last so long!

"All right, Perine," he conceded aloud, motioning for Rosine to pass him the bowl of gravy. "We'll change the subject. What would you have us talk about instead?"

"The convent," Perine replied quickly. "Mother Hyacinthe has asked if we could spare another five hundred."

"What! We've already laid out fifteen hundred this year to build those new classrooms."

"The right hand should not know what the left hand giveth," Perine smiled sweetly, but Gassion recognized the reproof and refused to be chastised.

"In times like these, a man had better keep track of his money! We've had a few good years here in the fifties, but we are in for worse troubles than we have ever had. I tell you…" His eyes had been on the gravy ladle, but he could *feel* her tense up again as he strayed back onto his favorite subject. He tried another tack.

"Besides, we've already given far more than anybody else in the state for the support of the mother convent. It seems to me that instead of asking us for more, Mother Hyacinthe should appreciate how generous we have been."

"Oui, cher," Perine agreed smoothly. "She does. Just this week, when she came upriver to check the progress of the workmen, she mentioned again the financial woes at the mother convent, and she was full of praise for us. Over and over, she told me how the devotion of our people has inspired her and her sisters."

"Well, it should!" That subject was another sore one for Gassion. In the two years since the Daughters of the Cross had announced its creation of a mission school on the Isle of Canes, it had not put one dollar into the building or its operation, while it had mortgaged itself to the hilt to provide a school for white parishioners down at Avoyelles. Here on the Isle, St. Augustin's parishioners had donated a building, then renovated it and furnished it in every way the Order said it needed. His people provided board, food, and medical care for the nuns who had been sent to staff the school. Yet there seemed to be no end to Mother Hyacinthe's pleas for five hundred for this and eight hundred for that. On his less-charitable days, Gassion had even found himself wondering whether their money wasn't being used to keep afloat the school that served those white Creoles at Avoyelles, though he knew better than to broach that suggestion to Perine!

"We promised the order that we would provide all the financial support," Perine reminded him. "You and I personally guaranteed Bishop Martin that after Grandpère died."

"*You* promised!" Gassion corrected, as he attacked another leg of rabbit.

"With your blessing, *cher.*" It was, in fact, on the basis of that promise that Bishop Martin had gone to France and persuaded the Order of the Cross to send nuns to the Isle of Canes. The problem was that St. Joseph's Convent had immediately outgrown itself, just with the girls who lived close by on the Isle, while their mushrooming family had spread so far, as each new generation had gobbled up more and more of the fertile farmland of the Cane River Valley. There was no way their girls could ride even ten, much less twenty miles and back to school every day. "The families from Cloutierville and Monette's Ferry," she went on aloud, "have asked Mother Hyacinthe to make the convent a boarding school."

"The additional tuition from those families should take care of that."

"It should," Perine agreed, "but first we have to add space, and enlarge the herd of stock to provide more milk and meat, and order more textbooks. Besides the good sisters want so badly a little chapel where they can pray in their spare moments…"

Perine's voice grew huskier, more persuasive. "It wasn't easy for Reverend Mother to ask for this, *cher.* You know the sisters have never asked anything for themselves, and they have done so much for us. Already, two of our girls are thinking about the sisterhood! We must encourage them, *cher.* There has never been a girl in all Natchitoches to take religious vows. Think how proud it would have made Grandpère for one of our girls to be the first."

Gassion swallowed the lump that choked him every time Perine mentioned his papa, and he managed a wry smile.

"All right, *chien-chien*. You know you win every time you invoke Papa's name. Tell me, which St. Augustin do you pray to?"

Perine just smiled. "We will all win from this, *cher*. The Creole girls from all the families along Cane River have needed a convent school for so long, to give them the type of religious education that molds Christian ladies."

Gassion's face twitched. "If Bishop Martin had been more adamant about our Christian rights when he opened Sacred Heart Convent at Natchitoches, we could have sent out daughters there. Instead, he backed down when all the good white townfolk raised their howl of protest."

"Not even Sacred Heart would have been the answer to our need, *cher*. Not all our people could afford to board all their daughters at Natchitoches. No, it's far better that we have our own school. In fact…"

"In fact, *what?*" Gus interjected sharply as Perine broke off and her thought was left unspoken. St. Joseph's Convent for the girls of the Isle meant little to him one way or the other. His babes were too young to attend. But the newest thrust of his stepmother's remarks brought to mind snatches of another conversation he had overheard after Mass that morning. He had, in fact, been meaning to ask Perine to clarify what he had heard.

Intuitively, she sensed his sudden tension and smiled back. "In fact, our people are not the only ones on the Isle with this problem. Just this morning, Mrs. Collins asked my advice on what she should do with her daughters."

Gus's eyes hardened and he sipped slowly, deliberately, from his tall glass of tea while he waited for Perine to go on.

"You know, there are four of the Collins girls who are now school-aged," she continued, addressing herself casually in her husband's direction rather than her stepson's. "But there is no public school in this area and the Collinses are just small farmers. They can't afford to board four daughters in Natchitoches, although it did embarrass Mrs. Collins to have to tell me that. She is a genteel lady, and went to school herself in Alabama. It really troubles her now that her daughters have had no formal education."

"What concern is that of ours?" Gus demanded.

"Our neighbors' problems are always our concern," Perine answered him evenly. "Isn't that the Christian way?"

"Well, there are white Christians and there are colored Christians," her stepson shot back. "Papa just reminded us of that. The white Christians of

Natchitoches set the example when they shut our girls out of Sacred Heart. I say if they don't want us mixing with them, then we sure as hell won't invite them to come mix with us!"

"Mrs. Collins had nothing to do with the decision at Sacred Heart."

"She's white, isn't she?"

"Gus! Since when do we condemn anyone on the basis of their color? You have been reared better than that!"

"I also was brought up to believe in the Biblical rule 'an eye for an eye'!"

Perine sighed and her eyes sought her husband's for support, but she found none. Gassion picked doggedly at the fried okra crumbs on his place, refusing to raise his gaze to meet her own.

"Gus… son…" she began again and then stopped again, weighing exactly how to proceed. "You can't hate the white man. He's as much a part of you as the black man is. More so. Your mother's father, her mother's father, your papa's grandfathers, all of them were white. Oh, Gus, don't you see? When whites and blacks war now, you cannot let yourself become the victim of their hatred. You'll fight yourself more than you will any other man, and you'll tear yourself apart."

"Oh?" her stepson retorted. "Does not the Bible also tell us that if our right eye offends us we should pluck it out?"

"Only if your right eye leads you from the path of God. Loving and respecting all parts of your heritage is a good thing, Gus, not a sinful one."

"*Zut,* Perine!" Gus's sarcasm was caustic. "Are you trying to tell me *that* part of our heritage had no sin involved? How do you think we got here? Only Christ was conceived immaculately, you know."

Across the table from him, a flock of children, restless and bored as always by the conversation of their elders, showed sudden interest in the turn the conversation had taken—but their mother gasped. This time, Gassion did intercede for her. "All right, son. You've gone too far now. I suggest you apologize to Perine for your disrespect!"

"No, *cher,*" she sighed. "I'm not his mother. I'm the one who is out of place for lecturing him as though I were." Just for a moment, she thought she saw the harshness soften in Gus's face. Gambling that she could bypass this stepson who now battled daily with his father and knowing that his father was weary from those battles, she pressed on.

Reaching across the table to take Gassion's hand, the one picking at the okra, she silently willed him to look at her. "Gassion, it's because I *am* a mother, that I can feel the worries of other mothers. That is why I'm asking for your permission to let the Collins girls come to the convent this fall. If you consent, I know the rest of our people will."

"By God, no!" Gus bellowed, throwing his napkin into the center of the table as he sprang from his chair. "The land St. Joseph's stands on will one day be mine. If I have any say-so, no white child will set foot inside our school until the whites let my sisters go to theirs!"

Stricken, they sat there at the Sunday table, even the babies Annice and Augustin, agog at the furor in Gus's voice, agape at the thought that anyone had spoken so to the man who had inherited the mantle of Grandpère Augustin. Eventually, Gassion spoke—nay, ruled—but it was clear from the droop of his shoulders that the mantle was one he did not want.

"No, son, you do not have a say-so, not so long as you express yourself in such uncivil terms. I have considered your opinion, but this is still my land. If Mrs. Collins can afford the tuition, then her daughters are welcome."

⟨⟩ 3 ⟨⟩

February 1862

Dr. Jean Napoleon Burdin's crisp commands rang sharply across the field. "Squadron front! Form columns! Close up ranks!" In unison, Augustin's Guards responded to their drillmaster, executing every movement with grace and precision, and the murmur of appreciation that rose among the spectators soon ripened into open cheers.

"M'sieur Metoyer, I am impressed." The concession came reluctantly from the lanky newspaper editor, new to the parish, whom Gassion had invited out to the Isle. "I will admit, I came to these maneuvers armed with skepticism. The Hertzogs told me I would be pleasantly surprised at the expertise your cavalry has developed in so short a time. But my friends, they have spent their lives on the frontiers of Louisiana, *n'est-ce pas?* They have never known a war. So I asked myself, what do the Hertzogs know of military skill?"

Gassion smiled noncommittally. "While you, Editor Le Gendre, are a man admirably qualified to pass on such performances, or so I hear."

"Merci," Ernest Le Gendre replied, with a measure of wistfulness softening his nasal French. "Alas, M'sieur, that is why I am here in this country. My participation in the Revolution of '48 made me not so welcome in *la France.*"

"Then your praise is doubly valued."

"You are kind, M'sieur, but I am truthful. I am amazed at the uniformity and precision of this squadron. The captain's commands are firm and in good cadence. The drillmaster certainly knows his business. But the superb horsemanship and the intelligent enthusiasm of your soldiers are amazing! I assure you, I have seen many troops train in Europe, and I marvel at how this squadron of yours could have achieved such perfection in so short a time."

"Perhaps the answer, as you have put it yourself, M'sieur, is their intelligence and enthusiasm," Gassion suggested pointedly.

"Eh? *Donc!* The men are enthusiastic, *certainement.* In fact, the whole parish has been quite impressed with your people's fervent support of our war."

"With all due respect, M'sieur, it is *our* war, too. Louisiana has been our home for a century and a quarter. My family has fought in every conflict—the Indian wars, the Anglo fight for independence, the War of 1812, the Mexican War. In fact," Gassion added proudly, "one of our number was breveted a United States major on the battlefield in that conflict."

"Really? I thought… ah… I thought that colored people did not serve as officers in American armies."

"This cousin did not volunteer here. Nor did he volunteer the fact that he was colored."

"Ahhh," Le Gendre smiled conspiratorially. "My apologies, sir, if my remarks have offended you. I mean only praise. Your patriotism is inspiring. I, for one, was pleased when Governor Moore finally authorized the colored men of this state to form militia units."

At our own expense, Gassion thought caustically. The white militia has been given arms, horses, uniforms, and ammunition. We have to supply our own. That way, the good people of this state can sleep easier knowing that only the *better class* of free coloreds will be armed.

"Oui," Le Gendre continued on enthusiastically. "With the enemy prowling the Gulf, your men will be most valuable in the defense of our homefront."

"If the situation becomes grave enough that the governor calls us out."

"Ah, but the situation, it is grave already. The enemy vows to take New Orleans before the end of spring. The other militias of this parish, they have been ordered to mobilize. They will be leaving Monday, I am told."

"How interesting!" Gassion mused aloud. "Neither the Augustin's Mounted Guards nor the Monette's Infantry has received any such order."

"Hehn? Well, they will. *Certainement.* Our Parish Police Jury, it has already appropriated the funds to send your people down to *la ville."*

Sur ma foi! Gassion muttered to himself, having heard that news a week or more before. Six hundred dollars for the mobilization expenses of their two squadrons, plus a twenty-five-dollar bounty per man—exactly half the bounty appropriated by the police jury for the *white* militiamen. The bitterness that burned his craw so much of late began to seethe again.

In a way, this war he had opposed from the beginning had brought his people closer to their white neighbors, but in too many other ways it underscored the widening chasm. He had meant it when he told Le Gendre it was *their* war, because Louisiana was their home. They had no choice but to serve its cause—doomed or not—even though some of them, himself included, felt that cause was wrong. And he, for one, was damned glad he was too old to be expected to volunteer, even for the militia.

"Form single rank!" Burdin commanded sharply from the field, and the columns wheeled in obeyance. "Prepare to charge! Charge!"

"Hé!" Le Gendre chortled as the line of cavalrymen pummeled past a split-rail fence, and each man slashed the stuffed figure that was tied astride. "Is that Abe Lincoln's name I see scrawled across that effigy?"

"None other," Gassion answered curtly. "That's Burdin's doings. For an *émigré* who has never taken out citizenship here, he has become a Confederate of the first order."

"An admirable man," Le Gendre nodded. "You are lucky to have a man of his experience drilling your men."

"Frankly, we had no other choice." Gassion did not bother to elaborate. The editor of the parish paper, having published lists of every man in every Confederate unit and every militia company as each was formed, should well know how few men were left in the parish. The laws of the New Regime in Louisiana had not changed since the Anglo usurpers made them back before the War of 1812. Colored Creoles could form militias, under state authority, only if they had *whites* to fill all the officerships—and the Confederate draft had taken up every able-bodied white male citizen between eighteen and forty-five. Knowing their predicament, Burdin volunteered. He appeared to be qualified—he was white and had seen his share of military action as part of the French army, or so he claimed. Ergo, the man became their drillmaster.

Le Gendre's eyebrows were raised quizzically, and a hint of a smile played around the corners of his mouth. "M'sieur, do I detect disenchantment in your remark?"

"Not disenchantment, disrespect. Mutual."

"*Tiens!* How so?"

"M'sieur Editor, when a man leaves his own dirt-floored cabin, mounts his half-blind mare, and rides up to my Big House, where he proceeds to address me with less civility than I show my field hands, then I'd say there is no love lost on either side."

"*Sur ma foi*, M'sieur! What a good thing it is you are not in his command! That kind of attitude in a soldier would undermine discipline."

"You are quite right," Gassion agreed tersely. "It's a good thing I'm not under his command."

"Dismount!" Burdin barked again. "That's all for today, men. Be back here tomorrow. Three o'clock sharp! Anybody who's tardy will have to answer to me!"

"*Pardonnez-moi*, M'sieur," Le Gendre excused himself. "I should interview the drillmaster also for my *Chronicle* account of these maneuvers. Good luck to you and your men, Metoyer."

"Of course," Gassion responded, to Le Gendre's back as it was, since the editor had pushed his way so quickly into the crowds. *Oui*, M'sieur Drillmaster must be interviewed, since M'sieur Editor's readers will surely wonder how the colored guard units now protecting them could execute their drills with such a display of horsemanship—not to mention precision.

"*Hé*, cousin!"

Gassion relaxed and turned an indulgent smile toward the sound of Manuel's voice, wordlessly taking in the once-crisp uniform that was now withered and clinging damply to Dupré's stocky frame, the stolid face that was flushed as much from excitement as from the exertion that was too strenuous for a man past forty-five. Not that Manuel would ever admit the strain, of course.

Joseph Emanuel Dupré

C. S. A. Militiaman
Augustin's Mounted Guards

"So, what did you think, Gassion? We're getting better every day, *non?*"

"*Oui,* Manuel," Gassion retorted, making no effort to hide his cynicism. "It's just a shame it's only fun and games."

"Ah, cousin! You don't let up, do you? I tell you, we'll be called. When we are, we'll be ready."

"For what? Pageantry duty again at another white hero's funeral? Like the one last Sunday? We were all impressed, Manuel. Two companies of white militia escorting the white body into Cloutierville, with two companies of colored militia falling *respectfully* behind, as the *Chronicle* put it. The captains of the white companies firing their final salutes into the grave of the stricken hero; while the two companies of colored militia fired their salutes *respectfully above* the grave."

Manuel colored from even more than the flush of the heat. Still he stubbornly shook his craggy head. "Cousin, I don't understand you any more. With every day that passes you grow more sarcastic."

"More disillusioned, Manuel. Disillusioned. When I wake up every morning and ride out over my place, and I look at my sheds bulging with cotton I can't sell because of the blockade of New Orleans, when I send my hands out to the fields to plant a new crop, knowing that I probably can't sell that one either, then I ask myself, *what is all this for?*"

"For freedom, cousin."

"Whose?" Gassion demanded. "Ours or our slaves?"

"For the South's freedom. For every working man's right to run his own life, without some outsider telling him he has no right to do this or that!"

"*Every* working man's rights, Manuel? Slaves are working men, too."

"You know what I mean!" Manuel muttered. "I'm talking about men of property, *citizens.*"

"Ah, then that excludes us, because we are no longer citizens no matter how much some of you delude yourselves. Even in the Confederacy, we don't vote, and we can't serve on juries—or in the white man's army."

Manuel pounded the sides of his head in frustration. "You just like to argue, Gassion. You know damned well there's a difference between us and slaves. You have to admit, too, the Confederacy's been a lot nicer to us than you predicted. There's been a new constitution, but where are all those laws against us you thought they'd write into it? Hunh?"

"*Oui, oui,*" Gassion conceded, grinning fondly at this cousin dressed out, in spite of the heat, in full dress uniform with a velvet collar, gold buttons, and a cocky feather in his hat. All that's missing, he noted, were the epaulets and the medals that the new Confederate States of America would never approve for its colored militias. His smile faded faster than it came.

"Sure, Manuel. I'll allow, I was wrong about the laws, but that's all the consideration we'll get from this new government, mark my words."

"No, I won't, cousin. What about public attitudes? Didn't I tell you that all the hostile rhetoric and threats of reenslavement would cease once we were out of the Union?"

"Ask yourself why, Manuel. It's because we're needed now. All the able-bodied white males around us are riding off to war, leaving their women and children and old men at the mercy of the slaves who outnumber them—not to mention all the poor free *nègres* whose blood and poverty have tied them to the slaves. That makes the slaveowning *Créole de couleur* the buffer now, Manuel. Our wealth, culture, and education is simply the salt that makes the crow palatable, now that they have to eat it."

"We always have been the buffer."

"We were *once* the buffer," Gassion shot back. *Oui,* he added to himself, we were definitely that for our old friends. *Creole* friends. Jean Prudhomme, Louis Derbanne, and their generation—they understood how crucial it was to society for us to stand between blacks and whites as a neutral caste. But those who have taken their places over the past quarter-century have grown up with Anglo scorn for Creole ways. They may not call us *niggers* yet, but they no longer stand up to those who do, like Jean and Louis and Ben used to.

Manuel, he realized, was just standing there shaking his head, and it was that perplexed look on his cousin's face that threatened to send Gassion over the edge. He steeled himself before he spoke again, but when he did, his voice still seethed.

"I suppose you've heard, Manuel, that Gus has had nine offers so far from white planters along the river? Now that they have to leave their business in the hands of inexperienced wives, they come begging to hire our sons as managers—happy to have hard-working, responsible, free men of color around. But you don't really expect that to last any longer than this war does, do you?"

"Yes, I do," Manuel answered matter-of-factly. "Gassion, sometimes it takes something catastrophic like war to remind all people that they need each other. It's God's way of teaching humility and charity and love."

"Then I'm not learning my lessons very well."

"Oh? Aren't you sparing a few of your hands this spring to help plant the crops of the poor soldiers' wives?"

"Of course. We all are."

"That's charity and love, cousin," Manuel grinned. "Two out of three virtues will do. None of us were very good at humility anyway."

Gassion gave up. *"Zut!* Will I never win an argument with you, Manuel?"

"Probably not. So why do you keep trying?"

"Because I keep hoping to penetrate that wall of complacency you hide behind."

"Some of us prefer not to torment ourselves, cousin, but that doesn't mean we're complacent," Manuel replied soberly.

"Torment? When does the truth become torment, Manuel?"

"When a man cannot decide for himself what the truth is. That's your problem, Gassion. You are at war with yourself. One part of you is every bit as tied to our way of life as the rest of us are, but the other part of you is a dreamer. You look to a world that doesn't exist, and never will exist, and that part of you can't accept reality either."

"For a man who never finds time to read, Manuel, you're quite a philosopher."

Dupré shrugged. "Some people study books. Others study people."

"Ah, ça!" Gassion grinned at last, but it was not really a smile. "That reminds me, Le Gendre says the Pied à Chausseurs and the Cloutierville Home Guard have received orders to move out Monday for *la ville."*

"Hehn?"

"That's what I thought. You didn't know. The colored Guards obviously won't be going with the white ones."

"But we're ready! We showed everybody that today!"

"Sur ma foi, you showed them, Manuel. It's been a dull time here on the home front. The novelty of daily sacrifices has worn off. People are restless and bored. So you did your duty. A crowd turned out, eager for entertainment, and you put on a good show."

"Now, cousin! There you go again!"

Gassion did smile then, cynically, as he slid Manuel's new saber from its sheath, turning it admiringly, watching the afternoon sun glow softly upon its burnished steel.

"Take my advice, Manuel, and have your picture made in that fine uniform before it gets worn out from drilling. You'll want a nice memory from this war to share with your grandchildren when you get old."

Still smiling, Gassion resheathed his cousin's sword and walked away.

∽ 4 ∽

New Orleans fell that spring, 1862, while Augustin's Mounted Guards and Monette's Infantry chafed at home, ostensibly needed to keep peace and order along Cane River. Then the occupation of Louisiana's capital by "Beast" Ben Butler and his bluecoats tightened the chains of fear and deprivation that already choked Louisiana.

For Creoles of color, the fall of *la ville* actually offered an opportunity to escape the South's defeat. Butler's Army opened its arms—at least one of them—to Louisiana's free Negroes, but its other arm blatantly held up all the social and racial barriers between white Northern soldiers and free colored ones. Of all the free Negro militiamen in the state, the only ones willing to exchange their gray uniforms for blue were those in the occupied city, and even they soon learned that Northern "liberation" did not mean *equality*. In the backcountry of Louisiana, the free men of color remained carefully neutral or staunchly Confederate.

For Creoles of all colors, many of whom shared Gassion's conviction that the war was wrong, the fall of New Orleans sent old Louisiana to its deathbed. Its governor had already decreed that no planter could harvest more than five bales of cotton per year until the blockade could be breached. Then the fall of *la ville* itself closed Louisiana's only port to all crops. Northwestwardly from the fallen city, the broad, open river wound enticingly through the heart of the richest cotton-producing region of the state, the valleys of the Red and the Cane, where one year's entire crop was stored and another already had sprouted. Louisiana's invaders now lounged in the plush city homes they had commandeered and laid plans to ravage the upriver harvest.

On the first of May 1862, Manuel sat dejectedly in his store, alone and staring at his half-bare shelves and his even emptier cash box.

"Ah, Manuel," Gassion greeted him at the door. "You look so glum. Don't you know it's every man's patriotic duty to suffer cheerfully?"

"Poppycock! How can I be cheerful when I haven't had a customer in two days? And that includes the Widow Hertzog just now. I had to let her walk out of here without the ball of twine she needed, because I couldn't give her change for her dollar and she couldn't afford to spend the rest of the only bill she had. How in the devil am I going to get small change if customers don't bring it in, hunh?"

"You haven't heard the half of our woes, Manuel. Since you normally have so little time for reading, I thought I'd ride over and share with you the latest news from the *Natchitoches Union.*"

"I have a feeling I don't want to hear it."

"You don't, but you need to. This is the governor's latest proclamation, and Thomas O. Moore does expect to be obeyed. Brace yourself."

> The extraordinary efforts of the enemy to capture our chief city have been successful. It is our duty now to deprive him of the fruits of victory. I therefore order the destruction of all cotton within the limits of Louisiana that is in danger of falling into the hands of the enemy, and I direct the militia officers in the several parishes to execute this order. In case those officers should not be able to act with sufficient promptitude, let the torch be applied by persons appointed by the several Police Juries.

"Burn our cotton?" Manuel exploded when he finished. "That's all most of us have left!" Manuel's plight was indeed grim. Since currency had become all but nonexistent, he and other merchants along the river had let their penniless customers pay for goods with the cotton they could not sell. Every storehouse had become, in fact, a *storehouse.* Bales were crammed under and on their porches and in their kitchens; and when all other nooks and crannies were filled, the merchants brought baskets of that white gold inside their shops to fill the shelves that were being emptied of other goods they could not replace for want of any cash of their own. If he burned this cotton, what would he have left?

"But it's our *duty,* Manuel," Gassion retorted, a mocking edge cutting through his crooked smile. "The Northern factories are running short of cotton now.

They are laying off workers. Northern families are going hungry. Our enemy is now feeling the pinch of war. We can't sit on our bales and let them steam straight upriver and take it to ease their own distress—and fill their pockets. Now can we?"

"I think you're being sarcastic again."

"Oh, I am." Gassion's smile grew broader. "We do have two alternatives."

"Only two?"

"Now you're being sarcastic yourself. First of all, Manuel, we have to build this river's defenses. Note that the governor's proclamation to burn becomes effective only if this cotton is in direct danger of being seized. If we can keep the Yankees out of Red River and the Cane, then our cotton is in no danger. There's already a call for volunteers for this defense."

"Volunteers? All the strong-backed males of this parish have already left."

"The *whites* have. Or they've fled to the hills or to Texas. That leaves us and the slaves. We're both admirably suited for digging ditches and building earthwalls, wouldn't you say?"

"No, I would not. I've never dug a ditch in my life," Manuel grunted.

"Well, I have. Once. But only because I chose to. You can take my word for it, it is not our kind of work. I'll volunteer my hands, all they want of them, but they'll have a devil of a time trying to draft me or my boys for that kind of service."

"Then what's our other alternative?"

"We pray."

"Eh?"

"For the blockade runners, Manuel," Gassion grinned. "They are setting up operations around the Río Grande and Matamoros, and their agents are already here on the river to buy up cotton."

"Aha!" Manuel nodded appreciatively. "So we do have a viable option."

"Perhaps. Things are never as simple as they seem, of course." Gassion's grin stayed in place, belying the caveat of his words. Nothing was ever simple, but the latest turn of events had renewed his faith in the ingenuity—and perfidy—of his fellow man. North and South, the disunited states of America were filled with French and English *émigrés* who had long proclaimed themselves to be American although they had never bothered to swear their allegiance in a court of law. Now, with France and England vowing to remain neutral, the non-American

Americans were perfectly poised to profit from the needs of true Americans, North and South. Although the Union forces had the Gulf blockaded, Louisiana's white gold could still be taken overland into Mexico for shipment to markets abroad as well as to the North. After all, any vessel loaded with cotton owned by a *neutral* citizen of France or Britain could not be seized by U.S. gunboats without violating international law.

Manuel still waited for an explanation, so Gassion gave the short version. "According to the agent who approached me yesterday, they aren't paying cash in advance—just contracting to buy, and we have to keep the cotton until the blockade runners can move it out of here. That might take as little as a month. Or a year. In the meanwhile, we still have to find storage space for new crops, and we still have to worry about the North seizing it or the South burning it."

"Frankly, I think we'd have done better if we had planted foodstuff this year instead of cotton."

"Now, you sound like my father, Manuel. Self-sufficiency. Self-sufficiency."

"Well, he was right."

"Oh, I won't dispute that. Only, food crops require seed, too, and there's none to be had, and if any more of my hogs get the thumps, I'm liable not to have any meat, either."

"The thumps? What have you been doing for it?"

"Everything everyone suggests, Manuel, and so far nothing helps."

"Well, there was this man in the store last week who swore he'd found a surefire cure. He says he puts shelled corn in a trough and covers it with tar water, then he stirs it good and turns the hogs loose on it. Have you tried that one?"

"Corn stewed in tar water? *Non.*"

"He swears it works."

"Then I'll try it. I'll try anything at this point."

"Oh, by the way, Gassion. Perine asked me at Mass Sunday if I thought I'd get any fresh quinine in stock for the summer and I told her not to expect it. This same fellow tells me that he uses the dogwood berry. One pill per dose. Maybe she ought to try it."

"Thanks. I'll pass it on… "

"The *berry?*" Perine exclaimed when Gassion relayed Manuel's message to her that night.

"That's what he said."

"Just pop a berry? Like a pill?"

"Oui."

"Man, do you know what I've been doing all day?"

"Cooking apparently. Your hair's still damp around the edges. It nice and kinky when it's damp. Did you ever notice that, Perine?" he teased, settling back into the old rocker that still sat on the gallery where Augustin had used it.

Perine plunked herself down beside him, pursed her lips, and vigorously blew a fresh puff of air upward to cool her still-flushed face. "I've been *brewing,* that's what!" she said wearily, as she eased herself into the porch swing and drew out a torn shirt, a home-whittled needle, and a twist of thread from the mending basket at her side.

"Week before last, the *Union* carried this new recipe for a quinine substitute, and after Manuel told me he didn't expect any fresh stock I decided to try this other concoction. That's what I've been doing all day."

"I gather the recipe wasn't quite as simple as popping a berry."

"And a far cry from the flatroot Mama used to work with, but that's just about gone on the Isle. Along with the red dogwood, which is what this recipe calls for. I found one tree on Papa's back forty, then I had to strip off the inside bark, chop it all up small and boil it until it was as thick as molasses—stirring nonstop the whole time. All while you were gossiping with Manuel at the store, of course."

"Ah, but *ma petite,*" Gassion grinned, "women were made for chopping and stirring. It makes their breasts ride high."

"Well, you'd better put your mind elsewhere, because I'm in no mood tonight. Rosine and I had to strain that cauldron four times. Then after we cooked that concoction until it was as thick as jelly, we had to work in a peck of flour and roll it all out into a thousand tiny little pills and spread them out on the roof to dry—all while you were gossiping with Manuel at the store, of course," she jibed again.

Gassion was about to add that the climbing was good for her legs, too, but she cut him off. "Man, when I climbed down the last time, I was ready to collapse, but I still felt good inside, knowing we'd have medicine for the slaves and the children when swamp fever sets in. Now you tell me all I had to do is go out and pluck the berries!"

Gassion decided to be serious. "Look at it another way, *chien-chien.* You have double protection now. If one doesn't work, you can use the other."

"Some consolation, now that I've used the last of our flour."

"*Hehn?*"

"And soda. I've been soaking corncob ashes to make an acid I can substitute. And we're out of coffee. Tomorrow, I'll be roasting and grinding peanuts to brew for you. Or would you prefer that I use the *Union* recipe for brewing beets?"

"*Nom de Dieu,* Perine! A Creole's got to have his coffee!"

"Then go tell that to Beast Butler. You can bow down on your soft knees that have no callouses from field work and say, 'Mista Butler, suh, I's a good feller an' I's do luv de Union. Please, suh, ken I hev some coffee?'"

"That's not funny, Perine."

" Just don't tell him your wife and her friends are having a musical Sunday to raise money for our sick and wounded soldiers. Or that our Ladies' Aid Society just shipped out a wagon load of underdrawers and socks, and summer clothes, and guava jelly, and vinegar, and pickles, and dried pumpkin, and tallow, and…"

"No wonder we're starving!" Gassion groaned. "You're sending it all off to the army!"

"They would starve if we didn't," Perine said quietly. "At least those of us who are here at home can grow more."

"There's a limit to what even you can do, Perine."

"None of us know the limits of our strength," she sighed, wearily pushing at a damp curl that kept falling into her eyes. "We're just beginning to learn."

Gassion rose from his rocker, gently tucked the curl back under her cap, and began to rub her shoulders and neck in the old, gentle way that never failed to soothe her whenever life tied her nerves into knots.

"Sometimes, *chien-chien,* your strength amazes me." In fact, sometimes when he watched her labor, hours on end, never complaining, it brought back memories of his old grandmother and the little cabin where he had sometimes spent the night—back before she became ill and his papa brought her down to Yucca Bend to live with them. *Oui,* she would work until she looked as though she would collapse any minute, but she always insisted she wasn't tired. She'd do everything for the little ones—and for her slaves, too.

Thinking on that, he chortled, prompting Perine to raise quizzical brows.

"Oh, I was just thinking of Mère Coincoin. It's funny. Sometimes I used to wonder, when I was a very little child, if they were her slaves or if she were theirs. She always seemed to be working more than they did. Always doing for them. If they were sick, she sat up and nursed them. All night, even. As many as she had, too, it seemed as though there always was one sick or birthing or something."

"No wonder she gave them away to her children!" Perine laughed. "Sometimes I think I'd rather give all ours away, too. Like today, when I was making all those pills they'll need."

"Are you serious, Perine?" Gassion asked, and Perine turned sharply at the gravity in his voice.

"No, but you sound like you are."

"I may be, *chien-chien.* Sometimes I really think it would be better for us as well as the *nègres* if we farmed with free labor. Since you let the houseservants go, I've noticed a real difference in the children. This younger set of ours is growing up more independent, more self-reliant, than my older boys—than Gus was the day he married and moved out."

"Aha! I hear someone taking my name in vain!" A voice spoke tartly behind them. "Evening, Cousin Perine, Papa."

"Gus!" Perine smiled as her stepson bent to kiss her hello, past arguments forgotten—or at least ignored. "We didn't see you ride up. Where's Estelle?"

"She's visiting Mama Morin, and I didn't ride up. I walked over the back way. I needed to see your blacksmith about doing some work over at my place, so I came up by way of the quarters. Where is everyone? The house is quiet for once, and I know you didn't put all the babies to bed this early."

"Rosine took them over to the school. The sisters and the students are putting on some sort of children's play tonight. I know I should have gone," Perine interjected quickly, but then her voice trailed off wearily.

"*Why* should you?" Gus challenged from his perch on the railing, as he brushed off his father's offer of a cigar.

"Oh, I don't know," Perine stammered, momentarily surprised at the questions. "Mothers are just supposed to."

"Even after as hard a day as you've obviously had? Pardon me for saying so, Cousin Perine, but you look like you just slaughtered, skinned, and salted down a whole hog by yourself."

Her hand flew abashedly to the lank corkscrews that were again straggling from her cap.

"So why should you feel guilty about letting Rosine take the children tonight while you stayed home?" Gus insisted. "I swear, I don't know what's happened to the people around here. *Everyone* seems to want to be a martyr. Women as well as men."

"Son, have you been drinking?" Gassion asked sharply.

Gus pretended to jest, but his tone was still edgy. *"Sapristi,* Papa! Since when have you found fault in drinking?"

"In moderation, never. To excess, always. You seem to be tottering on the line, son."

"Papa, the older you get the more you remind me of old Grandpère."

"What's wrong with that?"

"In his time, nothing, but today a man like him would be out of place."

"He only died six years ago, Gus."

"The whole world has changed in those six years. How do you think he'd deal with those changes?"

"Which ones, specifically?"

"This war, for one thing—this long overdue war we're in."

Gassion eyed him curiously from the rocker, his papa's rocker, its old runners creaking as he began to bob back and forth. "Are you being facetious, Gus? Or are you saying now that you favor the war? You, who have steadfastly resisted every attempt to draft you into one of our Guard units?"

"Ah, Papa, that's the problem. Our Guards aren't fighting on the right side."

"Hehn?" Gassion's pipe sputtered onto his lap as his jaw fell, and he furiously beat at the hot embers that smoldered through his pants. "Boy, you know I did not approve of secession, and I did not want to see this war—but that's the course Louisiana decided upon, and we're bound to see it through!" *What was it is his papa had said?* Back in the forties when they had made that steamboat run down to New Orleans and he had ventured to mention his idea about leaving Louisiana in hopes of a better life in Mexico. *This is your heritage, boy! No matter how Louisiana changes, this is* our home. *We Creoles built this state, and we will not forfeit it!*

"Maybe I should go on down to New Orleans," Gus proposed. "By signing up with the Union Army, I could help end this mess sooner."

Veins bulged across Gassion's temple, but he checked his anger before he spoke. "You would fight against your own people?"

"The way I see it, Papa, it would be fighting *for* my people. For justice. For equality. That's what the Union promises us, you know."

"The promises of Yankee Anglos aren't worth a tinker's damn!"

"They're better than what we've got! You'd rather spend your life bowing and scraping before every white man, no matter how trashy?"

"By God, son, that is one thing I've never done!"

"Oh, then what do you call it? Remember the time that scum at the dog fights knocked off your top hat just to see what you'd do about it?"

"What could I have done." Gassion replied miserably. It was a statement, not a question. Gus knew as well as he that the laws of this New Regime in Louisiana—these Anglo laws—did not permit a colored man to strike a white. And Gus knew what it had been like before. The boy had heard enough of his Grandpère's stories of life under the laws of Spain, when a free colored Creole could even challenge a white man to a duel if an affront deserved avenging. Gus had heard his *grandpère's* account of the time that first English Negro in the parish was being whipped unmercifully by an overseer, and how the man had "accidentally" axed his attacker to death and still had received no punishment at all from old Commandant De Blanc. In fact, Mère Coincoin's sister Tante Jeanne, had been the witness in that case. She had told what happened, straight and honest, and De Blanc had valued her word, right along with the *nègre's* right to defend himself. *Mon dieu!* How times had changed.

"Like I said, Papa," Gus repeated unmercifully, "you now bow and scrape."

"Gus," Gassion began heavily, then stopped again, trying to marshal his arguments into a battle line even he knew was defenseless. "There's a lot that needs changing, but there are times when changes can be made and times they can't."

"Face it, Papa," Gus cut in rudely. "You grumble, but it doesn't *gall* you the way it should. You can endure it all, just as long as you can dress up like Grandpère and swagger around the race track like Lord Chesterfield in blackface."

Mon dieu! The boy had gone too far! Gassion purpled, and struggled to regain some semblance of control before he gave Gus the dressing-down that was long overdue. He could forgive the boy's sass; boys grow out of that, but *never* had he allowed criticism of his papa in his presence! Not by anybody. Never mind that he and his papa had had their differences, just as he and Gus now. That still gave Gus no right to…

His son heard the thoughts he didn't really have to say, and simply laughed. "Papa, Papa. Save your anger for the enemy, if we ever decide who the enemy is. What I say is true and you know it. That's why you're so touchy. The old man was always the courtly Lord Chesterfield. Perfectly upright. Impeccably tailored. His nose up in the air like he was better than everyone else, and if they didn't agree, then to hell with them—as if they were beneath his soiling his hands on them."

"Which they were!"

"The shitty truth, Papa, is that he didn't dare soil his hands on them!"

That did it!

"Boy, no colored man ever stood up for his rights more than your Grand-père did!" Gassion thundered back. "When old François Roubieu tried to take a chunk of relatively worthless back land from him, he spent forty thousand dollars fighting him in court. And he won. In fact… " In fact, had Gassion been less angry, he would have slapped his knees and cackled as he recalled Augustin's biggest triumph in that case. "In fact, he even hired Roubieu's attorneys away from him! The very lawyers who filed Roubieu's suit against Papa were the same lawyers who won Papa's case for him in the end!"

Gus was not impressed. "Courts! Courts are for old men and women who can't fight. Or chicken-livered young ones who are afraid to challenge offenders to their face."

"Gus. Oh, Gus." Like a long-festering canker that, when pricked, spouts its purulence and then collapses flat, Gassion's outburst left him even more depressed. *Why did he bother? Why did he keep trying to make Gus see that their hopes for the future lay only in restoring the past?* "That's not how the system works for colored men," he said at last. "The courts are the only place left where we have equal rights in Louisiana."

"Then we're back to my original argument, Papa. It's time the system was overthrown."

Gassion had found yet another boil. "Overthrown? *Sacrebleu,* boy! This family has never overthrown any system. We work *within* the system to get what we want. Peacefully. It's been a damned effective system for us. It's gotten us out of the slave camps and up here into the Big House."

"Yet it won't keep us here, Papa. You know I'm right, too. I listened to your arguments with the rest of the family often enough before this war started. You said then what I'm saying now. Things will never be like they were before, and it's up to us to change them for the better. If we don't, those who hate us will change them for the worse."

"Yes, Gus," Gassion replied heavily. "I've long argued for change. I've squarely faced our prospects for the future, and they scare me, but war is no time for internal dissension. We're in the midst of a *war*. Louisiana has to remain unified to stand against the enemy, because a house divided against…"

"…itself will fall," Gus finished mockingly. "I know. I memorized that proverb at Grandpère's knee. The real question is *who's the enemy?*"

"The enemy is whoever invades our land."

"Even if they have come to enforce our rights, Papa? To bring us freedom and equality?"

"Freedom? Equality? Don't you read the papers, son? Haven't you heard the kind of equality the bluecoats brought to New Orleans? Colored Creoles have had their property confiscated and destroyed, at whim! If they own slaves, the Yankees justify their villainy by claiming our class of people has no right to the fruits of slave labor. Then when they want something a poor colored man has, they claim he stole it!"

"Hogwash!" Gus sniffed. "You know how those newspapers exaggerate."

"Certainly they do. Sensation sells copies. But my friends in *la ville* write me the same, and I know they speak the truth."

Gus shrugged, tossed his cigarette butt into the night, and then pulled from his hip pocket the flask he had been craving a taste of for most of that evening's argument. Staring down the disapproving look he got from both Gassion and Perine, he took a swig, but his sneer stayed in place. Gassion tried again.

"Son, the real truth is that neither side is our friend. There are a half-million of us free coloreds in America now and nobody wants us. They especially don't want those of us who have worked and made something of ourselves. We're the gravel stuck in everybody's craw, North as well as South. Each side has its own ideas about slavery and race relations and we spoil it all."

"Then why are you supporting the Confederacy?"

"Not the Confederacy, Gassion—Louisiana. That's what we're fighting for now. Our homes and everything we've worked for. That's what we'll lose if

Louisiana falls to the Yankees and the Anglos who run their government. It's not only us they are determined to bury. It's the whole Creole way of life that gave us the opportunity to prosper."

⚹ 5 ⚹

Summer 1863

"Well, I'll be Gawd-damned, Joe. You wuz right. This here Big House is owned by high-yallers. Lookee, here's one sleepin' right in the bed."

For a moment, Perine stirred fitfully. The coarse Anglo accent pierced the stillness of the quiet Sunday afternoon, and she flounced onto her back, subconsciously fighting an unwelcome dream. Another rough voice rudely snickered. "Whaddaya s'pose this yaller *lady* had to do, Sam, to git herself a house an' a bed like this?"

Perine's eyes opened then, widening in horror, and she fought her initial impulse to scream at the two leering, sunburned faces atop a pair of filthy, tattered gray uniforms, with pistols tucked ominously in their beltless pants. A cry for help, she knew, would only wake the children from their naps and bring them running—if, *Lord, have mercy!*—the intruders had not found them already. Donning an air of calmness she did not feel, she reached across the big four-poster to the spot where she had lain her dress carefully before she lay down to nap, but the runtier ruffian anticipated her move and snatched it from her.

"Naw, fancy lady. You don't need this," he cackled. His beady eyes glistened as he held the frock before him, trying it on for size. "Yas'm, fancy lady, it oughta jes' about fit my own woman. Course she's got a bit more meat on her bones than you has, but she ken allus split the seams."

Perine said nothing in reply, just reached instead for the coverlet to hide the nakedness her petticoat revealed. Her face was placid, but her mind darted furiously about for a means of escape. If only she had not foolishly let all her houseservants go! If only Gassion had not gone this weekend to Alexandria for the boys. *Dear God! Bring them back early! Or the hands! Why did it have to be Sunday, when she always gave them a pass?* Outside Perine could hear a chorus of loud guffaws and then a crash as more gray-coats, obviously, broke into her storeroom.

"Hey, Joe, lookee here," the taller rawbone grinned wonderingly, plucking from

510

Perine's dresser a small, silver music box that Gassion had given her on their first happy frolic together in New Orleans. As he turned the key curiously, the soft strains of Schubert's *Ave Maria* tinkled melodiously into the tepid summer air. "Jeez! That's right purty!" The grin grew broader. "A thang like this could put a feller to sleep right nice when he ain't got no woman handy."

"If you want it, soldier, you may have it," Perine said quietly, stalling for time. "I've made many donations to the cause. I've always been willing to give anything I have that would ease the lot of our brave soldiers."

"Izzat so?" Joe paused midway through the drawer he was rifling and grinned, suggestively hitching his sagging pants.

"Hell, Joe!" his friend cackled. "That don't qualify us. We ain't soldiers!"

"Oh?" Perine inquired casually, taking great care not to let anything they said or did arouse obvious emotion from her.

"Naw, fancy lady," Sam cackled. "Oh, we wuz. The rebels come an' got us like they wuz gittin' ever body whut warn't fool 'nuf to join up. They politely stuck their rifle up my nose an' they say all nice an' courteous like, 'Now, Mista Ivy, kiss yore wife bye-bye. It's time to go now.' Well, I done like they says, but it warn't a month 'fore I kiss a couple of rebel guards bye-bye with this here gun they gimme."

"The conscription officers haven't found you?"

"Naw!" Sam crowed. "They keep comin' back to the house, as if'n I'm fool 'nuf to stay there. No, sirree. We all got our l'il places back up in the hills an' we come down jes when we gets hungry—all us pore men whut thinks this war ain't none of our bizness 'cause we ain't got no slaves no how."

"Slaves aren't the only issue at stake," Perine said quietly, seething as the men continued to ransack her dresser, her armoire, her trunks. The little gown that each of her children had been christened in, that she had painstakingly stitched together and lavishly embroidered, went into one grimy pocket, obviously destined for one of Sam's own brood by some sullen, pinch-faced woman who would never wash or iron its delicate lace.

"Izzat so, fancy lady? Well, it shore as hell's whut yo're rootin' for. If ol' Abe turns yore slaves loose, you won't be any better than all the rest o' the niggers."

The silver-plated hairbrush that matched Perine's music box went into another of Sam's pockets, and Joe was already rolling into a bundle the trousers and shirts he had pilfered from Gassion's wardrobe. "That doesn't worry me, frankly," Perine responded coolly. "In fact, my husband and I have seriously considered freeing the slaves we own."

Joe froze, and his weasly face turned ugly. "Damned abolitionists!" he hissed. "That's 'bout the onliest thing I know whut's worse than an uppity high-yaller!"

"Why would you feel one way or the other about abolition?" Perine countered evenly. "You've just said that you have no slaves yourself."

"That don't mean I'm fond of the idea of turnin' all them animals loose on civilized folks. They'll be rapin' an' plunderin' white folks instead of lookin' fer honest work."

"Oh?" Perine retorted, and then hastily prayed that her voice did not reveal the sarcasm she felt when the remark slipped from her.

It didn't. Sam seemed not to have noticed, as his eyes raked back across the room in search of plunder he might have missed. "Well, ain't these the purtiest l'il beads, Joe?" he snickered, fingering the Rosary that always hung on the bedpost at Gassion's head—the string of exquisitely carved beads, ebony black now with age, that his old Grandmère had wrapped his little fingers around when he was too young to understand why they were more special to him than any other Rosary beads in all the world.

"This oughta make a right nice neckpiece for yore li'l gal, Joe, if'n you break off this Popish cross."

The fear and caution that had stilled Perine until now turned to rage as the renegade profaned Gassion's twice-sacred Rosary. She bounded from her bed, oblivious to the skin she exposed, and snatched the heirloom from his paws. The slender strand of leather on which the African artisan had strung his intricate beads, so long before, snapped from age and the force of Perine's furor. Fifty-five priceless, wooden jewels strew themselves into a dozen hidden places.

"You *cochons!*" Perine hissed, her face contorted now by disgust that bordered on hatred. "You pigs! You thieving, murderous scum! You can take anything else in this house you want. If your wives need clothes, take mine. If your children are hungry, I'll give them my food. But you keep your filthy hands off what's sacred!"

"Filthy?" Sam snarled and advanced slowly upon her, one gnarled hand resting menacingly on the butt of his pistol. "You aging yaller strumpet! You dare to call me filthy?"

In a moment he was upon her, his face but inches from her own, and his free hand wrapped itself in the long brown curls she had loosed before lying down for her nap. Then he yanked, wrenching her head back violently, and in spite of herself she screamed.

The very thing Perine feared most then happened. Her wail woke her children. The smallest one began to wail in the chamber next to hers, but the older Rosine—just as her mother knew she would—flew to Perine's room. Fortunately, she had the foresight to come prepared. Just as Sam slapped Perine across the bed, Rosine appeared in the doorway, the practice pistol her father had given her shook nervously in her hands and, behind her, the younger Flavie cowered.

"M'sieur! Let Mama go!" Rosine tried to bark, but her girlish voice broke midway.

"Well, well," Joe drawled. "A whole flock of li'l yaller birdies. Looks like we got us one each, Sam, and an extra fer the boys outside."

"Mama?" Rosine whimpered, her pistol beginning to waver.

"For God's sake, Rosine, shoot!" Perine screamed; but the girl had frozen, and Sam cackled as he yanked Perine up from the bed and clasped her in front of him so tight that his stench almost made her gag.

"Why, Mama," he cooed in her ear. "She ain't about to shoot me. She jes might hit you instead."

"Mama... ?"

"Joe," Sam wheezed. "Won' you relieve that li'l gal of that toy of hers. If'n she wants to play with us, I ken think of a lot funner games."

"Non, non!" Rosine screamed, as Joe began to advance upon her. "I'll shoot you! I swear I will! Don't come any closer... don't..."

One thick hand clasped her wrist in a painful vise and Joe's other paw slapped her violently. The pistol thudded into the carpet beneath their feet. Behind them in the doorway, Flavie shrieked and ran screaming through the salon and out the big front door.

"Aw, let her go," Sam chuckled as Joe's eyes darted after Flavie and his clutch on Rosine momentarily wavered. "The boys outside'll catch the kid. 'Sides, it don't pay to be greedy, Joe. Two yeller birdies in the hand's allus better than three in the bush!"

Sam cackled at his own wit, but Joe's face was sober. "Sam?" he growled. "I don't hear nuttin'."

"Huh?"

"The boys outside. I don't hear 'em. List'n. Everything's quiet."

"Shit, Joe. It wuz quiet when we got here."

"Yeah, but the boys ain't never quiet, an' I don't hear 'em no more."

Sam's grip tightened on Perine, and his big hands inched upward from her breasts to her throat. "Okay, yaller bitch, who else you got 'round here?"

"No one," Perine croaked. "There's just us. The children and I."

"Whar's yore man? An' don't tell me he's off fightin' the war cuz I know better. We don't take yore kind."

"He's gone. To Alexandria."

"Fer whut?"

"To get his sons. They were conscripted to work on the fortifications."

"Aha!" Joe cackled from the doorway, his worry momentarily forgotten. "So they put the rich yallers to diggin' ditches! Gawd! I shore wish I could see that!"

"Well, you won't see it," Perine spat. "Our sons have been exempted now."

"Oh, izzat so?" Sam snarled, and his fingers tightened on her throat. "How come they git exempted?"

Perine stared at the renegade contemptuously and ignored his question. Whatever designs these *canaille* had in mind, there was little now she could do to stop them, except stall, and pray that the slaves came home early—or Gassion and the boys—and beneath the arrogance she now affected, Perine's scared soul was praying hard. Again, Sam's big paw wrenched violently at her hair and she winced; but this time, she refused to give him the satisfaction of a scream.

"I ast you a question, bitch. How do rich yallers git exempted from diggin' ditches with the rest of the niggers?"

"With money!" she spat at him. "Something you've obviously never worked for."

"Well, I'll be Gawd-damned," Sam swore. "The rebels make us fight, try to git us kilt, an' they let the rich yallers do nuttin'."

Before Perine could spit out the contemptuous reply she planned, Rosine recovered from her fright. Flinging herself against the brute who had pinioned her, she flailed furiously with her free arm and her unshod feet. For a moment, Joe's hold on her tightened, but then as her teeth sank into his forearm, his temper snapped and he threw her crashing into the corner. The rifle he had stolen from

514

Gassion's guncase was thrust ominously in her face.

"If you kick up a ruckus one more time, li'l gal, I'll blow yore purty face off. You unnerstand?"

Rosine stared back, biting her lip to hold back a flood of tears.

"I say, *do you heah me?*" The cold barrel of the rifle shifted to one of her budding breasts and then began to inch itself over her body, up and down, over and around, tauntingly, suggestively.

"Joe," his rawboned friend interrupted, his own nervousness showing through at last. "Maybe yore right. It's too quiet out yonder. The boys shoulda caught that li'l gal by now, but I don't hear her yellin' or their funnin' or anything."

Perine winced anew at the horror his words implied, and her lips began to move again, unconsciously, silently pleading... *O Mary, Mother of God, pray for us...*

"The slaves," Sam hissed as a fresh thought struck him, and he yanked her locks again. "Where's yore slaves, bitch?"

"Aw, now, Sam," Joe interjected. "You don't really 'spect them to raise a hand to help the yallers whut own 'em? Slaves all hate rich yallers."

"They do?" a deep voice inquired cynically from the doorway, and the pair of renegades froze.

"Turn slowly, dogs," the voice commanded. "I want to see your tails tucked under or you won't live to lead another pack of hounds."

The men obeyed, but the powerful arm that clasped Perine to Sam did not let up as he pivoted.

"As you can see, *canaille,*" Gassion taunted from the doorway. "There is an armed *nègre* at each of my elbows, and if you do not believe that one of them will shoot you, then I invite you to make just one wrong move. All three of us would take great pleasure in blowing out the brains of scum who would attack helpless women and children."

"Now, Mista, it ain't whut yo think," Joe whined.

"*Ain't* it?" Gassion retorted frigidly. "That's not what my daughter told me when she ran screaming from you into my arms."

"She jes didn't unnerstand, sir," Joe blustered.

"An' you don't unnerstand either," Sam echoed. "Behind the back of this here woman of yore's, I got a pistol pointed. We're fixin' to walk right outa here, and the li'l woman's gonna lead the way. Now, you jes step aside, Mista High Yaller."

515

"I would suggest that you first turn and look behind you, dog," Gassion replied calmly. "You will find a son of mine and two more servants at each gallery window, and at least one of them, I'll warrant, is properly positioned to pick you off without nicking my wife at all."

Sam did not budge, but his runty partner could not resist the temptation to look. He quailed. "Sam, the man ain't foolin'."

"I ain't foolin', either," Sam replied levelly. "My shot's ready in this barrel. If'n anybody picks me off, I'll take this yaller bitch to hell with me. You got yore choice, Mista. She goes with me alive or dead, whutever you prefer."

It was Gassion who wavered, and Perine could read the despair that washed over his face.

"I'll go," she announced.

"Perine, *non!*"

"Stand aside, Gassion. Let us through."

Sam grinned, as Perine began to lead him across the chamber, his elbow still crooked around her neck. But then, as they stepped off the edge of the carpet and onto Perine's polished hardwood floor, his age-slick boot soles found a pair of beads. As he slid, Perine drew up her knee quickly and her bare heel ploughed backwards, savagely, into his groin.

Sam crumpled, keening in his agony. Within minutes, the Rebel deserters were trussed and thrown into a wagon behind Gus and a coterie of armed slaves.

"It's all right, *mes poulettes,*" Gassion comforted his flock as the wagon rolled off toward town. "By dusk, they'll be in jail. My only regret is that their barnyard friends fled when we approached. The river would be better off with all that swine behind bars."

"What did they want, Papa?" little Théodore asked innocently, soot-blackened from the fireplace where he had hidden in his fear until he heard his father calling.

"Anything they could get," Gassion replied grimly. "From the looks of our storehouse, they got a heap of it."

"Were they hungry, Papa?"

"That kind of animal is never hungry, son. At least, they haven't been since the war began. They may have been hungry before, since they're too shiftless to work, but now they feed better than any of us by preying on the unprotected.

Even when their bellies are full, they steal and plunder for the fun of it."

"Don't people try to stop them?"

"Most of the menfolk in other homes are gone off to war, son, and the women are afraid."

"Then I should have stopped them," the child sniffed, guilt troubling him now because he had succumbed to fright. "I was the only man left at home, Papa."

"*Oui*, Théodore, you're our little man and you did exactly what a wise little man should have done." Tenderly, Gassion picked up the lad and turned to lead his family back into the house where the stench and fear the renegades had brought into it would hover for a long time to come.

Halfway up the broad stairway that led to the upper gallery, Théodore stiffened in his father's arms.

"Papa!"

"Eh?" Gassion paused, looking curiously at the boy.

"Behind you, Papa! There's more of them!"

Gassion wheeled on the step, and then his tense face eased as he saw the men approaching.

"It's all right," he smiled reassuringly to Théodore and set the boy down gently on the steps. "See the man in front, in the nice uniform? He has two bars on his shoulder. That means he's an officer, a lieutenant, in the Confederate Army."

The child's eyes still wavered.

"Tell you what son. Take your little brothers and sisters inside, and your mama and I will see what these good soldiers want."

"Yes, Papa."

Taking Perine's hand, Gassion descended the stairs again to meet the small squadron at the end of the lane.

"Good day, M'sieur, Madame," the lieutenant greeted them politely, as he removed his cap. "I'm Felix Poché, requisition officer of the Second Louisiana Cavalry."

"Requisition officer?" Gassion replied quietly. "I'm afraid you are out of luck, lieutenant. Renegades have just hit us."

The lieutenant's face tightened. "Renegades, M'sieur? You mean jayhawkers?"

"No. Renegades. *Confederate* deserters."

"I'm sorry, sir," the lieutenant replied sincerely, his soft eyes noting Perine's still-pallid face. "I hope, sir, that you are all unharmed."

"Oui," Gassion replied tersely. "Shaken. That's all. But then we all live daily with fear now."

"The good Lord knows that's the truth," Poché agreed. "Since the Union began raiding the river valley, even the women and children at home aren't safe. That's one reason why so many of our companies have been assigned to the area."

"To protect us?" Gassion asked caustically. "I thought the governor ordered you here to burn our cotton before it falls into enemy hands."

"Now, M'sieur," the officer stiffened, but Gassion loosed his cynical laugh before Poché could finish his defense.

"No offense meant, Lieutenant. I'm just trying to bring a little levity into an otherwise intolerable afternoon."

"Oui, M'sieur. I do understand and I almost hate to say this, but I have my orders."

"Then get it over with," Gassion commanded.

"M'sieur, my orders are to purchase at least one keg of flour from every plantation along the river."

"Purchase? With Confederate money?"

"Oui."

"Then why don't you say you have come to *take* my flour. That paper you call money looks too much like the label off an old bottle of olive oil."

"Hehn?" the lieutenant's brows knitted.

"They're both greasy, smell bad, have a fancy autograph, and are totally worthless."

Poché laughed nervously. "I do appreciate your humor, sir."

"I wasn't jesting this time, Lieutenant," Gassion retorted, but Perine touched his arm lightly and her eyes begged him to wait.

"Sir," Perine addressed the officer in her own way. "I have exactly one-half barrel of flour in my storehouse now. I also had two barrels of meal, but the renegades hauled that away, along with most of my corn and peas and bacon, before my husband came home and they ran off. If you take my flour, Lieutenant, I won't have anything left to make bread for my family."

"You have a large family, Madame?"

"*Oui.*"

"Then I'm truly sorry," Poché replied, and his misery was evident. "Still, I have orders."

"Now look here," Gassion broke in furiously. "I have sent food off this plantation by the wagon loads to feed you soldiers. I've helped the poor wives make their crops, and I've fed their families. I've given all but my last block of salt to workers on the fortifications. I've even furnished hands from off this place..."

"And you have generously donated five hundred dollars to a needy politician this weekend so that your own sons don't have to serve," Poché interrupted coolly. "Word travels fast, M'sieur Metoyer."

"*Mon Dieu!*" Gassion exploded. "My people have volunteered to fight this war, but you whites won't have us. We're good enough to dig your trenches, but not to shoulder a gun beside you!"

Poché stared at him quietly, his blue eyes steady over his aquiline nose. "M'sieur, I assure you, the decision not to let your people fight—to disband your militia—was not mine. I have no objection to fighting beside any man who loves Louisiana as much as I do. I'm only a soldier, though, and I have to take orders. Right now, my order is to get flour from every planter who has it. I must ask you for the keys to your storehouse."

"You don't need keys," Gassion said savagely. "The other raiders broke the door down. You and yours are free now to help yourselves!" With that, Gassion wheeled and furiously propelled Perine back up the long sweep of stairs into what once had been the sanctity of their home.

৬ 6 ৩
Spring 1864

In the year that followed, life on the Isle of Canes sank to the lowest depths anyone could remember. Confederate renegades and Northern jayhawkers kept up their raids, and the troops assigned to hold the river against the enemy continued to appropriate their own provisions from the homes and farms of private citizens. Families were left without grain, meat, fruit, and vegetables to feed themselves or corn, hay, and fodder for their animals. In desperation many fed their livestock the cotton seed that would be needed to plant spring crops; then the animals bloated and died. Worn-out carding combs had no replacements, and worn-out women found a brief respite from spinning, weaving, and sewing. The clothes their families and slaves wore now were worn thin as well and, as winter set in, many suffered from exposure and some died. Finally, amid that joyless Christmas of 1863, the colored Islanders had suffered their greatest blow. St. Joseph's Convent closed for want of money, and the Daughters of the Cross left the Isle.

At last the terrible winter was over. The honeysuckle and the bougainvillea burst into glorious bloom—God's sweet and eternal reminder that a barren earth will replenish itself. But on the Isle of Canes that promise was a cruel illusion. The Holy Season of Lent began, but there were few sacrifices left for the pious to make. Gaunt and haggard from the deprivations of the war, the older menfolk returned to the fields alongside their slaves, while the younger ones took their wives and children with them. Together they plowed and harrowed the fields with aged mules they would have retired to pasture in better years. Among the truly destitute, the menfolk made beasts of burden of themselves, donned the wooden yokes, and pulled their plows like oxen. They planted what seed and hope they had left, and then fertilized it with tears of pain and desperation.

By late March, the first tender shoots of the new season were beginning to push their way through the fresh-turned earth. The lingering chill of late winter lifted, and the warm glow of the sun fell upon the seedlings, nourishing them, coaxing them to seek their full potential.

But the seeds of defeat had also been sown downriver, and the parish of Natchitoches would reap a full harvest from them. During that dismal winter, the federal forces had seized control of the mouth of the Red and poured into her waters a fleet of transports and gunboats. Her banks turned into a sea of blue as forty-five thousand Union soldiers marched northward along the winding course that river wove through the heart of Louisiana. At the city of Alexandria in the parish of Rapides, some fifty miles below the Isle, the advancing enemy had been halted, not by the Rebels but by a perennial act of God. The rapids, from which the parish took its name, were uncrossable in the winter. So it was that the multitude of blue coats were bottled up below them, building a restless, volatile head of steam while they waited for spring to pop the cork.

Across the nation, the Red River Campaign was hailed as a holy mission. The opening of the Red and the Cane to Union traffic—according to the Grand Old Army and its propaganda—meant the glorious Stars and Bars would fly over all the Western theatre. But that holy mission was, in truth, a sordid cotton raid.

Despite the efforts of the blockade runners, the storehouses from the Rapids up to the bluffs of Shreveport and on into Texas bulged with the white gold Union factories needed to provide work and clothing for Northern families, as well as uniforms for Northern soldiers. On the market, when that precious fiber could be bought, it brought a dollar a pound in sound U.S. currency. No wonder it was that zealous Union officers in Louisiana dedicated themselves to the mission of personal enrichment under the guise of patriotism and duty.

Throughout the length and breadth of that fertile valley, eager squadrons fanned out, seizing in the name of the Union every bale they could find, showing no discrimination between planters who supported the Rebels and those whose sympathies lay with the Union cause. When loyalists protested to the general whom they had welcomed to Rapides that winter, he curtly dismissed them with the news, "We did not come to buy. We came to take!"

To hide their plundering of civilians, federal officers stamped every confiscated bale with the initials "C.S.A." on one broad side and "U.S.A." on the other—then claimed the bales had been seized as the property of the enemy government. Here and there among the ranks, the conscientious and disgruntled began to quip that the letters stood for the Cotton Stealing Association of the United States Army, but their superiors quickly squelched the quibbling.

Meanwhile, Governor Moore's proclamation of 1862 was activated, and the Second Louisiana Cavalry became the "cotton burning brigade" along the Red and the Cane. In the last week of March 1864, as Union gunboats prepared to mount the rapids and federal soldiers began their own march up the broad banks of the river into the parish of Natchitoches, farmers were ordered to roll their bales into the open and shovel their seed cotton out of the cribs. Otherwise, their gins, their sheds, their porches, and their kitchens would be fired, along with any other buildings in which cotton might be stored. Most families complied. They had no choice. But then a dry and angry tempest blew in from the west, hurling sparks and smoldering lint upon split-rail fences, into the trees, and onto the rooftops. Woods, fields, and homes went up in flames as well.

As March gave way to April, the enemy advanced up Cane River like the ancient Israelites, led each day by a cloud of smoke and by a pillar of fire at night. Amidst a blackened sea of ruin, Negro slaves swarmed into their arms and followed them northward—thousands on foot, thousands more on mules taken from their masters, and yet more thousands of sassy pickaninnies and their mothers piled onto purloined wagons.

Jubilantly, relentlessly, their advance continued as they pursued the fleeing Confederate Army, past Ambroise Lecomte's three-storied Big House, now collapsed into a smoldering heap, victim of a Confederate torch. Through the heart of the Isle, where Yankee soldiers laughed at the *ignorance* of the people who still spoke French and delighted in the fear their presence caused. Into the town of Natchitoches, where they commandeered the newspaper and printed their own propaganda. And on to Grand Écore and Mansfield where the unthinkable happened. The retreating Rebs suddenly turned and crushed the enemy's advance.

The bluecoats fled. The pursuer became the pursued, as the Rebels now drove the Federals back down the river. A buoyant Yankee bard composed his own lighthearted ditty to cheer his fellow soldiers—*In eighteen hundred and sixty-four, we all skedaddled from Grand Ecore*—but few of his compatriots appreciated his humor. The bluecoats were demoralized by their defeat and vengeful in their anger. With the sanction, indeed the orders, of their officers they launched a terrible scourge.

On the Isle of Canes, Dr. Jean Napoleon Burdin went berserk. All the personal demons he had brought with him into his exile from France, he unleashed upon the Isle when a runner announced that forty-thousand and more bluecoats were headed back downriver, and that this time they were pillaging and burning everything in their broad swath.

"Morbleu!" he raged all the way through lunch, that fateful twenty-second of April. "We need that militia to protect this Isle! I should never have let the men disband."

"Now, *cher,*" his sweet-faced wife consoled him. "You had no choice. After the white militias disbanded for want of men, the colored guards were ordered to do the same. Here, *cher,* would you put another helping of sweet potatoes on Joseph's plate?"

"Well, they're damn sure needed now," he swore again, his pale face livid, and he stormed from the table, ignoring the child's empty tin that this wife still held out to him. Furiously, the doctor yanked his hat from off the wall peg and headed for the door.

"Jean?" she asked timidly. "Where are you going?"

"To do something! No blue-bellied Yankees are going to burn my home and run off with the gold I've saved through all these years of hell. I wouldn't let the Rebs have it, and I'll be six feet under before the Feds'll get it! These Creoles may be too chicken-livered to defend what's theirs, but I'm a soldier of France!"

River Road was filled with horses and riders, carriages and wagons, when Burdin stormed to his barn to hitch his buggy. Clambering onto the driver's seat like a man possessed, he snapped his whip above his old mare's head, and careened down the lane to the public thoroughfare.

"Whoa!" a passing rider called sharply to his own mount, and drew up short to avoid colliding with the doctor, who veered now from his dirt lane onto the hard-packed road. Politely, the rider tipped his hat, and Burdin's buggy screeched to a halt.

"Dupré! Hold up there, boy!"

"Of course, M'sieur," Manuel's son Joseph replied civilly. *"Bon jour."*

"Like hell it is. It's a rotten day! What's going on here, boy? Where are all these people going?"

"To a funeral." Joseph gestured toward the somber, telltale armband of wide black lace that girdled his forearm, as it did those of all the passersby who wound past them, nodding soberly.

"Eh? Who died? Never mind, it doesn't matter. There will be a lot more dead this day if we don't do something!"

"Tiens?"

"The jayhawkers are coming, boy!"

Joseph made no reply. Indeed, he struggled to contain himself, while Burdin went on with his harangue. For two years, he had jumped every time this drillmaster ordered their militia to jump, until their old captain died and Burdin took control of the company himself. With no other white officers to rein him in, the man had been unbearable. When the decision to disband was forced upon them, they were actually glad. All had suffered too much of the doctor's bullying, his wild threats.

"We have to stop them, boy! It's our duty!" Burdin thundered, his nose bobbing excitedly. "Pass the word to all the militiamen to meet me at the church at six. And bring all your weapons!"

The "boy" lost his struggle. His temper flared as he stared contemptuously down a nose that was almost as pale as Burdin's own.

"There *is* no militia, Burdin, and our family is burying a beloved aunt today. We will not discuss jayhawkers, weapons, or war at her funeral!"

"Don't you backtalk me, boy! We're going to be wiped out this time! Destroyed! Are you capable of understanding that? You'd better do some talking at that funeral. You tell your people that any man jack who fails to show had better spend the rest of his life with his gun in his hand, because if the jayhawkers don't burn him out and get his family, I'll do it myself!"

Joseph sobered. The man was crazy. "You don't mean that, Burdin! You *can't* mean that!"

"Like hell, I can't! We have to stick together on this Isle if we're going to survive those jayhawkers. Any yellow-bellied yellow man who won't fight doesn't deserve to live here. Six o'clock, boy. You hear me?" he added, jabbing the stock of his buggy whip under Joseph's nose for emphasis.

Joseph backed off. "Burdin, the services won't be over by six."

"Then make it half-past!" the doctor snapped as he loosed his whip, zinged it over his old mare's head again, and left Joseph in a cloud of dust.

Funeral or no, Joseph passed the word to all the mourners who had come to bury Susette Metoyer Rocques Morin, the last of Grandpère's daughters. At six, the chapel bells pealed the evening Angelus as the weeping women and children dispersed. At half-past, Burdin rolled into the churchyard, his buggy's reins clutched tautly in one hand and a rifle in the other. At the barrel end of that weapon there sat young Gus Metoyer who had been driven, feverishly, from his sickbed.

Curtly, the doctor nodded toward the men assembled and marched Gus into the church, assuming that all the others would dutifully follow. They did not. When Burdin wheeled before the altar to face them, in his full dress uniform, his pistol in its holster, his sword in its sheath, and his rifle still leveled at the flushed Gus, the lone, black-robed figure of Père Galop stared him down.

"My son," the priest began. "We do not bring weapons into the House of God."

Burdin glared back, startled momentarily from the frenzy that had mounted all that day. *"Hehn?"*

"Come, M'sieur, let us have our meeting at the rectory. It's a much more appropriate place."

Fires flared in the pits of Burdin's eyes, and he snapped. "There's nothing wrong with right here! It's a holy mission we have ahead of us this night!"

"What's wrong with the rectory, my son?" Father Galop persisted quietly. "I have already told the men to await us there."

"I didn't ask for your interference!"

"No, but my people asked for my intercession with you. Some fear... "

"They all fear!" Burdin sneered. Still, he yielded to the priest's entreaties. Jabbing his rifle again in Gus's direction, he marched him from the chapel, across the yard, to the parish rectory. "Where in blue blazes are the weapons I told all of you to bring?" he greeted the sullen assemblage.

"Weapons?" young Dupré spat back. "Almost all we had left, the Yankees took on their trek upriver. How, pray tell, did you manage to save yours?"

"With brains, boy!" Burdin bellowed.

"Then if you're so smart, *you* fight the jayhawkers!" someone from the crowd retorted, and Burdin's focus jiggled wildly across the room in search of the source.

"I'm not just talking now about jayhawkers. The whole Union Army's headed this way."

"The Bluecoats?" It was an incredulous chorus. "You expect us to take on forty thousand armed soldiers?"

"You have no choice. They're raping and stealing and burning and murdering. There's not a jackanape upriver who has stood up to them yet. You think they'll spare you and your women? They don't care if your skin's yellow or if you're as black as a coon. If you don't give into them, they'll slaughter you, too!"

"What are we to stop them with?" Joseph protested.

"Boy, you are always canting about something! Look around you, fool! Every one of you has weapons at home you can use—hoes, axes, sticks!"

"Burdin, you're crazy!" Gus spoke the mind of all of them. "You really think a hundred of us can take on forty thousand soldiers with *sticks?*"

Burdin's eyes squinted into angry slivers, and his rifle barrel jerked up again. "You bet your fat ass we will. We're marching. Now!"

"Fool!" Gus swore, glaring back at the doctor with eyes as feverish as Burdin's own.

The Frenchman shrieked in fury. "You'll do as I say, or I'll blast a hole through you big enough for your yellow guts to spew everywhere!"

Gus stood his ground defiantly, and Burdin fired, but in his frenzy he missed his mark. The ball ripped harmlessly through the leg of Gus's pants. Frantically, the doctor fumbled for his pistol, but it never cleared its holster. From the edge of the crowd, one of the few militiamen who still owned a weapon raised it, took aim, and fired. Burdin crumpled, and it was his own blood that spilled onto the polished hardwood floor of the rectory of St. Augustin Parish.

A pall descended upon the gathering as the impact of that moment sank in. The war had wrought many changes upon Louisiana. A Union government had even been established in the occupied southern reaches of the state. In the parish of Natchitoches, however, the law was still that of the Anglo South. Men of color could not kill a white and hope to escape retribution.

As a hundred of his best parishioners stood staring numbly at the bloody form in the center of his salon, Père Galop assumed command. Quickly, he ripped off his cassock and used it as a shroud.

"Take his feet, Gus, and help me lay him on the table."

"Hehn?" Gus responded numbly, and Père Galop quietly repeated his order.

"Oui, oui, Père." Gus echoed woodenly.

"Now, my children," the priest turned to face them calmly. "What has happened is unfortunate, but I do not feel you have cause to worry. We must call the authorities, but you will have my testimony on your behalf."

"A lot of good that'll do!" Joseph muttered. "No offense, father, but you're new here. Murder's murder, and when a colored man does it, he goes to the gallows."

"It was not murder," the priest said firmly.

"Well, it wasn't self-defense," Gus argued. "It was me he threatened, but it wasn't me who shot him."

"How could you? You were unarmed. The poor, disturbed man fired upon an unarmed person and your cousin was only protecting you. He had every right to do so."

"But, Father…"

"Enough said, son. Your people have always lived peaceful, God-fearing lives on this Isle. That's what everybody tells me. You're respected by everybody who knows you." The priest paused, struggling for a way to say what had to come next, "However…" He hesitated yet again as his eyes sought out the man who had pulled the trigger.

"What, Père?" that man asked hesitantly.

Misery spread across the good father's face and he squared his shoulders before he continued. "Son, I would suggest that you leave the parish quietly. Tonight. If, by any chance, some unchristian soul should be disappointed in the course of justice, it would be safer for you if you were not here."

The man nodded soberly, and Père Galop bowed his head. "Let us ask God's mercy on all of us. Then you must go and let me take the doctor's body home to his poor widow."

ᐧᐧ 7 ᐧᐧ

Hell dawned upon the Isle of Canes that next day, as vengeful bluecoats invaded the remains of the world Augustin and Louis Metoyer had built as both a refuge and a future for their people. In the dark hours of the morning, the advance guard swept upon Yucca Bend, and it was not the soft chirp of birds but the thunder of men, the distant and ominous crackle of burning wood, and the dancing shadows of a thousand breakfast fires that woke Perine and Gassion that April morn.

"Oh, my God!" Perine screamed as she pulled the drapes, opened the shutters, and then ran from one window to the other, gaping at the carnage that sprawled below them, on all sides. Nothing remained of the neat, whitewashed picket fence that had surrounded their estate, except a few jagged edges protruding, as yet unconsumed, from an endless row of fires. As far as the eye could see, where broad green fields had stretched the day before, a horde of wagons were rolling in, trampling the tender seedlings that were this year's crop.

Beyond them, an army of soldiers axed the fine split-rail fence that had enclosed all their fields, and another chased every chicken, guinea, and goose. Hogs lay slaughtered across the garden that stretched between the Big House and the slave quarters that had already been raided by the Union's upriver advance. Laughing soldiers now carved hunks from the fatter swine, letting the lean ones lie in their own blood, unwanted by those who had butchered them so wantonly.

"Oh, my God!" she prayed again, desperately, her soft voice barely audible.

"It's no use to pray, Perine," Gassion responded woodenly. "It's all over for us now."

For a moment, she stared in wonder. At the blankness of his gray-green eyes that used to dance with firelight. At the slackness of his once-firmly molded jaw. At the limpness with which he slumped onto the chaise, drained of all his will, purpose, or dreams.

"It's no use," he repeated, to himself as much as to his wife. "There is nothing left now. Not even hope."

"Don't say that!" she shot back. "There is always hope!"

Flinging off her nightgown, she snatched a day dress from her armoire. Like all her clothes now, this one was worn and mended, but it was clean and freshly ironed. Deftly, her fingers fastened the row of buttons that slashed its front—never had she made for herself one of those silly gowns that opened down the back, so no woman could fasten herself into it without a servant's help.

He said nothing more while she hastily pinned her hair into some semblance of respectability and slid her feet into her worn-soft shoes. Then she left him there, staring dully at the fresh dawn that mocked them through the gallery windows.

Below her, as she crossed the broad salon, she could hear the guffaws of the soldiers pilfering the above-ground basement of her Big House. Casting her face into a mold of determination that was no charade, she wrenched open the front door and a soldier crashed inside, shoulder first. The mix of surprise and guilt that flashed across his face clearly said that in another moment his burly frame would have splintered open the door, etched glass and all.

"Beg pardon, auntie," he stammered, straightening to his full height. "Is your missus up yet?"

Perine stared him coldly in the eye, as he had never before been stared at by any colored woman. Indeed, until this war erupted and he dutifully marched southward from his native Iowa, he had never seen any woman before whose skin was not white or red.

"This is my house," she snapped, "and normally my guests knock before they enter."

The soldier's eyes widened. "The white folks up and left the place to you?"

Perine did not know whether to laugh at his ignorance or fume at his insult. Instead, she breathed deeply and then replied as impassively as she could manage. "My great-grand-uncle built this house and lived here for fifty years before he died."

"You're joshing me!"

Perine said nothing.

"You mean he owned this place? Outright? The whole thing?"

"Two thousand acres at one time, and eighty-seven slaves."

"A colored man?'

"Of course."

"Well, I'll be hanged!"

"I hope you won't be," she retorted evenly, "but if you continue this habit of breaking into people's houses, it might come to pass."

"Now, auntie," he grinned. "This here's war."

A fresh chorus of whoops rose from the yard, peppered by a rapid series of shots, and the soldier hung his long head out the door to share the revelry. With a show of great indifference, Perine opened the venetian blinds that shaded the salon windows and seethed anew at the sight of another soldier taking potshots at the matching *pigeonnières* that had been Augustin's pride. He had drawn the plans himself, patterning them after the finest he had seen in France, and he had paid more taxes on them each year than any common man in the parish paid on the house he lived in.

"Step aside, soldier!" A sharp voice commanded from the open door, and the lanky Iowan gave way. The officer who strode in surveyed the room and then cast a scornful look upon Perine.

"This is your place?"

"*Oui.*"

"How's that? Don't you speak English?"

"Certainly. Also Spanish and Latin. Which language would you prefer?"

The lieutenant shrugged. "English will do. This *is* America, although you Rebels seem to have forgotten. Is there a man around?"

"There is, but he is ill this morning. May I help you?"

"Yes, your keys," he commanded.

"My keys? To what?"

"Your storerooms, woman! What else?"

"Sir, if you insist, I have no choice. I would hope, though, since you are the first Union officer I have had the opportunity to speak with, you would first enlighten me on a point that has troubled me for some time."

The lieutenant stared, puzzled, but then he shrugged again. "Make it quick, woman. The Rebels are on our tail."

"Why are you fighting this war?"

His look clearly said he deemed her stupid. "For right, of course. And to help the oppressed."

"Who are the oppressed, sir?"

The lieutenant's brows knotted, as he told himself that these coloreds were even more simple than he had been led to believe. "Why, the colored man, of course."

"And woman?"

"Well, of course."

"And children?"

"What are you getting at?" he challenged.

"Sir, look at me. My skin is brown. To most people, that makes me colored. I assume you consider me colored, too?"

The lieutenant merely stared.

"Well, I am also oppressed, sir! Two armies have fed themselves out of my family's storehouse since this war began. Rebel deserters and Yankee jayhawkers have pillaged us. Your army has now destroyed my crops for the coming year, and it is too late to replant. You have burned my fences, slaughtered my animals, and you ask me for the keys to my storerooms so you can take the last food I have put up for my family. Sir, there are a dozen *oppressed coloreds* in this household. You say you fight for us—and you'll leave us starving?"

The disdain on his face told Perine, from the moment she began her plea for mercy, that she was wasting her breath. She had to try, but the officer did not yield.

"Your keys, woman. I have no sympathy for Negroes who enslave their fellow man."

Wordlessly, Perine relinquished her ring of keys, and the lieutenant mockingly saluted her in return. Wheeling sharply in his dirty dress boots, he stalked toward the door, but then he drew up short as his eye caught, in the gilded mirror above the mantel, a reflection from the opposite wall, where there long had hung the portrait Augustin had commissioned the artist Feuille to paint in the years before depression hit the Isle of Canes.

Slowly the lieutenant turned and stared directly at the full-length oil, at the old and distinguished *homme de couleur libre,* dressed as fine as the Prince of Wales, standing on the pillared veranda of his Big House, as he gestured with pride toward his church.

The hooked nose of the officer rose derisively as he approached the oil.

"He was a slaveowner?"

"Oui," Perine replied defiantly. Then the pit of her stomach collapsed as the lieutenant unsheathed his sword, lifted it high, and slashed the portrait from Augustin's soft and gentle eyes to the parqueted floor on which he stood.

"That," he sneered, "is what I think of colored slaveowners!"

Forever after, Perine Metoyer Metoyer, Mme. François Gassion Metoyer, chatelaine of Augustin Manor, would count that sacrilege, that moment, as the end of the world that had always nurtured her, challenged her, inspired her, and sheltered her—and the moment that, at the age of forty-two, she learned what it felt like to *hate.*

"Officer! You are a disgrace to our uniform!"

The voice that barked behind them startled both Perine and the lieutenant from the wedge of time in which each was pinioned by the glare of the other, and they pivoted, almost in unison, toward the doorway. The voice had been deep, but the man was short, slender, graying and… and *almost Latin,* Perine thought suddenly, as she took in his elegantly chiseled face and skin of the palest olive. But his English was unmistakably Anglo in accent. Yankee Anglo, crisp and quick.

"Madam, my humblest apologies," the officer said as he swept off his cap and bowed deeply. "I assure you that this unpardonable insult will not go unreprimanded. You, lieutenant! Return to your duties. But, first, give me those keys!"

"Yes, *sir!"* the younger man snapped obediently, his heels clicking on the worn carpet as he exited furiously across the salon.

"Madam, Colonel Anthony Lewis of the Illinois Volunteers. What can I do to reassure you that the Army of the United States is not your enemy?"

"You've done much just now to reassure me that *not all* the Federals are my enemy," Perine replied, breathing deeply from her gut in an effort to regain some semblance of self-control. "In return, I offer you the hospitality of my home. My husband is ill and my children are still in their rooms, but I would be happy to prepare your breakfast."

"That won't be necessary, Madam. I have already eaten, and I am now sorry that I did so off one of your hogs. I had no idea that this plantation did not belong to another Southern sympathizer."

Perine made no attempt to correct his assumption. What could she say? For a year at least, she had found it hard to convince herself that she felt any sympathy for either side. What could she do, indeed, but accept the man's apology?

"You are forgiven, M'sieur Colonel." She forced a smile. "I must say that had I met you elsewhere, out of that uniform, I would have had no idea that you were not a true Southern gentleman."

The little officer's eyes twinkled. "Perhaps that is because I was born in the South, Madam. I must confess, though. I have had little exposure to the Southern way of life. I've lived in Illinois since I was a babe."

"Then that is the South's loss, M'sieur."

"Madam?" he interrupted her. Hesitantly.

"*Oui?*"

"Is there a plantation around here known as Yucca Bend? I think it is owned by people of color like yourself."

"Yucca Bend?" Perine echoed, puzzled. "It's a place, Colonel, not a planta-tion. It's that bend out there in the river. This plantation and the next one both share the general address."

A strange look came over the colonel's face. Enigmatic, Perine thought. Then he began again, caution clearly evident.

"Madame, may I ask your name?"

"Metoyer. Mme. François-Gassion Metoyer..."

Perine's disconcertment was growing even more intense. Something about this man troubled her deeply, but there was nothing tangible for her to grasp. Whatever it was, it eluded her like the gay yellow and green butterflies she had often tried to capture as a child.

"Yes, that is the name," Colonel Lewis murmured, almost inaudibly.

"I beg your pardon, M'sieur?"

Lost in his own thoughts, Lewis answered her question with another of his own.

"Madam, there was once a man from here who... who befriended me when I was small, or so my mother always said. I think his name was Lewis Metoyer. Did he ever own this place?"

"Oncle Louis? The first Louis? *Non,* he owned the other plantation that I mentioned." Again, Perine was caught in that time warp, deep in the woods, and the butterflies were flitting from sweet-gum tree to sweet-gum tree.

"But he's dead, sir," she added lamely. "He died many years ago. *Oui,* I was but a child."

"Oui," the colonel echoed softly, and for a moment his eyes hinted of a time in which he, too, was lost. Then the veil lifted from them, and he spoke impassively.

"Who owns that place now, Madame? Out of respect to his memory, let us say, I would like to visit it when I pass. Perhaps, too, I can spare the present owner some of the harsher aspects of this war."

"Why, the Hertzogs own it now." Perine hesitated. "They're white, sir. Oncle Louis's grandson lost the place back in the big depression."

The colonel's wince was almost imperceptible.

"I'm sorry, Madame—for your family's sake, of course. I assure you, though, the color of the present owners makes little difference. It is just a whim I have had, ever since I was assigned to the expedition. My unit bypassed this Isle on the trip up; but since I have come this way today, I'd like to satisfy my curiosity."

"Of course, I understand, Colonel," Perine murmured, but she did not understand at all.

"Madame?"

"Oui?"

"That man in the portrait. He was part of your family?"

"Oui. He was the brother of both my grandfathers, and he was my husband's father as well. Nicolas Augustin Metoyer was his name," she added proudly. "He was born in slavery, but he built this place and brought his younger brother Louis—the one you inquired about—out here to the Isle to build the place next door." Then her voice trailed off softly. "He died only eight years ago. Our Grandpère Augustin."

For a shadow of a moment, the colonel stared at the wounded portrait as though he had seen a ghost, a wisp of a world and a people he should have known but never would. Then his shoulders braced, and the look was gone. He was, once more, every inch an officer in the Grand Army of the Republic known as the United States. And Perine, herself, became once more the chatelaine of the home he had invaded.

This time, the colonel's bow was stiff. "My apologies are sincere, Mme. Metoyer. Believe me, I would have my men do nothing to worsen the lot this war has inflicted upon you. There will be no more pillaging or burning along the Isle by the men under my command."

The colonel kept his word. Descending the staircase, he ordered his forces to mount and march, and Perine was left with the questions that still plagued her and the havoc his army had wrought.

Behind that force of soldiers there came another and yet another. All day and all that night they came. Upon the center pillar of her house, the colonel had posted his command that this residence must be spared, and his order was respected—in letter, though not in principle. Each new wave of soldiers looted every chamber, every shed, until there was nothing left to loot. Frolicking bluecoats donned her faded gowns and the hats she had loved in gayer times. They danced like milkmaids in the lane, while other soldiers filled the yard with puddles of fresh, sweet milk and cream she had stored in the springhouse for her babies.

Still, the torch was not put to the walls that Grandpère had raised from the bare earth of what once had been a pestilential canebrake. Nor were his offspring harmed. Beyond the Big House, though, Colonel Anthony Lewis had failed, or forgotten, to post a similar notice on the Church of St. Augustin. The last of the retreating bluecoats, denied of plunder from the Big House by those who had come before them, looted the sacristy of the church of its golden vessels, filched the holy vestments for use as blankets on their sore-back horses, and torched the building as they pulled out.

Then in their wake, the darkened sky rent itself asunder, and a sympathetic God poured the torrents of heaven upon the Isle, upon the tongues of flame that licked hungrily at the sacristy walls. The unholy bonfire that vengeful soldiers had left to forever remind the Islanders of their presence now sizzled and died, leaving blackened, tortured walls standing amidst the Gehenna that both armies had made of the Isle of Canes.

∞ **8** ∞

Fall 1866

"Cousin Perine?"

"Yes, Joseph? Come on in." Resignedly, Perine pushed back the graying curl that straggled across her forehead and plunked her pen upon the account ledger she had tried futilely to balance for the past two hours.

"Struggling with the books again?" Dupré teased.

"Struggling is the word, for sure. I never was much at math, and Gassion did not give me much practice at bookkeeping."

A look of raw pain flashed across Perine's face as she said that. It always did when her thoughts drifted back to the grievous year of 1865 when the Confederacy lost the war and she lost her husband.

"You've done well at it, Perine, in spite of that," Joseph reassured her. "He would be proud of the way you have kept up your mettle. Not to mention the way you have kept this place out of debt."

Perine nodded soberly. "I do think he would, Joseph. The good Lord knows, plenty of other plantations around us are going up for taxes or debt. There's a new sheriff's sale advertised in the paper every week, it seems."

"At least that's one worry I don't have," Joseph quipped. "A man can't lose what he hasn't got, and maybe it's a good thing I have nothing because I'm no good at managing money. Books of no type ever appealed to me."

"But you are very good at managing people." It wasn't idle flattery. Perine never wasted her energies on such as that. She truly owed Joseph Dupré a debt. "With all the labor problems planters are having now, I honestly don't know what I would have done if you had not agreed to oversee this place for me."

"Well, it's been my pleasure, Boss Lady," he grinned. "By the way, that brings up the reason I came by this morning. I'll be bringing in a few new families to sharecrop come the first of the year. I've drawn up a labor contract I think will fix some of the problems we had this season, but I need you to approve it."

"You really think a contract will mean anything to unschooled field hands who have never dealt with such things? I declare, Joseph, I get so exasperated at the way these freedmen move out in the middle of cotton picking and leave us without labor, or disappear for a week in the middle of planting season, or spend their nights carousing and then show up in the fields at noon, too hung over to work!"

Joseph pondered her quizzically from the corner chair where he had settled. "You've changed since the war, Perine."

"Hehn?"

"Weren't you and Gassion the ones who used to talk about freeing your slaves, about farming this place with free labor, before the war?"

"Free labor's changed!" she said testily. "Or else we were fools. I've only had two dependable families on this place since the war ended. Most of these people seem to think that freedom means no commitment, no responsibility."

"Ah, give them time, Perine. They're all like eighteen-year-old bucks now. They're testing their independence, asserting their manhood. Sure, some of them go a bit to extremes; but they'll settle down."

"If they don't starve themselves first, and everybody else as well. The way the war destroyed the economy, we've got to all pull together to survive and rebuild."

"If they don't turn everyone against *all* colored people in the meanwhile!" Joseph added.

The long lines of worry that furrowed Perine's face grew taut. "That really does trouble me. It's not only the *nègres* that have changed. The war took so many of our old white friends. Now when this new generation of whites looks at us all they see is more free coloreds. It doesn't matter to them that we were free before the war, that we *earned* our freedom, that we've spent a century earning citizenship instead of having it given to us overnight by the enemy."

"We can deal with that, Perine. Once the Fourteenth Amendment is ratified, it won't matter whether whites see any difference or not. They will have to give us equal rights."

"Do you really think it will pass?" Perine asked wearily. "As many Democrats as we have in our state legislature, I see little hope for ratification in Louisiana."

"It will pass," Joseph declared. "In spite of our legislature. In fact, that's about to change, too. Mind me, Perine, we're going to oust those Democrats in next year's election!"

"We? You've joined the National Republican Union Club, too?"

"You bet I have! There are a dozen of our people in it now."

"How many hold an office, Joseph?"

"Eh?"

"How many *Créoles de couleur* are in a position of leadership in your club?"

Joseph shifted in his chair in obvious discomfort. "Well, at this moment, none, but..."

"There won't be, either," Perine retorted. "Oh, they appoint a token freedman to one committee or another. Or the freedmen themselves, once they get the vote, just might elect some of their own to office. But *our people* won't have a chance. Your white Republicans won't accept our leadership, and the freedmen won't either."

"You're in a pessimistic mood today, Boss Lady."

"Not pessimistic. Realistic. Joseph, we are in the very situation right now that Grandpère feared. There is no longer anyone we can depend on to help us but ourselves. Our only hope for survival is total self-sufficiency. Total independence from society in general!"

Joseph made no reply, but Perine could see indulgence wash over his face. It infuriated her that he could sit there smugly dismissing her opinion, just because she was a woman. It was the same look she always got from Gus and every other male she tried to talk some common sense into nowadays. Her voice rose.

"Joseph, let the freedmen and the whites and the Democrats and the Republicans all fight their political battles among themselves. Our involvement is not going to make one jot of difference. There are too many black freedmen who resent us because we have always been different from them. There are too many whites who no longer see that difference. We cannot win, Joseph. *We cannot win!*"

Joseph's mask of tolerance never left his face. "Perine," he responded softly, "Did anyone ever tell you that you are quite attractive when you get emotional?"

"Ooomphh!" she fumed. "Give me that contract and let me look it over! We both have better things to do than to sit here arguing when you are too bullheaded to listen to reason!"

"Whatever you say, Boss Lady," he grinned, his blue eyes dancing.

Quickly, she scanned the paper, then settled back in the big oak chair that had always stood behind Augustin's old desk. This time, she studied each provision carefully.

"Hmmnh..." she mulled, and then read the first two provisions aloud as she carefully considered each of them.

1. Employees shall work in common on the lands of the employer, doing whatever labor necessary to the operation of the farm.

2. All hands shall be expected to labor from 6 a.m. to noon and from 2 p.m. until 6, or until dark in the winter months. No labor shall be required on Sunday.

"Good!" she nodded. "I'm glad you included that."

3. Employer shall supply land, provisions, medicine, teams and wagons, seed, implements, rope, bagging, and all other items necessary to the operation of the farm.

4. Rations for a full hand shall be four pounds of pork or six of beef per week, plus one peck of meal. All laborers will be provided with garden ground to grow their own vegetables and shall be permitted to cut firewood off designated timberlands.

5. Laborers will be held responsible for loss or abuse of animals or any property of the employer that stems from the negligence or willfulness of the laborer.

6. In consideration of faithful performance, the employer binds himself to pay over to said laborer, after deducting all necessary expenses for producing the crop and for the laborer's support, the following share of the net proceeds: one third of the cotton crop; one fifth of the corn, hay, and fodder; one third of the peas and pumpkins; and one half of the potato crop.

"Hmmnh…" she mused again. "Only one fifth of the corn, fodder, and hay? What's the reasoning?"

"We're coming out on the short end with those this year, Perine. We can't give a third as we do with cotton. We're the ones… you're the one," Joseph hastily corrected himself, "who has the animals to feed. Most of the families we get here have nothing more than a mule, if that. They've ended up this year with corn and hay to sell, and we will end up having to buy."

Perine nodded silently and read on.

7. Laborers are expected to obey all rules and regulations of the plantation and to perform all duties promptly. Failure to do so shall result in immediate dismissal, which will entitle the laborer to no share of the proceeds. Specifically, the causes for which laborers may be discharged are as follows:

(a) Open disrespect or violence to employer or superintendent.

(b) Refusal to obey plantation orders.

(c) Continued neglect of duty.

(d) Stealing, pilfering, or destruction of plantation property.

(e) Continued absence from plantation without permission.

"Actually, Joseph, there's another item that should go here."

"Eh?"

"Under reasons for discharge," she instructed, "add in 'Disorderly conduct on plantation.' Of course, I will not tolerate violence toward us and our property, but fighting and continuous bickering among the workers have to be controlled, too. They are bad for morale."

"So far, that hasn't been much of a problem."

"Then we're lucky, judging from complaints the other planters have. So put it in anyway. It will serve as a warning in case you do hire a troublemaker."

Brusquely, Perine tapped the sheets of paper edgewise on the desk to straighten them and handed the contract back to Joseph.

"All in all, it is quite satisfactory—on paper. It remains to be seen whether it will have any effect on the actual behavior of the croppers. Do you plan to have the newspaper office print it?"

"If you approve. It will only cost a few dollars."

"All right then, Joseph," she sighed and picked up her pen again. For a moment she almost looked dismayed as she stared once more at the ledger.

"Well, I guess it's back to the books again for me, unless there is something else you need to discuss."

"Actually there is." Joseph paused, debating the best way to broach the issue. "Cousin Barbe came to me before I left home this morning. She wanted me to ask you something."

"Oh?" Perine rejoined, her curiosity piqued. "Why did she not come ask me herself?"

Joseph shrugged. "Maybe it was pride or something. You know Cousin Barbe."

Indeed. Better than Joseph would ever suspect.

"Perine, she needs help," Joseph went on quickly. "She just couldn't bring herself to admit it to you face to face. Barbe's homeless, Perine! She and her girls. You know how hard the war was on widow women... "

Sur ma foi! The war was hell for everybody. As for widow women, they came in all kinds. When old Nerestan Rocques died in 1859, he left his young widow a fortune. Perine *knew*. The 1860 census taker had come to her house right after he went to Barbe's and right there in his book, when he asked her to check the accuracy of her own entry, she saw just how much the widowed Barbe was worth—real estate *and* personal property. Even though the old man's children by his first wife had taken their share of his estate, Barbe's fortune was more than double what she and Gassion had to their names.

But, of course, Barbe had lived high on the hog. When goods became scarce after the blockade, the young Widow Rocques would pay anybody any price to get what she needed to maintain her *position*. When they could no longer sell their crops and Perine darned and patched the family clothes to keep from spending money they might be desperate for later, the young Widow Rocques kept right on ordering new frocks, laughing to all that dressmakers needed to feed their families, too, and she was just doing her Christian duty by helping them.

"Perine," Joseph went on. "She's penniless. Utterly destitute. All she has to her name is one old mule she rides to work." Joseph's voice lowered, almost to a whisper. "She's doing day labor, now, Perine. *Field* work."

Why am I not surprised? Perine thought, then chastised herself for her lack of charity.

"Perine, it occurred to me that you have one slave cabin that's still empty. So, I thought maybe you might be willing to let her and her girls live there—until they can get back on their feet, at least?"

Perine sighed. "Of course, Joseph. I'll see, too, if I can't find her some better work to do. I know she can at least cook. At least once upon a time she could."

"Thanks, Perine. I knew you wouldn't disappoint us."

Us? Perine's eyebrow cocked despite herself. Joseph obviously noticed.

"Actually, I didn't say that right. I knew you wouldn't disappoint *Cousin Barbe*," he added hastily. Perine could have laughed then. Joseph looked so much like a lovestruck boy thinking of his heart's dream! Apparently, he read in her face those thoughts she didn't say.

"I just feel sorry for her, Perine. I know she's just your age, but she looks *sixty* from all that field work, and it just breaks my heart to think how *pretty* she used to be." Joseph sheepishly grinned for a moment, offering up a confession.

"I keep remembering back when I first started noticing girls. *Coo-lee!* I thought Cousin Barbe was queen of the Isle or something! I never saw a picture of the Queen of England, but every time somebody mentioned her, the image that came to mind was Cousin Barbe."

Somehow, this didn't surprise Perine either.

"Life just isn't fair," Joseph muttered in conclusion. "It just isn't fair."

Au contraire! At least, that was what Perine was tempted to say, but she held her tongue. Joseph would not understand. No man would.

"Is there anything more, Joseph?" She asked politely, noticing the day's lengthening shadows and remembering that she still had not finished reconciling her accounts, or gone out to check on the sick wife of that new family they had hired, and she *had* promised to look in on the woman this afternoon, and then…

"As a matter of fact, there is something else," Joseph replied softly. "Will you marry me?"

"What!"

"You heard me, Perine." Casually he leaned back into the big, overstuffed chair and stretched out his long legs before him.

"Joseph, that's not funny!"

"Am I laughing, Boss Lady?"

The proposal took Perine completely by surprise, and she gaped at him in shock. Never, in the more than a year since Gassion gave up living, had she had the first romantic thought about young Joseph Dupré. Or any man for that matter. It wasn't that Perine's nights weren't lonely, or that she had consciously ruled out the thought of marrying again some day. She simply had never found a man who measured up to the husband she had loved, and every passing day now left its impression that she never would.

"Perine?" Joseph's voice, quiet but insistent, startled her from the soul-searching he had forced upon her.

"Hehn?"

"Am I that repugnant, Perine?"

"Non," she protested quickly, not wanting to hurt his feelings, but she was stalling desperately for time to sort out her own emotions. Joseph? As a husband? He was younger than her eldest stepson! Of course, Gus was not *that* much younger than she was, but… but Joseph's father had been her husband's best friend and she had always thought of the young Duprés as children! Of

course, that's foolish. They were all grown now. Still, there were too many years between her and Joseph, especially since she was the older one. *Non,* it would never work!

"Joseph, look at me!" she said aloud. "Tell me honestly. What do you see?"

"I see a good woman, Perine. Sensible, though a little peppery at times! Charitable. Virtuous."

"My God, Joseph! You make me sound like your mother, not a prospective lover. When young men start looking for romance…"

"Not all young men are irresponsible," he interjected patiently. "I'm no hot-blooded young fool, Perine. I've gone through romance and marriage and come out the worse for it. Now I've got babies who need a good mother, and I'm looking for a wife I can respect even when youth and beauty are gone."

"But, Joseph," she went on miserably. *"Look* at me! *Hard!"* Perine jumped quickly and ran to the windows. Opening the blinds wider, she let the bright, late-autumn glare pour in on her face unmercifully.

"Now *look,* Joseph Dupré!" she commanded. "I'm old beyond my time, too! My hair is just about totally gray. My daughters are courting already! In another year or two they will be married, and I'll be a grandmother!"

"I've looked, Perine—for quite some time now. The lines I see are lines of strength. Lines of laughter. They tell me that you know how to live and love."

Perine closed the blinds again, laboriously. "Maybe I have already used up all the love God put into my heart. That kind of love. I just can't forget so quickly a man who owned every inch of my heart for almost twenty years."

"I know that," Joseph said gently, keeping to his chair in the corner. Perine noticed. As she had said, Joseph *understood* people, and he knew she would feel threatened if he did not keep his distance while he pushed his case.

"Perine," he pressed on quietly, evenly. "We both have good memories that we will never forget. We should not forget them. Still, life goes on, Perine."

"And yours will go on longer than mine will!" she shot back harshly, fighting herself as much as his proposal. "Go find yourself a young woman, Joseph!"

Perine's eyes, her voice, were almost pleading now. For more than a year, she had struggled to put this new life of hers into some semblance of order, to accept the awesome responsibility of making every decision alone, of raising her orphaned children as firmly but gently as their father would have done, to keep her plantation out of debt, to open again—and, this time, *keep* open—the convent doors. Now, just when she thought she had created some measure of stability, Joseph Dupré had to come and *complicate* things!

He stared back, reading the misery in her plea, understanding the burdens that had threaded her locks with silver. At last he rose, but not to leave. Instead, he wrapped his arms around her as she stood, planted determinedly, by the window.

"Perine, I can help," he argued tenderly. "We'll be good for each other. You're carrying too heavy a load alone. Let me carry it with you."

"What will you get in return?" she asked despondently, fighting a sudden impulse to wrench herself from his touch, his closeness, his maleness.

"A wife who is mature enough to accept life the way it is, not a pampered young one who expects me to serve the world to her on the china plate she ate from before the war. No husband today could live up to that expectation."

Perine's mouth crinkled wryly as he continued to gaze straight into her soul. "No more romance and roses for us, eh, Joseph?"

"No more adolescent dreams, Perine. Just hope and determination. Is it a bargain?"

She was silent. Then she sighed, her taut muscles slackened, and a soft, almost reluctant smile washed across the face that he had cupped between his hands.

"Okay, Joseph. It is a bargain. But I'm still the Boss Lady."

He chuckled and then murmured confidently, drawing her closer, "Shall we seal it with a kiss?"

Perine actually laughed back, then, though she pulled herself quickly from his arms. "I thought you said you were no hot-blooded young fool!"

"So I did, Boss Lady," he winked, before retrieving the contract on the desk and striding confidently toward the door with the infectious grin that few females had ever been able to resist. "I'm still a man, though… as you'll very soon find out!"

৩ 9 ৩

Perine was right. The Louisiana legislature refused to ratify the Fourteenth Amendment, as did almost all the Southern states. Angry Radicals in the nation's Congress then passed their Reconstruction Acts of 1867, declaring the elected governments of ten still-rebellious states to be illegal. Martial law replaced police power. Former Confederate leaders were stripped of the vote and it was given, instead, to newly freed blacks, proud and eager, but unschooled and easily swayed.

In the fall of that tempestuous year, General Philip Sheridan marched his peacetime army into Louisiana and ordered new elections throughout the state. The freedmen turned out en masse, electing scores of their number as delegates to write the constitution that would govern their new society. Fearful whites predicted rape and rebellion, plunder and extermination, while the newly elected delegates envisioned a utopia in which all would be equal, education would be free, and they would be rich.

"Hogwash!" Perine scoffed in March when her jubilant husband returned from his National Republican Union Club meeting with a copy of the new Constitution of 1868 clenched exultantly in his fist.

"Free education? Maybe. Equality? *Never!*" she declared shortly. "They can pass all the laws they want, but they will never change men's hearts. People who don't like those laws will find a way to get around them. They always do."

"No, not here, Boss Lady." Joseph exuded such confidence, she almost shook her head in wonder. "At Opelousas or Alexandria, you may be right, Perine. The racists are in power there. But not here at Natchitoches. We are still the frontier of Louisiana and the people here have always been free thinkers. Besides, there are still enough of our old friends with influence. We'll work together now. You'll see."

The skepticism was clear on Perine's plain face. Checking the rest of the dire predictions she was sorely tempted to utter, she turned and drew a long, worn, nightgown of flannelette from the war-scarred armoire and mechanically, wearily, unbuttoned her work-soiled frock and let it slide to the floor.

"Don't you believe me, baby?" Joseph asked softly behind her, wrapping his arms around her when she shivered suddenly from the chill of that spring evening.

Perine still did not answer. She wanted to believe. Not so much for herself as for the children she had brought into this world. For the flock of daughters she had wanted to raise as fine, well-educated young ladies, embroidering delicate petticoats, humming dulcetly as they sat at the pianoforte in their salons, tripping through a light air from Schubert. Instead, the Isle now had no school for any of their children past the sixth grade, and her daughters now sang as lustily as the field hands while they reddened their knuckles against the wash board and calloused their knees while mopping the floors. If this were *equality*, then equality definitely wasn't all it was cracked up to be!

"Hey, baby," Joseph coaxed softly as she continued to stand there silently, stiffly, in his arms. His lean body began to sway rhythmically, rocking her gently in front of him as his hands strayed over her, trying to tease into her some of the excitement he had felt ever since they had announced the new constitution at that night's meeting. Soon, Perine's own body began to tremble and he spun her around, crushing her mouth to his, but then he tasted salt and realized she was crying.

Gently, Joseph lowered her upon the coverlet of the big, ancient, four poster and wiped away the wet trails that glistened over her furrows of care and worry.

"You want to tell me what's wrong?" he asked softly.

"I'm pregnant again, Joseph."

"What!" He sat upright on the bed beside her. "I'm about to have a son, and you're *crying?*"

"Yes!" She answered him furiously. "I don't *want* to bring another child into this crazy, hate-filled world, for people to treat as if he were a hybrid mongrel—another *nothing*, as Sukie used to call us, because we're neither black nor white!"

"Oh, baby, how can you say that? Do you think I'm a nothing?"

"It's not what *I* think that matters," Perine muttered, choking back a new flood of tears. "It's the reaction of this insane world that doesn't know—doesn't *care*—who we are. When we walk into our own church now and sit in the pews that have always been ours, I can *feel* some of the white women glaring at my back as though I have no right to seat myself in front of them."

Joseph said nothing, struggling to find a logical answer.

"Non!" she went on savagely. "Don't tell me that the people of Natchitoches are different from any of the rest we read about. I know fear and hostility and revulsion when I see it, and I have seen more of it in the three years since the war ended than I've seen in all my life."

"Maybe you're imagining it, *chérie*. People who have been your friends don't suddenly start to hate you. Things just can't change that fast."

"It hasn't been fast, Joseph. Distrust and envy have been simmering here for years. From there, it's been a short slide into the hate that some are now openly preaching. The war was all the push needed. Gassion said it would happen and he was right!"

Joseph winced. He always did when the spectre of her first husband loomed between them.

"Look, Perine." His tone was grim. "I respected Gassion as much as you did, but I can't agree with the way he thought. Sure, we're different from most people. We're neither black nor white, as you keep saying. But that doesn't mean the world hates us. Look baby, I know women get moody in your condition. God knows, Elise used to get all upset over the most trivial things."

"Nom de nom!" Perine pushed him aside and flung herself to the far reaches of the bed. "I am not Elise! My 'condition' has nothing to do with the issue. And I am tired of hearing men's smug platitudes about all women this and all women that! I'm not just a woman. I'm a person. Every person is different!"

"Yas'm, Boss Lady," Joseph grinned in mock contrition, but Perine was far from mollified.

"That's what's wrong with this world," she fumed. "It always tries to force people into categories. Everyone has to be either this or that, and when all the sheep are lined up in their own little pastures they stare out at the people who dare to be different and say, 'Hey, you're strange. We don't want anything to do with you.'"

"Well, I want you," Joseph teased. "Although I will admit I think you are a little strange at times, too!"

"Hmmph! You always want me," Perine snorted, relenting just a little. "It's a darned good thing I didn't marry a young man twenty years ago. I'd be plumb worn out by now!"

"Complaining?"

"No." She fought back a smile.

"Feel better now?"

"Non!" she retorted. "I still think you and Gus are pie-eyed fools if you think the politicians in this parish are going to give either of you a chance. The white Radicals don't trust you because you're too intelligent for them to control. The white Conservatives don't want you because they can't see past the tint of your skin. And the freedmen will never let you lead them because they remember what you once were—their master!"

"There's another way of looking at things, baby. Gus and I might be the bridge between all the different factions here."

"Poppycock!"

"Ah, such words of wisdom from a sage old woman."

"Well, you knew I was old before you married me."

"*Oui.* Wise and worldly, with lots of experience at living and loving, I think I once said. Tell you what, baby. Let's forget the living for a while and concentrate on the loving."

"Hmmph! You can't solve disagreements that way in politics, man!"

"Oh? Seems to me I've heard something or other about political bedfellows."

"Well, if you're looking for a *fellow* to bed with, maybe I made a mistake in marrying you!"

"Baby, I'm not looking for anybody else to bed. I have all I can handle right here."

He silenced her then. Yet the months ahead frustrated Joseph far more than he would admit. Perine's predictions proved damnably accurate. The Louisiana Constitution of 1868 made bold promises of equal rights to all public facilities, but when a bold black or colored in the state capital stepped onto the formerly white street cars, the whites deserted them. Then the drivers shrugged and parked their cars, declaring that street car lines could not afford to run for the benefit of one or two passengers.

Nor did Natchitoches prove to be any different. In that same summer of 1868, two freedmen celebrated their victorious election to the city council, but then the council delayed convening until night visitors persuaded the two black members to resign.

"Don't you dare say 'told you so,' Boss Lady," Joseph growled morosely at Perine when Gus rode over to bring him that piece of news from town.

Perine didn't say it, but Gus's penetrating gaze bounced knowingly from his stepmother to her new husband and he smiled sardonically.

"Oh? Don't tell me, Joseph, that Perine lectures you, too, on the perfidy of politics? I thought she only exercised her maternal instinct when I was around."

"Maternal instinct has nothing to do with it, Gus!" she retorted. "I'm just cautious, like Grandpère tried to teach us all to be."

"Ah, Perine! Won't you learn? That argument never worked on me like it did on Papa." Gus's smile grew broader, and Perine shivered deep inside herself. Once she really had cared for Gus, many years ago when she had been an unsure bride and he had accepted her in his mother's place with no resentment. Somehow, though, the years, the war, and all the hostility around them had twisted and bent Gus into a man that scared her. This smile of his never left his face now, and it was a sad, hurtful smile that left Perine scared inside.

"By the way, Perine," Gus continued blandly. "How's the convent faring?"

"Marvelously well!" she exclaimed, grateful that he had changed the subject. "We are almost out of debt. Estelle tells me that you two are planning to enroll little Ellie."

"Yes, since we'll be sending the boys to public school, we can afford tuition for her at the convent."

"What?" Surprise, suspicion—or was it foreboding—gripped Perine and she groped for a chair. "Gus, are you serious?"

"Quite serious. In fact, I came over to discuss this with you and Joseph. I'm taking my boys tomorrow to the public school that's opened here on the Isle. I thought you two might want to start Théodore."

Joseph's pale brows shifted inward, but he spoke quickly, forestalling as much as he could the protest he knew Perine was about to make.

"I don't know that it's my place to decide, Gus. Théodore is Perine's son. That would be more her decision than mine. Hers and yours. After all, the judge appointed you underguardian when your father died. I should think you and Perine would have to reach an agreement on his schooling, but if you merely want my opinion…"

"That's why I asked, Joseph," Gus purred.

"Then you know that I agree with you completely. Under our new constitution all children have an equal right to a public education. Of course, Perine feels strongly about the girls attending the convent where the nuns will influence them, but I see no reason why the boys of the Isle should not attend the public school. All of them."

"You know I disagree completely," Perine declared.

"I suspected that," Gus replied offhandedly, "although I do find it hard to understand. If I recall correctly, you and I had another disagreement once over the subject of our family's children going to school with whites. On that occasion you favored it. Your ideals have changed, it seems to me."

"Not at all! It was *our* school that was involved then, Gus. *We* were in control. We respected the Collinses, and they respected us. No one minded their daughters attending St. Joseph's. No one except you. This time there will be no respect between the students and our children. The whites don't want us."

Perine's eyes moved urgently from one to the other, pleading with both her menfolk to understand. She was Théodore's mother, but she was still only a woman. Under the law it was the men of her family who would have the final say-so over her own son's life.

For once, Gus did seem moved—but not enough. "I have already spoken to the schoolmaster, Perine. He has no objection to our children attending his classes, and he assures me that if anyone protests he will stand behind us solidly."

"But he's just one man!"

"Perine," Joseph interceded quietly, "when injustices are righted, it almost always begins with just one man who is willing to stand up for his principles. It also has to begin with someone among the oppressed who is willing to take a chance and fight for his rights."

"The two black councilmen in Natchitoches stood up for their rights when they ran for office! How far did it get them?"

"They're freedmen, Perine," Joseph argued. "We're not. It's like I keep telling you, baby, our people can be the buffer between the freed Negroes and the whites who fear them. It is far better that we take the first step to bring the races together. The whites here will accept us. Once they see that the plague does not descend upon their schoolhouses when colored children step inside, they'll be willing to show more tolerance to the black children as well."

Perine was losing the argument and she knew it. Still, it was never easy for her to concede defeat. "Ah, Joseph!" she sighed. "Will you never quit dreaming?"

"Grandpère was a dreamer. Old Coincoin was too," he reminded her.

It was a reminder she did not want to hear, but it was a truth she could not deny. Had it not been for them, their dreams, their audacity, the Isle would not exist—at least *their Isle* would not exist, the world they had built on the Isle would not exist. *Oui,* had it not been for their dreams, their visions, their plans, and the courage they had to execute those well-laid plans, all of their offspring—a thousand and more of them by now—would have been slaves right up to the day the Union Army loaded them onto wagons and rolled off with them atop everything else the Army confiscated. Where would they be now? Drifting whichever the Army had deposited them. Homeless. Penniless. Illiterate. No way to feed their children except the backbreaking field work that held no future. Angry, fighting for their rights without the knowledge of how to do it successfully, too naive to know when political opportunists were using them instead of helping them, and, worst of all, hating those who once had owned them.

Oui, Perine had to admit to herself, Grandpère and Mère Coincoin not only dreamed of a better world for us, they fought for it, legally, within the system. That's all Gus and Joseph were proposing now. The law of Louisiana, in this era of Reconstruction, now gave them the right to send their children to public school. They would be unworthy of citizenship if they did not use that right to make a better world for their offspring.

Perine had lost, and in her heart she knew there would be no winning, regardless of what the law now said.

When the autumn sun rose across Cane River the next morning, Gus rode into the yard with his three sturdy teenage sons and Joseph was waiting with Perine's Théodore. Glumly, she watched them swing their horses into River Road, joking as heartily as old Grandpère always had when he mounted for a hunt. As they turned the bend and disappeared from sight behind the corner of the house, she scurried to the back gallery and stared anxiously across the field that stretched between their plantation and the one old Louis had built and young Théophile-Louis had lost to Henry and Hypolite Hertzog.

Barely a half-mile lay between her and the long, rambling bousillage cabin that the Hertzogs had offered for use as the Isle's first public school—not that the Hertzogs would send their children there. No, she snorted, theirs would be sent to the boarding school in Natchitoches. Theirs would not share desks with the common rabble of whatever color who could not afford tuition. In truth, it was the thought of that "common rabble" that now bothered Perine, and tears of worry blurred her vision so badly she scarcely could see the forms of her menfolk as they dismounted and disappeared inside.

The minutes crept by. Ten. Fifteen. Time ceased to exist for Perine as she waited for the first sign of the trouble she had predicted and prayed would not come... *Ave Maria, gratia plena, ora pro nobis!...* In an eon, the two men appeared alone in the doorway. Like actors on a distant stage, they were slapping each other on the back, silently congratulating themselves on the smooth accomplishment of their mission, and Perine leaned against the gallery post to steady her trembling knees. Her eyes closed as her lips moved in gratitude, and so it was that somewhere between her *Gloria in excelsis deo* and her *Gratias agimus tibi*, she missed the brief flash of motion as a skinny lad darted from the rear doorway of the schoolhouse and disappeared into the backwoods.

Joseph and Gus's jocose laughter grew stronger as their horses trotted back up the road, and Perine quickly forced a mien of indifference onto her face in anticipation of the we-told-you-so's she knew would come. They had been right. Her fears had been foolish. Still, she could not make herself feel better about what the two of them had done.

Annoyed as much at herself as she was at them, Perine grabbed an armload of firewood from the pile and plunked it beneath one of the racks that held the two iron washpots in the yard. As her husband and her stepson hitched their horses to the fence, she disappeared into the house to fetch the big basket of laundry that had accumulated since the last wash day. While her menfolk jubilantly reported the schoolmaster's welcome, she furiously poked the soiled clothes around in the boiling kettle, then drained the first shirt and slapped it onto the rub-board of the cold-water pot.

In another minute, or two at most, Perine would have conceded the foolishness of her fears. Indeed, she would have preferred that prospect, infinitely, to the reality that followed. As Joseph's glowing praise for the schoolmaster at last wound down, there came into the void a distant, ominous hum of voices, a buzz that grew rapidly louder, shriller.

"Oh, my God!" she screamed, and the two men loped for their horses, leaving her alone with the rising chant that throbbed across the cotton field:

> Niggers, niggers, kinky-haired yellows!
> Go back home! We don't want you fellows!

A sudden flash of pain knotted her swollen belly, but she dashed heedlessly into the field. Her skirt snagged on empty, brittle, cotton bolls as she scrambled between the rows of waist-high stalks, between the field hands who had forgotten their tasks and stood gaping at the drama that was unfolding.

The angry chant now spilled onto the schoolyard. Frightened girls, their white faces paler than ever, ringed around the yard while a dozen husky boys tumbled through the opening that they left. Brown fists, white fists, angry curses, vile oaths that innocent young lads should not even know—all blurred into a kaleidoscope of sound and motion as she ran wildly toward the school. Then, beyond her on the other side of the senseless mêlée, there came an angry group of men, echoing the same curses their sons were using; and she froze in disbelief as she saw, at the head of the approaching mob, the unmistakable forms of Jake Collins and the skinny, whining boy that he had at last fathered after his long string of girls.

A lifetime of inner fury and resentment that Perine had heretofore subdued with long self-lectures on Christian love and charity now exploded. Fear and anger, as well as pain, clawed at her abdomen. Her eyes darted about her in search of a weapon and she found one—a long, three-tined pitchfork that a careless hand had abandoned beside a haystack in the Hertzog pasture. Her weapon jabbing menacingly before her, she descended then upon the screaming cluster of children, upon the marching gang of riffraff, upon her own pair of defiant menfolk who had reined their horses onto the path between the schoolyard and the armed mob in the road.

Whether it was the flash of murder in Perine's eyes or a twinge of remorse on the part of Jake Collins as he faced the woman who had befriended his family, no one could ever say, but the angry crowd fell back warily. With her pitchfork holding the whites at bay, Perine sharply ordered her son and Gus's off the boys whom they had pinioned to the ground. Muttering reluctantly, they straddled their horses and headed for home, just as Perine's world began to spin.

Joseph caught her as she crumpled. His muscular arm shot out quickly and swung her onto the horse in front of him. Then, deliberately, he turned his mount into the middle of the mob and it parted as he and Gus took her home.

10

Fall 1874

The years that followed were the bitterest the parish of Natchitoches, or the Isle of Canes, had ever known. Joseph, Gus, and other *Créoles de couleur* along Cane River needed no further convincing that the past was gone forever, that the whites whom they had befriended before the war—even the white Creoles who had once called them *mes amis*—now considered them untouchable. The young activists of the Isle, who had wanted nothing so much as to bridge the differences between white and black, between the old regime and the new one, were now driven into the camp of the radicals and the freedmen, as all armed themselves for almost a decade of rancor and violence.

It was a struggle neither side would win. Energies and obsessions that could have been spent in economic recovery were funneled into political strife and class warfare. The uncivil war already had turned neighbor against neighbor, but on the war-scarred homefront of the Cane River Valley—as elsewhere in the South—the internecine struggle called Reconstruction plunged everyone, black and white, further into the abyss of debt.

The children Perine had borne to Gassion grew to adulthood and married. Then the cycle of life began anew as the young couples started their own families and struggled to feed them. Troubled over their prospects, Perine called together her first set of offspring—and Gassion's sons by his first two wives—dividing between them all the land and houses their father had left.

Around them on the Isle, other once-prosperous estates were also split and then subdivided yet again. Large plantations became small farms. Still the times grew even worse, and scores of these homesteads went on the auction block when owners could not pay their taxes. Here and there a few plantations re-mained intact, but their owners paid a dreadful price for the land's salvation. Women and children wept but still held their heads high, as they moved into the crude cabins once occupied by their slaves and then tore down their Big Houses and sold the bricks for whatever cash those slave-baked blocks of mud would bring.

As, one by one, the majestic symbols of their proud heritage disappeared from the Isle, the people grew more bitter. More discouraged. They had tasted the equality the victorious Union gave them and they found it as galling as the acrid vetch some now forced themselves to eat. The new laws had made them equal only in penury, not in privilege. The political dominance of the old white planter class, who had been so closely akin to them in generations past, had been replaced by the tyranny of Radicals and opportunists who felt no affinity for anyone, not even each other. Blacks exploited blacks, whites reviled whites. The land that had been often called a paradise during the era of slavery now became a hellhole of poverty and turmoil.

But worst of all, the Isle's own people were now divided. The unity that

Augustin had forged for three-quarters of a century had been rent asunder.

"Papa, I just can't figure you out!" Joseph exclaimed to old Manuel in exasperation one evening in the fall of 1874. "You were one of the first colored Republicans in this parish and you have been one of the most active, even though the party has never given you an office. Now, with the new elections coming up tomorrow, you tell me you don't even care to go to tonight's rally! Has the White Man's League intimidated you?"

"Nobody intimidates Manuel Dupré!" his father retorted hotly, blue eyes flashing beneath once bushy brows now scraggly with age.

"Then what is it, Papa? Why this disloyalty to the party?"

"The party no longer deserves our loyalty! Its leaders have betrayed all the promises they ever made. The only thing we have gained from these wretched years has been the vote—but what good is that if we don't have decent men to vote for? Our Radical leaders are either ignorant or corrupt, every one of them, or they lack the guts to stand up to devils who are."

"Then those of us who believe in the Radical Republicans and their ideals should oust the crooks."

"Who are you going to replace them with? Look at the slate of candidates we have right now. God help us if we put those men in office!"

"All right, Papa. I'll admit, they may not be all we'd hope for. Nonetheless, it's too late for us to change our candidates for this election, and we have to keep the party itself in power. If we win this election, then we win another two years to work toward improvement. If we lose tomorrow to the White Man's League, then we have no more chance at all."

"Frankly, I think we'd have a better chance under the old white politicians. Life was a hell of a lot better when they ran things."

"You've got to be kidding, Papa! Are you content to be treated for the rest of your life the way we were before the war? My God! Perine! What did you do with that Natchitoches newspaper I was saving? Never mind, here it is."

Joseph's finger jabbed excitedly at a heavily circled passage. "Right here, Papa. Cosgrove printed the platform of his party. Let me read you how the White Man's League actually feels about us..."

> We recognize and faithfully uphold all the *constitutional* and *legal* rights to which the colored citizens of this State are entitled, yet we

are firmly convinced of *their incapacity to perform the duty of legislators and the management of public affairs.*

Manuel's craggy brows twitched almost imperceptibly, but his burly frame stayed planted in the worn-out chaise, his arms folded obstinately across his chest.

"That is an insult!" Joseph fumed, lowering the paper just momentarily. "But that's not the half of it! Listen to this…"

> We believe that the prosperity and improvement of the colored people themselves will be promoted by the restoration of the government to *their more intelligent, experienced, and competent white fellow citizens.*
> It is, then, because *the one race is superior to the other…*

This time, Joseph slammed the newspaper and its offending article onto the mantel where he had found it, but his father was unmoved. "I read the article myself, son. And if I recall correctly, you stopped too soon. What Cosgrove actually said was that one race is superior to the other in point of education and capacity, and he's completely right."

"He's *what?*"

"He is right. The White Man's League has plenty of educated men. The black ranks don't. Most of the Radicals have never been anything but laborers. All the high hopes and ideals in this world are not enough if black leaders are not educated enough to operate the government efficiently—or if black voters aren't worldly enough to elect honest officials. Until that day comes, yes, we'd be better off with the old-time whites."

Joseph turned his eyes away, in frustration and helplessness, from the big square face that glowered at him and refused to relent.

In a way Papa's right, Joseph conceded to himself in a flash of introspection he seldom permitted himself to suffer. In a way, Perine's right. I've tried grazing in both political pastures since the war ended, and both have made it clear that I don't belong with the rest of the herd. But how else can a man accomplish his dreams? Even Perine says I'm a good leader, that I can manage people. God knows I heard her often enough before the war telling her children that our people are special, that we can be anything we set our minds to being. Well, I've set my mind to this, and I could be good for this parish. I'm educated. I care about both sides. If only *they*, if only *someone,* would give me a chance…

"Troubled, son?"

The sound of Manuel's voice, low and still commanding in spite of his age, startled Joseph from his reverie.

"No. No, of course not, Papa," he stammered quickly in protest. "Look, Papa. I do see your side. Can't you see mine? Hang in there with me Papa, just for a couple of years. Let's make one last try to straighten out the party. The people need you, Papa. Our people look up to you."

"We'd be wasting our time, son," Manuel persisted. "We're just little minnows in a little bucket here on the Isle. The party and its problems are far bigger than what we see around us here, or even in the parish."

"Improvement has to start somewhere, Papa."

"You really think there is hope?"

"There has to be. Always."

"All right, son," Manuel sighed. "I'll stay on with you for a while more. But if we're going to change things, then *Mon Dieu!* Let's get on with it!"

"Right, Papa!" Joseph grinned excitedly. "Just let me get my hat. We can still make it to that rally in time."

Old Manuel's idea of reform, however, proved to be considerably more immediate and far more aggressive than the vague dreams of his son, as Joseph was soon to discover.

"Well, we must be early after all," Joseph observed as their old stallions trotted into the yard of what once had been the Jerome Sarpy plantation.

"Hey, Papa! There's old Carroll Jones over by the grandstand. *Tiens!* Look at that row of whiskey kegs. I'll have to say, Carroll does know how to throw a shindig!"

"It's not that he knows any more than anybody else," Manuel growled. "He just came out of this war with more wherewithal than most of us. Besides, we aren't early, either. Our folks aren't coming."

"Ah, Papa," Joseph retorted good-naturedly. "You shouldn't be jealous of Carroll. It was a good thing for all the Isle when he moved up here from Alexandria. He's pumped new life back into this place since the war, and this race track of his is something else…" But then he frowned, his brows knotting, as the implication of his father's last remark sank in.

"What do you mean, our people aren't coming?"

"Just what I said, son. I've talked to everybody on the Isle this past week, and our men are tired of politics. Tired, disillusioned, and fed up. You may still have hope. You and Gus and a few others like you who think you're still young warriors. But the rest of our people are ready to forget those fancy ideas of yours and concentrate on making a decent living again."

"You can't make a decent living as long as you are oppressed."

"You can't make a decent living as long as you have fools or crooks in office who keep the state bankrupt!" Manuel snapped back.

"Shhhh, Papa! Not so loud! Listen, I have a few matters to discuss with Senator Blunt, if you'll excuse me."

"*Senator* Blunt?" his father snorted again. "Don't you mean Rafe, the field hand with the fancy airs?"

"A. Rayford Blunt is now our senator, Papa. Possibly our next governor. He's an ambitious man."

"With fools following him as well as leading him."

"Then he could use a good, honest, sensible man to advise him."

"Like you?"

"Perhaps."

Manuel shook his wild gray mane, his broad face a study in perplexity. "Son, I've just about reached the point that I cannot go along with this mixed-up world any longer! Our people have always *told* the field hands what to do. Not *advised*. Not *suggested*. We don't get down on our knees before a black clodhopper—or a white one either!—and say 'Yassuh, Mister Blunt. Whatever you say, Mister Blunt.' Boy, where's your pride? You have noble blood flowing in those veins of yours! You weren't born to bow before rabble!"

"There is no nobility in America, Papa," Joseph smiled indulgently. "We're all equal now."

"Only on paper, Joseph. Blood still counts. Blood and brains. But go on, pay your homage to your politician. I have some things I want to discuss with a few people tonight myself."

The rally eventually called itself to order. Amid the fanfare of his band that drummed up followers, Senator A. Rayford Blunt and his fellow Radical leaders ascended the grandstand and seated themselves in the row of waiting chairs, the senator in the center, the party's key leaders flanking him, while a flock of minor acolytes, Joseph included, fanned out into the wings.

"My fellow citizens," the senator began as the drums and the cheers faded into the night. The crowd hushed and a sea of black faces, dotted only here or there by a white or tan one, looked up expectantly at the leader whose polish and rhetoric always held them spellbound.

"Citizens," he continued. "Ah! What a beautiful-sounding word that is to men who have been deprived of human rights for all their lives. Yes, *citizens!* That is what we are today, I and all of you, and I will humbly admit that I owe it all to the great Radical Republican Party!" Blunt paused, expectantly, and from the grandstand behind him the party leaders raised their fists and their cheers.

"But I have to tell you tonight, citizens—to *warn* you tonight—that we are in grave danger of losing it all tomorrow. The White Man's League has sworn to exterminate our glorious party in this election, not through honest politics, not on serious issues, but by fanning the flames of hate!"

"Hear! Hear!"

Blunt smiled acridly. "In the newspapers of this parish, they have spoken of our saintly leaders in the vilest of terms! Shall I tell you men what they have said?"

From the shadows of the crowd, beyond the torchlights and lanterns that ringed the grandstand, there rose the roar of assent he had expected.

"They have dared to call our dearly beloved friend and governor, William Pitt Kellogg, and our own heroic P. B. S. Pinchback, and all their faithful workers *a hybrid pack of lecherous pimps!* Yes, my fellow citizens, that is what the White League calls them! And worse! In their scurrilous attacks they have branded these fine, honorable men as *dogs conceived in sin, brought forth in pollution, and nursed by filthy harpies.*"

"Yes!" Blunt went on, his voice booming over the crowd. "They have accused our leaders of showing the world the depths of corruption, disgrace, and infamy that human nature is capable of when the flesh is weak and the spirit willing! But tonight I say—yea, I say unto you, fellow citizens—that God is on our side! The White League itself has only begun to show the world how corrupt and immoral it really is!"

Again, the roar of the crowd reassured the senator that he was arousing all the fury he needed from them, and he plowed on.

"If the White Man's Party wins the election tomorrow, then we will really see how vile humanity can be. What will they do, my fellow citizens? I'll tell you what they will do! They will close the Negro schools of this parish and drive our teachers out of the state. They will burn our churches and hang our preachers in the evil hours of the night. They will take away our right to vote. They will drive away the soldiers of the United States who protect us! And then they will *enslave* us again, my friends. My fellow citizens. Yea, they will put us—God's children—back into chains."

Blunt paused to let the force of those dire words prey upon the minds of his followers, but this time he paused too long. In that stunned interval, the old Manuel, ever blunt, lost the temper he had bridled throughout that evening's earlier disagreement with his son, and he stormed onto the platform. A sudden hush descended upon the crowd as the burly, ancient, freeborn quadroon confronted the younger, slighter, black freedman whose fist was still thrust dramatically toward heaven.

"*Mister* Blunt!" Manuel snorted contemptuously. "I am glad you brought up the subjects of morality and corruption. I have a few things of my own that need to be said, before the election, about our schools and our churches and the United States Army."

"Dupré, I believe?" Blunt queried condescendingly.

"You know damned well who I am," Manuel roared. "I was in this party before you ever joined it, and I've done my damnedest to keep you and your riffraff from getting control of it!"

"So you have, Dupré," Blunt agreed smoothly. "There is a Judas Iscariot in every group of disciples."

"And a Pontious Pilate who tells the crowd what they want to hear, whether it is just or not! Well, I'm a member of this party, and I want to tell this crowd a few things, too."

"Are you a scheduled speaker tonight, Dupré? If so, you'll have your turn."

"You know blasted well that nobody's a scheduled speaker unless he's your mouthpiece! Are you afraid, Blunt, for your own crowd to hear what I have to say?" Manuel challenged.

"Of course not!" the senator snapped. "Say anything you want, Dupré. I am a man of honor. I believe in free speech."

"And free education?"

"Of course."

"And big, fat checks to your cohorts when you give them teaching jobs—even when they don't know how to read and write and never show up at the schoolhouse?"

"Now, Dupré. I assure you, I don't know what you are talking about."

"Then you're either lying or you're dumb. You put J. G. Lewis on the public payroll as the teacher in your own school, the one you started in that church of yours. And everybody knows he hasn't shown up in the classroom yet."

"Mr. Lewis is a busy man, Dupré. After accepting the post, he realized he would not have time to fulfill all the duties of that office, as they deserve to be filled, so he has employed a substitute."

"*Zut!* He hired a substitute because he's not qualified to teach, and he pays that substitute exactly half of what the state gives him. The rest of it he pockets. Or spends on that loose woman he's living with. How do you justify that, Mister Preacher? You and I were both at that meeting in Campti when your fine, uprighteous, Mister Lewis denounced Jerry Hall for living with a woman here when Hall has a wife and children up in Cincinnati. Now *Mister* Lewis has abandoned his own wife and child, right in the town of Natchitoches, and is living with some other man's wife. And you tell us that your *Mister* Lewis is a fine, moral leader of your church and our party? He's not fit to teach our children. The vigilantes would do the public a favor by hanging him!"

A deadly silence crept over the racetrack as the black senator warily eyed his lighter-skinned opponent.

"Dupré," he began slowly, his voice as sharp as a sliver of steel. "You are beginning to sound like a *White Leaguer.* Indeed, when I look at you and listen to you, I find it hard to convince myself that you should even be allowed to attend a black meeting."

"It's not my color that bothers you, Blunt!" Manuel challenged. "It's my guts. Your type of leech feeds on the weaknesses of others. You've been doing that all week among my people here on the Isle. Your dirty, lying henchmen have not been to see me because they knew it would do no good, but don't think I have not heard about the visits they've made to the rest of my people— the *threats* they have made. It seems the vigilantes come in all colors in this parish!"

Blunt's face grew tighter as he continued to stare at the old man planted stubbornly before him. "Dupré, I have tolerated your interruption and your insults tonight because, after all, you're nothing but a harmless old fool. But I warn you…"

"Which is exactly what your men have been doing to my people all week," Manuel retorted, his face flushing in anger. "You dare to stand here and tell this crowd that the Yankee soldiers are the friend and protector of the colored man and that their white neighbors would enslave them—when all week long your henchmen have gone up and down this Isle telling my people that if they don't vote for your party, your blue-bellied Yankee friends would take them to New Orleans in chain gangs to work for the army! Blunt, you are a double-talking, double-dealing crook!"

The crowd began to buzz again and Blunt smiled in satisfaction, telling himself it had been no mistake to let the old man have his say. Dupré was too white. He had been the master when all these men were held in slavery. He could say almost anything here tonight, and it would make no difference at all. Few of his own people were out there to hear him, and that herd of black freedmen would never side with him against their own beloved senator, A. Rayford Blunt.

Still, Blunt mused to himself, it wouldn't do to let this little scenario go on too long. Or to let the old man talk too much.

"Dupré," he began again, his voice purring. "Obviously, *Mister* Dupré, your own people do not agree with you. Your son sits at my elbow tonight, and I do not recall any soldiers forcing him to mount this platform with me. But I am worried about you, sir. Your face is flushed. Your eyes are hot and heavy. Obviously you are ill. Perhaps your son would like to see you home?"

Joseph rose hesitantly, his face darkened with embarrassment, but his father's glare riveted him to his spot in the wings of the platform.

"I'm no blind, doddering old fool, Blunt. I know my way home and I can get there on my own two feet. I don't need anybody to lead me, which is more than I can say for the spineless, gutless cowards who follow you!"

The buzz grew louder. Still, the crowd parted as Manuel stalked off the platform and out to his horse. Just as he swore, his course was steady and his head was held high by all the majesty that had been bequeathed to him by Fanny and the African king who sired her.

∞ 11 ∞

"Joseph, what time did Papa Manuel say he'd be here?" Perine asked worriedly the next morning as she dried the last of her long-chipped dishes and set them carefully in the cupboard. "Wasn't he supposed to go with you to the polls?"

"After last night, he may not even talk to me," Joseph ruefully replied.

"I wouldn't blame him!"

"Ah, Boss Lady, don't you fault me, too. A man's got to do what he's got to do. Papa and I both want what's best for all of us. He's just going about it his way, and I'm going about it mine."

"Well, it's high time all of us remembered Grandpère's counsel and started pulling together instead of working at odds. I declare, Joseph, I just don't see how you could have sat there last night and let that riffraff, *Rafe,* treat your own father as though he were a fool!"

"He didn't really."

"Well, it sounded that way when you told it to me!"

"Then maybe I didn't tell it so good. Look, baby, I'll admit it bothered me. Every word Papa said was the truth. Still, it's just the way he said it. He did not help the party at all."

"Then maybe the party is past helping. Or else it does not want our kind of help because it is not the kind of party you think it is."

"Come here, baby," Joseph responded softly, ignoring her reproof.

"Hehn?"

"Here. Sit down."

Perine shrugged, then complied. As she settled onto the indicated spot on his lap, her tense face eased a little and then ruefully, almost like a loving mother with a willful son, she gently ran her fingers through his hair.

"Joseph, you keep telling me I'm just a woman and don't understand politics. Still, it seems to me that the Radical Party is getting out of hand. Look at all the threats it has made this week!"

"I know, baby. That stuff was really ill-advised. The party's leaders are badly worried, though. The opposition this time has done a damned good job of registering men to vote. It's going to be a mighty close contest. Our people are likely to hold the balance in the election in this parish, and that's why the party firebrands got so upset when they heard that some of our people might be switching allegiance."

"Well, we have every right to! What good is the right to vote if a man's not free to vote the way he believes?"

"None," Joseph conceded miserably. "Look, baby, you just don't understand politics. This is going to be a fierce election. The White Man's League is determined to whip the Radicals, and there is no telling what measures they might use. Those few little threats last week from our side are nothing compared to what the opposition might do today. Even the governor is worried about the Isle. He has shipped over five hundred rifles up here to the Radical movement to help us protect our right to vote if anyone tries to stop us."

"What!"

"They arrived yesterday afternoon, down at Twenty-four Mile Ferry. The party passed them out last night."

"Lord, have mercy!"

"Well, the black man has the right to vote, and the right to bear arms in defense of his rights if someone tries to deny them."

"And the colored man here on the Isle has the right to vote the way he sees fit without black Radicals and Yankee carpetbaggers threatening to enslave him! Joseph, I've said it a hundred times before and I'll keep saying it until you listen to me or the dear Lord himself shuts me up. We have no place in politics! We just don't belong to either side."

"You know, baby, I'm beginning to think you're right." Joseph's admission was barely audible.

"Hehn?"

He did not say it again.

"Well, for God's sake, Joseph, if you agree with me, why have you hung on with the Radicals?"

"For hope, baby," he said, in utter dejection. "A man has to have hope."

"Have you tried prayer, Joseph?"

"Not for quite a while," he confessed ruefully.

"Prayer is a form of hope, too, Joseph. The best kind. If you have just hope without prayer, then you are putting your trust in man. In a world in which it's every man for himself, that means you have nobody but yourself to count on. But if you pray, you have the best help of all. That's what Grandpère did, and

Elizabeth Shown Mills

look where it got him."

"Grandpère! Grandpère! His spectre will rule this Isle forever!"

"Well, it should," Perine exclaimed defensively. "He saw this day coming, Joseph. He tried to prepare us, to teach us to be self-sufficient, to work together, to be charitable to the outside world but not to let ourselves be ruined by the problems and the hatreds of the outsiders. That's where we have gone wrong, Joseph. That's why we are suffering now. Our people are forgetting Grandpère's advice on everything."

"I don't know, Perine. Life just isn't so simple any more."

"It never was! But we have always been smart enough to lick its problems. We still are. *You* are," she added softly, encouragingly. But then she tensed again, and the pensive look on her face turned to worry. "What's that?"

"What?"

Without waiting for his answer, Perine scurried from his lap and darted to the door. Wrenching the bolt back, she flung it open quickly, and the old Manuel slumped into her arms, his clothes ragged, his face battered and bleeding. A black ring was already forming under one of his steel blue eyes, and the curious angle of his arm mutely testified to the strength of the man who broke it.

"Joseph!" she screamed, as the force of the old man's heavy frame made her stumble backward.

"Papa!" Joseph cried behind her. Easily, tenderly, he lifted the weight from off Perine and helped his father to the couch where they had sat and argued less than a day before.

"Who did this, Papa?"

"Some of those hybrid mongrels we heard about last night," he sputtered, trying to force a smile between his swollen lips. "Nothing but a crossbreed between cowardly jackals and scared jackrabbits. Blue-bellied ones!"

"The federal soldiers?"

"Of course," Manuel grimaced. "Maybe now you will believe me. There are only two kinds of Yankees..."

"I know Papa," Joseph interrupted wryly, as he watched Perine sponge away the blood crusting on his father's face. "I know your joke, Yankee civilians are Damned Yankee Sons-of-bitches and Yankee soldiers are Damned *Blue-bellied* Yankee Sons-of-bitches."

"Well, do you believe me?" Manuel demanded.

"Papa, we can't condemn all men because of what a couple of bad ones do."

"Not a couple, a whole half-dozen!"

"Lord, have mercy!" Perine breathed.

"Hmmph!" Manuel retorted. "Any less than that and they'd never have done this to me!"

"Papa," Perine began hesitantly. "I have to set your arm."

"Well, what are you waiting for?"

"You want a bottle of rum, Papa?"

"Zut! Non! I don't drink before I vote."

"What?" Joseph interjected in disbelief. "You're in no shape to go to the polls!"

"I'd go now if I had to crawl there. The Conservatives are going to put the Radical scum out of office this time, and they're going to need every vote they can get to do it."

"You're still going to vote against the party, Papa?" Joseph asked, incredulity stamped across his face. "This was a warning, you know. If the soldiers would do this to you for what you said last night, aren't you afraid of what they'll do when you walk up to the polls and ask for a White League ticket?"

"Boy, you don't hear very well. I told you last night that *no one* intimidates Manuel Dupré!"

"So you did, Papa," Joseph sighed. "So you did."

"You're damned right, I did. I'm a free man. I have the right to vote the way I see it. That's what I'm going to do even though my ballot won't do a blasted thing but cancel out yours."

"No, it won't, Papa." Joseph's voice was quiet, but firm.

"Hehn?"

For a long moment, Joseph made no response as he stared out the window beside them. His troubled gaze swept across the road to the crumbling ruins of the *pigeonnières* that had been Grandpère's pride, to the church his people had been unable to rebuild amid the poverty of the Radical regime. Then he stared across to the fields, where a small patch of verdant cotton swayed gently in the late summer breeze.

There *is* hope, Joseph thought suddenly. It's in that field. It's in my sons who will help me raise more crops. It's in this Isle, in our people, in our church that has to rise again from those ruins, by God!

Slowly, almost magnetically, his eyes were drawn then to the sacred relic that still hung above the mantel. There, captured forever between the past and the present, the timeless face of Augustin Metoyer still smiled gently, promisingly, even though the canvass that transfixed him had been rent asunder.

"What did you say, boy?" Manuel repeated gruffly.

"You heard me, Papa. You have convinced me. Perine has convinced me. The world has convinced me. It's time our people pulled together again. It's time we put our trust in God again, instead of the perfidy of politics."

Impulsively, Joseph wrapped one long arm across his old father's shoulders, those gargantuan shoulders that had held up Joseph's world for as long as he could remember. It's time I carried some of his load myself, instead of adding to it, he thought guiltily, and Perine intuitively read his thoughts. Lines of worry softened in her plain, careworn face, and she slipped quietly, reassuringly, into the crook of her husband's free arm.

Together, they surveyed their world—or what was left of it—through the broad, open, window whose shutters were already beginning to sag. Then in silent unison, their eyes swept the row of pillars that lined the gallery just outside and riveted on the center one where the auction notice had been posted two days before by the parish tax collector.

"We'll survive!" Joseph swore fiercely, as much to himself as to his old papa or to Perine. "We *will* survive. We may lose this place, but we can build others—or our children can. *Oui!* As long as we *believe* in ourselves, as long as we respect *who* we are and *what* we are, then Grandpère's Isle will live on in our hearts and Coincoin's destiny will be our bridge to a better world."

Perine Metoyer and Joseph Dupré

Age and poverty had taken their toll upon the couple before their children took up a collection and had this likeness made on their last anniversary. But Joseph's face had not lost its gleam of hope and Perine still clung to her sources of strength—her prayerbook and her Rosary.

EPILOGUE
Circa 1900

The Rekindling

↪ EPILOGUE ↩
Circa 1900

"Tante Perine?" Gustin tugged gently on his old aunt's arm. She had been quiet for so long now, her eyelids closed, as though she had drifted off into another world. Even her old rocker had ceased to groan.

"Tante Perine? You sleepin'?"

"Non, Gustin," she replied at last, trying to smile at this child who was one of the few joys she had left in life. She had never been ruled by vanity, but the loss of her teeth to age and the poverty that kept her from replacing them had turned her wide and happy smile into a tight pinch of embarrassment.

Wearily, she straightened her shrivelled frame. The old hand-carved rocker creaked back into action as she fought the exhaustion of that long evening and the heartache that inevitably came when memories of the past engulfed her.

"That warn't really the end of Reconstruction, was it, Tante?"

"Non, child. Not quite. But it did not last much longer, though."

Gustin nodded eagerly. "I know. We studied 'bout that in school las' year. Mr. Conant, he taught us all 'bout the Presidential 'lection of '76 an' how the politicians made a deal that the soldiers would leave the South if'n the South would let Mr. Hayes be President."

"Oui, but even then it was not over, Gustin. In the '78 election, there was another fight in this parish, even worse than the fight of '74. Only, in '78, our people knew better than to get involved in other people's wars. We had our hands full enough, just fighting the mosquitoes and the cocoa weeds and the floods and the boll weevils. *Oui,* we had enough troubles just hanging onto our homes and lands."

"That's when you los' Grandpère's Big House?"

"That and a lot more, child. But we kept right on working, your Oncle Joseph and I, God rest his soul, until we had the money to buy back some of it. Only, not enough for Grandpère's house…"

Her voice faded for a moment as she dealt privately with the fact that she never could regain that now. Then her old soul rallied, and she plunged on.

"That's what it takes, *cher*. When you're down you cannot give in. You must keep trying. You must keep working, until you pull yourself right back up again!" For a long minute she paused, searching the boy's eyes, hoping to find in them that vital spark of fire that she saw now in too few of her people. She saw it, and she would not let herself believe that she imagined it.

"Gustin," she went on urgently. "Everyone in this world has the right to be *somebody*. But we have to *seize* that right. We have to set our mind to it and work at it like Mère Coincoin and Grandpère Augustin. *You* can be a *somebody*, if you believe!"

The spark gave way to misery. "Mista' Mackey's boy, he treats me like a *nobody*. He takes my marbles anytime he wants 'em, an' yestiddy he tried to make me wipe his nose when it got runny."

Perine's steely gaze locked the boy's own, with no sign of the droop that, ever since her stroke, tended to close her right eye. "What are you going to do about that, *cher?*" she challenged.

"I dunno," he muttered.

"You *don't know!*" she corrected sharply. "Well, I'll tell you what you can do, Gustin! First, you have to quit using that fieldhand talk you pick up from the freedmen and the poor whites who never had the chance to learn better. Your parents have taught you to speak English correctly, and you will earn no respect as long as you fail to do so."

Her voice rose testily, more so than she had intended, and the child hung his head, staring contritely at the shining hearth that Perine still scrubbed faithfully every morning.

"You really should be ashamed, Gustin, talking like that! Your poor mama has not had a new Easter dress in years, and your Papa walks everywhere he goes so he won't have to buy and feed a horse. That's how they keep you in school instead of putting you in the field to pick cotton."

"Yes, ma'am." Gustin's shoulders drooped guiltily now, and Perine felt a twinge of pity stir inside her brusque old soul.

"Come here, *cher*." Again she patted the big old chair beside her. "If I come down on you hard, Gustin, it is only because I think you are worth the trouble. You don't know it child, but I have been having some serious talks about you with your teacher."

"Huh?" He blurted in surprise.

"Ma'am," she corrected, but then she winked at him reassuringly. "Mr. Conant tells me you are very good at science, *cher*, and your papa has told me all about those sick cows of his that you have been doctoring."

"Yes, Ma'am," he interrupted eagerly, ready to spiel off a dozen stories of his own, but then the strange look on his old aunt's face hushed him. It was the same look she had every time she had reverently spoken Grandpère's name—or Coincoin's.

Gustin's blond brows knitted again, and Perine patted him fondly on the knee. Laboriously, she heaved herself from the old rocker and made her way across the room to the finely carved, leather-strapped, but timeworn chest in which she kept all the treasures she had accumulated in eighty-odd years of living. The big lid groaned, and she rummaged in its endless depths, past the restrung Rosary beads François had carved, past the last lone mug from the set with Napoleon's bust, past Manuel's sword that he never got to use, until at last a satisfied grunt announced to Gustin that she had found what she sought. Again, she shuffled slowly back, her knees aching although her spine was still straight and proud.

"I've been saving this, Gustin," she announced as she sank back into the broad expanse of the rocker.

"This letter came to me over four years ago, *cher*. I've been saving it until I found the right boy for it. This is too important to waste on just anyone."

Gustin's eyes widened as he took in the impressive letterhead, the fine ivory stationery, the neat black print of the letter. Never had he seen a letter that had nice bold type like a book instead of script or scrawl.

"This is from a lawyer, Gustin. In Chicago. Now you listen carefully…"

Mrs. Perine Metoyer Dupré
Cane Island
Natchitoches, Louisiana

Dear Mrs. Dupré:

For some years I have been both a friend and an attorney to a gentleman whom you met briefly during the war and whom you may have cause to remember, Mr. Anthony Lewis.

Gustin's eyes bulged in excitement. "That wuz the name of the army officer, Tante Perine! The nice Yankee!"

"Was," she retorted sharply, but then smiled at the child, nodded assuringly, and continued—her voice heavy with emotion.

> During our acquaintance, Mr. Lewis spoke to me on several occasions about his humble origins and, although his reminiscences were vague, he did indicate that he owed his education to the benevolence of a gentleman of your family. Mr. Lewis also expressed deep concern over the suffering and destitution that was forced upon your community by the war, and it has pained him that political and economic conditions have made it difficult for you to recover your losses.

Perine's voice broke momentarily, but she swallowed hard and plowed on before Gustin could interrupt again.

> To the sorrow of all who knew and loved him, Mr. Lewis passed away last week. He left no wife or children to benefit from his considerable estate; and in his last will and testament he concerned himself with the needs of others, just as he had done throughout his life.
>
> Among the many generous endowments Mr. Lewis left is one bequest of $10,000. It is his wish that this sum be used to provide the best education available, in the best schools of our country, for a deserving young man from your family. The sum is to be held by me in trust, and expended as necessary; but Mr. Lewis has left it to your discretion to choose a student worthy of this bequest.
>
> I trust I shall be hearing from you in response, but I wish to impress upon you that there need be no rush to make your decision. The bequeathed sum will be held at interest, in Mr. Lewis's own bank, until you are satisfied that you have found the right young man.

The letter fell slowly to Perine's lap, as she gazed intently at the child beside her.

"Me, Tante?"

"If you want it, child."

Gustin's eyes began to mist—a pair of robin's eggs at first dawn, Perine thought wistfully—but his young voice was steady. "I would have to leave home?"

"*Oui, cher.* You cannot get that education here on the Isle. Our school only goes through the sixth grade now."

"Next year?"

"*Oui.*"

The child grew silent again, his face pensive. Slowly, Perine caught him under the chin with one crooked finger and tilted it back up until he stared straight into her probing eyes.

"This is your chance, Gustin. All of us have chances in life, of one kind or another. If we don't seize them boldly when they come, if we don't reach way past all our fears, then our dreams will never come true."

Gustin swallowed and then his soft eyes seemed to harden, aging far beyond his years.

"This is my chance. To be *somebody?*"

"*Oui.*"

"As good as the Mackeys?"

"Better!" she responded vehemently.

The strange look still lingered in Gustin's eyes. "Tante Perine," he began hesitatingly. "Was Colonel Lewis a nigger, too?"

"The word is *Negro,* Gustin," Perine said slowly, stalling for time in which to frame the most difficult thing she would have to say that night. Gustin's eyes stayed on hers, waiting for an answer.

"Colonel Lewis was what he wanted to be," Perine continued at last. "Remember, child, I said that you, too, could be anything you wanted?"

"Yes, Ma'am."

"In your case, *cher*—and in the colonel's case—those words are true in every way. You have a heritage any man should be proud of. You come from three races, three worlds that are different but equally good. God blessed you Gustin, you and Colonel Lewis both, because he made you in such a way that you can choose which world you want to live in. You don't have to make the choice now, Gustin, but if you leave the Isle you will find that one day, just like Colonel Lewis, you will have to choose between those worlds—at least between black and white."

The old iron clock on the mantel above them struck nine, reminding her of the lateness of the hour and the chores still to be done before she turned in for the night. "You'd best run on home now, Gustin. Your Mama and Papa will be worried."

"Yes, Ma'am."

The child slipped slowly out of the chair. Then, as always, he wrapped his slender arms around his ancient aunt and kissed her gaunt cheeks good bye. Both her eyelids closed softly now. The old rocker went back into action, and something deep within her lit Perine's face.

Softly, Gustin tiptoed to the door, but then his gaze fell on the massive oil—the war-torn heirloom—that he had passed by a thousand times before. This time, his face broke into a grin. His back straightened and his right hand flew to his forehead in a sharp salute. Then, winking mischievously to his old Grandpère, the lad eased the door shut behind himself and strode jauntily into the night.

Augustin's Final Home

In this quaint Creole mausoleum, behind the Church of St. Augustin, there rest the remains of Sieur Nicolas Augustin Metoyer, f.m.c., his wife Marie Agnes Poissot, their son François-Gassion Metoyer, and the daughter-in-law who became Tante Perine to all the Isle.

A Note about Sources

Historians and archivists working with colonial Spanish records often jest that Spanish bureaucrats created six copies of everything. The jest is not far off the mark, creating both a boon and a nightmare for researchers. Multiple copies mean a greater likelihood that at least one copy survives. On the other hand, when multiple copies of the same document—each of them independently penned—are found and compared, researchers often find variations in content. One or more may be drafts, while another may be the intended final copy, and it is not always clear which is which.

Novelists who attempt to weave these documents into their narratives face other challenges as well. The language of our forebears often seems archaic by modern styles and standards, befuddling those who are not familiar with records of the time and place. In other cases, a single extracted document may make only an elliptical reference to a circumstance that is explained more fully in a companion record. Yet, presenting readers with all versions and all nuances is no way to present a clear and fast-paced narrative.

As a rule, the translated documents woven into this account follow the original records as closely as clarity permits. In some cases or passages, where the presentation of verbatim transcripts or multiple versions would be counterproductive, I have sought clarity by faithfully paraphrasing or summarizing the overall content of a document or a file. In other cases the original documents or newspapers do not appear to have survived but are described or discussed in extant records; my narrative borrows from those to present the essence of the original. Finally, in some cases where letters once held by the family have fallen victim to fire or the other ravages of time—as with the letters penned by Ben Metoyer, Pope Pius IX, and Colonel Anthony Lewis—the content of those letters has been reconstructed herein from family recollections of their content.

The events and characters that have been woven into *Isle of Canes* are chronicled in thousands of documents maintained at local, state, and national levels in the United States, Mexico, Cuba, Canada, France, and Spain. It is impossible to cite them all. However, the key documents presented in this story are identified in the following notes and illustration credits, so that readers, who wish, may personally consult the originals as a beginning point for their own probes.

Notes

P. 12
Baptism of Marie Thérèse *dite* Coincoin, 1742. Register 1 (unpaginated), Church of St. François des Natchitoches, Archives of Immaculate Conception Church, Natchitoches.

P. 90
Baptism of Claude Thomas Pierre Metoyer, 1744. Parish Registers of St. Sauveur de la Rochelle, Archives Departementales de la Charente-Maritime, La Rochelle, France.

P. 128
Quintanilla's Bill of Complaint, 1777. Document 1227, Colonial Archives, Office of the Clerk of Court, Natchitoches. The last part of the narrative's English rendition has been edited to reflect multiple documents by Quintanilla on the same subject.

PP. 204-05
Will of Claude Thomas Pierre Metoyer, Acts of Leonardo Mazange, vol. 78, pp. 187–91, Notarial Archives, New Orleans.

P. 208
Manumission of Marie Louise, by Marie Thérèse Coinquin, 1786, Old Natchitoches Data 2: 289, Cammie Henry Collection, Northwestern State University Archives, Natchitoches; and 1795, Document 2596, Colonial Archives, Office of the Clerk of Court, Natchitoches.

P. 214
Spanish Survey, Homestead of Marie Thérèse, *Négresse Libre,* File: February 1794, Opelousas Notarial Archives Collection, Louisiana Archives and Records Service, Baton Rouge.

P. 216
Clipped from *Le Marsellais,* the popular battle song of the French Revolution.

P. 231
Manumission of Thérèse and Joseph Maurice, summarized from several longer documents executed by Marie de St. Denis de Soto in favor of Marie Thérèse *dite* Coincoin between 28 September 1790 and 16 October 1797. Coincoin's copies are filed as Document 2804, Colonial Archives, Office of the Clerk of Court, Natchitoches.

P. 238

Manumission of Nicolas Augustin, Mulatto, by Claude Thomas Pierre Metoyer, 1792, Document 2409, Colonial Archives, Office of the Clerk of Court, Natchitoches.

P. 255

Manumission of Marguerite by Widow Lecomte 1794. Document 2551, Colonial Archives, Office of the Clerk of Court, Natchitoches.

P. 352

Frederick Law Olmsted's observations on the Isle of Canes. Extracted from Olmsted, *Journey in the Seaboard Slave States in the Years 1853–1854* (1956; reprint, New York: Negro Universities Press, 1968).

P. 422

Distribution of Proceeds among Heirs of Marie Susanne Metoyer, 1838. Succession 355, Office of the Clerk of Court, Natchitoches.

P. 440

"Adieux," by Bernard Dauphine. Published posthumously in *Les Cennelles* (New Orleans, 1845). Translation by Dorothea Olga McCants, in Rodolphe Lucien Desdunes, *Our People and Our History* (Baton Rouge: Louisiana State University Press, 1973). Reprinted in its entirety, with permission of the publisher.

PP. 535–36

This labor contract is drawn from several filed in the Chaplin, Breazeale, and Chaplin Collection [the papers of a Natchitoches law firm] in the Special Collections Department, Louisiana State University Archives, Baton Rouge.

Illustration Credits

P. 9

Augustin's Manor—In Decline, ca. late nineteenth century. Pen and ink sketch by Deanna Douglas, commissioned by the author from a photograph donated to the author in 1972 by the late Lee Etta Vaccarini Coutee.

P. 12

Baptism of Marie Thérèse *dite* Coincoin, 1742. Register 1 (unpaginated), Church of St. François des Natchitoches, Archives of Immaculate Conception Church, Natchitoches.

P. 14

St. François Church, 1738. Sketch by Charles Normand for Elizabeth Shown Mills, *Natchitoches, 1729–1803: Abstracts of the Catholic Church Registers of the French and*

Spanish Post of St. Jean Baptiste des Natchitoches in Louisiana. New Orleans: Polyanthos, 1977. Used with permission of the publisher.

P. 47
Fort St. Jean Baptiste des Natchitoches, reconstructed 1979. Sketch by Auseklis Ozios. Photo by Robert Buquoi, Louisiana Office of State Parks. Used with permission.

P. 247
Isle of Canes and Cane River, from Grande Ecore to Le Court's Bluff. Drawn to rough scale by the author.

P. 343
Coincoin's cabin. Pen and ink sketch by Carrie Starner Mills, commissioned by the author, from a photograph taken by the author in 1978.

P. 368
Yucca House, built ca. 1800 by Louis Metoyer on the plantation now known as Melrose. Charcoal sketch by Carrie Starner Mills, commissioned by the author, from photographs taken by the author in 1972.

P. 396
Nicolas Augustin Metoyer, f.m.c., and his Church of St. Augustin, life-sized oil on canvas, painted ca. 1836 by Feuille. Photograph made by the author, 1972.

P. 416
Louis Metoyer's African House. Pen and ink sketch by Bert Bertrand, provided by Bertrand to the author, 1976. Reproduced with permission.

P. 418
Melrose, Louis Metoyer's Big House. Pen and ink sketch by Bert Bertrand, provided by Bertrand to the author, 1976. Reproduced with permission.

P. 420
Auguste Metoyer and wife Marie Carmelite "Melite" Anty, oils on canvas, painted ca. 1836 by Feuille. Photographs supplied by Cammie G. Henry Research Center, Eugene P. Watson Library, Northwestern State University, Natchitoches.

P. 495
Joseph Emanuel Dupré Sr., C. S. A. Militiaman, Augustin's Mounted Guards. Photograph supplied 1972 by the late Lee Etta Vaccarini Coutee, Dupré's great-granddaughter.

P. 567
Perine Metoyer and Joseph Dupré. Photograph supplied 1975 by Harlan Mark Guidry and Jackie Rideau Griffin.

P. 577
Augustin's Final Home. Photograph taken 1972 by the author.